# Blood Seed

By Greg Park

THE EARTHSOUL PROPHECIES
Book One: *Veil of Darkness*
Book Two: *Cleansing Hunt*
Book Three: *Children of Ta'shaen*
Book Four: *Death's Third March*
Book Five: *Blood Seed*

# BLOOD SEED

---

BOOK FIVE

of

THE EARTHSOUL PROPHECIES

# Greg Park

BLOOD SEED

A Bladestar Book
Published by Bladestar Publishing
Orem, Utah


www.BladestarPublishing.com


Maps and sketches by Matthew Furner Broderick
Cover art and design by Nui Silva

Printed in the United States of America

ISBN-13: 978-0-9787931-4-2

**For Tilly**

*atanami en koires*

# Acknowledgments

There were times during the past ten years when I wondered if this day would ever come. But now it's here, and I'm experiencing a strange mix of emotions. I'm pleased and relieved to be finished, but I'm also sad that the Earthsoul Prophecies has come to an end. I've come to think of many of the characters as family—they are a part of me—and it's difficult to say goodbye.

So, instead of goodbye, I'll use the words 'see you later.' That leaves the door open for joyful reunions through follow-up stories or, perhaps, even a second series.

I want to thank all of you for your enthusiasm and support of the series. You are the reason I write. A special shout-out to the following: Bladestar Publishing; Nui Silva for cover art and design; Lori Humpherys and Chani Boyce for beta reading and editing; my colleagues at Timpanogos High School for their support and encouragement (specifically Brian Saxton); and to the many students I've had the privilege of teaching.

But most importantly, I want to thank my dear, sweet wife, Chantilly and my amazing children, who slow the writing process from time to time because spending time with them is always more enjoyable than sitting at a computer. Without family, none of this would have been possible.

# CONTENTS

# Seven Gifts of *Ta'shaen*

THE NINE LANDS

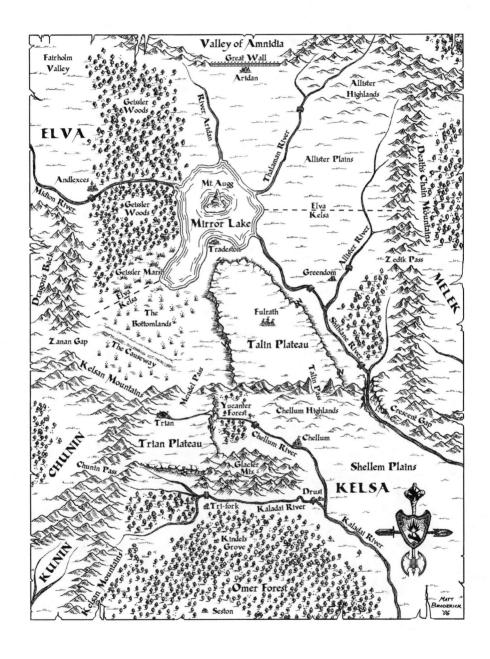

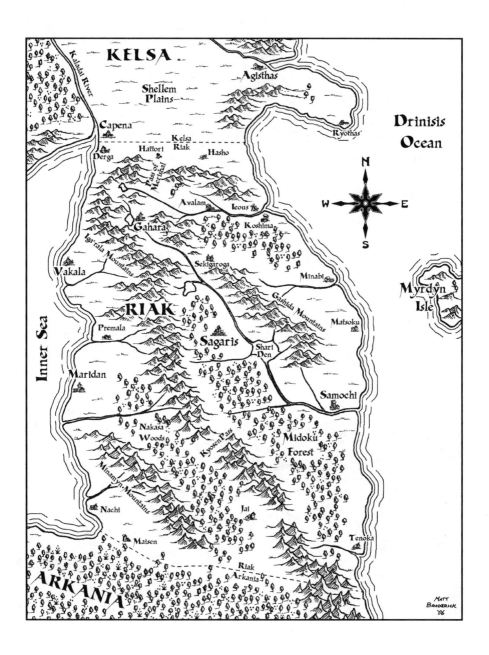

xvi

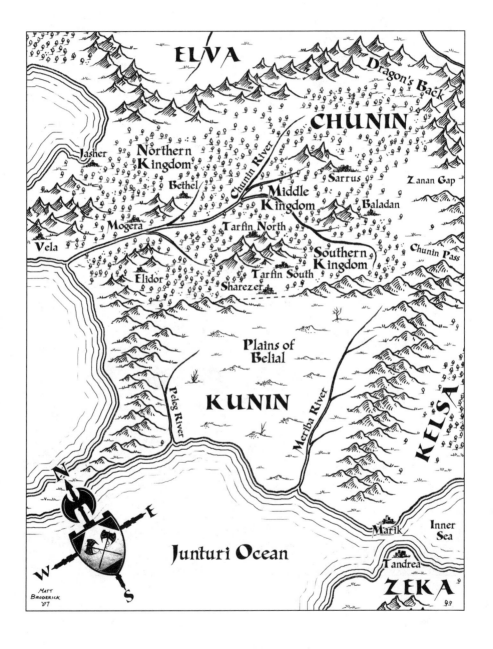

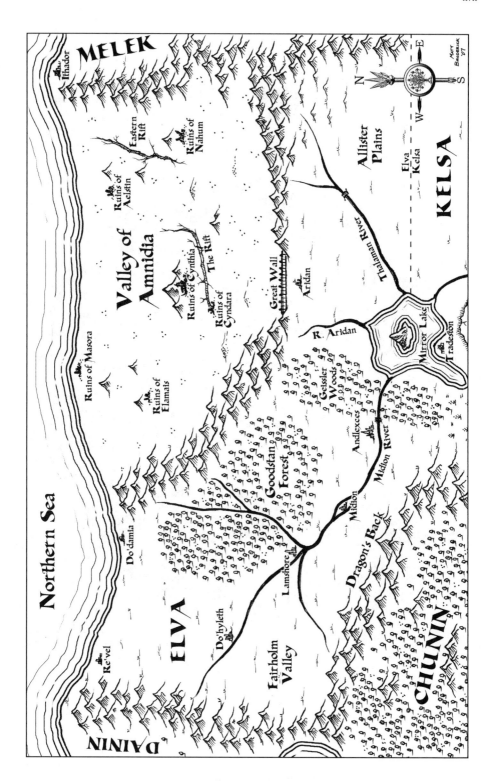

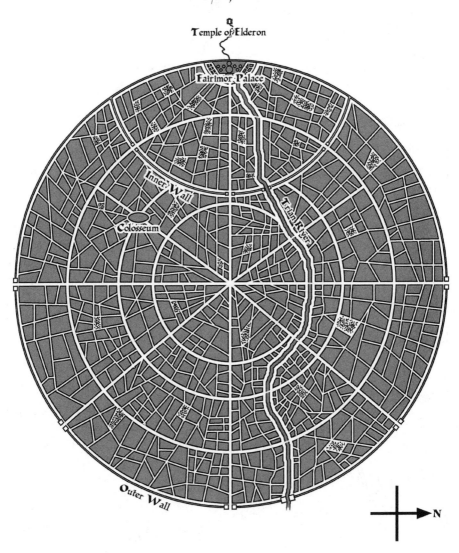

# The City of Trian
### and its Major Routes

Temple of Elderon

Fairimor Palace

Inner Wall

Colosseum

Trian River

Outer Wall

N

*And a voice spoke to me out of the Void, saying: Look!*
*And I looked and beheld a Veil of Darkness descending upon*
*the world as the Lord of Chaos besieged the nations, sowing the*
*Seeds of the Apocalypse and bringing about the End of Days.*

~ From an unabridged copy of the *Eli'shunda Kor.*
Credited to the Agla'Con Tarach Hadishar,

# PROLOGUE

## The Bride of Maeon

WITH TWO SQUADS OF TAMBA'S elite Deathwatch marching at his heels, Ibisar Naxis, Supreme Commander of the Tamban military, approached the entrance of the grand throne room of Berazzel. He stopped while a pair of grey-faced *Maa'tisis* pulled the doors open for him, then pointedly ignored the two refleshed beings as he awaited *Frel'mola*'s invitation to enter. Aside from the refleshed Dreadlord, the *Maa'tisis* were beneath him. Especially those who'd been destroyed during the coup to dethrone Wellisar Oagrem, former Emperor of Tamba.

He frowned inwardly. Bloody weaklings, all of them. In death and in their former lives when they'd so foolishly thought they could stand against him and the *Jeth'Jalda* loyal to the Bride of Maeon.

If the two *Maa'tisis* were aware of his disdain for them, it didn't show in their faces, and they resumed their posts without speaking. He continued to ignore them, turning his attention instead to *Frel'mola*.

Sitting straight-backed in her throne, she wore a shimmering dress of purple and gold and had a short reddish-gold scepter resting in her lap. The delicate crown gracing her raven-colored hair was complemented by an array of bracelets and rings. All sported blood diamonds and rubies which glittered brightly in the light of dozens of glowstone chandeliers and the Power-wrought orbs of light being channeled by *Jeth'Jalda*.

In addition to the *Jeth'Jalda*, six *Maa'tisis* lined the far wall and two dozen Deathwatch stood at attention opposite them. Ibisar took it all in with a glance, then returned his gaze to *Frel'mola*.

Her eyes shone a bright red as she watched the men and women dancing before her. All were scantily clad, their movements suggestive yet graceful as they performed a traditional Tamban courtship dance. *Frel'mola* seemed mesmerized by the performance, and it took her a moment to realize the doors had opened and Ibisar was waiting to enter.

With a wave of a jeweled hand, she motioned him forward, and the two *Maa'tisis* at the doors fell from his peripheral as he strode up the center aisle toward the throne. He dismissed them and everyone else in the room from his thoughts. Only *Frel'mola* mattered now. As always, he would need to step lightly around her, Supreme Commander or not.

Fortunately for him and all the rest who served in Berazzel, the female Dreadlord had been decidedly less volatile since being visited by Maeon three nights ago. The sudden change made Ibisar wonder if the Dark Lord had specifically instructed *Frel'mola* to stop destroying her subjects or if she was simply in a better mood because of the visit. Whatever the reason, the unnecessary destruction of those who displeased her had, for the most part, ceased. And that was the break Ibisar had been looking for.

As the man charged with uniting Tamba's forces, his efforts the past few months had been hampered by *Frel'mola's* temper and her obvious favoritism of the newer of her two religions. Her bias had deepened the division between the warring factions and had pushed Tamba to the brink of civil war. In the past few weeks alone, dozens of high-ranking officers, mostly those in the Tamban Navy, had chosen to serve Throy Shadan instead of *Frel'mola*.

And according to his sources, the rebellion had started at Kashilka Spike and had been influenced by an outsider. A Kelsan by the name of Aethon Fairimor. Apparently he was to Shadan what Ibisar was to *Frel'mola*: first among the living in Maeon's forces in that half of the world. The very thought rankled him badly. A duel to see who stood higher in Maeon's eyes might be in order. And in the very near future, if the newest reports of Aethon's meddling were accurate. He simply couldn't allow an outsider to undermine Tamba's military might any longer.

He reached the throne and turned to watch the performers even though he had no interest in what they were doing. He wouldn't speak until bidden to do so by *Frel'mola*. Instead, he concentrated on the large fiery-edged hole rippling in the air behind him. It framed *Frel'mola's* throne like a window pressed upon by night. The air around it was chill, and every so often an icy breeze flowed over him, pressed outward from the hole by a power only visible in his mind's eye.

Reaching into himself, he opened his Awareness and found threads of darkness snaking outward from the rent, bearing the realm of Con'Jithar into the living world. The luminescent fabric of the Veil shimmered a bluish-white around the rent as the Earthsoul worked to repair the damage, but this was a losing battle. Con'Jithar held sway here now. Hell had very literally come to Berazzel.

The hole had been rent by Maeon himself, and though the demon god hadn't actually entered the living world, it was clear his power had grown. It was only a matter of weeks now, if not days, and he should be able to overpower the Earthsoul completely.

Ibisar pressed his Awareness nearer the rent and found the wards *Frel'mola* had set in place to keep demons from entering the palace. The bloody creatures were no respecters of persons, and several Deathwatch and two *Jeth'Jalda* had died in the moments following Maeon's departure when four scaled monstrosities took advantage of the rent to enter the living world. *Frel'mola* had destroyed them easily, but their sudden appearance had put the entire palace on edge.

"Admiring my work?" *Frel'mola* asked, and Ibisar came back to himself in a rush. "Yes, Empress."

He turned to face her. And as always when he was this near, he found it difficult to look away. Unlike the rest of the Refleshed, *Frel'mola's* face was not grey and gaunt and sickly looking. It was beautiful. Undoubtedly the most beautiful female face Ibisar had ever seen. Only the unnatural glow of her eyes showed that she was something other than human.

She noticed his stare, and her lips curled into a smile. "I'm spoken for, my pet," she said, and Ibisar stiffened at the amount of levity in her voice. Maeon's visit truly *had* changed her demeanor.

He lowered his head. "My apologies if I offended."

She smiled again. "I would be offended if you didn't find me beautiful," she answered. "I worked hard for this body."

Ibisar allowed himself a tight smile as he returned his attention to the performers. *Worked hard for this body.*

It was an accurate statement, just not in the sense anyone but he or *Frel'mola* would understand. The truth was that in order to maintain the physical appearance of the host body, the refleshing had to take place at the exact moment of the chosen person's demise. Otherwise their appearance—in this case, their beauty—would change, resulting in the hideous, corpse-like face worn by all *Maa'tisis*.

That was why he'd spent more than a year preparing for *Frel'mola's* refleshing by seeking out and recruiting the most beautiful women he could find. He'd selected fifty in all, each in her early twenties, each a sworn member of *Frel'mola's* dark religion. And every one of them had been so eager to offer her life for a chance to become the new face of the Tamban Empress that Ibisar had made them draw lots to see who would go first.

He remembered how those with the lowest numbers had celebrated their fortune at being selected to go first, but in reality those with the higher numbers had the most reason to rejoice. With each failed attempt, the odds grew more and more in their favor that it would be one of them. Plus they'd had the added pleasure of watching the prior girl's beauty wither into nondescript ugliness—an ugliness he and the other *Jeth'Jalda* under his command had destroyed with Fire, sending *Frel'mola's* spirit back into Con'Jithar to await the next attempt. The face *Frel'mola* now wore had belonged to the thirty-third volunteer.

And what a face it was, Ibisar thought. It made the five days he'd spent refleshing then destroying the less-than-perfect attempts all the more rewarding. And he'd been allowed to keep the remaining women as payment for his efforts.

One of the male dancers clipped the foot of one of the ladies, and they both lost their balance, disrupting the flow of the performance. Their eyes went wide with fear as they hastily regained their momentum, and Ibisar braced himself, fully expecting a violent reaction from *Frel'mola* due to the lack of perfection.

To his surprise, she simply narrowed her eyes at the man and continued to watch the performance. It ended a few minutes later with each of the couples locked in a variety of intimate poses.

*Frel'mola* surprised everyone further when she lifted her hands from her lap to applaud.

"Very nice," she told them. "You are all dismissed." As the performers hurried away, she turned her red gaze on Ibisar. "Have the fool who tripped his partner executed," she told him. "He ruined the entire performance with his clumsiness."

So, Ibisar thought. *She hasn't changed after all.*

"It will be done, Empress," he told her.

*Frel'mola* looked as if she might say more, but a disturbance in the Power stayed her tongue. A heartbeat later, a rent opened in the Veil a short distance away and General Kantor of Tel'Haalaf's first battalion stepped through from beyond. He immediately went to one knee and let the rent snap shut behind him.

"I bring news of Death's Third March," he said. Keeping his head down, he waited.

"Rise, General Kantor," *Frel'mola* told him. "And tell me what that fool Throy Shadan has been up to."

General Kantor stood straight as he looked his Empress in the eyes. "His forces have taken the eastern rim of Talin Plateau," Kantor said, "but it was done at the expense of the *Jeth'Jalda* you sent to him yesterday. Obviously Shadan views *Frel'mola te Ujen* as expendable, and he recklessly used them as a diversion for the main assault."

He waited for a response, but when none came, he continued. "Shadan has a powerful new weapon at his disposal. It is a type of Veilgate, but it is more than a mile wide. He used it to place the Tamban army behind Kelsa's forces. The entire army was able to move through as one. The Kelsan army has been routed and is in full retreat."

*Frel'mola* narrowed her eyes skeptically. "Shadan did this?"

"No, Empress. Those who opened the gate were not men. Living or refleshed."

"What were they then?" Ibisar asked.

"Dragons," General Kantor replied, his tone almost reverent. "And it seems they have sworn themselves to Aethon Fairimor."

"Dragons," *Frel'mola* mused. "So, the legends are true."

"It would seem so, Empress. And these Dragons—they call themselves Rhiven—they are wielders of *Lo'shaen.*"

*Frel'mola* nodded as if she had expected as much. "What else do you have to report?"

General Kantor seemed hesitant to continue. "There is one among Kelsa's forces who rivals even Shadan in strength. He is only a boy but those who follow him are calling him the *Mith'elre Chon*. He single-handedly held off our forces, as well as numerous attacks by Shadan, and allowed the Kelsan army to escape."

"They are headed for Fulrath?" Ibisar asked. He knew little about the military city save for its name and location on the Kelsan map, but it seemed the most likely place.

"I don't think so, Supreme Commander," the general answered. "The city lies desolate. Left so by a powerful strike of Earthpower. I felt the detonation from ten leagues away. It obliterated the forward ranks of Shadan's army as they were attacking the city. A third of his troops vanished in a single instant. Fulrath's population appears to have been destroyed as well."

"Shadan's loss shall be our gain," *Frel'mola* said. "We will continue to assist with Death's Third March as is Maeon's will. Then, when the time is right, we will take Kelsa and her neighboring lands for ourselves. Trian shall become a second seat of power for *Frel'mola te Ujen*, and I will reign supreme on two continents."

Her voice had risen by the end, and her eyes flared brightly. For a moment she seemed more like the *Frel'mola* of old, vicious, ruthless, and hungry.

She calmed herself almost immediately. "You shall receive additional *Jeth'Jalda* shortly," she said. "They will join you through Veilgates by end of day tomorrow."

"And troops?" Kantor asked, directing the question to Ibisar.

"We've assembled an army to rival Shadan's forces and those of Kelsa's combined," he answered. "We will send them to you once Death's Third March reaches Trian."

"And then," *Frel'mola* said, her beautiful features twisting into a smile. "We will see who sits higher in the world to come—the Destroyer of Amnidia or the Bride of Maeon."

# CHAPTER 1

## Cutting Losses

LIGHTNING CRACKLED DOWN THE EDGES of Jase's shield, and the hair on his arms and head stood on end. The points of light obscuring his vision grew brighter, but it had little to do with the lightning strike. The amount of Earthpower coursing through him was well beyond what he was capable of on his own, and he had long since turned to the Blood Orb he possessed to boost his strength.

But that strength too would fade. And soon. And when it did, it would likely leave him as weak and helpless as a newborn babe. If it didn't kill him outright.

A second barrage of lightning hammered his shield, and the Blood Orb flared to life in his hand, warm and pulsing and alive. In his mind's eye, he could see the threads of corruption left by the lightning, and he used them as his guide as he channeled streamers of *Sei'shiin* back toward the Agla'Con who'd launched the attack. The men vanished from existence in flashes of white, and the cultist troops with them were left unprotected.

Idoman Leda and Tuari Renshar tore a number of them to pieces with thrusts of Flesh and streamers of Fire. The remaining cultists fled the area like sheep fleeing before wolves.

Jase didn't stay to celebrate. With great effort, he opened a part in the Veil, and he and Idoman and Tuari moved through to another section of the battlefield. It was an area where the heaviest fighting had already taken place, and bodies littered the ground like autumn leaves. Most were Tamban, but hundreds of Kelsans lay among them. Shadowhounds were moving among the corpses sniffing for survivors. They looked up as Jase and the others appeared in their midst, then died in bursts of superheated gore as Idoman struck them with the Power.

Jase turned his attention east to the wall of black marking the forward ranks of the third column of Shadan's army. Less than a half mile away, they were making their way through the tents and wagons of Kelsa's hastily abandoned camp. Most of the army had arrived at the top of the plateau through Veilgates or on the backs of shadowspawn. Some—Shadowhounds and hundreds of creatures Jase didn't have names for—had scaled the steep slopes on their own.

It was a terrifying sight, and Jase tightened his fist on the Blood Orb for strength. Even with a third of his army gone to Fulrath and the Tambans pursuing the routed Kelsans, Shadan had enough of an army here to lay siege to Trian.

And he had Dragons. Creatures capable of wielding *Lo'shaen*. Creatures capable of moving an entire army dozens of leagues in a single step. Creatures who had been hunting him relentlessly since the battle began.

Jase allowed himself a grim smile. Which was exactly what he wanted them to do. For despite their tremendous power, they bled and died like any other animal, and he'd killed one and injured two others in just the past hour. And still they kept coming for him, sometimes in human form, sometimes as glittering, sinuous serpents. It mattered little to him what they looked like so long as they died.

"Here they come," Tuari said, but the warning wasn't necessary. Jase had sensed the hellish corruption of *Lo'shaen* just as Tuari had. A heartbeat later, the sky came alive with crackling tendrils of darkness. Night Threads, Gideon had called them. The demonic equivalent of lightning.

Jase turned them aside with *El'shaen te sherah*, and an odd scream-like thunder echoed across the plateau as the deflected threads tore up the corpse-covered ground. Dirt and ash and flesh rained to the earth in dark sheets, obscuring Jase's view of Shadan's army. With his natural eyes, at least. In his mind's eye, the expanse of scales and armor was as clear as a summer's morning. And there on the edge of the mass of bodies was a Dragon in human form.

Wearing a stately uniform of black and silver, the creature had long white hair and chiseled, Elvan-like features. His yellow eyes shone with amusement as he prepared another strike. Jase recognized him as the one who'd been with Aethon in Zedik Pass.

"Time to go," he said, then wove a white-hot bar of *Sei'shiin* and sent it lancing at the creature as Idoman opened a Veilgate to another part of the battlefield. Jase followed him and Tuari through as the bar of *Sei'shiin* struck the Dragon's shield, and the area they'd left behind flashed bright as the sun.

A mile to the north, the same flash of light from the attack was visible, and Jase marveled at being able to see it from both sides of the Veilgate. The *boom* from the resulting explosion reached him through the Veilgate as it was sliding shut, and he nodded in satisfaction at what it meant. Even if the Dragon survived—and it probably would—all those around it would have been reduced to ash.

A moment later the same *boom* arrived from the north.

"I'm still getting used to that," Idoman commented. "It really messes with one's perception of time and distance."

Grunting in agreement, Jase lessened the amount of *Ta'shaen* flowing through him as he looked around. He could feel his exhaustion pressing heavily upon the protective cloak of *Jiu* he'd wrapped himself in, and the points of light flickering in his natural vision had brightened. Both were warning him that he was nearing his breaking point. Idoman and Tuari were as well. Neither had wielded even a fraction of what he had, but they hadn't enjoyed the added boost from the Blood Orb either.

"What's next, Jase?" Tuari asked, her Riaki eyes shining in spite of the weariness in her voice. Jase smiled fondly at her. This morning's battle aside, he hadn't seen much of her since the night she and the rest of *Ao tres'domei* had arrived at Fulrath, but she had endeared herself to him the moment they'd met. Not only did she remind him a great deal of his grandmother, she was practically the only person outside of his immediate family who would call him by his given name.

Jase looked across the battlefield as he considered. To the southwest, the bulk of the Kelsan army had made it beyond the reach of Shadan and his Agla'Con, but they were still being pressed upon by a number of mounted K'rrosha and *Jeth'Jalda* from the Tamban army.

The Tamban army itself had given up pursuit, content, it seemed, to regroup after being split by the roves Captain Galahan had led through their midst. Ten roves had ridden into the mass of bodies. Only five had emerged on the far side.

With a quick thrust of his Awareness, Jase found the survivors angling toward the rest of the Kelsan army. With a second thrust, he located the cavalry he'd sent through Veilgates to hit the Tambans on their southern flank. Led by Captain Brommis, they'd succeeded in turning back the Tamban pursuit and were now riding hellbent for the rear of the Kelsan army, eager to rejoin their companions. Obviously they didn't realize there were K'rrosha and *Jeth'Jalda* between them and their destination.

"We need to eliminate the Power-wielders between our cavalry and the rear of our army," he said. "Brommis and his men are about to ride right up on them."

"And the Tamban army?" Idoman asked.

"They seem content to let us go for now," Jase said, still studying the sprawling mass through his Awareness. "They've won the day, and they know it."

"If there is good to be found in this disaster," Tuari said, her eyes distant as she stared eastward, "it is that the Tambans are between our army and the Meleki scum Shadan commands. Those blood-thirsty fools wouldn't have given up the chase so easily."

"Some of them haven't," Jase said. "Come, we have K'rrosha and *Jeth'Jalda* to destroy." Reaching deeper into the Elsa talisman, he allowed it to boost his strength once more, then opened a part in the Veil and stepped through to the chaos beyond.

*Ta'shaen* seethed with dozens of wieldings, both pure and defiled, and peals of thunder rumbled overhead. A short distance to the west, explosions shook the ground as *Jeth'Jalda* struck at the Dymas protecting the rear of Kelsa's forces and the Dymas retaliated. North and east, vast stretches of the grassland were in flames, and smoke darkened the sky, making breathing difficult.

Jase cleared the smoke away with a rush of Air, then wrapped himself and the others inside a protective bubble of Spirit. That would help with breathing. It was also akin to lighting a signal fire for the enemy. This time he would let them come to him.

"To the left," Tuari said, and a moment later three Shadowlancers appeared from out of the roiling haze. Lances lowered, they sent streamers of sizzling death streaking forward.

Tuari turned the corrupted Fire aside with a thrust of Spirit, and Idoman sliced the heads from the Power-wrought horses with thin blades of Fire. Legs buckled as the horses collapsed, and the Shadowlancers were tossed head over foot. Jase burned them to ash while they were still airborne.

But this fight was just beginning, and lightning ripped up the ground at the edge of Jase's shield, shaking the earth and swallowing everything in flashes of blinding white.

"That bloody hurt," Idoman muttered, shaking his head. *Ta'shaen* surged into him as he prepared a return strike, but somewhere out on the battlefield another Dymas beat him to it. The tremor of corruption tickling Jase's Awareness vanished.

"It's about time we had some help," Idoman said, then hurriedly redirected his attack toward a pair of *Jeth'Jalda* who materialized out of the smoke to the right.

Idoman's strike crackled down the edge of a shield channeled by one of the men, and the ground around the two erupted into sprays of super-heated grit. Standing safely inside, the other *Jeth'Jalda* raised his fist and released a crimson bar of corrupted *Sei'shiin*.

It lanced through Jase's shield with a sound like breaking glass, and Jase and his companions were thrown to the ground as the shield unraveled. A second bar of *Sei'shiin* streaked past his head, and Jase flinched at the heat of the near miss.

Lurching to his feet, he tightened his grip on the Blood Orb and raised it before him, unleashing a stream of *El'shaen* that snuffed the *Jeth'Jalda's* shield and incinerated the two men beneath. The points of light in his vision grew brighter, and the sounds of battle faded beneath a roaring in his ears. He felt his exhaustion beginning to seep through the insulating wall of *Jiu* he'd placed around him.

Whirling toward a wave of corruption he felt streaking in from the north, Jase opened a Veilgate as if raising a shield, and the bar of *Sei'shiin* which had been meant for him streaked through into the midst of Shadan's army far to the east. He let the Veilgate close before those on the other side could react, then sent a barrage of lightning toward those who'd attacked him.

Somewhere out in the smoke and chaos, other Dymas joined him, and an area the size of Fairimor Dome flared red with Fire. Five more threads of corruption vanished from his Awareness.

"There can't be many left," Idoman commented, and Jase extended his Awareness outward as only he could. It was dangerous in the middle of such chaos, but he wanted to know how much longer this might go on.

As the battlefield came into focus in his mind's eye, the sounds associated with the viewing merged together into a thunderous roar so great it nearly drove him to his knees. He reached deeper into the Blood Orb for strength and fought through the pain.

Only seven *Jeth'Jalda* remained, three in a linked group to the north, four fighting separately to the south. Five Shadowlancers were riding in from the east.

The four *Jeth'Jalda* to the south wouldn't last much longer, but those who'd linked their abilities could hold out indefinitely unless something happened to tip the balance. As for the Shadowlancers—creatures that had once immobilized him with fear—they were nothing more than a nuisance to him now. A nuisance he could use to his advantage.

He reigned his Awareness back in and turned to Tuari and Idoman. "You two are on defense," he said. "I'm going to finish this."

Reaching out with his Awareness once more, this time in a much more controlled probing, he located the Shadowlancers, then opened a Veilgate immediately in front of them. They rode through without breaking stride, and lances shattered as they plowed into the invisible shield of the linked *Jeth'Jalda*. The shadowspawned horses struck next, and they and their riders went down in a tangle of bodies.

Surprised and outraged, the *Jeth'Jalda* lashed out at the K'rrosha with streamers of Fire, setting them and their mounts ablaze. Horses screamed. Lancers lurched to their feet as flaming columns of ruined flesh. The shields of the *Jeth'Jalda* wavered.

Jase struck with a powerful thrust of pure Flesh, and the *Jeth'Jalda* burst apart in sprays of crimson gore.

It had been more brutal than necessary, but Jase was way past caring. The men weren't any more dead than if he'd sliced their heads off with blades of Fire or torn them apart with lightning. Dead was dead, after all. It mattered little how it was accomplished. And the brutality might serve as a reminder to any *Jeth'Jalda* who might stumble upon the carnage that they could meet a similar end. Fear was a powerful weapon, and he could use it just as well as the enemy.

"Well, that was different," Idoman commented, and Jase turned to find him staring off in the direction of the attack.

"If you are referring to the destruction of the *Jeth'Jalda*," Jase said, "I did the same thing to an army of Darklings attacking Fairimor Dome. Only that was much messier and much less controlled."

Idoman wasn't fazed by the admission. "I was referring to how you used the Veilgate to attack the *Jeth'Jalda* with the Shadowlancers. It was bloody brilliant."

Jase shrugged tiredly. "That, I just thought of."

"This battle is over," Tuari commented, her gaze on something beyond the smoke to the south. "The last of our enemies have fallen there as well. The Kelsan army is free of pursuit."

"For now," Jase said. "I doubt Shadan will let those at the rim rest for long."

"But won't he send them to Fulrath to join those there already?" Idoman asked.

"Undoubtedly," Jase answered, letting the amount of Earthpower coursing through him drop to a trickle. He would have released it completely but for the fact he would likely drop dead from exhaustion. His link to *Ta'shaen* through the Blood Orb was the only thing keeping him upright. He couldn't afford to let it go until he was somewhere safe enough to sleep for a day or two.

"As for Fulrath," Tuari said, "should we go help Gideon?"

"Yes," Jase said. "Assuming Fulrath still stands." He checked the angle of the sun. It hadn't changed much since the attack began. "How long have we been at this?"

Idoman pulled a gold watch from his pocket. "Three hours."

Jase grunted. "Feels like a week." He spotted a column of horsemen approaching through the smoke and turned to face them. "You two can open a Veilgate ahead to our army if you wish," he told Tuari. "I will ride with Captain Brommis and his men. I want a report of how they fared."

Idoman shook his head. "We're staying with you."

Tuari nodded her agreement, and they waited for Brommis to reach them.

"I wondered if we would find you here," the captain said as he neared. He was a large chested man with long brown hair and a thick mustache. Tamban blood slicked his armor from the waist down, and his horse's hide was wet and matted with it. The rest of his men were similarly covered, but their faces were bright with the killing fury of battle. Surprisingly, very few of them appeared injured, though a third of their original number was missing.

"Wondered or knew?" Jase asked, his eyes moving to the Dymas sent to accompany Brommis' men.

The captain chuckled. "Ranishan Dymas may have given me a heads-up," he answered, shooting an amused glance at the aging Riaki woman. "But I could have guessed by how quickly things quieted here. One minute all hell was stomping about, the next minute silence."

"Any number of Dymas could have accomplished the same thing," Jase told him.

"Maybe," Brommis said, but he didn't sound convinced.

"If you have an extra horse or two," Jase said, "Idoman and Tuari and I would like to ride with you."

"It would be an honor, *Mith'elre Chon*," Brommis said, and horses were brought forward by some of his men.

Jase hoisted himself into the saddle and watched as the others did the same. Then they all started forward with Jase and Captain Brommis in the lead.

"We could have hit them again after turning them back," the captain commented, "but we decided to cut our losses and hightail it back to the main group. I hope you don't disapprove."

"Not at all," Jase told him. "Cutting our losses this day was as much as we could have hoped for. Thank you for doing what you did. Turning the Tamban army back saved thousands of lives."

"Don't underestimate what you did this morning," Ranishan Dymas said as she moved her horse up alongside his. "I doubt any of us would have survived if not for your efforts."

Jase tightened his grip on the Blood Orb. "I had help."

"I can see that," she said, her gaze on what he held. "Now just imagine what you could do with one still linked to its reservoir of Power."

"I don't have to imagine," he told her, and she chuckled.

"Oh, that's right. I don't know why I keep forgetting it was you who brought the Night of Fire to Shadan's army." She looked again at the Orb in his fist. "Is that the Orb you used then?"

"No. I gave that one to Gideon to use in Fulrath. But this one..." he added, holding up the eagle's claw for her to see, "is the one Gideon Dymas used in the Soul Chamber twenty years ago to end Death's Second March." He blew out his cheeks wearily. "He cut our losses that day and paid dearly for it."

Ranishan moved her horse nearer and looked up into Jase's face. "The way you said that... you were there, weren't you?"

"You're very perceptive," he said. "Yes, I was there. And I will need to go back if the world is to be saved."

"You will—" she began but cut off as a sudden powerful tremor rippled the entire spiritual fabric of *Ta'shaen*.

Jase opened his Awareness toward it, but it vanished as quickly as it had come. Still, he'd felt enough to know it had originated at Fulrath. Judging from the faces of Ranishan and the other Dymas, they knew so as well.

"Blood of Maeon," Idoman hissed. "What was that?"

"The ward on the Seal of Fulrath," Jase answered, a feeling of dread washing over him. "The city has fallen."

# CHAPTER 2

## Limitations

"THAT'S IMPOSSIBLE!" Captain Brommis said, and around him his men nodded. Career soldiers, all of them, they were numbered among the finest Rove Riders Fulrath had ever produced. To them, Jase's announcement that Fulrath had fallen wasn't just impossible, it was unthinkable.

And yet Jase knew it was true. Even before he finished extending his Awareness toward the great city, the Earthsoul confirmed the truth of it to him. Even now, as his spiritual eyes moved over a city left desolate, Her now familiar whispering was confirming to him that he was witnessing the fulfillment of prophecy.

It wasn't a prophecy he was familiar with—he certainly didn't remember reading anything about Fulrath's demise—but the builders of the city must have foreseen this day as evidenced by the construction of the Seal and its destructive wards.

Wards, Jase realized with no small sense of awe, which had been powerful enough to leave the Freezone desolate as well. Nothing remained of Shadan's army but a carpet of weapons and armor interspersed by towers and siege engines. Everything made of flesh had vanished, burned from existence by a powerful flash of Spirit, Fire, and Flesh.

"Lord Fairimor speaks the truth," Tuari Dymas said. "The city and the Freezone are empty."

"Empty?" Captain Brommis said, disbelief heavy in his voice. "What do you mean empty?"

"As in devoid of life," Ranishan Dymas answered. "The part of Shadan's army that went to attack the city is no more. The city's wards destroyed them."

"And everyone else in the city as well," Tuari added. "Unless they somehow managed to escape ahead of the detonation."

"They escaped," Jase told them as he reined in his Awareness. "But that is a tale best told elsewhere." He glanced pointedly in the direction of the Tamban army. "I don't want to risk the enemy learning the reason for Croneam Eries' sacrifice."

Captain Brommis' eyes went wide. "He's dead?"

"He decided long ago that he would be the one to stay behind to activate the wards," Jase answered. "He told me it was his way of spitting in Soulbiter's eye one last time." He smiled, his admiration for the old general growing.

"He certainly did that," Idoman said, his spiritual eyes still fastened on Fulrath. "He destroyed a third of Shadan's army." He came back to himself and turned an excited eye on Jase. "We have a chance now," he said.

"To do what?" Tuari Dymas asked.

"To hold the plateau," Idoman answered. "We can regroup in Fulrath and launch our attacks from there. Shadan will certainly come against us. Even with two to one odds, we could hold our own for weeks."

"Yes," Captain Brommis said, but Jase waved him off.

"No," he said, drawing confused and angry looks from the Rove Riders. "Fulrath is no longer strategically important in this war. It isn't what Shadan wants anyway. His sights are set on Trian."

Captain Brommis' face pinched into a frown as he spoke. "But Lord Fairimor—"

Jase talked over the top of him. "I doubt Shadan will even go near Fulrath now," he said. "A third of his army destroyed in an instant...." He shook his head. "He will not risk that it might happen to the rest of his army." He turned a smile on Brommis and his men. "General Eries knew what he was doing when he activated the fortress' final line of defense. It's our job to implement the rest of what he had in mind."

Captain Brommis' expression softened somewhat. "Which is?"

"To join those who made it out of Fulrath and set our next line of defense at Mendel Pass."

"And if Aethon's pet Dragons use Veilgates to put his armies there ahead of us?" Ranishan Dymas asked.

"I won't let that happen," Jase told them, though in truth he had no idea how he could stop the ancient creatures from doing anything. Especially if they acted soon. He was so bloody tired right now he was having trouble sitting up straight in the saddle.

Feigning confidence, he rode on in silence, and it wasn't long before the rear of the Kelsan army came into view beyond the smokey haze left behind by the battle. He felt the brush of numerous Awarenesses and was grateful to be back in the company of so many Dymas. He may have borne the brunt of Shadan's wrath as the Kelsan army escaped, but the Dymas would need to see everyone safely off the plateau.

He needed time to recover. He also needed to meet with Joneam Eries and any of the other generals who had survived this morning's debacle so they could decide the next courses of action. God send he would have someone to meet with.

The ranks of men and horsemen bringing up the rear of the army paused as he drew near, then made way for him to pass. He found a wide range of emotions in their faces, but the most common seemed to be anger and frustration. None of them had anticipated being so soundly outmaneuvered by Shadan's forces. Nor had they imagined that they might be running for their lives in the battle's opening moments.

Jase shared their frustration, but staying to fight would have cost all of them their lives, and Shadan would have been able to march on Trian with little or no resistance. Those who were frustrated about running would come to understand that in the days ahead. And they would have the opportunity to stand and fight. But it would be according to the terms that Jase and the leaders of Kelsa's army would set and not those orchestrated by Aethon's Dragons.

*Dragons*, he thought. *How is it possible?*

Urging his horse into a trot, he continued riding in silence, ignoring the soldiers' stares as he angled toward the banners of Kelsa's generals. They were near the center of the retreating throng, and squads of Rove Riders had formed up around them, a literal wall of swords and spears formidable enough to repel any attack not wrought of *Ta'shaen*.

Ever vigilant, the Rove Riders saw him coming and opened a path into the now mobile command center. It was then that he noticed the singed edges of General Chathem's banner and found his lifeless body draped over his horse. The left side of Chathem's body was badly burned, and his uniform clung to him in scorched shreds. The bodies of two female Dymas lay over the saddles of two nearby horses.

"Blood of Maeon," Jase muttered, and the spots of light flickering in his vision intensified with the sudden rush of emotion. The protective layer of *Jiu* he'd wrapped himself in was starting to fail. He would need to conclude things here quickly lest he collapse in front of the Kelsan High Command.

"Lord Fairimor," General Gefion said as Jase rode up next to him, "I'm so glad to see you alive and unharmed."

Jase grunted. "I'm alive anyway," he said, then glanced at Chathem's body. "I'm sorry about Thad," he said. "He was a good man."

General Gefion nodded. "And a good friend."

"What happened?"

"He was killed by *Jeth'Jalda* while sending a message to Trian by way of Communicator Stone." He gestured to the bodies of the slain Dymas. "Kiria and Sofila Dymas were killed as well, and the Stone was destroyed." He turned to look at Jase, his eyes troubled.

"Is it true about Fulrath?" he asked. "I've gotten reports from some of our Dymas that the city has been destroyed."

Captains Tarn and Dennison moved nearer, and Jase motioned for Idoman to channel a ward against eavesdropping.

When it was in place, Jase answered. "The city itself is intact," he said. "The warding Croneam released when he activated the Seal destroyed only flesh. The army Shadan sent to attack Fulrath was destroyed to the last Darkling. Our men escaped via the Tunnel and will join us at Mendel Pass."

"So we are abandoning Fulrath altogether?" Captain Tarn asked.

Jase nodded. "Yes. The city no longer has any military value. And as we so painfully learned today, we cannot stand toe to toe with Shadan's army in the openness of the plateau. Our best chance will be at Mendel Pass before we fall back to Trian."

"Don't you mean *if* we fall back to Trian?" Captain Dennison asked.

"No," Jase said. "I mean when. The prophecies are clear that the final battle in this war will take place inside Trian's walls. Which means our efforts here and elsewhere aren't about defeating Shadan in battle—they are about delaying him long enough for me or Endil to rejuvenate the Earthsoul. It is my prayer that it will happen before too many more people lose their lives."

"I don't suppose the prophecies give us any hints about who will win the battle at Trian, do they?" Captain Tarn asked.

Jase gave an unamused laugh. "No, but if you are a betting man, put your money on Shadan. The odds are obviously in his favor right now."

Captains Tarn and Dennison exchanged surprised looks, and General Gefion raised an eyebrow at him. "That's not funny, Lord Fairimor," he said, making it sound as much like a rebuke as he dared.

"I wasn't trying to be funny," Jase told him. "I'm simply stating a fact." He turned and looked the general in the eyes. "A fact I intend to do something about. The odds might currently be in Shadan's favor, but I plan on changing them before the day is out."

"How?"

Jase shrugged. "I don't know yet. As always, I'm making this up as I go."

"That isn't very reassuring," General Gefion grunted.

Jase would have grinned at him if not for the lights flickering in his vision. They were gradually growing brighter and were now accompanied by pinpricks of pain in his mind. It felt as if a thousand tiny needles were being driven into his skull. He lessened the amount of Earthpower he was holding through the Blood Orb until the pinpricks faded. It was a temporary reprieve at best, but it would have to do.

"The first thing we need to do is put some more distance between us and our enemies," Jase said. "Idoman, contact our Dymas and tell them to assemble themselves at the head of our army. We'll send the wounded through Veilgates first, followed by our infantry. If they still have strength after that, they can send our cavalry through as well. If not, those on horseback will have to ride for the rendezvous point."

"And where is the rendezvous point, *Mith'elre Chon*?" Idoman asked.

"The grasslands north of the Mendel Pass Waypost," Jase told him, then turned back to Gefion and the others when he felt Idoman open his Awareness.

"Croneam sent supplies and a crew of fifteen hundred men there four days ago to set up a secondary camp. We should have everything we need to regroup and rearm."

General Gefion smiled. "The old wardog thought of everything, didn't he?"

"Yes," Jase said, "but I don't think he intended for the secondary camp to be used quite this soon."

"Are we conceding the plateau to the enemy, then?" Captain Dennison asked.

Jase shook his head, an act he immediately regretted when the pinpricks of pain flashed into daggers. Squinting, he reached up and rubbed the side of his head, then blinked the sudden rush of pain away.

"Not at all," he said once he could form the words. "We will hit Shadan and his scum just like we did when they were crossing the Allister Plains. They will pay dearly for every step they take."

"Assuming they don't just open another one of those mile-wide gates and step right into our midst," Captain Tarn said. "Or worse yet, step right into the heart of Trian."

"Something tells me there is a limit to how far they can travel using a gate that large," Jase said, and felt the reassuring tickle of the Earthsoul affirm the truth to him. "I think—I know—they were right at the limit when they sent troops to Fulrath."

"And you know this how?" Captain Tarn asked, then stiffened when Jase leveled a stare at him. The man actually swallowed nervously. "Right," he said quickly. "I'll take your word for it."

Jase grunted. "I'm so glad."

"Our Dymas have been contacted," Idoman said, drawing all eyes back to him. "They should all be at the head of our army in the next few minutes."

"Good," Jase said. "Let's join them." He leaned over and offered his hand to General Gefion. "Until we meet again, General," he said. "Good luck."

Gefion's grip was strong as he nodded. "You too, my lord."

Jase heeled his horse forward, and Idoman and Tuari followed. As word of his arrival continued to race ahead of him, Kelsa's soldiers made room for him to pass, and shouts were raised in his honor. *Hail Lord Fairimor* and *Long live the Mith'elre Chon* were but a few of them. He acknowledged the cheers with a nod of his head and continued without slowing.

He was just short of reaching the cluster of Dymas when Elam Gaufin and Taggert Enue rode up to him. Elam held the reins to a second horse, and Jase smiled when he realized they belonged to A'shan.

"Nothing against the horses of Talin," Elam said, handing over the reins. "But I thought you might want a real horse."

Jase accepted them eagerly. "I do indeed. Thank you." As he moved onto A'shan's back, he took a moment to study Elam and Taggert. Both were spattered with blood, and their uniforms bore a number of slashes edged with crimson. That they were upright and well showed that they had been healed by Dymas. The bright, wetness of the blood showed the healing was recent.

"You've been through it, I see," Jase said, indicating their uniforms.

"The Chellum army took the brunt of the Tamban attack until the cavalry arrived," Taggert said, his voice filled with frustration. "I lost a lot of good men."

"But more would have fallen if not for the cavalry," Elam said. "Thank you for sending them to our aid."

Jase studied Elam for a moment without speaking. He knew of the miraculous circumstances which had been following Elam and his men from battle to battle. To date, the Chellum Home Guard hadn't lost a single man, though many had been wounded. It was part prophecy, part faith on the part of Elam. Jase didn't want to believe that either of the two had failed.

Hesitantly, he asked, "How many of the Home Guard did we lose?"

Elam glanced sympathetically at Taggert before answering. "None. But we lost nearly a thousand from Chellum's regular army."

"I'm sorry," Jase told Taggert. "I wish there was more I could have done."

"You did more than anyone expected, my lord," Taggert told him. "As Elam said, we would have lost a lot more than we did without your help."

"Still," Jase said, "Chellum has borne more than its fair share in this war. That's why I've decided to send them back to Chellum."

"My lord—" Taggert began, but Jase silenced the protest with a raised hand.

"I know what you are going to say, but I've made up my mind. And before you think I am putting you out of harm's way, consider this: There are no guarantees Shadan won't send troops through Talin Pass to come at Trian from the east. If he does, I need someone there to stop him."

"And if they don't use Talin Pass?" Taggert asked.

"You can join us on Trian Plateau once we know for sure that will be the case." He turned to Elam.

"I'm sending the Home Guard back to Chellum to resume their duties in the palace," he said. "And this, too, has nothing to do with moving you out of harm's way. After learning of Elliott's dealings in Riak, I'm convinced the southern clans have pinned a target on House Chellum."

He looked at Tuari for confirmation. "You witnessed some of what Elliott did in your country. What do you think of this?"

"I think sending troops to Chellum is wise," Tuari said. "Lord Chellum made enemies with most of the southern clans. Clans Kyoai, Gizo, and Maridan most of all. There are rumors that all three have put a price on the young man's head."

Elam dipped his head in acceptance. "We will go wherever you send us, of course."

"Thank you," Jase said, "I'm counting on you to keep Chellum safe." He turned to Idoman. "I know you are tired, but would you do the honors?"

"It would be my pleasure," the younger man replied, "but I think it will be the last thing I am able to do today."

"We all have our limits," Jase told him. "Which is why I will need Tuari to open me a Veilgate to Trian. I would drop dead if I tried, and I need to speak with the Queen about what happened here today. First, though, I want to speak with the rest of our Dymas."

He turned A'shan toward the Dymas, but Elam moved his horse near and reached over to take Jase by the arm. "Keep the faith," he said quietly. "And we will emerge victorious."

Jase looked the Chellum captain in the eyes. "Thanks for all you have done, my friend. Not just on the battlefield but in the hearts of those who follow you. I've said it before, but Norel was right to call you *Ael'mion*. You truly are a shaper of fate. For yourself and for those around you. I sense that your ability will become even more evident in the days and weeks to come."

Elam gave an amused grunt. "And here I was hoping for words of encouragement."

Jase grinned at him, then nudged A'shan toward the gathering Dymas.

Aethon Fairimor let the Veilgate snap shut behind him, but he didn't release the dark river of *Lo'shaen* coursing through him. Not only did it sharpen his senses, it deepened the terrible rage he'd been carrying since the death of his brothers. He embraced that rage and rode the darker feelings the Void inspired within him.

Extending his Awareness to probe the way ahead, he moved down the deserted narrow street of one of Talin's nameless villages and stopped at the edge of the Freezone to study the dark grey walls of Fulrath rising against the northern sky line.

He'd felt the sudden titanic detonation of Power which had originated deep inside the city, but feeling it had in no way prepared him for what he would find in person. His army of shadowspawn was gone. Burned from existence in a manner which was as unfathomable as it was incredible.

He stared at the sea of weapons and armor in disbelief, and his rage deepened. It was accompanied by the unfamiliar feelings of worry and doubt, but he crushed both the way he planned on crushing the skull of Jase Fairimor—with a cold and merciless disinterest. Only his rage mattered now. Only blood and vengeance and death.

And yet it was hard to deny that the sudden loss of so many of his troops would hinder Death's Third March. Not only would it weaken the morale of his remaining troops, it called into question his ability to effectively lay siege to Trian.

He clenched his hands into fists. More troops would be needed. And soon. And that meant he had two choices: One, he could pull troops from their posts in Melek. Or two, he could rely even more heavily upon the Tambans. Both were unsavory prospects with known as well as unseen risks.

With Lord Nid working to reclaim his kingdom, pulling troops from the cities they occupied would essentially give the Meleki King the victory without a fight. And that would expose the rear of Death's Third March to attack when, not if, Lord Nid decided to come to the aid of Kelsa.

Turning to *Frel'mola* for even more assistance was just as dangerous. He knew enough of the female Dreadlord to understand that she would not be content until she had claimed Trian for herself, Shadan's wishes be damned.

The Tamban soldiers he and his brothers had recruited were loyal to his cause, but *Frel'mola te* Bloody *Ujen* couldn't be trusted. He would need to watch his back every step of the way.

He narrowed his eyes in disgust as he weighed his options. He didn't like it, but enlisting more Tambans would be safer than giving Melek back to Lord Nid. And he might just be able to extend his reach into Tamba. *Frel'mola* wasn't the only one who could deal treacherously with pretended allies. And this was pretense, he knew. *Frel'mola* was no more his ally than Jase Fairimor was. She was vicious, cunning, and greedy.

*But so am I*, he thought with a smile. And there was no reason the throne of Berazzel couldn't be a second seat of Power for him. It would require but a single wielding of *Sei'shiin* to destroy *Frel'mola*. And then maybe a second wielding to get rid of Shadan. If Berazzel and Trian were in his possession when the Earthsoul failed, it was very likely Maeon would allow him to keep them in the world to come. If not... well, it would be a pleasure to destroy the refleshed Dreadlords anyway.

A disturbance in the Power alerted him to the arrival of Agla'Con, and he stretched forth his Awareness to investigate. Three streets over in the same abandoned village, Jamik Hedron and Asherim Ije'kre were moving cautiously through a rent in the Veil. Several more Agla'Con were visible behind them, but they vanished as the rent snapped shut.

Both men turned and looked in his direction, and he felt the brush of their Awarenesses as they investigated the disturbance his wielding of *Lo'shaen* had created in the spiritual fabric of the Earthsoul. He didn't like either of them any more than he liked Shadan, but they'd helped Kameron and Dathan keep the Meleki army together after Jase Fairimor had scattered it during his attack with the Blood Orb all those nights ago. Now that Dathan and Kameron had been lost and the deaths of Jothor and Vedrin had reduced them to K'rrosha, these two were the highest ranking Agla'Con in the army, second only to him. It made them both useful and dangerous.

Asherim seized the Power again and the two men joined him through a rent that opened a short distance away. The rent was still open when another more powerful wielding split the air and Krev and two of his Rhiven companions strode through in human form. They moved to join Aethon at the edge of the Freezone, their golden eyes alight with curiosity as they stared out across the expanse of soldierless armor and weapons.

Asherim let his rent snap shut, and he and Jamik moved near.

"Blood of Maeon," Jamik said, his Riaki face lined with surprise. "What happened?"

Krev answered, though he addressed the comment to Aethon. "An unforseen blow to Death's Third March," the Dragon said. He sounded both envious and impressed.

"Unforeseen by us," Aethon said. "The builders of Fulrath obviously knew this day would come."

Asherim narrowed his eyes at him. "What do you mean?"

"This wasn't wrought by any living Dymas," Aethon told them. "This was a warding created centuries ago and held in place by crux points."

"Then it's possible it could have reset itself," Jamik said.

Aethon nodded. "Yes, but I think it highly unlikely."

Krev turned his yellow gaze on him. "What makes you say that?"

"Just a hunch," he answered, then turned to look at the Dragon. "But it matters not. Fulrath was to be nothing more than a layover, anyway. Trian is the real target, my friend. Let's not forget that."

He turned his attention back to the dark walls rising in the distance. "Croneam Eries may have struck a blow to Death's Third March, but he struck himself one as well. His fortress is empty. His troops have fled through Veilgates or were destroyed as surely as those whose armor lies before us. Kelsa paid dearly for this surprise."

"They paid dearly at the rim as well," Asherim said, running his hand over his blood-red Mohawk. "Their army is in full retreat. Even now the survivors are fleeing through Veilgates or riding hellbent for the western rim. And the so-called *Mith'elre Chon*," he said, twisting the title derisively, "is nowhere to be found. We believe he fled with the rest of his rabble."

"But not before dealing a significant blow of his own," Krev said, his voice deathly cold in spite of the anger in his eyes. "He killed another one of my brethren and injured two others. I hunted him all morning with no success. Scoff at his title all you want, but that boy is the most dangerous enemy I've ever faced."

"He won't be troubling us again for a few days," Aethon said. "Not after the amount of Power he wielded this morning. He will need to rest before he comes at us again, figure of prophecy or not."

"Good," Asherim said. "Because our Power-wielders are at the breaking point as well. Some of them will need a week to recover, if they live through the healing so many of them need."

"Heal those you can," Aethon told him. "Kill the others and bring them back as Refleshed. I want Agla'Con in the Pit working nonstop to see that it happens."

He turned to Jamik. "Take the Agla'Con under your command to Kunin. There are warrens near the *chorazin* gate we discovered there. Empty them. We will replace the shadowspawn we lost today with the demonspawn our *Shel'tui* cousins have been breeding."

"Won't the *Shel'tui* resist?" Jamik asked.

"Undoubtedly," Aethon said. "But they belong to Maeon and would do well to remember that. Reflesh all those who are destroyed."

The aging Riaki gave a bow. "Yes, my lord."

"What of Fulrath?" Krev asked.

Aethon studied the dark walls a moment before speaking. "Leave it. It is no longer a threat to us. Our next battle lies to the west. Mendel Pass, most likely. I want our army rested and resupplied."

He seized a river of *Lo'shaen* and tore a hole in the Veil. It opened in a wide cobblestoned street lined with multistoried buildings. It was night, and lamps glowed on street corners and in a few of the windows. In the distance a glittering palace rose against the backdrop of stars.

"Is that what I think it is?" Asherim asked.

"Yes," Aethon answered, then looked to Krev and his companions. "Come. It's time to pay a visit to *Frel'mola*."

# CHAPTER 3

## Myths Dispelled

"I ASSURE YOU, MY LADY," Ammorin said gently, "that she can be trusted." His large weathered face was calm, but there was a hint of pleading in his eyes. Beside Ammorin, Pattalla nodded his agreement.

Brysia studied them both for a moment, then turned to Elison to find him frowning. Undoubtedly he was thinking the same thing she was: *Trust a Dragon? Had the world gone insane?*

Across from Elison, Talia wore a worried frown, but Brysia suspected it had little to do with the Dragon. She was concerned about Jase. The distant look in her eyes showed she was trying to feel for Jase through the *sei'vaiya* love-bond.

She watched Talia for a moment longer, then returned her attention to Galiena'ei to ul'Morgranon. The woman—the Rhiven, as she called herself—stood a few feet away, wrapped in a ward against eavesdropping which Ammon had put around her. She seemed unconcerned by the cautionary measure and stood with her head high, a patient smile on her face. Her striking yellow eyes were bright as she waited for the ward to be dropped.

"I do not doubt your sincerity, my friends," Brysia told the Dainin. "But I'm having trouble getting my head around this. We trusted Dragons once, and they betrayed us. The world was nearly destroyed because of their involvement in the wars leading up to the First Cleansing. And now their involvement with Shadan's army... it is most troublesome. Galiena's arrival at this time is even more so. What if her motives aren't as pure as she claims?"

"But she is a Dymas," Ammorin insisted. "She opened her mind to me. I saw her thoughts."

"All of them?" Brysia asked. "Or just those she wanted you to see?"

"A Dymas can hide nothing when opened to a Communal link," Pattalla said. "Mindwards are breached; everything is laid bare."

"For humans," Brysia countered, still hesitant to believe that the creature standing a few feet away might be an ally. "We know nothing of the abilities of Dragons. They kept their thoughts and intentions hidden from our ancestors, and the Old World was destroyed as a result."

"I understand your concern," Ammorin began but cut off as a Veilgate opened in front of the fireplace. Everyone in the room turned toward it as Jase moved through from the grassy expanse of Talin Plateau. Behind him stood a Riaki woman and a young Chellum soldier who held A'shan's bridle. They vanished from view as the gate slid shut.

Brysia was on her feet and moving toward her son in an instant, concern and relief washing through her in turns. Talia was even faster and reached Jase before Brysia could take more than a couple of steps. Jase smiled as she neared and opened his arms to receive her. He grunted as Talia hugged him tightly, then kissed her when she looked up at him.

Brysia moved up to her son. "Thank the Creator you're all right," she told him. "After we lost contact with General Chathem, we feared the worst."

"And you were right to do so," he said, sounding so tired she was amazed he was still upright. Talia heard it too and took a step back to look him over. Brow furrowed, she bit her lip in concern, tempted, it seemed to Brysia, to heal him.

"General Chathem is dead," Jase continued. "So is Croneam Eries."

Brysia felt as if she'd been kicked in the stomach. "Croneam? How?"

"Fulrath has fallen," Jase said, his bitterness evident. "Our army is in full retreat." He looked as if he might say more, but his eyes fell on Galiena, and he stiffened. The Blood Orb flared brightly in his fist.

"What is she doing here?" he asked, his voice suddenly edged with death. Face hard, he took a step forward.

Ammorin and Pattalla came to their feet in a rush, their large hands raised in a placating manner. "It's not what you think, Lord Fairimor," Pattalla said. "She's one of us. Please release the Power."

Jase turned a disbelieving stare on the Dainin. "What do you mean, one of us?"

"They claim she is a Dymas, my son," Brysia said, putting a hand on Jase's arm. The Blood Orb dimmed in his fist as he turned to look at her.

"You said *claim*. Do you doubt them?"

"I don't know what to think," she answered. "Maeon's power has grown these past few weeks. Toss in creatures out of legend, and it's possible that even the *Nar'shein Yahl* can be deceived."

"Possible," Jase said, "but not likely." Tucking the Blood Orb in his pocket, he stepped around Brysia and moved toward the raven-haired beauty standing within the ward. Galiena's eyes glimmered like Kelsan Marks as she watched him approach. If she was afraid to be face to face with the *Mith'elre Chon*, it didn't show.

"Please release the ward, Ammorin," Jase said. "I would speak with our guest."

A moment later Galiena went to one knee and lowered her head in respect. "It is a pleasure to meet you, *Mith'elre Chon*," she said, then looked up expectantly.

Jase offered his hand, and helped Galiena to her feet. Smiling, she met his gaze without blinking. She was tall for a woman, even taller than Talia. Knowing *what* she was made her seem taller still. Brysia held her breath as she waited to see what would happen.

Jase didn't release her hand, and the two stared at one another in silence for several moments. Finally Jase said, "You know who I am."

"My people might live apart from mankind, but we are not ignorant of world events. We know of your dealings in Melek and elsewhere. We know of the prophecies that name you as the one who is to rejuvenate the world. I have come to pledge my support to you. I have come to serve the *Mith'elre Chon*." She bowed her head. "If you will allow it, of course."

"I might," Jase said. "But first I want answers. And I want proof that you are what you claim to be."

Galiena smiled. "Of course, but first you must allow me to heal you. You are too weak for a Communal link. The weight of what I would share would be too much for you." She glanced at where he'd tucked away the Orb. "Even with the aid of the Blood Orb."

Brysia took a step forward, panic rushing through her. They couldn't allow Galiena to use the Power on Jase. She might kill him instead of healing him. It might be the very purpose for which she had come: To destroy the *Mith'elre Chon*.

"I cannot allow that," she said, failing to keep her mistrust from her voice. "Talia or Ammorin or Pattalla can heal him."

"It's all right, Mother," Jase said, his eyes never leaving Galiena's. "I want to believe she is telling the truth."

*And if she's not?* Brysia thought. Body tense with worry, she went cold inside as Galiena reached up and took Jase's head in her hands. Talia stepped near and took Brysia's arm, and she glanced over to find the young woman's face pinched with fear. "This isn't a good idea," she whispered, but she made no move to intervene.

"Watch carefully," Galiena said to Ammorin and Pattalla. "I'm going to show you the highest form of healing. Like *El'shaen te sherah*, it uses all Seven Gifts of Power. In this wielding, Flesh and Spirit are woven together, then used to bind the rest. Anything less than all seven would leave Lord Fairimor unconscious for days or weeks. A traditional healing using Flesh alone would kill him outright."

She turned a critical eye on Jase. "You've pushed yourself beyond the limits set by the Earthsoul. Honestly, I do not know how you didn't burn the ability to wield completely out of yourself. I can feel what you did, how close you came to dying from such an obvious overexertion of your abilities. You are lucky I came when I did, young man. Had anyone else attempted to heal you, Maeon would have had his victory."

Jase smiled at her, seemingly amused. "That sounded like something Norel would say," he told her. "Remind me to tell you about her after this is over."

The corners of Galiena's lips curled in a smile. "I will. Now brace yourself. This might take your breath away."

Jase stiffened as if he'd been stabbed, and Brysia took an unconscious step forward. Only Talia's hand on her arm stopped her from taking another. She took the young lady's hand in hers and watched as Jase's body jarred several times and his hands clenched into fists. After one final convulsion, he inhaled sharply, then relaxed, and Galiena put her arm around him to steady him.

"It's not as much as you deserve," she said. "But anything more would leave you incapacitated for a week. As it is, you won't be back to full strength for at least a day, maybe two."

Smiling, Jase put his arm around Galiena and allowed her to help him to a nearby sofa. Talia raced to his side as he settled in.

"Are you all right?" she asked, reaching up to touch his face.

"Just a little woozy is all," he said, then looked up at Galiena who had taken a step back to make way for Talia. "Thank you," he told her, gesturing to the chair across from him. "Please, have a seat. I am most eager to hear your story."

"And I am eager to give it," the Rhiven said as she seated herself. Straight-backed, and head held high, she placed her arms on the armrests and smiled serenely.

For the second time since meeting her, Brysia had the unmistakable feeling she was looking at a Queen.

"Open your Awareness, my young friend," Galiena said, "and you shall have the proof you seek."

Jase chuckled. "I already have proof," he said. "Now I want answers."

Focusing on the warm spot in her mind that was Jase, Talia felt the Communal link between him and Galiena take shape. She wasn't sure if the *sei'vaiya* would allow her to hear what was being communicated through the link, but she might be able to get a sense of things simply by what Jase was feeling.

When he glanced over at her and smiled, she knew he had sensed what she was thinking.

Galiena raised an eyebrow in wonder. "A *sei'vaiya* love-bond," she said, directing the comment to Talia. "How remarkable." She smiled warmly, then looked back to Jase.

Talia could feel how eager he was, but that eagerness morphed quickly into surprise and then to complete and utter shock. It was followed by a sense of remorse which grew into anger. That anger continued to fester for several minutes, but with it came a deep and expanding resolve. This was both good and bad, Talia realized. And she could feel that Jase believed what he was hearing.

A moment later Talia felt the severing of the link.

Jase lowered his head toward Galiena. "Thank you, Galiena'ei to ul'Morgranon, Queen of the Rhiven," he said, his tone formal. "I welcome whatever aid you and your people can give us."

He let his eyes move over the rest of those in the room. "She is what she claims," he said. "And you have no idea how wrong we have been about her and her people. What little we know of them from our histories has been corrupted. Malicious lies and half-truths which were obviously written by those who serve Maeon."

He gestured for everyone to sit. "Come. I want you to hear what Galiena revealed to me. And I want you to hear it from her."

They did as they were told. Brysia settled in next to Jase and Talia. Elison took a seat to the right of Galiena. Ammorin and Pattalla sat cross-legged on the floor to her left. Jase motioned for Gavin to join them also.

"We will need a ward against eaves—" Jase began, but cut off as a Veilgate opened near the fireplace. Gideon strode through from what appeared to be a military camp, and Elliott and Seth followed. A small, grey-haired old woman with bright blue eyes came next. She was followed by two Shizu in *komouri* black.

The gate slid shut the moment they were through, and the entire group paused to take in the scene before them. Their surprise at finding a Dragon in the Fairimor home was evident in their faces, but the only other reaction that Talia could see was the Shizu placing their hands on their sword hilts. It was possible that Gideon had embraced the Power, but she had no way of knowing unless things erupted into Fire.

"I trust there is an explanation for her presence," Gideon said. His eyes as he studied Galiena were both curious and wary. And understandably so, considering he'd just been battling Galiena's Rhiven brothers.

"There is," Jase answered. "And you are just in time to hear it."

As Gideon approached, Galiena rose to meet him. Face smooth, she offered her hand in greeting. "It is a pleasure to meet you, Guardian of Kelsa," she said, gripping Gideon's hand and offering a deep bow. "Your legacy as *El'kali* is well regarded by my people."

The look of curiosity in Gideon's eyes deepened. "Thank you, lady..."

"In the Old Tongue I am called, *Galiena'ei to ul'Morgranon*," she said. "Please, call me Galiena."

"Or Queen Morgranon," Jase added. "If you prefer using a title."

Gideon nodded. "So," he said, "you are the Queen of the Dragons."

"We prefer the name Rhiven," she said. "Dragon is the name given to us by men."

"My apologies if I offended," Gideon said.

Galiena smiled as she released his hand, then turned her golden-eyed gaze on Seth. "I know a great deal about you as well, *shent ze'deyar*. Or do you prefer the title of *Zele'elre Shizu?*"

Seth's smile didn't reach his eyes. "Those names are of Riaki origin," he told her. "Captain Lydon will suffice for as long as we are in Kelsa."

Galiena nodded. "As you wish, Captain." She returned to her chair and settled in.

Elliott helped the gray-haired Dymas ease herself onto one of the sofas, then took a seat next to her. The two Shizu moved to stand behind them, dark eyes vigilant.

"I'll get right to it, then," Galiena said. "In A.F. 1000, my people and I arrived in this world through a type of Veilgate called *Eloth en ol'shazar to eryth*. Translated, it means 'The Paths of Life and Creation.' It is the same type of gateway Elderon used to bring the Elvan people to this world during the Second Creation. Obviously, they allow travel between any of the worlds Elderon has created."

"The Elvan Histories make mention of them," Gideon said. "If I understood what I read, they allow passage when a Veilgate is opened into Eliara or Con'Jithar and then a second Gate is opened from beyond the Veil into another world."

"It's a bit more complicated than that," Galiena said, "but close enough for today's purpose. But be warned, it takes more strength in the Power than mortal man can possess." She looked pointedly at Jase. "And that includes you, my young friend."

Jase grinned at the Rhiven Queen, and Talia felt a powerful, unmistakable feeling of affection flowing through the love-bond. Under any other circumstance Talia would have been jealous of the feeling, but this was the kind of love reserved for a mentor. She'd felt the same thing from Jase when he'd been in the presence of Norel.

"I have no intention of opening a gate to another world," he told her. "Especially if it means I need to touch the afterlife first."

"Who opened the way for you to come here?" Ammorin asked, his dark brown eyes filled with wonder.

"My father and a number of our elders," Galiena said. "And they perished because of it." She spoke matter-of-factly, her face smooth, but Talia sensed the terrible bitterness beneath the facade. Only then did she realize it was coming to her from Jase. He had felt all of Galiena's emotions during their Communing, and the Rhiven's pain had become his and was seeping through the *sei'vaiya*. "They were overrun by demons as our world was destroyed by Maeon."

"So the reenactment performed during the Festival of the Dragon is true?" Talia asked.

"There is some truth in it," Galiena said. "Most of what is written is a lie. It was written by an Agla'Con, Tarach Hadishar, and was originally published in the *Eli'shunda Kor*."

"I read the *Eli'shunda Kor* from cover to cover just last week searching for prophecies that might involve Jase," Talia told her. "And I didn't see it in there. Are you sure we are talking about the same book?"

"I have an unabridged copy in my personal library," Galiena answered. "Your copy, it contained some three hundred pages or so?"

"About that, yes."

"The unabridged version has nearly seven hundred. And every page filled with corruption, lies, and nonsense. The Dragon Day ceremony is no exception." She looked to Jase. "Permission to embrace the Power?"

"You don't need to ask," Jase told her. "We are here to be enlightened. You do whatever you feel is necessary."

"Thank you," Galiena said, and a Veilgate opened a short distance away to reveal a library. A massive leather-bound volume stamped and carved with various Old World symbols slid off one of the shelves and was pulled through the opening by an invisible grip of Air. A second, much smaller book followed, and the two settled in Galiena's lap as the Veilgate slid shut.

"This copy of the *Eli'shunda Kor*," she said, opening to a page near the middle of the larger book, "is written in the Old Tongue. Are there any here who can read it?"

"I can," Brysia said, and Galiena rose and handed her the book.

"I wrote the translation in the margin. Please tell me if you think it is accurate."

Everyone waited silently as Brysia compared Galiena's translation against the original. After a moment, she nodded and began to read.

> *It is during this time that Dragons enter the land. They come as refugees, claiming to have been driven from their home world by the Lord of Darkness.*
>
> *The Dragons are welcomed into the world of men. They are peaceable and friendly, truly the refugees they claim to be. The people of the land accept them as friends.*
>
> *But behold, deceit lies in the hearts of the Dragons. They seek dominion over those who took them in. Winter covers the land as the Dragons rise up in war, striking down the defenseless and murdering the innocent.*
>
> *But lo, brave men and women rush to the aid of the Dymas. With swords and weapons of Earthpower they strike back against the evil serpents, killing many and driving them from the land.*

"Sounds familiar, yes?" Galiena asked, then held up the smaller book. "This is the personal journal of Dymas Xavelor Palinshar, and the following excerpt is dated the 26th of Morshe, A.F. 2016." She paused for emphasis. "The one year anniversary of the First Cleansing." Opening to a page near the middle, she read:

> *It was during that time that the Rhiven entered the land. They came as refugees, having been driven from their home world by the Lord of Darkness.*
>
> *The Rhiven were welcomed into the world of men. They were peaceable servants of the Earthsoul, eager to share their knowledge of Ta'shaen.*
>
> *For a thousand years, men and Rhiven lived in peace.*
>
> *But alas, darkness lay hidden in the hearts of some men, and they sought dominion over those who served them. With winter covering the land, those who took upon themselves the name of Agla'Con rose up against the Rhiven in war.*

> *But lo, brave men and women rushed to the aid of the Rhiven.*
> *With weapons of Earthpower they struck back against the servants*
> *of darkness, cleansing them from the land.*

Silence ensued as everyone in the room considered the discrepancy between the two texts. Finally Gideon spoke.

"Are you saying that the First Rise of the Agla'Con was an attack against the Rhiven?"

Galiena nodded. "Yes. And while many Rhiven perished before Xavelor and his fellow Dymas came to our aid, it wasn't nearly as devastating as the Second Rise of the Agla'Con." She shook her head sadly. "For seven hundred years the Agla'Con gathered in secret. Guided by Maeon. Mentored by some of my people who had forsaken the light and turned to the shadow. I didn't know it at the time, but my own brother, Krev'ei to ul'Morgranon taught many of them how to wield *Lo'shaen*."

Tears gathered in the corners of her eyes, but her face remained smooth and her chin high. "In A.F. 2790, they attacked. It was a widespread, carefully coordinated, simultaneous strike against my people. Before we realized what was happening, thousands of Rhiven had been slaughtered. Only two hundred and twenty-six of us survived. We fled the mainland continents and took refuge on a cluster of tropical islands far out in the Drinisis Ocean. It was there that we waited out the Gathering and the destruction of the Old World."

"And the Second Creation?" Gideon asked. "Did you witness it in person?"

"Some of it," Galiena said, and a profound reverence fell over her. Her golden eyes sparkled as she added, "Elderon was magnificent."

Talia's heart leapt in her chest. "You saw him?"

Galiena smiled. "I spoke with him. He counseled me to keep my people apart from the new races until they were sufficiently established. I agreed, but before we left, I was privileged to witness the Solemnizing of Imor and Temifair." She glanced around meaningfully.

"I watched as Elderon wrought the *chorazin* of this beautiful palace as a gift for the child Fairimor."

"And then?" Gideon asked.

"I returned to my people and we waited while the nations established themselves. Five hundred years after the Solemnizing, we made our return. After a conversation very much like this one—in this very room, I might add—we were welcomed by the ruling families of Trian and Andlexces."

She shook her head sadly. "But it didn't matter. The superstitions brought about by the Dragon Day verses in the *Eli'shunda Kor* were too much to overcome. Hundreds of years of performances had done their work. In the minds of the people we were monsters. We were feared and mistrusted by everyone outside the ruling families. Even worse, it wasn't long before the people's mistrust of the Rhiven began to transfer to the Fairimors. That was compounded when my brother and those who follow him resurfaced as the leaders of a growing number of Agla'Con."

"Tell me more of this brother," Gideon said. "I assume he is among those fighting for Shadan."

"He is," Galiena said, and there was a definite edge of anger in her words. A rush of anger reached Talia through the love-bond and she looked over to find Jase frowning.

"Apparently," Galiena continued, "he joined—I suppose I should say *rejoined*—the cause after he was freed from his imprisonment by Aethon Fairimor."

The feeling of anger in the *sei'vaiya* spiked, and with it came a sense of frustration. "That was my fault," Jase told them all. "When I defeated Aethon in the Meleki camp by shoving him through a Veilgate, he ended up at Earth's End. It is a frozen continent on the northernmost tip of the world. Literally uninhabitable by anyone other than the Rhiven."

"Even then, we require shelter from the fiercest storms," Galiena said. "The hostile environment makes an excellent place for a prison. Those of my brethren who had given themselves over to Maeon have been held there for the past eighteen hundred years."

"Held?" Gideon asked. "How?"

"With *da'shova* collars," the Rhiven Queen answered. "After they revealed themselves as traitors in A.S. 531, I was forced to sever them from the Power. They were sheltered and fed, and we checked on them monthly to provide for them, but they were no longer allowed to wield."

"Why didn't you just kill them?" Seth asked. "Instead of going to such lengths to keep them alive."

Galiena was quiet for some time before answering. Finally she said, "Because they are my people, my family, and I love them." She sighed. "For eighteen centuries I've held out hope that they might be brought back to the light. I see now that my hope was in vain."

"You said earlier that they resurfaced in A.S. 531," Brysia said, "Where were they during the eight hundred years between then and Second Rise of the Agla'Con?"

"I do not know where they waited out the Great Destruction," Galiena said. "Or where they were during the Second Creation. I can only tell you that they destroyed any chance we had of rejoining the races of men."

"Well, now they are working to destroy the world," Gideon told her, and Talia flinched at the sharpness in his voice. "They must be stopped, and I have no intention of taking them alive. There will be no *da'shova* collars this time, Queen of the Rhiven. I mean to kill them all."

"I know," Galiena said. "That is why I have come."

Gideon's eyes narrowed. "To stop me?"

"To help you."

# CHAPTER 4

## *Reluctant Allies*

WITH NO SMALL SENSE OF WONDER, Gideon watched Galiena'ei to ul' Morgranon and tried to come to terms with what he had learned. This woman, this creature of legend, was a living, breathing witness to the history of the world. And not this world alone, but the Rhiven home world as well. It was mind-boggling.

"There is more I would like to know," he told her. "I'm sure the others would as well."

Galiena spread her arms in invitation. "Such as?"

Gideon grunted. "Everything. How old you are. What your abilities are with the Power. What your true form is—I saw your brethren take the form of the serpents of myth and legend. How your world was destroyed. Anything you would like to share."

"The glittering serpents you saw on the battlefield are our true form. We are at our strongest in the Power when we take that shape. But as you have already guessed, we are shape-changers. Those of us who serve the Earthsoul can take any form we wish so long as it is a creation of Elderon. Shadowspawn and demons are forbidden. On our own world we preferred the true form—what you call a Dragon—but here we walk as humans. We do not breathe fire, though we can wield it in its purest form."

She glanced meaningfully at Seth's swords. "Your *kamui* blades were forged in Fire wrought by my people. If I might see the blades sometime, I can tell you the name of he who forged them."

She looked back to Gideon. "I saw the ladies in the room bristle when you mentioned my age, but Rhiven women are not offended by that question. We are proud of our age. I have walked this world for forty-three centuries. And before that another thirty-seven on my home world."

"Seven thousand years," Talia whispered in awe, then blushed when she realized she had spoken aloud.

"Seven thousand and eight, to be exact," Galiena said, seemingly amused by Talia's surprise. "Not many beings can claim to be older than the world itself."

"Not many beings can claim to have lived on more than one, either," Gideon added. "What happened on your home world to bring about destruction?"

"To put it simply," Galiena said, her voice steady in spite of the sorrow in her eyes, "our savior, the equivalent of your *Mith'elre Chon*, failed to rejuvenate the soul of our world. The Veil collapsed. Con'Jithar swallowed everything."

There was a horrified silence as everyone considered what they'd heard. Talia glanced over at Jase, and he took her hand reassuringly. There was no sign of what he might be thinking, but Gideon could posit a couple of guesses. Jase had no intention of failing in his duties as the *Mith'elre Chon*, but there was always that possibility. And now he knew of a surety what awaited them all if he did.

"What happened to him?" Talia asked. Her hand was tight on Jase's, and concern lined her face.

"That, I cannot speak about," the Rhiven Queen said. "It has been forbidden by Elderon. Knowing too much about our fate could alter the fate of this world by influencing the choices Jase must make in the near future. He must act on his own, without insight into the choices of others."

She turned her gaze on Jase, and her tone was apologetic as she continued. "That is the part of my mind which is warded even when Communing. I know you sensed it. Thank you for not pressing me on it. Thank you even more for not mistrusting me when you sensed it was there."

Jase smiled. "I thought about it," he told her. "But I've learned the hard way that ignoring the whisperings of the Earthsoul can be hazardous to my health."

"So the Earthsoul confirmed Galiena's faithfulness?" Brysia asked.

Jase nodded. "She did."

"That's good enough for me," Brysia said. "I'm sorry for my suspicions, Galiena. Please forgive me."

Galiena gave a light, pleasant laugh. "Not at all," she said. "I would have questioned your sanity if you hadn't been suspicious."

Brysia turned to the Dainin, her face hard. "So, you either missed seeing the part of her mind that was warded or you lied to me. Which is it?"

Ammorin shrugged. "Considering how your suspicions of Galiena have been rendered moot, I would prefer not to answer."

"So what do we do now?" Gideon asked, heading off whatever comment Brysia was preparing for the Dainin. "We have a war to fight. One that, at the moment, we are losing."

Brysia eyed Ammorin a moment longer to show she wasn't going to forget what he'd done, then turned to Gideon. "What happened at the rim?" she asked. "We lost communications with General Chathem, but what little we heard was bleak. We learned from Jase that Generals Chathem and Eries are dead and that Fulrath is lost. How on earth did it fall so quickly?"

"Dragon Gates," Gideon said. "At least that's what those out at the rim are calling them."

"That's what the people of the Old World called them, too," Galiena said. "They were used during the First Cleansing to surround the armies of the Agla'Con in what amounted to our final battle with them. They can only be opened by Rhiven in true form. They are really nothing more than an extremely large Veilgate, but as you saw at the rim, they can be *rent* open as well."

"Your brothers appeared to breathe fire at the rending," Gideon told her.

"For show only," she said. "They were trying to frighten you."

"Well, they bloody well did that," Elliott said, speaking for the first time. "But that wasn't nearly as terrifying as fifty thousand Tambans coming upon us as one. We're lucky any of us made it out of there alive."

Gideon gave Elliott a disapproving frown due to the sharpness of his tone, then looked back to Brysia. "A second Dragon Gate was opened to Fulrath," he said. "They filled the eastern side of the Freezone in an instant. Cultists, shadowspawn, K'rrosha—an army of darkness seventy thousand strong. We were quickly overwhelmed."

"How long did you hold?" Elison asked.

"Long enough to get everyone out through the Tunnel and by Veilgate. But only just. The fortress was crawling with the enemy as I took the last group out. Moments later, Croneam activated the wards of the Seal." He shook his head in awe at the memory.

"We watched the detonation from afar," he continued. "I've never seen anything like it. In one gigantic flash, the city and the Freezone were cleared of the enemy. Nothing survived."

"And the city itself?" Elison asked.

"Intact," Gideon answered, "but no longer important to us strategically. For two reasons. One: the Tunnel has been permanently sealed so there is no way out of the fortress but by Veilgate. And two: Shadan will not risk a second attack on Fulrath. Not after suffering such heavy losses during the first attempt."

"Did the wards reset themselves?" Brysia asked.

"No," Gideon told her. "But Shadan doesn't know that. He'll order his troops to march straight for Mendel Pass."

"What's to keep Krev and the rest of the Rhiven loyal to him from opening another Dragon Gate directly into the midst of our army?" Brysia asked. "Or worse, directly into Trian itself?" Her face was serene, but Gideon heard the fear in her voice.

"Those of my people who have come with me will deal with my traitorous brothers," Galiena said, and Gideon stiffened at what she'd just implied.

"How many are with you?" he asked. "And where are they?"

"Forty-one," she answered. "They are waiting for me in the Fairimor Gardens. I didn't think it wise to bring them all into the palace until I'd spoken with the High Queen. And some of those with me wished to pay respect to those of your family who have gone before."

"Your people are welcome in our home," Brysia told her. "I'll have the *Bero'thai* escort them in."

Galiena gave a nod of gratitude. "Thank you." She turned her attention back to Gideon. "We needn't worry about the enemy opening a Dragon Gate for a few more days yet. Not only will my brothers be exhausted from their part in the battle, but there are limits on distance for Dragon Gates. To put it simply, they are out of range."

"And what is the range?" Elison asked.

"Fifty miles," Jase answered. "Give or take a few. They were right at the limit this morning when they sent troops to Fulrath."

Galiena seemed impressed. "You felt that, did you?"

"Everyone on the plateau felt it," Jase told her. "Or rather, they felt the earthquake it caused. When the second gate shook the plateau, I figured it had to do with distance."

The Rhiven Queen nodded. "You are perceptive," she told him, then locked eyes with Gideon once more. "I will lead the attack against my brothers," she said. "You are welcome to join me, of course, but it will be dangerous. We will need to wait for them to start the rending before we strike. They will be most vulnerable at that moment, and it will allow us to know exactly where they are, which will make hitting them easier."

Gideon saw the wisdom in the plan and nodded his approval. "And those who aren't in the act of opening the Dragon Gate?" he asked.

"They will present more of a challenge," Galiena said. "Krev most of all. He is among the most powerful of all the Rhiven, and he will die before he allows himself to be collared again."

"Which suits our purposes just fine," he told her, "because as I said earlier, I have no intention of taking him alive."

"Regardless of what he believes our intentions to be," Galiena said, "he will be most formidable. If we encounter him on the battlefield, it would be best if you let me engage him. I know how he thinks. I know his tendencies in using the Power. Of all the Rhiven, I have the best chance of defeating him."

There was more to Galiena's words than was spoken, and Gideon studied her for a moment without speaking, unsure if he should voice his suspicion. Finally he said, "Krev is your brother, isn't he? Literally. You share the same blood."

"We are twins," Galiena answered. "A rarity among Rhiven births. Even more rare was the fact that we were conjoined and had to be separated by Healers. Our birth was heralded as an omen of destruction by some, a promise of redemption by others." She shook her head sadly. "It seems the first was correct—for my world at least. Here, I hope the second theory will come to pass."

"And to do that..." Talia began softly.

"I must kill my brother," Galiena finished. "Those who came with me will support me in this, but the majority of my people will want to see him and the others collared and returned to Earth's End. When one's race is facing extinction, it is difficult to justify capital punishment."

"Even if those who are sentenced to die are working to bring about that extinction?" Brysia asked.

Galiena smiled tiredly. "That was my argument as well," she said. "And it convinced those who came with me that it is our only course of action. But the rest of my people didn't see it that way and have chosen to sit this one out."

"How many of your people remain?" Talia asked.

"Including the forty-one who came with me, one hundred and seventy-eight. Those who had been collared and exiled numbered twenty-seven. I'm not sure how many remain."

"Nineteen," Jase said, and everyone turned to look at him in surprise. "At least that's how many were hunting me on the battlefield. There were twenty to start, but I killed one and wounded two others."

"That sounds about right," Gideon said. "I killed one in Zedik Pass, and our spotters reported that Norel destroyed six."

"Nineteen it is," Galiena told them. "We'll assume that the two Jase wounded have been healed by now. I'd rather estimate high and be pleasantly surprised."

"What will you need from us?" Jase asked.

"Nothing but your blessing," the Rhiven Queen answered. "You have enough to worry about with Shadan and his armies. Let me and my people deal with our traitorous brethren."

Gideon watched Galiena with curiosity, not sure how much he should hope for from her. "And when that is accomplished," he asked. "Then what?"

"We shall see," she said. "Those of my people who opposed my involvement in stopping Krev are even more opposed to the Rhiven becoming involved in Death's Third March."

"But the Rhiven are already involved," Joselyn said, and Gideon turned to find the old woman watching Galiena with anger in her bright blue eyes. Not anger toward Galiena specifically, but anger at the situation. She'd engaged the Rhiven in battle, and had nearly lost her life because of it.

"Your brethren," Joselyn continued, "facilitated an attack that ended with the routing of our armies and the destruction of Fulrath. Dozens of my sisters in the Power were cut down by *Lo'shaen* wielded not by Shadan or his minions, but by Rhiven."

"And I will make amends for all of it," Galiena said. "But I cannot compel my people to arms any more than Brysia Fairimor can. The forty-one who came with me will have to suffice. They came to your aid against the wishes of the rest of our kind. And they did it knowing that many of them might not survive. Considering that they comprise nearly a quarter of our dwindling population, it wasn't an easy decision for them."

"And the rest of your people," Gideon said softly, "do they understand if we fail in our efforts to rejuvenate the Earthsoul that extinction will find them anyway?"

Galiena's expression was pained as she answered. "They do."

"And they still insist on sitting this out?"

"It is a complicated issue for them," the Rhiven Queen replied. "I don't expect you to understand. Some of my people still harbor resentment toward mankind. They feel betrayed by you. A few even hate you enough that they are willing to die if it means the end of your race as well." She pinched her lips together in frustration. "Others believe the claims made by a few of the more eccentric among my people that we will move on to another world should Con'Jithar truly arrive here. They are delusional, of course. We haven't the strength to open *Eloth en ol'shazar to eryth*. Even if we did, I don't know where we would go."

From the corner of his eye, Gideon saw Brysia shaking her head. "I would have believed a race as ancient and noble as yours would be above harboring such petty feelings."

"Most of us are," Galiena said. "But others have spent millennia brooding over lost opportunities. Whatever wisdom they could have gained has been overshadowed by anger and regret and jealousy. The only thing that has kept them from joining Krev and the others is they hate Maeon even more than they hate you." She dipped her head in apology. "I'm sorry, but the Rhiven aren't all that different from humans, in spite of our age."

"We'll take what we can get," Jase said, drawing all eyes to him. "Thank you for bringing as many as you did."

"It was their choice *Mith'elre Chon*," she said. "As I said, I cannot compel my people to do something against their will."

"All the more reason to thank them," Jase said. "And I would like to do so in person. As soon as we finish here, we will bring them into the palace through a Veilgate. There's no need to make them walk all the way in from the gardens."

"Thank you, Lord Fairimor. I'm sure they will appreciate that."

"Not as much as I appreciate them coming to help," he told her, then turned to look at Gideon.

"I saw the rendezvous point through the Veilgate you used to come here," he said. "What is the status?"

"Joneam Eries is there with the rest of the High Command," Gideon answered. "They will see to our battle plan while our Dymas tend to the wounded. About half of our troops arrived from the plateau through Veilgates before the strength of our Dymas gave out. The rest, mostly cavalry, will arrive in the next couple of days. Sooner if they ride hard."

"And those in the Tunnel?"

"Most are on foot," Gideon said. "So I expect they will arrive about the same time as our cavalry."

"And what is the battle plan General Eries and the others will be seeing to?" Elison asked.

"More of what worked in the Allister Plains," Jase said, sounding pleased. "As they march, we will harass them through Veilgates and lay Power-wrought traps in their path. We can't stop them, but we can slow them down. They'll earn every step they take."

"What's to keep them from using the same tactics against us?" Brysia asked.

"Probably nothing," Jase admitted, "but if we hit them hard enough and often enough, their Agla'Con won't have the time or the strength to go on the offensive. They will be busy keeping their shadowspawn in check and the cultists from fleeing."

"Jase is right," Gideon agreed. "It will take everything their Power-wielders have just to keep Shadan's army moving forward. Yes, they still outnumber us more than two to one, but the loss of so many of their comrades at Fulrath will weigh heavily on their minds. There will be many who wish to abandon Death's Third March and slip away. The Agla'Con will have to watch them carefully. And the Agla'Con themselves will be wary about engaging us where we have entrenched ourselves for fear of triggering more traps."

"And there will be traps," Joselyn said. "Idoman and I will be overseeing their placement and construction. That boy is a genius with crux points."

Jase nodded, smiling. "He is indeed." He looked at Seth. "Which reminds me," he continued. "I have given the men of Chellum a new assignment. Taggert and his men are going to defend Talin Pass should any of Shadan's forces seek to use it. Elam and the Home Guard will be returning to their duties in Chellum Palace."

Seth's face remained smooth, but Gideon saw a hint of relief glimmering in the captain's blue eyes. "I think that is a wise move," he said. "Because truth be told, I am more worried about the threats we can't see. Especially those which might originate in Riak."

Gideon watched Raimen and Tohquin exchange a knowing glance, and he was grateful Elliott had his back to them. The prince wouldn't have appreciated what he saw in their eyes.

Elliott leveled a stare at Seth. "You're never going to let it go, are you?"

Seth's smile held no amusement. "No. And neither should you."

The sour smile Elliott directed at Seth was interrupted by Talia. "What did you do?" she asked.

Elliott blinked his surprise. "You don't know? I was certain Gideon or Jase or Seth would have blabbed it to the entire world by now." He glared at each of them in turn before looking back at his sister. "It's a long story. I'll tell you later."

"You most certainly will," she said. "Especially if Jase and Seth think it might bring some kind of calamity to Chellum."

"It brought good things, too," Elliott said in his defense. "An alliance with Clan Gahara for one. Not to mention *Ao tres'domei*."

"The good definitely outweighs the bad," Gideon said. "But having the Home Guard back in Chellum is wise." He waved his hand to dismiss the topic. "But enough of Riak. We need to focus on the dangers we can see. And right now they are marching across Talin Plateau."

"But not at breakneck speed," Jase said. "We have time to regroup and rest and heal. With Joneam at the rendezvous point, our army is in good hands. We can join him tomorrow. Right now, I would like to meet the rest of the Rhiven." He pushed himself slowly to his feet, his weariness evident in his movements. He paused, taking hold of the back of the chair to steady himself.

Talia took him by the arm, concern glimmering in her eyes. "Are you sure you are up to this?" she asked softly.

He smiled at her. "I wouldn't miss this for the world," he said, then looked at Gideon. "If you would be so kind as to open a Veilgate," he said, "I would like to meet our new allies."

光

Aethon ignored the surprised looks on the faces of the Tamban soldiers fronting the palace gates, turning instead to address the man wearing the mark of captain in *Frel'mola's* elite Deathwatch Guard. He exited the gate's tower with five more Deathwatch on his heels. Faces hard and hands on swords, they looked him over as if contemplating an attack. They seemed very aware of the fact that he wore no weapons of his own but had somehow managed to enter the city unchallenged.

*So they are smarter than they look*, he thought. *It might just keep them alive.*

He opened his mouth to greet them, but a powerful, unfamiliar Awareness brushed across the area before he could speak. He smiled inwardly.

"Your Empress has felt my arrival," he told the captain. "You would do well not to delay me."

The Deathwatch captain looked from Aethon to Krev and the other two Rhiven, then back to Aethon. "No one is allowed to enter the palace without express permission from *Frel'mola*," he said. "Especially not at this hour."

Aethon sighed patiently, then sliced the man's head from his neck with a blade of *Lo'shaen*. His body crumpled into a heap as the rest of the Deathwatch drew their weapons. Smiling to conceal his anger, Aethon caught the men in strands of corrupted Air and held them fast.

"Do you really think I couldn't have entered the palace already on my own?" he asked, then shook his head and turned to Krev. "See what I get for trying to pay a proper visit. What's the use in knocking if they won't answer the door?"

He looked back to the five Deathwatch. They were struggling against their invisible bonds but to no avail. He was tempted to simply kill them and rip the gates from their hinges, but knew that such a demonstration would anger *Frel'mola*. And he hadn't come here to anger her—well, not more than a little bit, anyway. He simply wanted to talk.

"I'm going to let you go now," he told them. "Stand down or I will kill you." He released the Power and waited, ready to strike if they pressed him. Slowly, grudgingly, they sheathed their swords, but their eyes burned with fury as they did.

Aethon smiled at them. "See, I'm here just to talk. Please send word to *Frel'mola* that Aethon Fairimor, first among the living in Death's Third March, would like a word with her." *Frel'mola's* powerful Awareness withdrew.

One of the men, obviously the acting captain now that his superior was dead, nodded to one of the regular soldiers who slipped into the guard tower then appeared in the street beyond the gate a moment later. He needn't have bothered.

*Ta'shaen* stirred as a Veilgate opened just outside the gate and an aging soldier wearing the rank of commander appeared in the fiery-edged hole.

He dipped his head in greeting, but it was decidedly void of respect. "I am Ibisar Naxis, Supreme Commander of the Tamban military and First Fist to *Frel'mola*," he said. "My mistress is expecting you."

He stepped back to make way for them, and Aethon stepped through into the throne room of Berazzel. Krev and the other two Rhiven followed, and the gate snapped shut behind them.

Aethon looked around, impressed. *Frel'mola's* seat of power was large, well-lighted and clean—a far cry from the poorly lit, smoke-filled pit of death and decay that was Shadan's throne room. And where Shadan chose to surround himself only with Greylings, *Frel'mola's* servants were made up mostly of the living. A full contingent of Deathwatch Guards lined both walls, and young men and women wearing dark green livery waited on bended knee near the service entrance. No K'rrosha were visible anywhere.

*I've been working with the wrong Dreadlord*, he decided, then started up the aisle toward the dais and the fiery-edged hole framing *Frel'mola's* throne.

He didn't need to extend his Awareness to know the hole opened into Con'Jithar—he could feel the coldness of death seeping from it well enough with his physical senses. He knew if he looked through the eyes of *Ta'shaen* he would find the Earthsoul working fruitlessly to close the rent, and a rush of jealousy swept through him. Having such a hole in the Pit would have aided in his efforts to create an entire army of Refleshed.

Shaking the thought away, he continued up the aisle toward the dais. Situated on a circle of polished stone, *Frel'mola's* massive high-backed throne faced the hole in the Veil, so all Aethon could see of her was her jeweled hands positioned daintily on the armrests. The flesh of those hands, he realized, wasn't the dead, sickly grey of the Refleshed he was used to, but the vibrant, cream-colored skin-tone of a Tamban.

He kept his surprise in check—if just barely—but it nearly broke free again a moment later when the throne rotated around to face him and he found himself staring into the face of the most beautiful woman he had ever seen. If not for the fiery red glow of her eyes, he might have been able to spend an eternity gazing upon such beauty.

The corrupted glow, however, destroyed the illusion, showing her for what she really was: a Greyling. And though the grey had been camouflaged, this kind of beauty truly was nothing more than skin deep, hiding one of the most vicious, murderous beings ever to walk the earth. The facade wasn't what he had expected, and for a moment he couldn't find his voice.

"Speechless in my presence?" she cooed seductively. "That's good. I worked hard for this body." She smiled, her perfectly formed lips parting to reveal a row of straight, white teeth.

"I'm sure you did," he told her. "How many attempts did it take?"

"Just one, darling," she said. "In Tamba, we do things right the first time." Still smiling, she fingered the short reddish-gold scepter lying across her lap.

"So it would seem." He knew she was lying. Avoiding the Greyling effect was nearly impossible to accomplish no matter how skilled the Agla'Con. Likely it had taken dozens, if not hundreds, of attempts. Evidence of the vanity she'd been so famous for in life.

"So," she continued. "You are the one I've been hearing so much about. Shadan's pet Fairimor."

Aethon's rage ignited within him, but he kept it contained. "I serve Maeon," he told her. "Just as you do. Shadan and his K'rrosha are simply a means to an end. Allies in a cause that's larger than any of us."

Her eyes flared with amusement. "I hear you challenged him."

He stared at her, his rage warring with curiosity. "How do you know of that?"

"The dead are not silent, dear," she said, an air of condescension in the words. "I know more about... well, everything, than you ever will." She looked at Krev and the other two Rhiven. "Including the history of the Dragons and Krev'ei to ul'Morgranon's part in that history."

"You will speak nothing of that here, K'rrosha," Krev said, twisting the name insultingly. Behind him, Ibisar tensed as if he might reach for his sword, but Frel'mola waved him off.

"Now, now. There is no need to be unpleasant. After all, we are allies in a cause larger than ourselves." She smiled again, apparently pleased with herself for twisting Aethon's words.

Her smugness made him want to burn her from existence. Not with Sei'shiin, since it would be much more rewarding to know she would spend weeks trying to replicate the refleshing she currently enjoyed. If she could replicate it at all.

She must have sensed some of what he'd been thinking because her eyes narrowed. She fingered the scepter again, then took it in one hand and rose. Moving down from the dais, she stopped next to him and offered her arm.

"Walk with me, my friend, and tell me what brings you to Tamba."

# CHAPTER 5

## *Paying the Butcher*

THORAC'S MUSCLES BURNED WITH FATIGUE, but he kept his shield up and his axe swinging as Kunin soldiers swarmed in from all sides. A spear clanged loudly off his shield, and a black-fletched arrow hissed past his head. His axe shattered a Kunin sword, and his hands stung when shards of steel peppered his skin. He ignored the pain and kept swinging, fueled by his rage.

Blackish-red blood sprayed the air as his blade again found its mark, and another Kunin fell. Then another. The ground was strewn with their dark bodies, the earth muddy with their blood.

But where one fell, it seemed two more appeared to take his place. Grimacing with disgust, Thorac set his jaw and braced himself for the long fight. He might be outnumbered, but these black-hearted vermin were going to pay the butcher before they felled him. And a steep price it would be, too. Bloody, filthy traitors to the Earthsoul.

One of his Kunin opponents flinched as Fire and lightning heated the air to the west, and Thorac seized the opportunity to split the man's skull. Pulling his axe free, he followed the Kunin's dead-eyed gaze and saw that Emma and the other Dymas were continuing to hammer the entrance to the underground warren of the Sons of Uri, killing the enemy as they emerged.

They'd been at it since the battle began, and demonspawn littered the area in front of the entrance, their hulking, misshapen forms twisted and broken. The walls of the building had long since collapsed, and the roof was in flames, but the demonspawn kept coming. They clawed their way from the burning ruins with snarls of rage, their eyes glowing red with demonic light.

Those who could seize *Ta'shaen* had wrapped themselves in auras of shadowed red for protection but had yet to strike back. They simply crouched beneath their shields and watched the Dymas with hungry, rage-filled eyes. *Chisa'mi* in the Kunin tongue, they were a lesser form of the Sons of Uri, if somewhat more powerful than *Shel'tui*. And there were eight so far with more sure to come.

Thorac had no idea what the foul creatures were waiting for, but he was grateful their attention was centered on the Dymas. Any one of them could have crushed him and the rest of the Chunin with barely any effort. Very likely they were waiting for Emma and the others to tire. When that happened—and it would—this battle would be over. Darkness would swallow light.

For now, though, Emma and her companions were holding the *Chisa'mi* at bay and tearing to shreds those who couldn't seize the Power. The women were fighting in pairs, he knew, with one channeling a shield while the other attacked. And it was working. They might be small in stature, but they were formidable. As the Light-blasted *Chisa'mi* and other demonspawn were learning the moment they appeared. Some thirty or forty lay dead. Heaven only knew how many more had yet to emerge.

Thorac felled another Kunin, then cast about for Endil and Jeymi. He hadn't seen either of them since the fighting started, but he refused to believe they were among the dead. Perhaps they'd made a break for it. He hoped so. This battle might be lost, but if Endil survived, their reason for coming to this godforsaken place could still be realized. The war could still be won.

A few paces to Thorac's left, Shen Halaf cried out as a Kunin spear took him in the side. Eyes wide with pain, he staggered and went to his knees. The Kunin who'd struck him grinned in triumph and hefted another spear.

Thorac leapt forward and knocked the spear aside with his shield, then chopped the Kunin's head from his neck with a vicious swing that sprayed the air with dark, foul-smelling blood.

Howling his rage, he stood over Shen and continued to deliver death to every Kunin who approached. There were too many for him to stand indefinitely, but they would know the strength and honor of the Chunin people before they felled him. The butcher's bill would be high indeed.

Culdin and two of his men appeared out of the mayhem to join him, and the four of them took up positions around their fallen friend. Kunin moved in from every direction, yellow eyes feral and hungry. There were too many, he realized. The last stand was upon them.

The sickening sound of rending flesh filled the air as the Kunin were ripped apart by some unseen force, and their gore wet the ground around Thorac and his companions.

"It's about bloody time we had some help," Culdin muttered.

Thorac nodded, but saw that the help had drawn the attention of some of the *Chisa'mi*. Four had turned away from Emma and the others and were moving to attack. Dozens of Kunin made way for them, then followed in their wake, weapons at the ready, leathery faces eager for blood.

"Brace yourselves," Thorac said, feeling the cold inevitability of death settle over him. "This will be the end."

"Not if I have anything to say about it," a female voice said, and Jeymi appeared as if stepping from thin air. Endil was beside her, spear in hand.

Thorac eyed Jeymi with relief. "Was that you?" he asked, glancing at the remains of the Kunin.

"Did you even have to ask?" Endil said, his face pinched with disgust.

Jeymi grinned at him, then raised her hands and sent streamers of green Fire streaking toward the approaching demonspawn. Reddish auras darkened around them, and the streamers crackled harmlessly away. The creatures stopped their advance, but retaliated with threads of sizzling red.

Jeymi turned them aside with an invisible shield of Spirit. "I'd wondered if they could attack," she said, sounding oddly satisfied. "All they've done thus far is defend."

"They're waiting for you to tire," Thorac told her. Then he deliberately looked her over and added, "Are you?"

"Am I what?"

"Tiring?"

"I'm just getting warmed up," she said. To prove it, she hammered the four *Chisa'mi* with a barrage of lightning that shook the entire outpost and left spots of light in Thorac's vision. When the spots faded, the demonspawn were gone. Only their smouldering remains showed they'd been there at all. The Kunin who'd been trailing them—those who'd survived the lightning—pushed themselves to their feet and tried to flee. They blew apart in sprays of blood and flesh as Jeymi finished them off.

"It's Emma and the others we need to worry about," the young lady said as if nothing had happened. "They've used a lot of energy attacking the demonspawn. I don't know how much they have left. I doubt it will be enough to get us out of here by Veilgate. We are going to have to fight our way clear."

She turned toward an area where some of Culdin's men were fighting, and the air turned to blood once again as she tore the Kunin soldiers apart with the Power. The brutality of the strike might worry some of those in Thorac's party—Emma most of all—but he appreciated the young woman's unbridled savagery. It was quick and effective, if a bit more messy than if he were to kill them.

"Gather your men," Jeymi ordered. "I want everyone inside my shield. I've already made contact with Emma. She and the others will be joining us shortly."

"And then what?" Thorac asked.

"You're the general," she said. "I was hoping you would tell me."

Under any other circumstance Thorac's frown would have brought a smile to Jeymi's face because it meant she'd just bested him in a bout of teasing. But her words had not been delivered in jest. She was dead serious. He *was* the general. Attacking this outpost had been his idea. True, there had been no way he could have known the outpost had been built on top of a demon breeding ground, but he'd always had contingency plans in place before. Surely he had a plan for getting them out of this mess. That he seemed at a loss was not at all comforting.

She motioned to the Chunin, gesturing them near. "Keep close," she told them. "A smaller shield is easier for me to maintain." And it would be small, she saw. Nearly a third of Culdin's men lay among the dead.

It broke her heart that she hadn't been near enough to save them when the fighting had been at its fiercest, but she'd been acting on orders from Emma to get Endil to safety. She realized now, that doing so had been a mistake. If she'd stayed, the loss of life would have been so much less.

When the Chunin were all safely inside her shield, she went to one knee and took Shen's head in her hands. Wielding Flesh for healing while maintaining the shield was tricky, but she managed enough of a healing to stop the bleeding and close the wound. A full healing would have to wait until they were away from here. And that was looking less likely by the second.

The rubble of the warren's entrance erupted skyward in a burst of corrupted *Ta'shaen*, filling the sky with stony missiles that rained down upon the outpost like oversized hailstones. Dozens thumped hollowly against her shield.

A moment later five monstrous demonspawn scrambled into the open. They had the appearance of wolves, but were roughly human-shaped and walked upright on heavily muscled legs. They wore armor fashioned from steel and bone and carried swords set with Jexlair crystals. All five were wrapped in shielding auras of corrupted Earthpower.

"Well," Thorac said, his voice filled with dread. "At least we got a look at who is really in charge of this place. The flaming *Chisa'mi* you killed were bloody hamsters compared to these guys. The Kunin call the big ones *Odai'mi*."

"And this knowledge helps me how?" Jeymi asked, channeling more Spirit into her shield as the *Odai'mi* took note of where she was and started toward her. Before Thorac could answer, streamers of Fire enveloped her shield, and the world vanished beneath a sea of red. Her Awareness trembled from the effort of holding the shield in place.

And then she felt it—a taint unlike any she'd ever felt before. It was darker, colder, and more filled with malice. It felt like...death.

Jeymi looked at Thorac, a cold feeling of dread settling in her heart. "The *Odai'mi*," she said, "their abilities are being enhanced by the power of the Void. I can feel it...like an eighth strand coursing through the other seven."

She would have said more, but the Fire vanished, and the *Odai'mi* halted their advance. That had been a test, she realized. The bloody creatures were feeling her out. Judging by the toothy grins on their wolf-like faces, they had liked what they found.

*Ta'shaen* came alive with a powerful wielding of Light, and stabs of silvery-blue crackled to life among the five creatures.

*Emma*, Jeymi thought with a smile, then added a barrage of her own. The Sons of Uri drew in on themselves, and the auras shielding them darkened. The lightning sizzled harmlessly away, setting corpses ablaze and filling the area with greasy smoke.

*Blood of Maeon!* she thought but didn't voice her shock aloud. She didn't want Thorac and the others to worry. Instead, she channeled even more Spirit into her shield and prayed for inspiration on what to do next.

The *Odai'mi* didn't move. Eyes glowing with understanding, they watched her with what could only be described as amusement. Thorac was right—they were waiting for her to tire. And being demonspawn, they could wait forever. This was a contest she could not win, and the *Odai'mi* knew it.

Movement in the smoke to her right pulled her attention from her enemies, and she looked over to find Emma and Lizette hurrying toward her. Aierlin, Kelby, and Gwenin were only a few paces behind and to the right. When all were near, Jeymi opened a hole in her shield and let them in.

Emma's face was a mask of fury. "I thought I told you to see Endil safely out of here. Why are you back?"

Jeymi flinched at the harshness in the smaller woman's voice. After a quick look at Endil, she answered. "I lost an argument."

Endil stepped near, poised to defend her. "An argument that should not have been necessary," he said. "This is my mission, Emma. I will decide where and when I go."

"But if you die," Emma countered, "there is no mission."

"Precisely why I am back," Endil said, his patience starting to slip. He jabbed a finger in the direction of the demonspawn. "How far do you think we would have made it before those bloody things caught up with us? Our best chance of survival is to stick together."

"It's a convincing argument," Thorac added, then flinched when Emma turned on him.

"Shut it, General," she snapped. "We're in this mess because of you."

Thorac bristled but said nothing. He did tighten his grip on his axe handle, though, as if he had momentarily considered using it on Emma.

The tiny Dymas pretended not to notice. "Kelby and Gwenin link with Jeymi," she ordered. "Lend her your strength as she holds the shield. Aierlin and Lizette, you link with me. I'm going to open us a Veilgate out of here."

Jeymi did as instructed, and the amount of Earthpower flowing through her spiked dramatically as soon as the Communal link was in place. She pressed the shield outward to make room for a Veilgate, watching in her mind's eye as it swelled like a giant luminescent bubble to more than twice its former size. And it was strong, far stronger than anything she could have managed on her own, even if she hadn't already exerted herself.

*Why don't we do this more often?* she asked.

*Because,* Kelby answered, *it is dangerous. If one Dymas should falter, the sudden loss of Power can shatter the link, and the others can lose their hold on* Ta'shaen.

*Oh,* Jeymi said, focusing more intently on what she was doing.

The Sons of Uri still hadn't moved, but their sword-like talismans continued to brighten with corrupted Earthpower. They were preparing a strike, Jeymi knew, and she braced herself for whatever it might be.

A river of *Ta'shaen* surged into Emma as she prepared to open a Veilgate, and Jeymi watched through her Awareness as the tiny woman channeled Spirit into the spiritual fabric of the Veil.

Snapping and sparking in protest, the air split to reveal an empty stretch of land far away from the outpost.

"Go," Emma shouted, and Culdin and his men started for the fiery edged square.

Jeymi's Awareness shrieked as a sudden powerful wielding of Earth erupted from the Sons of Uri. It struck somewhere well beneath the sheltering bubble of Spirit she held around the group, and her stomach lurched as the ground dropped from beneath them.

Time seemed to slow as she fell, and she watched the outpost disappear from view as a wall of dirt and rock rose around them. Instinctively, she strengthened her flows of Spirit, and the shield fell with them, an invisible barrier that scraped against the sides of the quickly expanding hole.

Emma shouted a warning and released the Power, but the last remnants of the collapsing Veilgate sliced through the shield like a fiery razor. The inside of Jeymi's head flashed into pain, and the shield began to unravel at the point of contact.

She fought through the pain and managed to hold onto the Power even as Kelby's mind disappeared from the Communal link. In desperation, Jeymi channeled even more Spirit into the shield and closed the shimmering gash. But they were still falling. The sky was a circle of light some thirty or forty feet above, creating the illusion that she was peering up from the bottom of a well.

The earth inside her shield began to break apart around her feet, but it was that loosening which saved them all as they crashed to a stop a moment later.

Fighting to get air back into her lungs, Jeymi blinked against the dirt in her eyes and pushed herself to her feet. Points of light danced in her Awareness, but the shield was still intact. Miraculous considering that Gwenin had lost her hold on the link as well. She lay face down a few feet away and wasn't moving.

As Jeymi's eyes adjusted to the dim light, a coldness settled over her when she saw a vast cavern stretching away in all directions. Sickly firelight from copper urns cast flickering shadows across the pens and cages of the breeding stock the Sons of Uri used to create more demonspawn. And there, lurking in a pulsating aura of darkness, was the demon whose warren this was.

Roughly the size of a bear, it sported an odd mixture of fur and spikes and leathery skin. It stared at them as if unsure what to make of the new arrivals, then started forward to investigate. Only then did Jeymi see that it was chained and collared. The chains, heavy enough to hold a Dainin, were secured to a reddish column of what looked like *chorazin*.

Groans of pain pulled Jeymi's attention from the demon long enough for her to see Emma pushing herself to her feet. Thorac was beside her and had a hold of her arm. Concern glimmered in his eyes as he checked to see if she was all right.

*Not that it will matter for long*, Jeymi thought, returning her attention to the demon. It had reached the end of its chains and was hunkering down to watch. It seemed curious. Eager. Perhaps it thought they were the newest group of breeding stock.

*Perhaps we are*, Jeymi thought, then shivered in disgust and pushed the thought away.

Endil took her by the arm. "Are you all right?" he asked, his hair spilling dirt as he moved.

"As well as can be expected after that," she said, looking up at the circle of light some fifty feet above. Dark shadows moved at the edge. Hulking wolf-like shadows.

*Ta'shaen* came alive with another Void-laced, corrupted wielding, and lightning hammered the top of her shield. The inside of her head went white with pain, and spots flashed in her spiritual vision. She staggered, but Endil caught her in his arms.

Jeymi felt the brush of Emma's Awareness and opened herself to a Communal link. "Let me take the shield," the smaller woman said aloud, and Jeymi transferred control via the link. But she didn't release her hold on the Power or break the link. Emma smiled fondly as she sent a rush of communication across the link.

*You did well, young lady. But you are not finished yet. Our lives cannot end the way our enemies intend. I'll do it if you can't, but we cannot allow the Sons of Uri to claim the Fairimor bloodline. They would use it to create demonspawn of unimaginable power. I'll tell you when it is time.* The words were simple, but the meaning, conveyed directly into Jeymi's mind, tore her heart from her chest.

Tears welled up in her eyes as she nodded that she understood. *I'll do it*, she said. *But I want you to send me with him.*

Thorac narrowed his eyes at Emma. "So that's it?" he asked. "We're just going to stand here until your strength gives out?"

"I'll hold the shield until Aierlin and the others are strong enough to open a Veilgate out of here," Emma told him. "I've already done a probe of the ground beneath. It's solid. Our enemies won't be able to use that trick again."

Jeymi reached over and took Emma by the hand. She'd felt how sharply the lie had pained her. But Thorac, like Endil, didn't need to know that there would be no Veilgate. He didn't need to know that none of the Dymas, including Emma, had enough strength left to open an escape. Emma was simply buying some time for them to say goodbye.

*Yes*, Emma told her through the link. *So make the most of it.*

The area went white with another barrage of lightning, and the ground shook. The creatures in the pens cringed away in fright. The demon backed up until it was next to the *chorazin* post. Even if its chains had been long enough to allow it, the creature likely wouldn't enter the fray. It didn't need to. Its masters would see that the Chunin intruders were subdued. All it had to do was wait.

Jeymi put her arms around Endil and hugged him tightly. He had no idea what she was preparing to do, but she loved him too much to let him fall into the hands of the Sons of Uri. Hopefully he would forgive her when they met again in the afterlife.

He hugged her back and pressed his lips against the top of her head, flinching only slightly as corrupted lightning struck the shield once more. "I love you," he whispered, and the dam on her tears burst. She hugged him even tighter, steeling herself to do the unthinkable as Emma's shield continued to weaken.

Green light flashed atop the chasm, and the threads of corruption staining the luminescent world of Jeymi's Awareness cut off. Fearing a trick, she braced herself for an attack and risked a quick upward probe with her Awareness.

She gaped in wonder. Veilgates were opening all across the outpost. Pure, undefiled Veilgates with edges of shimmering blue. And there, striding through with spears and nets in hand, came a dozen or more *Nar'shein Yahl.*

Her emotions overcame her and she sagged into Endil, weeping openly, grateful for reinforcements. Grateful that she'd been spared from ending Endil's life.

# CHAPTER 6

## Course Corrections

EMMARENZIANA ANTILLA FELT THE ARRIVAL of the Dainin just as Jeymi had, and she stretched her Awareness upward to find a dozen or more Keepers of the Earth rushing through purely wrought Veilgates to engage the enemy. *Arinseil* nets hurled from within the shimmering blue squares materialized as if from thin air, and the *Odai'mi* went down in crackling flashes of green.

Jexlair talismans went dark, and snarls of rage rose above the tumult of battle as the snared demonspawn thrashed against the Power-wrought nets. *Nar'shein* rushed from somewhere beyond and speared the fearsome creatures through the head, silencing their rage.

Other *Nar'shein* met the suicidal charge of dozens of Kunin and hewed the wretched creatures down like reapers gleaning stubble from a field. That task accomplished, they turned their attention to the demonspawn scrambling from the ruined buildings. The nightmarish creatures launched themselves at the Dainin but were met with spears and clubs and sometimes bare fists. Within seconds, grey-green blood ran in rivers across the muddy earth.

A larger Veilgate opened, and a column of *Bero'thai* rode through on horseback, arrows hissing ahead of them like locusts, felling Kunin and demonspawn alike. A white-haired Kelsan strode through after the *Bero'thai*, and the Veilgate slid shut behind him. He took note of the situation, and Emma felt the reassuring brush of his Awareness.

A heartbeat later the air split wide in front of her, and the man stepped into the cavernous underground warren. He took one look at the demon chained to the *chorazin* post, and a white-hot bar of *Sei'shiin* lanced from his fist, burning the creature from existence. His eyes moved over the cages and pens, and the look of disgust on his face turned to pity. Opening himself more fully to the Power, he unleashed a wave of Fire that burned the pen's inhabitants to ash. When the fiery light faded, he turned to Emma and motioned for her to drop the shield.

"I am Thex Landoral," he said, moving to kneel next to Gwenin. He placed a hand on her head and sent a rush of healing into her. She gave a cough as she came to and rolled over onto her side. Her face was smudged with dirt, but her eyes were bright. She looked at her healer in surprise.

Thex rose smoothly to his feet. "I was sent by the *Mith'elre Chon* to aid you in your quest to rescue the Blood Orb from the Sons of Uri," he continued, then offered a bow to Endil. "Please, allow me to open the way out of this filthy place."

Endil nodded. "By all means," he said. "And thank you for coming."

"My pleasure, Lord Fairimor," Thex said, and *Ta'shaen* came alive once more as he opened a Veilgate to the surface.

This time Emma saw how it was done, and she marveled at the complexity of the wielding. All Seven Gifts woven together. Magnificent. And it made perfect sense now that she'd seen it.

"How did you learn to do that?" she asked.

"We'll talk *after* I get you out of here," he said, motioning her forward.

Emma led the way through into the midst of the Dainin, and the giant warriors dipped their heads in greeting. Aside from one final skirmish at the far side of the outpost where *Bero'thai* archers were mercilessly shooting down the remaining Kunin, the battle was over. The outpost and its secreted warren had been destroyed.

She felt Thex release the Power, and turned to face him as the Veilgate slid silently closed. Thorac and Endil moved to stand beside her as Thex approached.

"I know you have many questions," Thex said. "But we dare not linger here any longer than necessary. Heaven only knows what kinds of godforsaken creatures might have sensed our use of *Ta'shaen*. The rest of our party is awaiting our return some distance to the north. We will take you there so that we may speak at our leisure."

He nodded to the Dainin, and they wove the Seven Gifts together once more and opened Veilgates for themselves and the *Bero'thai*. Thex opened a gate for the rest of them, and Thorac took the lead. Emma followed, eager to be away from the carnage.

The place beyond Thex's gate was wide and flat, but had piles of stony rubble at regular intervals. Some fifty yards to the right, stood a large stone fountain. Acidic waters spurted skyward in spasmodic bursts, etching the stone of the fountain and the broken benches surrounding it. A small stream flowed away from the fountain, snaking away through the ruins.

"Is this where I think it is?" Emma asked, and Thorac nodded.

"We were here yesterday," he said. "Which puts the warren about fifteen miles to the south-southwest of here." He pointed, and Emma thought she could see wisps of dark smoke rising from one of the larger hills.

"We tracked you to this point," Thex told them, letting the Veilgate close and releasing the Power. "We had just arrived when we felt your use of *Ta'shaen* at the outpost. We'd have been here sooner, but getting past the northern watchtower proved a bit more difficult than we had anticipated because of what you did there."

"My apologies," Thorac said, "but I needed to turn Kunin's attention away from me and my group."

"Well, you certainly did that," a familiar voice said, and Emma and Thorac turned to find General Kennin approaching with his Krelltin. Not far behind him stretched a literal army of Krelltin-mounted Chunin soldiers. Emma estimated them at more than two hundred. Some twenty or so near the front sported armbands marked with the symbols for *Ta'shaen.*

"That little maneuver," General Kennin continued, "all but painted a bull's eye on us." He dismounted and stepped forward to shake Thorac's hand. "But it was bloody brilliant, even if it did slow us down by a good two days." He slapped his friend on the shoulder, then turned his attention to Emma. Taking her hand in his, he pressed it to his lips before releasing it.

"It is a pleasure to find you in good health, Dymas," he said, offering a bow. "I know firsthand how hazardous it can be traveling with this old wardog."

"We've had our moments," Emma said and left it at that.

General Kennin raised an eyebrow at her. "The way the Dainin and the others rushed away through Veilgates makes me think you were having one of those moments just now."

"It wasn't anything we couldn't handle," Emma lied. "We were just about to flee through a Veilgate when Thex arrived. Your timing simply allowed us to join you sooner. Otherwise I would have taken us some miles to the south of the outpost."

She felt Jeymi's gaze but didn't turn to acknowledge it. The young lady knew the truth of what had been about to happen, but there was no need for Thorac or Endil or the others to know how close to death they'd been. Someday Jeymi might tell Endil what she'd been prepared to do, but it didn't need to come to light here in this awful place.

"What's done is done," Thex said, and his tone coupled with the way he looked at Emma and Jeymi hinted that he knew the lie. "We found you, and the world is a better place for your safety and for the destruction of the warren."

"Warren?" General Kennin hissed. "Blood of Maeon! No wonder the Dainin raced to your aid. Whose idea was it to attack a bloody warren?"

"We didn't *know* it was a warren," Thorac told him. "We wouldn't have gone anywhere near it if we had. But after how easily we destroyed the first outpost, we decided it was easier to attack our enemies head on than it was trying to sneak past them."

General Kennin shot a skeptical look at Emma. "And you agreed with him?"

Emma shrugged. "Like he said, it worked the first time."

"That it did," the general laughed. "Maybe a little too well. All of northern Kunin believes a full scale invasion is underway."

"I'd say that isn't far from the truth," Emma said, looking pointedly at the army of Chunin and *Bero'thai* stretching away among the ruins. And that was to say nothing of the twenty-five Dainin she had counted—they were the equivalent of the rest of the army combined.

"Courtesy of the *Mith'elre Chon*," Thex said. "He wasn't convinced that a small party could wrest the Orb away from Loharg. No offense, General Shurr."

"None taken," Thorac said.

Emma's heart skipped a beat. "The *Mith'elre Chon* has come?" she asked. "When? Who is he?"

"Jase Fairimor," one of the approaching Dainin answered, and Emma turned to face him as he neared. Four others followed close on his heels, two of whom were women. None of them carried *arinseil* nets, but each had a large quiver-like container of spears.

The one who had spoken went to a knee in front of Endil. "I see you, Lord Fairimor," he said, his weathered brown face intense as he gazed into Endil's eyes. "I am Dommoni Kia'Kal, Chief Captain of the *Nar'shein Yahl*."

"I see you, *Nar'shein*," Endil said, returning the formal greeting. "Please, tell me about Jase."

"I will," the Dainin said. "But first I have been tasked with delivering news that will rend your heart. Are you prepared to hear it?"

Endil's face tightened, and his body grew stiff. Jeymi reached over and took his hand. "Is anyone ever ready for such news?" the prince asked.

Chieftain Kia'Kal smiled sympathetically. "Not usually," he answered, then seated himself cross-legged on the ground.

One of his companions brought over a large chunk of stone from one of the ruined buildings and offered it as a chair for Endil. He thanked the Dainin but motioned for Jeymi to sit instead. Still holding her hand, Endil nodded for Dommoni to continue. "You may deliver your message."

Endil tightened his grip on Jeymi's hand as word of his father's death hit him like a hammer. A rush of pain and sorrow swept through him, then took him by the heart and began to squeeze, a cold jarring ache that made him wish he had chosen to sit down.

His legs felt weak, and the world around him felt distorted as he wrestled with his grief. Closing his eyes for a moment, he held himself straight and tall, the way his father would have expected.

His father... dead? It didn't seem possible.

He opened his eyes to find Jeymi's face wet with tears as she tried unsuccessfully to hold back her sobs. Thorac's face was pinched with a frown, and he was shaking his head in disbelief. Emma and the rest of those who'd been his companions the past few weeks watched him with concern. No one had anything to say. Endil included.

He stood silently for quite some time, trying to come to terms with the sudden loss. That his father had died more than a week ago only made it that much more difficult to comprehend.

When he finally found his voice, he asked quietly, "How did it happen?"

"To answer that will require some time," Chief Kia'Kal replied, motioning everyone to sit.

Endil settled in next to Jeymi while Thorac and the others picked spots on the ground. Weary as they were, they didn't even bother to lay out a cloak first but just plopped down in the dirt.

"Fairimor Palace was seized by an army of Agla'Con," the Dainin began, and Endil listened with a mixture of horror and pride as Dommoni revealed the last few hours of the High King's life. His pride deepened when he learned of his father's sacrifice and how it had been the blood-stained banner of his death shroud which had rallied the people when Elison Brey raised it before them.

He was relieved to hear that the city had been cleared of the enemy and that all the rest of those he cared about had survived.

"There is much more to the story of Trian's cleansing, of course," Dommoni said, "but the details will be best told by those who were there. You can ask them yourself once our mission here is complete."

Endil nodded, his throat still tight with emotion. "And what exactly is that mission?" he asked.

"The same as it was when you entered this Light-blasted land," Dommoni answered. "We will take the Blood Orb from the creature Loharg and, if possible, we will destroy the Sons of Uri."

"And who heads this mission going forward?" he asked.

"You do," Thex answered. "Nothing has changed but the number of troops you lead, my lord. General Shurr and Emmarenziana Dymas will continue to act as your advisors. The rest of us are here to assist in whatever way you deem necessary."

Endil hadn't expected to feel relieved, especially since he'd never asked to be in charge of the mission, but a feeling of calm settled over him. This was what the Earthsoul wanted. And, strangely enough, he realized it was what he wanted. Hopefully he would be up to the challenge.

"And the leadership structure?" he asked.

"I will be acting as your advisor as well," Thex answered. "The Chunin will report to General Kennin. The *Bero'thai* to Captain Haslem. The *Nar'shein* are under the direction of Chieftain Kia'Kal. All three will answer directly to you."

Endil nodded. "Before I make any decisions about what to do next, I need to know what our options are? I know enough about Veilgates to realize those you opened for our rescue are not like those we've been using. How are they different?"

"They're pure," Thex answered. "They don't harm the Earthsoul the way the others did." He glanced at Emma as he continued. "And because they are pure, the point of arrival cannot be as readily felt by our enemies. We can get much closer to them without them sensing us."

"And we can open them in ways the enemy can't," Dommoni added. "Those of my companions who were sent to us yesterday by Ohran Peregam brought with them the knowledge of several new wieldings which will prove useful in the coming days."

"I thought you said the *Mith'elre Chon* sent you," Emma said.

Dommoni smiled. "He did. It was he who opened the way for me and my team to join Thex Landoral and his men in Chunin. But at that time only we five were sent, and the manner of opening Veilgates at the time was still corrupted. Just recently was the new method discovered." He paused and his voice took on a tone of reverence as he continued.

"Jase Fairimor learned it from the Earthsoul Herself. He and other powerful Dymas traveled to all the major cities of our lands and taught the wielding to all those who stand with him against Soulbiter. Chieftain Peregam felt we could benefit from it as well, so he sent twenty more *Nar'shein* to join my squad."

"Your squad," Thorac said, eyeing Dommoni and his four companions. "None of you are carrying *arinseil*. I take it Loharg isn't to be captured for trial."

Dommoni's face grew hard. "No. His trial is over. This Cleansing Hunt will end with his death or ours. No prisoners will be taken."

"And the rest of the *Nar'shein?*" Thorac asked. "Those who just saved us at the warren?"

Dommoni shrugged his massive shoulders. "They will do as Lord Endil commands, of course, but they do not intend to take demonspawn back to Dainin for trial either."

"Good," Endil said, a fiery determination igniting within him. "Creatures like Loharg and his *Shel'tui* deserve nothing more than a speedy destruction."

"If I may," Jeymi said, "I need some clarification on the different types of demonspawn. I noticed that all had been branded, but there were different marks. They seemed to have different abilities with the Power as well. The *Odai'mi*, as Thorac called them, wielded a form of corrupted *Ta'shaen*. But it wasn't the corruption of an Agla'Con. It was something worse than that. It felt like it was coming from Con'Jithar itself."

Chieftain Kia'Kal looked Jeymi in the eyes, an appreciative smile on his face. "Your powers of discernment are impressive for one so young," he told her. "And you are correct. The *Odai'mi* wield *Ta'shaen* mingled with a single strand of *Lo'shaen*, the power of the Void."

Endil was intrigued. "Which strand?"

"Fire."

"And the others?" Jeymi asked. "I saw at least three more distinct markings."

"There are four categories of demonspawn," Dommoni answered, looking from Jeymi to Endil and then back. "Thus the four different symbols the Sons of Uri use as brands. The *Tsuchi'mi* are the lowest form and are unable to wield the Power. Their demon blood is weak. The *Chisa'mi* can wield *Ta'shaen* with the aid of a Jexlair talisman as the *Shel'tui* do. The demon blood of the *Odai'mi* is strong, enabling them to enhance their corruption of *Ta'shaen* with the Fire of the Void."

"And the fourth category?" Endil asked even though he'd already guessed at the answer.

Dommoni's expression hardened. "They call themselves *Vakesh'mi ke Uri*," Dommoni answered. "Or in our tongue: The Sons of Uri. And the strength of their demon blood allows them to wield *Lo'shaen* in its entirety."

Endil nodded. "Then it is well that you do not intend to take them to Dainin for trial. We will kill them all. No mercy. No hesitation. Just a much deserved death."

"There is much of your cousin in you," Thex said, sounding pleased. "He destroyed the Agla'Con and their Con'Kumen army to the last man in a mass execution in the Colosseum shortly before he sent me to join you."

"That wasn't an execution," Dommoni said. "It was a Cleansing. People can be executed. Filth can only be cleansed."

For all the fire burning in him, Endil was shocked. "How... many?" was all he could manage.

"Several thousand," Dommoni answered. "But the events at the Colosseum pale in comparison to the destruction he unleashed on Shadan's forces at Zedik Pass."

Endil stiffened at what Dommoni's words implied. "Death's Third March is underway?"

"It is."

"And?"

"Shadan's army entered Kelsa four days ago. By now they will have reached Talin Plateau, but we do not know how either side has fared since the enemy reached Greendom. It was on that evening that Chieftain Peregam sent the twenty *Nar'shein* reinforcements."

"And the new wieldings they brought with them," Emma began. "They work here in Kunin? Even with the taint blackening our spiritual eyes?"

Dommoni's face split wide with a grin. "They do. And like I said, they give us great advantage." He looked at Endil. "If you will permit me to demonstrate..."

Endil motioned for him to proceed.

"Look right there," Dommoni said, pointing to a spot a short distance away. A split second later a small hole, like a window, opened in the air about shoulder height to Endil. Rimmed with blue, it was obviously a Veilgate but was smaller than any Endil had ever seen.

Curious, he moved to it and peered through. It was difficult not to hiss in surprise at what he found. The window—for that was what it was—looked down on the ruined outpost from several hundred feet in the air.

"What do you think?" Dommoni asked.

"I think this gives us great advantage," Endil answered, then turned to Thorac. "One I think you could put to good use."

Thorac snorted. "If I could see through it."

"I can get a stone for you to stand on if you wish," one of the Dainin offered.

"Or Chieftain Kia'Kal could open one at a more appropriate height," Thorac said, doing little to hide his irritation.

Dommoni chuckled. "I most certainly can," he said, and the window in front of Endil vanished. A second one opened at Chunin eye-level a short distance away. Thorac and Emma moved to peer through it together.

"Light of heaven," Thorac breathed. "Is that us?" He turned and looked skyward over Endil's shoulder.

Endil followed the little man's gaze and found an odd-looking square some hundred feet above. It would have been impossible to pick out had he not known exactly what he was looking for.

"It is," Emma said, still peering through the window. "And Endil is right: This gives us great advantage. With this we can spy out our enemies without using our Awareness. The taint on this land can no longer hide them from our view."

"It is how we found you at the outpost," Chieftain Kia'Kal told them. "We could feel your use of the Power, of course. But the taint is particularly strong in this area and worse at the outpost. We could not see you through the eyes of *Ta'shaen*. These *windows* allowed us to see what we were leaping into when we came to your aid."

Endil could tell by the way Thorac was stroking his beard that he was already coming up with a plan.

"What do you propose, General?" he asked.

"We've been doing this wrong," Thorac said. "Trying to overtake Loharg has been giving him the advantage. This is his land. He knows the layout, the snares and dangers, and where the taint blinds us from seeing him. He's used all of it to play us for fools right from the start. That bloody warren—" he cut off, hissing in disgust. "We played right into his hands." He shook his head. "*I* played right into his hands."

"And?" Endil prompted.

"And I'm wise enough to learn from my mistakes. I'm done chasing Loharg. We'll use these windows to scout the way ahead. When I find what I'm looking for, we'll jump ahead of Loharg and wait for him to come to us."

"And what are you looking for?" Endil asked, a sudden apprehension rising within him.

Thorac's eyes narrowed. "The Shrine of Uri."

# CHAPTER 7

## A Throne Reclaimed

THE EXPLOSIONS OF POWER ROCKING Kamoth's outer wall quieted, and Hulanekaefil Nid reached out carefully with his Awareness. The rest of the Dymas with him did likewise, but none pressed near enough the wall to alert the Agla'Con stationed there that the real attack was yet to come. And it would come from within the city, not from without as they were being led to believe. By the time they learned the truth, it would be too late.

Hul studied the Agla'Con for a moment, a bird's eye view that allowed him to see beyond them to the army fronting the city. It was his army, rallied from all the eastern cities who'd remained loyal to the Crescent Moon. Some had marched here, others had been brought near the city through Veilgates.

Hul smiled at the thought. Pure Veilgates—the knowledge of which had been brought to him by Joselyn Rai and young Idoman Leda. A gift from the Earthsoul which had sped up his campaign here by weeks. *Praised be the Creator for that*, he added. *And praised be Jase Fairimor.*

Thoughts of Jase and the others made him wonder how they were faring in their war with Shadan. Four days was a bloody long time to have to stand against a nightmare as monstrous as Death's Third March. There was no telling what could have happened in that time. *I'm coming, my friends*, he told them. *As soon as I finish here.*

He returned his attention to the Agla'Con on the wall. There weren't more than twenty-five or thirty of them, but most held the Power in anticipation of another strike from the Dymas in Hul's army. Few seemed to possess any real strength as Agla'Con went, but they were accompanied by fifty or sixty K'rrosha and twice that many Shadowhounds. Those bloody creatures moved along the top of the wall like patches of liquid night, their greyish-green spikes bright in the afternoon light.

Below the wall, stretching away into the city, some four or five thousand cultists held weapons at the ready, columns of black-robed, black-armored traitors he would be only too happy to kill. They were a fraction of the army that had taken the city all those weeks ago, and they were hopelessly outnumbered.

*But I'm not complaining,* Hul thought with a smile. Shadan had done Melek a favor by pulling so many of his troops out of Kamoth in order for them to take part in Death's Third March. Obviously he had underestimated Hul's chances of rallying an army sufficient to retake the city. That, or there was more to all of this than Hul realized. In which case he would need to be careful.

He reined in his Awareness and glanced over his shoulder at the line of soldiers and Dymas stretching away down the sloping corridor behind him. Glowstone lamps lit the small army at intervals, pools of soft white in a seemingly endless darkness. This was the very same passage he'd used to escape the Agla'Con invasion which had captured the city. Fitting that he was using it now to take the city back.

From its entrance more than a mile outside the city, the passage dropped deep into the earth via a spiraling stairwell, then ran straight as an arrow to a large chamber beneath the city proper. An intersection of sorts, the chamber had a number of passages leading to key points in the city. The path he'd taken led to the heart of Crescent Palace. And he was almost there.

Motioning Captain Plat and Kelithor Dymas near, he spoke in a whisper. "It's possible the Agla'Con have troops stationed in the throne room and throughout the palace," he told them. "Remind your men to be cautious as we near the exits."

He looked Vol in the eyes and smiled. It was good to see him without that blasted Mohawk. "Tell your men to spare any who surrender," he told his friend. "Kill all who resist. Hopefully we can separate the enemy from those who might have been held here against their will."

He looked at Kelithor. "Instruct the Dymas not to embrace the Power until I give the signal. If we can take the palace without using *Ta'shaen*, it would be well. *I* want to be the one to let the vermin out at the wall know we have returned."

"Yes, my lord," both men said, and Captain Plat smiled, curious as to what such an announcement might look like.

Hul took the lead once more, and they continued on up the passage. As they went, squads of Crescent Guard escorted by Dymas vanished into side passages, eager to reach their exit points, eager to engage the enemy. By the time Hul reached the small chamber inside the walls of the throne room, only Captain Plat's squad and Kelithor Dymas remained.

Hul brought them to a halt with raised fist and motioned for silence, then he moved the last few feet to the door and took hold of the lever that would release the locks of the hidden doorway. Behind him, Vol and his men extinguished the light of their glowstones, and the chamber plunged into darkness.

Pulling the lever, Hul eased the door open a couple of inches and peered out. A short distance beyond stood a decorative screen of tightly woven lattice and beyond that the Crescent Throne. There were flickers of movement out in the throne room, dark shadows against the light streaming in through the balcony windows at the far end of the chamber. There was a mumbling of voices, but Hul couldn't make out what was being said.

Steeling himself for what might follow, he eased the door the rest of the way open and moved out into the throne room, ready to embrace the Power should it come to that. For now, the latticed screen would shield him from the view of those in the room as it had so often shielded the Crescent Guard when they'd stood watch here. He wanted to hear what was being said. He wanted to know who these people were and if they were friend or foe.

"I told you the rumors were true," one voice said. "Lord Nid is in command of that army. He's come to reclaim his throne."

"Gelliston Dar," Captain Plat whispered, stepping near, and Hul nodded.

Gelliston was a member of Hul's political cabinet and was one of the highest ranking members in the Meleki government. For the past fifteen years he'd acted as the head of the Trade Commission and was an expert in Riaki customs and goods.

"Do you think he knows?" another voice asked, and Hul identified the speaker as Serifalin Inolt, another high-ranking member of the cabinet.

"Knows what?" Gelliston asked.

"About us," Serifalin answered.

"It won't matter," a female voice said, and Hul looked to Vol for help. Frowning, the captain shook his head. He didn't recognize the voice either.

"Because it's highly unlikely," the woman continued, "that he will trust any but those who died and those who escaped the attack with him. All who remained here under the cultist occupation, willingly or not, will be suspect. Regaining his trust will be most difficult."

*Not as difficult as you might think*, Hul thought, pleased to learn that some of those who'd been loyal to him still lived. And if these few had survived, others might have as well. Nodding for Captain Plat to follow, he started for the end of the screen, eager to reveal himself.

"It's worth a try," another voice said, and Hul paused as he tried to put a face to the speaker. Lonalisafin Jorn, he decided finally. Former Crescent Guardsman turned politician. He was a junior member of the cabinet, with less than three years of service, but he had made a name for himself as one of the more outspoken opponents of the Shadan Cult.

"Which is why," Lonalisafin continued, "I ordered my men to silence all those who might wish to discredit our names."

Hul knotted his hands into fists, a sick feeling washing through him. And he'd been about to reveal himself to these people. These traitors! He shot a look at Vol to find him frowning.

"I guess we know whose side they're on," the captain whispered.

"Under whose authority did you do this?" Gelliston asked. Hul couldn't decide if he sounded angry about the killings or just irritated that Lon hadn't consulted him first.

"Mine," a deep voice said from the throne room's eastern entrance.

Hul listened as booted footsteps echoed loudly in the silence as the man made his way to the others.

"Lord Shup," Gelliston said. "I thought you were out at the wall with the rest of the Agla'Con."

"I was," the other replied. "And it was painfully obvious that this battle is already lost." The sound of his feet ceased as he reached the others. "The fools at the wall just don't know it yet," he continued, his tone disgusted. "The only chance we have now of surviving this is if Lord Nid believes we were here against our will. Which is why it became necessary to silence those who might turn from us now that Lord Nid has returned. All those who know the truth about our involvement are dead."

*Not all of them,* Hul thought, his heart burning with anger. He exchanged a quick look with Vol and found that the captain's expression mirrored his own. Panishern Shup. Heir to the throne of Kamasin. Veteran of the Battle of Greendom. And now a Dymas turned Agla'Con. Hul shook his head in disgust.

"Now what?" Vol whispered.

"Nothing has changed," Hul whispered in return. "You and your men will arrest Gelliston and the others. I will deal with my traitorous cousin." He looked at Kelithor. "Be ready to defend us if my actions draw the attention of those out at the wall."

Kelithor nodded, and Hul took a steadying breath, steeling himself for battle. When he was calm, he moved around the end of the screen and strode into the open.

Lonalisafin spotted him first, and the former captain's mouth dropped open in surprise. He looked as if he'd seen a ghost. His companions followed his gaze, but Hul ignored them. His eyes stayed on Panishern, anger and disgust at his cousin's betrayal washing through him in turns.

For Panishern had betrayed more than Melek and the Crescent Moon. He'd betrayed the Earthsoul. He'd sold his soul to Maeon in exchange for promises of power and glory in the world to come and for a bloody Jexlair crystal. Hul spotted the crystal on Pan's wrist, a large ruby-like gem in a bracelet of silver.

Panishern turned as well, and surprise flashed into horror in an instant. The Jexlair crystal flared as he seized the Power, then winked out as Hul sliced the traitor's head from his neck with a blade of Spirit. Panishern's corpse toppled into a heap as the others looked on in terror.

And there were more than just the four whose voices Hul had heard from behind the screen. Ten others looked on as Melek's rightful King strode toward them.

Hul studied them all with contempt. Biladorian Kel and Habalishean Dio of the Trade Commission. Padikashi Vop and Quentifael Drim of the Cabinet of the Crescent Throne. Judges Raem and Gil of the High Court. And four women wearing small silver crowns bearing the Crimson Nightingale of Kamasin. Hul didn't recognize any of them, but it was likely they were nobility loyal to Panishern.

"Lord Nid," Lonalisafin said, dropping to one knee in respect. "Thank the light you've returned. And just in time to save us from this Agl–" He cut off as Hul knocked him senseless with a fist of Air that sent his limp body skidding away across the polished stone.

"Enough of your pretense," Hul told them. "I know you for what you are. The next one who speaks to me dies." He gestured to Vol. "Captain Plat, have your men hold these traitors here until the battle is ended. At which time I will be back to question them."

With Captain Plat and Kelithor Dymas at his side, he started for the balcony as the Crescent Guard formed up around the nine traitors. A small part of him hoped they would object so Captain Plat's men would have a reason to kill them. It would lighten his load considerably—the fewer trials the better. He had more important things to do now that Death's Third March had left his kingdom. The most pressing of which was sending aid to the Fairimors.

A gentle breeze welcomed him as he moved out onto the balcony and gazed down at his city. The Agla'Con and shadowspawn atop the outer wall still had their attention fastened on the Dymas outside the city, which wasn't all that surprising. There was so much Earthpower being held or wielded down there on both sides that his actions in the throne room would have amounted to nothing more than a whisper in a hurricane.

Smiling, he let his eyes move over the rest of the city. Aside from the thousands of cultist soldiers in the outermost parts of the city, the streets of Kamoth were empty. The majority of citizens had either fled during the first attack or were holed up in their homes and businesses. They'd already been through one battle to take the city—they were probably hoping to sit this one out. It was time to find out how many of them would take up arms to join him once they learned he had returned.

Opening himself to the Power, he channeled currents of Air and Spirit and sent his words to the far reaches of the city. "Enemies and allies of Melek," he began, "this is Hulanekaefil Nid, High King of Melek. I have retaken Crescent Palace and have reclaimed my throne." For emphasis, and to prove his words to those who couldn't sense his use of the Power, he opened himself to the Gift of *Shiin* and sent a brilliant column of Light lancing skyward from the balcony.

Down in the city, *Ta'shaen* came alive with a dozen corrupted wieldings, and crimson stabs of lightning crackled along the edge of the shield Kelithor pulled around them. Dozens of pure wieldings followed, and Fire and lightning erupted along the top of the outer wall. The attacks on Hul ceased as the Agla'Con went on the defensive. Several threads of corruption vanished from his Awareness as the Agla'Con who'd wielded them died.

"I and those who have come with me will now retake the city of Kamoth," Hul continued. "To those of you still loyal to the Crescent Moon, I say take up your swords and join me in battle. To my enemies, I say farewell. You shall not see the sun set on this day. *Dro'shen Kandekor!*"

Redirecting the column of Light toward the outer wall, he combined it with a powerful wielding of Spirit and sent several bars of *Sei'shiin* lancing into the midst of the enemy. Three Agla'Con and four K'rrosha flashed from existence while those around them dove for cover.

Two Agla'Con tried to retaliate but were ripped apart by Dymas the moment they lowered their shields. The rest hunkered beneath their shields, so hopelessly outnumbered that all they could do was defend while a second army led by Kelithor's Dymas emerged from the depths of the city to attack them from behind.

K'rrosha burst into flames. Shadowhounds blew apart in bursts of superheated gore. Cultist soldiers died on the swords and spears of the soldiers rallied from all the eastern cities and at the hands of the Crescent Guardsman who led them.

Not content to watch from the palace, Hul opened a Veilgate atop the wall, and Vol and Kelithor followed him into the midst of the fray. Wielding blades of Fire and Spirit as deftly as Croneam Eries might wield a Dragonblade, Kelithor Dymas cut his way through the terrified Agla'Con like a reaper, slicing through shields and men alike.

Hul watched him go, then turned and sent sizzling green tendrils of Fire sweeping down the top of the wall in the other direction. Black-cloaked figures, both living and refleshed, blew apart in smoking chunks and bits of flaming cloth.

*Ta'shaen* came alive as pure Veilgates opened around him and Dymas came through with soldiers and archers on their heels. The archers took positions along the inner edge of the wall and loosed a storm of arrows into the cultists below.

Hundreds fell dead or dying. Hundreds more fled, seeking refuge deeper in the city. They were met by the Crescent Guardsmen Hul had led into the city. Silver breastplates shining in the sun, they fell on the cultists in a flurry of steel. And they weren't alone—hundreds of Kamoth's citizens had joined them. Armed with swords and clubs and whatever else they could find, they'd answered their King's call to arms.

Heart filled with admiration, Hul watched them for a moment, then returned his attention to those atop the wall. Most of the Agla'Con were dead or incapacitated, but the few who remained had linked to enhance their abilities. Wrapped in a shield strong enough to deflect *Sei'shiin*, they were some fifty yards ahead near a tower and were hurling balls of Fire and stabs of lightning into the army below. It was a desperate act, a last ditch effort to inflict as much death as possible before they fell.

Hul spotted Kelithor just ahead and called to him, motioning him near. He had to shout to be heard over the rumble of Agla'Con thunder.

"Let's end this!" he said, then drew in all Seven Gifts of Power and opened a Veilgate inside the Agla'Con's shield.

Startled, the three men turned to face him but vanished in flashes of white as Kelithor burned them from existence with *Sei'shiin*.

"That is indeed a useful weapon," Kelithor commented as Hul let the gate slide shut. "You say Gideon taught you?"

"That and a lot more," Hul told him. Sensing corruption in his Awareness, he turned and sent killing tendrils of blue-green Fire lancing into a pair of Shadowhounds racing toward him. Both creatures blew apart in chunks of sizzling flesh that slicked the top of the wall with foul-smelling gore. "Although some of his tricks are messier than others."

"I don't mind messy if it means a dead enemy," Kelithor said. Turning on another pair of Shadowhounds racing up the side of a building inside the city, he channeled a tightly woven spiral of Flesh, and the creatures blew apart in fountains of greyish green blood. The sticky mess fell like rain on the cultists below. "Besides," he added, "certain methods leave the real estate intact."

"Still," Captain Plat said, stepping near, "I hope you two plan on cleaning up after yourselves. Especially if you're trying to preserve property values for our citizens." Grinning, he drew fletchings to cheek and loosed an arrow at another rooftop. The razored shaft took a Shadowhound through the head, and the beast's legs dropped from beneath it. Its limp corpse slid down the roof tiles and dropped into the street below, crushing an unsuspecting cultist.

"See," Vol said, taking aim at another Shadowhound. "It's much more tidy my way." The arrow left with a hiss and the hound dropped as if poleaxed.

"So it is," Hul told him with a smile.

He glanced over the edge of the wall at the army fronting the city. With the Agla'Con and K'rrosha destroyed, the approach to the city gate was clear, and the forward ranks had started forward. Banners from each of the eastern cities marked the various columns, and Hul smiled at the show of strength and unity. But it also awakened a touch of sadness. If only Melek had been this united a few years ago, Shadan's forces never would have gotten a hold like they did. It was a lesson he wouldn't soon forget. First, though, he needed to finish what he'd started.

"We need to get the gates open," he said. "Don't bother being gentle. We'll repair everything after this is over."

"Yes, my lord," Kelithor said, and Hul felt him stretch out with his Awareness to contact the Dymas leading the assault. A moment later a powerful surge of Air struck the gates, an invisible battering ram that knocked the massive metal doors from their hinges and sent them toppling onto the cultists beyond. Dozens were crushed beneath thousands of pounds of polished steel.

Meleki soldiers charged into the city, and their booted feet rang hollowly as they swarmed over the fallen gates and into the midst of the Shadan Cultists. A clash of swords followed and with it came the cries of the wounded and dying. Most were cultist scum, but Hul knew that many good and loyal men would be found among the dead. It was the cost of war, and it pained him that he'd grown accustomed to paying the bill.

And yet he would do what he could to minimize the loss of life—on his side, at least. The filth of Shadan's Cult would be killed to the last man.

"Send your Dymas among the wounded," Hul told Kelithor. "Have them heal all they can. Leave the killing to our soldiers." He turned to Captain Plat. "Come, Vol," he said. "This battle is over. I wish to speak with those who sought to claim my throne."

"As you wish, my King," Vol said, his eagerness to confront the traitors evident in his eyes.

Taking one last look at a battle which was now well in hand, Hul wove the necessary strands of Earthpower and opened a Veilgate back into his throne room.

Gelliston and the rest of the prisoners looked up as he appeared, and expressions of fear or worry painted every face. Lonalisafin had regained consciousness, but one of his eyes was swollen shut from where he'd struck the floor. His good eye was wide with fear, and he tensed as Hul approached. The movement prompted the Crescent Guardsman nearest him to raise a sword in warning.

"My lord..." Lon began but trailed off as Hul's eyes bored into him.

"The battle is over," Hul told them. "But my investigation into this treachery has just begun. It will go easier for all of you if you cooperate. No more deception. No more lies. A speedy confession of the truth may earn you a speedy and relatively painless execution. Toy with me further and you will regret it."

Gelliston opened his mouth to speak, but Hul silenced him with a look. "Captain Plat," he said, turning to Vol. "I would speak with each of the prisoners individually that I might weigh their words against the others. Hold them all here and keep them silent. We'll begin with the women."

He strode across the floor and up the steps of the dais to the Crescent Throne. Seating himself, he beckoned the first of the women forward. "This court is now in session," he said, glaring meaningfully at Judges Raem and Gil. They might be the two highest ranking judges in Melek, but today *he* was the High Court in this land.

The woman reached the foot of the dais, and Hul wove an invisible shield against eavesdropping around them. "You may speak," he told her, watching her face for some sign of what she might be thinking. She looked to be approaching middle age, and there was a softness to her face. Her eyes, however, were hard. Darkness lurked behind that gaze, he realized. Darkness and a terrible anger.

"Praised be Maeon," she said. "May the Crescent Throne burn beneath his feet and all that you love die at his coming."

Hul gave an unamused grunt. "Much of what I loved has already died," he told her. "As will you." He leaned forward and looked her in the eyes. "Just not in the manner you might think."

Embracing more of the Power, he parted the Veil directly behind her and used a rush of air to shove her through to the grasslands beyond. The shimmering blue hole closed before she could speak, but Hul knew from the look of horror that washed over her face that she realized where he'd sent her. The question now was how many of her companions would be joining her.

He motioned for Captain Plat to send the next woman forward. She, too, was in her middle years, and, like the first, there was a hardness to her that was evident in her eyes. He knew before she spoke where her allegiance lay. Still, he wanted to hear it for himself.

"You may speak," he said.

"And you may fling yourself into the fires of Con'Jithar," she answered, then sneered and added, "my *lord*."

Hul shook his head sadly, then parted the Veil and sent her through to join the first. Before the gate closed, he caught a glimpse of dark shapes cresting a nearby hill.

The third woman was young and strikingly beautiful, with some of the most intricate lines of maturation he'd ever seen, a spider-webbed pattern of lavender that crisscrossed her nose and touched both cheeks. Her snow-white mane reached almost to the middle of her back.

"You may speak," he said once she was inside the ward against eavesdropping.

"I have nothing to say that you don't already know," she said, meeting his gaze. Her face was set, but there was a hint of sadness in her eyes. "I sold my honor, my birthright, and my soul for a chance to elevate my status in this kingdom. It was a vain and foolish decision based on reasons too many to name. Reasons I don't fully understand myself. I... I was deceived, my lord. By people I thought I knew. By people I trusted."

She went slowly to one knee and lowered her head. "With hope that I might find forgiveness in the afterlife, I accept the consequences of my actions. But please, my lord, I beg you: spare the life of my sister. She, too, was deceived by Lord Shup's enticings. She knew nothing of his nature as an Agla'Con and journeyed to Kamoth just this morning. She is innocent of any wrongdoing."

"And you?" Hul asked. "Are you innocent as well?"

"No, my lord," she said, lowering her head even more. "I knew what he was, and I chose to ignore it. But I did not plot against you or those who serve you. I...."

She sighed. "I thought you were dead. I never would have put my name in their book had I known the truth."

Hul's pulse quickened. "What book?"

"The Con'Kumen Book of Names," she answered. "It is a record of those who've pledged themselves. Lord Shup keeps his in his coat pocket."

"I'm so glad I didn't kill him with Fire," Hul muttered, then motioned for Captain Plat to come near. After whispering instructions, he returned his attention to the young woman while Vol went to fetch the book.

"What is your name, young lady?" he asked.

"Persyvonella Fim, my lord."

"Well, Persy," he said, shortening her name to show the formalities were over. "I think you have redeemed yourself for the time being. Only time will tell if I should pardon you completely."

She looked up, tears glistening in her eyes. "I shall do my best to earn that pardon. Thank you, my lord."

"Thank *you*," he told her, then motioned for her to rise. "You may wait with your sister while I speak with the rest of Shup's lackeys." He turned to Vol who had returned with the book. "Thank you, Captain," he said, then thumbed through the pages, scanning the lists of names.

After finding what he was looking for, he looked up and smiled at Persy. "Please distance Lady Fim and her sister from the others," he said. "I would keep them safe from retaliation should anyone be displeased with them."

"Yes, Lord Nid," Vol said, taking Persy by the arm and leading her to a spot well away from Gelliston and the others. Her sister joined her and the two embraced, their faces wet with tears.

"Bring me Lonalisafin," Hul ordered, and two Crescent Guardsmen urged the man to his feet with the tips of their swords.

The former Captain of the Crescent Guard stopped at the foot of the dais, his good eye wary. "What did that little tramp tell you?" he asked, his voice harsh. One of his escorts stepped forward and whacked Lon across the back of the knees with the blunt edge of his sword, driving him to his knees.

"You will address the High King in a civil tone," the guard snapped.

"He is no king to me," Lon replied, and Hul motioned the guardsman to stand down when his hand tightened on his sword once more. Dipping his head in a bow, the guard complied.

Hul stared down at Lon, disgust warring with anger as he contemplated just how far the man had fallen. To go from a Captain in the Crescent Guard to a notable and powerful politician and then to end up as a traitorous cur loyal to Shadan... such a fall from grace was beyond Hul's comprehension.

"It's what she didn't tell me that should concern you," Hul told his former friend. "For instance," he continued, thumbing through Shup's book of names, "she said nothing about your name being in this book, and yet here it is. Along with the names of the rest of your constituents in this rebellion."

He looked up from the book, his eyes boring into Lon. "What have you to say about it?"

"You can't win, *my lord*," he said, twisting the words derisively. "Nothing can stop Death's Third March or the collapse of the Veil. Maeon will claim this miserable world, and I will be there at his side when he does, watching you suffer."

Hul chuckled mirthlessly. "In the meantime, enjoy your Brotherhood." Opening another Veilgate, he shoved Lon through to join the women. The dark shapes he'd spotted on a nearby hill had taken the form of mounted K'rrosha and knots of armored Darklings. They were near enough now that they spotted Lon standing framed by the Veilgate, and a howl went up as they drew swords and broke into a run.

To his credit, Lon turned to face them, his head held high. The women dropped to their knees, weeping.

Hul let the Veilgate close and rose from his throne. Moving down the steps of the dais, he crossed to where the other prisoners waited. They watched him warily, their eyes flitting about as if they were contemplating running for their freedom. *I can help you with that,* he thought and opened another larger Veilgate behind them.

"We are done here," he told them, holding up the book for them to see. "I will hear no more from those who so willingly pledged themselves to Maeon." Channeling a large rush of Air, he pushed them through to join the other three. "Give my regards to the K'rrosha," he told them, then released the Power.

As the part in the Veil slid shut, he turned to Captain Plat. "As soon as the city is secure, assemble the War Council. We need to plan our next move."

"Any idea what that might be?" Vol asked, his trademark smile eager.

"We retake Kamasin," Hul told him, looking out the window at the Death's Chain Mountains rising to the northeast. "And then we go after Shadan."

Lonalisafin Jorn watched the approaching army of Darklings with a great deal of trepidation. The bloody creatures had the temperament of wild dogs and wouldn't be easy to reason with. The K'rrosha weren't much better, though they might listen to him long enough for him to plead his case.

A hole opened in the air to his right and Gelliston and the other prisoners tumbled through with the help of an invisible rush of Air. They scrambled to their feet in panic and looked around in horror. Startled cries and gasps escaped several of them when they spotted the quickly approaching army.

"On your feet," Lon ordered. "And stop your sniveling. We have one chance to survive this."

They did as they were told, but huddled together like terrified sheep facing an onslaught of lions. *Well aren't we?* he thought, his eyes on the nightmare bearing down on them.

When they were near enough to see him clearly, he flashed a series of Con'Kumen hand signals identifying himself as a *Mae'rillium*. It wasn't the highest rank in the order, but it might buy him some time to speak.

Two of the five K'rrosha raised their lances skyward and sent short bursts of corrupted Fire into the air. The Darklings slowed and lowered their weapons, but their animal-like faces watched Lon and the others hungrily.

The K'rrosha brought their shadow-wrought mounts to a halt in front of Lon, and each stared down at him with eyes of fire. The silence that followed was broken only by the snorting and stamping of their demon-like horses and the feral grunts of the Darklings.

"Speak, *Mae'Rillium*," one of the Shadowlancers said at last, its voice harsh and demanding.

"I am Lonalisafin Jorn, sworn servant of the Agla'Con Panishern Shup, Lord of Kamasin."

"And yet here you are," the refleshed being said. "On the fringe of a battle between Kelsa and the armies of Death's Third March." Pausing, eyes flaring, the K'rrosha leaned forward menacingly. "Brought here through a Veilgate wrought by a Dymas."

"It was High King Nid," Lon explained, a knot of fear tightening in his chest. "He has retaken Kamoth. He killed my master and exiled my companions and I to... to...." He looked around. "Where are we?"

"Talin Plateau," the K'rrosha said, then turned his fiery gaze on the other four. "What should we do with them?"

Lon went cold inside as the four K'rrosha considered. Gelliston and two others dropped to their knees next to the women, their faces terrified.

"They failed their Agla'Con master," one K'rrosha said. "That doesn't speak well of them."

"But they brought word of Kamoth's fall," another said. "Lord Shadan will want to know of that."

"Perhaps they would like to be the ones to tell him," said a third.

The final K'rrosha leaned forward, his grey-fleshed face visible inside his hood. "I say we just kill them and move on."

"No," the first said. "I have a better idea."

Turning to a knot of Darklings, it gave several quick signals in the language of the Brotherhood, and Lon's heart sank as he did his best to make sense of them.

It sank further when he realized that he'd been right in his interpretation, and he watched helplessly as a dozen or more Darklings moved forward and tossed a variety of weapons at his and the others' feet.

"You march with us," the K'rrosha said. "Fall behind and I will feed you to my Shadowhounds." He nudged his shadowspawned mount into a trot and Lon had to jump out of the way to avoid being trampled.

Six Shadowhounds flowed out of the midst of the Darklings and hurried to take point for their masters. Spike-backed monstrosities of grey and black, they glanced at Lon and the others as they passed, eyes flaring hungrily.

*Maeon help us*, Lon thought, taking up a sword and falling into step with the Darklings. From the corner of his eye, he saw Gelliston and three others do the same, but the rest dropped to their knees and put their hands over their faces, weeping.

True to the K'rrosha's threat, two Shadowhounds broke from the pack ahead and raced back the way they had come.

Lon quickened his pace, but he was still within earshot when the sounds of slaughter began.

He shuddered. *Burn you, Nid*, he thought, doing his best to shut his ears to the screaming.

# CHAPTER 8

## Homecomings

As Elam Gaufin led his men through the northern gate and into the city of Chellum, he glanced up at the blue and silver banners flapping gently atop the palace towers, and a feeling of peace washed over him. He was home, and with him every member of the Chellum Home Guard. Not a single man had been lost. *Praised be the Creator*, he thought, smiling.

The lane leading to the palace was a thoroughfare of commerce with two- and three-story shops and businesses on both sides. People bustled about, buying and selling and visiting with neighbors, but all of them moved aside as he neared, taking a break from what they were doing to watch him and his men pass. Many appeared in doorways and on balconies. Some exited the buildings to join the throng. Cheers and shouts of welcome were raised, giving a parade-like feeling to the situation.

Elam's smile deepened. This is why he'd had the Dymas in Cro—in Joneam's army open their Veilgates outside the city instead of directly into the palace grounds. It was important to him that he and his men enter the city the same way they had left. It brought the journey full circle. It felt... right.

He'd wanted the people of Chellum to know the Home Guard had returned. Even more important, he'd wanted his men to see that they were valued and appreciated by those they served. The people of Chellum didn't disappoint, and the cheers and shouts followed them all the way to Festival Lane.

Elam turned his men south and followed the park-like road around to the palace's main gate. Once there, he was met by Tarasin Ebirin and a squad of Home Guard.

"Welcome home," the acting captain greeted, moving up to take the reins of Elam's horse. He looked down the line of horsemen as if expecting more. "Is it just the Home Guard you bring?"

"General Taggert has a different assignment," Elam said, leaving it at that. "I need to debrief Lord Chellum on the change of plans for us and for the general."

"Of course," Tarasin said, then flashed a smile and added, "Oh, by the way, word of your return rushed ahead of you as if driven by the wind. Your wife is waiting for you in the Royal Ballroom. I believe you'll find her beneath the silver oak."

Elam smiled. *Which is where we said goodbye,* he thought. Things really had come full circle.

"Thank you, Tarasin," Elam said. "I've instructed the men to visit their families before returning to duty. Can those under your command continue their assignments for one more day?"

"Of a certainty," Tarasin answered. "You will be taking command, I assume?"

"Not unless you would like to volunteer for it."

Tarasin grunted in amusement. "Not on your life," he said, then brought his fist to his chest in salute. "Home Guard, attention!" he shouted, and all across the lane, backs stiffened and heads came up. "Captain Ebirin transferring command of the Home Guard to First Captain Elam Gaufin. May he lead us here at home as he has led you on the battlefield. For the honor of God, the Flame of Kelsa, and the liberty of our people, let it be so."

"Let it be so," the men repeated, their voices filling Festival Lane like thunder.

"I'll take your horse to the stables," Tarasin said. "Don't forget to stop and speak with your wife."

*Not a chance of that,* he thought, hurrying through the gates and onto the bridge spanning the moat. He glanced down as dark shapes glided effortlessly under the water, moving in both directions. He had just reached the other side, when one of the lumtars emerged, sliding its massive forebody up onto the rim of the moat and bracing itself with the hooked claws of its flippers. It chittered excitedly in its language.

"It's good to see you, too, Mauf," Elam called, but he didn't stop to engage the massive creature. There would be time for that later.

Still chittering, Mauf bobbed his head up and down a few times before disappearing into the depths once more.

Once inside, Elam quickened his pace, his heart racing with excitement as he prepared to greet his wife. She should be very close to delivering their baby, he realized. If she hadn't already. *No,* he thought. *Tarasin would have said something.*

Those who worked in this part of the palace—the bureaucrats and lawyers and judges—stepped hastily aside as he approached, stifling any attempt to speak to him because of the look in his eyes. He had somewhere he needed to be, they realized. Best not to delay or interfere.

The guards fronting the entrance to the royal ballroom pulled the doors open as he neared, and he strode through into the massive dome beyond. And there, sitting on a bench beneath the giant silver oak, was Jaina. She had one hand resting on her belly—so much larger than when he'd last seen her—and with the other hand she was fingering a leaf which had fallen from the tree. She hadn't seen him yet, and he took advantage of the moment to look at her.

She was beautiful. She was more than beautiful—she was radiant. She had a glow about her which could only come from the wondrous knowledge that she carried inside her a new generation, a new hope for the future.

"Hello, Jaina," he said as he neared.

Her head snapped up, and she smiled even as tears welled up in her eyes.

"Elam," she said, reaching out a hand.

He helped her to her feet and they embraced. And just like that, the loneliness he'd felt during the weeks they'd been apart vanished. He smoothed her hair as she cried tears of happiness, then lifted her chin so he could kiss her gently on the mouth. It was some time before he released her and stepped back to look her over.

"You've gotten—"

"Big," she said.

"I was going to say more beautiful."

"Perhaps," she said. "But I've also gotten big. Jonnil Dymas says it's because I'm carrying twins."

Elam blinked. "Twins? That's wonderful."

"Boys," Jaina said, then tears welled up once more. "Oh, Elam. I'm so glad you are home safe."

"Me too," he said, hugging her once more. He held her for a long time, enjoying the scent of her hair and the warmth of her body. Finally, he stepped back and took her hand.

"Will you accompany me into the inner palace?" he asked. "I need to speak to Lord Chellum about what transpired at Talin Plateau."

Her face grew immediately worried. "It's bad, isn't it?"

"Nothing we can't overcome," he said, surprised by how strongly he believed it.

The belief had nothing to do with the miracles he'd seen on the battlefield, impressive as those had been. He simply refused to believe the Creator would allow children to be born into a world that had no future.

His confidence reassured Jaina, and together they made their way into the Chellum home.

え

Lounging in one of the high-backed chairs at the table of the Kelsan High Tribunal, Elliott listened intently as Jase addressed the forty-one Rhiven who'd come to Trian with their Queen. They occupied the first few rows of tiered seats facing the table, and Jase stood before them the way a professor might stand in front of a class of eager college students—he had their complete attention.

Elliott suspected it was due in part to the fact that Jase was the *Mith'elre Chon*, but he suspected, too, that there was more to it than feelings of awe for fancy titles of prophecy. Jase had a presence about him now that invited respect without demanding it. In ways too many to name, he was the most important and potentially the most powerful person in the world. He'd stood toe to toe with Death's Third March and had delivered a blow that likely had a large portion of Shadan's army second guessing the Dreadlord's choice to invade Kelsa.

*Not that it will change anything*, Elliott thought. Shadan's minions, whether they liked it or not, would continued their westward march.

And that's where the Rhiven came in, which was what Jase was explaining to them at that very moment.

"If we can take away Shadan's ability to move entire armies through Dragon Gates," Jase said, "we can buy ourselves the time we need to find a viable Blood Orb and bring about the Rejuvenation."

"We will deal with our wayward brethren," one of the male Rhiven said. He was well-muscled, with dark red hair and neatly trimmed sideburns and pointed goatee. Those, combined with his bright yellow eyes, made him look like a type of songbird Elliott had seen in Riak. Flamebursts, Raimen had called them.

Jase nodded to him. "Thank you..."

"Yavil to al'Jagulair," the Rhiven said. "Warder Advisor to Queen Morgranon. And from this day forward, ally of the *Mith'elre Chon*."

Jase acknowledged the pledge of support with a smile.

"As for the Blood of Orbs of Elsa," another Rhiven began, and Elliott turned to regard her curiously. A woman with even sharper features than her Queen, her hair was the same golden hue as her eyes. "Do we have any clues as to their location?"

"One," Jase answered. "At least we think it's a clue—a relationship of some kind between the *chorazin* T'rii Gates of the Old World and the Temples of Elderon. Wherever we've found one, the other was nearby. The Dainin are searching for more as we speak."

"Your assumption is correct," the yellow-haired woman said. "T'rii Gates fronted all the major cities of the world, and a good many of those cities would have housed temples."

"But not all?"

"No," a raven-haired male said, drawing all eyes to him. "I lived in Fas'Drolma for a time. There was no temple there. Tre'Ledarius, however, had two."

Elliott sat up a little straighter, a rush of excitement washing through him. *Two temples in the same city?*

"This Tre'Ledarius," Jase asked. "Do you know where it is?"

Elliott's excitement vanished when raven-hair shook his head. "When we emerged from hiding after the Great Destruction, nothing of the world we had known remained. Entire continents had been broken up or had disappeared entirely. The entire face of the world had been altered."

"But we know where several T'rii Gates are located," red-haired Yavil said. "We will send some of our people to investigate." He shot a quick look at Galiena. "If my

Queen approves, of course."

Galiena smiled. "I do."

Elliott cast a sideways glance down the table at her. She sat next to Brysia and had remained silent until now, content, it seemed to Elliott, to let Jase do the talking.

Rising now, she left her seat and moved around the table to stop next to Jase. Elliott still couldn't believe the woman was seven thousand years old—she looked no older than Talia.

"Stop oogling her like you would a pretty girl at a ball," Talia whispered from beside him.

"I wasn't oogling," Elliott told her, offended. "I just can't get past the fact that she is older than the world itself."

"And not at all what she seems," Talia said in return. "What are they like? In their true form, I mean."

"Terrifying," Elliott told her, then shook his head. "At least the evil ones are. I'd say Galiena and those who follow her would be magnificent."

"The days ahead will be difficult," Galiena told her people, and Elliott turned to regard her once more. He *wasn't* oogling. He was just... well, fascinated. It was the kind of fascination one might have for a ruby-spotted adder or a blue-fanged spider. Both were beautiful, but they were also extremely deadly.

"Some of us," the Queen continued, "won't survive the conflict with our wayward brethren. But it is a battle which must be fought. It is my hope that we can spare this world the fate we ourselves suffered. For the honor of God, the Flame of Kelsa, and the salvation of our races, let it be done."

"Let it be done," her people echoed.

"Thank you," Jase told them. "I will leave all decisions about confronting your brethren to you. Let me know if there is anything you need. In the meantime, the palace and Overlook are open to you. My home is your home."

He turned to leave, and the Rhiven came to their feet in a show of respect.

Jase smiled, but didn't turn back. He was tired, Elliott knew. He could see it in his friend's face.

Those at the table rose to follow, and Elliott and Talia fell in beside Seth as Gideon and Brysia hurried to catch up to Jase. Elison, however, hung back, waiting to speak again with Galiena.

"He needs to sleep," Talia said, concern heavy in her voice as she studied Jase.

Elliott followed her gaze to Jase. Gideon and Brysia had reached him, and each had taken him by an arm to act as escorts. *Probably to keep him from falling on his face.*

"Gideon and Brysia will see that Jase finds his way into a bed," Seth said. "And Ammorin has prepared an herbal tea that will ensure he sleeps until tomorrow morning."

Elliott couldn't keep from smiling. Jase might be the *Mith'elre Chon*, prophesied savior-warrior of the Earthsoul, but in the eyes of Gideon and Brysia he would always be their son. His smile deepened. *Parents.*

"Good," Talia said, sounding relieved. "He pushes himself too hard." She glanced pointedly at Seth. "Like some others I know."

Seth's eyes narrowed but he said nothing, and they walked the rest of the way into the Fairimor home in silence.

The smell of warm food greeted them as they entered, and Elliott's stomach growled as he made his way to the dining table. He was greeted by an assortment of meats and breads prepared for them by Allisen.

Inhaling deeply, he took a plate and began helping himself. Seth and Talia joined him, but Gideon and Brysia guided Jase up the stairs into the north tower without slowing. They were serious about getting him to rest.

"This looks good," Elliott said as he sat. "Much better than the slop they were serving on the front lines."

Seth grunted as he started layering smoked meats onto a thick slice of bread. "Allisen doesn't have to cook over a measly little fire surrounded by soldiers and horses."

"Acknowledged," Elliott said, "but you might think soldiers would expect a bit more from their cooks considering that it could very well be their last meal."

When Seth didn't respond, Elliott let the topic die, and each was left to focus on their food in silence. As he ate, he felt Talia's eyes on him and knew what she was thinking. It was confirmed the moment he pushed his plate away.

"So," she said, her tone conversational, "what *did* you do in Riak?"

Elliott related the tale as nonchalantly and as straightforward as possible, but Talia's eyes were wide and her expression one of disbelief as she listened. She interrupted a few times with questions about what might happen as a result of some of the events—those concerning clans Kyoai, Gizo, and Maridan—and he was forced to admit that he didn't know. *Nothing good*, he told her silently, then finished with how he passed the Shizu trials and was granted Riaki citizenship.

Talia was quiet as she contemplated what she'd heard. After a while she spoke. "It was indeed wise for Jase to send Chellum's troops home." Her eyes moved to Seth, but she looked away quickly as if trying to squash an unpleasant thought.

Elliott stiffened when he realized what that thought had been. *Elisa... Seth's young wife murdered by Shizu in retaliation for things Seth did in Riaki.*

He went cold inside. The similarities between his experiences in Riak and Seth's were uncanny. Both had become Shizu. Both had started a war and fought on the side of Clan Gahara. Both had made numerous enemies.

*But that's where the similarities end*, he thought. *I will not lose Tana the way Seth lost Elisa.*

Fortunately, Seth hadn't seen his or Talia's reaction. His attention was fastened on a pair of *Bero'thai* who had entered from the Dome and were making their way toward the dining table.

"It was," Elliott agreed. "In fact, I've been thinking about sending—escorting—Raimen and Tohquin to Chellum as well."

The comment pulled Seth's eyes away from the approaching *Bero'thai.* "Why?"

"To keep an eye on Tey Eries," he answered, then added a silent, *And Tana.*

"They're quite fond of that little girl," he continued, "and she them. Besides, they promised Croneam they would keep her safe. They can't do that if they are here. It is what they and Croneam would want."

*And Joneam,* he thought, but decided not to speak it aloud. The younger Eries hadn't specifically mentioned Raimen and Tohquin when he'd asked Elliott to deliver a message to his wife, but he'd made it clear that he wanted Alesha and the children kept safe. This was just the best way to do that *and* allow the Shizu to keep their promise.

Talia nodded. "I think that is a great idea." She rose and moved around the table, offering him her arm. "I think I would like to accompany you."

Seth stood as well. "We'll all go," he said. "Just give me a moment to speak with the *Bero'thai.*" Stepping past them, he acknowledged the men's salutes with a nod.

"What did you find?" he asked.

"Cheslie Brandameir is alive and well," one of the Elvan soldiers said. "She fled the palace during the Agla'Con attack and has been staying with family in the outer city."

Seth nodded, looking greatly relieved. "Thank you."

"Yes, Captain," the *Bero'thai* said and headed back the way they had come.

"Cheslie," Elliott said, "is that the woman you—"

"Yes," Seth said, and Elliott knew by the look in the older man's eyes not to make a big deal out of it. He glanced at Talia and found that she was trying—very unsuccessfully—not to smile.

Seth noticed it too, and a scowl moved over his face. "Raimen and Tohquin are in the Dome," he said. "And I'm sure we'll find Dymas capable of parting the Veil. We'll leave from there." Still scowling, he strode away.

Grinning at Talia, Elliott took her arm in his and they hurried to catch up.

# CHAPTER 9

## New Assignments

"IT'S GOOD TO HAVE YOU BACK," Decker Chellum said as Elam and Jaina entered the Chellum home. The King motioned for them to join him and Rhea at the dining table. The Queen, Elam noted, was starting to show her pregnancy. On Rhea's right, sat a young woman, a slender, brown-haired beauty Elam had never seen before. She looked about the same age as Talia.

"It's good to *be* back," Elam replied, helping Jaina ease herself into one of the high-backed chairs. *Twins*, he thought again, looking at her belly. *Amazing.*

He took the chair next to hers so he could hold her hand, and she smiled as they interlocked fingers. He'd almost forgotten how soft her skin was.

"This is Tana Murra," Rhea said, introducing the young woman. "Elliott's fiancee."

Elam blinked. "Well, I have been away for a while, haven't I?"

Tana gave a pleasant laugh. "It's a recent development."

"Tana is from Kindel's Grove," Decker added, his expression growing solemn. "You heard what happened there?"

"A little," Elam answered, watching Tana for some sign as to what she might be thinking. Undoubtedly she would have lost friends, possibly even family to the vicious attack. "Similar attacks were made against villages in the Allister Plains."

"Is that why the Home Guard has returned?" Rhea asked. "Does Gideon fear that Chellum might be attacked as well?"

"It wasn't Gideon that sent us," Elam said. "It was Jase. And I don't think he considers Shadan to be the only threat."

Decker's brow pinched down as he frowned. "What does that mean?"

"It means," Elliott said, exiting the stairwell of the north tower with Talia, Seth, and two Shizu, "that he thinks there are some in Riak who might be holding a grudge against me."

"Elliott!" Tana squawked.

Leaping to her feet, she raced across the room, where Elliott caught her in his arms and hugged her tightly. Talia waited until they were finished, then opened her arms for a hug as well. The two young ladies exchanged a series of excited whispers as they embraced.

Seth started to move past, but Tana released Talia and grabbed the captain by the arm, pulling him close.

Surprised by the show of affection, Seth stood stiffly for a moment, then slowly brought his arms up and returned the hug.

Talia and Elliott exchanged amused smiles while Rhea said softly, "I told you she would be good for this family."

Decker chuckled. "I never doubted it for a second."

The moment ended when the doors to the ballroom opened and a middle-aged man in a grey cloak strode in with a four young people close behind. Each wore the blue *kitara*-style jacket of a *Dalae*.

"Ah, Jonnil Dymas," Decker said. "You felt their arrival, I see."

Jonnil nodded. "I did," he answered, then looked expectantly at the new arrivals. "You bring word from the front?"

"And from Trian," Seth answered. He moved to the table and took a seat next to Elam. "Please join us," he told Jonnil. "And ward the immediate area against eavesdropping. I would like a shield of Spirit or Air as a barrier against physical intrusion as well."

"Is that really necessary?" Rhea asked, sounding worried. Obviously, she understood what such wards implied.

"In light of all that has happened of late," Seth told her. "Yes."

"You guys have fun," Elliott told them. "We'll be out in the ballroom with Tey Eries and her family."

"The Shizu, too?" Decker asked, studying the two black-clad warriors.

Elliott shrugged. "Raimen and Tohquin are Tey's uncles. She adopted them while she was in Riak. They are here on assignment from Joneam Eries and will be acting as the child's warders for the next few weeks."

Both Shizu faces remained perfectly stoic, but the brief look they exchanged practically shouted of surprise. Neither had expected this. Either that, or Elliott was being entirely untruthful about something. Elam sighed inwardly. *How shocking.*

"Make sure you let the Home Guard know," Seth told Elliott. "I don't want a war breaking out in the palace should anyone believe we've been infiltrated by the enemy."

Jaina tightened her grip on Elam's hand. "But there are only two of them," she whispered. "How could anyone believe we were under attack?"

Seth smiled at her naivety. "They are Shizu," he said simply, leaving it at that.

Elliott took Tana's hand, and they started for the doors. Raimen and Tohquin followed, but Talia came to the table and sat next to her father. Jonnil Dymas excused the four *Dalae* and came to the table also.

Elam nodded a greeting, then turned to find Decker smiling fondly at Talia as she adjusted her dress. "I understand you had a rather close brush with death a few days back," Decker said, stopping her cold. "Is it true?"

Talia remained still for the barest of moments, then finished adjusting her dress before looking up. She smiled disarmingly.

"Who told on me?" she asked.

"Everyone," Decker said, the gruffness of the reply tempered by the tender way in which he reached up to touch her face. "Care to elaborate?"

"Not really," she told him. "Not now, anyway. There are more important things to discuss."

Decker grunted. "More important to them, maybe," he said. "Nothing is more important to a father than the well-being of his daughter." His eyes misted as tears threatened to form.

Talia smiled as she took his hand. "I promise to tell you everything after we are done here."

Decker started to smile, then coughed to cover his embarrassment at showing so much emotion. "Well, let's get to it," he said, sounding as impatient as ever.

Elam turned to Seth, but his friend shook his head. "You are in command here, Elam," he said. "My duty lies with the *Mith'elre Chon* until the war with Shadan ends."

"Of course," Elam said, but it was difficult not to feel disappointed. Being in command meant he would have less time to spend with Jaina. At least until he could delegate some of the less pressing matters to Tarasin and the others. He wasn't going to *completely* abandon his wife.

He fastened his attention on Decker. "As Elliott said when he arrived, Jase sent the Home Guard back to Chellum because he fears retaliation by some of the clans in Riak. Several have issued death warrants for Elliott, and will stop at nothing to see them carried out. Jase sent me and my men here to keep that from happening."

"And the rest of our army?" Decker asked.

"Are stationed in Talin Pass," Elam answered. "With lookouts at strategic points along the highway leading from Fulrath to Chellum. Jase assigned enough Dymas to General Taggert to make moving the Chellum army through Veilgates possible. If any part of Shadan's army attempts to approach Trian by way of Chellum, we will be prepared to meet them."

"Is that a legitimate threat?" Rhea asked. She sounded worried.

"I don't think Shadan will risk dividing his forces again," Seth said. "Not after losing a third of his troops at Fulrath."

Decker's brows turned down on themselves in a scowl. "I thought Death's Third March assaulted the rim just this morning. How the blazes did they reach Fulrath so quickly?"

"Through a new type of Veilgate," Elam answered. "A very large Veilgate. And not just one, but two. We were routed in the opening moments of the battle."

"So *that's* what I felt?" Jonnil Dymas said, then looked embarrassed that he had spoken. Smiling apologetically, he added, "It sent a shockwave through *Ta'shaen* that, for a moment anyway, made me think the Veil was collapsing."

"Not all that far from the truth," Elam told him, then looked back to Decker. "One army attacked Fulrath while a second attacked our forces from the rear. It was retreat or be annihilated."

Jaina's hand tightened on his and Elam looked over to find fear in her eyes. Fear and the unmistakable worry all soldiers' wives felt for their husbands. He smiled reassuringly before turning his attention to Decker.

The King was shaking his head as if having trouble comprehending what he'd heard. "Blood of Maeon," he said. "Then what happened?"

"We lost thousands of men." Seth told him. "But it would have been tens of thousands if not for Jase and the Dymas."

"Mostly Jase," Elam said, forever in awe of the memory. "He kept the enemy busy while our army escaped." When Jaina's grip tightened further, he decided not to elaborate on just how narrow that escape had been. At least not here in front of the others. She deserved to know the truth of what had happened to him. All of the truth, including his appointment to *Ael'mion* by the Earthsoul. She'd hear of everything eventually. It would be best if it came from him.

"And Fulrath?" Decker asked.

Elam shrugged, looking to Seth for the answer. "You were there," he said. "I'll let you answer."

"They held long enough to evacuate everyone," Seth said. "Croneam stayed behind and activated the city's wards. Every living thing from the Seal to the perimeter of the Freezone was destroyed. Shadan lost some seventy thousand troops. Most of them Darklings and other shadowspawn."

"Croneam?" Decker asked, his face growing solemn. He knew.

"Took his rightful place among the heroes in Eliara."

They spoke of other things for a while, mostly Jase's plans for confronting Death's Third March in the days to come, and the ongoing search for a Blood Orb of Elsa. The conversation ended, much to Elam's chagrin, with Decker pressing Seth for a report of what transpired at Zedik Pass. He also wanted more information about the battle at the rim. Fortunately, Seth wasn't the storyteller Elliott was so the report was business-like and not terribly graphic. Even so, Jaina, bless her heart, had turned white by the end and was trembling.

Elam brought her hand to his lips and kissed it. "But it's over now, and my men and I are home safely."

"The Home Guard didn't lose a single man," Seth said. "Many, including myself, attribute that to Elam's faith and inspiring leadership."

"Many things contributed to our survival," Elam told them. "I witnessed miracles within miracles that are beyond my limited understanding."

"You understand enough," Seth told him, his eyes even more intense than normal. "I'll rest easier knowing you are warding Chellum in my absence."

"Thank you, Captain," Elam said, moved by the show of confidence.

Seth's eyes moved to Jaina. "I'm not due back in Trian for a few hours yet," he said. "Why don't you two find a quiet place to visit while I make the rounds. I'm sure there is much you would like to discuss."

Elam smiled. *Yes*, he thought, looking at his wife. *Names for the twins.*

With Raimen and Tohquin in tow, Elliott led Tana toward the giant tree rising in the center of the ballroom. The room was unusually crowded for this time of day, but Elliott suspected it was due to the Home Guard's return. The palace residents, mostly members of the lesser houses judging from their apparel, had gotten word of the return and had congregated to speculate and to share gossip.

*Well, this will give them something to talk about,* he thought, but it wasn't clear to him if the looks of wonder on their faces were due to the presence of the Shizu or to the fact that he was holding Tana's hand.

*Some of both, probably,* he decided.

The real question was which of the two was more shocking? Shizu had a reputation as assassins—he had a reputation for spurning the young ladies of the other Houses who were constantly fawning over him. *Fawning over my status as prince*, he thought sourly. He'd never met a single one of the supposedly love-sick girls who could look much further than the crown he would someday wear. It had been a pleasure disappointing them then—it would be even better now because it would put the foolishness to rest. Forever.

"I know that look," she said. "You're showing me off to your subjects."

He feigned surprise. "Showing you off? I'm not sure what you mean."

The right side of her beautiful mouth turned upward in a sort of half-smile. "I'm flattered, of course," she said, "but there is a story here that I would very much like to hear."

Elliott chuckled. "And I will tell it," he said. "Later. Right now I want to savor the moment."

Tana studied the crowd as they walked, taking note of the young ladies who were about their age. "There are a lot of beautiful young women here," she said. "How did none of them catch your eye?"

Elliott nodded to Kranston Fillista, head of House Fillista, father of one of the girls Tana was studying. "I thought we agreed to talk about this *later*," he whispered when they were out of earshot of the man.

"No, *you* agreed. I'm curious now."

"It was my duty to dance with them at celebrations," he said. "So I did. Beyond that, I kept my distance."

"Duty, huh?" she said, smiling mischievously. "Does that mean parading me around in front of them is part of that duty?"

"No, my love," he said, looking into her beautiful eyes. "This is a pleasure." He was pleased to see color rising in her cheeks.

They reached the base of the great oak a moment later, and Elliott paused and scanned the area for the Eries family. He found them near one of blue-marble pillars further to the right. Alesha Eries occupied one of the cushioned, high-backed benches with her son Garrick. Both held books, but neither was reading at the moment. Garrick's eyes were on a group of young women across the way from him. Alesha was watching the Eries children as they played a game at her feet.

Several children from various houses had joined Tey and her siblings, and the group was clustered around a circle they'd formed with a length of string. Marbles of various sizes and colors were scattered about within, and Tey's brother Cam was preparing to shoot a marble. A sharp click sounded and was followed by a chorus of cheers. Tey bounced to her feet and scurried to retrieve the marble Cam had freed from the circle, giving chase as it rolled across the floor toward Elliott.

As she scooped it up, her eyes found Elliott, and she squealed with delight. "Elliott," she said, rushing forward. "Did you come here on the giant bird?"

Kneeling, he caught her in his arms, then leaned back so he could look her in the eyes. They were bright with excitement. "No, little one," he said. "But I brought some friends. He turned her so she could see the Shizu.

"Raimen!" she yelled. "Tohquin!"

Wriggling free of Elliott, she raced into their waiting arms as they knelt to embrace her. It was undoubtedly an odd sight for all those looking on, but Elliott just smiled as he watched the tenderness with which the two greeted the little girl. Tohquin kissed her on the top of her head, then brushed her hair back behind her ears so he could look at her.

She grinned at both of them. "Did you come on a bird?" she asked, then continued before they could answer. "Where is Aimi? Is she coming too?"

"I'm afraid not," Tohquin answered. "At least not yet. Perhaps later."

"Okay," Tey said. Pulling on their hands, she started toward her aunt.

Alesha had risen from the bench and was watching the Shizu with curiosity. Elliott had explained Raimen and Tohquin's involvement in rescuing and sheltering Tey, but seeing her niece's love for the two men had brought it home for Alesha. Setting her book on the bench, she walked forward to greet them.

"I've heard a great deal about you two," she said, extending her hand. "I'm Alesha, Tey's aunt. Thank you..." she hesitated as tears formed in her eyes. "...thank you for saving my brother's children."

Both men bowed deeply in the Riaki tradition. "We would have your forgiveness for not returning her sooner," Tohquin said.

"And for failing to save the others," Raimen added.

The tears gathering in Alesha's eyes ran down her cheeks as she shook her head. "It is enough that she is here now," she told them. Stepping forward, she hugged each man to show her gratitude.

"We have come to fulfill a promise we made to Croneam Eries," Raimen said when Alesha released him. "We shall watch over you and the children until our debt to this family is paid in full."

Alesha smiled through her tears. "And how long might that be?"

"That is for you to decide," Tohquin told her, "but it cannot be less than the number of days Tey was in our custody."

"Forever, it is then," Alesha said, and Elliott stiffened in shock. Beside him, Tana's surprise escaped as a hiss. Raimen and Tohquin, however, simply glanced at one another, then looked back to Alesha.

"It will be a pleasure," Tohquin said.

Alesha studied both men as if seeing them for the first time. "You are serious about this, aren't you?"

"They are Shizu," Elliott told her. "They don't take Reckonings lightly."

"I can see that," Alesha said. "And my heart is touched by the offer. But I will release you once the minimum has been met. Or sooner if the *Mith'elre Chon* has need of you. My niece, however, might not be so understanding." She glanced down at Tey who had been following the conversation as best she could.

"I think forever is best," the little girl said, then took each Shizu by the hand and led them over to meet her siblings and friends.

"They are good men," Elliott told her. "They fought alongside Croneam and your husband as Fulrath was overrun."

Alesha's face paled. "Overrun? Then that means...." She was unable to finish.

"Your husband is well," Elliott said. "He asked me to deliver this to you." He took the note from his pocket and handed it to her.

She pressed it to her chest without looking at it. "And Croneam?"

Elliott pursed his lips sadly. "He went home."

# CHAPTER 10

## Taking Command

BIDDING TAGGERT ENUE FAREWELL, Idoman Leda moved through a Veilgate to join the army gathering north of Mendel Pass. He released the Power, then glanced back at his friend as the gate slid silently closed. Taggert was already moving away, issuing orders to the men of Chellum as they continued to set up camp in Talin Pass.

The edges of the Veilgate came together in a flash of blue, and Idoman was left to stare at the greens and yellows of the Bottomlands. The bright warmth of the afternoon sun was a stark contrast to the cold, shadowed stone of the pass, and he shivered at the abrupt change in temperature. Taggert had elected to make camp where the mountain road began its steep climb between the Dragon's Fangs because it offered the best view of Talin Plateau. Add the large spyglasses provided by the Dainin, and Taggert's ability to track the enemy's movements was enhanced an hundred fold. It was a good tactical position.

"I thought that might be you I felt," a familiar voice said, and Idoman turned to find Kalear Beumestra striding toward him. The former Sarui smiled as he stopped to look Idoman over. "You look tired."

"I am," he admitted. "Moving the Chellum army into position took longer than I thought." He glanced at the spot where he'd arrived. "I'm afraid that was my last Veilgate for the day."

"We're all spent," his friend said. "I barely had enough strength left to assist General Eries with his announcement."

Idoman arched an eyebrow at him. "What announcement?"

"The death of Croneam and the fall of Fulrath," Kalear answered. "Most of the men in this camp were at the rim when it happened and had no idea. He wanted to put rumor and hearsay to rest quickly. And per military protocol he officially took command of the Kelsan army."

Idoman nodded. "Good. The men need to know we will continue to function as normal in spite of losses and setbacks."

"Those were my thoughts as well," the Sarui said. "But there is more."

The way he said it put Idoman on edge. "How much more?"

Kalear smiled. "He announced that you will be taking command of the army's Dymas," he answered. *"Ao tres'domei* included. He wanted me to be the one to tell you." He brought his fist to his chest in salute. "What are your orders, General?"

Idoman stared at him, waiting for him to laugh or do something else to give away the lie. When Kalear did nothing but hold the salute, Idoman felt a heavy weight settle over him. "You're serious."

Kalear nodded. "Come, my friend. General Eries would hear your report."

As they made their way toward the center of camp, Idoman tried to ignore the newfound weight by taking note of the progress Joneam's men had made. Most of the tents were up, and smoke rose from cookfires as soldiers prepared for the evening meal. Picket lines had been erected for the horses of the roves and cavalry which were yet to arrive. Supply wagons were positioned at evenly spaced intervals among the rows of tents. To a casual observer, it might seem as if all was well and ready for the next fight. Not so.

Nearly all of the men were foot soldiers and had arrived with nothing more than what they were carrying when they'd fled here through Veilgates. Extra weapons, spare clothes, blankets and bedrolls—all had been left behind to be claimed or destroyed by the enemy. This camp was a bare-bones refuge for men who, at the moment, looked more like refugees than soldiers.

*But at least we had a place to fall back to,* Idoman thought. *Thanks to the wisdom of Croneam Eries.*

"Do we know when additional supplies will be arriving?" he asked Kalear.

"Tomorrow," his friend answered. "At least, that's what Gideon said."

"Where is Gideon?"

Kalear nodded a greeting to a group of men clustered around a cookfire before answering. "Trian. He went to report to the High Queen and to check on Jase."

Idoman nodded. "Good. About checking on Jase, I mean. He overdid it this morning."

Kalear grunted. "He overdoes it every morning."

"But aren't we glad he does," Idoman said, his eyes on a group of soldiers exiting a tent which had been set up for healing. The bloodstained gashes in the men's uniforms were evidence of the seriousness of the wounds they'd sustained that morning. Faces tired, they made their way to one of the cookfires to eat.

*But they are alive,* he thought. A credit to Jase—and to all the Dymas—for 'overdoing' it.

They continued on toward the center of camp and were met along the way by Joselyn Rai. The aged Dymas fell in next to Idoman.

"What did Taggert have to say about his new assignment?" she asked.

Idoman laughed. "He used words like *abandoned* and *forsaken*—as well as a few other words I won't repeat in your presence—but you know Taggert. Grumbling is his way of showing he takes the assignment seriously. It's backwards, I know."

"How do you feel about *your* new assignment?" Joselyn asked.

"Overwhelmed," he answered before he could stop himself. He shrugged uncomfortably. "And... flattered. It's nice to be trusted so. I just hope I don't disappoint."

Joselyn smiled. "You won't. I have complete faith in you, Dymas General Idoman Leda."

"Thank you," he said, but inside he was as jittery as a goldfish in the Chellum Palace moat. Joselyn and Kalear were generals—experienced in years *and* on the battlefield. "I have to admit," he said after a moment, "that I feel a bit young for the title."

"Age has nothing to do with being a general," Joselyn said. "If it did, then anyone with grey hair and wrinkles could lay claim to it." She shook her head. "Being a general is about leadership. It's about understanding *people*. A prowess with weapons and a knowledge of tactics is helpful, but none of that means anything if people won't follow you."

"Joselyn Dymas is right," Kalear said. "You have a gift, Idoman. And it extends well beyond your abilities with *Ta'shaen*. Joneam was right to put you in charge of our Dymas."

Idoman nodded, feelings of inadequacy racing through him in spite of his friends' words. *I'll take your word for it.*

They reached the command tent a moment later, and two soldiers pulled the tent flaps aside to allow them to enter. Idoman motioned for Joselyn to go ahead of him, then took a deep breath and followed. It was time to learn what taking command of the army's Dymas would mean.

The interior of the tent grew bright as the tent flaps were pulled aside, and Teig Ole'ar looked up as Joselyn Rai entered. The aged, little woman was followed by Idoman and Kalear, and then the tent flaps dropped back into place, throwing the interior into a sudden, short-lived darkness.

Teig rose from the collapsible stool he'd been using and moved to greet the new arrivals. Joselyn smiled as he took her hand and kissed it. "It's good to see you again," he told her, then nodded to Idoman and Kalear. "And you two as well."

Joneam Eries turned from the table where he, Erebius Dymas, and General Gefion had been poring over maps of the area. "Ah, Dymas General Leda," Joneam said. "Welcome back. I take it Chellum's forces are in position."

"Yes, General. I arrived from Talin Pass just a few minutes ago."

"Excellent," Joneam said, motioning Idoman and the other two to the table.

Teig followed, and looked over Idoman's shoulder as Joneam pointed out the coins and pewter figures he'd placed on the map. "We've begun to lay out plans for the next stages of the war," the general said. "But we could use a second opinion. Please look things over and tell us what you think. Obviously our biggest concern is Shadan's ability to move an entire army at once." He pointed to two lengths of red string he'd placed along the rim of Talin Plateau and at the rear of the Kelsan army. "My guess is they will attempt to open gates here," he said, pointing to the strings, "in hopes of pinning us against the cliffs."

"That would be my guess," Idoman said, studying the map. "If they intend to engage us at all. They could just as easily use Dragon Gates to move all the way to Trian Plateau, bypassing us altogether. Yes, it would leave them exposed in the rear once we managed to get our army through Mendel Pass, but they would clearly have a head start in attacking Trian." He shook his head. "Any way you look at it, Dragon Gates make this a bad tactical position for our armies."

"What do you propose we do?" Erebius asked.

Idoman's eyes never left the map. "We eliminate the Dragons before they open another gate."

"How?" Joselyn asked. "We can't very well attack them while they are in the midst of Shadan's troops. They'll be too well protected. Any attempt to kill them would be nothing short of suicide for those we send."

"And that's assuming we can even identify them among so many," Kalear added. "The only time we saw them *not* in human form was when they opened the gates."

"That's our answer," Idoman said, placing a finger on each end of the string and pulling it tight. "We can use our current position to bait Shadan into using gates against us here in the Bottomlands. He will believe we made a mistake in remaining here, and, as General Eries said, he will undoubtedly attempt to use gates to surround us and pin us against the plateau."

He smiled. "We'll strike the Dragons as they begin to shape shift. They will have revealed themselves and will be preoccupied with opening the Veilgate. That's when we will kill them." He lifted his fingers and the taut string snapped back on itself in a tangle.

Joselyn shook her head. "It's too risky," she said. "If we fail to kill the Dragons and gates are opened, we will be faced with the same nightmare we encountered at the eastern rim. And this time there is nowhere for us to flee. Mendel Pass would become a bottleneck."

"Then we don't fail," Idoman said simply.

Teig watched Joneam carefully as the general considered. Frowning thoughtfully, his hazel eyes darted from point to point across the map. Finally he nodded. "See to the details," he told Idoman, sounding very much like his father would have. "I'll be back shortly to hear your report."

"Yes, General," Idoman said, then returned his attention to the map as Joneam started for the entrance.

"Teig," Joneam said, "I need you and Erebius Dymas to come with me."

"Yes, General," Teig said, then squinted against the sudden brightness as he followed Joneam and Erebius outside.

It was nearing evening, and the sun was a red-gold orb in the sky above the Kelsan Mountains. It painted Zanan Gap in hues of orange, but beyond the pass storm clouds stretched away into Chunin, dark and heavy with rain. It wouldn't be long before they prematurely dimmed the light of the waning day.

*Not an omen I hope*, Teig thought, then followed Joneam north through the camp. The general offered words of encouragement to all those he passed, but Teig could see in the men's faces that they were troubled. Not only had they been thoroughly routed in the opening battle, they'd lost Fulrath and its legendary general. It had shaken their faith that this war could be won.

Just shy of the perimeter of the camp, Joneam stopped at a line of horses. Two of the animals, Teig noted, had been saddled.

"I have a mission for you two," Joneam said as he untethered the horses. "I need you to intercept Fulrath's forces before they exit the Tunnel."

A knot tightened in Teig's stomach. The Tunnel? Blood of Maeon, but he'd thought he'd never have to set foot in that awful place again. All that stone and stale air... the feeling of being slowly crushed by some unseen force...

He pushed the thoughts away, hoping his fear hadn't shown in his face. "Of course, General," he said, taking the reins of one of the horses.

Erebius accepted the other set. "I assume this means we are not to use Veilgates to get there."

"Correct," Joneam said. "I don't want to do anything that might draw the attention of the enemy should they have shadowspawn in the area."

"It's just as well," Erebius told him. "I don't have strength enough to open one tonight anyway."

"The other Dymas said the same thing," Joneam told him. "Six in all, they will be waiting for you at the West Rim Waypost at the bottom of the rampway. They left one at a time over the past few hours so as not to be noticed. They will assist you in opening the Veilgate to bring our troops out of the Tunnel and directly to this camp. It will speed the rebuilding of our army, and it will preserve the secret of the Tunnel."

"Is such secrecy necessary now that Fulrath has fallen?" Teig asked, then flinched under the hardness of Joneam's stare.

"I'm fighting this war under the assumption that we will win," Joneam said. "And *when* we win, Fulrath will be reclaimed. I want all its secrets intact."

"Of course, General," Teig said. "I meant no disrespect."

"And I did not mean to sound harsh," Joneam said, his voice softening somewhat. "And it's not just about secrecy. We need to intercept our people before they exit the Tunnel in order to keep them safe. Can you imagine what would happen if the enemy spotted them as they were exiting? I can. They'd jump in through Veilgates to attack. With so many pinned against the cliff face—or worse: trapped inside the Tunnel—it would be a bloodbath."

Erebius nodded. "We'll bring them out, my friend," he said. "Expect us sometime tomorrow morning."

"Thank you," Joneam said, then looked back to Teig. "Do you remember where it is?"

Teig nodded. "Yes."

Joneam relaxed visibly. "I'm glad. Aside from my father's warders, who are *in* the Tunnel, you and Lord Nid are the only other people who have been there recently. I don't think I could find it if I had a week to look." He withdrew a medallion and handed it to Teig. "You'll need this to get past the wards."

Teig ran his thumb over the image of the Fighting Lion of Fulrath, then turned it over and examined the raised, jewel-like crystal on the other side. It looked like the same silver disk Croneam had used weeks earlier to unlock the Tunnel, but Teig knew it wasn't. This crystal was the color of amber. Croneam's had been blue.

He tucked the talisman in his pocket. "We'd best get going," he said, climbing into the saddle. Erebius did likewise, and his horse stamped its feet excitedly.

"God's speed, my friends," Joneam said. "And good luck." With that he turned and started back toward the center of camp.

Teig watched him go, then turned his horse northward and urged it into a trot. He could see where the highway leading to the rampway cut through the grasslands a half mile to the east and angled toward it. In the distance, just visible in the last rays of the setting sun, the rampway was a ribbon of black as it snaked up the cliff face.

It would be dark long before they reached the Waypost at the bottom of the rampway, but that would be for the best. It would allow him and the others to slip off the Highway unnoticed when the time came to seek out the entrance.

He'd spoken true when he'd told Joneam he could find it—he had an uncanny memory for such things. He was less certain about what would happen *after* he found the entrance. He honestly didn't know if he could go inside again.

Which was completely irrational, he knew. Not to mention stupid. It was just a tunnel. And Power-wrought at that. It was no different than being inside Fulrath or Fairimor Palace.

Unfortunately, some part of him refused to believe it, and the imagined weight of the plateau grew heavier with each passing mile. By the time the lights of the Waypost came into view, his back was tight and his shoulders hunched. When he realized how tense he was, he forced himself to relax, arching his back to stretch angry muscles.

"Not many lights on for a Waypost this size," Erebius commented as they rode into the compound a short time later.

"Most of the Highwaymen have left to join Joneam," Teig told him. "This is a skeleton crew at best. Tasked with ushering people off of Talin Plateau and away from the area."

"The Dymas are waiting for us in the main barracks," Erebius said, pointing.

"How did you..." he started, then smiled sheepishly. "Oh, right." He should have known Erebius would have probed the way ahead with his Awareness.

They stopped in front of the barracks, and Teig swung down from the saddle. Wrapping his reins around a hitching post, he glanced around the compound. It looked abandoned. Aside from the lamp at the entrance, the only other pools of light came from a pair of glowstone lamps fronting the stables and a swath of light emanating from the barrack's front window.

"Aside from the Dymas, it makes you wonder if any one else is home," he said, stepping up onto the boardwalk and reaching for the door.

It opened before he could take the handle, spilling light across the boardwalk and framing a slender silhouette in the doorway.

"Welcome, Master of Spies," the silhouette said, then materialized into Tuari Renshar as she came outside. "Erebius Dymas," she said. "I thought that was your Awareness I felt. It's nice to see you. I'd wondered who else Joneam might send."

Glancing back to Teig, she gestured through the door. "The others are waiting inside. Captain Welliston of the Waypost had food prepared for us. We can leave as soon as you two get something to eat."

The mention of food made Teig's stomach growl. "Great," he said, following her inside. "I'm starving."

A dozen uniformed Highwaymen looked up as he entered. Some sat with plates of food at tables, others lounged on cots along the far wall. If they were surprised by the fact he was Elvan, it didn't show in their faces.

Five Dymas in *kitara* jackets sat at one of the nearest tables, but Teig only recognized Gristen Lobadar, the round-faced woman who had accompanied Idoman into Melek to teach the new wieldings to Lord Nid. Gristen smiled at him as he drew near, and for the briefest moment he had trouble imagining her as anything other than a wife and mother. Her gentle demeanor was at odds with the stories he'd heard about her dealings on the battlefield. Today, and during the Battle of Greendom.

Teig returned Gristen's smile, then listened as Tuari made introductions. The two women, Hemishi Kiora and Yoso Basivi were Riaki and had helped liberate Sagaris. The men, Jax Gorbon and Calim Dorsey, were from Agisthas. Both were young and had been soldiers under General Crompton's command before their Gifts had manifested and they'd joined the Children of *Ta'shaen*.

They made small talk while he and Erebius ate, careful not to say anything about where they would be going next since it was obvious that the Highwaymen within earshot were listening to every word.

Teig couldn't blame them for being curious—seven Dymas and an Elvan Scout gathering in such a clandestine manner would make anyone wonder what was going on. To the men's credit, however, they didn't ask any questions, and they appeared to quit listening after just a few minutes.

When Teig had eaten his fill, he pushed his plate away to show he was finished. Erebius mopped up the last of the gravy on his plate with a piece of bread, then pushed his plate away as well.

"We'd best get going," Teig said as he stood, and the Dymas rose with him.

Across the room, Captain Welliston set down the stack of papers he'd been reading and hurriedly crossed the room. Smoke from his pipe scented the air as he drew near.

"Leaving so soon?" he asked. "You just got here. And, uh, beggin' your pardon, you all look like you could do with a good night's sleep."

"We could at that," Teig told him. "But Shadan and his *chael'trom* don't sleep, so tonight, neither do we. We must make Tradeston by morning."

"Tradeston?" the captain said, failing to conceal his surprise. "That's quite a journey to begin at this time of night, especially on horseback. Are you certain it can't wait till mornin'? You could rest and then go by way of one of those holes in the Veil I've been hearing about."

"I'm afraid not," Teig said. "A Veilgate would draw the kind of attention we're hoping to avoid. We appreciate your concern, but we must go now."

"Then God's speed on your journey," Welliston said and gestured to three of his men. "Fetch their horses from the stable."

Teig offered his hand. "Thank you, Captain," he said, then he and the others followed Welliston's men out into the night. Within minutes they were riding between the pools of lamplight at the Waypost's entrance and out into the darkness of the highway.

The road forked almost immediately, but Teig and his companions stayed on the stretch heading north. To the right, a few hundred yards away, the West Talin Rampway began its snake-like climb up to the rim. Lit at each switchback by glowstone lamps, it cast odd shadows across the cliff face. It looked deserted now, but that was likely to change tomorrow as the inhabitants of the plateau fled ahead of Shadan's army.

Teig studied the zigzag pattern of lights a moment longer, then turned his attention to the road before them, keeping watch for anything that might hint of trouble. He didn't think there was any real danger on the highway, but old habits died hard. Undoubtedly, Erebius and the others were doing the same with their Awarenesses.

Teig kept to the road until it started to bend westward, then angled across the grasslands toward a point eight or nine miles distant. "All this land is off limits to civilians," he explained, gesturing with a sweep of his arm. "The Fulrath High Command oversees the restriction with patrols. It not only keeps a certain secret safe, but Croneam was quite proud of the fact that it provides undisturbed habitat for wild game."

Miles of open grassland passed quickly, and Teig kept track of the distance by watching the contour of the plateau's rim high overhead. A dark outline against a backdrop of stars, it cast a deep shadow over the lowlands. That would change once the moon crested, and Teig wanted to be out of the grasslands before that happened. Fortunately they were close to their destination, and a half mile further on, he spotted what he'd been looking for.

"This way," he said, turning his horse toward a line of paperbarks at the base of the cliffs. He lost sight of the rim as they passed through the trees, but it didn't matter. He had his heading. That he was still on course was confirmed when they passed through a small clearing and the rim came into view once more.

The moon had become a bright glow just beyond the rim's edge and would be visible in the next few minutes. *Perfect timing,* he thought. The added light would make it possible to find the keyhole for the medallion without using Light wrought by the Dymas.

The paperbarks gave way to dense stands of willows taller than the horses, and Teig selected a narrow pathway between them. Fifty yards further on, the path emerged in a hollow fronting the cliff face.

Teig dismounted and moved forward to investigate. "This is it," he said, and his stomach tightened at what the announcement implied. He'd been so focused on *getting* here that he hadn't given much thought to what would follow.

The Tunnel. Thirty-six miles of...

*Stop it!* he told himself sharply. *Stop being such a coward. You've done it twice already. You can do it again.*

Taking the lion medallion from his pocket, he moved to the small outcropping Croneam had shown him and felt around the underside until he felt what he was looking for. Pressing the medallion's crystal against the stone, he heard it click into place.

The Tunnel opened with a faint whisper of stone on stone, revealing a blackness that seemed to stretch away to eternity.

"Dymas," he said, gesturing them forward. "Our army awaits."

As they started inside, he added, "Hold off on wielding Light until I close the doors behind us."

When they were all inside, Teig took the reins of his horse, then removed the medallion and hurried inside as the doors began to swing shut.

*Heaven help me,* he thought as darkness closed around him.

# CHAPTER 11

## *Premonitions*

THE SKY OVER TRIAN GROWS DARK *as the light of day suddenly begins to dim. The sun is still visible overhead but is diminishing to a sickly-looking orb of orange-red amid a background of deepening grey. The air grows heavy. Green things begin to wither and die. The sky grows darker by the moment, as if layer after layer of dark cloth is being stretched across the heavens.*

*The Veil is collapsing. The Earthsoul is being swallowed by Con'Jithar.*

*Standing on the small railed platform atop Fairimor Dome, Jase Fairimor gazes out across Trian Plateau and knows in his heart that the battle taking place there has already been decided. Hundreds of thousands of soldiers representing every nation in the world are bleeding out their lives in futility.*

And it is my fault, *he thinks.* Because I failed.

*He continues to watch men die, powerless to stop the slaughter. Through his Awareness he sees the spirits of the righteous leave their bodies only to stand in stupefied horror when they realize they are trapped on the wrong side of the Veil. Eliara is out of reach for them. Their fate is the same as the wicked.*

*The world shifts around him, and he finds himself on the battlefield. The combatants are gone, but a sea of bones spreads before him, stretching from horizon to horizon. The eyeless sockets of millions of skulls stare up at him while the accompanying rows of teeth grin with macabre humor.*

*It is then that he realizes this is only a dream.*

*No. A nightmare.*

*And perhaps even a vision of the future.*

*The earth groans deep inside Herself as an earthquake shakes the plateau, and Jase braces himself against it. Around him, a tumultuous clattering fills the air as the bones are tossed about by the quaking. Here and there they form the skeletal shapes of men, some of which rise up to walk only to fall quickly back into disarray. Overhead, bizarre horizontal tornados of Fire* form, spiraling away in every direction, their fiery glow painting the sea of bones the color of blood.

The heat of the fires vanishes as a sudden cold wind buffets him, seemingly from every direction at once, and he pulls his cloak tightly about him. Ghostly cries ride the winds, and dark, ephemeral shapes tease the edges of his vision.

One of those shapes coalesces into a hulking, insect-like creature the size of a horse. As the creature orients itself, its eyes burn red with the corruption of Con'Jithar, then flare brightly when it sees Jase.

A demon, he realizes, and opens himself to Ta'shaen.

It isn't there. He searches, but his Awareness finds only darkness. A cold, horrified, sadness washes through him at what it means:

No Earthsoul means there are no Gifts of Ta'shaen.

He is Power-less.

Defenseless.

Helpless.

As if sensing his plight, the demon scrambles forward on a dozen spidery legs, its massive wedge-shaped body sprouting an array of spikes and whip-like tentacles. A mouth opens inside of a mouth, and a proboscis tipped with barbed needles begins to extend. Jase watches it come, knowing it is only a dream.

The world shifts.

He stands on the balconied edge of the cliff fronting the Temple of Elderon high above the city of Trian. Much of the outer city is in flames, and the wall of the inner city has been breached in a dozen places. Demons are pouring through the gaps by the thousands, streams of fiery-eyed abominations the color of pitch.

And they aren't alone.

Spectral shapes of greenish-white move with them, and Jase recognizes them as the fleeting images which had teased him on the battlefield. With the Veil no longer in place, the spirits of those damned to an eternity of misery and servitude to Maeon are taking a hand in the battle.

Elvan archers line the top of the Overlook, and a steady stream of arrows hisses into the approaching darkness as it enters the courtyard fronting the palace. Demons fall dead or wounded, and are trampled by their own kind, but the dark river of bodies doesn't slow. The courtyard is quickly overrun, and demons reach the palace entrance. The sounds of splintering wood and shattering steel echo across the courtyard as the gates are ripped from their hinges.

The dead have a different approach. Not bound by the laws of nature, they swarm up the sides of the Overlook and into the midst of the Bero'thai. Elvan blood spatters the rapidly wilting foliage of the gardens as living flesh is rent by apparitional frenzy.

Jase stretches out his hand to shield the Bero'thai, but Ta'shaen remains out of reach. He can only watch as the Elvan soldiers continue to fall before the ghostly figures.

They are nearing the entrance to the Dome when Jase's Awareness comes alive with a powerful surge of Earthpower. Brilliant light lances from the Dome's entrance, a radiant burst of energy that strikes the apparitions and hurls them out into the dusky sky like leaves blown *by a gust of wind. They vanish into nothingness as they plummet earthward.*

*Gideon appears from out of the Dome, face like a thunderhead as he strides through the gardens toward the eastern edge of the Overlook. In his hand, shining like a miniature sun, is a Blood Orb of Elsa. Its brilliance bathes the whole of Fairimor Palace in life-giving light, and Gideon wraps the Overlook in a sheltering bubble of Spirit.*

*When he reaches the eastern rim, he attacks again, unleashing a firestorm of Sei'shiin into the demons and shadowspawned creatures swarming below, burning them from existence in curt flashes of bluish green. For a moment it looks as if the palace might be spared.*

*But the reservoir of Earthpower flowing through the Orb isn't endless, and the glow in Gideon's hand begins to dim. The shield over the gardens falters. As it does, Night Threads lance out of the sky, sizzling flashes of black that tear the Bero'thai to shreds and send Gideon tumbling to the ground. The light of the Blood Orb winks out as something monstrous swoops in on leathery wings and lands amid the carnage.*

*A robed figure sits atop the winged demon, but its face is hidden. It scans the gardens casually, triumphantly, and the air turns dark around it as sizzling tendrils of Lo'shaen snuff the lives of the surviving Bero'thai.*

*Gideon tries to rise and is seized in an invisible grip by the demon rider.*

*The world shifts.*

*Jase finds himself in the Soul Chamber, standing next to a bloodstained altar. Beyond the altar lie the bodies of his friends. Seth. Elliott. Talia. They've been killed with the Power. Their sightless eyes stare at him accusingly. Their mouths, open from their last breath, bear witness against him. This is his fault. They are dead because of him.*

*His heart bursts with agony at the sight, and he falls to his knees at the altar. The bloodstains swell wetly, like water welling up from a spring, and flow over his hands and arms and down the sides of the altar.*

*The world fades.*

Jase opened his eyes to darkness, but there was just enough moonlight coming through a gap in the curtains that he could tell he was in his room in Fairimor Palace. He didn't know how long he'd slept, but he suspected only a few hours. He didn't want to believe he could have slept through an entire day. Not and still feel this bloody tired.

He tried to sit up but only managed to lift his head. And that just barely.

"I wouldn't do that if I were you," Ammorin said, his voice floating out of the dark like a rumble of distant thunder. "One of the ingredients in the tea I gave you has a narcotic effect. You can no more control your movements than a newborn baby."

Jase managed to turn his head enough to see the Dainin's outline against the lighter *chorazin* of the wall behind him. The outline shifted, and Ammorin's face moved near. His large eyes reflected the moonlight brightly. "It was the only way I could ensure that you would stay put long enough to heal properly."

"Ha lung vaiiii bin ssleep?" Jase asked, forcing the words through lips which refused to cooperate.

"Not long enough," Ammorin told him.

"Iiiimm ffffiiine," Jase told him, his anger rising. Ammorin *drugged* him?

"You think you are fine because the drug doesn't affect certain parts of your mind," Ammorin said, sounding amused. "Just your body. Oh, and your ability to wield *Ta'shaen*. We can't have you whacking about with the Power if we want you to regain your strength, now can we?"

*I don't whack about*, Jase thought irritably. He tried to say as much, but his mouth wouldn't respond.

A small orb of Light appeared bedside, and Jase watched as Ammorin crushed some leaves with his fingers and dropped the powder into a cup. The cup filled with water and was stirred by an invisible finger of Air.

"But I obviously didn't add enough of this or you wouldn't have awakened so soon." He tipped Jase's head forward with one hand and held the cup to his lips with the other. "Drink up," he said.

The concoction went down without too much trouble, and Ammorin used a handkerchief to wipe away what little had dribbled down Jase's chin.

"Good night, *Mith'elre Chon*," the Dainin said, and Jase felt himself sink into oblivion.

---

*He finds himself inside an immense chamber, the walls and ceiling of which are beyond the reach of the light emanating from a single lamp near an altar of stone a dozen paces away. A figure kneels at the altar—is it him? No. It is someone else. A sharp-faced man with dark hair and green eyes. Face wet with tears, his body shakes with the sobs he is unable to hold back. Clutched tightly in his hand is a red-gold orb.*

*Jase starts, then takes a closer look at the altar. It is shaped like a Dragon, intricate and ornate. It is then that Jase realizes this is the Soul Chamber—or its equivalent, at least—on the Rhiven home world. But the altar is free of blood, which means there has been no sacrifice. No attempt at rejuvenation.*

*The world shifts.*

*He's back in the same chamber, but the view has changed. So has the altar. Not only is he looking at it from the other side, but it is no longer shaped like a Dragon. It is a simple block of stone with slightly rounded edges.*

*A strange, ambient half-light allows him to see that the chamber is empty. He moves to the altar and looks around, knowing instinctively that time has reversed itself. He is here before the time of his last visit.*

*A figure approaches out of the dark, and Jase moves back to make way for the man at the altar. It is the same man as before, and he seems not to notice Jase. He appears hesitant, as if his mind is elsewhere. Slowly, woodenly, he kneels next to the altar and removes the red-gold orb from a pocket of his military uniform. From the sheath at his waist he draws a knife. He stares at the items in his hands but does nothing with them. Time drags slowly on.*

*Suddenly the man's head snaps up and his eyes fasten on something in the distance.*

*It is then that Jase realizes the altar has morphed into the shape of a Dragon.*

*The world shifts.*

*Fire falls from the sky like an avalanche, but the combined strength of the remaining Rhiven turns it aside with a shield of Spirit. They are in their true form, glittering, sinuous shapes that flow like water across the battlefield. The sky is dark, but it is not night. A sickly red orb hangs above the mountains to the east.*

*The Veil over this world is collapsing—has already collapsed completely in many places, and Maeon himself walks the battlefield, a singularly dark figure crowned with fire. At his advance, the Rhiven have retreated to their capital city for one final stand against him. That city, a lone mountain filled with vast caverns and interconnecting passages, bears on its face smaller structures suitable for Rhiven in human form.*

*Suitable for* humans, *Jase amends. Those lining the battlements are not Rhiven. They look— He resists the thought. They look... Elvan.*

*With weapons in hand, they gaze down at the battlefield, their expressions resigned. This is the end, and they know it.*

*Jase follows their gaze down the slopes of the mountain-city to a particularly frenzied part of the battle. Demons from Con'Jithar have reached the entrance to the city and are on the verge of breaking through the Rhiven defenses. Glittering, serpentine forms of all colors rush to the area, and lightning and Fire tear massive holes in the enemy ranks. Thunder echoes up the mountain's slopes. The demon attack stalls.*

*A swirling vortex of Fire wrought of Lo'shaen rends the air in the midst of the Rhiven, and Maeon steps through from beyond. With a casual flick of his wrist he sends Rhiven tumbling head over tail through the air. One, a ruby-red female with a mane of black, manages to land on her feet, then rears up to face the demon god, her yellow-eyes flashing. El'shaen te sherah leaves her in a white-hot burst powerful enough to crack the mountain, but Maeon snuffs it as if it were a candle.*

*The black-maned female is seized in a grip of Lo'shaen and Maeon's laugh echoes across the battlefield.*

*There is a flash of light as someone or something arrives through a Veilgate, then the area turns white with unprecedented brilliance. The Rhiven flee into their mountain home as the new arrival engages Maeon in battle.*

*The world shifts.*

*He's in the Soul Chamber again and the scene is the same as when he first arrived here. A single lamp burns a few feet away. The green-eyed male is here, too, kneeling at the altar. He really does look Elvan, though Jase suspects it is just coincidence. Like before, his face is wet with tears, and his body shakes as he sobs.*

*And there, clutched tightly in his hand, is a small red-gold orb. It is dark, its reservoir of Power spent.*

*As Jase watches, the darkness in the chamber grows more pronounced even though the flame within the lamp continues to burn just as brightly as before. The circle of light it throws across the floor shrinks inward as something dark approaches, a midnight shadow, thick and palpable.*

*The man turns toward the darkness, his face grey, his eyes sunken and hollow. He is dead but not dead, alive but devoid of vitality. He continues to wither before Jase's eyes but forces himself to his feet to face the approaching darkness.*

*Jase follows his gaze as the darkness coalesces into a black-robed man sporting a crown of fire.*

*The world fades.*

Jase opened his eyes to daylight streaming in through an open window. He lay on his side, a sign that the paralysis caused by Ammorin's drugs had worn off, but he still felt so weak that he stared at the window without moving. The angle of the sunlight spoke of midmorning, and a cool breeze rippled the curtains. The air was fresh with the smell of rain.

The bright freshness of it all did little to lighten his mood as images from the dreams—the nightmares—bounced around inside his head. Blood welling from the altar. Talia and the others lying dead. Gideon using a Blood Orb as Trian fell to an army of demons. The dead marching into battle.

He closed his eyes, but the images had burned themselves into his mind. Especially the sight of Talia lying dead in the Soul Chamber.

Could they be visions of things to come? Or were they simply manifestations of his own fears about the future? There was no way to tell.

And what of the things he'd seen of the Rhiven home world? Could *they* have been a vision? Or was it simply his subconscious coming to terms with the things he'd learned during his Communing with Galiena? Considering that part of her mind had been warded, this might be his way of trying to fill in the gaps.

He opened his eyes again and stared at the window. No. It had been too vivid, too *real* to be his own invention.

And that meant it had come from the Earthsoul. But why? What was the connection?

Sighing, he rolled onto his back and pushed himself up on his elbows. As he did, Ammorin sat up from where he'd been lying on the floor, and the sofa he'd been using as a pillow creaked as the weight of his head left it.

"How are you feeling?" his friend asked.

"Better," Jase answered, though in truth he felt like he'd been trampled by a horse.

The sound of the door opening caused him to turn, and pain lanced through his head, blurring his vision with blinding points of light. *Make that twenty horses,* he thought. *And all of them at once. For a week.*

"How is he?" Gideon asked, taking a seat on the edge of the bed.

"Healthy enough to lie about his condition," Ammorin answered. "But I would advise against him using the Power for another day or two. Galiena was right that he nearly burned the ability to wield out of himself."

"It's rude to talk about me like I'm not here," Jase told them, squinting through the fading points of light. Blood of Maeon, but his head hurt. "And next time I would appreciate a head's up about intentions to drug me."

The two exchanged amused looks. "That was your mother's idea," Gideon said.

"Whatever," he said and eased himself back down onto the pillow. The room felt like it was spinning, so he closed his eyes and waited for it to stop. When it had slowed to a wobble, he opened his eyes. "And for the record, I do feel better."

Gideon grunted. "Which is the equivalent of claiming it hurts less to have an arm sliced off than it does to lose a leg. In the moment, pain is pain, and I can see by your face that you are hurting."

"At least I'm still standing," he countered, then added, "metaphorically speaking of course."

Ammorin chuckled. "Well, it's obvious he gets his stubbornness from you," he told Gideon.

Jase would have laughed at the comment if not for the fact it would hurt. "Is Galiena still in the palace?" he asked.

"She is," Gideon answered. "Why?"

"I would like to speak with her." He paused, unsure if he should continue. "I need to ask her about some of the dreams I had."

Gideon's face grew serious. "What kinds of dreams?"

"The kind that let me know we better find a Blood Orb soon," he answered and left it at that.

Gideon wasn't satisfied. "What did you see?"

"The fall of the Rhiven home world," he said. He'd already decided not to share what he'd seen of the fall of Trian until he could decide if it really was a premonition or just another bloody nightmare.

"Residual images from your Communing with Galiena?" Ammorin asked.

"I don't think so," Jase said. "She didn't show me anything that took place before her arrival in this world."

"Could it have been a vision?" Gideon asked.

Jase closed his eyes then opened them. "I don't know. Maybe. That's why I would like to speak with Galiena."

"I'll fetch her," Ammorin said, and his enormous frame filled the room as he stood. The dining hall and library might accommodate his size, but he dwarfed the smaller rooms in the palace.

Jase looked at Gideon who hadn't moved. "Alone," he added. "I would like to speak with her alone."

His father's face remained smooth, but Jase knew as soon as he spoke that he was irritated. "Of course," he said. Rising, he followed Ammorin to the door. "She'll be here shortly."

When they were gone, Jase eased himself into a sitting position and propped several pillows behind his back. If he moved slowly, the room didn't spin as much, but he still needed to close his eyes for a moment once he was situated.

A few minutes later, a knock sounded at the door and Galiena entered.

"You're looking better," she said. She wore the same dark red dress as yesterday, but she'd braided her long raven-colored hair, and it hung over the front of her right shoulder like a thick rope. He felt her embrace the Power, and a chair slid across the floor to stop bedside.

"I feel better," he said as she sat. "Thanks to you."

Her yellow eyes glittered with fondness as they studied him. "I can see in your eyes that you are troubled," she said at last. "What is it you wish to discuss?"

"The fall of your world," he said. "I think I may have witnessed it last night by way of a dream."

There was a long moment of silence before she spoke. "I see," she said at last. "May I ward the room against eavesdropping?"

"Please," he said and waited until the ward was in place. When she released the Power, he began.

He told her everything as he remembered it. Of both dreams. He spoke of this world first, his throat tight with emotion as he described the open-eyed stares of Talia and the others lying dead near the altar. Then he moved through the out-of-order-events he'd seen of the Rhiven world. She listened without a hint of what she was thinking or feeling until he began describing the last moments of the green-eyed man at the Rhiven altar. It was then that tears formed in her beautiful eyes and she closed them against the pain.

*So, it was a vision of actual events,* he thought, watching Galiena closely. Somehow the Earthsoul had shown him that part of her mind which was warded.

"That was you who faced Maeon at the gates of your city, wasn't it?" he asked. "You were the red Dragon I saw."

Eyes still closed, she nodded. "Yes," she said, her lips trembling, her voice filled with pain and sadness. "My foolishness brought about the fall of my world."

Jase stared at her. "Foolishness?" he said at last. "I've never seen anything so brave."

Her yellow eyes fixed on him once more. "Facing Maeon was an act of desperation," she said. "The foolishness I speak of came much earlier."

Suddenly Jase understood, but he was hesitant to go where his thoughts were leading him. Finally, he said, "The man at the altar... the one who looked Elvan... he sensed you were in danger and came to help. You two shared a *sei'vaiya* love-bond, didn't you?"

Galiena wiped the tears from her glistening cheeks and forced a smile. "His name was Alashon, and he was a member of the Rhayn race. And I loved him more than I've ever loved anyone else." She hesitated as a look of fondness moved upon her face. "I spent nearly a hundred years with him in human form. He knew what I was, of course, but love had blinded us both. There were times I almost forgot I was Rhiven."

She sighed as she continued. "Relationships between my people and the Rhayn were forbidden, but I didn't care. Heaven help me, but I loved that man." The tears threatened to return, but Galiena continued before they could.

"When prophecy revealed that Alashon was to be the healer of our world, I took him under my protection. I barely knew him at the time, but as the years passed, my role as his warder grew into something more. Duty turned to love. Protection turned to companionship."

A gust of wind made the curtains billow inward, and they both turned to stare at them for a moment. The smell of rain was still strong in the air. When the curtains settled once more, Galiena turned back to Jase.

"I should have been with him in the Soul Chamber," she said at last. "It was stupid of me to remain outside with my people. It distracted him."

Jase blinked his surprise. "The Soul Chamber was inside the mountain city?"

"Yes."

"And Alashon had an undefiled Blood Orb?"

She nodded. "He did. It..." she paused, and it was clear she wasn't sure if she should continue. "On my world the Soul Chambers and the temples housing the Blood Orbs were one and the same."

Jase's surprise deepened. Soul *Chambers*? Plural? With Orbs already present?

"Then why—" He cut off, so upset he could barely form the words. "Why didn't he bring about the Rejuvenation when he first learned who he was? Why wait until the Veil was collapsing?"

"Because on my world the Rejuvenation couldn't take place until the Veil had collapsed completely." She shook her head in disgust. "That's what happens when mere mortals take it upon themselves to play god."

Jase arched an eyebrow at her. "I'm not following you."

"A thousand years before the fall of my world, a number of Soul Chambers were attacked and destroyed by servants of Maeon. In response, a group of *A'dala*—what you would call Dymas—took it upon themselves to set wards on the altars in each of the remaining Soul Chambers to protect them. They were the most powerful wards our world had ever seen, but they were also fatally flawed. The crux points holding them in place refused to respond when Alashon and I tried to undo them.

"Somehow those who'd wrought them had tapped directly into the life essence of the world itself to hold the wards in place, and nothing short of her demise could bring them down. That's what Alashon was waiting for when you saw him kneeling at the altar with Orb in hand. That's why my people and I went to battle against Maeon. We were trying to buy time for our world to die."

"And it did," Jase said. "In the very moment Alashon came to your aid. That's why the altar shifted into the form of a Dragon—the wards had collapsed."

"Yes," Galiena said, and Jase flinched at the bitterness in her voice. "Which brings me back to where we started: my foolishness in indulging in a forbidden love and then thinking I could better protect that love by separating myself from it. Had I been there with him..." She was unable to finish.

"You don't know that," Jase told her. "There is no way of knowing *what* would have happened. Besides, we can't change the past. For either of our worlds." Leaning forward, he placed his hand on hers and looked her in the eyes. "We do, however, have a chance to save this one."

He kept his hand on hers for a moment longer, then leaned back against the pillows. The act of moving caused the room to start spinning again, but it was considerably less than when he'd first awakened. A sign he was getting better. Hopefully.

"I want your opinion about what I saw of this world," he said. "The images were just as vivid and the emotions just as powerful. But they seemed..."

"Less certain?" she finished for him.

He nodded.

"The future," she said, "unlike the past, is not set in stone. It is constantly being shaped and reshaped moment by moment by what we do today. The decisions we make, the things we do—all have an effect on things to come. As for the images in your dream, vivid though they were, they are nothing more than possibilities."

"And their meanings?" he asked, not completely sure if he agreed with everything he was hearing. Still, if he could trust anyone's opinion about the differences between past and future events, it was hers.

"Should not be over analyzed," she told him. "They might be glimpses or premonitions of the future—a possible future, anyway—or they could be nothing more than manifestations of your fears."

"They certainly were that," he said. "My friends dead, Gideon captured by... something. I can't allow those things to happen."

Galiena was quiet a moment, her eyes sympathetic. "You might not be able to stop them."

# CHAPTER 12

## Fortuitous Arrivals

JONEAM STUDIED THE MAP OF Talin Plateau and considered what he'd just heard. Across the table, Idoman waited expectantly. He'd stayed up most of the night working out the details of his plan, and Joneam could see in his face that he was tired. His exhaustion had been compounded by the storm which had pummeled the camp shortly before dawn. Torrential rains, gusty winds, and roaring thunder had cheated the young man—had cheated them all—out of the precious few hours of rest they could have gotten otherwise.

Joneam eyed the young Dymas General a moment longer, then looked back at the map with its pewter figures and detailed notes. Idoman was a genius when it came to wielding the Power, but Joneam feared his tactics might be a little *too* aggressive. Committing so many of their strongest Dymas to a single maneuver....

He frowned inwardly. And that was to say nothing of leaving the Kelsan army here as bait. It showed how desperate their situation had become that he was even considering saying yes to the plan.

"Estimate on casualties?"

"It will cost us," the young man admitted. "Which is why I suggest it be a volunteer mission only."

Joneam looked to Joselyn. "Your thoughts?"

The tiny, white-haired woman scrunched her lips thoughtfully. "I don't think we have any other choice," she said at last. "We simply can't stand toe to toe with—" She cut off, and her head swivelled to the right as she looked at something beyond the walls of the tent. Idoman and Kalear did likewise.

"Blood of Maeon," Idoman whispered, his eyes wide.

"What is it?" Joneam asked, immediately on alert. His hand moved to the sword at his waist—his father's sword—and the Dragon etchings glittered as he started to bare the blade.

"New arrivals," Kalear said, placing a hand on Joneam's arm. "You won't need that."

Joneam slid the blade home, then turned as the tent flap moved aside and Elison Brey entered. He was accompanied by a man with bright red hair and yellow eyes. Joneam's hand tightened on his sword again, and Idoman's words echoed in his mind. *Blood of Maeon!*

"General Eries," Elison said, moving forward and offering his hand in greeting. Joneam hesitated, then released his sword hilt to accept the captain's hand. "I am glad you are well," Elison continued. "I am sorry to hear about your father."

Joneam kept his face smooth as he answered. "Thank you, Captain," he said, then turned his gaze on the Dragon. "I trust there is an explanation for this."

Elison's excitement was evident. "There is indeed," he said, moving farther into the tent. "And you are going to like what you hear." He gestured to his yellow-eyed companion. "This is Yavil to al'Jagulair," he said. "Warder Advisor to Galiena'ei to ul'Morgranon, Queen of the Rhiven."

"It is the true name for our race," Yavil said. "Dragon is the name given to us by men."

"Yavil has come to assist in the war effort," Elison said. "He and those who serve Queen Morgranon will confront the Rhiven who serve Maeon."

"Excellent," Joneam said, still trying to come to terms with the sudden turn of events. *Dragons fighting Dragons? Could the world get any stranger?*

He gestured to Idoman. "Our young Dymas General has a plan you might be able to help with."

Yavil turned his golden eyes on Idoman. "Gideon spoke highly of you, Idoman Leda," the Rhiven said. "And I can see through the eyes of *Ta'shaen* that you are highly favored of the Earthsoul as well." He brought his fist to his chest in a show of respect. "What would you have me and my people do?"

Idoman stared at Yavil for a moment without speaking, then pointed to the table. "You could look this over and tell me what you think."

"I'll leave you to your work," Joneam said. "There are things I need to attend to elsewhere." Moving to the tent flap, he motioned for Elison to follow.

Idoman didn't answer. He and Yavil were already discussing the marks on the map. The young Dymas' weariness had vanished, replaced by the same enthusiasm which had kept him up for most of the night.

"Keep an eye on them," Joneam whispered to Joselyn, then he and Elison stepped out into the brighter light of day.

The ground was soft from the overnight rains, but the grasses held the soil together enough to keep his boots from getting muddy. The air smelled fresh and clean. He waited until they were away from the tent before turning a skeptical look on Elison.

"Is this for real?" he asked. "Giving a Dragon access to our battle plans? How do we know they can be trusted?"

"Jase and Gideon trust them," Elison said. "The Dainin in the palace confirmed that Queen Morgranon and those who follow her are Dymas. The title is *A'dala* in their language."

Joneam's misgivings lessened at the mention of the Dainin. If the *Nar'shein* approved, who was he to argue? Still, it was unsettling. "How many of these *A'dala* are coming to help?"

"Forty-two," Elison said, "counting Yavil and the Queen. They swore allegiance to Jase yesterday in the Dome." He paused, and Joneam could tell the captain was impressed by what he had witnessed. "They are going to remain in Trian to keep their involvement hidden from those in Shadan's army. When the time comes for them to attack, it will be swift and hopefully unexpected. In the meantime, Yavil will act as liaison between Idoman and Jase."

The mention of Jase prompted Joneam's next question. "How is he? From what I've heard of him from Idoman and the others, he nearly killed himself on the battle field."

"An accurate assessment," Elison said, "but he is doing better now. He was healed by Queen Morgranon and has gotten some much needed rest."

"He really does trust them," Joneam commented, "if he let their Queen use the Power on him."

"He does," Elison said. "So much so, that he's asked Queen Morgranon to act as one of his advisors."

"And sent her advisor to act as one of mine."

Elison smiled. "Exactly."

They continued walking, weaving through clusters of tents and skirting lines of horses until they reached the northern edge of the camp. It was there that Joneam found the spyglass he'd ordered to be put in place. The lieutenant on duty at the spyglass saluted as he and Elison drew near.

"The first of the roves reached the western rim this morning," he said. "And they have started their descent down the rampway."

"They must have ridden hard," Joneam said. "Any sign of the enemy?"

"A few bladehawks," the lieutenant answered. "Our Dymas kill them if they get too close to the camp." He swung the spyglass to the northwest. "But you might want to take a look at this."

Joneam stepped up to the spyglass and peered through. Two or three miles distant, dark patches had appeared among the light yellows and greens of the grasslands. As he watched, they continued to grow larger, spreading outward from dozens of specific points rimmed with blue light. Those spreading outward the fastest sported flashes of fiery-red plumage among shimmering chain mail and armor.

Joneam smiled at the sight. *Krelltin. Thousands of them.*

"They began arriving through Veilgates about twenty minutes ago," the lieutenant said. "I sent a messenger to inform you, but you likely passed him on the way here."

"Are they riding Krelltin?" Elison asked, squinting at the rapidly expanding army.

"You have good eyes," Joneam commented, watching the birds darting out of the gates.

"Take a look at the causeway," the lieutenant said. "Ten or so miles north."

Joneam did, and an army of mounted *Bero'thai* came into view, silver armor glittering in the morning sunlight. And there, flapping gently in the breeze, was the Tree of Life banner of Elva and the Golden Eagle banner of the *Bero'thai*.

"That is a beautiful sight," Joneam said, then stepped aside so Elison could take a look. "If those are standard columns, I'd say we are looking at ten thousand men."

"Nice," Elison said. "Jase said they'd be coming."

"I expected them to arrive by Veilgate," Joneam said. "I wonder why they came the old-fashioned way."

"Riding isn't old-fashioned," Elison said. "It's practical."

He swung the telescope back in the direction of the Chunin army. "Most of Andlexces' Dymas are already among us. Jase brought them with him when he liberated Trian. Apparently, the Chunin had quite a few more in reserve."

Joneam nodded. "And we are going to need every last one of them."

He reached for the spyglass and Elison stepped aside for him. He watched the Chunin army for a moment longer, then swivelled the glass back to the rampway to study the descending roves. "Now all we need is for our own forces to arrive so we can get back to fighting this war."

He lowered the spyglass and turned to Elison. "Those on the plateau I'm not so worried about. Those exiting Fulrath should have been here by now. I do hope nothing has happened to them."

Teig Ole'ar opened his eyes to the sight of stone looming overheard and a line of glowstones trailing away into what looked like the depths of hell.

*Right*, he thought. *The Tunnel.*

Suppressing a shudder, he sat up in his blankets and looked around. Tuari and the rest of the Dymas were still asleep, which was understandable considering all they'd been through yesterday. Their fatigue was the main reason he'd insisted that they make camp here at mile-marker three instead of riding through the night to meet Fulrath's forces somewhere further on. They would all need to be at full strength if they hoped to hold Veilgates open long enough to evacuate ten thousand men.

He watched them silently for a moment, unsure if he should wake them, then rose and quietly rolled up his blankets. He felt refreshed even though his back was stiff from sleeping on solid rock, and the combination made him believe he'd been asleep for a while. But he wasn't willing to wake the others until he knew for sure, so he moved to his saddlebags to retrieve the pocket watch Joneam had given him. There was no other way for him to tell what time it was inside this bloody place.

His horse snorted softly at his approach, and Teig ran a hand down its neck to soothe it before flipping open the watch. He stiffened in surprise at the time. It was almost noon. They had, all of them, slept much longer than planned.

"It's got to be the lack of air in this bloody place," he muttered softly. Tucking the watch into his pocket, he moved to kneel next to Erebius.

"Dymas," he said, nudging Erebius gently. "We've overslept."

Erebius' eyes snapped open, and he sat up. "What time is it?"

"Almost noon," Teig answered, then turned his attention to Tuari and the others as they stirred and came awake. "Fulrath's forces should have been here by now," he continued. "Something's wrong."

Erebius pushed himself to his feet, and his eyes grew distant as he stared eastward down the Tunnel. He was quiet for a long time, and his face grew darker by the minute.

Finally, he shook his head and looked back to Teig. "Bloody earthquakes," he mumbled. "The Tunnel has been damaged in several places, the worst of which is only five miles outside the city. They're past it now, but they're still fifteen miles away from here."

Teig managed to hold back the string of curses brewing on his tongue if for no other reason than that there were ladies present. "Well, saddle up," he said. "We need to make up for lost time."

"We won't be riding," Erebius said. "The Tunnel suffered similar damage just a few miles ahead. The only way to get to them now is by Veilgate."

"And you're sure you are up to that?" Teig asked.

Erebius grunted. "We overslept, remember? I've got strength enough now to open dozens of Veilgates." Behind him, Tuari and the others nodded that they did as well.

"Good," Teig told them, then glanced around at the walls nervously. "Because the sooner we get out of this hellhole the better." *Power-wrought stone, indeed!*

As soon as they were all ready, Erebius embraced the Power and opened a shimmering blue hole in the air. "After you, Master of Spies."

Trying not to hunch his shoulders, Teig led his horse through into the semi-lit darkness beyond.

Lenea Prenum grimaced in disgust as the wounded wolfrat ran headlong into the wall and blood splattered across the Power-wrought stone of the Tunnel. The soldier who'd loosed the arrow—a young lieutenant named Carson—nocked a second arrow and stilled the creature's thrashing. The blood pooling beneath it caught the light of one of the glowstone lamps in a brief reflection of reddish light, and Lenea shuddered and turned away.

"We're getting low on arrows," a second soldier scolded as he moved near with a glowstone lamp in hand. Although a captain, he didn't appear all that much older than Carson. His eyes told a different story. This was a man who had seen his share of combat. He placed a handful of arrows in Carson's quiver as he continued. "Make sure you kill the next one with your first shot."

"Yes, Captain," the younger man said, nocking another arrow and studying the break in the Tunnel's wall for his next target. Like the others they'd passed, the break opened into the natural caverns, a seemingly endless maze of caves with a seemingly endless population of wolfrats.

Suppressing another shiver, Lenea turned her attention back to the Tunnel ahead of her. It stretched away into a darkness so complete, it was hard to imagine there was an end to it. *Maybe there isn't,* she thought then pushed it away.

She refused to believe they were trapped in here. No matter how badly damaged some sections of the Tunnel seemed to be, there would be a way out. Even if that meant being rescued by Veilgate once Joneam realized they were in trouble.

It was difficult not to hiss loudly in frustration. If only they had brought Dymas with them. They could have sent for help and been out of here by now. It was an oversight she would never make again. Not that she had intentions to ever come back into this awful place.

She was still staring into the dark abyss ahead of her when she heard Havim Polomar approaching from behind. She turned toward the sound of his voice and spotted the glowstone lamp he carried atop a pole. It swung to and fro as he made his way through the crowded passage toward her.

Tall and lean with dark hair and pale-blue eyes, Havim had been one of Croneam's warders and, like the other five with him, had attached himself to her now that Croneam had passed to the other side.

She still found it hard to believe Croneam was gone, and tears threatened to break free every time she thought about him. Now was no different and her vision blurred wetly as she fought them down.

"What is the status at the rear?" she asked when Havim reached her.

"The last of our men are across the chasm," he answered. "But we lost a number of men and horses when part of the ledge collapsed as the last group was coming across."

"How many?"

"No one knows for sure," he answered. "Maybe fifty men. Ten or so horses."

"Burn this place!" Lenea said, not caring how angry she sounded. She'd had it with this hellhole. They should have been to the exit by now, not fumbling their way through the dark no more than ten miles out from the Seal. Knee deep in wolfrats and rubble... their only source of light from the makeshift lamps they'd fashioned from glowstones salvaged from the Tunnel's ruined mechanisms... limited weapons... no Dymas—it was enough to make her want to scream.

Havim looked like he was about to agree with the sentiment, but stopped as the advanced scouts came into view further down the Tunnel. They were on horseback and carried glowstone lamps, and the *clop-clop* of their horses grew louder as they neared.

"They're back sooner than expected," Havim said, shaking his head. "Blood of Maeon, now what?"

"I guess we'll find out," Lenea said, her frustration rising. Blood of Maeon was right. If they'd had Dymas with them, none of this would have happened. Bloody fine oversight that was.

Watching the light of the lamps increase as the warders approached, Lenea braced herself for whatever bad news they were bringing. And it would be bad, she knew. Nothing had gone right since they'd entered the Tunnel.

The two warders swung down from their saddles but kept hold of the bridles as they faced Lenea. Both horses were skittish, and snorted and stamped in agitation.

"More wolfrats ahead," Framis Coleston said, shaking his head. He was a head shorter than his companion, but much more heavily muscled. He wore two short *kamui* style blades and had a bow and quiver of arrows hanging from his saddle.

His companion, Ilishar Brem, also had a bow and quiver, but favored a longer Shizu style blade. His face was pinched in a frown as he added, "And like this stretch of the Tunnel, the mechanisms that activate the glowstones in the next two sections have been damaged as well. It's darker than Maeon's soul up ahead."

"But it's passable," Framis said. "It's the two sections beyond that which will give us trouble. The walls have been opened up in dozens of places and there are hundreds of wolfrats stomping about. Cutting our way through them won't be easy. Bloody things almost overran us before we could hightail it back here."

"Your recommendation?" Lenea asked.

"Keep pressing forward," he answered. "There's not much else we can do. We'll send archers and spearmen ahead to clear out the wolfrats."

"Or we could just hold tight here," Framis suggested. "Joneam will send someone looking for us once he realizes we have been delayed."

"But that could mean waiting here for two or three days," Lenea countered. "And we are getting low on supplies." She glanced at Lieutenant Carson. "Arrows as well as food and water."

"At this rate," Havim said, "it's going to take us two or three days to reach the exit anyway—assuming it's even reachable. There could be worse damage ahead."

"So, why didn't we bring any Dymas with us?" Lieutenant Carson asked, then flinched when everyone turned to stare at him. Embarrassed that he'd been eavesdropping and mortified that he'd spoken aloud, he lowered his eyes. "Uh, if you don't mind my asking?"

"They were needed to evacuate those we left behind when Croneam closed the Seal," Lenea told him, then looked back to the warders. "Havim is right," she said. "There are no guarantees we can even reach the exit. We'll wait here for Joneam to realize we aren't coming."

Havim nodded. "I'll inform the captains," he said. "We'll divide into camps and ration what food and water we have. God send help arrives soon."

"Amen to that," Lenea said and watched Havim disappear among the crowd.

"Uh, what's that?" Lieutenant Carson asked, and Lenea followed his gaze to the break in the wall. A pair of fiery red eyes stared out at them from the darkness. A sound like leather rubbing on stone followed, and a massive snake-like creature emerged, its forked tongue flicking the air as it looked around. Hooded like a cobra and sporting a pair of arms, it held its thick torso area upright and carried a sword in each of two clawed hands.

Before anyone could answer Carson's question, the creature attacked.

As Teig moved through the Veilgate opened by Erebius, he was greeted by screams and the clash of steel on steel. They echoed down the Tunnel from a spot some seventy or eighty yards distant. Flames danced along the floor on one side of the commotion where a broken lamp had spilled its oily contents. Beyond the flames, a massive serpentine shape lunged to a fro, striking with fangs and swords alike.

"Demon," Teig shouted, then stepped aside as Tuari Dymas raced through the Veilgate and ran toward the melee.

She snuffed the flames with a rush of Air, and the use of *Ta'shaen* drew the attention of the demon. It turned toward her with a hiss and started forward in great slithering lunges. Those who'd stood against it watched the creature go with a mixture of relief and horror. Teig spotted a number of bodies on the ground and prayed their injuries weren't severe.

Tuari slowed as the creature advanced, and Teig held his breath as he waited to see what she would do. Some demons, he knew, couldn't be harmed by *Ta'shaen*. Hopefully this wasn't one of them.

Erebius and the others led their horses through the Veilgate, and Erebius stopped beside Teig as the Veilgate closed behind them. Teig looked over at him. "Aren't you going to help?"

"Tuari can handle this," he answered. "And if I know her, she has something special in mind."

Intrigued, Teig watched as the creature continued to bear down on the Dymas. When it had closed to within a dozen yards, a Veilgate opened beneath it and the creature dropped away into the brilliant light of day. Squinting against the brightness, Teig spotted only empty air and blue sky. It vanished as the Veilgate closed, and the semi-lit darkness of the Tunnel returned.

Erebius chuckled. "She never disappoints."

Teig arched an eyebrow at him. "Where did she send it?"

"Death's Third March," the aging Dymas answered. "She dropped it right in the middle of a column of Tambans."

Teig nodded in appreciation. "Why kill it when you can use it against the enemy, eh?"

"Exactly. Come, we have wounded in need of healing."

They joined Tuari, then made their way to those who'd stood against the demon. Governor Prenum greeted them as they arrived.

"Are we glad to see you," she said. The bottom of her dress was torn, and her hands were covered with blood, but she appeared unharmed. "I've bandaged their wounds as best I could," she said, pointing to the injured men, "but they are in need of healing."

Teig studied the men as Erebius knelt to look them over. Two were warders. The other five were soldiers of Fulrath.

"They saved my life," Lenea said, seemingly oblivious to the blood on her hands. "What was that thing?"

"A demon from Con'Jithar," Tuari answered. "Somewhere in the natural caverns a hole opened in the Veil. It's happening all over the world now. As the Earthsoul continues to weaken, it will become more frequent. And in areas much more populated than the caverns."

"I'll bet that's why there are so many wolfrats in here," one of the warders said. "They were trying to get away from the demon."

Erebius finished healing the last of the wounded men, then looked pointedly at the break in the wall. "It might not be the only one down there," he said. "We'd best get going." He turned to Lenea. "The Tunnel ahead is impassable. We're taking everyone out through Veilgates. We'll divide your people into seven equal-sized groups, and each Dymas will open a gate for them. We'll all leave at the same time."

*Good,* Teig thought. *I hate this bloody place.*

As the Dymas rode away down the Tunnel to take their respective places, Teig stared into the abyss of the natural caverns and felt the weight of the world begin to settle on him once again. He'd momentarily forgotten about it due to the excitement with the demon, but now that things had quieted, the feeling of being suffocated was once again real.

The only thing that kept him from hyperventilating completely was the realization that because the Tunnel was damaged beyond any immediate repair, he would *never* have to come back inside.

*Thank the light,* he thought, and waited for Erebius to open the way to freedom.

# CHAPTER 13

## *Core Decisions*

JASE FAIRIMOR WOKE to the sound of thunder.

Thankfully it was real thunder from real storm clouds and not the ear rattling cracks that followed strikes crafted of *Ta'shaen*. Pulling back his blankets, he sat up and looked around his room. It was empty, which was a first. Hopefully it meant he was well enough that Ammorin no longer thought he needed a nursemaid.

Lightning flashed outside, and a few seconds later thunder rolled across the palace. A rush of wind followed, and fat drops of rain pounded the windows to run in uneven streaks down the glass. Beyond, the sky churned with roiling, low-hanging clouds, and the light of day had been reduced to gloom and grey.

*Matches my mood*, he thought.

The darkness in him was due in part to the dreams he'd had of the Rhiven home world and the death of Talia and the others in the Soul Chamber. But mostly it was because he'd had two days to think about what the dreams might mean. Worse, Galiena's words still echoed in his mind that he might not be able to save his friends.

He coughed loudly, waiting to see if Ammorin would burst into the room to check on him. When nothing happened, he coughed again, louder this time. Still nothing.

He nodded in satisfaction. *It's about time he left me alone.*

Pushing himself to his feet, he moved to the wardrobe to find something to wear. So far, he hadn't been allowed out of bed for anything other than visits to the chamber pot, and he'd been wearing this same pair of nightclothes for two days. No wonder he was grumpy.

He pulled open the wardrobe and began picking through his clothes. Most were uniforms and other stuffy, stately-looking clothes, but he found what he was looking for and pulled them out. A pair of soft pants, a short-sleeved shirt, and a loose-fitting riding jacket. Yes, they were more suited to Kindel's Grove than the palace, but they were comfortable and helped brighten his mood. Somewhat.

He was pulling on his boots when the door opened and Ammorin ducked into the room. "Talia said you were up and about," he said, his broad face breaking into a smile. "I had my doubts, of course. I was starting to wonder if you would ever recover."

"I recovered *yesterday*," Jase told him. "You were the one who insisted I take it easy for a while longer."

Ammorin's smile widened. "So I did," he said. "But it was really just a test to see if the *Mith'elre Chon* could be ordered about."

Jase stared at him, trying to decide if the Dainin was joking. "I'm going to pretend I didn't hear that," he said, then finished with his boots and stood.

Even before Ammorin had mentioned Talia, Jase had sensed she was near. He could feel the increased proximity through the *sei'vaiya*. He could also feel that she was agitated about something. "When did Talia return from Chellum?" he asked.

"This morning," Ammorin answered. "Apparently she had a difficult time convincing her father that she should be allowed to return to the place where she nearly died." He shrugged. "As least that's the way she tells it. I think she just wanted to spend some time with her family. There wasn't much for her to do here anyway, with you incapacitated and all."

"I'll ignore that last comment as well," Jase mumbled. "Did Seth and Elliott come with her?"

"They did," Ammorin said, then laughed. "Apparently Elliott had an even more difficult time leaving than Talia, but for different reasons."

Jase smiled knowingly. "Tana."

"Anyway, everyone is gathering right now in the private library. Your mother called for an assembly of the Core Council, and she and the others are pleased that you are up. She would like you to join the discussion."

"First things first," Jase said, then opened his Awareness to the luminescent world of *Ta'shaen* and embraced the gift of Air. It was the first time he'd touched the Power since collapsing two days ago, and it was like a cool drink of water after a sojourn in the desert—a sweet elixir of life-giving energy.

Careful not to drink too deeply at first, he channeled only what was necessary to open the small chest on the table next to his bed. Inside were the two Blood Orbs he and Gideon had used during their respective battles with Death's Third March. Using another tendril of Air, he pulled them into his outstretched hand, then released the Power as he tucked the Orbs into the pockets of his jacket.

Lightning flashed behind him, and thunder rumbled across the city.

"Some storm," he said, moving to the door. "Another sign that the Earthsoul is failing?"

Ammorin nodded. "Yes." He held the door open for Jase, then followed him out into the hall. "And reports are coming in from all over the Nine Lands about similar incidents. Most are much worse than this storm. Trian is being shielded by the Earthsoul as much as is in Her power to do."

"What's happening elsewhere?"

"The earthquake that rocked Talin Plateau during the battle was but one of many. The Tunnel was damaged so severely it was rendered impassable. Governor Prenum and those with her had to be rescued through Veilgates. And they were lucky to have gotten out when they did. This morning all thirty-six miles collapsed, and a rift opened in the plateau along the same path. It's hundreds of feet deep and a hundred feet across, and it stretches for almost twenty miles."

"The Tunnel served its purpose," Jase said. "No use mourning over what we can't fix. Besides, the rift will keep Shadan's army from turning north to Tradeston. What else has been happening?"

"Another collapse of the sea cliffs west of Thion," Ammorin said. "Dozens of coastal cities and villages swallowed by the resulting waves. Not that it really mattered—most were destroyed as a result of the first collapse. Similar destructions in Melek and Riak as a result of tremendous earthquakes and storms. A little closer to home, a massive tornado touched down yesterday afternoon in Omer Forest. It was on the ground for nearly a hundred miles and ripped a swath of devastation more than a mile wide."

Just felt a sudden stab of panic. "Kindel's Grove?"

"Fine," Ammorin answered. "The storm was to the east. So far it looks like no villages were affected."

"Thank the Creator," Jase said, relieved.

They reached the stairwell and started down. His legs still felt a little weak, but he refused to use the handrail out of stubborn pride. He didn't want to give Ammorin the pleasure of knowing that he wasn't *fully* recovered.

"The same storm that tore through Omer Forest," Ammorin continued, "dropped hailstones the size of melons on the grasslands north of Capena, destroying crops and killing livestock. But there have been no reports of human casualties." The Dainin shook his head in disbelief. "And there are dozens more reports like these. It's getting worse, Jase. The Earthsoul is literally on the edge of collapse."

"How much time do we have?"

"A week maybe."

The stab of panic returned, but he crushed it determinedly. A Blood Orb would be found. And it would be found soon. There would be enough time to rejuvenate the Earthsoul. To believe otherwise was to surrender to Maeon right now. And he would never surrender. Even if it meant standing toe to toe with him as Galiena had done on her world, he would fight until his last breath.

Still, he couldn't stop himself from asking, "How goes the search for a Blood Orb?" It wasn't doubt that prompted the question. It was hope. Hope, and a belief that the Creator still had a hand to play in all of this.

"Two more *chorazin* T'rii Gates were located in Kelsa and a third was found in

Chunin. All three were within a mile or so of ruins that could have once been a Temple of Elderon, but no altars or Orbs were found." He glanced down at Jase, his eyes glimmering with the same look of hope. "It's only a matter of time before we find a viable Orb, my friend. I can feel it."

Jase nodded. "Anything else I should know?"

"Arkania entered the war," he answered. "And I don't just mean the trivial raids along the Riaki and Zekan borders. Dozens of tribes along both borders have banded together and have attacked cities and villages deep inside both countries. They are being led by the Power-wielding priests and priestesses who serve Maeon. They have loosed many Con'droth to help in the battles, and Riak and Zeka are taking heavy losses. I'd like to think it is simply a result of Maeon extending his hand to more of his servants, but I fear this sudden alliance between the various tribes is a result of *our* actions there. The destruction of the village during the rescue of your mother, may have been perceived as an act of war."

"It was an act of war," Jase said. "But the first stone was not cast by us." He turned and looked his giant friend in the eyes. "But we will bloody well cast the last. I will send Dymas to Zeka to reenforce those fighting there. I'm confident the Riaki can handle themselves."

They were making their way down the last bend in the stairwell when the sound of voices became audible. It didn't sound serious—just idle chatter among friends—and Jase smiled as he picked out the voices of his mother and Talia and Cassia amid the deeper voices of Elison and Elliott and Seth. But there were other voices he didn't recognize, and he cocked his ear toward it, listening. The newly appointed members of the Core, he decided, curious to see who his mother had selected.

They came into view a moment later, seated with everyone else in the library half of the room. Joel Korishal and Rosil Eraiadin of the lesser houses, he recognized. So too with Kustin Landar of the Merchants Guild and Lyndon Ryban, First Captain of the City Guardsmen. The two women, however, he'd never seen before. Both were in their mid to later years and held themselves with an air of intelligence.

He studied them for a moment, then let his eyes move over the others who had gathered. In addition to those whose voices he'd identified in the stairwell, he found Ladies Hadershi and Korishal, along with Bornis, Zea, and Velerie. The Dymas were clustered around a stack of books on an end table. Bornis stood behind Zea who held a sleeping Kindel. Gideon and Galiena were noticeably absent.

Elison and Lavin occupied chairs next to Seth, and all three had their chairs turned backwards to keep their swords free. Seth spotted him and Ammorin as they entered, and smiled warmly. Talia spotted him a heartbeat later, and a rush of warmth reached him through the *sei'vaiya* as she sprang to her feet and rushed forward to embrace him.

He welcomed the hug with a smile, but holding her reawakened the dread of the nightmares.

"What is it?" she asked, sensing his mood through the love-bond.

He knew better than to lie to her—she would sense that as well. "Just a bad dream," he told her. Taking her hand, he led her back to the collection of sofas. The newly appointed members of the Core watched him with a mixture of awe and curiosity as he approached.

"Jase," Talia said by way of introduction, "this is Daphney Mabela, Dean of Religious Studies at Jyoai College."

Daphney rose and offered her hand. "It's a pleasure, *Mith'elre Chon*," she said, offering a bow.

"The pleasure is mine, Dean Mabela," Jase told her, then turned to the other woman as she rose.

"And this is Asbella Belaris," Talia said. "Professor of politics and law."

"A wise choice," Jase said, taking her hand. "We will need your expertise now that most of the former members of the government are dead."

If Asbella was fazed by the comment, it didn't show. She simply smiled. "I was at the Colosseum," she said. "I will do my part to make sure a repeat cleansing isn't necessary."

"Thank you, Professor," Jase said, then moved to stand behind his mother as Talia and the others returned to their seats. Yes, his legs felt weak, but it was so nice to be upright again he ignored the weariness. He also wanted to send a message to the newly appointed members of the Core that he had his mother's back. Literally as well as figuratively.

"I understand the Core has been called into assembly," he said. "What are the items of business?"

"There are several," Brysia said, "but the most pressing is the evacuation of Trian and her surrounding areas. We need to decide if it is to be mandatory or voluntary. Any thoughts?"

"If I may," Elison said. "I think it needs to be a little of both. Women and children and the elderly must be evacuated. For their safety and to free those of us who will remain to concentrate on the enemy. We cannot engage Death's Third March and protect the powerless."

"I agree," Seth said. "And I would add that any men who aren't truly capable of wielding a sword be sent to oversee the exodus."

"And those who are capable?" Cassia asked.

"Can choose to stay and fight or to escort their families to safety," Elison answered.

"What of those women who don't have children or families?" Asbella asked. "I know many women who are expert archers and some who can wield a sword. Will they be allowed to stay and fight if they wish?"

Jase could tell by Elison's expression that he wanted to say no. It wasn't that he believed women were incapable of handling themselves in battle, he simply wanted to eliminate the distraction women soldiers would present to some of the men. After a short deliberation, he nodded.

"They will."

An unmistakable feeling of relief flooded through the *sei'vaiya* and Jase glanced at Talia to find her smiling. Ladies Hadershi and Korishal were smiling as well. So was Velerie Kivashey. Of course they would want to stay and fight—they'd already fought several battles within Trian's walls. He caught Talia's eye and winked at her.

"All Power-wielders, male and female alike," Jase said, drawing all eyes to him, "are free to choose for themselves, but I'm fairly certain where they will be when Shadan's forces arrive."

"But if some do desire to go with their families," Asbella began, "you will allow them to leave?"

Jase grunted with amusement. "They answer to the Earthsoul," he told her. "Not to me. They will go where She directs."

"Where are the evacuees to go?" Kustin Landar asked. "They can't very well live in the fields and farmlands of the plateau. And none of the outlying villages are big enough to house so many. Even if we send them off the plateau, there isn't enough housing for everyone."

"Spoken like a true merchant," Brysia said, sounding pleased with her choice to put Kustin on the Core. "Does anyone have an answer for Kustin?"

"Begging your pardon, High Queen," Lavin said. "I know I do not sit on this council, but I have a thought on this matter."

"Please, Captain," Brysia said. "We would hear all ideas, not just those of the Core."

"We could just evacuate the northern half of the city, or on a minimum, just those neighborhoods bordering the main thoroughfares. Once the enemy reaches the city, they will most assuredly assault North and Northeast gates and River and East Gates, then seek the most direct routes toward the inner city. Their goal is to capture Fairimor Palace—they won't waste time going door to door looking for slaughter."

"Probably not," Seth said, "but they might set fire to those areas they don't intend to conquer. They burned Greendom to the ground for no other reason than that it was there."

"Evacuate the northern half of the city," Jase said, not caring if it sounded like a directive. "Seth is right: The enemy will destroy whatever they can. Those in the southern half can flee through the southern gates if it comes to that. Just leave enough of a buffer between East Road and our people to keep them out of harm's way."

"What's to keep the enemy from sending troops to attack the southern gates?" Rosil Eraiadin asked. "It seems to me they would seek to exploit every entry point into the city."

"Numbers," Lavin said. "They don't have enough troops to assault all the gates at once. Not and have strength enough to make a push through the outer city. Remember, they will need to breach the inner wall as well once they make it that far.

They won't risk spreading themselves too thin in order to make that second assault at the inner wall. I am certain they will attempt to bring most of their forces along North and Northeast Roads."

"We know they will eventually make it into the city," Lyndon Ryban said. "They are simply too large a force for us to hold off indefinitely. If we present the two northern gates as weaker points, but hold River Gate and East Gate, we can use the Trian River as a natural barrier to corral them in the city."

"I like the sound of that," Seth said. "And we could have our Dymas set up a perimeter of wardings involving crux points. Something similar to what Idoman created in Zedik Pass. We could place them along the river and then again just south of East Road should the enemy make their way toward the southern half of the city."

"The crux points Gideon created in Fulrath were capable of resetting themselves after destroying the enemy," Jase said. "I saw how it was done. I can set up similar wardings here."

"I don't know," Cassia said. "I worry that having any civilians in the city is a mistake. I know our dear captains believe they will be out of harm's way, but there are no guarantees the enemy will leave them be. If the wards are breached and the southern half of the city is overrun, the two southern gates will become a bottleneck. Our people will be slaughtered."

"The enemy doesn't have the numbers for a citywide attack," Lavin insisted. "They will be focused on taking the inner city and the palace."

"I agree," Lyndon said.

"I have seen it," Jase said, and a hush fell over the room as everyone turned to look at him in surprise.

"Several times," he continued. "In dreams and visions. Shadan wants Fairimor Palace, and he will throw everything he has at us to get it. Will civilians be killed? Probably. But we can minimize that by evacuating the northern half of the city. Evacuation of the southern half can be voluntary if you choose, but those who stay should be made to understand that they are not safe. As Cassia said, there are no guarantees. If things proceed as I have seen, nowhere in the world will be safe in the final moments before rejuvenation or death."

Brysia nodded. "I propose we put this matter to a vote. All in favor of proceeding with both the mandatory evacuation of Trian's northern half and all outlying areas in the path of Death's Third March, please signify."

All twelve hands went up.

"All in favor of the evacuation of the rest of Trian and its surrounding areas being voluntary but encouraged, please signify." Again all twelve hands went up, but there was hesitation on the part of Joel and Rosil.

"Thank you," Brysia told them, then turned to Elison. "In light of this endeavor, we will table the other items for now. Captain Brey will oversee the military preparations for the evacuation. Kustin will see to the evacuation side of things. Ladies Hadershi and Korishal will head the Dymas who will be preparing the wardings." She paused and looked at each of them in turn.

"This is not going to be easy, my friends, but thank you for your thoughts and for the fine job I know you will do in seeing this through. For the honor of God, the Flame of Kelsa, and the liberty of the people, let it be done."

# CHAPTER 14

## Executive Orders

JASE WATCHED THE MEMBERS of the Core Council exit the Fairimor home, then turned to those who remained. "I don't know about you, but I'm starving." Taking Talia by the hand, he stood and started for the dining half of the room. "Gavin," he called, "please have Allisen bring in something to eat."

Elliott and Seth followed him to the table, but Brysia hung back for a moment to speak with Ammorin and Elison before joining them. Cassia and Andil came as well, and for a brief moment things felt normal once again, a glimpse of quieter times past. It was refreshing—he'd almost forgotten how emotionally powerful something as simple as eating with friends and family could be.

"I'm going to address our citizens after lunch," Brysia said, drawing all eyes to her. "If we are going through with the evacuation, there is no better time to start than now."

"I agree," Jase said, pulling a plate close as he waited for Allisen to arrive. "I'll join you on the Overlook when you go out." He adjusted his silverware fastidiously for a moment, then glanced across the table at his mother. "So, where are Gideon and Galiena? Or the rest of the Rhiven, for that matter?"

"The Rhiven are still here in the palace," Brysia answered. "Gideon and Galiena went to the front. Gideon wanted to assist Dymas General Leda in setting booby traps for the enemy. Galiena went to keep an eye on her brother so as to assess when they might seek to open another Dragon Gate."

"How far has the enemy advanced in the two days I've been under house arrest?" He asked it simply, but the look he directed at Ammorin let the Dainin know what he thought of his nursing skills.

"They passed Fulrath this morning," Seth said. "As you might imagine, they gave it a wide berth. At their current pace, they will reach the western rim in two, maybe three days."

Jase nodded. "Which is when they will probably attempt the Dragon Gate." He caught sight of Allisen as she entered from the kitchens, then took a deep breath as she set a tray of warm bread on the table. She pulled back the covering linen to reveal an assortment of sliced meats and mustards, as well as jams, jellies, and butter.

"Fresh out of the ovens," Allisen said. "Eat while it's still warm."

Jase's stomach knotted with hunger at the smells. "Thank you, Allisen," he said, and was echoed by the others. The aging cook smiled as she returned to the kitchens.

Everyone helped themselves to the food, and for a while not much was said as they ate. Then thunder rumbled loudly once again, and talk turned to the obvious signs of the Earthsoul's imminent demise. As Jase listened, he realized that Ammorin had mentioned only a fraction of the natural disasters plaguing the Nine Lands. Things were worsening much more quickly and were much more widespread than Jase had imagined.

It darkened his mood and stifled his appetite, but he finished what was on his plate because eating was necessary, if no longer pleasurable.

Pushing his plate away, he rose. "I'll wait for you out on the Overlook, Mother," he told her.

He helped Talia to her feet, and together they made their way out of the Fairimor home and into the Dome.

The massive chamber was empty but for a handful of tribunal members and three squads of *Bero'thai*. They watched quietly as he and Talia made their way across the Blue Flame rug and out the doors onto the Overlook.

The smell of rain greeted them as they entered the gardens, and the pathway was wet from the earlier downpour. The darkest clouds had moved off to the south, but there was still a slight mist-like drizzle falling across the city. The coolness felt good on his skin and was a nice contrast to the warmth of Talia's hand.

She smiled, tightening her grip. "I was just thinking the same thing."

"I've been thinking about the last time we were out here in the gardens," he said, "and it terrifies me when I think about how close I came to losing you."

"Then we're even," she said. "Because it terrifies me every time you go off to battle. I almost lost you this last time. If Galiena hadn't arrived when she did, I would have. She saved your life, Jase. I hope you know that."

"I do," he said. "And I promise to be more careful in the future."

She grunted. "If only that were true."

They reached the eastern edge and stopped at the wall to gaze down at the city. "There are a lot of people down there," she said. "Do you really think we can evacuate them all?"

"No," he admitted, "but we'll do our best."

She leaned close, searching his face. "Have you really seen the fall of Trian in a vision?"

He nodded. "Yes," he said softly. "And it wasn't pretty. A lot of people are going to die here. Some who are dear to me." He felt bitterness seeping toward Talia through the *sei'vaiya* and tried unsuccessfully to squelch it. Finally, he added, "And the worst part is: There isn't much I can do to stop it."

She stared at him, her bright green eyes sparkling with concern. "What makes you say that?"

"Because I won't be here."

She squeezed his hand reassuringly. "You'll stop it when you rejuvenate the Earthsoul."

He knew she could feel his dread and doubt through the love-bond, but she didn't press him on it, and together they stood quietly, gazing over the city.

The clouds continued to move eastward amid flashes of lightning and the rumble of distant thunder. The light mist ceased falling. In the streets below people began venturing out of their homes, eager to be about the day's business.

Brysia arrived a few minutes later with Ammorin as her escort. Her face was set. Her eyes, like emeralds, shone with determination. She didn't like what she was about to do, but she would do it anyway because it was best for her people. She nodded to Ammorin and Jase felt him embrace the Power and channel streams of Air to amplify Brysia's voice.

"Citizens of Trian," she began, and Ammorin urged her words to the far reaches of the city. In the streets below, people stopped what they were doing and turned their attention to the Overlook. "This is Brysia Fairimor, High Queen of Kelsa. I come to you now with heavy heart, and I pray that you will listen closely to my words." Her tone was authoritative yet warm, and Jase marveled at how perfectly she wove the two together.

"Our armies have suffered a significant defeat at the hands of Throy Shadan," she continued, "and the forces of Death's Third March have taken Talin Plateau. The city of Fulrath has fallen."

She paused to let her words reach all who were listening, and Jase stretched out with his Awareness to search the faces below. They were etched with horror and disbelief. Here and there a woman brought hands to mouth to stifle a gasp.

"And while our armies have since regrouped and are preparing to meet the enemy at Mendel Pass," Brysia continued, "it is unlikely they will be able to hold indefinitely. This is the reason I speak to you now."

She paused again, collecting her thoughts as Ammorin urged her voice outward.

"Death's Third March *will* reach Trian. In weeks or days, no one can tell, but Shadan's arrival is inevitable. Because of this, the Core Council voted unanimously to evacuate Trian and her surrounding areas. The northern half of the city is under a mandatory evacuation order. The southern half is voluntary to an extent."

She shook her head sadly before continuing, and Jase listened carefully as she issued instructions as had been decided upon by the Core. When she finished, she waited for the people to process what they had heard, then added, "This directive is effective immediately. The City Guard will be moving among you to assist where they can. *Bero'thai* will be distributing written copies of this order and its accompanying instructions.

"There is no need to panic, but please heed this directive in a timely manner. Once Death's Third March arrives, any who remain in the city will be in harm's way, and our soldiers might not be able to adequately protect you from the enemy."

Smiling as if those in the city could see her, her voice grew warm as she added, "As dire as the situation might seem, I still have hope for a victory over the servants of darkness. I have hope because the *Mith'elre Chon* fights for us. Pray for him, my friends. Pray for the soldiers who fight alongside him. Pray for the Earthsoul. Pray that She might have the strength to hold on until a Blood Orb can be found. And lastly, pray for those of us who will defend this great city after you leave."

Tears leaked from her eyes as she finished. "For the honor of God, the Flame of Kelsa, and the liberty of us all, let it be done." She nodded, and Ammorin released the Power.

"Well said, Mother," Jase told her, then put his arm around her and pulled her close to him. "We *will* win," he whispered, pressing his cheek against the top of her head.

She nodded, but her eyes remained on the city below. "But at what cost?"

Jase couldn't answer as images of the dreams flickered through his mind.

"They are just about there," Idoman said, stepping back from the tiny Power-wrought window so Gideon could have a look.

He stepped forward and peered through, impressed as always with the view the windows provided. A thousand feet below, the front lines of Death's Third March looked like a line of ants marching across the grasslands of Talin. At their current pace, they were still two or three days away from the western rim, and Idoman was determined to stretch it to four or even five.

"There are burnt patches marking the crux points," the young Dymas General continued. "They don't look like much from the ground, of course, but I put them there for us to measure distance."

"Smart," Gideon said. "You think of everything." As he watched, those on the ground continued their steady march westward, drawing ever closer to the unseen trap that would obliterate them. Mostly Darklings and Shadan Cultists, they were being escorted—he supposed herded would be a better word—by Shadowlancers and a handful of Agla'Con riding scaled reptiles the size of horses.

The reptiles, he realized, were Zotam, which meant the array of unfamiliar-looking shadowspawn with them weren't shadowspawn at all: They were nightmares bred in the warrens of Kunin.

He pictured Endil and Thorac on their quest to recapture the stolen Blood Orb from Loharg, and a sudden rush of panic filled him that Aethon had learned of the mission. He shook it away as quickly as it had come. No. If Aethon knew of the Blood Orb, he would have attempted to take it for himself, and every Dymas in the world would have felt the resulting cataclysm. His traitorous nephew was simply exploiting a new resource, albeit one that might be just as dangerous to him as it was to Kelsa.

"Aethon has been to Kunin," he said, shaking his head in disgust. "Those new mounts are Zotam. The creatures with them are demonspawn."

"Let me see," Galiena said, and Gideon stepped back to allow her to peer through. She nodded. "Yes. Those are Zotam, but there aren't any *Shel'tui* among the riders. Aethon hasn't formed an alliance with Kunin. He's plundering it to rebuild his army."

"Shadowspawn. Demonspawn," Idoman said, waving his hand dismissively. "All the same in my book. And the same to my crux points, if you get my meaning."

"I do," Galiena said, "and they are right on top of them."

Not wanting to miss the detonation, Gideon opened a second small window next to Galiena's and peered through. A few seconds later the first of the Darklings passed through the invisible trip wire of Spirit linking the crux points, and a dome of Spirit sprang into place to cover an area two hundred feet wide. That triggered the next crux points, and lightning crackled upward from the ground, blowing Darklings and cultists apart in superheated bursts of white-hot energy. The bolts danced along the inside of the dome, then sizzled downward, tearing up the ground and tossing lifeless bodies around like rags.

When the lightning had run its course, the dome collapsed, and those who'd been on the outside were left to stare in horror at the smoking remains of their comrades.

Some of the cultists backed away and looked around as if contemplating fleeing, but the tips of the K'rrosha's lances flared to life, changing the would-be deserter's minds. They started marching again as the demonspawn moved into the area of ruined flesh to steal a quick meal.

Turning to Idoman, Gideon released the Power and let the window slide shut. "That was brilliant," he complimented. "And you say you've laid other traps elsewhere along their path?"

Idoman nodded. "This was just the first one. And a small one at that. The largest are nearer the rim."

Nodding, Gideon scratched his cheek thoughtfully as he gazed about the command tent. Large enough to be comfortable but not so large as to draw attention to itself, it was sparsely furnished on the inside and without banner or ornamentation on the outside. Only those of the High Command knew it was the nerve center of Kelsa's army. For added precaution should Shadan seek to eliminate Kelsa's leadership, the High Command was never here all at once but spread throughout the camp. When it was necessary for a full assembly, they gathered at another location well away from camp.

The members of the High Command now present were Idoman, Joselyn, and

General Gefion. Joneam was somewhere with the leaders of the newly arrived Chunin and Elvan armies. Captains Tarn and Dennison were with Governor Prenum somewhere on the south side of camp making arrangements for Fulrath's civilian staff to journey to Trian.

Gideon smiled at Lenea's tenacity and strength of spirit, impressed with how well she had handled her underground ordeal. Teig Ole'ar, on the other hand, refused even to enter a tent. He'd slept outside last night under the stars. He was still a fierce warrior and the finest scout Gideon had ever met, but his experiences in the Tunnel had unhinged him in some way. He'd taken to standing guard outside the command tent so he could be outside.

Gideon glanced at the shadow Teig threw on the tent wall, then turned to the map on the table. "What else are you doing to disrupt the enemy?"

"Hit and run attacks through Veilgates similar to what we did in the Allister Plains. The only difference is we are launching the attacks from the plateau instead of from camp. I didn't want Agla'Con tracing our Dymas back here."

"Have they attacked here at all?" Galiena asked.

"Three small strikes is all," Idoman answered. "And they were repelled easily. The Agla'Con are limited in their abilities with Veilgates. And as you saw just now, they are busy keeping the cultists and other cowards from deserting. It's why I've kept the booby traps small. I enjoy leaving survivors to wonder if they might be next."

"Have any Rhiven been engaged during your attacks?" Galiena asked, and Idoman shook his head.

"Thankfully no," he answered. "I've had about as much close contact with them as I care to. Present company excluded, of course."

Galiena exchanged an amused look with Yavil, then looked at Gideon. "The Rhiven's absence in battle means they are conserving their strength for a Dragon Gate." She moved to the map and looked it over. Yavil joined her, indicating some of the marks.

"We think they will attempt the gates somewhere about here," he said, pointing to the red line Idoman had inked on the map of Talin Plateau. "With exit points to the north and west of the united armies. Here and here."

"That would be my guess as well," Galiena agreed. "Too far a leap and they risk opening up another rift in the plateau. They care nothing for the geography, of course, but they won't risk losing more troops."

"The only troops being risked in this maneuver are our own," Joselyn muttered, and the look she directed at Idoman showed what she thought about the young man's plan. "We should be fortifying Mendel Pass instead of sitting in the open waiting to be attacked."

"If we were to move into the pass now," Idoman said, not looking up from the map, "Shadan would use gates to leap to Trian Plateau, bypassing us altogether. And there isn't time to move all of our army to Trian Plateau before Death's Third March reaches the red line."

He turned and smiled at her in spite of her frustrated stare. "We must make our stand here while we have the element of surprise. It will give us a chance to kill as many of his troops as are stranded here when the gates collapse behind them."

Gideon stepped up to the map, then turned to Idoman. "Your plan for the coming days is a good one," he said. "But I didn't come to discuss your tactics. I came to be part of them. What are your orders, Dymas General Leda?"

Idoman failed to cover his surprise.

"I... uh... I can't give orders to you. You are the Guardian of Kelsa."

"And a servant and soldier of the Earthsoul," Gideon said. "But I do not head this army of Gifted, Idoman. You do. What would you have me do?"

The young Dymas still seemed uncertain, but after a moment he shook it off. "Kalear is heading an attack against the Tambans on the northern flank. They have many *Jeth'Jalda* with them. I'm sure he would appreciate the help. He and his strike team have gathered— Oh, I'll just take you there. It will be faster than explaining it."

"Spoken like a true Dymas General," Gideon said, smiling. He nodded to Galiena. "I'll be back after the attack. Are you staying here?"

"Yes. Yavil and I need to discuss how best to move against our traitorous brethren."

"Until then," Gideon said, giving a bow of respect. Nodding for Idoman to open a gate, he followed the young man onto Talin Plateau.

と

Aethon Fairimor let the rent from Tamba close behind him, but he didn't release *Lo'shaen* as he made his way toward the line of Shadowlancers fronting Shadan. He let the dark river of power flow through him, strengthening him even as it darkened the air around him. It would serve as a reminder to the K'rrosha and their Dreadlord that the last of the Fairimor Three was not to be trifled with.

The line of Shadowlancers watched him come, then grudgingly parted in the middle to allow him to pass. Krev and the other Rhiven stopped short of the K'rrosha, and Aethon moved through without breaking stride, his eyes intent on Shadan, his contempt for the refleshed being growing with each step.

The Dreadlord sat atop another one of his pet K'sivik, scepter in hand, his good eye burning red with irritation.

"What took you so long?" he rasped, his ruined voice the sound of steel on stone. Tapping his K'sivik with his scepter, he brought the creature to a halt and glared down at Aethon. The air turned foul as the K'sivik's rancid breath washed over him.

"*Frel'mola* insisted that I join her for a tour of her kingdom," he answered. Using a tendril of *Lo'shaen* to touch the K'sivik's mind, he turned the creature's attention toward a knot of Darklings marching to the south. When the air was mostly breathable again, he continued. "Then I took a second one of my own to meet with the generals and *Jeth'Jalda* who belong to the Fist of Con'Jithar. Their loyalties are to

Maeon and Tamba, not to *Frel'mola*."

"And where do your loyalties lie?" Shadan rasped.

"With Maeon," Aethon told him. Without intending to, he allowed the river of *Lo'shaen* coursing through him to increase and was pleased when Shadan's hand tightened on his scepter. *So*, he thought, *the Destroyer of Amnidia is wary of a rematch, is he? Good to know.*

Shadan's eye narrowed. "And this Fist of Con'Jithar, they agreed to help?"

"Another forty thousand troops have sworn to the cause."

Shadan leaned forward eagerly. "Where are they?"

"Coming."

"Do not betray me for the female Dreadlord," Shadan hissed, and the tip of his scepter flared sharply.

"Not to worry," Aethon told him. "I trust her even less than I trust you." With that he turned his back on Shadan and strode away, moving the Shadowlancers aside with nothing more than his presence. He didn't need to look back to know Shadan was fuming.

"You enjoy taunting him, don't you?" Krev said as he fell in beside him.

Aethon grunted in amusement. "Very much. But it's more to remind him and his K'rrosha that I am first among the living. They would do well to remember that in the eyes of Maeon I am on an equal standing with Throy bloody Shadan."

Krev laughed, a strange sound coming from him. "Which justifies my use of the word taunt."

Aethon cast a sideways glance at the Rhiven. "You're unusually chipper all of a sudden. Anything I should know about?"

"My sister is near."

Aethon stared at him. "Your sister?"

"Galiena'ei to ul'Morgranon," Krev said. "Queen of the Rhiven." He laughed again, but it sounded much darker this time. "I told you my people would eventually notice we were missing from our icy prison. Apparently, my sister has come to investigate our dealings here."

"Is she a threat to our cause?"

"Galiena?" Krev said with a derisive snort. "Hardly. My people have given up on this world. They will not involve themselves in this war. They hate humankind almost as much as you hate Throy Shadan."

"But she will want to recapture you—to return you to Earth's End?"

Krev smiled, his yellow eyes eager. "I'm counting on it."

"So long is it doesn't interfere with the war effort," Aethon told him. "How do you know she is near?"

"I can feel her presence in my mind. We are twins so we share a birth-bond—something similar to a *sei'vaiya*, if far less intimate and precise. I can tell you only that she is near, perhaps within fifty or sixty miles."

Aethon still wasn't convinced Galiena didn't pose a threat. "Will she have other

Rhiven with her?"

"A few, perhaps," Krev answered. "Enough to try to take us back into custody."
He looked over, his yellow eyes shining. "It is their weakness. They do not believe in
capital punishment. They will use the Power, of course, but only as much as is
necessary to recapture us. It will be a pleasure disappointing them."

They cut across the ranks of soldiers until they reached a line of horsemen. Jamik
Hedron and Asherim Ije'kre were there along with several other Agla'Con
commanders. Two of the lesser Agla'Con dismounted and offered their horses to
Aethon and Krev. When they were seated, Aethon moved his horse alongside Jamik
and Asherim.

"What did I miss?"

"Aside from Shadan ranting about your absence?" Jamik asked, his contempt
obvious. "Not much."

Asherim turned in his saddle to stare at Jamik, his Meleki face unamused. "I
disagree," he countered. "The attacks coming at us through Veilgates have been most
troublesome. Especially the one which dropped a demon into the midst of the
Tambans."

"Demon?" Aethon asked. "Kelsa is using demons against us?" That didn't sound
right. How would a Dymas come into possession of a demon from Con'Jithar?

"The bloody thing was immune to the effects of *Ta'shaen*," Jamik said, his hard
Shizu-like persona crumbling slightly. "The *Jeth'Jalda* were powerless against it.
Tamban archers and spearmen eventually brought it down, but nearly a hundred
men, including a number of *Jeth'Jalda* were killed in the process."

Aethon cared little for numbers, especially where the Tambans were concerned.
He was concerned, however, that his enemies might have gained some new
advantage. Newer than their horizontal Veilgates, anyway. Those blasted things were
infuriating. Particularly because he couldn't duplicate them, not even with *Lo'shaen*.
It wasn't fair.

"A fluke," Asherim said, referring to the demon. "It was already wounded when
it arrived. The Dymas who sent it here obviously sent it through a Veilgate as a last
resort."

"And was clever enough to use it as a weapon against us," Jamik said, his
irritation rising. "Demons don't care what side of the war you are on. Being mortal
makes you their enemy." He sat up straight as if something had just occurred to him.
Frowning, he turned to Aethon. "Speaking of demons, what is to stop them from
turning on us once the Veil collapses?"

"Nothing," Aethon said. "But then it won't really matter, will it? Con'Jithar will
have arrived. The victory will be ours regardless." He waved his hand, dismissing the
matter. "Tell me more of the attacks."

"Small, quick, and precise," Jamik answered, business-like once more. "Just like
in the Allister Plains. Whoever is leading them knows what he is about."

"Gideon?" Aethon asked.

"Maybe," Asherim answered. "The *Jeth'Jalda* reported that he was part of the most recent attack. But they said he acted less like a general and more like a soldier. He bloody well enjoys killing our Power-wielders. The attacks happened just before you arrived."

"Which is why Shadan's bellyaching was so bad," Jamik added. Gripping his reins, he fought to control the rage threatening to break free. After a moment, the Riaki noble in him won out and he continued. His voice, however, was laced with scorn. "He sits on his K'sivik like he's Maeon himself and yells at us to do something about it. Con'Jithar forbid he get off his grey-fleshed backside and fight."

Asherim stiffened. He'd been a Shadan Cult Priest before accepting the charge to help lead the army, and Aethon suspected there was a part of the Meleki that would remain loyal to the Dreadlord in spite of Shadan's obvious failings.

"Shadan's time will come," Aethon said, hoping to diffuse the situation. He shared Jamik's sentiment, but there was no need to fuel the discord already rampant among the troops. Yes, he and Shadan had become rivals, but he didn't want the situation here to deteriorate as badly as it had in Tamba between the Fist of Con'Jithar and *Frel'mola te Ujen*. He needed the cultists no matter how badly he hated them.

"What of Power-wrought traps?" he asked. "They're still happening, I assume."

"Yes," Asherim answered. "But they have been small and relatively ineffective. The enemy hasn't had as much time to put them in place as they had before."

Aethon gazed westward. "They'll get worse the closer we get to the rim," he said. "What of the Kelsan army? Have they retreated through Mendel Pass?"

Asherim shook his head. "No. They haven't moved at all. It looks as if they are preparing to meet us as we make our descent from the plateau. They probably think to attack while we are exposed on the precarious terrain."

Aethon grunted in satisfaction. "Then they are playing into our hands," he said. "Just as I hoped they would." He turned to Jamik. "Did your trip to Kunin prove fruitful?"

"We emptied the warrens as you directed," he said. "It was surprisingly easy because there were no *Shel'tui* present to protest the acquisition."

"Where were they?"

"None of the Kunin soldiers we interrogated knew," Jamik answered. "At first I thought they were lying, but I always get the truth. Aside from the fact that the *Shel'tui* took Zotam and rode south, they really had no idea."

Aethon arched an eyebrow at him. "You used Thought Intrusion?"

Jamik chuckled. "I'm pretty sure the Dainin are too busy right now to invoke a Cleansing Hunt for me."

Several of the nearby Agla'Con laughed at the comment, but Aethon silenced them with a look before facing Jamik once more.

"Since the warrens are unguarded, perhaps we should empty a few more. Take as many Agla'Con as you need. There are warrens to the south and west of the northern watchtowers."

"Yes, Lord Fairimor," Jamik said. Turning his horse, he rode away across the trampled grassland toward a line of black-robed horsemen.

Aethon watched him go, then turned to Krev. "Come, my friend. I want to inspect the demonspawn Jamik commandeered from our *Shel'tui* brethren. If any are proving too unruly for our purposes here, I will find a use for them elsewhere."

Krev smiled, but his earlier levity had been replaced by the assassin-like coldness Aethon had come to expect from the creature. "I like the sound of that," he said, his yellow eyes deepening to the color of gold. "Anything particular in mind?"

Aethon chuckled. "A message for the *Mith'elre Chon.*"

# CHAPTER 15

## *Plausible Deniability*

SHAVIS DAKSHAR WATCHED THE HIGHSEATS and leiflords of Riak's two newest clans make their way toward the exit of the Imperial Clave Chamber, and he couldn't stop from smiling at how quickly they had proceeded in claiming the rights of aggregation afforded them by Article Four. Rights which had just been ratified by the Imperial Clave.

Leifs Chisei, Rento, and Ansa, formerly of Clan Gizo, had joined together to form Clan Chisei and had selected Roalir Boka as their highseat. A wise choice, Shavis knew. Highseat Boka would do more with three leifs than Gizo would do with the six who remained. Chisei would be a powerful clan in spite of being half as numerous as their former clansmen. That they would remain here in Sagaris under the watchful eyes of Tereus Dromensai would ensure they would be able to conduct their affairs without interference from Clan Gizo.

He was a bit more concerned about the three former leifs of Matsoku. They'd banded together to form Clan Duroma, but Matsoku Prefecture was a considerable distance away. Should the four disgruntled leifs of Clan Matsoku decide not to honor Article Four, Highseat Gahashi's fledgling clan might be in danger.

None of the leifs who'd opposed Dromensai had come to enact their rights, but Shavis suspected they would eventually. Leif Vantoru might even decide to remain part of Clan Samochi in spite of their leiflord's irritation with Highseat Roliar. Clans Ayame and Daoshi of Koshima might have a change of heart as well, but if not, Koshima Prefecture was rural enough that land disputes likely wouldn't erupt. *Thank the Creator for that*, Shavis thought. *We've got enough to deal with right here.*

Shavis followed the highseats with his eyes as they filed out of the room. When they were gone, he approached the dais where Dromensai still sat on the throne-like chair of the Emperor. Railen Nogeru occupied the chair next to Tereus, and the young Dymas nodded a greeting as Shavis drew near, then promptly returned his attention to Sheymi Oroshi.

Shavis frowned inwardly at what he was seeing. It was clear from the way the two were looking at one another that their relationship was no longer strictly professional. Hopefully there wasn't a law prohibiting members of the Imperial Clave from courting one another.

"With your permission, Emperor," Shavis said, "I would like to send a couple of striketeams and a Dymas or two to keep an eye on Clan Duroma until we are certain things have settled in Matsoku." From the corner of his eye, he saw Railen and Sheymi break off their conversation to listen.

"Granted," Tereus said. "It might also be a good idea to have a few of your men watch Tenoka and Maridan. Just in case they should decide to take up arms as part of their rebellion against this administration."

"Already in place, my Lord," he said. "Sorry that I forgot to mention it."

Tereus eyed him, unamused. "Why do I get the feeling there are several other things you have failed to mention?"

"It's called plausible deniability," Railen said, entering the conversation. "It's Shavis's way of keeping you out of the Circle of Reckoning."

Tereus's lack of amusement turned to suspicion, then alarm. "What exactly have you done?" he asked, then shook his head. "Never mind. I don't want to know. Just try not to act too much like Lord Chellum."

"I'm not even remotely that reckless," Shavis told him.

"No," Tereus agreed. "Your mischief is wrought on purpose."

The comment drew a laugh from Railen. Beside him, Sheymi turned away to cover her smile. Shavis was glad she'd only briefly toyed with the idea of pursuing Elliott Chellum. The two were about as compatible as an executioner and a jester. Elliott would not have survived the relationship.

Shavis grunted. "Everyone has a gift. Mine is doing what needs to be done even if it isn't popular."

"Or legal," Railen added, then flinched when Shavis narrowed his eyes at him. Sheymi put her hand on Railen's arm to reassure him, and the young man smiled at her. Tereus stared at them, and Shavis could tell by his tight smile that he had finally noticed the way the two were looking at one another.

"This will complicate things," he said.

"What will?" Railen asked, seemingly oblivious to the love-struck smile on his face.

Tereus opened his mouth to answer, then closed it again and shook his head. "Never mind," he said. "I'll just pretend not to have noticed."

Shavis grunted. "Plausible deniability can only be stretched so far," he said. "A blind man could see the two are in love." He was pleased when both of their faces flushed red with embarrassment.

"Is there some law against being in love?" Railen asked.

"Intimate relationships between clave members is strictly forbidden," Tereus told him. "It always has been."

"Well, that's it," Railen said. "I'm resigning my position as Gahara's representative, effective immediately." He smiled at Sheymi who looked as if she wanted to kiss him right then and there. Instead, she turned to Tereus, arching an eyebrow at him.

"Why are intimate relationships forbidden?" she asked, and Shavis could tell by the look in her eyes that the young woman already knew the answer but wanted to hear it from Tereus.

"Because..." Tereus began, then paused as he thought about it. After a moment, he looked at Shavis and started to laugh. "Because up until now all the members of the Imperial Clave have been men."

"Then it might be safe to assume," Sheymi began, "that intimacy between a man and woman would be allowed."

"Why?" Shavis asked. "Are you two sharing moments of intimacy?"

Sheymi's face went red once more, but she met his gaze without blinking. "We most certainly are not," she said indignantly. "In my family we were taught to wait until after marriage." She looked at Dromensai. "Are intimate relationships allowed if said man and woman are married?"

Tereus shook his head. "The law also addresses nepotism. No two people from the same family can fill positions at the same time."

Railen's face pinched into a frown. "Then amend the bloody law," he said. "Because I was serious about resigning."

"No need to be hasty," Tereus said. "It's unlikely anyone in the current government even knows of the law. We'll only address it if it comes up. Until then, just don't be so obvious about your affection for one another."

"Yes, Emperor Dromensai," they said together. Railen stood and offered his arm, and together they made their way across the Clave Chamber to the door.

"Would you really amend the law?" Shavis asked.

"To accommodate marriage between a man and a woman, yes. I'll let you use your imagination as to what I wouldn't change."

"I think I can guess," Shavis told him, then changed the subject. "As you know, Raimen and Tohquin stayed in Kelsa to make their Reckoning with the Eries family. With your permission, Highseat Tynda and I would like to send Tohquin's wife and daughter there as well. It will be good for Aimi and Tey to spend some time together. And I know Tohquin would appreciate having his wife near."

Tereus nodded. "You have my permission. Will you be sending them by Myrscraw or Veilgate?"

"Both," Shavis told him. "I want to see how the birds react to flying through a hole in the air. Think of the tactical applications this will have. Flights of hundreds of miles will be a thing of the past."

"Intriguing," Tereus said. "But those Veilgates will need to be big."

"Yes," he agreed. "But we have Dymas who are capable. And for now they will open the gate just outside the entrance to the Imperial Aviary. The stonework will shield the birds' wings from the edges of the gate as they exit."

"I like it," Tereus said, "but I sense you have more in mind than just ease of travel. You gave it away with the use of the word *tactical*."

"Eventually, I would like to have Dymas open Veilgates while the birds are in flight."

"Isn't that risky without the tower's stonework to shield the Myrscraws' wings?"

"Not if the birds are folded in a dive."

Tereus' brow furrowed in thought as he considered. "But if they miss the hole by even a little, bird and rider will be sliced in half."

Shavis grunted. "When was the last time a Myrscraw missed *anything?*"

"Good point. But the Veilgate will still need to be larger than normal, even if the birds are folded. And you are talking about opening a hole horizontally instead of vertically. Is that even possible?"

"Yes," Shavis said with a smile. "Kalear and Tuari have been sending regular reports on their whereabouts and activities. They have learned several new wieldings, and they have General Eries' permission to teach them to other Dymas." He glanced around the room to make sure no one was within earshot, then lowered his voice anyway before continuing. "Which leads me to my next request."

Tereus narrowed his eyes at him. "Go on."

"I need to borrow Railen and Sheymi for a day or two so they can learn the new wieldings."

"They are members of the Imperial Clave," Tereus said, a trace of irritation in his voice. "Their responsibilities are in politics now. Not warfare."

"Is there a difference?" Shavis asked, failing to keep his own irritation in check. "Railen and Sheymi's responsibilities are to the Earthsoul. As two of the most powerful Dymas in Riak, they need to learn these new wieldings and teach them to others."

Tereus's eyes narrowed. "And then what?"

Shavis kept his face smooth. "And then we put those new wieldings to use."

Tereus closed his eyes, then rubbed them with the palms of his hands. When he looked up once more, he sighed. "Why do I get the feeling this is going to lead to bloodshed?"

"Because we are at war with Soulbiter and those who serve him," Shavis said. "And I'm not going to wait for them to come to us. I intend to hunt them wherever they may be."

"Then God's speed, Dai'shozen Dakshar," Tereus said. "Railen and Sheymi are yours for as long as you need them. But have them check in with me regularly in case I need to call the Imperial Clave together."

Shavis forced a smile. "And so they can keep you up to date on my dealings with the enemy?"

Tereus shook his head. "Plausible deniability, remember? I'd rather not know what you are doing. Just don't do anything that might lead *you* into the Circle of Reckoning."

"And take all the fun out of things?" Shavis asked. "I make no promises."

"God help us," Tereus said, and Shavis bowed deeply before striding away.

He found Railen and Sheymi speaking with Derian Oronei in the rotunda fronting the Clave Chamber. The Shizu captain looked over as Shavis entered the room, but Railen and Sheymi seemed to see only each other. The two weren't even trying to conceal their feelings for one another. Shavis frowned inwardly. All the more reason to get them out of the palace.

Derian's face was a picture of Shizu calm, but the light glittering in his eyes told a different story. He had something urgent to report.

"What is it?" Shavis asked.

"Not here," Derian said, glancing around at those in the room meaningfully. "We need somewhere more private."

Sheymi gave a slight laugh. "With a ward against eavesdropping, anywhere can be private. You make speak freely, Derian. Maeon himself couldn't hear you now."

When Railen nodded, Shavis turned back to Derian. "What did you find out?"

Derian kept his voice down in spite of the ward surrounding them. "Clan Maridan is planning a Deathstrike on Lord Chellum," he said, and from the corner of his eye, Shavis saw Sheymi and Railen stiffen.

"Are you sure?" Railen asked, and his love-struck smile vanished beneath a mask of steely-hard Shizu intensity.

*There's the Railen I know*, Shavis thought.

Derian directed his answer to Shavis. "The men we put in place overheard it with their own ears," he said. "They also sent me this." He opened his hand to reveal a small silver bracelet sporting a bright red crystal.

A rush of anger warmed Shavis' blood as he took it. "And the Agla'Con?"

"In custody," Derian answered. "Minus the arm that once sported that bracelet."

Shavis tucked the bracelet into his uniform. "Where is he now?"

"She," Derian corrected. "This one is a woman. More importantly, she is the wife of Demiso Unosei, the late Highseat of Clan Maridan."

"Unosei," Shavis said with disgust. "I always wondered how that worm rose to the position of Highseat. Undoubtedly his wife had a hand in things."

"It seems you removed the wrong head," Derian said.

"A mistake which can be remedied," Shavis told him. "Tell me, what was Lady Unosei doing in Maridan before she was captured?"

"Pulling the strings of her husband's successor," Derian answered, his voice filled with disgust. "Like Demiso, Highseat Galashin has given himself over to her enticings."

"Given himself over to Maeon," Railen growled.

Derian ignored the younger man. "In addition to the Deathstrike on Lord

Chellum," he continued, looking Shavis in the eyes, "Lady Unosei ordered one on you as well."

"Did she now?" he asked. "Were there any striketeams foolish enough to accept the assignment?"

"There was only one who didn't," Derian said. "I believe you know them. Deathsquad Io. They were present when you killed their highseat."

Shavis nodded. "And heard him confess himself a servant of Maeon. I was hoping some good would come from letting them go. Where is Deathsquad Io now?"

"A good number of them are dead," Derian replied. "Lady Unosei killed them with the Power. Those who survived went into hiding."

"You can drop the title for that wretch," Sheymi said, her face pinched with disgust. "She is no more a lady than a K'rrosha. Women Agla'Con are vile, black-souled abominations deserving of a swift and permanent death."

"And male Agla'Con aren't?" Derian asked.

"No offense to your gender," Sheymi said, "but men don't have as far to fall as women do. We live closer to the whisperings of the Earthsoul so it isn't in our nature to rebel as readily as men do. That's why there are so few female Agla'Con. But those who do turn are worse than any man could be."

Derian stared at her for a moment, then shook his head. "I'll take your word for it." He looked back to Shavis. "After Deathsquad Io refused to be part of the Deathstrike, La—Agla'Con Unosei attacked them at their stronghold. That's how our men discovered what she was. Our Dymas felt her use of the Power. They waited for her to return to her estates and captured her there."

"And Highseat Galashin?" Shavis asked, even though he already suspected what the answer would be.

"Preparing to carry out deathstrikes against you and Lord Chellum."

"Does the Highseat know his Agla'Con mistress has been captured?" Railen asked.

"Not likely," Derian said. "She lives alone on her estates and our men reported that she doesn't entertain guests. It might be some time before she is missed." He reached into his uniform and withdrew a small leather-bound book. "Our men found this in Unosei's library," he said, handing it over. "It is another Con'Kumen book of names. Maridan's treachery runs deep, it seems."

"Well done," he said as he thumbed through a few of the pages. This would allow him to target the evil within Maridan without attacking the clan as a whole. Remove the infection, spare the patient. It had worked in Samochi. Hopefully it would work with Maridan as well.

"If there are Agla'Con in that book," Railen said. "Sheymi and I can help."

Shavis shook his head. "Not this time," he told them. "You are members of the Imperial Clave now. Your involvement in this would jeopardize your standing. Besides, I have a different mission for you."

They frowned at him, so he added, "Don't worry, I have the Emperor's permission."

"Well, in that case," Railen said, "what would you have us do?"

"Go find Kalear and Tuari in the Kelsan camp," he said. "They will teach you several new wieldings of *Ta'shaen*. Once you've mastered them, return to Riak and begin teaching them to the Dymas here."

Railen did little to conceal his excitement. "Yes, Dai'shozen," he said. "It will be a pleasure."

Shavis took the younger man by the arm. "And Railen," he said. "Be careful. I suspect Lord Chellum and I aren't the only ones with a price on our heads."

Railen nodded, then he and Sheymi moved away down the corridor.

Shavis looked back to Derian. "Joshomi Dymas will open us a Veilgate to Gahara," he said. "I'll launch the attack from there."

"I was wondering when I would see you again," Akota Tynda said as the Veilgate slid closed behind Shavis and Derian. Pushing himself from the chair of the highseat, he excused himself from the conversation he'd been having with Gahara's leiflords and moved to shake his friends' hands. Keeping his voice low, he continued, "I can see in your eyes that things did not go as planned."

"On the contrary," Shavis said. "Emperor Dromensai responded favorably to my request to send Railen and Sheymi to Kelsa."

"What is it then?" he asked. "I know that look. You are planning on killing someone."

"Several someones, actually," Shavis said, handing over a small leather-bound book.

Akota went cold inside. "Is this what I think it is?"

"Clan Maridan is still under the influence of the Hand of the Dark," Shavis said. "I would like to remove the evil from their midst."

"They issued deathstrikes for Elliott Chellum and Dai'shozen Dakshar," Derian added. He sounded like he wanted to stick a knife in someone.

"Then by all means, do whatever is needed," Akota said, and for a moment he wished he wasn't the Highseat of Gahara so he could join Shavis and Derian in the attack.

"I always do," Shavis said.

Akota couldn't stop himself from smiling. "Isn't that the truth." He reined in his smile before continuing. "Tell me, what was Emperor Dromensai's answer regarding Raimen and Tohquin?"

"He gave his permission," Shavis answered. "I will inform Kailei and Aimi of the good news on my way to meet with Iga's strike teams."

"Not just Iga this time," Akota said. "Clan Maridan threatened your life, and you are the Dai'shozen of Riak. You should take Shizu from *all* leifs for this strike."

Shavis allowed himself a slight smile as he brought his fist to his chest in salute. "It will be as you say, Highseat."

"And, Shavis," Akota added, dropping the formalities. "Be careful. There might be more to this than you suppose."

Shavis grunted. "Isn't there always?"

# CHAPTER 16

## *Friendship Fortified*

"THEY ARE IN WORSE SHAPE than I imagined," Railen whispered as he and Sheymi stepped into the midst of the Kelsan camp. Letting the Veilgate slide closed, he released *Ta'shaen* and offered Sheymi his arm. She took it and together they started in the direction of what looked to be the center of camp.

All those who'd witnessed their arrival nodded a greeting, then promptly returned to their duties. He saw men cooking, sharpening swords, adding fletchings to arrows, and dozens of other tasks that soldiers did to occupy their time while they waited for the fight to reach them.

In spite of all the activity, however, Railen could see that a good number of these men were tired. Not physically but emotionally. Being so thoroughly routed in the open battle had rattled them. Kalear had mentioned that morale was low among some of the men, but he'd downplayed how serious it might be. That they didn't really seem to have adequate supplies likely only added to their frustration.

"They do look a little down-trodden," Sheymi whispered back. "Do you think there is anything we can do for them?"

"Short of ending the war with Shadan..." Railen said, "not much."

"They didn't even flinch when we arrived," she said. "Did you notice?"

"They are getting used to having Gifted in their midst," he told her. "I see that as a definite improvement over even just a few months ago."

She looked at him out of the corner of her eye. "Is that when your Gifts first manifested?"

He nodded. "We were on our way back from a Deathstrike in Kelsa," he told her. "I felt Jase Fairimor light the night sky over Trian with Fire. Not long after that I met Kalear and he began to train me."

"You are lucky," she said, shaking her head sadly. "My Gifts first manifested when I was sixteen, and I was on my own to learn how to use and control them. It didn't always work out so well."

He searched her face a moment before asking. "What happened?"

"Let's just say that the wooded area beyond my family's estates looked like the Battle of Greendom had been fought there. And that was *before* an Agla'Con showed up and tried to recruit me to Soulbiter's cause."

Railen was intrigued. "What did you do?"

"I killed him with a barrage of lightning that set two homes on fire and destroyed my uncle's cherry orchard. As you might imagine, I couldn't stay there after doing something like that—I feared I might harm someone I loved. So to protect my family from any more mishaps, I left. Jyosei Dymas found me living on my own in the woodlands south of Avalam and took me in and trained me."

"And your family..." Railen began. "How did they react to you leaving?"

"We've never really talked about it," Sheymi answered. "But I suspect they were both saddened and relieved. When I finally returned home, they were visibly nervous for the first few weeks. But when I didn't set anything on fire or kill anyone, they relaxed."

"Derian and Shavis seemed nervous around me at first as well," Railen confided. "Especially after I blew the front wall off of Samochi Castle when I killed an Agla'Con."

"That was you?" Sheymi asked. "The rumor I heard gave credit to an Agla'Con."

"And I am completely okay with that," Railen said. After a moment, he looked over at her. "Did you hear anything about who killed the Byoten Leiflord?"

Sheymi smiled. "No. But I can see in your eyes that it was you."

He grunted. "Now you know why Shavis and the others were nervous at first."

They continued on toward the center of camp, passing through the midst of innumerable men and horses. Railen was starting to worry that they might not ever find the command tent when his Awareness alerted him to the presence of a Dymas. Somewhere not far ahead, all Seven Gifts were being used to open a Veilgate. Only this one felt different. It felt small.

"I feel it too," Sheymi whispered, then pointed to a large nondescript-looking tent beyond a line of horses.

As they neared, an Elvan scout rose from where he'd been crouching beside the tent flap and moved to intercept them.

"Can I help you find something?" he asked. His tone was neither friendly nor unfriendly, but it was obvious he wouldn't be allowing them any nearer the tent until he knew what they were about.

"I am Railen Nogeru of Clan Gahara," Railen told him. "My companion is Sheymi Oroshi of Clan Ieous. We wish to speak with Kalear Beumestra. Is he here?"

"He is," the other replied, but before he could say more, the tent flap pulled aside and Gideon stepped out.

"I thought I recognized that voice," he said, moving near to shake Railen's hand.

"It's good to see you again, my friend."

He released Railen's hand, then turned to face Sheymi, offering a Riaki bow of greeting. "It's good to see you again too, young lady." Straightening, he looked back to Railen. "What brings you two to Kelsa?"

"We would like to learn the new wieldings we've been hearing about," Railen answered. "Particularly the new variations on Veilgates."

"We also bring word from Dai'shozen Dakshar," Sheymi added. "But that would be best shared behind a ward against eavesdropping."

Nodding, Gideon moved to the tent and pulled the flap aside. "After you," he said, then followed them inside.

Gideon listened intently as Sheymi relayed the news regarding Clan Maridan's plot to assassinate Shavis Dakshar and Elliott Chellum. It was difficult to control his anger, but he fought it down, then asked a few follow-up questions as he contemplated what he should do. Part of him wanted to join Shavis on his raid so he could help put down the Hand of the Dark, but he also felt like he might be needed in Chellum should striketeams show up there. Unfortunately, neither was an option right now, but for different reasons. Still, he had to do something.

"You don't need to worry about Chellum," he told Sheymi when she finished. "Kalear will send Dymas from *Ao tres'domei* to watch over them. Their understanding of your nation's customs will allow them to deal with any striketeams in more appropriate fashion than if I were to go." From the corner of his eye, he saw Kalear nodding in agreement.

"And how would you deal with them?" Sheymi asked.

"I don't take kindly to people trying to kill my friends," he told her. "Use your imagination."

Railen chuckled. "I don't have to imagine. I've seen firsthand what you can do."

Kalear grunted in amusement. "What Gideon did in Riak was nothing more than child's play compared to his actions on the battlefield of Death's Third March," he said. "His title of Guardian of Kelsa is well-founded."

"Amen to that," Idoman said, his eyes bright with his usual excitement. "And what he did today against the Tambans was no exception. He's a flaming army unto himself."

Gideon smiled at the compliment, but kept his eyes on Railen. "Aside from Maridan's stupidity," he began, "how goes the restructuring of the disaggregated clans?"

"As well as can be expected," Railen said. "Emperor Dromensai expects everything to be settled in the next few weeks. Shavis has put the newly formed Clans under his personal protection should Gizo or Kyoai have any ill intentions toward them."

"And the Earthsoul?" he asked, not needing to elaborate on the question.

"Failing quickly," Sheymi said. "Earthquakes and storms abound, but it is the holes in the Veil which are most troublesome. Jai isn't the only clan to suffer an attack by demons. Doroku Dymas heads the team tasked with killing them."

Gideon nodded. "An excellent choice." He'd only met Doroku the one time in the Imperial Aviary after the debacle Elliott had caused there, but he'd been very impressed with the man's abilities. As a Dymas and as a Shizu.

"He's also keeping an eye out for *chorazin* T'rii Gates," Sheymi added. "As are all the Dymas in Riak."

"I appreciate that," Gideon said. "Because truth be told, we don't have much time left before the Veil collapses completely. A week, maybe. Two at most."

"Which leads us to the reason we came," Sheymi said.

Gideon nodded, then turned his attention to Kalear and Idoman. "Our brothers and sisters in Riak would like to learn the new wieldings," he said. "Please teach them everything you know."

"Yes, *El'kali*," Kalear said, but Idoman frowned at him.

"Wait. Where are you going?"

"To Trian," he answered. "The Queen has asked for regular reports on Shadan's progress. Galiena will remain here with Yavil so she can continue to monitor Krev."

Railen's brow furrowed. "Who's Krev?"

"A Dragon," Idoman said, seemingly amused by the shock value the announcement held. "And he isn't alone."

"No," Gideon said, "but he is outnumbered by those who joined our side."

"You mean..." Railen began, looking from Gideon to Idoman and then back to Gideon, "you mean to tell me Dragons are *real?*"

Gideon smiled at the younger man's incredulity. "Yes. Their real name is Rhiven, and they are a force to be reckoned with. One of the new wieldings you will learn is one of the only weapons we have against them."

"You did all right with your sword," Idoman said, trying unsuccessfully to hold back a smile as Railen's Shizu persona crumbled further. Eyes wide, the young Riaki shook his head as if that act alone might rid the world of this new and completely unexpected threat.

Finally, he found his voice. "You killed a Dragon with your sword?"

"He was in human form at the time," Gideon answered, directing a look at Idoman which he hoped would still the young man's tongue. Now wasn't the time for this. "Kalear and Idoman will fill you in on all the details. If you desire further information about the Rhiven, I suggest you speak with Galiena. She is their Queen."

He offered his hand to Railen. "If I don't see you again before you leave, give my regards to Shavis and Emperor Dromensai."

"I will," Railen said. "And thank you."

Gideon arched an eyebrow at him. "Thank you for what?"

Railen smiled. "For being a friend to Riak."

He returned the smile. "Take care, Railen," he said, then bowed to Sheymi. "You too, young lady." With that, he opened a Veilgate along the tent wall and moved through to the gardens of the Overlook.

Derian looked over his shoulder at the shimmering hole hanging in the air, then briefly met Kailei Nagaro's wide-eyed stare of wonder before facing forward once more. He wasn't sure if the awe in that stare was due to the Veilgate or to the fact that she and Aimi had been permitted to ride on a Myrscraw. Veilgates and civilians riding Myrscraw would have been unthinkable just a few short weeks ago, but Riak had been turned on its head by Shavis Dakshar just as surely as the world had been upended by the arrival of Jase Fairimor as the *Mith'elre Chon*.

Derian smiled. If Kailei's look of wonder and Aimi's squeals of delight were any indication, the changes had been good. Now the *Mith'elre Chon* just needed to put an end to Death's Third March and bring about the Rejuvenation so those changes could be permanent.

Such thinking would label him a traitor in the eyes of most of Riak's Shizu, but he was glad Shavis was trampling parts of the Shizu Code, especially where the Myrscraw were concerned. Yes, they had been the keystone to the Shizu way of life for millennia, but now, considering Aimi's utter delight, it seemed wrong to have kept them secret.

Looking down to where she was lashed to the saddle in front of him confirmed what he was thinking. He could only see the side of her face, but he could tell she was grinning from ear to ear.

*The world is changing, little one,* he told her. *And it is changing for the better.* Hopefully it would last long enough for all of them to enjoy those changes.

Returning to the task at hand, he glanced down at the Kelsan landscape far below. The Veilgate Joshomi Dymas had opened for him had deposited them above the Glacier Mountains to the southwest of Chellum where it was unlikely anyone would see or feel their arrival. For all his excitement at sharing the secret with Aimi and Kailei, he wasn't about to let just anyone catch a glimpse of a Myrscraw. He would keep that part of the Code until ordered by Shavis to do otherwise.

All he had to do now was keep one of the peaks at his back to break up Shotei's silhouette as she made her descent. If anyone in Chellum was looking this way, it would be impossible to pick the bird out against the dark grey-brown slopes. But it meant they would be walking once they landed.

He pointed between two of the peaks. "See that city there in the distance," he asked and Aimi nodded.

"Yes," she said.

"That's Chellum. Where your daddy is."

"And Tey?"

Derian smiled. "And Tey." He spoke over his shoulder to Kailei, shielding his mouth against the rush of wind with his hand. "I'll get us as close as I dare, but we will be walking the last few miles."

"That's fine," she said. "I thought I would enjoy this, but I'm anxious to have my feet on the ground again."

Derian grunted, amused. So, it wasn't wonder in her eyes. He'd completely misread her expression. "We're perfectly safe," he assured her. "Riding a horse is far more dangerous."

"I'm not worried about safety," she said. "I feel like I'm going to throw up. All this swaying and weaving is making me sick."

"Are you sure it's the bird," he asked, trying for some levity. "It could be morning sickness."

"It is morning sickness, Derian," she said, sounding very irritated. "But I'll stick a knife in you if you leak a word of it to anyone. I want to tell Tohquin the good news myself."

"Silent as the dead," he told her. "You have my word."

"What's morning sickness?" Aimi asked.

"Never you mind, sweetheart," Kailei told her. "Just look at the pretty mountains and enjoy the ride."

Shotei sailed between the last of the rugged peaks, then angled to the right and dove for the timbered foothills far below. With her keen eyes, the bird would find a suitable landing site. All Derian had to do was keep Aimi from being jostled during the landing. As the ground raced up toward them, he felt Kailei tense and offered a silent prayer that she wouldn't empty her stomach all over his back.

As the shapes of individual trees came into focus, Shotei's wings extended and Aimi squealed with delight at the sudden deceleration. The Chellum Lowlands vanished from view behind a wall of evergreens as Shotei settled gently to the ground.

As the bird bellied down to let them dismount, Derian loosed the straps he'd used to secure Aimi to the saddle. Behind him, Kailei flung her straps away and leaped clear before Derian could offer to help. Holding her hand to her mouth, Kailei raced to the nearest clump of scrub oak and dropped to her knees. Heaving sounds followed as she painted the ground with her breakfast.

Derian lowered Aimi to the ground, and the little girl moved around to look Shotei in the eye, seemingly oblivious to her mother's condition.

The bird watched Aimi intently, then blinked, and Aimi took an unconscious step backward even as she continued to stare in awe at her reflection in the shining mirror-like surface.

"She likes you," Derian said as he climbed out of the saddle. Shotei stood up but kept her eye fastened on Aimi, clearly fascinated by the little girl. And why not? Derian thought. Until today, the bird had never carried anyone other than Shizu.

"Is she going to leave now?" Aimi asked. Her face was solemn, and she sounded sad.

"Yes, little one," he answered. "Shavis will want to know that we made it here safely. I left him a note in Shotei's saddle." He made a series of hand gestures to signal the bird to return to Gahara, and the clearing was filled with a powerful rushing of wind as Shotei lifted into the air.

"Goodbye, Shotei," Aimi said, her sadness evident as she watched the bird disappear above the treetops.

Kailei joined them a moment later. She followed her daughter's gaze, but there was no sadness in her eyes. If anything she seemed pleased to have Shotei on her way.

"Are you feeling better?" he asked, and she turned a flat stare on him.

"As well as can be expected after being jostled about like that."

He stifled the smile he felt creeping over his face, then bent to lift Aimi onto his shoulders. "Good. Because it's a five mile walk to the city."

"I'd be willing to walk all the way back to Gahara if it means never riding another Myrscraw," Kailei muttered.

Keeping his face smooth, he handed her one of the water skins he'd brought, then waited as she rinsed her mouth. When she was finished, he led the way into the trees and angled down the broad slope toward Chellum.

The afternoon sun painted the Chellum family's private garden with hues of orange and yellow, and the checkerboard framework of windows separating the gardens from the Chellum dining room threw prisms of light across the flora without and the furniture within. Squinting against the brightness as he exited the palace, Elam Gaufin pulled the glass door shut behind him, then made his way past the fountain toward the moat.

Three pairs of Chellum Home Guard stood at intervals in the gardens and watched him pass in silence. Keeping watch in the gardens was so serene, so completely opposite from the chaos they'd experienced at Zedik Pass and the Rim, that he'd been worried they might find it too mundane. Not so. These men knew the fight could come to them here, and they were as vigilant as any *Bero'thai* would have been. He appreciated their dedication.

He reached the edge of the palace moat and started along the walkway leading around the edge of the palace. With soldiers at every watch point, the afternoon rounds were more of a formality than anything, but he wanted his men to know he took his command seriously. It's what Seth would have done. It's what he would do until Seth returned to assume command.

He was nearing the courtyard fronting the palace's entrance when a lumtar slid out of the water and onto the walkway to block his path. Chittering excitedly, it bobbed its head up and down in greeting.

Elam smiled. "Hello, Mauf," he said, bending to rub the lumtar's snout.

Mauf stuck out his tongue and chittered again, then humped his massive body backward into the water with a splash and disappeared into the depths of the moat.

Elam shook his head in admiration. "Magnificent creatures," he whispered, starting on his way once more. He reached the courtyard and strode up onto the bridge stretching across the moat to the guard towers framing the palace entrance.

The gates were open, but three pairs of Home Guard had moved to bar the way of a Shizu in *komouri* black. A sword was strapped to his back, but he appeared relaxed as he spoke to the six men barring his way.

Curious more than concerned, Elam hurried toward them. It was then that he spotted the little girl. She held the Shizu's hand and looked to be about five years old. A woman, possibly the little girl's mother, stood next to her. She spotted Elam and smiled.

The six men of the Chellum Home Guard followed her gaze.

"Captain Gaufin," Lieutenant Femil said, "these three just arrived. They claim to have been sent by the Highseat of Clan Gahara."

Elam looked at the Shizu. "You wear the mark of Gahara, I see."

"Derian Oronei of Lief Iga," the Shizu said, offering a bow. "Striketeam companion of Tohquin Nagaro and Raimen Adirhah. These two are Kailei and Aimi Nagaro, Tohquin's wife and daughter."

Elam motioned the Home Guard aside. "Welcome to Chellum," he said, offering the Shizu his hand. "I am Elam Gaufin, Captain of the Home Guard." He dipped his head in greeting to Kailei. "If you will come with me, I will take you to Tohquin."

"And Tey?" the little girl asked.

Elam smiled down at her. "And Tey." He offered her his hand and she took it without hesitation. As they started across the bridge, dark shapes became visible in the water below, streaking toward them from the left.

Aimi saw them and pointed. "What are those?" she asked, her eyes wide.

"Lumtars," Elam told her. "They protect the palace." He looked over his shoulder at Kailei. "If it's all right with your mother, I can introduce you to them."

Her eyes sparkling with curiosity, the Riaki woman nodded. "We can spare a few minutes."

"You won't be disappointed."

He led them around the end of the bridge and knelt next to the moat. Reaching down, he slapped the water a few times with his open palm, then stepped back as three lumtars slid from the water to surround them.

Heads bobbing, they chittered excitedly, showing pink tongues and rows of sharp, white teeth. Aimi squealed with delight, but Derian and Kailei stiffened as if Shadowhounds had appeared instead of lumtars.

"This is Mauf," Elam said, rubbing the creature's head. "These two are Shom and Philo."

Grinning, eyes bright with excitement, Aimi reached out and touched Mauf's tongue. "It's prickly," she said, then touched several of his teeth before reaching up to run her hand along the side of his head. "I like him."

"And he likes you," Elam said. What he didn't say was that Mauf now had her scent and would keep her from drowning should she ever happen to fall in the moat. He'd done the same thing for Tey Eries and her siblings as a precaution as well.

Standing, he motioned with his hand, and the lumtars slid back into the moat and disappeared into the depths.

When they were gone, he turned to Kailei. "Let's go find your husband."

Standing beneath the great tree in the Chellum Ballroom, Tohquin Nagaro watched Tey Eries as she used a length of string to tease the kitten Raimen had given to her. The tiny feline flopped over on its back after missing a pounce and Tey giggled with amusement. Tohquin glanced over at Raimen to find him grinning.

Tey's aunt sat a few feet away on one of the benches, her eyes on Cam and Hena as they scampered about in a game of tag with some of the other palace children. Home Guard stood at attention at the ballroom's entry points. Here and there, nobles and politicians were conversing in small clusters. Tohquin sighed inwardly. It was another routine day in Chellum Palace.

A sudden hush fell upon the ballroom, starting near the entrance, and Tohquin turned to investigate the cause of it. Elam Gaufin had entered with a Shizu at his side—and not just any Shizu, but Derian Oronei. And behind him came Kailei and Aimi.

Tohquin started forward to greet them, but Aimi broke free of her mother's hand and rushed forward to greet him.

"Daddy," she shouted as she ran, and he knelt to catch her in his arms.

"Hello, gorgeous," he said, kissing the top of her head. He ran his fingers through her hair, then kissed her on both of her cheeks. Picking her up, he stood to greet his wife as she stepped into his open arm. Tears wet her face as she wrapped her arms around him and held him tight.

"This is a pleasant surprise," he told her.

"You can thank Shavis," Derian said as he drew near. "He thought you might be getting lonely."

"Hey," Raimen said, moving up to tickle the back of Aimi's neck, "he's had me for company."

Derian ignored the comment. Turning to Elam Gaufin, he said softly, "I bring a message from the Dai'shozen for you, Captain. One that would best be delivered in private."

Tohquin heard the tone of seriousness in his friend's voice so he released Kailei and set Aimi down. Kneeling, he pointed to Tey. "Why don't you go say hi to your friend," he said and watched as she moved away. Kailei started to follow, but Tohquin caught her hand and stopped her.

"You are an honorary member of Deathsquad Alpha," he told her. "You can hear whatever it is that Shavis would say to Captain Gaufin."

Smiling, she squeezed his hand. "And then when we are finished with that, I have a message of my own for you." The way she said it sent a rush of warmth through him, and he found himself grinning like a fool. He sobered as Elam motioned for a young woman wearing the mark of Dymas to join them.

"We need a ward against eavesdropping," he told her when she reached them.

"Yes, Captain Gaufin," she said. "You make speak freely."

Elam turned to Derian. "What is the Dai'shozen's message?"

"He wants you to put your men on alert," the Shizu said. "Clan Maridan has ordered a deathstrike on Elliott. One we fear may be attempted in the coming days or weeks."

Tohquin stiffened. "Then why did he send my wife and daughter here?" he asked. "They would be safer in Gahara."

Derian shook his head. "Not necessarily. Maridan also issued a deathstrike for Shavis and all those associated with him. Iga's estates are being fortified as we speak, but we did not think it wise for Kailei and Aimi to remain there on their own."

Tohquin glanced down at his wife briefly before nodding. "Thank you," he said. "I feel better about having them here."

Derian turned his eyes on Elam. "If you wish it, Captain, we have Shizu available for deployment here in Chellum. They would be under your command and report directly to you."

Elam seemed baffled. "Why would you do this?" he asked.

"Elliott Chellum is one of us," Derian replied. "And we protect our own."

# CHAPTER 17

## *To Wage War*

THE STUNNED LOOK ON HIGHSEAT Galashin's face as Iga's striketeams entered the room was all the proof Shavis needed to know the man was guilty. The leiflords occupying the chairs on both sides of Galashin looked equally stunned, but there were varying degrees of outrage as well. Faces tight, they watched Iga's Shizu fan out across Maridan's Clave Chamber with swords bared and arrows drawn.

"What— what is the meaning of this?" Highseat Galashin finally managed. He pushed himself from the throne-like chair, but stopped cold as three dozen Shizu leveled arrows at his chest. Glaring at Shavis, he tried to find courage in his anger. "This is an outrage. Invading the sovereign territory of a rival clan is an act of war."

Shavis grunted. "So is issuing a deathstrike on the Dai'shozen of Riak."

Moving to the foot of the dais, he motioned for Agla'Con Unosei to be brought in, then watched with a smile as Galashin's courage evaporated at the sight of the woman.

Leashed like a dog, and with a second set of chains shackling her feet, the black-hearted mastermind behind Maridan's rise to power shuffled forward, eyes burning with an insane rage, mouth bound with the Power to stifle her curses. Her missing arm was obvious to all who looked on.

Shavis eyed the Agla'Con with disgust before leveling a stare at Galashin. "But that is the least of your concerns, you traitorous piece of filth," he continued. "Your allegiance to Soulbiter is a crime for which there can be no forgiveness."

He tossed the Con'Kumen book of names at the Highseat's feet and added, "In this life or in the life to come."

Galashin stared at the book as if a spotted viper had landed in front of him. After a moment he shook himself mentally and huffed himself up once more. "That proves nothing," he managed at last. "Anyone can keep names in a book."

"Yes," Shavis agreed. "But no one keeps them quite as well as the Con'Kumen." His eyes moved from Galashin to the three leiflords who were also guilty of Con'Kumen treachery.

Kanso, Shoden, and Maifo weren't the largest of Maridan's nine leifs, but the information in the book of names showed how the Con'Kumen had helped them become the three most powerful. Both Unosei and Galashin had headed Kanso before being raised to Highseat.

Shavis shook his head in disgust. "Arrest them."

Four pairs of Shizu moved up the steps of the dais, and Shavis watched while they shackled the men's hands behind them.

When they were secure, Shavis turned to the six leiflords who remained. They were watching him the way a fox might watch a wolf, wary but willing to fight if pressed. "My fight is not with Clan Maridan," he told them. "But with the treacherous scum of the Con'Kumen. Refrain from interfering with this raid, and your clan sovereignty will remain intact. Resist and you will be destroyed."

"So that's it?" the Heilin leiflord asked. He was one of the oldest of Maridan's leiflords and probably would have been appointed highseat if not for the Con'Kumen's meddling. "You're simply going to take those you believe are guilty of serving Soulbiter without warrant, evidence, or trial?"

Shavis glanced pointedly at the book of names. "That is my warrant," he said, "and should you choose to examine it, you will see it contains all the evidence I need to take these men. Sadly, they are but four of many who will be arrested this day."

"Just how deep does this conspiracy go?" another leiflord asked. He wore the mark of Kaishi and had the mannerisms of one who had once been a Shizu.

Shavis did nothing to hide his disgust. "Every leif in Maridan is infected with this disease," he answered. "Some worse than others." He looked pointedly at Galashin before continuing. "But since I would prefer to keep the arrests limited to those who allied themselves with Soulbiter, I would advise you to order your men to stand down."

"And if we choose not to?" the Heilin leiflord asked.

"You already know the answer to that," Shavis told him. "I have swords enough to bring this clan to extinction, and the blessing of the Emperor should that be necessary." He looked from face to face to let the statement sink in. Finally, he added, "But I do not desire more bloodshed. And I am willing to overlook the plot to have me assassinated because I believe you were misled by the Con'Kumen. They are the enemy here. Not Maridan. How many more good people have to die before you will see that?"

He turned and pointed at Lady Unosei. "That woman is an Agla'Con. She's been manipulating this clan through her former husband for years. Upon Highseat Unosei's death, she started working through Galashin. The Deathstrikes issued for me and for Lord Chellum of Kelsa were ordered by her. When Deathsquad Io refused the order, she went to their stronghold and attacked them with the Power.

Many good men were killed. The rest are in hiding."

"Not all of us," a voice said, and Shavis turned to find a Shizu exiting a narrow slit in the wall near the bamboo racks used to hold the cushions and stools used for clave meetings. Ten more Shizu exited behind him, hands on swords, *koro* masks in place.

Several squads of Iga's Shizu turned to face them, weapons at the ready, but Shavis raised a hand. "Stand down," he ordered. "These men are not enemies."

As the eleven Shizu drew near, the one who had spoken removed his *koro* mask and brought fist to chest in salute. "I am Strikecaptain Shikei Manzo of Deathsquad Io of Leif Kanso," he said. "It is a pleasure to be in your presence once again, Dai'Shozen. The last time we met you had just removed the head of Galashin's predecessor."

Shavis nodded. "My thanks to you for cleaning up my mess that day," he said. "I take it you came here today to clean up another one?"

Captain Manzo shook his head. "Actually, we came here to make one." He glanced pointedly at Galashin. "Your arrival kept the Clave Chamber from being painted with this man's blood."

"I heard what Io did in defying the order to assassinate me," Shavis said, changing the subject. "We came here in part to avenge you. It pleases me that you are alive."

"Some of us are," Manzo said. "Two thirds of my striketeam never made it out of our stronghold." He pointed at the Agla'Con with his sword. "Thanks to her."

"I would allow you to remove her head," Shavis told him, "but she would likely return to this world as a Greyling." He turned a hard eye on the woman. "Our Dymas, however, have a much more permanent means of execution."

For the first time since being brought in, the woman's muffled curses stopped and a look of terror washed over her face.

Shavis smiled at her. "You've heard of *Sei'shiin*, I see. Good. Tell me, how does it feel to know there will be no second chance for you?"

With her mouth bound shut by the Power, she couldn't speak, but Shavis didn't really want an answer anyway. It had been a rhetorical question, as much to taunt her as it was to remind the Maridan leiflords that there was more to Iga's army than Shizu and Sarui.

He turned back to the Heilin leiflord. "Amifin Polodar, you are the senior member of the clave now," he told him. "Emperor Dromensai wishes to make you steward until things can be sorted out and a new highseat elected. What say you to this?"

Polodar looked to the other leiflords who nodded. Finally he nodded as well. "I accept," he said. "And Clan Maridan will cooperate with the Dai'shozen's investigation."

"Good," Shavis said. He'd expected Polodar to accept, and not simply to avoid a potential bloodbath. He was ambitious enough to believe being steward would increase his chances of being raised to highseat. And it might... assuming his name didn't turn up in a Con'Kumen record book.

He turned back to Strikecaptain Manzo. "Leif Kanso is in need of a leiflord," he said. "The job is yours if you want it."

Highseat Galashin pulled against his shackles but was restrained by the Shizu holding him. "You have no authority to make such an appointment!" he snapped, his earlier anger returning. "It is for the ruling members of the leif to decide."

"Considering how all the ruling members of Leif Kanso are currently being arrested for Con'Kumen treachery," Shavis began, "a new procedure is in order." He turned back to Manzo. "What say you?"

The Shizu captain hesitated before answering. "I appreciate the offer, but I do not have the manpower to hold onto the title should Kanso's other striketeams object. "

"Thirty-five Deathsquads from seven different clans will remain here to keep an eye on things," Shavis told him. "They are yours to command."

"This is a wise move," Polodar said. "And as the newly appointed Steward of Maridan, I wish to endorse it."

"As do I," the Jyosho Leiflord added. The other four leiflords followed with endorsements of their own.

Manzo looked from face to face, then took a deep breath and gave a slight bow to Shavis. "In that case, I accept."

"Excellent," Shavis said. "As for Leifs Shoden and Maifo... they will be free to select new leiflords once the Con'Kumen among them have been apprehended." He motioned for Manzo to join him. "Come. I wish to check on the status of those arrests."

He started for the doors, and Gahara's Shizu formed up around him. Those escorting Galashin and the rest of those who'd been arrested brought up the rear. Polodar and the remaining leiflords hung back as if uncertain about following, but Shavis caught Polodar's eye and motioned for him to come.

"I want your new steward to see this," Shavis whispered to Manzo as they reached the doors. Smiling, he pushed them open and moved outside.

Manzo hissed in surprise at the scene, and Shavis' smile deepened as he followed the strikecaptain's gaze. More than a thousand Shizu and Sarui representing the twelve clans of the Imperial Clave filled the city's central plaza.

They stretched from the stairs at the foot of the Clave Chamber to the gates of Maridan Keep on the far side of the expanse. Some held Con'Kumen prisoners at sword point. Others were clustered in striketeams, ready to engage any who might prove to be a threat to Shavis' mission. Still others had formed a protective wall around Dymas who were in the process of moving prisoners out of Maridan through Veilgates.

When Polodar and the other leiflords exited the Clave Chamber, their surprise was even more marked than Manzo's had been. The newly appointed steward stopped as if he'd walked into a spear. Eyes wide and mouth open, he could only stare at the spectacle before him.

"There won't be trouble in Maridan for a while," Shavis told him. "The force I will be leaving behind will see to that. Not only will they continue to root out the Con'Kumen, they will maintain the peace as you and the others rebuild Maridan's High Clave."

Polodar shook himself free for speech. "So Maridan is to be occupied by Gahara?"

"I prefer to think of this as a peace-keeping operation," Shavis told him. "And if you'll take a closer look at the insignias, you'll see this isn't a unilateral force. The Imperial Clave is acting as one to combat the Con'Kumen. These men represent the Emperor, not Gahara."

Polodar frowned at him. "Then why do I get the feeling *you* are calling the shots here instead of Emperor Dromensai."

"Because I am," Shavis told him. "The privilege of being Dai'shozen of Riak."

He turned and let his gaze move across the plaza before looking back to Polodar.

"I will be leaving a number of Dymas here as well," he told the newly appointed steward. "They will assist you in communicating with Emperor Dromensai and will provide Veilgates for transportation should you wish to visit Sagaris in person."

"We have Myrscraw for that," Polodar said.

"I'm taking Maridan's Myrscraw with me," Shavis said. "All of them."

Polodar finally fought through his shock enough speak. "Why?" was all he could manage.

"To wage war against the enemy," he answered. "Wherever they might be."

と

Standing on a grassy hilltop a few miles outside of the Kelsan camp, Railen Nogeru peered through the small horizontal Veilgate he'd opened above Shadan's army and marveled at how easy it had been. It was simply a matter of channeling the threads of Spirit into a different part of the Veil. It was ever-present, after all, stretching horizontally as well as vertically across the spiritual landscape of his Awareness.

*Holding* the gate open, however, was much more difficult than he'd anticipated. He had strength enough to do it, of course, it was just a bit more... well... slippery. It was the only word he could think of to describe how the edges kept trying to slip free of his Awareness.

*The feeling goes away with practice,* Kalear told him through the mindlink. *The first couple of times I tried, I couldn't hold it open for more than a few seconds.*

*And believe it or not,* Idoman added, *the larger the gate, the easier it is to hold. I have no idea why.*

Railen let the opening close, then opened another one over a different part of the enemy army. As Kalear had said, it was slightly easier this time. He let that gate close as well, then repeated the process five more times, each time opening a gate a little larger than the last. The final gate was large enough to drop a house through, and as the edges settled into place, the wielding didn't feel any different than any other Veilgate he'd ever opened.

*See,* Kalear said. *The slippery feeling goes away.*

*Gideon says it's really just your Awareness adjusting to a new dimension of the Earthsoul,* Idoman said. *Ta'shaen hasn't changed, just your perception of it.*

*It makes sense,* Sheymi said, nodding. Her eyes moved from the gate to Railen and a smile spread over her face. *Well done, my love.*

Railen blinked in surprise. She wasn't even trying to conceal her emotions, and the pride she felt for Railen's accomplishment flowed through the Communal link for all to feel. It was accompanied by a rush of love and desire and passion, but it was the series of intimate images flickering through her thoughts that made Railen's face go red and his ears turn hot.

Idoman and Kalear exchanged amused looks, and Kalear cleared his throat to bring Sheymi back to the moment. She glanced over at him but did nothing to still her emotions. *What?* was all she asked.

Kalear shook his head. "No wonder Emperor Dromensai wanted you two out of the palace," he said, and his Awareness withdrew from the link. Idoman followed a heartbeat later, and Railen and Sheymi were left alone in their thoughts.

*I'm sorry that I embarrassed you,* Sheymi told him. *Will you forgive me?*

*For the untempered emotion, yes,* he said. *But you might want to keep your intentions for our wedding night a bit more hidden. Particularly because I haven't even proposed yet.*

Sheymi's face flushed red. *You saw that?* she asked, her emotions exploding into a jumbled mess that zipped around through the mindlink like hailstones in a tempest. Fear and shame were the most prominent of those stones, but a sudden, terrible sadness followed, and tears began to form in her eyes. She was worried she had crossed the line, possibly jeopardizing their relationship. Her concern only made him love her that much more.

He took her hand to comfort her. *I said, yet. I haven't proposed yet.*

A wave of relief stilled the tempest inside her, and she smiled. *If we were alone, I would kiss you.*

*I have no doubt,* he said, then let the Communal link fade as her face turned red once more.

He turned to Idoman. "Now that we have a feel for the new wieldings, I would like to take a closer look at Shadan's army. I saw something earlier that I didn't like the look of."

"By all means," Idoman said. "Do you know where it was?"

"Northwestern corner," Railen answered. "It looked like they were forming shadowspawn into columns."

"General Eries will want to know about this," Idoman said, opening a Veilgate into the command tent. "Come. Let's look at this together."

General Eries looked up from the maps he was studying and motioned them to join him. "How did the training go?"

"Great," Idoman said, letting the gate slide shut behind them. "These two are very talented."

They stopped at the table, and Idoman pointed at the map indicating the position of Shadan's army. "Railen saw something he thinks might be an issue."

He opened himself to *Ta'shaen* once more, and Railen watched as a small horizontal window opened just above the map of Talin Plateau. Idoman kept it smaller than the table so that none of them would inadvertently lean into it and be sliced by the razor-sharp edges of Spirit. They all peered through together.

"There," Railen said, pointing to a spot near the edge of the mass of bodies. "What do you make of that?"

"Those look like Shadowlancers and Agla'Con at the rear," Joneam Eries said. "What are they doing?"

"They are forming an army of shadowspawn into columns," Railen answered. "At least that's what it looks like to me."

"Those aren't shadowspawn," Idoman corrected. "They're demonspawn from the warrens of Kunin."

Railen raised an eyebrow. "Is there a difference?"

"A big one," the young Dymas General answered. "Shadowspawn are creatures wrought of corrupted *Ta'shaen*. The abominations bred in the warrens are the literal offspring of demons. Some can even wield the Power."

"That is a problem," Railen said, a shiver of disgust running up his spine. He looked down at the columns. "So what do you make of that?"

"They are getting ready to attack," Idoman said. "My guess is through Veilgates."

"Alert the camp," Joneam ordered. "And send word to the Elvan and Chunin armies as well. I want every available Dymas ready to engage them when they arrive."

"You think they are coming here?" Idoman asked. His eyes were still on the scene below, but Railen felt him stretch out his Awareness to contact several Dymas to set the chain of communication into motion.

Joneam nodded. "Where else would they go? We've been making things difficult for them of late. Actually, I'm surprised they haven't done something like this sooner."

"Our Dymas have been contacted," Idoman announced. "They'll be ready for them when they arrive."

"It will be soon," Railen said. "They are breaking the columns into smaller attack groups. They'll be arriving at multiple locations."

And he was right. A moment later rents began opening, and knots of demonspawn vanished to somewhere beyond. But it wasn't to the Kelsan camp. At least not within range of Railen's Awareness. *Ta'shaen* remained as quiet as a summer morning.

Idoman and Kalear looked as surprised as he felt.

"What is it?" Joneam asked.

"They aren't coming here," Idoman answered.

Joneam's eyes returned to the enemy army. Veilgate after Veilgate opened and closed as demonspawn rushed through in waves. Hundreds vanished from the plateau as they watched. When the last Veilgate closed, Joneam looked up, his face lined with worry. "Well, they sure as blazes went somewhere. Where?"

Before anyone could answer, Railen's Awareness shrieked in alarm as a rent sliced through the wall of the tent and demonspawn poured through from beyond.

# CHAPTER 18

## A Message Delivered

JASE SET THE BOOK OF PROPHECIES back on the table and reached up to rub his eyes. All this reading was getting them nowhere. Even with all the new volumes recovered from Jyoai's archives, he was no closer to discovering the location of a Temple of Elderon than he was a month ago. If anything, the abundance of useless information made him feel as if he were sifting through a mountain of rubble with nothing more than a spoon. And a tiny spoon at that.

When Talia looked up from her reading, Jase knew his frustration had made it through the love-bond.

"What is it?" she asked.

"This," he said, making a disgusted gesture at the pile of books. "I doubt we'll ever find anything in all this—" he cut off, shaking his head. His frustration kept him from finding a suitable swear word.

"Patience," Beraline said, marking her place in the volume she was reading. "It's a lot to go through. There's bound to be something in one of these books." Beside her, Marithen Korishal read without interruption, her eyes moving over the words with a fixation only she could achieve. It made Jase wonder if it might have something to do with her uncanny ability to remember everything she read. Odd, since she couldn't seem to remember a scrap of what had happened even five minutes earlier.

Jase pushed the thought away and met Beraline's gaze. "I just can't shake the feeling that we are looking in the wrong place."

She arched an eyebrow at him. "Where else would you look?"

Jase shook his head. "I don't know." Standing, he stretched his back until it popped. "Somewhere other than books. I'm sick of books."

"We could go to Elldrenei College," Beraline suggested.

Jase turned to stare at her. "Why? So we could read *more* books. No thank you."

"The Elvan people have more than books in the Old World collections," Brysia said, and Jase turned to find her standing at the foot of the south tower stairs. How long she had been there was anyone's guess. Gideon was with her, a thoughtful smile on his face.

"Yes," he added. "They have a large collection of maps. Nothing recognizable to us, of course, but we might be able to use the location of the recently discovered T'rii Gates to piece something together. At least enough to make a guess at where a temple might be."

Jase was quiet as he considered. It wasn't a bad idea, really. T'rii Gates were immovable so even if the landscape had changed, they might be able to get some idea of where to look. He shrugged. "It's worth a try I suppose."

"They might have other artifacts as well," Talia said, and Jase could feel her excitement through the love-bond. "Carvings or paintings which might contain something useful."

"Elldrenei it is, then," Brysia said. "And I will accompany you. I know that library well."

"Marithen and I would like to come," Beraline said.

Jase nodded. "That will be fine. I welcome any and all hel—" He cut off as *Ta'shaen* came alive with a powerful corrupted wielding.

Instinctively he embraced the Power and channeled a shield of Spirit around himself and Talia. Gideon did the same for himself and Brysia. Beraline and Marithen were only seconds behind with shields of their own.

"What is it?" Talia asked, sensing his alarm.

A quick thrust of his Awareness gave Jase the answer. "Shadowspawn," he told her. "Arriving through rents in the Veil."

She was on her feet in an instant, and *Ta'shaen* surged into her as she embraced her Gift. "Where?"

"In the Dome," he answered, starting for the door. Before he could reach it, *Ta'shaen* reeled again as a rent opened in the dining area not twenty feet away and five armored creatures scrambled through. Their arrival triggered a release of Power from the wards Gideon had set in place, and tendrils of *Sei'shiin* materialized as if from thin air, burning the creatures from existence.

But five more followed on their heels, entering the palace before a second release of Power from the ward collapsed the gate behind them.

Roughly man-shaped, they were armed with blades and clubs and their own clawed limbs. But they weren't Darklings. In fact, they didn't resemble any shadowspawn he'd ever seen before. Even the fiery glow of their eyes was different. And their faces—they were less animal and more... he balked at the thought. They were more demonic. These were the demonspawn Gideon had seen in Shadan's army.

Snarling, the five monstrosities rushed him but slammed into the invisible barrier of his shield.

Talia struck the nearest creature with a quick thrust of Flesh, and it staggered away as its heart exploded inside its chest.

Enraged by her use of the Power, the remaining four attacked the shield in a frenzy, filling the inside of the protective dome with a series of hollow thumps as they hacked at it with their weapons. Jase sliced the heads off of two of the creatures with a blade of Fire while Talia burst another one's heart. The final creature vanished in a flare of white light as a bar of *Sei'shiin* channeled by Gideon took it in the back.

"To the Dome," Gideon shouted, racing for the door. "Beraline, you and Marithen protect the Queen."

Leaving the two Dymas behind to do as ordered, Jase took Talia by the hand and followed. He knew what he would find in the Dome—he'd seen the chaos through his Awareness. It was what awaited him on the Overlook that put a knot in his stomach. Especially since whatever it was had the ability to disrupt his spiritual vision. Even now as he pressed it with his Awareness, he could see only darkness.

Seth pulled his blade free of the creature's neck, and it dropped lifeless at his feet, its red eyes dimming as its sword clattered noisily across the floor. Whirling away from the hairy corpse, he engaged a second beast but found himself retreating down an aisle of tables almost instantly. Not only did the creature have a long reach, it had four arms like a K'tyr, and each clawed fist gripped a short blood-blackened sword.

The mark burned into its neck was a brand used by the Sons of Uri, but Seth would have known the creature had been bred in the warrens of Kunin even without the mark. It had the look of a demon—feral and vicious, yes, but intelligent. Far more intelligent than a Darkling.

*And inhumanly strong*, he added, barely turning aside a thrust that would have spilled his guts on the floor. His hands stung from the effort, and he retreated further, kicking over a chair in attempt to slow the creature. It smashed the chair beneath an armored foot and kept coming, its red eyes burning with demonic rage.

Steeling himself for a long fight, Seth was about to re-engage when an arrow took the demonspawned creature in the head, punching through its skull with a loud *crack*.

It dropped as if poleaxed, and Seth turned to see Bornis nocking another arrow. The young blacksmith-turned-warder nodded grimly, then turned and loosed again, killing a wolf-like creature angling toward Elison.

Seth snatched up one of the demonspawn's four swords and hurled it at a creature doing battle with Taka O'sei. The sword took the creature in the back, and it snarled in pain. It was cut down by Taka a moment later.

With no enemies within range, Seth took a look around the Dome. Some twenty or so creatures remained, about half of which could wield the Power as evidenced by the dark reddish-black auras surrounding them. They'd killed two Dymas and a number of *Bero'thai* before retreating into their protective shields to defend against the remaining Dymas in the room. So far they'd turned aside everything hurled their way.

Velerie Kivashey appeared at his side. "I've got you, Captain," she said, bidding him to follow. "Come. I want to bring Bornis into my shield as well." She glanced at a bear-like monster lumbering toward them, and the creature's head burst apart in a flash of superheated gore.

The demonspawn who could wield turned to stare at her in a fury, but none of them attacked. They couldn't without weakening their defenses. They might be strong, but they were outnumbered, and more Dymas were arriving by the minute.

Bornis exhaled in relief as Velerie took him by the hand. "No more arrows for a minute, my love," she told him. "You're inside my shield. The rest of our men are being sheltered now as well."

Bornis pointed at the Power-wielding creatures. "So that's it? We're in a stand off against those bloody things?"

"Just until more Dymas arrive," she told him. "We'll make quick work of them."

"Which makes me wonder why they are here at all?" Bornis said. "There was no way they could win such an assault. This was a suicide mission."

"I agree," Seth said. "This attack has some other purpose. Best be on your guard."

Velerie turned to look at him, but before she could speak, the doors leading out of the Fairimor home flew open and Gideon rushed into the Dome. Jase and Talia were only a step behind.

Gideon took one look around the Dome, and his face hardened into a mask of death. A moment later the demonspawn not cloaked in corrupted *Ta'shaen* burst apart into chunks of seared flesh as Fire tore them apart from the inside.

The Power-wielding demonspawn leapt to their feet and raced toward the big Dymas, knocking over tables and chairs in their rush to reach him. They stopped cold as some unseen force suddenly barred their way, and Seth glanced at Jase to find him with arm extended. His face, pinched with concentration, wore a tight smile.

"Enough of this," he said, and Veilgates opened beneath each of the creatures. They dropped away as if they'd fallen through holes in the floor, and Jase lowered his arm as the Veilgates closed. "Let's see how they deal with a drop of ten thousand feet."

"Where did you drop them?" Gideon asked.

"The middle of the Junturi Ocean," Jase answered. "If the fall doesn't kill them, drowning will." He turned his attention to the doors of the Overlook and Seth followed his gaze, suddenly on edge at what he'd seen in his young friend's eyes.

"This isn't all of them," Velerie said, moving up to Jase. "I felt at least a dozen other groups arriving at locations throughout the inner and outer cities."

Jase nodded. "I felt them too," he said, then motioned to several nearby Dymas. "Rally as many Gifted as you need," he told them. "I want every last one of these creatures destroyed. If you encounter Ammorin and Pattalla, tell them they are needed in here."

The two had left the palace earlier in the day to assist Captain Dium with the evacuation of Trian's residents. They most certainly would have felt the arrival of the demonspawn and had likely engaged whichever group was unlucky enough to have arrived near them.

"Yes, *Mith'elre Chon*," they said, and a Veilgate opened into the city. When they were gone, Velerie looked at Jase expectantly.

"You're not going with them?" she asked. It sounded like an accusation.

If Jase was offended by her tone, it didn't show. He simply shook his head, his eyes still on the doors leading out to the Overlook. "No. The demonspawn are a diversion. The real fight is out there."

The feeling of dread flowing toward Talia through the love-bond was so strong it nearly stopped her heart, and she tightened her grip on Jase's hand to comfort him. To comfort herself.

Velerie's face pinched into a frown as she gazed at something beyond the doors. "I can't see anything," she said. "It's as if *Ta'shaen* has been nullified. How is that possible? And why didn't I notice it before?" She sounded angry at herself.

"You were busy in here," Jase said. "I told you: The demonspawn were a distraction." He looked to Gideon. "Any thoughts on what is out there?"

"It feels like the void a K'tyr can create," Gideon said. "Only this is much bigger."

"So we can't touch the Power out there?" Velerie asked.

Jase shook his head. "No. But then neither can the enemy." He glanced at Talia, and the words *I hope* found their way into her thoughts. That and a heightened sense of anxiety. He really had no idea what he would find out there.

"Finally," Seth said, twirling his swords for emphasis. "My kind of fight."

"And I'm going to need you," Jase said. He motioned the Chellum Captain near and continued in a whisper. "You and Elison and Taka take as many *Bero'thai* as you can and use the catacombs to get into position behind the enemy. Whatever is out there is confined to the half nearest the doors. The gardens beyond the center fountain are clear at the moment."

Nodding, Seth sheathed his swords and motioned for Elison and Taka to follow. Talia watched them go and offered a silent prayer for their success. The three captains disappeared through the doors leading into the Fairimor home.

Jase motioned for a nearby *Bero'thai*. "I need your sword," he said, then held up a hand as he changed his mind. "Actually, I need a good long spear."

"Still prefer a long shaft over a blade, do you?" Bornis asked, stepping near. Jukstin came with him, a look of panic on his face.

"I always will," Jase said as he tested the spear. Then he noticed the looks on his friend's faces. "What is it?"

Bornis put a hand on Jase's arm. "Zea and Kindel are out there with Galam and Gillium," he said. "My..." he hesitated. "My little sister is with them." His voice was steady, but his eyes showed how worried he was.

Jase closed his eyes for a minute, then opened them and forced a smile. The anxiety and fear flowing through the *sei'vaiya* slowly gave way to steely determination. "They are going to be fine," he said, and Talia could feel how strongly he believed it.

Gideon's expression, however, was far less confident. "How do you want to play this?" he asked.

Jase looked around at the *Bero'thai* who'd drawn near to listen. "We'll keep the enemy focused on us until Seth and Elison are in position," Jase answered. "If whatever is out there was going to attack, it would have done it by now. Obviously, they are waiting for us to come to them. Either they want to negotiate or it's a trap."

"I'm betting on the latter," Gideon muttered. He stretched out his hand, and Talia watched as a sword from one of the fallen *Bero'thai* hissed toward him. He caught it by the hilt and inspected the blade, then looked pointedly at her and Velerie. "As Seth said, this is his kind of fight. The Power will be useless out there. You two wait here until whatever is causing the void in *Ta'shaen* has been neutralized."

Talia wanted to argue, but quickly decided against it. Without the Power, she would be worse than useless—she'd be a distraction. She nodded.

Velerie nodded as well, but Talia could tell she didn't like it. She took the young woman's hand in hers and squeezed it reassuringly. *We'll find some other way to help*, she told her silently, though in truth, she had no idea what she was going to do.

Jase hefted his spear, motioning for the *Bero'thai* to follow. "Let's go see what they want."

Racing through the catacombs on Elison's heels was a disorienting experience for Seth, but he tightened his grip on his swords and raced on. How Elison was able to find his way through the maze of narrow corridors was beyond him. The smooth, grey-green *chorazin* bore no distinguishing marks, and they had yet to pass any of the small signs Taka claimed were present. He glanced over his shoulder at Taka and found the captain's eyes narrowed with concentration. Behind him, Gavin and the dozens of *Bero'thai* strung out down the passage wore similar expressions.

"We're almost there," Elison said, raising a fist to signal those behind him. He slowed a moment later as the passage opened into a small chamber. A narrow staircase spiraled upward along the wall toward a small round door set in the ceiling some ten feet above. It reminded Seth of the Seal of Fulrath, if quite a bit smaller.

"The Creator thought of everything, didn't he?" Seth whispered.

Elison nodded. "This is the second time this chamber has come in handy," he said. He climbed the stairs, and Seth watched him trip the release that opened the door. It slid silently into the wall and disappeared.

Elison moved the rest of the way up the stairs and peeked cautiously over the edge. When he descended a moment later he wore a frown. "We have a problem," he whispered. "You better take a look."

Seth moved up the stairs and peered over the edge. The hole opened in the center of a small gazebo surrounded by a copse of trees and trellised rosebushes. It would have been the perfect place to exit the catacombs unseen if not for the Satyr standing near the trellis. Thankfully, the creature had its back to the gazebo. If it had been facing this way, Elison would have lost his head the moment he peeked over the edge.

Without taking his eyes off the Satyr, Seth quickly considered their options. There was really only one.

Motioning for the others to follow, he wrapped himself in *Jiu* and exited the catacombs.

Jase nodded to the *Bero'thai* taking point, and they pulled open the doors so he and Gideon could enter the gardens of the Overlook. Beyond, the sun was shining, and the gardens were bright with the greens of trees and shrubs and a brightly colored array of blooming flowers.

The view through his Awareness, however, was the black, darkness of hell. Even worse, his ability to embrace *Ta'shaen* ceased the moment he crossed into that darkness. He could no longer even sense the Power.

"I'd forgotten what it was like," he whispered to Gideon, "...to be without my Gifts. I don't like it."

Gideon grunted. "Try wearing a *da'shova* collar for twenty years."

They continued down the center pathway, and Jase scanned the gardens as if he were back in Omer Forest on a hunting excursion, suddenly grateful for the years he'd spent honing his natural senses. With his Awareness lost to him, his eyes and ears were all he had.

The center point of the darkness was easy to pinpoint since the creature was obviously not trying to hide itself. It stood in the middle of the path next to the stream some thirty paces ahead. As tall as a man on horseback, it resembled a K'tyr, with large, leathery wings and two sets of arms. But it was much more heavily muscled than a K'tyr, which were bred to be quick in the air and light on their feet. This thing—this demonspawned abomination—appeared to have been bred for brute strength. That, and its ability to create a void in *Ta'shaen*.

Jase gave it a cursory glance, then let his eyes move over the rest of the gardens.

"By the weeping mulberry on the left," he said. "Two Satyrs. There are two more in the shrubs near the fountain on the right and two in the shadows of the ivy archway of that gazebo."

"And you thought you would need your Awareness," Gideon said with a smile. He glanced pointedly to the left. "One more in the grasses beyond the cherry tree."

"And another near the northern wall by the coneflowers," Bornis said.

Jase nodded and glanced over his shoulder at the small army of *Bero'thai* trailing behind them. He could tell by their stern expressions that they'd spotted the creatures as well. Dozens of bows creaked as strings were drawn tight and arrows leveled at the targets. He just hoped they'd accounted for all of them.

He turned his attention back to the massive, winged demonspawn. "It isn't the Satyrs that concern me," he said. "It's that thing and its companions."

Gideon raised an eyebrow in alarm. "Companions?"

"Crouched on the far side of those raised beds just behind it," Jase told him. "I'd say at least six."

"What is the big one waiting for?" Jukstin asked.

"Probably a command from whoever that is," Jase answered, indicating the hooded figure who rose from one of the stone benches on the side of the path.

The figure—Jase decided it was a man—stopped in the path as if to bar their way. "That's far enough," he said as he reached up to lower his hood and reveal his face. He was Riaki.

"I am Jamik Hedron," he said. "Second in command to Aethon Fairimor in Shadan's army. I bring a message from the First to his nephew, the so-called *Mith'elre Chon*."

"I am him," Jase told him, curious but wary. This did seem like something Aethon would do, arrogant cur that he was. "What does the *so-called* First have to say?"

Jamik's eyes narrowed at Jase's twisting of his words. "It's simple really," the Agla'Con said. "He wanted you to know that the slaughter taking place in the streets of Trian at the hands of his newly acquired demonspawn is but a shadow of things to come. He also wanted you to know that the destruction of Kindel's Grove was his doing." He smiled. "And that he enjoyed it."

Jase's hand tightened on the spear in his hand as a rush of anger washed through him. *Aethon attacked Kindel's Grove? Of course it was him, the bloody coward.*

"There's more, of course," Jamik said, his tone conversational. "He wanted you to know that no amount of harassment through Veilgates by your armies will slow Death's Third March. If anything, it is providing a certain amount of motivation for our troops. They are most eager to engage your forces at Mendel Pass. And once that pitiful force has been destroyed, they will be joining you here. You will be here, won't you? The First would be severely disappointed if you weren't."

"If he is so anxious to meet me," Jase said, letting his disgust for Aethon color his tone, "why did the coward send you instead of coming here himself?"

"Your uncle has more pressing matters to attend to at the moment," Jamik answered.

"I'm sure," Jase said. He pointed the spear at the Agla'Con's chest. "Tell me, Jamik, now that your message has been delivered, what makes you or that traitorous scumbag who calls himself my uncle think you will be leaving here alive?"

Smiling, the Agla'Con pointed to his left where a Satyr was emerging from behind one of the larger oak trees. It held Zea Lyacon by her hair with one hand while its other hand held a curved blade to her throat. Twenty feet to Jamik's right, a second Satyr rose from a clump of ferns holding a blade to the throat of Bornis' five-year-old sister, Wytni.

Bornis hissed in alarm and started forward, but Jase put out a hand to stop him. "Not yet," he said, then added a silent, *Not if you want her to live.*

Anger coursing through him, he kept his eyes on Jamik. He *would* kill this man, and he would send his talisman back to Aethon as a message of his own. All he needed now was a miracle.

That, and a little help from Seth and those who were moving into position behind Jamik and his demonspawn. They should be poised to strike by now.

*Come on, Seth. Don't let me down.*

"And if that isn't sufficient," Jamik said, his earlier arrogance returning, "here is another little gift from your uncle." He glanced over his shoulder as Veilgates opened and a dozen more Satyrs and ten knots of Darklings rushed through and began spreading out through the gardens.

With his Awareness nullified, Jase could sense nothing of the wielding, but he suspected the gates had been wrought with *Lo'shaen.* He was suddenly aware of just how powerless he was should Aethon or one of the Rhiven choose to appear. Apparently the power of the Void could be wielded within a void, which meant he was completely overmatched here.

"They aren't here for you," Jamik commented as the Darklings continued to spread out. "They are here to look after the other hostages scattered about which aren't as visible as these two here." He glanced pointedly at Zea and Wytni. "Even you aren't so foolish as to think you can save them all." He chuckled, a low sound filled with malice. "Especially without the Power."

"I guess we'll find out," Jase said, but he didn't move. Neither did the Agla'Con. He simply stood there as if he had more to say. Or maybe he was waiting for Jase to attack so he could kill the hostages. Whatever the case, Jase didn't press him. The longer he waited, the more time Seth and the *Bero'thai* had to get into position. The more time he had to come up with a miracle.

"You are more disciplined than Aethon said you would be," Jamik said at last. "Pity. I was hoping to be here when—"

He cut off as something massive landed with a bone-shattering thud on top of the demonspawned creature behind him.

"*Bal'tei Nar'shein,*" a Dainin voice boomed, and the void over Jase's Awareness vanished as Ohran Peregam drove a spear through the beast's head.

The miracle had arrived.

# CHAPTER 19

## A Message Answered

EVERYTHING HAPPENED IN AN INSTANT.

*Ta'shaen* returned to Gideon's Awareness as Ohran Peregam drove a spear through the demonspawn's head. Arrows loosed by *Bero'thai* filled the air with hisses and were followed by the razored *shumps* of pierced flesh. Satyrs fell dead and dying. Demonspawn howled in rage and pain. Five more Dainin landed with ground shaking thumps amid the foliage. Jamik Hedron's eyes went wide as Jase used a thread of Spirit to separate him from his Agla'Con talisman by slicing off his arm. Then surprise and pain turned to agony as Jase seized him in a grip of Air and yanked him forward onto his outstretched spear.

Gideon would have enjoyed being privy to the conversation that followed, but a gasp of pain from Zea Lyacon called him another way. The Satyr which had held her was dead, but it had managed to use its blade as it fell. Zea knelt among the flowers, blood running from between her fingers where she was pressing them against her throat.

Gideon raced to her side and took her head in his hands as he embraced the Power. Zea gasped again as the Gift of Flesh rushed into her and the wound closed.

She was on her feet instantly. "My baby," she said, pointing to a hedgerow a short distance away.

Wrapping himself and Zea in a shield of Spirit, he took her hand, and they rushed to the area she'd indicated. What they found there was heartbreaking.

Little Kindel was fussing quietly in her blankets, but Gillium, her valiant young warder, lay next to a dead Satyr a short distance away. His eyes were open and vacant. His hands still clutched the sword he'd driven through the creature's chest. Gideon could tell just by looking that Gillium had stepped into the Satyr's path as it had lunged for Kindel.

Zea dropped to her knees and scooped her baby into her arms. Holding her close, she looked at Gillium. "Can you heal him?" she asked, tears streaming down her face.

Gideon shook his head. "Only the Creator can heal death," he answered. "I'm sorry."

Zea buried her face against her baby and wept.

Gideon would have wept, too, if not for the rage burning inside him. Keeping Zea inside his shield, he turned his attention back to the fight taking place all around him.

The Dainin had engaged the demonspawn that could wield the Power, but their unwillingness to use *Ta'shaen* as a weapon meant things were taking longer than they should have while they tried to reach them with their spears. Wielding shields of Spirit, they deflected streamers of Fire channeled by the creatures, sending them sizzling harmlessly into the air.

Gideon waited impatiently until he had a clear line of sight on one of the creatures, then drew in more of the Power and sent a white-hot bar of *Sei'shiin* lancing from his fist. It took the beast in the head, and it vanished in a flash of white as it was burned from existence. The Dainin who'd been engaging the creature turned and looked at Gideon in surprise, then selected another target.

Gideon destroyed that one with a thrust of Flesh and Fire that sprayed the Dainin with smouldering gore. "See how much easier that is," he shouted, then killed another of the creatures in like manner.

His use of *Ta'shaen* drew the attention of the rest of the demonspawn, and they broke from the Dainin and raced toward him, eyes glowing with rage, snarls filling the air.

"Time for you to go," he told Zea. Helping her to her feet, he ushered her through the Veilgate he'd opened into the palace. When she was gone, he let the Veilgate close and turned to face the demonspawn as streamers of corrupted Earthpower exploded all around him.

Elison Brey sliced the arm off a Darkling that leapt out of the bushes to attack him, then drove the point of his sword deep into the creature's chest. A second Darkling appeared behind the first only to drop lifeless as Gavin put an arrow through its head.

More arrows were loosed as the *Bero'thai* spread out across the gardens and attacked the enemy from behind. There were a lot more than he had expected, and dark shapes darted every which way. Still, battling Darklings was better than whatever was happening closer to the Dome, and he killed another one of the abominations as Fire erupted up ahead.

Stepping over the Darkling's corpse, he cast about for Seth, but the Chellum captain was lost somewhere in the melee to the right, a trail of decapitated Darklings the only sign he'd gone that way.

"Follow Seth," he told Gavin, "and make sure he doesn't try to engage any of the demonspawn on his own."

"You saw the look in his eyes, too, did you?" Gavin asked. Nocking another arrow, he disappeared in the direction Seth had gone.

Elison watched him go, then singled out another Darkling he intended to kill. It had taken an arrow in the shoulder and was hacking at the foliage in a frenzy, confused and enraged by the pain. The bloody creatures really were nothing more than animals.

Careful to stay out of the Darkling's line of sight, he slipped in behind it and quickly stilled the madness. The cat-faced creature dropped amid a colorful array of flowers, and Elison was struck by the odd contrast between beauty and filth. He didn't have time to dwell on it, though, as a flash of dark movement to his left caught his attention.

Whirling, he had just enough time to raise his sword as the Saytr lunged.

Jase shoved the spear deeper into Jamik Hedron's chest and was rewarded with the warmth of the man's blood on his hand. Jamik looked up, surprise mingled with agony spreading over his face.

"How does it feel to lose?" Jase asked. "Because you *have* lost, you filthy cur. Just as Aethon will lose."

Jamik tried to respond but couldn't. A gurgled moan was all that escaped his lips as his legs gave out and Jase let him fall backwards, spear still in his chest.

"Enjoy a permanent trip to hell," Jase told him, then burned him from existence with a streamer of *Sei'shiin*. "Because you won't be coming back as a K'rrosha."

Still holding the Power, he took note of where everyone was, then began killing Satyrs with blades of Fire. The Darklings he left to the *Bero'thai*, and the clash of steel sounded everywhere.

He caught sight of Bornis battling a pair of Darklings on the other side of the small stream, and saw that his friend was bleeding from a deep wound in his side. Little Wytni was a few steps behind him, her face a mask of terror as she watched the creatures come at her brother. Bornis' wound had likely come as a result of having his movement restricted due to protecting her.

Jase obliterated the Darklings with two streamers of *Sei'shiin*, then opened a Veilgate for Bornis into the palace. "Go," he shouted. "You need healing."

Pressing a hand to the wound, Bornis nodded, then ushered Wytni through to safety.

A powerful use of *Ta'shaen* rocked his Awareness, and he turned to see Gideon sending Zea Lyacon through a gate as well. When she was away, Gideon turned back to face a herd of demonspawn bearing down on him. Wielding swords set with Jexlair crystals, the apelike creatures sent streamers of Fire lancing forward, and Gideon vanished behind a wall of flames.

Jase sliced the head off one of the creatures, then watched a second one tumble to the earth in the crackling of an *arinseil* net. A third creature exploded into chunks of ruined flesh as Gideon, still somewhere amid the corrupted flames, lashed out with a violent thrust reminiscent of Jase's earlier days.

A Veilgate opened behind the remaining demonspawn and Marithen Korishal stepped through with Brysia at her side. Streamers of *Sei'shiin* lanced from the old woman's outstretched hands, and one of the creatures vanished in a flare of white.

Brysia held the Power as well, and another creature was seized by a rose bush that suddenly came to life. The writhing mass entangled itself around the demonspawn, then sprouted thorns as long as swords as it tightened its hold, piercing the creature from all sides.

Marithen and Gideon struck again, and the three remaining demonspawn were burned from existence by the cleansing white of *Sei'shiin*.

As *Ta'shaen* quieted in his mind, the sounds of clashing steel became more pronounced. Then those, too, began to fade. A moment later all was silence. The fight, it seemed, was over.

To confirm, he extended his Awareness across the whole of the Overlook, allowing it to take shape in his mind's eye. He was relieved to discover that aside from the demonspawn entangled in Dainin nets, no enemies remained alive. But relief turned to sorrow when he numbered the dead of his own people and found Galam and Gillium among them. There were dozens of wounded, too, including Elison. Bleeding profusely, he lay on his side next to Taka O'sei and a limbless Satyr. Taka, Jase realized, wasn't breathing.

He reined in his Awareness and forced his grief aside as best he could. There would be time to mourn for his friends later. Now was the time to care for the living.

"*Nar'shein*," Jase called, "please tend to the wounded. Elison Bray will need attention first. He's just beyond the fountain. Hurry, he's in pretty bad shape."

Bringing fists to chest, five of the six Dainin moved off to do as ordered. The sixth, which Jase now recognized as Ohran Peregam himself, pulled his spear from the head of the Power-voiding demonspawn and moved to kneel before him.

"I see you, *Mith'elre Chon*," he said.

"I see you, Chieftain of the *Nar'shein Yahl*." He glanced pointedly at the sky. "And I must say your arrival, and the manner thereof, was most fortuitous."

"You can thank Talia Chellum and Velerie Kivashey for that," Ohran said with a smile. "It was they who alerted me to your plight."

*Of course it was*, Jase thought with a smile. Even when Talia wasn't part of the immediate battle, she found a way to take part in the war. And Velerie also. The two had a knack for doing the right thing at the right time. And thankfully so. There was no telling what might have happened if he'd been forced to fight without *Ta'shaen*.

"Come, my friend," Jase said, bidding Ohran to rise. "I would speak with Gideon."

"As would I," Ohran said, and together they made their way to where Gideon was standing over the demonspawn laying powerless beneath the *arinseil* net. Brysia was with him, her face pinched with disgust as she gazed down at the creature. She looked up as Jase drew near and hurried forward to hug him.

"Thank the Light you are unharmed," she whispered, then stepped back to look him over. She saw the blood on his hand and her eyes widened slightly. "You *are* unharmed, right?"

"Not a scratch," he said.

"What should we do with this one?" Gideon asked, indicating the netted demonspawn.

"What we do with all creatures bred of corruption," Ohran answered. Hefting his spear, he drove it through the creature's head and held it there until it stopped twitching.

"And yet you won't use the Power to kill them," Gideon said.

"Our nets are wrought of *Ta'shaen*," Ohran said. "That will have to suffice." His large eyes narrowed as he looked at Gideon. "Besides, with *El'kali* on the battlefield, what need have we of the Power?"

"Speaking of the Power," Jase said, heading off whatever Gideon had been about to say, "the enemy used *Lo'shaen* to open Veilgates inside the void that creature created, didn't they?"

"Yes," Ohran answered. His eyes met Gideon's briefly, and the look that passed between them told Jase that they were both thinking about Gideon's—about Dunkin Fairimor's—transgressions with the Power of the Void. And why not? It had been Ohran who had invoked a Cleansing Hunt for the former High King. It made Jase wonder how Gideon had managed to evade the *Nar'shein* long enough to repent. A question for another time, he supposed.

"The void surrounding that creature," Gideon added, "was literally an extension of Con'Jithar, forcefully brought into the living world by reason of its demon blood. It's what the world will feel like if the Veil collapses completely. *Ta'shaen* will be out of reach for us. Only *Lo'shaen* will remain."

Jase went cold inside. "Which means only Aethon, the traitorous Rhiven, and certain demonspawn will be able to wield."

Ohran nodded. "Makes things a bit more difficult for us, doesn't it?"

"Difficult?" Jase asked. "How about impossible?"

Gideon put a hand on his shoulder. "Then let's make sure it doesn't come to that by rejuvenating the Earthsoul."

"Which brings us back to where we were before this thing arrived," Brysia said. "Searching for clues as to the whereabouts of a lost Temple of Elderon." She looked up at Ohran. "We are going to Andlexces," she said, "to see if we can find something in the Old World collections that might help."

"Maps, specifically," Gideon said. "With the number of T'rii Gates discovered in the past few days, we might be able to bridge the Old World with the New. At least enough to get an idea where to look."

"A good idea," Ohran said. "If you can delay your departure until this evening when my scouts return, I may have a few more T'rii Gate locations to add to your list."

"This evening will be fine," Brysia said, then looked at Jase as if to apologize. "If the *Mith'elre Chon* approves, of course."

He stared at her. "You're my mother. When have I ever disapproved of your decisions?"

She arched an eyebrow at him. "Do you really want me to answer that?"

"Not kicking the so-called *Noble Houses* out of the palace doesn't count," he told her. "I didn't disapprove; I disagreed. There's a difference."

Ohran got down on one knee and looked him in the eyes. "You wanted to oust Trian's ruling families from their home?" he asked. He didn't seem upset, just curious.

Jase shrugged. "Just the ones who deserved it."

"So all of them," Gideon said.

"You said it, not me," he said, then looked at his mother.

She stared at him for a moment, then made a motion with her hand to dismiss the matter and change the subject. "What are we going to do about this?" she asked, indicating the enemy bodies scattered about the gardens.

"I've got an idea about that," Jase said. After a slight pause, he added, "If you approve, of course."

Her eyes narrowed. "How can I approve until you tell me what the idea is."

"Aethon orchestrated this to deliver a message," Jase told her. "I was thinking about sending a message in reply."

"To what end?" Ohran asked.

Jase felt his resolve tighten. "To let that gutless coward know that I won't be intimidated." He looked around at the dead demonspawn. "And he is a coward," he said. "Otherwise he would have delivered the message himself."

"If he had come," Ohran said, "there may have been no message. He may have simply killed you with *Lo'shaen* and been done with it."

"But he didn't," Seth said, moving up to them. His uniform was speckled with Darkling blood, but as usual he appeared uninjured. "Which is why I'm inclined to agree with Jase. Aethon sent others in his stead because he was uncertain of the outcome."

"That or he'd grown weary of using *Lo'shaen* to control the *Ta'shaen*-voiding creature," Gideon said. "I can't imagine it behaved itself among the Agla'Con who can only wield *Ta'shaen*. Aethon might have simply needed to get rid of it and saw this as an opportunity."

"Whatever his reasons," Brysia said. "We are fortunate things turned out as well as they did. This could have been much worse." She looked at Jase. "Do whatever it is you have planned," she told him. "You have my approval."

"Thank you," he said. Opening himself to *Ta'shaen*, he channeled hundreds of streamers of Air and gathered all the enemy corpses and their weapons together into one big mass. He held them in the air above the pathway, then lifted the larger, Power-voiding demonspawn and Jamik's severed arm above them. The Jexlair crystal caught the afternoon sunlight in a flash of red as Jase placed the arm in the demonspawn's mouth.

Nodding in satisfaction, he opened a horizontal Veilgate and let the macabre message fall through onto the heads of part of Shadan's army.

Aethon watched as a tangle of bodies fell through a hole in the sky and landed amid a column of Shadan Cultists. Shouts of alarm and cries of pain followed as dozens of cultists were pummeled by the carnage, and Aethon ground his teeth in anger at what the avalanche of death implied.

Heeling his horse into a trot, he rode up to the disgusting heap in time to see cultists clawing their way out of the mess. Those who'd survived, anyway. Twenty or so had been killed, at least five of which lay beneath the bulk of the Power-voiding demonspawn he'd had such high expectations for.

Asherim Ije'kre swung down from his mount and moved to inspect the creature. "Stabbed through the top of the head," he said, and Aethon scowled at him.

"I have eyes," he said, then shook his head in disgust. It had to have been a Dainin, he decided. No one else was tall enough or strong enough to deliver such a blow. He sighed in disgust. He should have known there would be some hanging about the palace.

"Jamik is dead," Asherim said as he pulled an arm from the demonspawn's mouth and held it up for Aethon to see. Jamik's talisman was still fastened about the wrist.

"He knew the risks when he went," Aethon said. "Obviously, he stayed longer than he should have after delivering my message. No one to blame but himself."

"Indeed," Asherim said. He looked up at the spot where the Veilgate had opened. "But now I am wondering how well that message was received."

"Well enough for our purposes," Aethon said, but as his eyes moved over the corpses heaped before him, he had his doubts, fleeting as they might be.

"After all," he continued, "the attack in Trian was only one part of this operation. Once Jase Fairimor learns of the attacks that took place elsewhere, he will see just how long my reach is."

*And*, he added, *the little fool's heart will bleed for those he knew.*

Aethon smiled. Compassion was the boy's biggest weakness. A weakness Aethon fully intended to continue exploiting. Jase could play at being hard all he wanted, but in the end, his grief would catch up to him. And that would be his undoing.

# CHAPTER 20

## *Losses*

IDOMAN BURNED THE DEMONSPAWN from existence with a brilliant burst of *El'shaen te sherah*, then took hold of a rack of spears with a grip of Air and hurled them, rack and all, into a knot of Darklings. A number of the creatures fell, pierced and bleeding, and Idoman left the rest for the squad of *Bero'thai* racing toward the melee. He had more pressing enemies to destroy.

And they were everywhere.

A powerful burst of corrupted Earthpower tore at his Awareness as another demonspawn lashed out with Fire, destroying a supply wagon and killing a number of Kelsan soldiers. Holding a shield of Spirit around him, Idoman moved toward the fire, but another Dymas reached the area first. *Ta'shaen* came alive with a wielding of *Sei'shiin*, and he felt the brush of a familiar Awareness.

*Joselyn*, he thought with a smile, grateful she was still alive. He hadn't seen her since the opening moments of the attack when the command tent had been overrun by Power-wielding demonspawn and everyone had been scattered. He cast a quick look over his shoulder at the column of smoke rising from the ruined tent and breathed a silent prayer for the others.

Railen and Sheymi had fled one direction. Kalear and Joneam had gone another, the Riaki shielding the general with the Power as they ran. He hadn't seen or felt anything of them since.

*God help them*, he thought, then, quickening his pace, he hurried to join Joselyn.

Railen held a shield of Spirit around himself and Sheymi as a pair of wolf-like demonspawn lashed at him with the Power. The Jexlair crystals set in their swords glowed brightly, but he could feel that the beasts were weakening.

"Just another moment or two," he told Sheymi, and she nodded, her beautiful face set as she watched the creatures' frenzy. She'd tried striking them earlier, but they were strong and had easily deflected her attack. Letting them lash at him with such wild abandon would eventually take the edge off their ability to quickly switch between attacking and defending. Or so he hoped.

Channeling more Spirit into his shield to strengthen it, he settled in to wait.

This was the third pair of Power-wielding creatures they'd encountered in as many minutes, and he was starting to wonder just how many there were. He could feel surges of *Ta'shaen*, both corrupted and pure, being channeled all across the camp, and smoke rose from fires in a dozen places. Intermittent flashes of lightning lit the area and were followed by rumbles of thunder. The horrified cries of men being killed by demonspawn sounded loudly from almost every direction.

Railen did his best to ignore the tumult and concentrated on the enemies before him. The attack grew even more frenzied, but the streamers of Fire hammering his shield weren't nearly as powerful as when the attack began. And then one of the streamers sputtered briefly as the demonspawn's concentration slipped.

Railen squeezed Sheymi's hand. "Now," he said, and she channeled a swirling column of *El'shaen* that dropped on the creatures from above.

Their fiery attack broke off as they hurriedly cast up shields to defend themselves, but, as Railen had anticipated, they weren't fast enough. *El'shaen* burned them from existence in a flash so bright it left a column of white in Railen's vision.

"Nice," he said, blinking against the afterimage.

"We came here to learn and master the new wieldings, did we not?"

"We did, indeed," he answered. "But you are the master here, not me." Casting about, he asked, "Where to now?"

The fierce look in her eyes intensified. "Wherever the fighting is the worst."

He grinned at her. "You're starting to sound like Shavis," he said, then cast about for another enemy to engage. A sudden flare of corrupted Fire beyond a row of tents caught his attention, and he pressed his Awareness toward it. Joselyn and Idoman came into view in his mind's eye.

"There," he said. "Joselyn and Idoman need our help." Taking her hand in his, he started to run.

They'd only gone a few paces when the ground around them erupted in sprays of superheated dirt and they were sent tumbling through the air.

Idoman felt the demonspawn before he saw it. It moved through the camp as a void in his Awareness, a bubble of darkness that somehow threw back the luminescent world that was *Ta'shaen*.

He tracked it as it drew near, and when it came around the corner of a tent a moment later, the aura surrounding it was visible to his natural eyes as well, a shroud of reddish-black that moved and pulsated like something alive.

The creature inside the darkness walked upright like a man, and carried a long slender sword and a black shield. Its grey skin was covered with snake-like scales and rows of short rose-like thorns. Its face was pitted and scarred, and scars crisscrossed its chest and torso.

"We've got trouble," he said, and Joselyn turned from the demonspawn she'd just obliterated to study the approaching creature.

"It's creating a void in the Power," she said, and Idoman heard fear in her voice. Raising her palms, she sent two streamers of *Sei'shiin* lancing at the creature, but they vanished into nothingness the moment they encountered the sheltering aura. Her eyes went wide. "That shouldn't be possible."

She struck again, this time hurling a spear at the creature with a fist of Air. The deadly missile penetrated the dark aura but shattered harmlessly against the blackened shield. The creature showed a row of pointed teeth as it grinned at them.

But Joselyn had given Idoman an idea. Using tendrils of Air, he took up every arrow, spear, and sword in the area and prepared to fling them at the creature from every direction. There was no way the bloody thing could block them all.

The creature's shield flared red with the glow of corrupted Power, and the aura surrounding it expanded outward, voiding Idoman's Awareness and severing his hold on the Power. The assortment of missiles intended for the creature dropped to the earth in a clatter of steel and wood.

Idoman drew his sword. "I think you should run," he said to Joselyn. "Get beyond the void and continue the fight elsewhere. I will contend with this one." *So long as it can't use the Power in other ways,* he thought grimly.

Joselyn started away but was stopped short of exiting the void by a Darkling arrow that hissed in from the right and struck her in the side. Crying out in pain, the elderly Dymas staggered and went down, a rapidly expanding spot of crimson staining her dress. The Darkling who'd loosed the arrow appeared from behind a wagon and rushed forward with sword raised, intent on finishing her off.

Idoman got there first, fueled by a white-hot rush of rage. He caught the Darkling's sword on his, then punched the creature in the face, shattering cheekbones and knocking the cat-faced monster backwards. Before it could recover, Idoman sliced its head from its neck, and it dropped in a heap, spraying the ground with its greenish-brown blood.

Sensing movement behind him, Idoman whirled to find the demonspawn lunging with its sword. He managed to deflect the killing blow, but the creature followed with a thrust of its shield, and pain shot through Idoman's arm as he was knocked from his feet. He landed ten paces away and scrambled to his feet, his broken left arm throbbing at his side.

Gripping his sword in his good hand, he raced back toward the creature but could only watch as it buried its sword in Joselyn's chest.

Gasping, she stiffened then fell back and lay still.

The demonspawn pulled its blade free, then turned to stare at Idoman, a smile of evil satisfaction on its face.

Rage unlike anything he'd ever felt took hold of him, and he felt a previously unknown part of his Awareness awaken. Without realizing it at first, he found himself reaching for a river of dark energy flowing throughout the void around him. It moved toward him, a torrent of evil eager to make his acquaintance.

*Lo'shaen,* he realized, and it was his if he would surrender to it.

His eyes moved from the demonspawn to Joselyn and the temptation to give himself over to *Lo'shaen* dissipated when he realized how disappointed his sweet, old mentor would be if he did. She'd trained him better than this. He was better than this. He would not use the Power of the Void. Not now. Not ever.

Raising his sword before him with his good arm, he started forward to engage the demonspawn. It watched him come, its red eyes shining with what could only be described as amusement.

"It won't be as easy as you think, you miserable filth," he told it, not caring if it understood him or not. His tone would convey the meaning. "I'm going to cut your head off and send it to your master on a spear."

"*Broakosha vai mora sey,*" the demonspawn hissed, and the void around them darkened as its shield glowed an even brighter red.

Idoman suddenly felt as if he couldn't breathe, and his vision started to darken. The demonspawn started forward, but it was difficult for Idoman to track its movements as shadow blended into shadow.

One of those shadows moved on his left, and he slashed at it with his sword. The blade passed through the shadow with no resistance, and he momentarily lost his balance. Righting himself, he slashed at another shadow moving on his right with the same result. His vision dimmed further as shadows continued to move all around him, and he grew desperate, flailing wildly with his sword. Steel met demonspawned flesh, and the creature hissed in pain.

"Hurts, doesn't it?" Idoman said, but his satisfaction was short-lived.

The clash of steel sounded sharply as the demonspawn knocked his sword away, then Idoman's chest exploded into pain.

His vision cleared instantly, and he found himself looking his enemy in the eyes. Teeth bared with evil pleasure, the beast pushed the blade deeper, and Idoman hissed as the blood-blackened hilt came to rest against his chest. He glanced down to find it getting a fresh coat of red.

"*Voshomi ke tolo,*" the creature said, pulling the blade free.

Idoman's sword slipped from his grasp, and he fell, his strength, like his lifeblood, leaving him in a rush. He landed on his side and gazed across the trampled ground at his slain mentor.

"Forgive me, Joselyn," he whispered, then watched as the world began to dim once more.

Teig Ole'ar's arrow punched through the demonspawned creature's skull with a loud crack, and it staggered but remained upright. His second arrow took it in the neck as it turned to regard him for a moment, then it wobbled and fell, dropping both sword and shield as it collapsed into a heap next to Idoman Leda.

Teig rushed to kneel at his friend's side, but hope vanished when he saw the seriousness of the wound.

"Hold on," he said, then cut two strips of cloth from Idoman's uniform and pressed them against the wounds to slow the bleeding.

Idoman's eyelids fluttered but remained closed. His breathing was shallow and weak, his face pale.

"I need a Dymas here!" Teig shouted, but the battle was still raging, and no one heard his call.

No one, it seemed, but a knot of Darklings skulking along behind a row of wagons. They rounded the last wagon with swords raised, eager at the prospect of killing. Seeing him alone, they howled with feral pleasure as they rushed him.

Taking up his bow, he loosed arrow after arrow as they neared, felling one Light-blasted creature with every shot. But there were too many, and they were closing the gap faster than he could kill them. In the end he was forced to abandon his bow and engage them with his sword.

He killed the first one easily but was forced to give ground as the others arrived and started to flank him. One of the creatures glanced down at Idoman laying helpless in his own blood, and a cat-like mewing sounded as it raised its sword to finish him off.

Teig drew the last dagger from his belt and hurled it at the creature, striking it in the chest. It dropped its sword and staggered away, clutching at the hilt as it fell.

Two Darklings rushed him, and Teig sliced the arm off of the first one, then spun around behind it and removed the head of another before finishing the first one off with a thrust through the back.

But the rest had him surrounded, and there were seven of them.

Keeping his sword before him, he turned one way and then another, trying to keep eyes on all of them at once. They watched him with swords raised, their animalistic faces twisted with amusement. They had him and they knew it.

Still rotating to keep them at bay, his eyes lighted briefly on Idoman, and he clenched his teeth in anger and frustration at being unable to help his young friend—even if that meant simply being with him as he passed.

His eyes returned to the Darklings. They were preparing to rush him, he knew. When they did, the fight would be over. It would be interesting to see how many he could kill before they got him.

Tightening his grip on his sword, he attacked.

Railen seized the remaining Darklings in a grip of Air, then sliced their heads off with blades of Fire. Their headless corpses dropped at the feet of Teig Ole'ar who looked around in surprise. The Elvan Master of Spies was bleeding from several sword wounds, but he waved Sheymi off as she neared.

"There," he said, pointing to a body on the ground. "Idoman needs you worse than I do."

Sheymi hurried forward, and, as she did, Railen wrapped them all in a sheltering bubble of Spirit. The sounds of battle were fading rapidly, but he wasn't taking any chances until he knew for sure the enemy had been destroyed. Tremors in *Ta'shaen* told him that at least a few demonspawn remained and were being attacked by Dymas.

He was on his way to join Sheymi when he spotted a second body a short distance away. He hurried forward and found that it was Joselyn Rai. A quick probe of his Awareness revealed that she was dead.

Placing his fingers gently on her eyelids, he closed her eyes, then rolled her onto her side and covered her with an abandoned cloak he found lying nearby. He'd known Joselyn for less than a day, but his heart ached at her loss. The death of any Dymas was tragic, but the loss of this sweet old woman would be felt by many.

Leaving her to lie in peace, he joined Sheymi. She had a hand on Idoman's head, and her eyes were closed as she probed him with her Awareness and sent healing tendrils of Flesh to the most critical areas.

"How is he?" he asked, afraid of the answer once he got a look at the young Dymas General's wounds.

"He still clings to life," Sheymi answered. "But barely."

"Can you save him?" Railen asked, then turned to regard Teig as he limped near. The Elvan man's face was lined with pain, and he was pale from loss of blood. His eyes, though, showed that it would take a lot more than a few Darklings to kill him. The Elvan scout would have made a fine Shizu.

Railen considered healing him, but he still wasn't willing to drop the shield he was holding around them until he knew they were safe. Teig must have read his thoughts in his face because he shrugged.

"I'll live," he said, then dropped to one knee next to Sheymi. "How is Idoman?"

"I've stopped the bleeding," Sheymi told him. "But he is so close to death that I need to work slowly so as not to shock his system. Too much healing all at once would kill him." She shook her head. "He might die anyway if I can't remove the poison."

"Poison?" Teig asked, and Railen shared his surprise.

"The sword that stabbed him was tainted," Sheymi answered. "But it is unlike any poison I've ever encountered. It is tied to the Power somehow. It fights back."

"Gideon can help with that," Railen told her. "He healed Doroku Dymas of a similar wound."

"Fetch him quickly," Sheymi said. "We'll be all right until you get back. The fighting here is over."

Railen was hesitant to leave them, but a quick extension of his Awareness proved Sheymi right. *Ta'shaen* had quieted save for the Gift of Flesh being used to heal the wounded. That and the occasional burst of Water to extinguish a fire. He relaxed even more when a squad of *Bero'thai* came into view beyond the wagons.

He ran his fingers through Sheymi's hair. "I'll be back soon," he said, letting the shield of Spirit drop.

Turning to Teig, he placed his hands on his head and healed him of his wounds, then opened a Veilgate directly into Fairimor Dome.

Walking next to Brysia on the cobblestone path, Gideon watched with sadness as Jase used a blanket of Air to carry the bodies of Galam and Gillium toward the entrance to the Dome. Behind him, Seth and Elison bore the body of Taka O'sei on a makeshift litter they had fashioned from Dainin spears, their faces somber as they carried the slain captain. According to Elison, Taka had saved his life by stepping into the path of a Satyr lunging for him. The First Captain of the Palace Guard had served faithfully to the end. Glory would be his in the afterlife.

Out of reverence for the dead, no one spoke, and the silence gave him a chance to notice the pain and sorrow in Jase's eyes as he carried the bodies of his childhood friends. He also noticed the terrible rage smoldering just beneath that pain, and it was frightening to think what might happen if Jase failed to keep that rage in check.

And that more than anything made Gideon think Aethon's attack hadn't been a complete failure after all. Jamik Hedron may have been speaking the truth when he said they hadn't come here for Jase. At least not to attack him physically. They'd come here to harm him emotionally.

*And to some extent it worked*, he thought. *Just as it had with the attack on Kindel's Grove.*

He cast a sideways glance at Brysia and could tell from her expression that she was thinking the same thing. Reaching over to take her hand, he offered a smile of encouragement when she turned to look at him. "He'll shake it off," he whispered.

"I hope so," she said, but she didn't sound convinced. The manner in which she met his gaze and then looked away spoke volumes, and the realization of what she was thinking stung him deeply. She was worried Jase would give into his rage just as he had after the murder of Kio and Dace.

He forced the hurt away and squeezed her hand so she would look at him.

"He won't follow that path," he whispered. "He's a much better person than I was at that time."

Tears formed in her beautiful green eyes. "How did you know what I was thinking?"

He leaned near and his lips brushed her ear as he whispered. "Because I am your husband," he answered and squeezed her hand again.

Her tears increased, and she reached up to wipe them away with her other hand. "Forgive me," she said softly. "I should not be entertaining such thoughts. I hope I did not offend."

"Not at all," he told her. "I entertained those thoughts all the time when I first met the boy. But I soon learned that he is *not* his father."

She squeezed his hand in return, and the smile she gave him sent a rush of warmth through his chest. "He is like his father in the ways that matter."

They reached the doors leading into the Dome, and Talia and Velerie and the others were waiting for them inside. Talia's face was wet with tears—undoubtedly she'd felt Jase's grief through the love-bond—and she hurried forward to embrace him.

Hugging her tightly, Jase lowered the bodies of Galam and Gillium to the floor, then released the Power. But he didn't release Talia, and the two continued to hug one another without speaking. They didn't need words—the love-bond would convey their emotions much more purely and clearly than words ever could.

While Jase and Talia continued to hold one another in silence, Bornis left his little sister with Velerie and moved to kneel next to the bodies of his friends. Jukstin joined him, and they lowered their heads in grief, their eyes pinched tightly against the tears which threatened to come.

Zea handed Kindel to Velerie, then she, too, moved to kneel with Bornis and Jukstin. The dam the two young men had placed on their grief burst as Zea put her arms around them and pulled them close, and the three of them wept together while others looked on in awkward silence.

Gideon motioned for the Dainin to follow, then moved deeper into the Dome, not stopping until he'd reached the Blue Flame rug in the center of the room.

He was about to ask Ohran how Velerie had alerted him to their plight when *Ta'shaen* came alive and a pure Veilgate opened a short distance away.

Railen Nogeru stepped through, then stopped when he saw Gideon. A look of relief washed over his face. "I hadn't counted on finding you so quickly," he said, holding the gate open behind him. "Quickly, we need your help to heal Idoman Leda. He's dying of a shadow-tainted wound."

"The Kelsan camp was attacked?" Gideon asked as he released Brysia's hand and started forward.

"Demonspawn," Railen answered. "One of them had the ability to nullify the Power."

*Just like here*, Gideon thought and followed his young friend through to the bloodstained grasses on the other side of the gate. A Demonspawned creature with arrows through its head and neck lay a short distance away, and Teig Ole'ar stood over it with a third arrow nocked and ready. To the right of Teig, Sheymi Oroshi knelt next to Idoman and was sending healing tendrils of *Ta'shaen* into his body.

Gideon glanced over his shoulder as the gate slid shut behind him and caught one last glimpse of Brysia before she vanished. Her eyes, he noted, were brimming once again with tears. *I love you, too*, he thought, longing for the day when he could say it in the presence of others.

Maybe once the war with Shadan was over. Until then, he would just need to say it even more in private.

Moving to kneel next to Sheymi Oroshi, he focused on the matter at hand. "Let's have a look," he said as he opened his Awareness and delved into the young man's body. He found the poison almost immediately. It was a shadowwound all right, and it was as dark as any he'd ever encountered.

"We need to heal him of his physical wounds first," Gideon told them. "If we don't, he won't survive the removal of the poison. As you may have noticed, it fights back."

"Tell me what you want me to do," Sheymi said.

"I need you to boost his strength gradually," he said. "Try to do it at the same pace as the healing I'll give him. We'll address the shadowwound once I'm certain he is going to live. Attacking it now would only finish what its wielder started."

They worked carefully and quietly for the next several minutes, starting first with the hole in Idoman's heart, then repairing his damaged lung. When that was done, Gideon allowed Sheymi to strengthen Idoman's heartbeat until blood was flowing steadily through his veins once more.

By then, a crowd of soldiers had gathered, and many had taken a knee to watch Gideon and Sheymi work. Gideon glanced at them and found that most were Kelsan, but there were a number of *Bero'thai* as well. They knew who Idoman was and what he had done at the rim, and their faces were lined with worry as they waited for word on the young Dymas General's condition.

He hoped he would be able to tell them what they wanted to hear. Returning his attention to Idoman, he watched as color gradually returned to his face. A moment later, his eyes opened.

He seemed not to recognize them at first, but then he forced a weak smile. "It's good to see you," he said in a tired whisper.

"Don't speak," Sheymi told him. "You aren't out of the woods yet."

"That's comforting," Idoman said, then closed his eyes. A few seconds passed and he spoke again. "Joselyn?"

Sheymi looked at Gideon before answering, and his chest tightened with a sudden sharp sadness at what he saw in the young woman's eyes. He nodded that it was all right to answer.

"I'm sorry," Sheymi said, smoothing Idoman's hair with her hand. "She didn't make it."

There was a collective murmur of disbelief from the gathered soldiers, but Idoman simply nodded, his eyes still closed. Tears gathered in his eyes, then ran in streaks through the dirt coating his cheeks. "I saw it happen," he said. "And I couldn't stop it."

He opened his Awareness to them, and images of Joselyn's final moments flowed into their minds. They saw it as clearly as if they'd been standing there.

Idoman opened his eyes, and his rage at his helplessness flowed through the Communal link. Then a rush of frustration and horror and guilt followed, and Gideon felt Sheymi stiffen as the next wave of images washed over them.

*I could have destroyed the demonspawn,* Idoman told them. *If I had, I may have been able to save Joselyn.*

*And lost yourself in the process,* Gideon told him. *No, my young friend. You did the right thing.*

Sheymi's earlier surprise turned to admiration, and she added, *Gideon is right. There is no honor in using Lo'shaen. Joselyn would be proud. No. She IS proud of you.*

*Thank you,* Idoman said, then his Awareness withdrew and he slipped back into unconsciousness.

"Continue to boost his strength," Gideon said, and Sheymi nodded. "Railen and I will see to any others who need healing. When Idoman wakes, I will address the shadowwound."

He motioned for Railen to follow and they moved among the soldiers who'd gathered, healing all who needed it. Gideon had just finished closing a head wound on a *Bero'thai* when Joneam Eries appeared beyond the edge of the crowd.

A contingent of warders walked with him and the entire group was flanked by a squad of *Bero'thai*. The soldiers milling around Gideon parted as their general neared, and he made straight for Gideon. His face was speckled with Darkling blood and his hair and uniform were singed. But he was alive, and for that Gideon was grateful.

Railen looked past him expectantly. "Where is Kalear?"

Joneam's face tightened and he shook his head. "Kalear is dead," he answered. "He died protecting me." He pointed at the demonspawn laying at Teig's feet and added. "From that."

Gideon looked at Railen, worried about how he would react. Kalear had been more than a mentor to the young Shizu, he'd been a dear and trusted friend as well. He would be sorely missed by all who knew him, Railen most of all.

Railen kept his face smooth at the announcement, but there was a smoldering fury in his eyes that shouted of death and vengeance. He suddenly looked very much like Shavis.

"I'm sorry," Gideon said, placing a hand on his shoulder to comfort him.

The fury in Railen's eyes intensified. "Not as sorry as the enemy is going to be," he said, and the words sent a chill down Gideon's spine.

*And I was worried about Jase,* he thought, then forced a smile. "We will hunt those responsible," he said. "And we will do it together." *That way,* he added silently, *I can keep an eye on you.*

Railen nodded, but said nothing more. Gideon looked back to Joneam.

"Idoman was injured," he said. "We healed the physical wounds, but he suffered a shadowwound that still needs to be addressed." He let his eyes move over all the soldiers milling about and added, "But I'd prefer to do it somewhere a little more private. With your permission, I would like to take him to Fairimor Palace."

"Granted," Joneam said. "How long will he be gone?"

"A day or two at most," Gideon answered, then hesitated before adding, "If he survives the shadowwound, of course."

Joneam frowned. "It's that bad?"

Gideon nodded. "One of the worst I've ever seen. But Ohran Peregam is in Trian and will assist me."

Joneam's brow furrowed in surprise. "Ohran. But he never leaves Dainin."

"Your camp wasn't the only place attacked by demonspawn," Gideon told him. "Ohran's arrival very likely saved the *Mith'elre Chon* from a fate similar to Idoman's"

"Then God's speed, Dymas," Joneam said, "and thank you for coming to our aid." His eyes narrowed with curiosity. "How did you know we needed help?"

"Railen came for me," he said, then glanced at his young friend. "And you are welcome to come with me now if you want. You and Sheymi both." *That way,* he thought, *I can keep an eye on both of you.*

"I would like that," Railen said. "We aren't due back in Sagaris until tomorrow."

"Come along, then," Gideon told him.

When they reached Sheymi, Gideon explained the plan, then wrapped Idoman in a sheltering embrace of Air and lifted him gently from the ground.

"I'll be back soon," he told Joneam, then looked at Railen. "If you would do the honors," he said, gesturing at the spot in front of them.

Eyes still alight with anger at the death of Kalear, Railen embraced the Power, and the interior of the Fairimor home appeared beyond the shimmering edges of a Veilgate.

With one last nod of farewell to Joneam, Gideon carried Idoman through and laid him in the waiting arms of Ohran Peregam.

# CHAPTER 21

## *Spiritual Wounds*

WATCHING THROUGH HIS AWARENESS, Jase held his breath as Ohran and Gideon used tendrils of Spirit mingled with Flesh to attack the last of the demonspawned poison infecting Idoman Leda. Talia watched as well, but Jase knew from the frustration flowing toward him through the *sei'vaiya* that she could only see half of what was going on.

The poison and the threads of Flesh being used to corral it would be visible to her, but the tendrils of Spirit battling the spider-webbed darkness which was part of the Void were beyond the range of her spiritual eyes.

He suspected, too, that her frustration came from the knowledge that this was a wound only a Dymas could heal. Powerful as she was with the Gift of Flesh, shadowwounds were beyond her.

Truth be told, this wound was beyond him as well—a frightening prospect considering that he was the most powerful Dymas in the room. It was a good reminder that not every battle was won by brute strength. Sometimes finesse was the key. Unfortunately, when it came to many uses of the Power, finesse wasn't his strong point.

"Almost there," Gideon said, and Idoman nodded. The young man's eyes were closed, and sweat beaded his face, but Jase knew he was going to be okay. He'd had his doubts at first—they all had—but Idoman was a fighter, and Ohran and Gideon were skilled healers. The combination had brought Idoman back from the brink of death.

The darkness of the wound vanished, and Idoman let out a sigh of relief, then sagged deeper into the pillows of the sofa and lay still. Gideon and Ohran released the Power but remained kneeling as they inspected the young soldier through the eyes of *Ta'shaen.* When they were satisfied, they rose and the silence was broken by

Sheymi Oroshi.

"That was amazing," she said, and everyone turned to regard her curiously. In light of the urgency of Idoman's wounds, proper introductions hadn't yet been made. She moved onto the rug centering the ring of sofas and shook her head in wonder. "I never would have guessed that Spirit needed to be merged with Flesh to heal such a wound."

"It was the same with Doroku," Railen said, and Gideon nodded.

"Indeed it was," he agreed, then motioned the two Riaki forward. He addressed Brysia, but Jase knew the introductions were for everyone.

"My Lady, this is Sheymi Oroshi and Railen Nogeru of the Riaki Imperial Clave. They were instrumental in the liberation of Sagaris and in the rebuilding of the Riaki government. I'm also proud to call them my friends."

He smiled at both young people before continuing. "Sheymi, Railen, this is Brysia Fairimor, High Queen of Kelsa."

"It is a pleasure to meet you," they said, offering deep bows of respect. As Railen straightened, he turned to Jase.

"It's good to see you again, *Mith'elre Chon*," he said, stepping forward and offering Jase his hand.

"Likewise," Jase told him. "And I want to thank you for all you did today. Here and in the Kelsan camp."

"It wasn't enough," Railen said, sobering immediately. "We lost some good people today. And some dear friends."

Jase nodded as he glanced at the shrouded bodies of Galam and Gillium lying on the floor near the door. "Yes, we did."

A rush of sympathy reached him through the love-bond, and he smiled at Talia before turning back to Railen. "I would hear what happened in the Kelsan camp," he said. "Come, let's sit a moment."

As everyone moved to the ring of sofas, he took Talia's hand, and they squeezed in next to Cassia and Andil who had arrived midway through Idoman's healing. They'd been elsewhere in the palace when the attack commenced and had been out of harm's way. They seemed anxious to learn what had happened.

Jase gave them a reassuring smile, then waited for everyone else to be seated.

Sheymi and Railen sat together, as did Gideon and Brysia. Ohran and the Dainin seated themselves directly on the floor, while Gavin and a full contingent of *Bero'thai* took up positions just beyond the ward against eavesdropping. As usual, Seth and Elison took high-backed chairs and sat on them backwards to keep their swords free.

Gideon took a moment to finish the rest of the introductions, then looked at Jase. "Where are Beraline and Marithen?"

"Tending to the wounded out in the city," Jase answered, his earlier anger returning. "As you might imagine, there were many."

"And Velerie?"

"Doing what she can for Wytni." He shook his head in frustration. "The poor little girl was so traumatized by what she saw on the Overlook that she couldn't stop shaking. Velerie said she could use the Power to calm her. Afterwards, she is going to check on Zea and Kindel. Bornis and Jukstin are with her."

He turned his attention to Railen, but the image of Wytni's terrified face was burned into his memory. It made him hate the enemy that much more.

"What happened in the Kelsa camp?" he asked, knowing that he wouldn't like the answer.

"Like here," Railen began, his face hardening, "demonspawn arrived through rents in the Veil. The command tent was overrun in moments and we were scattered. Kalear and Joselyn were killed by the same creature that nearly claimed Idoman." He glanced at the young Dymas general lying inert on the sofa, and added, "It was the Elvan Master of Spies who saved Idoman. He killed the demonspawn before it could finish him off."

Jase was relieved to hear Teig was alive. He liked the Elvan scout a lot.

As Railen continued his account, Jase was even more relieved to hear that Joneam Eries had survived—Kelsa couldn't afford to lose another general. The loss of Joselyn and Kalear would be hard enough to bear.

"I'm sorry about Kalear," Jase said when Railen finished. "He is one of the finest men I've ever met. I'm not surprised he died protecting General Eries."

Railen could only nod as words failed him.

Sheymi placed a hand on Railen's arm, and the look that passed between them revealed the nature of their relationship. Jase smiled. It was exactly the same look he and Talia shared at any given moment. She squeezed his hand to let him know she was thinking the same thing, and a rush of warmth reached him through the love-bond.

They discussed the attacks for a while longer, each person contributing what he or she knew in order to paint a more complete picture. They learned that Velerie had contacted Ohran directly via a Veilgate, and that Railen and Sheymi had been the ones to save Teig as he was defending Idoman.

The random and chaotic nature of the attacks coupled with Jamik Hedron's message only confirmed that all of it had been nothing more than another attempt by Aethon Fairimor to instill fear into those standing against him.

By the time the discussion ended, Jase was so angry that he was tempted to open a Veilgate into Shadan's camp and lay waste to as much of it as he could. A few months ago he might have done just that. But now was a time for control. Aethon wanted him to act rashly. He was probably counting on it. Besides, he'd already given the traitorous Fairimor his answer. Kelsa would not be intimidated. By demonspawn, by Aethon, or by the Rhiven who served him.

That last thought prompted a question. "Did Galiena or Yavil take part in the battle?" He hoped not. He didn't want their presence to be known to the enemy until they attacked Galiena's brother. It's why none of the Rhiven here in the palace had participated in the fight.

"No," Idoman said, his voice not much more than a whisper. Jase, like everyone else, turned to look at him in surprise.

"I thought you were unconscious," Jase said. "How long have you been listening?"

"Long enough," Idoman said. His eyes remained closed as he added, "Galiena and Yavil returned to their people to see if they could convince any more of them to join our cause."

"Did they say when they might be back?"

Idoman shook his head ever so slightly. "No."

"It better be soon," Gideon said. "At the rate Shadan's army is moving, they will reach the western rim sometime tomorrow afternoon."

"What of the Rhiven here in the palace?" Seth asked, directing the question to Brysia. "They've promised to help."

"They won't act without their Queen," Brysia said. "But I trust she will be back in time."

"So do I," Jase said. "But with Kalear and Joselyn dead and Idoman out of the fight for the next few days, we are going to need to find Dymas who can stand toe to toe with a Rhiven."

"I'll be ready by tomorrow," Idoman said. "I'm not missing this one."

"We'll see," Gideon said, but when he glanced at Ohran, the Dainin shook his head.

"Sheymi and I will help," Railen said, and Jase turned to look at them in surprise.

Gideon seemed equally amazed. "Are you sure that is wise?" he asked. "I doubt Emperor Dromensai would approve of members of his cabinet taking part in such a battle."

"He sent us here to learn and master the new wieldings," Sheymi said. "He didn't specify how that was to be done."

Seth chuckled. "That kind of thinking will get you in trouble some day," he said. "It also sounds very much like something Elliott would have said. Just how much time did you two spend with him in Riak?"

"Too much," Sheymi said at the same time Railen said, "Not enough."

"Your help is welcome," Jase told them, "and thank you."

"Where is Elliott?" Railen asked, blatantly ignoring the warning stare Sheymi directed his way. "I was hoping to speak with him while we were here."

Sheymi's expression coupled with her earlier comment, let Jase know that something had happened between her and Elliott which made her eager to avoid him. He shot a quick look at Gideon to confirm and found him trying not to smile.

Sheymi noticed Gideon's amusement, and her face flushed red with anger or embarrassment or both. Knowing Elliott, it was probably anger. Whatever the reason, this was something best left unspoken.

"Elliott is in Chellum at the moment," Seth answered, but he didn't elaborate on why. "He is due back tomorrow." His face remained expressionless as he met Sheymi's gaze, but Jase suspected he knew something about what had happened. He would have to ask him about it when Sheymi was no longer around. Or better yet, he would ask Elliott when he returned. It would be fun to see his reaction.

"What do you make of the sudden use of demonspawn by our enemies?" Cassia asked, directing the question to Ohran. "Do you think it has anything to do with Endil and those with him?"

"No," Ohran said. "This is nothing more than coincidence. If the mission to obtain the stolen Blood Orb had been compromised, we wouldn't be having this conversation. We would be dead."

"Ohran's right," Jase said, meeting his aunt's worried gaze. "If Loharg felt he was in danger of losing the Orb, he would use it to bring down the Veil, whether he'd reached the Shrine of Uri or not. And it wouldn't matter if it was Endil or Aethon who threatened him."

"And therein lies the danger," Gideon said. "Aethon's plundering of warrens to replace the shadowspawn he lost at Fulrath might cause Loharg to react."

"Loharg knows he is being hunted," Ohran said. "But he is determined to take the Orb to the shrine and offer up its power there."

"How can you be sure of that?" Cassia asked.

"I've been receiving updates from the *Nar'shein* I sent to join Chieftain Kia'Kal," Ohran answered. He turned his dark eyes on Jase. "I considered it wise for them to know the proper method of opening a Veilgate," he added. "And the small windows used to spy on an enemy are most advantageous in a land where one's Awareness is obscured by the taint." His smile was unapologetic. "I knew you would have no objections."

Jase grinned at him. "None whatsoever," he said. "So what have you learned?"

"Just that Loharg is determined to reach the Shrine of Uri," he answered. "And that General Shurr is either a genius or a madman."

"Is there a difference?" Gideon asked, then leaned forward curiously. "What did he do?"

Ohran's smile was one of admiration. "His small group singlehandedly destroyed one of the northern watchtowers and turned the eyes of the entire Kunin army away from the path Thorac intended to take."

He sighed, and the look of admiration faded. "It worked so well that Chieftain Kia'Kal had trouble catching up to them." His eyes darted to Cassia momentarily, and he hesitated as if unsure about continuing. Finally he added, "But they are together now, and that is all that matters."

Jase decided not to pursue what had obviously just been omitted from the story. If Ohran thought it wise to leave it unspoken, there was a good reason for it. Instead he asked, "When did you last hear from them?"

"Yesterday," Ohran answered. "Which is well past the twelve hour intervals we'd agreed upon." He turned and gazed in the direction of Kunin. "Something big is about to happen," he said. "I can feel it."

"Do you know where they are?" Gideon asked.

Ohran shook his head. "No."

A short silence followed as those in the room considered what might be happening in Kunin. Nothing yet, Jase decided—he would know when the Orb was accessed. He might not have a lot of time to act if it were Loharg, but he would feel the Orb's awakening nonetheless.

The silence was interrupted by the return of Ammorin and Pattalla. They entered from the Dome with Beraline and Marithen behind them. Lavin and a contingent of *Bero'thai* brought up the rear. A smile spread over Ammorin's face as he spotted Ohran.

"I see you, Chieftain," he said as he neared.

"I see you, *Nar'shein*," Ohran replied, and like a mound of stone reassembling itself into a mountain peak, he rose to his feet and moved to take his friend's hand. "What word from the city?"

"The demonspawn have been destroyed," he said, directing the answer to Jase. His face grew solemn. "But there were many casualties among the citizens of Trian."

Jase's chest tightened with anger. "How many?"

"Almost two hundred wounded," Beraline answered. "A hundred and fifteen dead."

Jase closed his eyes and took a deep breath. He let it out slowly, as if that act alone might nullify the pain he felt for those who had been lost. It didn't, of course, but it kept him from unleashing a string of curses which would have offended everyone in the room.

He opened his eyes and smiled at her and those with her. "Thank you for helping those you could," he told them. "During *and* after the battle. It would have been much worse without you."

Ammorin nodded, but before he could speak, *Ta'shaen* came alive with a powerful but pure wielding as a Veilgate opened in front of the fireplace.

Galiena and Yavil stepped through from beyond, then stepped aside to make way for others. Jase watched with appreciation as twenty-five Rhiven entered the Fairimor home, their yellow eyes shining with wonder as they looked around.

When the last one was through, Galiena let the Veilgate close, and she and Yavil made their way to Jase. The smile she'd worn upon arriving vanished when she noticed the covered bodies of Galam and Gillium and Taka and the blood-spattered clothing of the *Bero'thai*. Jase left the ring of sofas to meet her.

"What happened?" she asked, her eyes searching his face to make sure he was all right.

"It's a long story," he said. "I'll tell you everything after we get your people settled in."

"The Kelsan camp was attacked also, wasn't it?" she asked, looking pointedly at Idoman. The young Dymas General had pushed himself into a sitting position and was watching Galiena with a tired smile.

"An even longer story," Jase said. "And a painful one. We lost Kalear and

Joselyn." Saying it hurt more than he'd anticipated, and he had to wrap himself in *Jiu* to stifle a sudden rush of tears.

Galiena's expression sobered further. "I'm sorry."

Jase squeezed her hand in thanks, then turned to her people. "Thank you for coming to our aid," he told them. "I know it wasn't an easy decision for you."

"We are with you, *Mith'elre Chon*," one of the female Rhiven said. Sharp-faced even for a Rhiven, she had a bluish tint to her raven-colored hair and flecks of green in her yellow eyes.

Jase smiled his thanks. "You must be eager to join those of your people who came here before you," he told them. "The *Bero'thai* will take you to them."

Jase watched them exit to the Dome, then offered Galiena his arm and led her to the sofas. He gestured for her to sit next to Talia, then moved around to stand behind the two before introducing Galiena to Ohran and his *Nar'shein.*

"I've heard a great deal about you and your people the last few days," Ohran said as he settled to the floor once more. "It pleases me that you are here."

"We should have come sooner," she said, her tone apologetic. "If we had, we may have been able to prevent my brother's alliance with Aethon Fairimor."

"The past is always easier to read than the future," Ohran said. "We all have things we should have done. You are here now, and that's what matters."

"And with more of your people," Gideon said. "May I ask what changed their minds?"

"Their reasons vary," Galiena answered. "Some of which I don't necessarily like. Still, I'm glad they are here."

"We all are," Jase said, "and—" He cut off as another Veilgate opened in front of the fireplace, and a female Dainin ducked through from the wooded area beyond.

"Chieftain Peregam," she said, dropping to one knee as the Veilgate closed behind her, "the last of our scouts have returned to Kavet de'Leflure."

"Excellent," Ohran said. "What is their report?"

"They discovered five additional T'rii Gates but found nothing resembling a lost Temple of Elderon."

Jase's excitement got the best of him, and he spoke before he thought better of it. "Where were these T'rii Gates found?" he asked, and Ohran's messenger turned a hard eye on him, obviously offended that he would interrupt her report to her Chieftain. The hard look vanished as soon as she realized who he was.

"I see you, *Mith'elre Chon*," she said, her tone suddenly apologetic. "I am Hallishoi Jommoki, and I beg your pardon."

"I see you, Hallishoi," Jase told her, smiling. "So, where were these gates?"

"Two of the gates were discovered in Rosda," she answered. "The other three in Glenda."

Jase turned to look at Ohran in wonder. "When you said you were going to expand your search, you meant it. How long have you been sending *Nar'shein* to the Jyndar continent?"

"Since the moment you revealed to us the proper method for parting the Veil," Ohran told him. "Elderon's influence wasn't limited to this continent alone, after all. At one time all nations worshiped him, and temples were erected in his honor." He turned his attention back to his messenger.

"I can see in your eyes, Hallishoi, that there is more to your report."

She nodded. "Chieftains Hammishin and Paddishor encountered a number of Gifted during their travels. They wish to join the armies of the *Mith'elre Chon* and are standing by as they wait for his blessing to enter the Nine Lands."

"They are from Glenda and Rosda?" Gideon asked, and the look he exchanged with Ohran sent a shiver of excitement up Jase's spine.

"They are," Hallishoi answered. "Prophecy, it seems, has been fulfilled."

"What prophecy?" Cassia asked.

"It's in the *Tei'shevisar*," Talia answered. "I don't remember the exact phrasing, but it says that all the nations of the earth shall be gathered for the final battle between light and darkness. *All* nations, not just those here in the Nine Lands."

"*Light and darkness*," Marithen said, her eyes distant, her tone that of the now familiar singsong. "*Hope and despair. The Blood of the sons and the Blood of the Void. The blood of all nations gathered. The blood of all nations shed.*"

A profound silence followed as everyone in the room regarded the old woman curiously. Then Beraline touched her gently on the arm. "Marithen," she said, where did you read that?"

Marithen smiled at her. "Read what, dear?"

Beraline patted her cheek affectionately. "Never mind." Looking back to Ohran, she shrugged.

"Sounds like something from the *Eli'shundakor*," Ohran said. "And dark prophecy or not, it supports what Talia paraphrased from the *Tei'shevisar*. Prophecy has been fulfilled. All the nations of the world will be represented in the battles to come."

Jase stared at Ohran with a newfound appreciation. "Why do I get the feeling you sent *Nar'shein* to the Jyndar continent in order to facilitate the fulfillment?"

"Because I did," Ohran answered. "As always, we show our belief in the prophecies by doing our part to bring them to pass." He leaned forward, his weathered face lined with conviction. "But in the end, the choice to unite with us rested on these new allies. I merely provided them with the opportunity."

Jase smiled his bewilderment. "Will I ever understand how all this works?" he asked.

Ohran chuckled. "Not likely. I've got nine hundred years of experience and it's still a mystery to me. Most of the time."

"I'd like to meet these new allies," Jase said. "Where would be the best place to do so?"

"Chieftains Hammishin and Paddishor had planned to bring them to the Grand Hall of the *Nar'shein*," Hallishoi answered. "But we can bring them here if you wish."

"The Grand Hall will be fine," he said. Moving around to the front of the sofa, he offered Talia his hand. The feeling of excitement flowing toward him through the *sei'vaiya* was evident in her eyes as she stood.

"I've always wanted to visit Dainin," she whispered as Ohran and the rest of the *Nar'shein* rose to their feet.

He smiled at her. "I know." He turned to Gideon. "I would like you to join us," he said. "They may have come to join the *Mith'elre Chon*, but it will be you who commands them in battle."

Gideon nodded his acceptance. "It will be an honor."

Jase looked at his mother. "This won't take long," he told her. "I'll be back shortly to tend to Galam and Gillium."

"The *Bero'thai* can do it," she said, her eyes full of sympathy.

He knew what she was thinking, and he appreciated her concern. She believed that by giving the task to the *Bero'thai* it would spare him additional heartache. But he *needed* to be the one to tend to them. Just as he'd needed to tend to Daris and Corom and Helem. It was the only way he could think to begin the healing process.

No," he said. "They were my friends. I will see that they are laid to rest."

"It will be as you say, my son," she said.

Jase gave her one last smile, then looked to the Dainin. "Come, my friends, let's not keep our new allies waiting."

"Yes, *Mith'elre Chon*," Ohran said, then embraced all Seven Gifts and effortlessly opened a Veilgate into the Grand Hall of the *Nar'shein* Chieftains.

Brysia watched the Veilgate to Dainin close behind her son, then turned to Galiena and the others. "I'm worried about Jase," she said. "He's hurting. I can see it in his eyes no matter how hard he tries to hide it."

"He'll work through it," Seth said. "He always does."

"Yes," Brysia said, "by internalizing it. It isn't healthy."

"Would you prefer he lash out?" Seth asked. "Because I've seen him do that, and it isn't pretty. Tetrica is still on edge after what he did to the Con'Kumen chapter house there."

"Of course I don't want him to lash out," she said, her frustration growing. "But I'm worried that if he internalizes too much, all the pent up emotion will eventually break free of its own accord, regardless of what we want or what Jase intends. And it might happen at the most inopportune time."

"I'm certain that is what Aethon Fairimor is hoping for," Ammorin said. He and Pattalla had chosen to remain in Trian instead of joining the other *Nar'shein* in the Grand Hall, and Brysia was grateful for their willingness to continue acting as her warders. She felt much safer with them in the palace.

"I have no doubt that is his intention," she said. "Which is why I want to know what we can do to protect Jase from more of this kind of harm."

"Short of ending the war," Seth said, "not much. Sorry to be a pessimist, but others he cares for will undoubtedly be killed in the coming days." He looked at the spot where Jase had departed through the Veilgate. "And that boy cares for everyone."

"His compassion is what qualifies him to be the *Mith'elre Chon*," Galiena said, her golden eyes sparkling with fondness. She looked at each of them in turn before continuing. "But he isn't internalizing this the way he once did, when he would blame himself for not doing enough or curse fate for doing too much.

"Is he hurting? Yes. But he is taking ownership of that pain. It's his way of recommitting himself to do what he can to keep things like this from happening again. Aethon Fairimor is a fool if he thinks he can break Jase. Be at ease, Queen of Kelsa. Your son is stronger than you are giving him credit for."

"I agree," Ammorin said. "And these recent events will only make him stronger."

Brysia sighed resignedly. The mother in her wanted to argue the point further, but she knew Ammorin was right. Jase had been through much the past few weeks, and had become a better person because of it.

"*Folomei suzu ke un mesho'liel*," she said in the Old Tongue, then smiled in spite of her doubts. "Daris used to say that whenever I felt things were more difficult than they should be."

"What does it mean?" Sheymi asked.

Brysia felt a rush of gratitude for her former warder as she answered, "The hottest fires make the best steel."

# CHAPTER 22

## A Gathering of Nations

TALIA'S HEART RACED WITH EXCITEMENT as she moved through the Veilgate into the Grand Hall of the *Nar'shein* and found it even more magnificent than she had imagined. She could feel Jase's wonder through the *sei'vaiya*, but none of what he was feeling made it to his face. He'd come here as the *Mith'elre Chon* to welcome newfound allies. There wasn't time to gawk at the surroundings, no matter how impressive they were. And they were impressive—never in her life had she seen such a perfect blend of nature and the domestic.

The Grand Hall wasn't a hall at all, but a forested expanse beneath some of the largest Laureola trees Talia had ever seen. The seven giant trees were evenly spaced around the perimeter of the expanse and had picket-like lines of smaller trees growing in the spaces between. The branches of those smaller trees had obviously been wrought upon by the Power and had grown together into a vibrant latticework draped with flowering ivies and vines. It was a sheltering, protective wall as impenetrable as any constructed of stone, and it was much more beautiful.

High overhead, the branches of the Laureola trees had also grown together in such away as to form a leafy dome-like canopy dense enough to shelter the area from even the heaviest of rains. Talia stared at the living ceiling in wonder, then dropped her eyes to take in the vastness of the Grand Hall itself. It was easily five times the size of Fairimor Dome.

There were a variety of flowers and ferns, shrubs, and small trees throughout the hall, but they weren't confined in beds or arranged in any particular fashion like those in the gardens of the Overlook. This place wasn't a garden so much as an extension of the natural environment. Aside from the Power-wrought walls and canopy, most everything on the forest floor had been left to grow where and how they would. The only exceptions were the bloodleaf oaks.

A ring of the beautiful trees grew near the center of the hall, and it was obvious that they, too, had been wrought upon by the Power. Already short and stocky by nature, their massively thick trunks had been further shaped into chairs and benches sufficient to hold a Dainin.

The wonder she could feel coming from Jase spiked when he noticed the trees, and some of what he was trying to conceal made it to his face. "Now that is awesome," he whispered.

Two of the chair-like trees were occupied, and Ohran started toward them, following a well-worn footpath through the undergrowth. The two *Nar'shein* —Talia supposed they were Chieftains Hammishin and Paddishor—rose as Ohran neared and dropped to one knee.

"We see you, Chieftain Peregam," the fiercer-looking of the two said.

"I see you, Chieftain Paddishor," Ohran said in return. "Rise so that we may welcome our new allies."

The two Chieftains did as instructed, and Paddishor turned to address Jase.

"I see you, *Mith'elre Chon*," he said, offering a deep bow to show his respect. Chieftain Hammishin did likewise.

"I see you, *Nar'shein*," Jase said, addressing them both. "And I want to thank you for your efforts these past few days. This new alliance comes at a critical time in the war."

"This was the Earthmother's doing," Hammishin said. "We simply followed Her whisperings as they came upon us."

"All the more reason for thanks," Jase told them. "Because those whisperings are growing fainter by the day as She weakens." His voice was calm, but the sudden surge of fear that reached Talia through the love-bond told her how much this terrified him. Even with all the recent talk of how the Earthsoul was nearing total collapse, it was now that she realized how desperate the situation really was. And that meant he'd done a better job of concealing his emotions than she'd thought possible.

"No," he told her, drawing surprised looks from Hammishin and Paddishor. "This is a newfound terror."

Ohran chuckled at the Chieftains' reactions. "They share a love-bond," he explained. "Apparently, Talia's whisperings are less faint than those of the Earthmother."

"Another thing for which to be thankful," Gideon said, and his voice made Talia jump. She'd become so engrossed in her surroundings that she'd completely forgotten he'd come with them. He winked at her as he added, "She keeps Jase from doing anything rash."

Talia gave Jase a disapproving stare. "If only that were true."

Jase grinned at her before turning back to the *Nar'shein*. "It is time to meet these new allies," he told them, and Talia watched excitedly as a shimmering Veilgate opened and the first of the Rosdans stepped through.

A slender, but well-muscled people, they had dark brown skin and eyes which ranged in color from a deep green to the palest grey. The women wore their long, jet-black hair in dozens of thin, beaded braids. The men's hair was short and had intricate patterns shaved along the sides and back. Both men and women wore tight-fitting clothing in a variety of colorful patterns. Some of the patterns resembled the spots or stripes of cats while others had an insect-like look to them. Like the Dainin, their feet were bare.

They fanned out through the undergrowth to make room for those who were to follow, and Talia marveled at how quick and precise their movements were. It was like watching brightly colored versions of Elvan *Bero'thai*.

"I was thinking the same thing," Jase whispered, and she squeezed his hand to acknowledge that she'd heard him. Her eyes, however, never left the Rosdans. They were some of the most beautiful people she'd ever seen.

When Jase squeezed her hand, she knew he'd heard that last thought as well.

Talia kept count as best she could, and by the time the Veilgate slid closed in a silent flash of blue light, she had reached seventy-three. Before she had time to consider what those numbers would mean in the upcoming battles, a second Veilgate opened into Glenda.

Even though the Glendan people shared the lower half of the Jyndar Continent with Rosda, they couldn't have been more different in appearance. With hair so blonde it bordered on Meleki white, they had bright blue eyes and pale skin. Tall and very heavily muscled, the men wore loose fitting shirts and trousers of a soft, lightweight material. The colors were soft as well and were without pattern or other ornamentation. The Glendan women were strikingly beautiful in spite of being almost as heavily muscled as the men, and each wore a light-colored blouse and skirts which had been divided for riding.

As the Glendans entered the Grand Hall, they sought out Ohran with their eyes and each touched two fingers to his or her forehead before tracing the symbol for Eliara above their hearts. The gesture was the highest show of respect in Glendan culture and served as both a greeting and a prayer.

As the Glendans moved away from the Veilgate, the Rosdans welcomed them into their midst with open arms. Yes, their nations had been staunch allies since the early days of the New World—united in their fight against Tamban aggression—but Talia knew that what she was witnessing went beyond political alliances and trade agreements. These people were brothers and sisters in the Power. They were Children of *Ta'shaen*.

When the Veilgate to Glenda finally closed, the number of Power-wielders in the Grand Hall had doubled. The sight sent a rush of excitement through Talia, and she looked at Jase to find him smiling. The pain and anger and frustration he'd been feeling earlier had been replaced by a feeling of hope. She could feel it as strongly as if it were her own.

"Welcome, Children of *Ta'shaen*," Ohran said, his strong voice filling the Grand Hall like a sudden rumble of thunder. "And thank you for answering the call of the

Earthmother. I am Ohran Peregam, Chief of the *Nar'shein Yahl.*" He let his eyes move over them briefly before continuing. "I know that coming to the Nine Lands was a sacrifice—for you, your families and friends, and your countries."

"No sacrifice is too great for the Earthsoul," one of the Rosdan women said. Her manner of speech and accent were strange to Talia's ears, but there was an element of beauty in the way the words seemed to bounce off the woman's tongue. She was older than most of those with her, as evidenced by the hints of grey in her dark braids. "But we did not leave our own people unprotected. Those of us who remained behind will use the new wieldings taught to us by your *Nar'shein* to protect our people from the demons being loosed by the collapse of the Veil."

"We would have joined you sooner," a Glendan male said, "if we'd had the knowledge of Veilgates. We had discussed coming to the Nine Lands by ship, but knew we would not reach you in time to help." His accent and manner of speech were as different from the Rosdan's as was his physical appearance. The words were sharper, crisper, and less musical sounding.

"You are here now," Ohran told them. "And that is what matters."

The Rosdan woman who'd spoken took a half step forward, her face bright with excitement as she looked from Ohran to Gideon and then back. "We were told by your Chieftains that the *Mith'elre Chon* has come. Is this him?" Her eyes returned to Gideon.

Ohran chuckled as he placed a hand on Gideon's shoulder. "This is Gideon Dymas," he said. "And while he has many titles—Guardian of the Blue Flame, *El'Kali*, the Soldier of God, and the Defender of Kelsa, to name a few—*Mith'elre Chon* isn't one of them."

He turned and gestured to Jase, a broad smile on his weathered face. "This young man is the *Mith'elre Chon.*"

If the new arrivals were surprised at how young Jase was, they kept it from their faces. Even the woman who had mistakenly assumed it was Gideon managed to keep her face smooth.

"All hail the *Mith'elre Chon,*" she shouted, and it was echoed by the rest of her people. The Glendans, however, simply repeated the silent show of respect they'd given to Ohran upon arriving, and seventy plus Dymas touched fingers to forehead before tracing the symbol for Eliara above their hearts.

Jase released Talia's hand and stepped forward to greet them. "Welcome to the Army of the Gifted," he told them. "And thank you for coming to our aid. It is not an accident that you arrived at this time. We've suffered serious losses in the past few days which your arrival will help to fill. You have restored our hope that this war can be won."

The two who had spoken left their respective groups and moved to stand before Jase. The Glendan offered his hand, then bowed deeply when Jase took it in his. "I am Keenan Nolan," he said. "Captain of the Glendan Blood Guard in the city of Raelvin. My life is yours to command."

"Thank you for coming," Jase said, then released his hand as the Rosdan woman stepped close. Smiling, she clasped him by the shoulders then kissed him on both of his cheeks.

"I am Quintella Zakeya," she said, her bright green eyes sparkling, "mother of seven and grandmother of twenty-eight."

"A noble profession," he told her. "Thank you for coming. It must have been difficult for you to leave so many family members behind."

She showed her teeth in a wide smile. "Not all of them stayed in Rosda," she said. "Two of my daughters and six of my grandchildren came with me. All of them are *Shomei*." Her grin widened. "'tis the Rosdan word for Dymas."

A mix of admiration and amusement reached Talia through the love-bond, and she cast a sideways glance at Jase to find him smiling at Quintella. "An even greater sacrifice, then," he told her. "May the Earthsoul protect your loved ones in the days to come."

"May She protect all of us," Quintella said in return.

Jase looked at Keenan. "What is the Glendan word for Dymas?"

"*Valhan*," he answered. "But we are in your lands, so Dymas will do."

Jase nodded, then looked at both of them in turn. "There is much I would say to your people," he said. "If they will hear the words of one so young."

When they both stiffened, he grinned at them, and the amusement present in the *sei'vaiya* grew stronger. "I saw how you were looking at Gideon," he whispered. "And I don't fault you at all." He leaned forward conspiratorially. "For the longest time I thought *he* would be the *Mith'elre Chon*. Imagine my surprise when it turned out to be me."

Quintella's broad smile returned. "That must have been quite a day for you," she whispered in return.

"It had its moments," Jase said, then looked beyond her and Keenan to their people. "May I?"

Nodding, they turned to face their people as Jase took a step forward to address them. There was a short silence before he spoke, during which time Talia felt the *sei'vaiya* grow quiet as Jase wrapped himself in the calming effects of *Jiu*. It didn't completely eliminate the emotional connection—it just softened the intensity of what he was feeling. Of what *she* could feel of what he was feeling.

"Children of *Ta'shaen*," he said, and the effect was immediate. Curiosity transformed into wonder, then into awe and a profound sense of respect. They knew they were looking at the *Mith'elre Chon* as surely as if they'd sensed it through the Power.

The thought sent a rush of excitement through her. *Perhaps they had.*

"I am Jase Fairimor," he continued, "son of Brysia Fairimor, High Queen of Kelsa. And as Chief Peregam has said, the *Mith'elre Chon*."

Then, just as he'd done with the Rhiven in Fairimor Dome, he held them captive with his presence as he explained the events of the past few days and weeks.

The feeling of pride Gideon felt as he listened to his son address the newly arrived Dymas very nearly brought tears to his eyes, and probably would have if the topic of discussion had been something other than Death's Third March.

Jase spoke matter-of-factly, detailing the defeat at the eastern rim, the loss of Fulrath, and how all of it had been facilitated by the Rhiven and their Dragon Gates. He spoke also of Tamba's involvement, the recent arrival of the demonspawn from Kunin, and Shadan's relentless march across the plateau.

"By tomorrow evening," he continued, "they will be in position to open another Dragon Gate, and we believe it is their intent to do so. They will be in range to put an army behind ours, thus pinning us against Talin Plateau. Or they might simply move directly to Trian Plateau, which would put the Kelsan Mountain range between us and them. If they do that, there is nothing to stop them from marching directly on Trian."

He paused briefly as he let his eyes move over them. "We need to prevent them from opening a Dragon Gate for either purpose," he said. "And that's where some of you come in." He turned and motioned for Gideon to join him.

"But since Gideon Dymas will be overseeing this operation, I will let him tell you what this is to look like."

Gideon stepped forward, slightly caught off guard by the invitation, but eager to address his new allies. "The Rhiven who have joined our cause will contend with their traitorous brethren. It will be up to us to keep the Power-wielders, K'rrosha, and demonspawn off them while they do. Stepping into the heart of Shadan's army is going to get really ugly really fast, so this is a volunteer mission only."

Quintella gave an amused laugh, her beaded braids clicking softly as she did. "None of us are here against our will," she said. "We volunteered the moment we stepped through the Veilgate." All across the gathering, people of both races nodded their heads in agreement.

"We are here to fight, El'kali," Keenan said. "Send us where you will."

"To the front lines, then," Gideon said, and beside him Jase nodded.

"I will join you all tomorrow," Jase told them. "Until then, you are in good hands."

Ta'shaen came alive as Jase opened a large Veilgate in the grassy area centering the ring of Blood Oaks. A second smaller wielding by Jase wrapped him and Talia and Gideon in a small ward against eavesdropping. "They're all yours, Father," he said.

A wave of emotion washed over Gideon at Jase's use of the word father. It was the first time since the truth came out that Jase had addressed him as such. The urge to hug his son warred with the need to keep things businesslike, so he simply reached over and placed a hand on Jase's shoulder. "I won't disappoint you," he said with a smile.

Jase chuckled fondly. "You never do. Worry me, yes. But never disappoint."

He gave his son's shoulder a squeeze, then lowered his hand and turned to the army of Dymas gathered before him. "Follow me," he said, striding toward the gate. "We have rogue Dragons to kill."

When the last of the Rosdans had passed through the Veilgate, Jase let it close and released the Power. He looked at Talia and found her smiling at him. The feeling of approval flowing toward him through the *sei'vaiya* was strong.

"What?" he asked, even though he'd already sensed what she was thinking.

"He needed to hear that," she said. "I'm proud of you for saying it." She glanced around guardedly. "I trust there was a ward in place to keep that from everyone else's ears."

"It's still in place," he told her, stepping near and taking her hands. "So if there is anything you would like to say, feel free."

She glanced at Ohran who was watching them with a quizzical stare. "It can wait," she said. "I wouldn't want the Dainin to think we were being rude."

"This is why I bring you with me," he said. "Without you I would have no manners at all."

*Without me you would be dead.*

"I heard that," he told her, then let the ward drop and turned to Ohran and the other Chieftains.

"Thank you for all that you have done," he told them. "Without the Dainin, this war would have already been lost."

"A bit of an overstatement," Ohran said. "But you are welcome."

He dropped to one knee and looked Jase in the eyes, his weathered face a mask of seriousness. "The *Nar'shein* will continue to seek out lost temples. Your assignment—and it comes from the Earthmother—is to make sure you are healthy enough to take up a Blood Orb when one is found."

"What are you saying?" Jase asked. "That I should not take part in any more battles?"

"That is exactly what I am saying," Ohran said. "At least not to the extent you have been. You are too valuable to risk in these lesser conflicts. Your death would give Maeon the victory in spite of what the rest of us do. But death isn't the only danger. If you are too weak to take up an Orb when one is found because you've spent yourself as you did the other day, Maeon's victory will be just as complete."

He knew from the feelings coming through the love-bond that Talia agreed with Ohran, and he glanced at her briefly before looking back at the Chieftain. The thought of sitting back while others fought and bled and died was abhorrent to him, but he knew there was wisdom in Ohran's words. "I will heed your advice," he said. "When an Orb is found, I will be ready."

Pacing slowly in front of the cabinet housing the Blue Flame Scepter, Brysia occasionally glanced at the talisman's shimmering blue gem and thought about how drastically things had changed since Jase had turned it over to her. In her short time as High Queen, she'd experienced the invasion of her nation by Death's Third March, the crushing defeat of the Kelsan army and the fall of Fulrath, the arrival of rogue Dragons and demonspawn—the list went on. And it was long and bloody.

She realized she'd balled her hands into fists and forced herself to relax.

*Look for the good*, she told herself. *Not everything has been bad.*

She and Talia had survived the assassination attempt by Stalix Geshiann. Jase and Gideon had survived the opening battles with Shadan's army. Galiena had arrived with an army of Rhiven. The Dainin had rallied Dymas from Glenda and Rosda. The evacuation of Trian was proceeding smoothly. And....

She sighed. And all of it could change tomorrow when Gideon led the attack against Galiena's traitorous brethren. It could change in the next minute should the Earthsoul suddenly fail.

"You look like you just ate a wormy apple," Seth said from beside her, and she jumped at the sound of his voice. She looked over to find him watching her from the end of the cabinet. How he managed to move so quietly gave her fits, and she frowned at him.

"You shouldn't sneak up on people," she scolded. "It isn't polite."

"I've been standing here for five minutes," he told her, the faint hint of a smile visible beneath his mustache. "Long enough to see that you are doing exactly what you were worried Jase was doing."

She stopped pacing. "And what is that?"

"Internalizing your emotions. I've seen that same look on Gideon's face when he was taking the troubles of the world upon himself. I've seen it in Jase's, too. Apparently it runs in the family."

"I wasn't internalizing," she told him. "I was just... thinking."

He grunted. "Those must have been some pretty powerful thoughts."

"Is there something you wanted to say to me?"

He didn't answer immediately but let his eyes move deliberately across the room. "Do you see that?" he said softly. "It is proof that we are not alone. Proof that *you* are not alone in this."

Turning, she followed his gaze. The library half of the room was quiet save for a whispered conversation between Railen and Sheymi. They sat side by side on one of the love-seats, so absorbed in their discussion that they were oblivious to Galiena and Idoman listening from across the Blue Flame rug. Idoman wore a smile, and Galiena's yellow-gold eyes glimmered with amusement.

A short distance away, Beraline and Marithen sat at a small table in contemplative silence as they searched the ancient texts for information about the lost Temples of Elderon. Cassia and Andil were at another table, doing the same.

On the far side of the room, Ammorin and Pattalla were at the dining table enjoying a meal with Lavin Dium and a number of *Bero'thai*. Dozens more *Bero'thai* stood watch throughout the room, their faces alert and protective. Medwin Tas and the Shizu Javan Galatea were also at the dining table, though when they had arrived, Brysia couldn't say. She could tell by the serious looks on their faces as they spoke to Elison that they were giving a report on the progress of the evacuation.

"This is just a glimpse," Seth said. "There are tens of thousands more who are helping bear the burden of this war. And these allies—your allies—come from every nation save Tamba, Arkania, and Kunin. When was the last time nine of the twelve races were united in a single cause?"

"Never," Brysia said, then smiled her thanks. "And there are ten if you count the Rhiven." She reached out her hand, and her smile widened when he took it. "Thank you, Seth, for readjusting my perspective."

"Considering all the times you've readjusted mine, it was the least I could do." He turned her in the direction of the dining table. "Come. I've noticed you haven't eaten much today. Gideon would never forgive me if I allowed you to faint for want of food."

As they passed by the sofas, Railen and Sheymi joined them and were followed by Galiena and Idoman a moment later. The young Dymas General was weak on his feet, but Galiena supported him with a strength that belied her slender human form. Idoman smiled gratefully as she helped him ease himself down into a chair.

"I'm starving," he said, his voice still not much more than a whisper. Eyes sparkling with fondness for the young man, Galiena took a seat next to him and began loading food onto a plate for him.

They were halfway through their meal, when a Veilgate opened in front of the fireplace and Jase and Talia walked through from beyond.

"Oh, perfect," Jase said as he and Talia started for the table. "I'm starving."

"I've never met a young man who wasn't," Sheymi said, casting a sideways look at Railen. He grinned at her from around a mouthful of ham.

When the Veilgate slid closed without anyone else coming through, Brysia felt a rush of disappointment. Her husband, it seemed, wouldn't be joining them.

Some of what she was thinking must have shown on her face because Jase spoke again. "Gideon took the Glendan and Rosdan Dymas to the Kelsan camp." Pausing, he pulled a chair out for Talia. "They will engage the Agla'Con and other Power-wielders in Shadan's army while Galiena and her people deal with the Dragon Gates."

"That sounded like you won't be taking part in the battle," Idoman said, some of the weakness gone from his voice. A bit of color had returned to his face as well, a result, perhaps, of the food.

Jase exchanged looks with Talia, then looked back to Idoman. "I've been counseled not to."

"By who?" Brysia asked, relieved by the announcement. "I must thank this person for finally talking some sense into you."

"I said I've been *counseled* not to," Jase said. "I never said I *wouldn't* participate."

Talia narrowed her eyes at him. "But you told Ohran—"

"That I would be ready to take up an Orb when one is found." He popped a piece of fruit into his mouth, and it bulged in his cheek as he smiled. "And I agreed not to risk myself in lesser conflicts. This isn't a lesser conflict."

The frown that appeared on Talia's face mirrored Brysia's, but Jase continued before either of them could speak.

"Don't worry," he said, looking at each of them in turn. "I'm not going to overexert myself or do anything dangerous. Well, overly dangerous. Just *being* the *Mith'elre Chon* is dangerous. Today's events are proof of that." He looked at the bodies of Galam and Gillium still wrapped in blankets near the door and his face grew solemn. "And being here didn't prevent them from dying. If anything, it put them in harm's way."

"Nothing of what happened here today is your fault," Brysia told him.

"Of course it isn't my fault," Jase said. "But Aethon targeted me specifically—no one here can deny that. Hopefully by making my presence felt on the front lines, I can turn his attention away from Trian."

"But even if you do," Brysia told him, "there are no guarantees that similar attacks won't happen here."

"Precisely why you and Talia will be going to Andlexces," Jase said. "You said yourself you want to search the archives. Now is the perfect time."

"I agree," Elison said. "And I think Cassia and Andil should join you. And Beraline and Marithen as well. They can help you in your search of the archives."

Brysia was tempted to argue if for no other reason than to show she wouldn't be bullied out of her home, but she knew there was wisdom in the plan. At least the part involving her going to Andlexces. She still wasn't convinced Jase should risk himself at the front.

"We will leave this evening," she said. "But I expect updates on everything that transpires here."

"You are only a Veilgate away," Elison told her. "Unless you prefer us to use Communicator Stones."

"Veilgates," she said. "I prefer speaking to you face to face."

"Then it's settled," Jase said. "I'll escort you to Andlexces once Galam and Gillium have been laid to rest."

"What is your plan for them?" Elison asked, his eyes sympathetic.

"They've earned a place in the Fairimor Gardens with the other heroes who've died for this family," Jase said. "Any who wish to join me are welcome."

"Galam and Gillium didn't die for this family alone," Brysia told him. She glanced at Railen and Sheymi, then let her eyes move over Lavin and the *Bero'thai*, before settling on Ammorin and Pattalla. "They were servants of the Earthsoul fighting for all our nations," she continued, turning her attention back to Jase. "It would be fitting if we all joined you to pay our respects."

"Thank you," he said, and Brysia didn't need the effects of a love-bond to know what he was thinking. She could see it in his eyes. Galiena had been right: This was

Jase's way of taking ownership of his grief and pain. This would help him heal. As his mother, helping him along that path was the least she could do.

# CHAPTER 23

## The Shrine of Uri

*THIS HAS TO BE IT.*

Frowning impatiently, Thorac stood in a sheltering cluster of rocks near the top of a steep ridgeline overlooking a boulder-strewn valley. He was too high to be seen by any of those below, but he kept a wall of rock at his back as he moved to a new vantage point, careful not to silhouette himself against the sky as he paced the now familiar trail he'd beaten with his impatience. This was the right place, he decided. It had to be.

Ringed all the way around by a spine of steep, rocky ridges, the valley looked like a bowl—a poorly-made ceramic bowl that had shattered in the kiln while being fired. And it was barren, even for this godforsaken country—as if that same fire had forever scorched away everything green. Nothing grew anywhere in the valley or on its surrounding slopes. No bitterbrush. No sawgrass. No thorny oak. Nothing.

And yet there was a surprising amount of cover for the *Bero'thai* even with the lack of foliage. Boulder fields, fins of twisted rock, fissures of various depths and lengths—all had allowed the light-footed Elvan soldiers to move down into the valley with ease. He'd lost sight of them just minutes after their departure yesterday afternoon.

*Yesterday*, he thought, his frown deepening. *They should have been back by now.*

His eyes moved to the southernmost end of the valley and the pyramid-shaped structure that might possibly be the Shrine of Uri. Chieftain Kia'Kal had found it yesterday with one of the small Veilgates he and the other Dainin used as peep-holes from the sky. The entire group had journeyed here through a regular Veilgate not long afterward.

The shrine—Thorac was certain it was one—butted up against a tower-like monolith of dark grey stone several hundred feet high. Like the rest of the valley, the monolith was broken and scarred, as if it too had shattered during the firing. Far out in the valley, chunks of rock that looked as if they might have once been part of the monolith were scattered about, and Thorac estimated that some were four, possibly five miles away from the source.

Something catastrophic had happened here, a literal wrath-of-God destruction that had forever altered the nature of this place, both physically and in the unseen world of *Ta'shaen*. He pursed his lips. *The Defiling. It has to be.*

He sighed. As convinced as he was personally, Emma had insisted that they couldn't proceed until the *Bero'thai* confirmed this was the right place. And for confirmation they needed a look inside the pyramid structure. Unfortunately, the Power-wrought peep holes were out of the question. There might very well be *Shel'tui* or demonspawn present who would sense the use of the Power. The *Bero'thai* were having to do this the hard way.

Thorac studied the shrine and tried to imagine what might be going on inside. Yes, the *Bero'thai* were good, but one misstep at any point during their investigation would alert the enemy. Loharg would know they were here.

He stilled his worries as best he could and continued to watch the shrine. That nothing had erupted into fiery chaos was good. It meant Captain Haslem's men had infiltrated the shrine successfully or that there were no *Shel'tui* present. Still, it was bloody-well taking them forever.

"Patience, Thorac," Emma said from behind him, and he shot her an irritated look before returning to his perusal of the valley. Behind him, Emma whispered something unintelligible, and Jeymi and Endil laughed softly.

Thorac kept his back to them, unwilling to give them the pleasure. Raising his spyglass as if he hadn't heard, he took another look at the shrine. *It has to be it.*

Pyramid in shape but terraced with broad landings at each level, it was seven stories high. What had once been the crisp edges and sharp even symmetry of ancient architecture was broken and worn, and there were gaping holes in the walls on nearly every level. It seemed a miracle that it was even standing—especially when it had obviously been the epicenter of whatever had destroyed the valley. *More proof this is the right place.*

A smooth expanse of black stone several hundred feet across fronted the entrance to the shrine. It had been cleared of the boulders littering the rest of the valley, and those had been stacked along the perimeter to form a wall of sorts. Further out, perhaps a half mile or so, four towers stood like sentinels, marking the corners of the shrine's grounds. Constructed of blocks hewn from pieces blown free of the grey monolith, they rose to a height of forty or so feet and were topped with misshapen, beastly statues reminiscent of the Sons of Uri.

"How much more proof do we need?" he mumbled, then cringed inwardly when he realized he'd spoken aloud. Behind him, the whispers resumed and were followed by soft laughter.

Thorac pretended not to notice. Instead, he swung the spyglass northward across the valley and the dark splotches where thousands of Kunin had gathered in camps. Clustered here and there among the boulder fields and fins of rock, each camp sported a tribal banner which rippled in the breeze above it.

And more tribes were arriving by the hour. Atop Zotam and on foot, they streamed into the valley through several narrow canyons to the north and west. Like dark water, they were slowly filling up the misshapen bowl. The first to arrive had stopped well short of the shrine's grounds, apparently wary of drawing too near. But why?

Even more important: Why were they here at all? And from so many different tribes? Did they know Loharg was coming and that he had possession of a Blood Orb of Elsa? If so, it meant there were *Shel'tui* or demonspawn among them and Loharg had used the Power to send word ahead of him.

*Or*, his mind whispered pessimistically, *they have gathered for some completely unrelated reason, and this is the wrong place.*

He shook the thought away. No. This *was* the Shrine of Uri.

Soft-soled footsteps sounded beside him, and he lowered the spyglass to find Thex Landoral. The Dymas could move as quietly as a *Bero'thai* when he wanted to, so Thorac suspected the noise had been deliberate so as not to startle him.

"Dymas," Thorac greeted.

"What do you think?" Thex asked.

Thorac studied the valley floor a moment before answering. "They know Loharg is coming," he answered. "This is the right place."

"I think so, too," Thex said, his eyes on the gathering Kunin.

Thorac kept his impatience in check. "Then what are we waiting for?" he asked, pleased with how calm he sounded. Apparently, Emma had heard Thex's agreement as well—evidenced by the lack of whispering and laughter—and she joined them a moment later.

"We need to know *exactly* where the altar room is," she said. "It will be difficult enough opening a Veilgate into that godforsaken place. We don't want to go in blind." She grunted sourly. "Well, more blind anyway."

Thorac arched an eyebrow at her. "Just how bad is it here?"

"The worst I've ever experienced," Emma answered, and Thex nodded. "Our spiritual vision isn't just obscured here like in other places in Kunin. It has been obliterated."

"I have never experienced anything so dark," Thex said. "We are indeed blind, General. None of us can see anything further than ten or so feet away. Even then it is murky. I..." he shook his head. "I will admit it frightens me."

A stab of dread washed through Thorac, but he fought it down and asked, "The Power?"

"We can still wield," Emma told him, placing a hand on his arm reassuringly. "And we can still feel when others wield. We just can't see anything through our Awareness. That's why I need to know where the altar room is. I will need to have

Loharg in view of my natural eyes when I strike."

Thorac frowned at her. "You said *I* that time. Who decided you were going in?"

"I did," Endil said, moving up to them. He held Jeymi's hand, and the look he wore showed that arguing the decision would be useless. Jeymi's frown confirmed it. She'd already tried and lost.

He looked back to Emma. "Who is going in with you?"

"That will be decided once we know if this is even the right place," Endil answered. "It will also be determined by how large the altar room is."

"But you are going, correct?"

Endil nodded.

Thorac looked at Jeymi. "And you?"

Her frown deepened. "Like Endil said, it depends on how much room there is inside."

"I see," Thorac said, then turned his attention back to the shrine below. So, Jeymi lost that argument too, did she? That would have been something to witness. Oh, he knew Endil was just looking to protect his young love, but he seemed to have forgotten that Jeymi was far more capable of protecting him than he was of protecting her. A little intervention might be necessary.

"If this shrine is the defiled Temple of Elderon, it will be fashioned similarly to those in Trian and Andlexces," Thorac began, "the altar room will be large enough to hold a small army of Dainin. You won't need to go in alone."

"Nor should he be allowed to," a voice said, and they all turned as Captain Haslem appeared with several of his *Bero'thai*. They slipped from among the boulders as silently as ghosts. "There is only one way in or out of the altar room," he continued. "If the shrine is overrun by the enemy, the only way out will be through Veilgate."

"So, this is the Shrine of Uri?" Endil asked.

Captain Haslem nodded. "Yes. We found prayers to Maeon in most of the rooms. Some were written in blood. Others were carved into the walls. All were signed by the Sons of Uri."

"That doesn't necessarily mean this is the right place," Emma said. "The Sons of Uri write similar things in their watchtowers and warrens."

"I know," Captain Haslem said, "but we found more than just their psychotic scribblings. There are Old World symbols carved into the stonework in nearly every room. Loharg and his illiterate filth would not have recognized them for what they were, which is probably why they are still there. They likely thought the carvings were for ornamentation."

"And if you want even more proof," Chief Kia'kal said as he materialized from the terrain, "there is a *chorazin* T'rii Gate in the midst of that boulder field." He pointed to an expanse of particularly large rocks a mile beyond the shrine's perimeter. Thorac watched the giant man in amazement. How the Dainin managed to move as quietly and secretively as the *Bero'thai* was beyond him.

Captain Haslem was watching Kia'kal with the same look of wonder. Finally, he smiled and looked back to Thorac. "We found the altar room," he said. "It..." he hesitated, looking at Emma and Jeymi before continuing. "It has indeed been desecrated. The Altar of Elsa lies in ruin and there are writings and... remains."

"Remains?" Endil asked.

"Human sacrifice," Emma said, then turned to Thorac. "You have your proof, General."

*I had my proof long before this,* he told her irritably. Smiling to cover the thought, he turned to Endil. "How would you like to play this?"

Endil scratched his cheek as he considered. He'd discussed several options with Thorac last night and again this morning, but now that the time had come to make a decision, he seemed to be having second thoughts. Undoubtedly, his hesitation had something to do with Jeymi. He looked at Captain Haslem.

"What are our chances of sneaking back in on foot?" he asked.

"Excellent now that the *Shel'tui* priests and their guards have been eliminated," the Elvan captain said. "We hid their bodies in one of the lesser chambers. I have men positioned at the shrine's entrance to intercept any others who might venture in ahead of Loharg." He glanced at the position of the morning sun. "I could have everyone inside by midday."

"I would advise against going in on foot," Emma said. "We cannot risk being seen by the Kunin. A Veilgate will be faster."

Thorac narrowed his eyes at her. "I thought you said you couldn't see anything in there. How exactly will you know where to go?"

"With this," she said, and a small hole opened in the air in front of her. "I can use one now that the *Shel'tui* are dead. Thank you, Captain Haslem, for that." Leaning close she peered through. "Where is the altar room in relation to the broken fountain on the ground level?" she asked.

"Almost directly above on the sixth level," Captain Haslem answered. "There are shafts cut in the ceiling and walls which allow light in."

The small Veilgate closed, and a second one opened almost immediately in the same spot. She peered through. "Found it." The tiny window closed, and Emma turned to Endil. "We have some decisions to make."

This time Endil didn't hesitate. "Emma, Jeymi, and I will wait for Loharg in the altar room," Endil said, and Jeymi relaxed visibly. The earlier look of worry on her face was replaced by steely determination. She *would* protect Endil, Thorac knew, as she had done so many times before.

Endil saw the look in her eyes and smiled at her. "Everyone else," he continued, "will take positions outside or wherever you think gives us the best tactical advantage. On the shrine's grounds or just beyond them where there is enough cover."

"It is unlikely that Loharg will enter the shrine alone," Chieftain Kia'Kal said, going to one knee so he could look Endil in the eyes. "The Sons of Uri are many, and Loharg's brothers will want to be part of this second defiling. Some of my *Nar'shein* and I will accompany you inside."

Endil smiled. "I would like that."

"A wise decision," Thex said. "The rest of the Dymas will take up positions to the east and west of the shrine's grounds. We will engage any *Shel'tui* or Kunin who attempt to come to the aid of their demonspawned masters."

"I will need a few Power-wielders to stay with me," Thorac told them. "And they need to be strong enough to open multiple Veilgates over a relatively short period of time."

Emma narrowed her eyes at him. "Why?"

"Because as well thought out as this plan may be," he said, "there will undoubtedly be something we haven't thought of. At the very least, Veilgates will allow the Chunin and *Bero'thai* to hit the Kunin camps from the rear. If we can turn their attention away from what is happening at the shrine by making them believe the entire valley is under attack, it will go better for those fighting at the shrine."

"I agree," Thex said. "You shall have the Dymas you need."

"Won't that be spreading our forces too thin?" Endil asked.

Thorac grunted. "We're already outnumbered a thousand to one," he said. "Thin is an understatement. But hitting them from multiple locations will give them the impression we are much larger than we really are."

"Well, it worked at the watchtowers," Endil conceded. "It might work here as well."

"If you do your job quickly enough," Thorac said, "our part in this battle might not even be necessary."

Endil grinned at him. "Is that a challenge?"

"A request," Thorac said. "As much fun as attacking a vastly superior force is for me, I would be just as happy to sit this one out."

"I'll do what I can," Endil said, then looked around at the others. "It is settled. Thorac will oversee the battle from up here, utilizing Veilgates as needed. Thex and his Dymas will guard the entrance to the shrine. Emma, Jeymi, and I will wait in the altar room while the *Nar'shein* take positions inside the shrine. As soon as I have possession of the Blood Orb we will retreat through Veilgates."

"Sounds easy enough," Jeymi said, putting some levity in her voice.

*Yes,* Thorac thought, *assuming that we overlook the part where some of us get killed.*

Instead, he turned to Emma. "When are you leaving?"

"Right now," she answered. "We'll take food and water enough for three days. If Loharg isn't here by then, he isn't coming."

Thorac took her by the arm and looked her in the eyes. "You be careful," he told her.

She took his hand in hers. "You too, General," she said, then released him and motioned for Endil and Jeymi to follow. "Let's get our things. We have an Orb to rescue."

Thorac watched them move back into the rocks, then turned to Chieftain

Kia'Kal. "God's speed, *Nar'shein*," he said. "And good luck."

"And to you, General Shurr," the giant man said, motioning for his people to follow. They disappeared into the broken landscape as if they'd never been.

Thex gave an impressed grunt. "Amazing people, the *Nar'shein*," he said. "I couldn't have been less visible if I used the Power." He turned to Thorac. "Which is why I will have our Dymas use the Power to move to the shrine through a Veilgate. I don't want to risk being seen by the enemy any more than Emma does." With that he moved away, and Thorac was left alone with Captain Haslem.

They stood quietly for a moment, staring down at the Shrine of Uri. Finally, Captain Haslem spoke. "What are you thinking, General?"

Thorac scratched his cheek before answering. "We'll need an area large enough for our cavalries to form up," he said. "We'll move our forces off the back side of this ridgeline and see what we can find down below. The way this valley is shaped, we'll have a pretty good vantage point wherever we set up."

"I'll have my men see what they can find," the *Bero'thai* captain said. "Is there anything else?"

Thorac let his eyes move over the rival clans of Kunin, the beginnings of an idea forming in his head. "We'll need Kunin arrows," he said. "A lot of them."

Captain Haslem followed his gaze to the massing tribes of Kunin. "Do you want my men to get them for you?"

"No," Thorac said. "I will get them. But not from where you might think. Come. I need to speak with one of our Dymas. I need a Veilgate."

"Where are you going?"

"The warren we destroyed had an armory. It should have all the Kunin arrows we'll need."

Captain Haslem's curiosity was obvious. "What are you planning, General?"

Thorac chuckled. "Something devious."

As Emmarenziana Antilla stepped into the altar room of the Shrine of Uri, what little remained of her spiritual vision vanished completely. She could still *feel* the Power coursing through her as she held the Veilgate open for Endil and Jeymi, but the eyes of *Ta'shaen* were blinded. Nothing of the luminescent world she was so accustomed to seeing remained. This was indeed the epicenter of the Defiling. This was true darkness.

"Blood of Maeon," Jeymi whispered as she and Endil came through the gate.

Emma nodded. "Now you know what hell looks like," she told the young Dymas. "A complete absence of spiritual light."

She let the Veilgate slide closed, then looked up at the shafts cut at angles through the stonework of the seventh level. "At least we still have daylight, sickly as it may be. It will be enough for me to confront Loharg."

Endil slung his pack off his shoulder and rested it on his foot, unwilling to let it touch the ground. His face as he glanced around the room was pinched with disgust.

"Well, this is bloody awful," he said, wrinkling his nose. "Captain Haslem failed to mention the stench when he gave his report."

"The Sons of Uri are nothing more than animals," Emma said. "They mark their territory like the feral curs they are."

Endil shuddered. "Lovely."

"That's not all they mark," Jeymi said, pointing to the scribblings on the wall opposite them, beyond the shattered altar. "Can you read what it says?"

"Yes," Emma answered, "but I will not repeat it. This place is dark enough as it is. No need to give voice to something so vile." She moved near the remains of the altar and gazed down at it. It was hard to believe that it had once held a Blood Orb and that this room had been used as a place of worship for those Kunin who believed in Elderon.

She pursed her lips in anger. Then came the Defiling, an act of sacrilege and rebellion so great it had destroyed the ancient temple and the entire Kunin nation along with it. Her eyes moved to a second altar constructed by the Sons of Uri, and her anger turned to disgust.

A single block of dark grey stone, the altar was streaked black with dried blood, and skulls and other remnants of Loharg's atrocities littered the floor around it. Emma gave them a cursory glance before turning to survey the room.

It was indeed large as Thorac had said it would be—at least fifty or so feet wide and some thirty feet high. Pillars at intermittent intervals supported the ceiling, but it was clear from the marks on the ceiling and floor, not to mention the rubble which was strewn about, that there had once been twice as many. How the place had not collapsed completely was beyond her. Not a comforting thought considering the amount of Earthpower which would shortly be unleashed in here.

"I hope the roof holds," Endil said, echoing her thoughts. "At least until we have the Orb. Then this place can crumble into dust for all I care."

"We'll get it," Emma told him. "But we are going to need a plan." She pointed to a cluster of pillars off to the right of the door. "And an ambush point. Follow me, and I'll tell you what I have in mind."

# CHAPTER 24

## *Beyond the Wall*

ELRIEN STARED AT THE EMPTY expanse of hard-packed earth behind the Great Wall of Aridan, momentarily unsure if he believed what he was seeing. The Shadan'Ko were gone. All of them.

"They left shortly after midnight," Captain Kium told him. "Just stopped their mindless attacking of the wall and walked away north. Captain Alleilwin took a squad of *Bero'thai* to follow them, but he hasn't yet returned."

Elrien looked in the direction indicated, but the only thing visible in the predawn darkness was the fiery wedge of Mt Tabor. The violent eruptions had ceased, but rivers of magma still flowed down its southern and eastern slopes, casting an orange glow across the broken foothills beneath.

He stared at it a moment longer, then glanced eastward along the wall, following the lights of the battlements and towers as they receded into the distance. Dawn would break soon, heralding a day of unprecedented bloodshed.

He'd seen it during the night in a vision sent by the Earthsoul. Only this vision had been different than any he'd experienced before. Instead of finding himself immersed in two or three well-structured images flowing smoothly from one to the other, he'd been bombarded by a barrage of image fragments, rough and raw and disjointed. The frantic nature of the communication had frightened him almost as much as the horrible images they'd conveyed, and for a short while after waking, he'd wondered if maybe it had simply been a nightmare whipped up by his own worries and fears.

Only after immersing himself in the Power did he realize that it had indeed come from Her. Only then did he realize what the barrage of images meant.

Today, Death's Third March would reach the western rim of Talin Plateau. Today, the creature Loharg would reach the Shrine of Uri and be confronted by those sent to recapture the Blood Orb. Today, tens of thousands of lives would be lost on both sides of the conflict. And that was to say nothing of the calamities which would continue to fall upon the people of the earth as the Earthsoul neared collapse.

*And now this new problem,* he thought, looking back down at the wasteland stretching away toward Mt. Tabor. Images of the Twisted Ones often haunted his dreams, so he hadn't given those from last night all that much thought. He knew now it had been a mistake. The Earthsoul had been trying to tell him something. He tried to recall what he'd seen, but the images were elusive and jumbled.

He frowned at the darkness. Where would the Shadan'Ko have gone? And why now after centuries of attacking the wall? It couldn't be an accident—some evil was at work here. Something new to have changed the game so drastically.

Opening his Awareness, he stretched it north toward the Rift. As expected, the radiant view began to dim almost immediately, darkened by the taint left by Throy Shadan's destruction of the valley. Only now it darkened at a much faster rate than ever before. He was still well short of the Rift when the last vestiges of the ruined landscape suddenly and completely vanished from his mind's eye. With the darkness came the cold, unmistakable feeling of death.

An icy fist took him by the heart when he realized what it meant. The Veil had collapsed completely in this area.

Con'Jithar had arrived in the Valley of Amnidia.

Steeling himself, he continued to probe the darkness like a blind man feeling his way through an unfamiliar room. His suspicions were confirmed a moment later when his Awareness touched the mind of a demon.

Instinctively the demon's Awareness lashed out, and images of blood and death and killing flooded into Elrien's mind. The torn and ruined bodies of people. Farmhouses, villages, and cities in flames. Hordes of demons roaming the earth, preying on the living and feasting on the dead—a holocaust fueled by primal, blood-thirsty rage. He knew instinctively that the images were part prediction of the future, part memory of peoples and worlds already destroyed.

Elrien ripped his Awareness free of the horrifying barrage and reined it in with a shudder.

"I can see that didn't go well," Captain Kium commented.

Still prickling with disgust, Elrien turned to answer but stopped as something dark brushed his Awareness. The demon, it seemed, had pinpointed his location. And it wasn't alone. In the seconds that followed, Elrien felt six more probings, and he didn't need to open his Awareness to them to know they had come from six different demons—the mind-signatures were varied and distinct and came at him in different ways.

The knot of disgust in his chest quickly tightened into an almost crippling fear as the six Awarenesses turned into several dozen and then grew to almost a hundred.

Even with his Awareness safely wrapped in its mind-ward, it was difficult for Elrien to find his voice. "Sound the alarm," he said. "Full combat readiness. The

Great Wall is about to experience its first real test."

Captain Kium's surprise was obvious. "By what?"

Elrien couldn't stop himself from shivering as he answered. "An army from Con'Jithar."

With Jase, Seth, and Elliott at his side, Gideon strode through the Veilgate into the Kelsan camp, then let the gate slide closed behind him and released the Power. The sky was bright and cloudless, but the morning sun was still concealed behind the plateau, and the deep shadow of the towering cliffs made the air seem colder than normal for this time of year. He pulled his cloak more tightly about him as he walked.

Last night after he'd gotten the Dymas from Rosdan and Glenda settled in here, he'd returned to Trian to report to Brysia, only to find her and all the other women gone to Andlexces. Aside from Elison and the *Bero'thai* tasked with warding the inner palace, only Jase and Seth and Elliott had remained. He'd found them swapping stories of the earlier, happier days when they'd been unaware the world was dying.

He cast a sideways glance at them, envious of the times they'd had together but grateful Seth had stepped in to help fill the role of father. Daris Stodd had done his part to fill that role as well. So had Randle, and to a lesser degree Elison and Breiter. Jase was the man he was today because of their combined influence.

Jase noticed the look and raised an eyebrow at him. "What is it?"

"Just thinking about how proud I am of you and what you've been able to accomplish," he answered, careful not to trip over a tent stake as they turned the corner on a row of tents. "And how worried I am about what the next few days will bring. I—" He hesitated, unsure if he should say more. "I had some horrible dreams last night."

"Dreams or visions?" Jase asked, instantly on edge.

"Hard to say," Gideon answered, but deep down inside he suspected that what he'd seen had come from the Earthsoul. "It was different from other visions I've had. More fragmented and frantic." He shook his head. "It could just be my subconscious getting the best of me."

"I don't think so," Jase said. "Because I had them too."

They stopped walking, and Gideon looked his son in the eyes. Seth, ever the warder, put his back to them and made it clear to any who might draw too near that they weren't to be interrupted. Elliott did the same, but it was clear from the cocked angle of his head that he was listening intently.

"What did you see?" Gideon asked, and the images which had plagued his sleep flashed unbidden through his mind's eye as he waited for Jase to answer.

"Demons," Jase said. "Roaming the land in droves, killing everything they encountered and feasting on the dead. Some..." He tilted his head to the side as he tried to recapture the image. "Some attacked the earth itself, tearing deep holes in the ground as if... as if they were preparing to plant something."

He came back to himself and looked Gideon in the eyes. "Any idea what *that* might mean?"

Gideon shook his head. "No. I didn't see that last part. Demons roaming the land and killing, yes. But not that. What else did you see?"

"What else did *you* see?" Jase asked.

Elliott gave up the pretense of warding them and turned to look at Gideon expectantly.

Gideon ignored the prince as he answered. "I saw an increase in earthquakes and storms and floods and everything else which is already happening as a result of the Earthsoul dying. But like the other images they were fragmented, and I couldn't determine where any of them would happen."

Jase nodded as if he'd seen similar things, but what he said next made Gideon stiffen as if he'd just been stabbed.

"I saw a Blood Orb being defiled. It was just a glimpse so I didn't see where it was or who did the defiling." His face was lined with frustration as he added. "In fact, I'm not sure if it is yet to happen or if I glimpsed something of the past."

"Let's hope it is past," Gideon said. "I'd rather not think about what will happen if the power of a Blood Orb were to be unleashed by our enemies."

"We are starting to draw a crowd," Seth said softly, and Gideon looked around to find that several soldiers had stopped what they were doing to watch them.

Gideon took Jase by the arm, and they started walking again. "We'll finish this conversation later."

They reached the command tent a few moments later, and Teig stepped forward to greet them. "Welcome back, *El'kali*," he said, then offered a deep bow of respect for Jase. "It's good to have you here as well, *Mith'elre Chon*."

"I was thinking the same for you, Master of Spies," Jase told him. "My thanks for keeping Idoman Leda alive."

"Just helping out where I can," he said, shrugging modestly. "The young Dymas General is inside, though if you ask me, he should probably still be in a bed in Trian."

"I won't argue with that," Jase said. "But some people just don't know when to rest." He looked at each of them in turn, his eyes lingering the longest on Seth, then he added, "Present company included."

Teig pulled the tent flap aside for them, and they moved inside to find Idoman leaning on a large, makeshift table for support. His was face concentrated as he adjusted pewter pieces on a map of Talin Plateau. Railen and Sheymi were with him, but seemed less concerned with the map than with Idoman's well-being.

As Gideon neared, he saw that it was the same map Idoman had been using before the attack. Charred along one edge, it was more than a little worse for wear, having also been sliced in half by a corrupted Veilgate before being trampled by the attacking demonspawn.

Most of the pewter pieces marking various elements of Shadan's army were back in place, and they were much nearer the western rim than yesterday. The pieces representing Aethon and his Dragons were almost to the line marking the spot where Idoman believed Dragon Gates would be utilized.

"They're moving faster than anticipated," Gideon said, and Idoman nodded.

"At this rate they'll reach that mark sometime around midday."

Jase moved up to the table and ran his finger down the line. "And you are certain this is the spot?"

"Galiena believes it is," Idoman answered. "And the way the enemy is forming up supports it. It's similar to what they did at the eastern rim."

"Where is Galiena?" Gideon asked.

"Giving final instructions to her people," Idoman answered. "They've gathered—" he cut off as the tent flap was yanked aside and Joneam rushed in with an Elvan captain at his side. Their faces were flushed, and they were breathing heavily as if they'd been running.

Joneam moved right up to them before speaking. "Thank the Light you two are here," he said, looking from Jase to Gideon before turning to the Elvan soldier. "This is Kavil Tamsin, First Captain of the *Bero'thai* from Do'hyleth. He brings word from Elrien Dymas. There is trouble at the Great Wall."

"What kind of trouble?" Jase asked.

"A large stretch of the Veil has collapsed in the Valley of Amnidia," Tamsin answered, sounding as if he couldn't quite comprehend what it meant. "The Great Wall is about to be attacked by an army of demons."

The barrage of images from last night's dreams flooded Gideon's mind, and he knew from Jase's expression that he was reliving them as well.

"You said, Do'hyleth," Gideon said, breaking the silence. "Have the western cities been mobilized, then?"

Captain Tamsin nodded. "Those of us not already mobilizing here," he said. "But I fear there may not be enough Dymas among those going to the Great Wall. As you know, most already came here to answer the call of the *Mith'elre Chon*."

"Which is why I won't let Elva face this new threat alone," Jase said, and the way he said it sent a wave of apprehension rushing through Gideon.

"What are you saying?" he asked, placing a hand on Jase's shoulder and looking him in the eyes.

"I'm going to the Great Wall," he answered, "and I'm taking whatever Dymas we can spare."

"But—"

"I know what you are going to say," Jase told him. "But this is the way it has to be. Think about what we witnessed last night and tell me it wasn't the Earthsoul crying for help. Whatever else happens today, we cannot let the demons get beyond the wall."

Gideon's steely silence put Jase on edge, and he braced himself for the objection he could see forming on his father's lips. He didn't want to argue in front of the others, but he had no intention of backing down from this. He was the *Mith'elre Chon*, and he would go where the Earthsoul directed. And this *was* Her directive. He could feel the stirrings of *Ta'shaen* in his heart as well as in his mind.

But it wasn't Her whisperings alone calling him northward—it was his sense of duty to Elrien and his *Bero'thai*. Without their intervention that dark night on the slopes of Mount Tabor, he would have died at the hands of the Shadan'Ko. He would help Elrien whether Gideon liked it or not.

The tension inside the command tent intensified as Gideon's silence stretched on, then dissipated when he nodded. "It shall be as you say, *Mith'elre Chon*," he said. "But you must be reasonable about your involvement. Your presence alone should be enough to inspire those defending the wall. You need not risk yourself in a battle with demons."

"You cannot risk it," Sheymi Oroshi said sharply, and Jase turned to find her staring at him with a disapproving frown. "I know little about the prophecies concerning your role as the *Mith'elre Chon*," she said. "But I don't need the words of men long dead to tell me what I can see through the eyes of *Ta'shaen*. You are key to this world's survival, Jase Fairimor. We cannot afford to lose you in a battle that may very well already be lost."

Captain Tamsin bristled at the comment. "You overestimate the demon's chances," he said, his voice and eyes hard. "The Elvan army will hold the wall."

Sheymi didn't seem convinced. "This Elrien must have his doubts about that or he wouldn't have sent you here to get help."

"And he shall have that help," Jase said, bringing the discussion to an end. "I'll leave as soon as we've gathered as many Dymas as this army can spare." He looked pointedly at Gideon. "But since I've been counseled to not overexert myself, I'd appreciate it if you would open a Veilgate for me."

Gideon smiled as if he'd just won a tremendous victory. "It would be my pleasure."

"I think I'd like to tag along," Elliott said, ignoring the hard look Seth gave him. "I've always wanted to see the Great Wall."

"In that case," Seth said, still scowling, "I'll be coming as well."

Jase smiled at both of them. "It will be just like old times."

"I very much doubt that," Seth told him.

"Sheymi and I would like to come," Railen said. "If the *Mith'elre Chon* approves, of course."

"I do," he told them, then met Gideon's gaze once more. "Would you like to notify our Dymas or do you want me to do it?"

"Also my pleasure," he answered. "How many do you want?"

"Thirty to start. We can always call for more if needed."

"Thirty it is," Gideon said, and Jase felt him extend his Awareness to touch the minds of several nearby Dymas. They touched the minds of others, and within moments they had their volunteers. Gideon had scarcely reined in his Awareness when the first few Dymas reached the command tent.

Erebius Laceda and his daughter Junteri were the first to arrive, and Jase stepped outside to greet them. They were followed by Tuari Renshar and two of her Riaki companions. A small group of Chunin women was followed by more than a dozen Elvan men and women. Two Dainin and a group of Kelsans brought the number to thirty.

"Thank you for answering the call so quickly," Jase told them, then nodded to Gideon.

"Be careful," Gideon said, then embraced all Seven Gifts and opened a shimmering doorway to the top of the Great Wall of Aridan.

Elrien smiled as word of the *Mith'elre Chon's* arrival raced along the top of the wall, bringing cheers to many and hope to all. It was like witnessing a powerful wind move across a field of wheat—the effects of its touch were immediately apparent. One after another, Dymas and *Bero'thai* alike stood a little taller, and spears and swords and bows were held with a little more confidence.

He hadn't expected Jase to answer the call for help personally, but he wasn't surprised he was here. For all any of them knew, his arrival may even be the fulfillment of prophecy. The boy had a knack for being where he was supposed to be *when* he was supposed to be there.

Opening his Awareness, he stretched it toward the point of Jase's arrival and found him in the same courtyard where he had destroyed the *Reiker's* scepter after escaping Amnidia. Captain Tamsin was with him, as were Seth Lydon and Elliott Chellum. They stood next to a Veilgate as Dymas of nearly every nationality moved from the shadows of the Kelsan camp into the sunlight bathing the top of the wall.

Elrien watched until the Veilgate closed, then drew in his Awareness and started for the courtyard. He was met halfway by Jase and those who'd come with him.

"It's good to see you again, my friend," Jase said, offering his hand in greeting. "I wish it were under better circumstances. What exactly will we be facing here?"

"An enemy unlike any we've ever seen," Elrien told him, knowing that sugarcoating his answer was pointless. Jase would see the truth for himself soon enough. "And a good number of them. I can't say for sure, but there may be as many as a hundred."

"And they are demons?" Jase asked. "Not demonspawn?"

"Yes," Elrien answered. "Which means many of them will be able to wield *Lo'shaen*."

"I see," Jase said, then moved to the battlements and looked out at the ruined valley. "Where are the Shadan'Ko?"

"No one knows," Elrien said. "They left during the night. I tried finding them through the eyes of *Ta'shaen*, but the curse on the valley has grown. It reaches nearly to the wall now."

"And the collapsed part of the Veil?" Jase asked.

"Runs the full length of the Rift," Elrien answered. "But unlike prior holes we've encountered that opened like windows into Con'Jithar, this one is three dimensional. It is miles thick and growing thicker by the hour. Fortunately, it is spreading southward toward the wall. For now, the Soul Chamber is still in the world of the living."

Jase nodded his understanding. "Let's pray it stays that way."

A horn sounded long and loud from atop the nearest watchtower and shouts were raised and relayed along the wall. Riders were coming. Elvan. And they were riding hard.

"That will be Captain Alleilwin and his men," Elrien said. He studied the landscape for some sign of the men, but without the aid of the watchtower's spyglass they were likely out of his range of vision.

A short time later, Seth Lydon pointed.

"There," he said, and Elrien and the others followed his outstretched arm to a tiny pinprick of movement.

"You've got good eyes," Elrien told him. "That is a long way away."

"Too long if they hope to outrun the creatures pursuing them," Seth said, his eyes fastened on something only he could see. It wasn't until Elrien extended his Awareness that he spotted the pack of demons chasing Alleilwin and his men. Less than a half mile separated the two groups, but the gap was closing rapidly. Seth was right: The Elvan soldiers would be overtaken long before they reached the wall.

"We can help with that," Jase said, then nodded to an aging Kelsan Dymas. "Erebius, if you would please."

Erebius embraced the Power and opened a Veilgate in front of Alleilwin and his men. For those atop the wall it was but a small flash of light in the distance. For Elrien, still watching through his Awareness, it was like witnessing a flash of lightning, the brightness thereof enhanced by the darkness of the taint. A dozen feet high and twice that wide, it allowed the Elvan horsemen to ride through as one, and they arrived on the south side of the wall without breaking stride.

The Veilgate slid shut as soon as they were through, and Elrien crossed to the southern battlements to look down at them. Alleilwin had already dismounted and was hurrying toward the nearest entrance. Elrien cut ten minutes off his journey by providing a Veilgate to the top of the wall.

"Thanks for that," Alleilwin said, sounding winded. "I wasn't looking forward to all the stairs." He took a few calming breaths, then looked northward and added, "An even bigger thanks for getting us out of the valley. You saw the demons, I presume."

"Yes," Elrien answered, taking the captain by the arm and turning him toward Jase. "But you can give your report to the *Mith'elre Chon*."

If Alleilwin was surprised that Jase was present, he didn't show it. He simply brought his fist to his chest in salute. "The approaching demons are only part of the problem, my Lord," he said. "The Shadan'Ko who were here at the wall are no longer in the valley."

The announcement brought a hiss of disbelief from nearly everyone within earshot, but Jase simply exchanged an unreadable look with Seth Lydon before turning back to Alleilwin. "How did they manage that?" he asked.

"We tracked them to a rent in the Veil," Alleilwin answered. "It opened into Con'Jithar, where a second rent was visible just a few feet beyond. That one opened into the Fairholm Valley and we could see Lamshore some miles in the distance. The Shadan'Ko literally passed through Con'Jithar to escape the valley. And they didn't go alone—we found *Mrogin* tracks as well." He shook his head. "Havilam Dymas—may God rest his soul—attempted to close the rent but triggered a warding in the process. Stabs of dark energy erupted out of nowhere and killed him and three of my men."

"And the rent?" Jase asked.

"Still open."

Jase motioned for the two Dainin who'd arrived with him. "Send word to Ohran," he told them. "Tell him *Nar'shein* are needed in Fairholm Valley. See if they can close the rent from that side. If not, tell them to hold the area against anything else that might arrive."

"Yes, *Mith'elre Chon*," the Dainin said, then moved a short distance away and opened a small window into Dainin to deliver the message.

Jase fastened his attention on Alleilwin once more. "What else did you learn out there?" he asked.

Alleilwin's reply was forestalled by a sudden cacophony of demonic howls and cries. Though distant, they echoed loudly off the towers and battlements, sending a visual ripple through the wall's defenders as soldiers and Dymas alike stiffened in alarm.

Jase moved to the northern battlements and extended his Awareness to view the approaching horde. They were near enough now not to be obscured by the taint, and Jase's expression hardened at the sight of them.

Elrien watched him for a moment, trying to determine what he was thinking, then opened his Awareness as well and extended it in the direction of the approaching demons.

Cloaked in pools of darkness, they thundered across the ruined landscape like a plague of nightmarish locust. No two were alike, and they were spread unevenly across several miles as the quickest among them outran their slower companions. The hellish menagerie was far less organized than Elrien would have suspected, but he wasn't going to complain. The disjointed attacks would favor the wall's defenders.

"I don't like the look of that," Jase said after a moment, and Elrien blinked in surprise at how different the statement was from what he'd just been thinking. Captain Alleilwin had been entertaining similar thoughts as evidenced by what he said next.

"But *Mith'elre Chon*," he said, "if they come at us in such an unorganized fashion, we can destroy them easily."

"That's what they want us to think," Jase said, then reined in his Awareness and turned to Seth who was watching the demons through a small spyglass. "What do you think, Captain?"

Seth lowered the spyglass. "I think you're right," he answered. "Those racing ahead of the others are likely the demonic equivalent of Shadowhounds. Vicious but expendable. Whatever sent them ahead expects our Dymas to attack them with the Power."

Jase nodded. "And by so doing reveal our locations and numbers. They're probably hoping to wear us down a little before they arrive." He turned and looked Elrien in the eyes. "Send word to our Dymas," he said. "Tell them to leave these forerunners to the *Bero'thai*. I want to see what we are really up against." Looking back at the ruined valley, he added, "I have a feeling it's going to be bad."

# CHAPTER 25

## Hell's Army

JASE WATCHED THE APPROACHING DEMONS with a great deal of trepidation. These animalistic forerunners may only be the equivalent of Shadowhounds when compared to a creature like the *Reiker*, but Shadowhounds weren't much more than mice when compared to these. And since no two were alike, the wall's defenders would need different tactics for each.

There were soft-bodied creatures wearing armor made of metal and bone; leathery and scaled reptilian beasts sporting an array of spikes and quills and patches of fur; and insect-like monstrosities with shimmering exoskeletons. They ran on a variety of legs and arms and pointed appendages ranging in number from two to ten. Some were roughly human-shaped, most were not; hulking creatures resembling everything from wolves and apes to lizards and beetles.

"Do you think they can walk up stone like Shadowhounds?" Elliott asked, stepping near. He wore his sword over his shoulder like a Shizu, blade still sheathed. His face, which just a few weeks ago would have been alight with boyish excitement at the prospect of battle, was a picture of Shizu calm. He suddenly looked very much like Seth.

"I guess we'll find out," Jase answered. He watched the demons for a moment longer, then embraced the Power and used a channeling of Air to carry his voice along the top of the wall.

"Defenders of Aridan," he said. "This is the *Mith'elre Chon*. What you see coming is only the first wave. Our Power-wielders will not engage them with *Ta'shaen* unless they make it atop the wall, and then only if conventional weapons are insufficient. We need to conserve our strength for what will follow. Stand to your duties, hold your positions, and trust those around you. We will make it through this."

"Very inspirational," Elliott said, the boyish smile momentarily visible on his face.

He reached up and pulled his sword from its sheath. "Except for the part where I get to face one of those things with a sword instead of lightning."

"That time will come," Jase told him. "And when it does, I want to see just how much the Earthsoul has boosted your strength."

The shocked look on Elliott's face was better than Jase had expected and he grinned at him. "I don't think Shizu are supposed to gape," he told him. "But, yes. The Earthsoul has increased the strength of your Gift. I can sense it through *Ta'shaen*. Just be careful not to tear down the wall when you destroy the demons."

"I have control of my abilities," Elliott said, and the Shizu persona slid back in place despite the glimmer of excitement in his eyes.

Jase turned to Elrien. "Are the access points at the base of the wall secure?" he asked.

Elrien nodded. "Made of Power-wrought stone and steel and warded against discovery. But we have soldiers and Dymas stationed inside the wall at each point just in case."

"Good," Jase told him. "The last thing we need is demons inside the wall."

He turned his attention back to the demons. They were near now, less than a half mile away, and their snarls and grunts and insect hissings were becoming audible. The rumble of the stampede reached his ears a short time later, like distant thunder announcing an approaching storm.

Along the top of the wall, archers raised bows and selected targets, and the creak of arrows being drawn sounded in near unison. The demons didn't slow, howling with frenzied eagerness. The archers loosed.

Razored heads caught the sunlight in flashes of silvery-white as a literal storm of arrows met the charging horde. Several of the soft-bodied demons staggered and fell, howling in pain and rage as arrows found the creases in their armor. A large wolf-like creature covered with thick scales and quills tumbled in a cloud of dust as an arrow took it in the eye and pierced its brain. It continued to thrash and howl as others intent on reaching the wall raced past.

A second volley was loosed, and two more demons fell wounded. Scrambling to their feet, they took the arrows in their teeth and yanked them from their bodies, crushing the shafts with their jaws. They tossed the splinters to the ground, then started forward again, eyes glowing with demonic rage.

Neither volley had an effect on the hard exoskeletons of the insect-like creatures, and they reached the wall before a third volley could be loosed. Most slammed into the wall like battering rams and were stopped cold, but ten or twelve continued upward, hissing and snarling. The raspy clicks of their feet as they scrambled up the face of the wall sent a shiver down Jase's back.

He looked at Elliott. "I guess that answers your question about their ability to walk up stone," he told him.

"We'll have something for them," Captain Alleilwin said, and motioned to the soldiers manning the spear-thrower atop the nearest tower. Essentially a giant crossbow, it was capable of hurling a spear more than half a mile.

The soldiers swung the weapon in the direction indicated, then waited. A few seconds later, a massive six-legged demon crested the battlements. Its wedge-shaped head swivelled this way and that as it was pelted with arrows, but its armor-plating deflected them as easily as a metal plate deflected hailstones. Hissing and clicking, it lashed out with its two front legs and three *Bero'thai* went down in sprays of blood.

A large *thrump* sounded as the spear-thrower was fired, and the demon was ripped from the top of the wall with a loud crack. The force of the shot carried the creature several hundred yards into the valley, its trajectory marked by a trailing mist of greenish-grey blood.

"Nice shot," Jase said, but the sense of accomplishment was short-lived as another demon crested a short distance to the left. Holes opened in its exoskeleton, and thorny tentacles shot out, a whipping, lashing maelstrom too quick to counter. A number of soldiers went down or were flung from the battlements to the demons waiting below.

Further down the wall, a bear-like monstrosity bristling with spikes and razored plates of bone came over the battlements like a grey-black avalanche. It was immediately hit by a spear from a spear-thrower, but the shot missed the creature's vitals. It killed four *Bero'thai*, before being brought down.

For miles in each direction, the scene was the same. Demons breached the top of the wall and were repelled or killed even as they managed to kill or wound *Bero'thai* in return.

Below the wall, the demons who couldn't walk up stone howled and snarled as they threw themselves fruitlessly against the Power-wrought fortress or were shot with arrows from above. After what seemed an eternity, they gave up and raced away northward out of range of the defender's arrows, leaving the demons atop the wall to fend for themselves.

Unfortunately, they were many, and in every place where they had crested, they were leaving injury and death. So much so that in several locations, Dymas were forced to use the Power to destroy them, revealing themselves to the demons who were yet to arrive. Jase felt the dark touch of dozens of demon Awarenesses as they briefly probed the wall then retreated.

"Those were some of the same ones I felt this morning," Elrien commented, shivering in spite of the growing warmth of the day.

Jase nodded but said nothing as he listened to the snarls and growls and hisses of the few remaining demons rising above the shouts of the men killing them. Several minutes passed and the sounds of battle finally subsided. A profound silence descended upon the wall as the Elvan soldiers considered what they had just faced and how insignificant it had been in light of what was still to come.

Jase addressed them again, urging his words to the far reaches of the wall with the Power. "Defenders of Aridan," he said, letting his fondness for them fill his voice, "this is the *Mith'elre Chon* again. I commend you for your efforts during this first attack. You handled yourselves with all the skill and fortitude I have come to expect from my Elvan brothers and sisters.

"But this was only the beginning. As anticipated, the demon vanguard has retreated to wait for the rest of their kind to join them. The true test is yet to come, and it will be unlike anything any of us has ever faced before. Many of the demons in the next wave are capable of wielding *Lo'shaen*, the Power of the Void.

"But fear not. This terrible power can be countered with *El'shaen te sherah*, and the Dymas I brought with me are the most capable wielders in all of the Nine Lands. With your help, we will meet this threat, and we will send this demon horde back to hell where it belongs. For the honor of God, the liberty of our peoples, and the salvation of the Earthsoul, it will be done."

As he released the Power, a cheer went up from the wall's defenders, and Seth nodded his approval.

"You sound more like your mother everyday," the captain said. "She would be proud of the way you are handling this situation."

"She would be furious to know I am here," Jase told him. "I'm supposed to be with Gideon, remember?"

"You are supposed to be where you choose to be," Seth countered. "Let's just make sure you leave here in one piece."

Jase grunted, then fell silent as he watched the demons milling out of arrow range. Their masters were yet to appear on the horizon, and he suspected it would be some time before they did.

He was right, and the next five hours passed slowly as those atop the wall watched and waited. Occasionally the relative silence was broken by growls and snarls from the hellish creatures milling out of range, but the demons did not advance on the wall, content, it seemed, to wait for reinforcements.

Jase watched them with the same morbid curiosity he'd once felt for Shadowhounds, then dismissed them and turned to watch Elliott instead.

His friend had produced his wallet of colored paper and was in the process of folding something resembling the insect-like creature which had breached the top of the wall. It was startlingly accurate and Jase marveled at his friend's talent.

"A souvenir," Elliott said, handing it to him. "So you won't forget what it looked like."

"Not much chance of that," Jase told him, then watched with fascination as Elliott produced five more foldings resembling other demons in the group.

"That's quite a skill," Elrien said, taking one of the paper demons to examine it. "Did you learn that in Riak?"

Elliott shook his head. "I'm self-educated," he said, then shrugged. "But it helped pass the time in Riak just as it is helping pass the time here." He set an ape-like creature on the battlement with the others. "Even so, this is bloody taking forever."

They fell silent again, and the minutes continued to drag on. An hour later, Jase spotted a hint of movement in the distance.

"Here they come," he said, pointing at the line of demons coming into view. They were still a long way off, but there were enough of them to stand out against the barren landscape of the valley.

Seth raised the spyglass for a look, then frowned. After a moment, he handed the spyglass to Elliott.

"Blood of Maeon," Elliott whispered, and the obvious fear in his voice turned the heads of all those within earshot.

Jase held out his hand for the spyglass. "May I? I'd prefer to keep my Awareness separate from that filth for a little while longer."

"By all means," Elliott said, handing over the spyglass. "But try to control your language once you get a look at them. There are ladies present."

Jase brought the spyglass to his eye and leveled it at the dark line on the valley floor. Elliott had been right about the kind of language the sight would inspire, but he managed to keep his thoughts to himself, if just barely.

Elrien had been way off on his estimate of how many demons were marching toward them. He'd said there were about a hundred—this looked more like a thousand. And unlike the undisciplined rush of the first wave, the second group was marching in formation.

They were human in form, but much more monstrous and grotesque than any Darkling Jase had ever encountered. And they were heavily armored, with shields and breastplates; steel boots, gauntlets, and shin-guards. Visored helmets obscured their faces, but the slits only served to focus the red glow of their demon eyes. Most carried some kind of weapon—a sword or axe or spear—but there were many with staffs or scepters, the ends of which glowed red with the power of the Void.

Jase handed Elrien the spyglass. "Any thoughts?"

The Elvan prophet raised the spyglass, and Jase waited patiently while he studied the demon army. "Quite a few more than I thought there would be," he admitted. "But I was pretty close on my estimate of how many can wield *Lo'shaen*. It is they who present the greatest danger. The rest likely aren't much more than soldiers."

"Demon soldiers," Elliott muttered. "I wouldn't downplay their abilities too much."

"I downplay nothing," Elrien told him. "But those who can't wield *Lo'shaen* are far less of a threat than those who can."

"Unless they make it atop the wall," Seth said. "In which case, we will have our hands full."

"Then let's make sure they stay below," Elliott said, locking eyes with Jase. "I say we hit them before they get close enough to hit us."

"I agree," Railen said. "We should thin their ranks as much as possible before they reach the wall."

Tuari and several other Dymas nodded their agreement, but Elrien shook his head. "I think defense is still our best bet against these creatures," he said. "We outnumber them and we hold the high ground."

"All the more reason to strike first," Elliott said, then looked pointedly at the spot where the insect-like demon had breached the wall. Healers had long since finished tending to the wounded, but more than a dozen Elvan soldiers had been killed. The bodies of those who hadn't been tossed from the wall by the demon had been covered with their cloaks and moved to the southern battlements where they would be out of the way until they could be properly tended to.

"Those men might still be alive if we'd killed the demons *before* they made it to the top of the wall," Elliott continued. "I know you wish to conserve your strength, but sometimes the best defense is a good offensive. Once the demons are here, defense will be the only option we have. We need to strike now, while we still have that option."

Jase studied his friend for a moment before answering. "What would you propose?" he asked.

"Attack them through Veilgates," Elliott answered, "but not from atop the wall. Send Dymas to another location first and have them attack from there. The demons will believe we have numbers beyond what they may have counted at the wall, and it won't open the wall's defenders to attack should a demon somehow make it through a Veilgate."

"I like it," Seth said, and beside him Railen and Sheymi were nodding.

"So do I," Jase told him. "But since I have been *advised* not to enter the fight, who would like to see this through?"

"I'll go," Railen said, stepping forward.

"Not without me, you're not," Sheymi told him, and her tone left no room for argument.

Tuari stepped forward and was followed by Erebius and his daughter. Two Elvan men who had the look of *Bero'thai* volunteered to go as well, and they were joined by two young women who'd been sticking close to Elrien. Likely they were more of his apprentices, and both looked younger than Talia.

Elrien must have read the thought in his expression, because he stepped forward. "Have no fear, *Mith'elre Chon*," he said. "They are more experienced than they look. Besides, I will be there to look after them."

Jase's surprise deepened. "You're going?"

"I know the wastes better than anyone," the aged prophet told him. "If we must attack as you propose, I will see that everyone returns safely."

"In that case," Elliott said, "I'm coming with you." He raised an eyebrow at Jase questioningly. "If the *Mith'elre Chon* approves, of course."

"Would it matter if I didn't?" Jase asked.

Elliott grinned at him. "Probably not. But as you said earlier, we can't have me tearing down the wall with my newly increased abilities."

Jase returned the smile. "We most certainly cannot." He returned his attention to Elrien. "You'll be leading this attack," he said. "As soon as you've hit them to your satisfaction, I want you to break off and return to the wall."

"Yes, *Mith'elre Chon*," Elrien said, a sudden glimmer of excitement in his eyes. For all his insistence that defense was their best bet, he clearly seemed eager for battle. It was a side of the aging prophet Jase hadn't seen before, but he was glad to see it now. Elrien was likely the most experienced Dymas in all of the Nine Lands.

"God's speed, my friends," Jase told them, then watched as they moved to a secluded corner at the base of the nearest tower and left through a Veilgate wrought by Railen.

"Are you sure this is a good idea?" Captain Alleilwin asked when they were gone.

"Absolutely," Jase said, then turned his gaze north toward the demons. He didn't want to miss Elliott's arrival.

With a gentle breeze rippling the knee-high grasses around him, Elliott drew his sword and waited for the Dymas to open Veilgates into the Amnidian wasteland. Railen's Veilgate had deposited them somewhere in the Allister Highlands, but there wasn't a village or homestead anywhere in sight.

*That way*, the young Shizu said upon arrival, *there will be no risk to life or property should any of the demons somehow fight their way through the Power-wrought openings.*

Elliott tightened his grip on his sword as he looked at those who'd come with him. *Yes. But what about the danger to us?*

"Is your sword some sort of talisman?" one of Elrien's apprentices asked as she stepped near. She was a slender young lady with bright blue eyes and a wry smile. The short-cut length of her hair made her Elvan ears that much more prominent a feature. She was cute, but not what Elliott would consider beautiful. Not like Tana was beautiful, he thought, his mind suddenly back in Chellum as an image of Tana's face appeared in his mind's eye.

She would be furious to know what he was getting ready to do, but it couldn't be helped. They were at war, after all. And this attack had been his idea. He let Tana's image linger a moment longer, then shook himself free of it and answered the girl's question.

"No," he told her. "It's just a sword. But it gives me something physical to focus on when I utilize my Gift."

"And what is your Gift?" she asked, still smiling. He wasn't entirely sure she wasn't flirting with him.

"Light," he told her, then looked expectantly at Elrien. "Are we going to do this or not?"

Elrien looked down the line of Dymas, and one by one they nodded. He looked back to Elliott. "On your command, Lord Chellum," he said.

Elliott pointed his sword at a spot in front of him. "Let's do it," he said, and the air split wide to reveal a column of demons.

They were facing away from the Veilgate but immediately whirled to face him, their demon eyes flaring bright with surprise. He struck before the Power-wielders among them could react, and a sizzling arc of lightning as thick as a tree lanced from his sword tip and ripped dozens of the hellish creatures to smoking shreds.

Jase had been right about the Earthsoul increasing his Gift, and the strike was larger than anything he'd ever channeled before and came much easier than he would have imagined. And he was nowhere near the limit of his abilities.

Reveling in his newfound strength, he struck again, and a dozen more demons vanished beneath the sizzling destruction.

To his left, Tuari struck the demons through another gate, and Elliott saw the fiery detonation of Power behind and to the right of the column he was attacking. The demons there whirled toward that attack, leaving them exposed to Railen who struck them through a gate he opened above their heads.

All across the demon army, the scene was the same—demons died as Veilgates opened around them and attacks were launched from the safety of the Allister Highlands. Fire and lightning, blades of Spirit and explosive thrusts of Flesh—each strike tailored to the strengths of the Dymas launching them. In the opening seconds of the attack more than a hundred demons were killed.

Then something dark struck the edges of Elrien's Veilgate, and the blue-rimmed opening crackled and sparked in protest as Elrien staggered away, both hands clutched to his head. One of his apprentices caught him by the arm, and it was clear from the look of horror on the young Dymas' face that her mentor no longer held the Power.

Elliott turned back to the Veilgate. It should have collapsed the moment Elrien lost his hold on *Ta'shaen*, but it hadn't. Tendrils of darkness, like the fingers of some monstrous beast, had curled around all four edges of the opening and were holding it open from the other side. Even worse, it seemed to be growing larger.

Opening himself even more fully to his Gift, Elliott sent a barrage of lightning streaking through the opening and into the demons beyond. Dozens more died, but the opening continued to grow bigger.

"We need to stop that," Railen shouted, sending white-hot bars of *Sei'shiin* lancing into the finger-like tendrils of darkness.

They recoiled when struck, but others replaced them immediately, and the Veilgate continued to expand. Elliott couldn't believe what he was seeing. The demons had somehow taken control of Elrien's Veilgate and were going to use it to escape Amnidia.

And this wasn't the only place it was happening. Two more Veilgates on his left had also been seized by the demons. The Allister Highlands were about to be invaded by an army from Con'Jithar.

And it was his fault. If he hadn't suggested this offensive....

He let the thought die, determined to keep an invasion from happening.

Striding forward, he continued to draw upon his Gift until he thought he might burst, and points of light appeared in his vision as he neared his breaking point. But, oh, what a point it was. Never in his life would he have imagined that such power existed.

He neared the edge of the now corrupt Veilgate and raised his sword, prepared to release everything he had. With a little luck, he would kill the creature who had seized control of the gate.

But before he could strike, the Veilgate moved, lurching forward so quickly that Elliott found himself standing in the Valley of Amnidia surrounded by a patch of knee-high Allister grassland. Almost as one, the grasses toppled around him. Their bottoms, cleanly sliced at ground level, briefly glowed a faint red before fading to charred black.

Elliott looked up from the fallen grass to find a very human-looking demon watching him from behind a glowing scepter. Their eyes met, and the world erupted into Fire and Light.

Jase smiled in appreciation as Elliott's lightning bathed the Valley of Amnidia in flashes of bluish-white, momentarily blinding those watching from atop the wall. With each burst, dozens of demons were destroyed. Several seconds after each titanic flash, a crack of thunder reached the Great Wall of Aridan, echoing along the stony monolith like an invisible ocean wave crashing on a shoreline.

*Ta'shaen* was alive with other strikes—Fire and Spirit and Flesh—as Railen and the other Dymas attacked, but it was the unbelievable strength and ferocity of Elliott's wielding that drew the attention of every Power-wielder on the wall.

Unfortunately, it drew the attention of one of the more powerful demons as well, and a torrent of *Lo'shaen* struck the Veilgate Elliott was using to launch his attack. The Dymas beyond the gate—Jase thought it might be Elrien—lost his hold on the Power, but the Veilgate, which should have collapsed the moment *Ta'shaen* vanished, remained open, held so by tendrils of *Lo'shaen*.

"That shouldn't be possible," Jase said, pressing his Awareness closer for a better look. Around him, other Dymas did the same, and murmurs of disbelief swept along their ranks.

"What is it?" Seth asked. He held the spyglass leveled at the battle, but there was no way for him to see what was only visible to those who could wield the Power.

Jase didn't answer him directly, but opened himself to the Power and sent his voice along the top of the wall. "Children of *Ta'shaen*," he called. "The demons have taken control of some of our Veilgates. Elrien and those with him need assistance." He pointed to six Elvan Dymas standing a short way off. "You," he said, getting their attention, "take ten or twelve Dymas with you and collapse the Veilgates from our side. I don't want a single demon getting through."

With hastily uttered acknowledgments, the six hurried to obey, and Jase felt a Veilgate open into the Allister Highlands.

Other Veilgates opened atop the wall, and Dymas dashed through to several hilltops to the east and west of the demon army. The gates closed without incident, but the Dymas who'd opened them came under attack almost immediately. Scream-like peals of thunder echoed across the landscape as Night Threads ricocheted off shields of Spirit and tore gashes in the hillside.

But the real fight was at the center of the demon army where the singularly powerful demon was enlarging the Veilgate he'd seized control of. Already it was half again as big as what Elrien had opened.

Pressing his Awareness closer, Jase tried to get a glimpse of what was happening beyond the gate, but could see only the green-yellow grasses of the Allister Highlands. For a moment he feared his friends had been lost. Then Elliott appeared, a white-hot pillar of Light in Jase's spiritual vision as he prepared to loose a barrage of lightning powerful enough to level a city.

Jase held his breath as he waited for his friend to strike.

The Veilgate moved, a sudden forward shift that left Elliott standing in the Valley of Amnidia.

"Blood of Maeon," Seth cursed, lowering the spyglass and turning to Jase expectantly. "You're going to help him, right?"

Before Jase could answer, his Awareness came alive with a wielding powerful enough to shatter the Great Wall. But it wasn't originating in the ruined valley. It was coming from somewhere in Kunin.

The stolen Blood Orb of Elsa had just been accessed.

# CHAPTER 26

## Altar of Defiling

"HE'S HERE."

Thorac lowered the spyglass and handed it to Thex Landoral so the Dymas could have a look for himself. *And it's about bloody time*, he added silently. Endil and those with him had been inside the shrine since yesterday, and Captain Haslem's men had been in position since early this morning. Everyone was on edge from waiting.

Well, the waiting was over. Chaos and death were about to engulf the valley below. Again.

Hopefully this time the outcome would be different. If not, and Loharg accessed the Orb's reservoir of Power, the Veil would collapse and Con'Jithar would arrive in this place in full. The rest of the world would be swallowed soon after.

Thex handed the spyglass back, and Thorac raised it to his eye once more. He picked Loharg out immediately.

A hulking, wolf-like monstrosity half again larger than a man, he towered over the Kunin who parted before him, knees bowed, heads lowered in fearful respect. And there, clutched in one of Loharg's clawed fists, was a leather satchel taken from one of the Dymas massacred at the Temple of Elderon.

"He has the Blood Orb in the satchel," Thex whispered. "I can see it in my mind's eye in spite of the taint." His voice was filled with awe as he added, "I can feel its power, and it is immense. And the Orb... it is pulses like something alive."

Thorac watched Loharg for a while longer, then scanned the path ahead of him through the valley. Word of their master's arrival was racing through the Kunin who'd gathered, and tens of thousands of voices were raised in shouts of praise and welcome. Tribal banners were waved in celebration, and throngs of Kunin eager to see their master pressed upon those who were trying to make way for the Sons of Uri.

But with so many rival tribes in such a confined area, Kunin blood soon spattered the rocky ground as scuffles turned deadly in several places. The bloodshed was exactly what Thorac had expected, and it made him confident that his plan would work.

"Now I see why you wanted all those Kunin arrows," Thex said, his eyes on a particularly large fight erupting in Loharg's wake. "Should I notify our archers to engage?"

"We have a while yet to wait," Thorac told him. "At his current pace, Loharg won't reach the shrine for at least another hour."

He fell silent as he watched the Sons of Uri slowly make their way across the valley. It was the longest hour of his life, especially when he occasionally lost sight of Loharg in a draw or behind a fin of rock. When that happened, he kept his eyes on the Kunin, measuring Loharg's progress by their movements instead.

After one particularly long stretch, Loharg came into the open one final time as he neared the shrine, and Thorac's impatience turned to anticipation as the Sons of Uri passed between the stone towers marking the shrine's boundary. The Kunin following in his wake stopped short of the markers, and Loharg and his brethren continued on alone.

There were nearly three dozen of them, all undoubtedly *Odai'mi*, all as massive and hideously misshapen as Loharg. But they seemed completely unaware that they were walking into an ambush.

Thorac's anticipation turned to all out excitement. Barring any unforseen complications, this might actually work. He found himself fingering his axe as he watched them cross the smooth, courtyard-like expanse of black stone and disappear inside the temple. When the last one was gone, he turned to Thex.

"Tell the archers to attack," he said.

Nodding, Thex moved down the back side of the ridge to give the signal, and Thorac turned his attention back to the shrine.

"It's in your hands now, Emma," he whispered. Drawing his axe from the loop on his belt, he gripped the handle tightly and braced himself for what would shortly follow.

Sitting on a block of stone a short distance away from the Altar of Uri, Emmarenziana Antilla closed her eyes and let the radiant power of the Blood Orb bathe her Awareness with much needed Light. It was small and still distant, but she could see it in her mind's eye like a single bright star shining in an endless night sky. Considering where she was, it was the most beautiful thing she'd ever seen.

She let the Light lift her spirits for a moment longer, then sighed and opened her eyes to the horrors which had surrounded her since yesterday. An unholy altar, the remnants of slaughter and sacrifice, the darkness of hell itself—each of them a stark contrast to the brilliant power being carried her way.

A moment later Dommoni Kia'Kal appeared in the entrance to the altar room, and she smiled at him as he went to one knee.

"The Blood Orb is in the valley," he said.

"I felt it as well," she told him. "It won't be long now."

Endil and Jeymi moved out of the shadows beyond a cluster of pillars, their faces expectant.

"How long do we have?" Endil asked. He was surprisingly calm. Much more calm than Emma would have expected considering what was about to happen.

"An hour at most," the *Nar'shein* Chieftain answered. "We'd best get into position." He offered a deep bow of respect. "May the Earthmother shelter and protect you should we fail to meet again at the end of this battle." Rising to his feet, he disappeared back the way he had come.

"Get into position," Endil said, forcing a laugh. "We've been in position for two bloody days." He took Jeymi's hand, and they picked their way carefully across the room, mindful not to disturb anything which might alert Loharg to their presence once he arrived.

Jeymi stared at the entrance, her lips pinched worriedly. Finally she spoke. "Chieftain Kia'Kal's farewell didn't exactly fill me with confidence," she said. "*Should we fail to meet again...* What kind of talk is that?"

"Realistic talk," Emma told her. "Not all of us are going to make it out of here alive. But then that has been the case since we first entered this Light-blasted land."

Endil shook his head. "And like fools we came anyway."

"No, Endil," Emma said softly. "Fools do things unwittingly or without consideration of the consequences. You know exactly why you are here. You know what needs to be done. And you know what will happen to us if we fail."

She stood and moved forward to take his hand in hers. Looking up into his face, she continued. "By definition that makes you a hero, not a fool."

"I'm not a hero," Endil said. "I'm just doing what has to be done because there is no one else who can do it."

Emma shot an amused look at Jeymi, then met Endil's eyes once more. Smiling, she squeezed his hand affectionately. "When this is over, promise me you will look the word up in a dictionary."

She released his hand and stepped back. "It's time. Whatever else happens, stick to the plan. As soon as you have possession of the Orb, we will open a Veilgate out of here."

"And you're certain it has to be me that takes possession of it?" Endil asked. "It's already been defiled. You or Jeymi or even one of the Dainin could carry it at this point."

They'd been over this before, but now that the moment was upon him, he wanted to make sure that putting the most powerful talisman in the world into the hands of one Gifted only with Water wasn't a mistake. Surely a Dymas was better suited to the task.

"You are a Son of Elsa," Emma said. "Jeymi or I could wield the Orb's Power, certainly. But this is your birthright. Only you are eligible to receive Elsa's guidance as you wield. Only you can hear Her voice. Do as She instructs and we will survive this."

Endil's face hardened determinedly. "I will do my best," he told her.

She smiled at him. "You always do." She pointed at the cluster of pillars. "Take your places. We'll do this exactly as we discussed."

As the two young people picked their way carefully back to their hiding place, Emma moved behind a large block of stone which had fallen from the ceiling some century past. It was in the shadows beneath a sickly bar of sunlight streaming at an angle through one of the shafts cut for that purpose. As luck would have it, the bar of light passed above the Altar of Uri and would be in Loharg's eyes as he neared the altar.

*Thank the Light*, Emma thought, pleased with the dual meaning the thought contained. It led her to believe that Elderon had foreseen this exact moment and had guided the temple's builders to cut the shaft just so. With the luminescent world of *Ta'shaen* obliterated as it was, she would indeed be using her natural eyes.

To make sure, she closed her eyes and extended her Awareness toward the altar. There was nothing but darkness—the eyes of *Ta'shaen* were blind. If she'd been anywhere else, the lack of spiritual vision would have terrified her. Now, oddly enough, it was a comfort because it meant Loharg would be just as blind. That coupled with the light which would be in his eyes, not to mention the mix of shadows beneath, should give her an advantage, however small.

She closed off her Awareness and took a calming breath. She knew what she needed to do and how quickly she needed to do it. If she missed her mark, the fight would be over. For all of them.

*God's speed, Endil*, she thought, then echoed Dommoni Kia'Kal's words. *May the Earthmother shelter and protect you should we fail to meet again at the end of this battle.*

At peace with the situation, she settled in to wait.

Accompanied by thirty of his most powerful brethren, Loharg Kala'peleg entered the Shrine of Uri with a sense of triumph. It had been a long and difficult journey, but he'd made it. He'd managed to elude the Chunin army who'd been hunting him, and he'd survived nine attempts by nine of his now-deceased brethren to take the Blood Orb from him so they could claim the glory for themselves.

He eyed the thirty who remained, and each lowered his head or looked away, unwilling to challenge him any further. Satisfied, he angled across the large, ground-level chamber and climbed the stairs to the second level. There, as he led the way down a long, narrow hallway, he passed a large hole in the wall and looked out at the valley spreading away north.

Tens of thousands of Kunin were still chanting his name and shouting praises to the Sons of Uri, but his disgust for them had never been higher. The fools had no idea what was about to happen, just as their ancestors hadn't had a clue about the first defiling.

He allowed himself a smile, a low growl of pleasure sounding in his throat. Only this would be more than a simple defiling. This would be complete destruction. It would be the end. Of Kunin and the Nine Lands. Of the Earthsoul. Of everything.

Then he and his brethren would at last be welcomed into Con'Jithar by Father Uri himself.

His growl of pleasure deepened as he turned into a stairway and began the climb to the third level. Here, part of the ceiling and outer wall had collapsed, and he was forced to climb over a pile of rubble to reach the chamber at the top. Once there, he slowed as he waited for his brethren to navigate the debris.

When most were through, he continued on up to the fourth level. As he passed a section of collapsed wall he glanced out through the jagged hole and saw something that gave him pause. On the north end of the valley, vast sections of the Kunin hordes were facing away from the shrine. Bursts of corrupted Earthpower flashed red, tickling his Awareness.

"*Krashevic polet vausen*," he ordered, and one of his brothers produced a spyglass and moved to the opening to investigate.

After a moment he lowered the spyglass, his boar-like face twisted with contempt. "*Chunin sholo kaveshin*," he said, his growl of anger and contempt echoing down the hallway.

Loharg shared the sentiment. So, the Chunin army had managed to close the gap, had they? It wouldn't matter. They would be destroyed along with the rest of those in the valley. Still, it would be wise to hurry. He didn't want to risk his enemies reaching the shrine before he was ready to unleash the Orb.

"Some of you take positions at the entrance," he said, switching to the common tongue. "Signal the *Shel'tui* to engage any who get too close to the shrine."

He turned to Inoshi Kala'zefin and Preniz Kala'joffeg. "You two prepare the sacrifice for the altar."

They glanced at one another in confusion. "What sacrifice?"

Stepping past them, Loharg bared the claws on his right hand and ripped the throat out of one of the largest of his brethren. Eyes wide, the cat-faced creature clutched at the wound, then teetered to the side and fell, its dark, grey-black blood spattering across the stonework.

"That sacrifice," he said, retracting his claws and turning away as if nothing had happened.

Grinning with anticipation, he tightened his grip on the satchel holding the Blood Orb and continued, eager to kneel at the Altar of Uri, eager to usher in his father's kingdom.

"Kunin arrows," Thorac said smugly. "I told you it would be spectacular."

"I think devious was the word you used," Thex told him, impressed by how well Thorac knew his enemies. Why attack them directly, when you could use their animosity for one another against them and spark a multi-faceted civil war between rival tribes?

Thorac continued to watch his handiwork, a grim smile on his face. After a few minutes he spoke. "The *Shel'tui* are regaining control of the first area we hit," he said. "Let's hit them again."

Thex extended his Awareness to the Dymas in charge of the Chunin archers and gave the command. To the north, two Veilgates opened in the air above rival tribes and a hail of Kunin arrows hissed through from beyond, killing Kunin on both sides and wounding many more. Ignoring their *Shel'tui* masters, the two tribes renewed their efforts to kill one another.

"That's it, you filthy, worthless vermin," Thorac said, "keep killing each other while we engage your master." He lowered the spyglass and looked at Thex.

"Speaking of Loharg, have you sensed anything yet?"

Thex shook his head. "No. But he has to be getting close to the altar room." He looked at the shrine and added, "Do you really think you will need me to tell you when Emma engages him? You know what she is capable of. The entire valley will probably know when that moment comes."

"True enough," Thorac said, "But since I can't tell the difference between her wieldings and Loharg's, I want to know if something goes wrong."

"You have my word," Thex said. "And if something does go wrong?"

Thorac's expression hardened. "I want a Veilgate into the shrine."

Keeping her Awareness well away from the Blood Orb so as not to come in contact with the minds of Loharg or his brethren, Jeymi watched as it drew near. A single, pulsating source of Light, it shone like a miniature sun in the midst of the endless darkness blanketing her mind's eye. And yet, brilliant as it was, it cast no light on those bearing it toward her. It was a very uneasy sensation.

She reached over and touched Endil on the arm.

*They're coming.* She mouthed the words silently, and he nodded.

They could see nothing of the entrance to the altar room, but they didn't need to—they could see the altar itself and Emma's hiding place a short distance beyond. That was all they would need. *I hope.*

A few minutes passed, and the sound of claws clicking and scraping on stone became audible, gradually growing louder as the Sons of Uri drew near. She held her breath as the sounds suddenly spiked, echoing off the walls of the chamber.

They were here.

A flicker of movement beyond the pillars confirmed it, and a moment later, Loharg and two more demonspawn came into a view. Those two were dragging the lifeless body of a third demonspawn which they unceremoniously threw upon the altar. Its throat had been ripped out, and symbols similar to those scrawled on the wall had been carved into its hide with a knife.

Loharg moved up to the altar and went to his knees. Even then he was the most frighteningly hideous creature Jeymi had ever encountered, shadowspawn, other demonspawn, and demons included. No wonder this creature held power in this land.

A rush of panic filled her. How could Emma hope to defeat a creature such as this? And not just one, but three. It was impossible! It was—

The Altar of Uri exploded into shards as Emma struck with a vicious thrust of Earth, and Loharg and his companions were thrown backward by the blast. The satchel containing the Blood Orb was knocked loose from Loharg's grasp and slid across the floor toward Jeymi and Endil.

Dazed by the explosion and bleeding from several deep wounds, Loharg and his companions lurched to their feet as Emma struck again, this time with streamers of Fire. Instinctively, the three wove shields of corrupted Spirit to defend themselves, but one of the creatures fell, a smoking hole burned through its head.

It all happened in an instant, but it was enough for Jeymi to do her part. Seizing the satchel in a grip of Air, she tore it open and yanked the Blood Orb toward Endil's outstretched hands. He caught it, and his eyes went wide in surprise or awe or both. Mouth open, he stood motionless, staring at the glowing sphere of light in his hand.

Jeymi reached for him, but her wielding had alerted Loharg to her presence. Howling in demonic rage, he whirled to face her, the air darkening around him as he struck with *Lo'shaen*.

She cast up a hastily woven shield as everything vanished into flame and heat.

The light in the *Odai'mi's* eyes dimmed as it died, and Dommoni Kia'Kal pulled his spear free of its chest and let it topple to the floor. All throughout the shrine, his *Nar'shein* were similarly engaged, and the Sons of Uri were being cleansed from the realm of the Earthsoul. Nine or ten had fallen in the opening moments of the attack.

But with the element of surprise lost, the contest had begun in earnest, and the Light-blasted creatures were holding their own. For now. In a few moments, it wouldn't matter how strong they were with the Power of the Void. Endil had possession of the Orb—the Blood of Elsa had been awakened. He could feel Elsa's power—he could feel her presence—resonating through the spiritual fabric of the Earthsoul.

A powerful surge of *Lo'shaen* originating in the altar room shook the shrine to its core, and part of the ceiling at the far end of the passage Dommoni was using collapsed in a rumble of shattered stone and dust.

He wrapped himself in a sheltering bubble of Spirit as the wave of grit washed past him, then started for the newly opened hole.

Emma or Jeymi should have opened a Veilgate out of the shrine by now. He could feel them wielding, but they were defending. Something was wrong. Endil still held the Blood Orb, but he was in danger of losing it.

"*Bal'tei Nar'shein!*" he shouted, then bolted for the altar room.

Endil was lost in a sea of radiant energy so vast and incomprehensible that he could only stand in wonder before it. The altar room, Jeymi and Emma and Loharg...everything about the physical world had been swallowed up in the Orb's brilliance. This was true power, he realized, beyond anything he had ever imagined. And he had no business trying to wield it, Fairimor birthright or not.

*Endil.*

A voice. It sounded like Jeymi's, but he knew it wasn't. It had come from everywhere and nowhere. It had sounded inside his head. Inside his Awareness.

But how was that possible? He wasn't a Dymas. He had no ability to Commune with other Power-wielders. His was the lowly Gift of Water, about as far from the defining Gift of Spirit as one could get.

*Endil. Son of Fairimor and blood of my blood.*

He strained toward the voice, trying to pinpoint its location. Once again it sounded as if it were coming from everywhere and nowhere.

And then, distantly at first, he became aware of the Blood Orb in his hand. He could feel its warmth. Warmth, and a gentle, rhythmic pulsing, like that of a beating heart.

*Endil.*

*Elsa?* he sent in return.

*Yes, my son,* the voice said. *Your friends need you. I need you. Cast aside your doubt and help us.*

*I don't know how,* he told her, then flinched as something dark appeared at the far edge of his vision. At the far edge of his Awareness, he corrected. He was witnessing a Power-wrought attack through the eyes of *Ta'shaen.*

The darkness sent a tremor through the brilliance filling his mind's eye, but the sea of Power reacted by channeling something akin to a lightning strike. It blew the darkness apart in a spray of blue and green.

Endil was stunned. *Did you do that?*

*We did it together,* came the reply. *Endil, focus on me. You've let your Awareness stray too far.*

*But I–*

*Focus on me.*

Blinking against the spots of light filling her vision, Emma pursed her lips in disgust as pieces of Loharg's companion rained down upon the altar room. One large chunk of flesh thumped against her shield, then left a streak of greyish blood on the invisible barrier as it slid to the floor.

Obviously the fool hadn't realized that attacking the wielder of a Blood Orb of Elsa was to attack the Orb itself. Alive as it was with the spirit of Elsa, the Orb would react accordingly. If only Loharg had been so foolish.

Still blinking against the spots of light in her vision, she looked for him among the shadows. She found him skulking around the edge of the pillars to come at Endil from the side. He'd released *Lo'shaen* but held a long dagger in one clawed hand.

He'd realized what had happened to his companion and had decided to kill Endil without using the power of the Void. With Jeymi down and Endil standing in a stupefied daze, it wouldn't be hard.

Redirecting the flow of Spirit she held, she combined it with threads of Light and sent a bar of *Sei'shiin* streaking toward Loharg. He whirled to face it as *Lo'shaen* surged into him once more, and streamers of darkness shot forth to intercept the killing strike.

The two powers exploded on contact and sent a shockwave through the room that shattered pillars into powder and knocked Emma off her feet. The blast flung her backwards into a block of stone, and flashes of color filled her vision as she struck her head. She felt herself slipping toward unconsciousness, but fought through it, focusing on the luminous spot of light that was the Blood Orb to keep from blacking out. As long as Endil had possession of it, there was still hope.

Using that hope as a lifeline, she pushed herself unsteadily to her feet.

Loharg stood over her, dagger in hand, the air around him darkening with *Lo'shaen.*

Emma tried to embrace the Power, but it wasn't there. Her Awareness was silent. Her connection to *Ta'shaen* had been severed.

Loharg took her by the throat and lifted her into the air until she was eye to eye with him.

"*Kroshten fel'shor Chunin,*" he snarled and buried the dagger in her chest.

# CHAPTER 27

## *Dragon Gates*

WITH JONEAM ERIES AND THE rest of Fulrath's High Command peering over his shoulder, Idoman watched Shadan's army through the small window he'd opened in the sky above the advancing horde. He was frustrated that he wouldn't be taking part in the upcoming battle, but he knew Gideon had been right to insist he sit this one out. The proof had come when he'd opened this tiny window and found the wielding almost more than he could muster.

But it wasn't just a physical weariness brought about by his near-death experience—his Awareness had been affected as well. He was simply...tired. Mentally and physically.

Quintella placed a hand on his arm to steady him, and he smiled his thanks. The grand-motherly leader of the Rosdan Dymas had attached herself to him the moment he'd returned from Trian, sensing, perhaps, that he would need someone to look after him now that Joselyn was gone.

*Joselyn*, he thought, haunted by the memory of her last moments and his own powerlessness to save her. *Forgive me.*

He felt Quintella's grip tighten on his arm, and he looked over to find her deep green eyes watching him intently. "Are you all right?" she asked, the words bouncing off her tongue with an almost musical sound.

"I'm fine," he lied. Quintella could have opened the window with barely any effort at all, but he'd insisted on doing it himself. It helped him feel like he was contributing to the battle even if he couldn't actually fight in it.

Using his sleeve for a rag, he wiped away the beads of sweat forming on his forehead, then returned to his study of the scene below.

Shadan's army had reached the point where Dragon Gates could be used to bypass the Kelsan army, and they were preparing to do just that. Two distinct columns had formed, each stretching nearly a mile wide.

"If Galiena and her people fail in this," Joneam said, "we are going to find ourselves caught in the middle of those two armies."

"They won't fail," Idoman said, surprised by how strongly he believed it. "The enemy should be worried about those who make it through before the gates collapse. They'll be outnumbered and have no way of rejoining their companions atop the plateau."

"That's the spirit," Captain Tarn said, and from the corner of his eye, Idoman saw Captain Dennison nodding his agreement. Both captains had overseen the positioning of troops around the Kelsan camp should the Dragon Gates prove successful, and they were confident in their placement.

Idoman trusted their judgement and knew that so long as only a limited number of enemies arrived, the united armies would win the day. If Galiena and her people failed to collapse the gates...

Irritated at himself for allowing doubt to creep in, he pushed the thought away and returned his attention to the enemy below.

Both columns were an even mix of Meleki and Tamban, and had an equal number of Darklings and other shadowspawn, with the more unruly and dangerous being corralled by Agla'Con and *Jeth'Jalda*.

"Do you think they will send Power-wielders through small Veilgates to try to disrupt our camp like they did at the eastern rim?" General Gefion asked.

Idoman shook his head. "No. That attack was meant to distract us while the Rhiven launched the real offensive. We know what the real threat is now. They will come at us as one, probably from two fronts, hoping to overwhelm us."

"Which will happen if Galiena and her people fail," Joneam muttered, then shrugged uncomfortably when he realized he'd spoken aloud. "My apologies for my pessimism," he added, "But it's hard to deny these bloody Dragon Gates put us in a bad tactical situation."

"Yes," Idoman agreed, "they do. But like I said the other day, this time surprise is on *our* side." He nodded to the scene below. "Quiet now, the Rhiven are moving into position. Things are about to get interesting."

乀

With the afternoon sun obliterated by the blood-red leaves of a particularly large Yucanter, the lower canopy of Yucanter Forest was even darker than usual for this time of day. Aside from one bar of amber-colored sunlight slicing through the giant branches far overhead, the light was diffused, an eerie hue of crimson that painted everything beneath the massive tree the color of blood. The shadows at ground level were deeper, darker, and provided more cover for the Dymas concealed among them.

Gideon looked around at the gloom and smiled. *Blood and shadow,* he thought. *A perfect combination for what will soon take place in these woods.*

The area he'd chosen looked a lot like the clearing he and Jase and the others had stayed in all those weeks ago—a small clearing surrounded by a wall of paper barks and hardwoods. Directly above the clearing, a sliver of pale blue sky was visible through a gap in the giant boughs of the Yucanter.

The ground cover among the trees surrounding the clearing was dense enough to hide in but not so thick as to restrict movement once the fighting started. The trees, however, were spaced closely enough together to restrict the movement of anything larger than a man. If any of the Rhiven arrived here in their true form—a form Galiena insisted made them more powerful when wielding—they would be confined to the clearing. And they would be surrounded. In essence, this clearing would soon become a forested kill box.

Or so he hoped. A lot could still go wrong with this plan. Galiena could fail on her end. Shadan could learn he and his team of Dymas were here and launch a strike of his own. Galiena's people could change their minds and leave him and the other Dymas to be slaughtered at the hands of Aethon's pet Rhiven. The list of potential disasters went on and on.

In fact, the longer he stood in the blood-red shade of the Yucanter, the more he began to fear something had happened to Galiena. She should have been here by now. Something should have happened—for better or for worse—to let him know the offensive was underway.

He closed his eyes and took a deep breath to calm his anxiety. He was just being impatient. A result, perhaps, of spending too much time with Elliott.

It was possible Shadan's army hadn't advanced as far as first thought and Galiena was simply waiting for the right moment to attack. Or she may have already attacked and had been so successful that this secondary location hadn't been necessary.

*Or,* he thought, worry and impatience creeping back into his heart, *this phase of the offensive has become obsolete because Galiena failed.*

Opening his Awareness, he was about to contact the other Dymas with him when *Ta'shaen* came alive with powerful wieldings. The color of the forest light changed as the sky above the clearing split wide with Veilgates, and the sinuous forms of Dragons landed among the foliage.

Wrapped in auras of *Lo'shaen,* the glittering beasts channeled Night Threads in every direction, and the stillness of Yucanter Forest was shattered by peals of horrific, scream-like thunder.

With Krev at his side, Aethon watched as the Rhiven assigned to open the Dragon Gates morphed into the serpentine creatures of legend. Triple the length of a horse, they moved along the front of the mile-wide column of this half of Shadan's army. Their movements were graceful and fluid in spite of their immense size, and their jewel-colored scales reflected the afternoon sunlight in a shimmer of colors. It was an incredible sight, and those waiting to attack the Kelsan army watched the creatures in awe as they passed. Even the shadowspawn recognized greatness when they saw it and took unconscious steps backwards.

Aethon smiled. He knew his enemies were watching in awe as well, using their silly little window-like Veilgates as peepholes from the sky. He wished he could see their faces as they braced themselves to meet the onslaught. They would likely be painted with a mixture of fear and dread and uncertainty. They knew what was coming. They just didn't know exactly where it would arrive.

That uncertainty had forced the Kelsan High Command to divide their forces into multiple fronts, spreading their forces thin and weakening their defenses. Once again they had played right into his hands. They would be overrun no matter where the Rhiven opened their gates.

Hurried movement to his right caught his attention, and he turned toward it. Warskel Hozekar, the Agla'Con he'd promoted after Jamik Hedron's demise, was approaching on horseback. He was in such a hurry to arrive, that he used the Power to sweep a knot of Darklings out of his way when the dim-witted creatures didn't clear a path for him fast enough.

Reining in hard as he neared, he swung down from the saddle before his mount was even fully stopped.

"What is it?" Aethon asked. "Don't you know we are about to open the gates?"

Warskel ran his hand over his blood-red Mohawk before answering. "The *Jeth'Jalda* of the second column and the Tamban soldiers they lead have decided not to take point for the attack," he said. "Someone put it in their heads that you and Shadan think they are expendable. They cite the near decimation of their countrymen during the battle at the eastern rim as evidence."

"Then have them switch with the cultists," Aethon told him, not even trying to conceal his irritation. "Those zealots *want* to go first. Who cares if they aren't as skilled? Their numbers will make up the difference."

"Yes, Lord Fairimor," Warskel said. Scrambling into the saddle, he rode back the way he'd come.

"Bloody Tambans," Aethon said, shaking his head in disgust. "Somehow they've overlooked the fact that I lost a third of my army in a single flaming instant."

"Or maybe they haven't," Krev said, his eyes thoughtful. "The Tambans in the second column are members of *Frel'mola te Ujen*. Perhaps they think to assume control of Death's Third March if your numbers continue to dwindle."

"I'm sure that's what they are thinking. And the idea probably came from their Empress."

"Then why involve her and her cult at all?" Krev asked. "With the Fist of Con'Jithar on our side, we have the numbers to claim Trian without the help of *Frel'mola* or her cult."

"Maeon's orders," Aethon said. "In his eyes, we are all expendable."

Krev smiled inwardly at Aethon's comment. *Not the Rhiven, my friend. We survived the destruction of our world, and we will survive the destruction of this one.*

He glanced at his brothers as they neared the end of the columns. *Well, at least those of us who serve Maeon,* he amended. Galiena and her people would perish along with everyone else in this miserable world, while he and the Rhiven who followed him would depart for another. And once there, they would start the process of destruction all over again. It was one of the privileges of having a life span tens of thousands of years long, and a master determined to exploit it.

But first things first. He would only be free to walk *Eloth en ol'shazar to eryth*—or as he liked to refer to it: 'The paths of death and destruction'—after this war was over. Best to speed things along.

Grinning, he turned his attention back to his brethren. They'd reached the ends of the columns and were opening themselves to *Lo'shaen.* As before, three on each end linked their abilities and channeled a combined torrent of dark energy into the fourth.

The spiritual fabric of the Earthsoul trembled as the fourth Dragon, imbued now with unfathomable power, opened its mouth and sent tendrils of Fire streaking along the front of the waiting armies. The Earthsoul's trembling turned to spasms of pain as the fiery tendrils met, then pulled back, tearing a mile-wide hole in the Veil.

Shadan's army disappeared behind the fogged, glass-like opening that was the back side of a Veilgate, but Krev could see them well enough through his Awareness. Weapons ready, tens of thousands of Meleki and Tambans and shadowspawn charged the opening.

Four powerful surges of *El'shaen* lit up his mind's eye like flashes of lightning on a dark night, and the Rhiven channeling the gates dropped away as if falling through trap doors.

The rivers of *Lo'shaen* being channeled ceased. The Dragon Gates collapsed in on themselves in a hissing of sparks, and the forefront of the nearest column came into view once more. Thousands of soldiers and shadowspawn had been sliced cleanly in two, the two halves of their severed corpses separated now by more than thirty miles. Thousands more were missing arms or legs or were holding spears or swords with missing ends. Wisps of smoke and the stench of seared flesh filled the air.

Krev shook his head in disgust. His sister, it seemed, had decided to take part in the battle after all.

When the Dragon Gates collapsed on the advancing hordes of Death's Third March, Idoman let his small Power-wrought window above Shadan's army close, then fought through his weariness and opened a second one above the Kelsan camp.

"There," Captain Dennison said, pointing to a thin line of troops a short distance to the west of Kelsa's soldiers. A second line was visible to the northwest. "Right where I thought they'd appear," he continued. "They were hoping to pin us against the plateau."

"Not many made it through," Joneam commented. "Our men will make quick work of them."

Idoman released the Power and dropped wearily into a chair. Blowing out his cheeks, he wiped the beads of sweat from his forehead with his sleeve. "Galiena timed her strike perfectly," he commented. "Let's hope the rest of this goes as planned."

"Aren't we going to watch?" Joneam asked.

"Not unless Quintella Dymas opens a window for us," he said. "I'm done wielding for today."

"It would be my pleasure," Quintella said. Her beaded braids clicked loudly as she moved to stand behind Idoman's chair. "I wouldn't miss this for the world."

Idoman grunted tiredly. "Let's just hope it's worth watching," he said. "Galiena and her people are about to leap into the heart of darkness itself."

Gideon deflected another barrage of Night Threads with a shield of *El'shaen*, then shielded his ears as thunder echoed upward through the boughs of the Yucanter. A moment later, the clearing was pelted by a hailstorm of broken branches and shattered bark, and a moment after that, a shower of blood-red leaves settled around the three remaining Dragons like puddles of blood.

The fourth Dragon, its head cleanly sliced from its neck by Galiena, lay in a pool of real blood. Its death had sent a clear message to the remaining three that their Queen had no intentions of collaring them, and they fought with a frenzy Gideon hadn't believed possible.

In the opening minute of battle they'd killed three of Gideon's newly acquired Glendan and Rosdan Dymas and had wounded nine or ten more. Parts of the forest surrounding the clearing had been reduced to kindling, and fires burned in several places.

But his plan to corral them had worked. In their true form they were too large to seek shelter among the trees. The clearing had become the kill box he'd expected.

And it wasn't just the forest or the Dymas hiding therein which held them here—six Rhiven loyal to Galiena surrounded them, magnificent serpents of legend filled with the Power of Eliara. Twice now, the rogue Dragons had tried fleeing through Veilgates, but Galiena's people had stopped them, unraveling the Veilgates with stabs of Spirit or pounding the area with lightning.

Now the three rogues no longer had the strength to open Veilgates large enough for a Dragon, and they were unwilling to change to human form. Doing so would only speed up their demise.

Not that it mattered. They would all be dead before long, and it would be time to hunt the others.

Apparently, Galiena was thinking the same thing because she joined him on the edge of the clearing.

"They are finished," she said, then turned aside a torrent of reddish-black fire hurled at her by one of the Dragons. The deflected blast scorched the ground and set one of the shattered trees ablaze. "They just don't know it."

There was no pleasure in her voice, just resignation and a profound sadness. Killing her own people, even those sworn to Maeon, was almost more than she could bear, but she would see this through to the end because it was necessary. Gideon admired her for her dedication.

He stole a quick look at her and found her face smooth in spite of the sadness he'd heard in her voice. Unlike the rest of the Rhiven, she had remained in human form throughout the fight and was wrapped in a sheltering bubble of *El'shaen*. Except for the strike which had killed the first Dragon, she'd channeled only as much of the Power as she needed for protection. She was conserving her strength for when she confronted her brother.

Another strike of corrupted Fire was hurled their way, and Galiena drew in more of *El'shaen* to deflect it. Gideon beat her to it, turning the raging torrent back on its wielder. Part of the creature's shield collapsed, and the Fire left a smoldering dark streak where glittering scales had been.

Howling in pain, the Dragon morphed into human form and used the last of his strength to open a small Veilgate to escape. He vanished in a flash of light as a tightly woven bar of *Sei'shiin* took him in the back.

Gideon looked to the source of the strike and found Yavil. In Dragon form, he was a brilliant green and shimmered like an emerald. His crimson colored mane was singed above his right shoulder, and he was favoring one leg, but he was otherwise unharmed. The other five sported superficial wounds or burns of their own, but each was filled with the righteous, cleansing power of *El'shaen*.

Seeing their chance, they struck in unison, and the final two traitorous Dragons vanished as *Sei'shiin* burned them from existence in curt flashes of white-hot energy.

A sudden profound hush fell across the clearing. This part of the offensive was over. Now the real attack could begin.

The look of horror on the faces of those who'd just missed being killed by the failed Dragon Gate told Aethon what was coming, and he channeled threads of Air to amplify his voice.

"Hold your positions!" he shouted, and for a moment no one moved, stunned to silence by the collapse and the sheer number of casualties.

Then a group of Meleki cultists turned away from the carnage and tried to retreat into the safety of the army. A knot of Darklings did likewise and were joined by more cultists. Within seconds the entire mass had started to pull back.

Uncertainty turned to fear and then to complete panic as those at the rear were pressed upon. Aethon shouted again, and Fire crackled along the rear of the army as a number of Agla'Con and Shadowlancers tried to stop the retreat and regain control of the situation. The terrified soldiers halted, but it was clear to Aethon that their obedience was tenuous.

He turned a furious stare on Krev. "What in the name of hell's pit happened?" he snarled.

"My sister has entered the battle," he answered. "It seems I underestimated her."

"You think?" Aethon growled, stretching out with his Awareness to touch the minds of several dozen Shadowhounds. Fiercely obedient, they formed a wall in front of a group of Meleki who looked on the verge of fleeing.

Next, he touched the minds of the Rhiven who'd been assisting with the opening of the Dragon Gates, and nine of the twelve raced away in undulating flashes of color, moving along the perimeter of the two columns to further corral the terrified soldiers. The remaining three stood still, their golden eyes vacant as they stared off into space. The sudden loss of *Lo'shaen* had been too much for them, and their minds had been destroyed when the Communal link failed.

Krev didn't seem to notice. His eyes, fastened on something in the distance, burned with unbridled rage.

"Brace for incoming," he said, then wrapped himself and Aethon in a protective shield of *Lo'shaen*.

A moment later dozens of powerful wieldings of *El'shaen* jarred Aethon's Awareness as Rhiven began arriving through Veilgates. Most were in their true form, glittering monstrosities that scattered Shadan's troops the way a wolf would scatter a flock of geese.

But it was clear Krev's sister and her people hadn't come here to scatter geese, and a literal storm of *El'shaen* was unleashed as they targeted Krev and his brethren.

Aethon barely managed to stay upright as a fist of *El'shaen* slammed into Krev's shield with enough force to punch a hole through Trian's outer wall.

His golden-eyed friend flinched beneath the impact, but it was slight. Eyes still raging, he channeled a barrage of Night Threads, forcing his Rhiven attacker to retreat behind a shield of its own.

Some of Krev's followers, however, didn't fare as well. Outnumbered four to one, they were quickly overwhelmed, and it was unclear if they'd been killed or collared.

*Ta'shaen* came alive with hundreds of corrupted wieldings as Agla'Con and *Jeth'Jalda* joined the fight, and pandemonium ensued as the regular soldiers of Death's Third March found themselves caught in the midst of something they were powerless to stop and fled in every direction.

A tremendous surge of corruption at the rear of the army showed that Shadan had taken a hand in the battle, but it might be too little too late if they were unable to stop the army from fragmenting.

"I'm needed on the perimeter," he told Krev. "Join me if you can."

With that, he opened a Veilgate beyond the edge of the army and channeled a wall of Fire to stop the cowardly retreat. A quick glance over his shoulder before the gate closed showed that Krev hadn't moved. Wrapped in the darkness of the Void, he stood perfectly still, waiting.

On what, Aethon didn't know. And right now it didn't matter. He needed to act before Death's Third March was scattered to the wind.

Drawing in even more of the Void, he launched a series of strategically placed strikes and slowly but surely began turning his fleeing troops back where he needed them to be. Not in the midst of the battle between the Rhiven—only a fool would stick his hand in that fire—but to where they could be easily gathered once the Rhiven were finished.

Regardless of what happened with the Dragons, he would see that Death's Third March would be ready to continue its invasion of Kelsa. Judging from the amount of Power being wielded by Throy Shadan near the rear of the army, the refleshed Dreadlord was working toward the same end.

The march on Trian would be more difficult without the aid of Krev and his people, but he'd been prepared to do it without them anyway. The use of Dragon Gates was simply a bonus.

A Veilgate opened a short distance to his right, and a bluish-green Dragon filled with the power of *El'shaen* started through from beyond. Aethon struck before the creature was fully through, and its hold on the Power faltered as it tried to shift to defense while still maintaining the Veilgate. The silvery-rimmed opening snapped shut, slicing the creature in two.

Aethon finished it off with a Night Thread, then turned his attention back to his troops and continued his efforts to hold Death's Third March together. It was proving more difficult than expected, and the maelstrom of Power being unleashed in the center of it all only made it worse.

He flinched as a stray lightning bolt struck nearby.

*Bloody Rhiven*, he thought, then flinched again as a sudden powerful wielding reached his Awareness.

He stretched his mind toward it but stopped when he realized the wielding was originating far away from the battle. Very far away from the battle.

So far away, if fact, it could only mean one thing: Someone had just accessed a Blood Orb of Elsa.

Breaking off his attempt to redirect his troops, he tore a hole in the Veil and moved through to a waiting Throy Shadan.

# CHAPTER 28

## Sibling Rivalry

KREV'EI TO UL'MORGRANON stood in silence as Shadan's army fragmented around him, irritated with himself for having underestimated his sister and her people. For them to strike with such precision to collapse the Dragon Gates showed that at least some of them had changed their minds about killing since they would have known the collapse would claim many lives.

He shook his head. Thousands of soldiers dead and seven Rhiven lost in an instant—it was bloody brilliant, he would give them that.

But it wouldn't stop him from fulfilling his oath to assist Aethon with the attack on Trian. And it wouldn't keep him from fulfilling his oath to Maeon to bring about the death of this miserable world. He would be victorious on both counts, and he would be rewarded with passage to another world where he would continue to serve the Dark Lord.

Weaving a shield of dark Spirit energy, he turned aside a pathetic attack by one of Galiena's followers, then sent the yellow-green female scrambling for cover with streamers of counterfeit Fire. A group of *Jeth'Jalda* took up the fight as the Rhiven retreated, and Krev left them to it. He had a more important enemy to face, and the birth-bond told him she was very near. Perhaps somewhere on the battlefield, though he had yet to feel her signature wielding.

Fire and lightning continued to crackle along the perimeter of the army as Aethon and his Agla'Con worked to corral the cowards who sought to flee. Their methods were far from gentle and hundreds were wounded or killed in the chaos.

Shadan was doing likewise at the rear of the army and the ground trembled as he pummeled the plateau with as much Earthpower as the rest of the Agla'Con combined. It was an incredible display. Too bad the refleshed Dreadlord was such a fool.

A sudden increase in the strength of the birth-bond alerted him to his sister's arrival, and he turned to see her approaching through the melee accompanied by Yavil and a number of human Dymas. Yavil was in his true form, his bright red mane and emerald-like scales alight with the Power of *El'shaen*. The Veilgate he'd opened from elsewhere on the battlefield closed behind him, and he shifted the river of Power he held into a shield which he placed around his Queen.

The Dymas walking beside Yavil held shields as well but were taking turns striking any who strayed too near. One of them bore a strong resemblance to Aethon and held nearly as much of the Power as Yavil.

Galiena, her long dark hair flowing freely down her back, wore one of the crimson-colored dresses she was so fond of. She held *El'shaen* as well but was doing nothing with it. He could tell by her expression, however, that her restraint wouldn't last.

He stood his ground, his curiosity about her intentions almost as strong as his unwillingness to flee. Fleeing would only delay the inevitable anyway. If he ran, she would follow. And she would find him. The birth-bond they shared would eventually lead her right to him. No. This millennia-old conflict would be settled today. One way or another.

When she had closed to within earshot he called to her. "You didn't bring a *da'shova*."

Her smile never reached her eyes. "I didn't come here to capture you," she answered, and Krev's Awareness trembled as she attacked.

Gideon waited until Krev had fully committed himself to warding off his sister's attack, then launched an attack of his own. Not at the traitorous Rhiven, but at those coming to his aid. Tamban armor blew apart in shards of green-laquered metal, and chunks of flesh fell across the battlefield like bloody hailstones. Yavil struck a split second later, and a group of *Jeth'Jalda* vanished in flashes of *Sei'shiin*.

Others rushed in to fill their absence but were met by several Dymas from Rosda. All attempts to interfere with the siblings' conflict were turned back. But, standing as they were in the midst of an enemy army, it was only a matter of time before enough help arrived to unbalance the playing field.

And it was balanced, he realized. Galiena and her brother were equal in every facet of their abilities. Aside from outside interference, only a mistake or a lapse in concentration by either of the two would tip the balance.

He was tempted to tip that balance himself, but Galiena had made him promise not to. And he would keep his promise... as long as no one tipped it in Krev's favor.

And so he and the others staved off all those who drew too near or sought to help Krev in his fight. Within moments, an arena-like clearing had formed, its perimeter littered with the ruined corpses of any who got too close.

He ripped up the ground beneath a pair of mounted K'rrosha, then incinerated their refleshed bodies as they toppled earthward. Their singed mounts screamed in pain, then bolted back the way they had come, stomping and kicking at everything in their path.

Yavil opened his mouth and sent a stream of pure Fire roaring into the midst of an advancing horde of Darklings, and the creatures crumbled to ash beneath the intense heat.

But it wasn't all attack, and he wove a shield of Spirit to deflect a vicious strike of Night Threads aimed at Galiena. The ground shook and the air trembled as thunder echoed overhead.

Galiena and Krev never even flinched, so intent on attacking one another that Shadan himself could have walked between them and not been noticed.

That last thought gave him pause, and he hurriedly thrust his Awareness in the direction he knew Shadan to be. He found the Dreadlord atop a K'sivik, wielding unimaginable amounts of corrupted *Ta'shaen* to stop his army from fragmenting. Aethon was with him, and together they were accomplishing their design. It wouldn't be long before they turned their attention from the edges of their army to what was happening in the middle of it.

Reining his Awareness back in, he redirected it toward Yavil, touching the Rhiven's Awareness. *We need to take this fight elsewhere*, he told him. *Any ideas on how we should do that?*

*Yes*, he replied, *but I will need your help. Watch closely.* The Rhiven's Awareness opened further, and a rush of knowledge spilled into Gideon's thoughts, showing him a new way of utilizing a Veilgate.

*That*, he said, *is amazing.*

Then applying the new knowledge, he drew in more of the Power and opened a Veilgate next to Krev. Expecting an attack, the white-haired Rhiven wrapped himself more firmly in a defensive shield of *Lo'shaen* and turned toward the opening. He saw nothing save an empty expanse of grassland stretching across the Chellum Highlands. A heartbeat later he was standing in those grasses as Gideon yanked the Veilgate forward and let it collapse.

*Well done*, Yavil said as he closed the Veilgate he'd opened for Galiena. *Now we hunt the rest of my traitorous brethren.*

*Aren't you going with your Queen?* Gideon asked.

*She can take care of herself*, Yavil replied.

*God's speed, then*, Gideon told him, severing the Communal link.

He watched Yavil's glittering green form race away into the midst of the chaos engulfing the center of Shadan's army. Yavil might think Galiena would be fine on her own, but Gideon wasn't about to risk losing such a powerful new ally. He also didn't want to risk that she might not follow through with her promise to destroy her brother.

Weaving the strands of Power necessary to open a Veilgate, he moved through to a hilltop overlooking the battle between the Rhiven siblings. The area below was in flames, and flashes of light warred with stabs of darkness as the powers of Heaven and the Void were brought to bear.

Crouching down in the grasses, Gideon wrapped himself in a shield of Spirit and settled in to watch. As much as he wanted to enter the fight to help Galiena, he wouldn't unless it became necessary to save her life. In the meantime, this was her fight, and he would respect her wishes to keep out of it.

But as the two continued to lash at one another, seemingly without weakening, Gideon's patience began to wane. At this rate, the confrontation could well last for hours. And with the sheer amount of Power being wielded, it was sure to draw the attention of someone or something which might tip the balance.

He sighed his frustration. Which is why he would remain here. He wouldn't risk a third party coming to Krev's aid.

A short time later, his paranoia proved justified when a corrupted tremor of Power beyond an opposing hill tickled his Awareness and something dark came into view. A quick glimpse through his spiritual eyes revealed a silver-scaled Dragon with a black mane. It bore several burn-wounds down the length of its back and it was limping, but it held a literal river of *Lo'shaen*. Angling around behind Galiena, it prepared to strike.

Gideon moved to intercept, channeling a spiraling vortex of *El'shaen* that stopped the creature cold. It managed to weave a shield to ward off most of the strike, but silvery scales turned black and peeled away from its forelegs as it was scorched further. Gideon struck again, this time with tendrils of *Sei'shiin*, but he'd lost the element of surprise, and the Dragon deflected them easily. Turning away from Galiena, it made its way toward Gideon.

*That's it*, Gideon thought, *follow me*.

Channeling a barrage of lightning, he hammered the creature's shield with sizzling, white-hot death as he continued to lead it further away from Galiena. Neither she nor her brother showed any signs that they'd noticed the exchange, but he was certain they had. One would have to be dead to not feel the amount of Power being exchanged.

*Hurry, my friend*, he told her as he deflected a vicious series of Night Threads. *Because if anyone else arrives, I won't be able to do much about it.*

Wrapped in the sheltering light of *El'shaen*, he continued to attack his enemy, probing for a weakness as he lured the Dragon further away from Galiena. Things were going well until a powerful tremor rocked the entire fabric of *Ta'shaen*.

Gideon knew instinctively what is was, and the sudden rush of fear it brought to his heart distracted him just enough for the silver-scaled Dragon's attack to have an effect. Part of a Night Thread breached his shield, and the ground exploded upward in a spray of superheated dirt.

Hands and face stinging, he opened a small Veilgate and dove through to a hillside behind the Dragon. The move caught the creature off guard, but it reacted quickly enough to deflect Gideon's counterattack of lightning and Fire.

But the maneuver had given him an idea.

He wasn't certain he had the strength or the skill to pull it off, but it was worth a try. Wrapping his mind in *Jiu* to steel his concentration, he opened another Veilgate a short distance behind the creature, and watched as it whirled toward the opening, strengthening its shield as it turned. Its confusion at finding nothing but empty air within the gate gave Gideon the edge he'd been seeking, and he opened a second, much smaller gate directly inside the Dragon's shield, mere inches from one of its great golden eyes.

"Goodbye," he whispered, and sent a silvery bar of *Sei'shiin* lancing into the creature's head. Its entire serpentine length vanished in a brilliant flash of white, and *Ta'shaen* quieted as the power of the Void collapsed.

With a weary but satisfied sigh of relief, Gideon let the two Veilgates close and released the Power. He kept his Awareness open, however, and turned his attention to Galiena and Krev. Still locked in mortal combat, they seemed unconcerned that a Blood Orb of Elsa had just been accessed far to the west.

He momentarily considered opening a Veilgate to the point of origin, but knew whatever was happening in Kunin would be beyond anything he would have strength for. Besides, he couldn't leave until the battle here was over. Galiena might still need his help. And in all likelihood, Jase had already gone to investigate things for himself. He just hoped his son would find the Orb in Endil's hands and not Loharg's. Or anyone else who might decide to bring down the Veil.

Keeping part of his Awareness fastened on the distant disturbance, he settled in to wait once more. *Hurry, Galiena,* he urged. *We might be needed elsewhere.*

*Your human friend is very talented. Too bad I'll have to kill him after this is over.*

Krev's thoughts reached Galiena's mind through the birth-bond, but she ignored them just as she'd ignored everything else he'd sent her way. She kept her own thoughts safely inside the warding on her mind, unwilling to give her brother anything of what she was thinking. She didn't want him to sense how conflicted she was about killing him. Instead, she sent a spiraling jet of *El'shaen* lancing into his dark shield. It burned away more than half the shield's thickness before exploding in all directions like a sunburst, ripping huge gashes in the earth and lighting the grassland for miles.

Krev forced himself back onto his feet from where she'd driven him to his knees.

*Still not talking to me?* he asked. *After all we've been through together. This isn't like you, little sister.* Focusing his energy, he retaliated with sizzling, red-black tendrils of corrupted Fire.

Galiena opened a Veilgate in front of her, and the Fire passed through to slam Krev from above and behind. The force of his own attack drove him to his knees, and she felt his surprise and pain through the birth-bond as he strengthened his shield and dove clear of the avalanche of dark power.

*Clever, little sister,* he said as he came to his feet. *Did you learn that from your human friend? Tell me, have you chosen him to replace Alashon?*

The words stung deeply, but she kept her face smooth and her thoughts hidden. That he would mention Alashon in an attempt to distract her proved she was winning the fight. He would never stoop so low otherwise. He must be weaker than he was letting on.

Then again, so was she. A fact that made her grateful Gideon had decided to tag along. If he hadn't been here to intercept the new arrival, she'd have already fallen. She was tempted to have him join the fight against Krev, but resisted. She would finish this on her own. And she would finish it now.

Drawing in as much Power as she could hold without destroying herself, she sent another jet of *El'shaen* boring into her brother's shield. The Light of Creation met the darkness of the Void in an explosive burst that shook the earth and threatened to set the air itself ablaze.

Krev stood his ground as she advanced on him, but she sensed his alarm through the birth-bond as the dark aura surrounding him was slowly burned away.

He attempted to launch a counterattack of Night Threads, but in his weakened state the task proved too difficult, and the dark aura shielding him wavered momentarily, leaving him partially exposed to the cleansing power of Heaven's Fire.

One shimmering thread reached him, and his right arm went from flame to ash in an instant. Howling in rage and pain, he staggered backward, his shirt and cloak smoldering. But then his sheltering aura of darkness sprang back into place, and he stood his ground once more.

Galiena pressed harder, ignoring Krev's pain and crushing the affection and sympathy she felt for him. He'd brought this upon himself. He deserved this.

With the last of her strength, she burned away his shield and dispelled the Void with *El'shaen te sherah*, severing Krev's hold on *Lo'shaen*.

Stunned, he dropped to his knees and could only stare at her as she moved to stand before him.

"I thought you weren't here to capture me," he said, his words laced with sarcasm in spite of the pain in his voice.

"I'm not," she said, then formed a blade of Spirit and sliced his head from his neck. His lifeless corpse toppled to the side and lay still.

She stood in silence, wanting to weep, but unable to find the tears. She was still staring at her brother's lifeless form when Gideon appeared beside her.

"I know that wasn't easy for you," he said, placing a hand on her arm.

She looked over at him and found his eyes filled with sympathy.

"No. But he was my responsibility," she said. "If I'd had the courage to do this eighteen hundred years ago, a lot of your recent troubles could have been avoided."

"Well, you did the right thing this time," he told her. "As the Riaki say: To Kill the Dragon…"

"One must cut off its head," she finished for him. She sighed. "Actually, it isn't a Riaki saying. It's Rhiven. My father used to say it all the time."

Gideon glanced at Krev, then met her eyes once more. "Can you feel what is happening in Kunin?" he asked.

She turned her gaze to the southwest. "Yes," she answered. "The Blood Orb Lord Endil went to retrieve is being accessed."

"And?" Gideon prompted.

"And what?" she asked.

"Are we going to investigate?"

She smiled tiredly. "Do *you* have strength enough for another fight?"

He shook his head.

She took him by the arm. "Neither do I," she told him. "In fact, I don't think I can even open us a Veilgate out of here, weak as I am right now."

"Allow me," Gideon said, and a small doorway opened into the Kelsan camp.

Holding onto Gideon's arm for support, Galiena took one last look at her brother's headless body and allowed herself to be led through the opening.

Aethon watched the last of the Dragons vanish through Veilgates, then released *Lo'shaen* and turned a hard eye on Shadan. The Dreadlord had finally joined the fight, but only when necessary, and mostly just on defense. Once again, the famed Destroyer of Amnidia had been more concerned with his own safety than for the well-being of his troops. *The flaming coward*, he thought disgustedly.

"What now?" Aethon asked.

Those who'd tried to flee the chaos had been corralled and were being herded back into position by Agla'Con and *Jeth'Jalda*, but it would be some time before order was completely restored. Even worse, every last one of Krev's people had been killed or captured and Krev himself had not returned. And with how targeted Krev's sister's attack had been on the Rhiven, Aethon suspected he had seen the last of Krev'ei to ul'Morgranon. It was a bloody shame, but one he could do nothing about.

Right now he and Shadan had more important things to worry about, not the least of which was how to move Death's Third March forward without the aid of Dragon Gates. He repeated his question and succeeded in drawing Shadan's attention away from the scene before him.

The Dreadlord's good eye shone with anger and frustration, and his K'sivik stamped its feet, sensing its master's mood.

"We march," Shadan said, his raspy voice filled with scorn. "Trian awaits."

"And the Rhiven who sided with our enemies?"

"If they return, we will run them off as we did this time."

Aethon grunted but said nothing. Of course the fool would have seen things that way. He was either too stupid or too arrogant to realize the Rhiven had left because they'd achieved their purpose.

Shadan tightened his grip on his scepter and leaned forward in the K'sivik's saddle. "Krev and his Dragon Gates were nothing more than a convenience we exploited while it lasted," Shadan said. "They shaved days off our march when they helped us bypass the eastern rim. Their loss at this point is of no consequence. We hold the high ground, and we outnumber Kelsa's forces more than two to one."

Straightening in the saddle once more, he pointed west with his scepter. "We will push them into Mendel Pass and fill it with their ruined bodies." He allowed himself a chuckle. "Trian will be mine within a week at most."

*Not without a lot more help*, Aethon thought. Instead he said, "I will contact our allies in Tamba and see to the—" He cut off as a powerful but distant tremor rippled the fabric of *Ta'shaen*. Even without extending his Awareness toward it, he knew what it was—he'd felt its exact likeness the night Jase Fairimor had scattered the Meleki camp.

A Blood Orb of Elsa was being used in battle. To what end, he couldn't say, but it was certainly worth investigating.

Without waiting for comment from Shadan, he seized *Lo'shaen* and tore a hole in the Veil. Warskel Hozekar and a number of Agla'Con turned toward the opening and brought fists to chest in salute. He could tell by their expressions that they'd felt the disturbance as well.

"A Blood Orb is being accessed in Kunin," he told them. "Find it."

# CHAPTER 29

## *Reservoir Unleashed*

AS ENDIL FOUGHT TO REIN in his Awareness, the sea of light surrounding him began to change. The all-encompassing brilliance changed to flickering spots that whirred and danced in his vision and were accompanied by a great roaring hiss—like the sound of gravel being driven over stone by strong winds.

Occasionally, one of the flickering lights would take shape for the briefest moment, giving him a glimpse of the person he'd just touched with his mind. A little girl in Arkania playing with a colorful bird. A man on a ship sailing the Inner Sea. A woman baking bread in Tetrica. Three faces amid the millions living in the Nine Lands.

It was almost more than he could bear. Would have been more if not for the sheltering power of the Blood Orb coursing through him. Man was not meant to have such an Awareness of the world. Only Elderon should be able to see and hear so much at once.

And so he continued to pull his mind inward, guided by Elsa, sheltered by her spirit.

Then all at once vast areas of the flickering lights dimmed. Much of the hiss and roar assaulting him vanished or was dampened. But it was sporadic, loud in one place but muted in others.

He felt a rush of excitement as he realized what it meant. He was experiencing the curse he'd been hearing so much about. His Awareness was moving across Kunin—he was almost back.

A moment later, everything vanished from his mind's eye save for one point of light shining like a miniature sun. He'd reached the valley of the defilement. A fact that was confirmed by the bursts of Earthpower he felt being wielded in battle. The Dymas in his group had engaged demonspawn and *Shel'tui*.

Amid all the surges, the single point of light that was the Orb drew nearer. The darkness of the curse grew more oppressive.

When at last he drew into himself, his natural vision returned in a rush and he found himself staring into the red-gold Orb of his birthright.

Movement beyond the Orb's sphere of light caught his attention, and he glanced past it to find Loharg holding Emma by the throat. Blood slicked the side of her head, and she was struggling to breathe.

*No,* his mind screamed, but before he could move, Loharg stabbed the tiny woman with a dagger, then dropped her the way a spiteful child might drop an unwanted doll.

Endil took a step forward, grief and rage washing through in him in turns, but he hesitated when his eyes fell on Jeymi. She was lying a few feet away, her eyes closed, her face and hands blistered and burned. He couldn't tell if she was alive or dead.

His rage spiked sharply, burying his grief and awakening a need for vengeance. Hefting the Blood Orb, he imagined a torrent of white-hot fire.

The Orb flared brightly, but nothing happened. The reservoir of Power he'd seen—the reservoir he could *feel*—remained distant and out of reach.

*Focus on me.*

Loharg turned toward him, his demonic eyes wary as he stared at the Orb. Hefting the dagger, he started cautiously forward. Clearly, he knew enough of the Orb's properties not to strike with *Lo'shaen*. He meant to kill Endil just as he'd killed Emma.

Reaching deeper into himself, Endil imagined the same killing fire.

Again nothing happened.

*On me, my son.*

Loharg stepped over the remains of his ruined companion, and his massive body shifted into a crouch, like a stalking cat ready to pounce as he circled around behind the pillars to come at Endil from the side.

Common sense said otherwise, but Endil closed his eyes and reached toward that part of himself that was his newly expanded Awareness. This time, instead of letting it expand outward, he focused it on the Orb. It was like peering into a keyhole on a door barring entrance to a very bright room—at first he saw nothing but the singular bright light beyond.

Then the light gave way and he found himself looking at the altar room through the eyes of *Ta'shaen*. Or perhaps even the eyes of Elsa herself. He'd become one with her Awareness, and no taint or curse was strong enough to dim the light of her spiritual vision.

He saw everything just as if he were looking with his natural eyes, only now his view of the world was painted with a shimmering, blue luminescence. He saw Jeymi, badly injured but alive. He saw the shattered altar, the psychotic writings and remnants of horrific sacrifices. He saw Emma's mortally wounded body and her lifeblood pooling on the floor beneath her. He saw the fissures and fractures in the temples walls and supporting pillars. He saw individual motes of dust, like miniature fireflies, floating in the malodorous air. He saw *everything.*

His eyes—his spiritual eyes—settled on Loharg. Dagger at the ready, the leader of the Sons of Uri had cleared the last of the pillars and was preparing to lunge.

Endil opened himself to the vastness of Power he could see shimmering all around him and felt it condense itself into a fist of pure, potent, cleansing energy.

*For Emma,* he thought, and Loharg vanished in a burst of unparalleled destruction.

Thorac watched in stunned silence as pieces of the Shrine of Uri rained down upon the ruined valley like monstrous hailstones. Blocks of stone the size of wagons pummeled the earth, crushing Kunin and demonspawn like insects and tearing fresh gashes in the already ruined landscape. Smaller fragments were still airborne and would land as far as five or six miles away.

Fighting all across the valley stopped at the sound of the explosion, and all eyes turned toward the shrine. The entire north face of the structure from the fifth level up was gone, as were the pyramid like cap of the seventh level and most of the sixth level's ceiling.

Thorac raised his spyglass toward the destruction, fear and uncertainty warring with hope. He found a single figure standing at the epicenter, holding a glowing Blood Orb of Elsa, but he was unable to make out who it was through all the dust filling the air in front of the temple. He held his breath while he waited for the air to clear.

A moment later a swirl of wind brought Endil's face into view.

"Thank the Creator," he said, then went cold inside as he got a better look at his young friend's face. Jaw clenched, a terrible light burned in his eyes.

"Something's wrong," he told Thex. "I need a Veilgate to the altar room."

Channeling just enough of the Power to cloak himself in bended Light, Elliott picked his way carefully through the ruined landscape of Amnidia and away from the pack of demons hunting him. Seven in all, they were furious with him for destroying their leader in an exchange of Fire and Light that had lit the valley from one end to the other and had transformed a half-mile wide stretch of black rock and sand into a sheet of glass.

His hair was singed from the encounter, and he had heat blisters on his face and hands, but he was otherwise unharmed. It was a bloody miracle, he knew, especially considering that his cloak had been so badly burned he'd had to discard it.

He reached the top of the hill he'd been climbing and looked back the way he had come. The demons were still trailing him, but he'd managed to increase the distance between himself and them. It wasn't clear which of the seven could wield *Lo'shaen*, but as long as he kept his distance, they wouldn't be able to feel his use of bended Light. Of all the things he could do with his Gift, this one required the least amount of effort and left the smallest Power signature.

Now all he had to do was stay hidden and wait to be rescued.

He frowned. Only it was taking much longer than it should have, especially considering that every Dymas atop the wall and all those who'd been with him before he'd been pulled through the Veilgate knew he was here.

"Come on, Jase," he whispered. "I could use a little help right now."

He studied the seven demons who were hunting him until he was satisfied that they'd lost his trail, then turned his attention to the Veilgates the demons had commandeered. Three were still being held open by fiery tendrils of *Lo'shaen*, but none of the demons had made it through the openings as of yet. That might change if something didn't happen soon to cut off the demon's hold.

He momentarily considered trying to sneak close enough to make a run for one of the gates, but knew it would be nothing more than suicide at this point. There was simply too much power being wielded by both sides.

Turning his attention back to those who were hunting him, he watched as one of them bent and fingered the ground. When it rose, it pointed in the direction he'd taken and all seven started forward as one.

Muttering a string of whispered curses, he moved down the back side of the hill and broke into a run, desperate to put as much distance between himself and the demons as possible. As soon as he was certain he was out of their line of sight, he released the Power, hopeful that someone atop the wall might spot him.

He'd gone about a mile when he spotted movement in the mouth of a fissure a few hundred yards to his right.

He immediately wrapped himself in bended Light and froze, unsure what it was he had seen. A few seconds passed and a *Mrogin* moved a short distance into the open. He knew what it was even though he'd never seen one—Jase's description had been spot on.

The *Mrogin* seemed wary, understandable considering that an army of demons had entered its valley, but Elliott could tell by its stance that it was also curious. And hungry.

And it was looking right at him.

*So much for trying to sneak my way out of here,* he thought and readied a strike as the *Mrogin* sprinted toward him.

"Can you see him?"

The fear Seth heard in the question caused him to lower the spyglass and turn to look at Jase. The young man's face was bright with panic. For Elliott, certainly, but it was what Jase could feel happening in Kunin that had him gripping the stone of the battlements as if he were trying to crush it into powder. The distant look in his eyes showed that he was searching for Elliott through the eyes of *Ta'shaen*.

"Nothing yet," Seth answered. "He must have wrapped himself in bended Light."

"If he made it out of that inferno, that is," Captain Kium added, and Jase turned a stare on him that made the captain take an unconscious step backward.

"He's alive," Jase insisted. "Keep looking."

Seth raised the spyglass, and Jase lapsed back into agonized silence as he wrestled with the choices laid before him.

A short time later he jumped as if he'd been kicked.

"Endil needs me," he said. Turning his back on the valley, he opened a Veilgate into Kunin.

As Thorac moved through the Veilgate into what was left of the altar room, he spotted Emma lying among the rubble and rushed to her side. Her face was ashen, her dress soaked with blood from the wound in her chest.

"No, no, no, no," he said, scooping her up in his arms. "Emma, talk to me. Emma." He turned to Thex, his throat tightening with pain, his heart breaking. "You have to heal her," he said. "Hurry."

Thex placed his hands on the tiny woman's head, then lowered them a moment later. "I'm sorry, my friend. She's gone."

Thorac shook his head, tears welling up in his eyes. No, he thought. Her life couldn't end here. Not after all she had done to serve and protect the Earthsoul. It wasn't fair. It wasn't—

His eyes fell on Endil standing at the edge of the massive hole he'd opened in the shrine, and he knew what he had to do. Cradling Emma against his chest, he rose and rushed across the room

Endil turned as he approached, his eyes alight with something only he could see. His face, his very countenance seemed to glow. He looked at Emma, then at Thorac.

"I'm sorry, Thorac," he said. "I couldn't save her." He looked back out at the bowl-like valley. Hundreds of *Shel'tui* had banded together and were approaching the shrine's outer courtyard, fists glowing red with corruption.

"But," Endil continued, "I can avenge her."

He raised the Blood Orb before him and sent a river of white-hot energy streaming into the midst of the advancing horde of Power-wielders. They vanished like gnats in a furnace, burned from existence with no understanding of what had killed them. The river of fire flowed northward, incinerating everything it touched. Thousands of Kunin died, but to Thorac it would never be enough to atone for the loss of Emma. Even if Endil killed every last one of them, it—

"Endil!" the shout turned everyone about, and they found Jase Fairimor striding through a Veilgate. At least Thorac thought it was Jase. He wore the young man's face, but something about him was different. No. *Everything* about the young man was different.

"This won't help the Earthsoul," Jase continued. "I can hear what Elsa is telling you to do, and this isn't it. Don't let your rage blind you to her wishes."

Endil lowered the Orb, and the rush of killing energy ceased. He seemed to come back to himself in a rush. "I'm sorry," he said, sounding ashamed. "I never should have tried to wield." He offered the Orb to Jase. "You should finish this, not me."

Jase shook his head. "No. The Earthsoul has chosen you. Finish it as She and Elsa direct. I will deal with our enemies."

Thorac gently laid Emma's lifeless body on the floor, then drew his axe as he stood. His heart still ached, but he was able to mask much of the pain with anger. Like Endil, he wanted nothing more than to avenge Emma. Fighting side by side with the *Mith'elre Chon* should provide the means for that vengeance.

Fingering his axe, he looked out over the valley. "Tell me how I can help."

Jase waited until Endil opened himself to the Orb, then followed Thorac's gaze out at the valley.

"I need to know where your men are positioned," he said. "I can't see a bloody thing through my Awareness, and I don't want to strike any of our people by mistake."

"Half of the Chunin are on the back side of the eastern ridge," Thorac answered. "They are loosing arrows through Veilgates. General Kennin is leading a Krelltin cavalry assault beyond that rock fin there." He pointed. "The one with the greyish top. Captain Haslem and his *Bero'thai* are hitting the Kunin nearest to us from both the east and the west. They are trying to funnel everything toward the front of the shrine so nothing gets around behind us. Our Dymas are exchanging blows with a host of demonspawn, and the *Nar'shein* are hunting the Sons of Uri in the lower levels of the shrine."

Jase nodded. He'd felt the exchanges between the Dymas and the demonspawn, and for now it seemed as if Thex's people were holding their own. Down below, Chieftain Kia'Kal and his men had the Sons of Uri on the run. Likely the filthy creatures had felt Endil's use of the Blood Orb and wanted nothing to do with it.

"So the center of the valley is clear of our men?" Jase asked.

"Yes," Thorac answered. "We felt it wise to avoid the demonspawn and *Shel'tui* who clustered there to welcome Loharg into the valley."

Jase nodded. "I knew I could feel an unusual concentration of wieldings in that area," he told Thorac. "They..." he paused, trying to get a feel for what they were doing. A tremendous amount of Power was being seized out there, but the absence of explosions and other displays of aggression was confusing. It felt like a fire was spreading, a great spider web of energy that—

"Brace yourselves," he yelled, opening himself to the Power and casting up a shield of *El'shaen* only a heartbeat before an avalanche of corrupted Fire struck the top of the shrine. It slammed Jase's shield with enough force to drive him to his knees, and the impact sent a sharp stab of pain lancing through his Awareness. His shield held, but barely.

It was a bloody good thing he hadn't taken a hand in the battle at the Great Wall. Any expenditure of energy there would have cost him his life here. He would need to thank Ohran for his advice once this was over. If he survived.

Thex appeared at his side, his aged face lined with concern. He'd healed the young female Dymas of her wounds, and she stood behind him. The fierce look in her eyes showed she was ready to reenter the fight.

Thex glanced at the fire raging overhead. "What was that?" he asked.

"The *Shel'tui* have linked their abilities," Jase said, forcing the words through clenched teeth. "They've given themselves over to one of the Sons of Uri. Obviously not all of them are here in the shrine. And the fool doesn't understand that the Orb could have reacted against his attack instead of me. But I won't allow the reservoir of Power to be squandered destroying him and his followers."

"The Son of Uri holding the link," Thorac said, "must have felt Loharg's death and is making a move to replace him as head of their brotherhood. He will stop at nothing to accomplish that."

"Jeymi and I will do what we can to draw his attention away from here," Thex said, then held up a hand when Jase started to protest. "Don't worry. We aren't going alone." Jase felt him embrace the Power, and a Veilgate opened to another location in the shrine. The two disappeared through without another word.

Jase forced himself to his feet and channeled every bit of strength he had into his shield. Overhead, the sky was being obliterated by swirling, red-hot death. And it was growing stronger as more *Shel'tui* added their strength to the wielding. If something didn't happen soon to disrupt their link, he would lose his hold on the shield, and the Orb's purposes would be frustrated when it reacted to defend itself. He couldn't allow that to happen.

Motioning Thorac to follow, he moved closer to Endil and decreased the size of the shield even as he increased its strength.

Endil didn't seem to notice. His eyes, filled with wonder at the amount of Power coursing through him, remained on the Blood Orb.

"What is he doing?" Thorac asked, his irritation obvious. Clearly he thought Endil's unleashing of the Orb's reservoir of Power should be evidenced by more god-like acts of destruction.

"He's strengthening the Veil," Jase answered, unable to keep the wonder from his voice. If this was what a defiled Blood Orb was capable of—

"So what do we do?"

The question brought Jase back to the moment, and he looked over to find Thorac fingering his axe.

"We make sure he isn't interrupted," Jase told him.

Directing more energy into his shield, he watched through the eyes of *Ta'shaen* as the pillar of light that was Endil Fairimor acted as a conduit between the powers of heaven and the fragile, spiritual fabric holding back the powers of hell.

Jeymi sent spears of *Sei'shiin* lancing into a cluster of *Shel'tui* and watched them flash from existence in bursts of white. Several *Shel'tui* near the cleansing strike cried out as their connection to the massive mindlink vanished, and Jexlair crystals winked out or exploded, killing those who held them.

Jeymi smiled grimly. This was too easy. With their will surrendered to their demonspawned master, the *Shel'tui* had neither the strength nor the ability to defend themselves. And it would continue to be that way until the Son of Uri holding the link released them.

She could see him, just beyond the towers marking the edge of the shrine's grounds. Wrapped in an impenetrable bubble of *Lo'shaen*, he continued to channel a literal river of Fire onto the shield of Jase Fairimor.

Jase was holding for now, but even the *Mith'elre Chon* couldn't hold back such an attack indefinitely. She and Thex and the others needed to do more to disrupt the link and cut off the demonspawn's flow of Power.

But there were *hundreds* of corrupted Power-wielders in the valley below, both *Shel'tui* and demonspawn, and those not already linked to their masters were venturing forth to engage her and the other Dymas. Scattered and outnumbered, it wouldn't be long before all they could do was flee or wield *Ta'shaen* for defense, as Jase was being forced to do.

Her attack on the *Shel'tui* complete, she nodded to Aierlin who opened a small Veilgate to another location overlooking the valley. Once there, she and Aierlin released the Power, trusting in the curse to keep them hidden from enemy Awarenesses.

"What now?" Aierlin asked, her eyes on the chaos below.

Before Jeymi could answer, *Ta'shaen* groaned in protest as a corrupted Veilgate opened not far below them and several Meleki Agla'Con moved through from beyond. And not just any Agla'Con either, but Shadan Cult priests. The proof was in their blood-red Mohawks and the crimson lightning bolts sewn on their uniforms.

Jeymi placed a hand on Aierlin's arm to keep her from embracing the Power. "They haven't seen us," she whispered, and Aierlin nodded. Together they crouched among the boulders and waited to see what would happen.

One of the Agla'Con pointed at the shrine. "There," he said. "The Orb."

"Fetch the others," said another, and the one who'd pointed out the Orb ducked back through the still-open Veilgate.

He reappeared after only a moment, and the Veilgate snapped shut in a hiss of angry sparks.

"Just what we need," Jeymi muttered as corrupted Veilgates began opening all across the ruined hillside.

"We've got company," Thex said as he stepped through the Veilgate he'd opened into the altar room. "They appear to be Agla'Con from Death's Third March."

"I felt them," Jase said. "Aethon is making a play for the Blood Orb. This might be exactly what we need."

Thex raised his brow at the young man in surprise. "I'm not sure what you mean."

Jase smiled as the raging torrent of Fire overhead lessened considerably. He pointed upward. "That," he answered. "The *Shel'tui* have a new enemy. One they likely consider to be more of a threat."

"But not all of them will be released from the link to engage the Agla'Con," Thex warned. "We are still extremely outnumbered." He quickly viewed Endil with his Awareness and found a river of Earthpower flowing through him. It didn't seem to be slowing down or weakening. "How much longer?"

Jase studied Endil a moment without speaking. "I don't know," he answered. "It could be minutes or it could be an hour."

A pure Veilgate opened just beyond Jase's shield and Jeymi and Aierlin hurried through. "There are Agla'Con all across the upper slopes," Jeymi said. "Maybe as many as thirty." She turned her attention to Endil. "Is he all right?"

"He's fine," Jase answered. "How much strength do you have left?"

"Enough to see this through," Jeymi answered, but Thex thought she sounded tired. Not surprising considering the healing she'd needed earlier. But she was one of the most powerful young Dymas Thex had ever met, and he agreed with her assessment of her abilities.

Apparently Jase did as well. "Good," he said. "You and your companion link with Thex. I'm going to turn the shield over to you."

Jeymi was shocked. "Me?"

Jase smiled encouragement. "Just until Chieftain Kia'kal arrives," he said. He and the other *Nar'shein* will be here shortly."

Thex stepped forward. "What are you going to do?"

Jase's face hardened. "I'm going to buy some time for Endil to finish with the Blood Orb."

"How?" Thorac asked, and Thex knew from the white-knuckled grip he had on his axe and the frustration in his voice that he wanted to be part of whatever Jase had planned.

"There is a Son of Uri in need of killing," Jase said. "I'm going to introduce myself to him." He looked at each of them in turn, then settled on Thorac once more, a look of understanding in his eyes. "I thought you might want to join me."

Thorac grinned. "With pleasure."

Endil gazed into the incandescent river rushing through his Awareness and reveled in the potent purity of the flow. It was originating from a reservoir on the Eliara side of the Veil as a single, titanic thread of *El'shaen te sherah*, but as it passed through the Blood Orb, it separated into the Seven Gifts of Earthpower, each of which spiraled away beyond the reach of his Awareness.

But he didn't need to see where they stopped to know what was happening. The Earthsoul was receiving much needed strength. She was being healed—here in the defiled valley and elsewhere throughout the Nine Lands. Where the Gift of Earth was weak, strands of *Ta* raced in to fill the void. And that was true for the other Gifts, as well. Fire for Fire. Air for Air. Flesh for Flesh. All were being strengthened and rejuvenated.

He couldn't say for sure, but it felt like an unusual amount of Spirit was being directed somewhere far to the north. He probably could have followed the threads with his Awareness, but he chose not to. *Focus on me*, Elsa had said. And so he would. He wanted to be ready when the reservoir was exhausted and it was time to leave this awful place behind.

And the awfulness was getting worse by the minute. He could feel the strikes of Earthpower, both pure and corrupted, surging across the valley. Only it was no longer limited to exchanges between *Shel'tui* and Dymas. Agla'Con had arrived to join the fight, and the valley had erupted into even more chaos.

*Focus on me*, Elsa cautioned, and Endil turned his attention inward once more. It was difficult to clear his mind, but he found a small measure of peace in knowing that Jeymi was nearby.

As the torrent of energy continued to flow through him, he sensed that the reservoir feeding it was nearing an end. Once exhausted, his god-like omnipotence would end with it. The thought gave him pause.

He hadn't expected to feel disappointed.

The Veilgate Jase opened into the midst of his enemies drew surprisingly little attention from the Kunin who couldn't tell one wielding from another, but the *Shel'tui* in the area went berserk. Breaking free of the mind-link, they hurled a multiplicity of attacks, all of which ricocheted off of Jase's shield and into the swarming Kunin. Bodies were hurled skyward, were incinerated, or were simply ripped to pieces.

With barely a glance at the carnage being wrought around him, Jase held his shield in place and continued his advance on the Son of Uri. He was somewhere just ahead, surrounded by a host of demonspawn.

Thorac had called them *Chisa'mi*, and like many of the *Shel'tui*, these lesser demonspawn were lending their strength to their master through a Communal link. As of yet, though, neither they nor their master had taken an interest in him or the other Dymas who'd entered the fray at various locations throughout the swarming mass of bodies. Their attention, fueled by demonic rage, was still fastened on what was happening in the Shrine of Uri.

That was about to change.

Reaching into his pocket, he withdrew the Blood Orb he'd received from Gideon all those weeks ago in Kindel's Grove. The foot and talons gripping the Blood Orb were a little worse for wear, but the Orb itself felt warm in his palm. It had been awakened by Endil's wielding of its sister-Orb, and though it no longer had access to any reservoir of its own, its very presence was a strength to Jase. Mentally as well as physically.

He tightened his grip on the Orb and continued to advance on the Son of Uri. He could see him now, a monstrous, misshapen creature that towered over those around him. His back was to Jase. His attention, like the *Chisa'mi* around him, was fastened on the shrine. The air around him was dark with the Power of the Void.

Jase pressed on, deflecting all his enemies' strikes back into the Kunin and carving a path of death through their midst. It was strange to have his Awareness blacked out by the curse and still be able to feel the Power being wielded, but the lack of spiritual vision wasn't a concern now that he had the Son of Uri in sight.

The number of pure wieldings was far fewer than he would have liked, but he was pleased that he'd been right about the *Shel'tui's* reaction to the Agla'Con—they were targeting them just as aggressively as they were the Dymas.

He smiled at the thought. Corruption killing corruption suited him just fine.

A powerful thrust of corrupted Spirit struck his shield hard enough to rattle his teeth, but he tightened his grip on the Blood Orb and pressed on. He was within fifty paces of the Son of Uri when some of the accompanying *Chisa'mi* noticed his approach.

A cacophony of sharp, feral cries filled the air as they called for the master, and Jase settled in as the Son of Uri turned to regard him with a mixture of surprise and contempt. Its wolf-like face twisted into a snarl as fangs were bared.

"*Droshem kala veskin,*" it said, and the torrent of Earthpower being directed at Endil was redirected into a thrust of sizzling death that hit Jase's shield with the force of a battering ram.

The impact knocked him back several paces, but his shield held and he remained on his feet. More importantly, he could feel that the Son of Uri had made no attempt to shield itself. Driven by its rage, it was instead channeling everything it had into its attack.

Jase smiled inwardly. *Just like I thought you would.*

Deflecting the flow of destruction into the surrounding *Chisa'mi*, Jase listened to them burst into flaming ruin, collateral damage of their master's anger. Dozens died, but still the Son of Uri attacked, strengthened by those whose minds it held, driven by blind rage to kill Jase and seize the Orb he held.

This wasn't a contest Jase could win, and the demonspawn knew it. It started toward him, eager to claim its prize.

Jase stood his ground. It wouldn't be long now.

"Is he just going to stand there?" Jeymi asked, then shifted her feet in embarrassment when Chieftain Kia'kal turned to regard her with a smile.

"He is fighting like a *Nar'shein*," the giant man told her. "A powerful defense is often the best form of attack."

Before Jeymi could form a rebuttal, another corrupted Veilgate opened into the altar room, and two Agla'Con rushed through from beyond with Jexlair talismans blazing.

Jeymi burned them from existence with spears of *Sei'shiin*, then sent several follow-up spears through the collapsing Veilgate. She didn't even try to hide her frustration as she looked back to Dommoni. "An attack is the best form of attack," she told him. "And Jase isn't doing *anything*."

"He won't need to," Thex said. "Patience. The conflict will be over soon."

Jeymi wasn't so sure, but she moved back to the gaping hole in the wall and raised the spyglass Thorac had given to her before he'd left with Jase. But where was he? Not anywhere on the battlefield that she could see. Wise since only a Power-wielder could survive in such chaos.

The Son of Uri came into view through the spyglass and just beyond him, the swirling vortex of Fire hammering Jase's shield. She frowned. *How much more of that can he take?*

A small Veilgate opened at an angle above and behind the Son of Uri's head, and Jeymi's heart skipped a beat when Thorac sailed through from beyond. Brass chain mail shining, he landed feet first on the demonspawn's back and drove a Dainin spear clear through the creature's massive body.

The force of the blow drove the demonspawn to the ground, and the torrent of fire assaulting Jase vanished.

All across the area, *Shel'tui* talismans winked out or exploded as the mind-link was severed and the flow of shared corruption was lost. Those not killed outright clutched at their heads in pain and confusion or simply stood in a stupefied daze.

Jase's shield vanished, and *Ta'shaen* came alive with a tremendous wielding of Spirit and Light as he channeled *Sei'shiin* into the mass of bodies. *Shel'tui*, demonspawn, and Kunin flashed from existence in flares of white.

Through it all, Jeymi kept the spyglass centered on Thorac, watching as the insanely courageous little man pulled his axe from his belt and split the Son of Uri's head like an overripe melon.

Pulling the blade free, he turned as if he intended to single-handedly take on the rest of the Kunin army, but Jase was there to meet him, and *Ta'shaen* came alive once more as Jase opened a Veilgate back into the altar room.

Endil felt Jase's return just as he'd felt everything else taking place in the valley. The arrival of the Agla'Con; the massive assault by, and then the death of, the final Son of Uri; the eradication of hundreds of *Shel'tui* and demonspawn by Jase—the Blood Orb had conveyed all of it to him through the spiritual consciousness of Elsa herself.

But as the final flows of *El'shaen te Sherah* began to ebb, that vast consciousness began to diminish with it. This was the end, he knew. His moment as the most powerful wielder on earth was about to end.

*There is one more thing,* Elsa's fading voice whispered. *Use your Gift to wash the filth from the valley.* A sudden powerful image of how to do that entered his mind, then she was gone.

Endil opened his eyes to find thunder rumbling overhead and his friends watching him with concern. The stabs of corrupted lightning stopping just short of killing him and the others told him they were under attack by *Shel'tui* or Agla'Con or both. That he could no longer feel the wieldings let him know that his moment of being a Dymas was over.

Jeymi stepped forward and took his hand. "Are you all right?" she asked.

Endil nodded, then changed his mind and shook his head. "I'm not. It's not easy to let go of such power. It makes me feel... insignificant."

"You did well," Jase said, and around him the others nodded. "But we should talk elsewhere. The rest of our people have already retreated through Veilgates. We should join them before the shrine is overrun."

"Let them come," Endil said. "I have one last surprise for them."

Opening his Awareness to the Gift of Water, he reached deep into the earth beneath the shrine, stretching it toward the underground lake Elsa had shown to him. Before the Defiling, its waters had flowed freely upward through cracks in the bedrock, filling Elsa's Font as well as dozens of fountains throughout the Temple of Elderon. A beautiful, tree-lined river once divided the valley as it ran northward to a pristine lake. The flow simply needed to be set into motion once more.

More than a thousand feet below the surface, the curse suddenly vanished and the reservoir of water came into view in his mind's eye as clearly as if he were still linked to Elsa's Awareness through the Blood Orb.

He didn't know if the area had been cleansed of the curse during his wielding of the Orb or if it had never been affected by the Defilement at all, and right now it didn't matter. He knew what he needed to do.

Embracing his Gift, he did as Elsa had shown and channeled a stream of Water into the underground lake, creating pressure and forcing water upward through the natural and Power-wrought aqueducts leading to the font and surrounding fountains.

But that pressure also pressed down on even deeper chambers of water, and Endil felt something break loose, as if an old channel had been sealed off by some ancient collapse. Just like that, an unfathomable amount of water rushed upward, increasing the pressure in the underground lake and sending water jetting through the aqueducts toward the font and fountains.

The ground began to tremble as the water rose, increasing to the intensity of an earthquake within moments. An explosion sounded in the lowest level of the shrine as the long-desecrated font erupted like a geyser, filling the cavernous room in an instant. Hallways became aqueducts channeling the water outside, carrying away the bodies of the slain Sons of Uri, scouring away their filth.

Endil channeled his Gift into the reservoir with even more intensity, and fountains of water erupted skyward all across the shrine's grounds and in hundreds of places across the valley, roaring towers of frothy white that fell upon the Kunin below, knocking them from their feet and sweeping them away in rivers of liquid death.

And still he channeled, dredging up every bit of strength he had left, determined to rid the world of the wretched creatures trapped in the rapidly expanding flood below. He would drown them all.

A hand on his shoulder brought him back to himself, and he looked over to find Jase watching him with concern.

"That's enough," he said. "You'll only injure yourself if you continue." He pointed out at the valley, and a grimly satisfied smile moved over his face. "Besides, you've set something in motion that will fill this godforsaken valley and bury the Shrine of Uri beneath hundreds of feet of water. You did well."

Endil released the Power, then studied the rapidly expanding lake. Kunin and demonspawn were drowning by the thousands or were being crushed against the rocks by swirling currents. Thousands more were scrambling for higher ground but were having trouble outrunning the rising waters. The valley would soon be swallowed by a massive lake.

He looked at the Orb in his hand, then tucked it into his pocket and moved to kneel next to Emma. He took one of her tiny hands in his, and the tears he'd been holding back blurred his vision and wet his cheeks.

The mission to recapture the Blood Orb had been a success, the Sons of Uri were no more, and much needed strength had been added to the Veil, possibly delaying an all-out collapse by weeks.

But he'd lost one of his dearest friends in the process. That alone trumped all the successes combined and left him feeling like a failure. He ran a finger over her cheek.

"Now I know what a hero looks like," he whispered. Taking her up in his arms, he turned to Jase. "Let's go home."

# CHAPTER 30

## *"Scattered From Hell to Breakfast"*

ELLIOTT DODGED A SIZZLING CHUNK of *Mrogin*. then lowered his sword and released the Power. The thunder from his lightning bolt echoed away across the rocky landscape, a clarion call for every demon in the valley.

He shook his head in disgust as he started running. Someone on the wall had to have seen *that*. The demons hunting him certainly had. He could hear their cries as they resumed the chase.

He didn't want to remove himself from the view of any who might be trying to spot him from the wall, but the demons crested the hill behind him much sooner than expected. He had no choice but to hurriedly wrap himself in bended Light.

When one of the demon's clawed fists went red with corruption, Elliott knew he hadn't been fast enough, and he dove behind a large rock as streamers of red-black Fire streaked toward him. The area where he'd been standing exploded with heat, and shards of rock and burning dirt pelted his backside. Sudden searing pain accompanied the sound of pierced flesh, and he grimaced.

And not just from pain. He was mortified about the healing such a wound would require. He didn't relish the thought of a Dymas, particularly a young, pretty, female Dymas, gaining such an up-close awareness of his rump.

Clenching his teeth against the pain, he pulled three dagger-length shards free and tossed them to the ground. Angry now, he hammered the hilltop with a dozen stabs of lightning. The entire area went white with the attack and the resulting rumbles of thunder echoed away for miles.

*Tell me someone saw that.*

Still cloaked in bended Light, he rose and limped away from the boulder, casting a quick look over his shoulder as he went. Five of the demons lay in smoking ruin, and one was writhing in agony, alive but missing both its legs. The one who could wield was hunkered beneath a shield of palpable darkness. Elliott hoped it was second-guessing its desire to continue the chase.

Night Threads tore up the ground behind him, but Elliott had put enough distance between himself and his previous hiding spot that the lethal strikes did little more than assault his ears with the strange, screaming thunder.

With his pride as injured as his rump, he clamped a hand over the wound and ran. When he was sure the demon was no longer trailing him, he stopped for a moment, trying to catch his breath. This was not at all how he had expected this day to go.

た

The ringing in Railen's ears was almost more than he could bear, but he kept his shield in place against the Night Threads streaking toward him and forced his way closer to the final Veilgate still being held open by the demons on the other side.

The demons who'd made it through were throwing everything they had at him and Elrien and the others, and they were bloody strong. Numbering almost forty, they were shaped like men, but that was as far as the resemblance went. Their grey, leathery faces were pitted and scarred, and eyes glowed red with the powers of hell.

A particularly powerful strike of corrupted Light hit the top of Railen's shield and the inside of his head went bright with pain. The ringing in his ears vanished—all sound vanished. He could feel the jarring hits of the Night Threads on his shield, but to his ears all was silence.

He reached up and touched his right ear, and his hand came away slick with blood. He blinked. *That can't be good.*

Another vicious stab struck his shield, and he was driven to his knees. If something didn't happen soon to even the playing field, he and the others would be killed.

A small but pure Veilgate opened inside his shield, and Sheymi ducked through to kneel next to him. She was speaking urgently, but he shook his head and pointed to his ears. Her eyes went wide with understanding, and she quickly gripped his head and sent a rush of healing into him.

The sound of the tumult raging overhead returned, and he cringed. Blood of Maeon, but it was loud.

"We need to fall back," Sheymi said. "This battle is lost."

"No. We cannot allow any more demons to escape the valley."

"Railen," she said, her tone surprisingly gentle. "We need to go. Elrien's orders."

He shook his head. "But Elliott—"

"There is nothing we can do for him here," she said. "He would want you to—" She stopped as a sudden influx of Spirit struck the edges of the Veilgate, severing the demons' hold on it and collapsing it in a shower of sparks.

Railen stared at the spot in wonder. "What was that?"

"I don't know," Sheymi said, pulling him to his feet. "We'll figure it out later." Opening herself more fully to the Power, she opened another small Veilgate and they ducked through to safety.

Sheymi sagged to her knees in exhaustion, then turned and looked northward. Five miles away, smoke rose from the smouldering grasslands where Elrien and the other Dymas were still engaging the demons in battle. Flickers of black destruction were followed by muffled rumbles of thunder, and flashes of red sparked new fires amid the grasses.

Around her, intermittent surges of Spirit announced the arrival of other Dymas who'd fled the conflict through Veilgates, and the number of strikes, both pure and corrupted, gradually decreased in the distance until *Ta'shaen* was quiet once more.

Sheymi pushed herself to her feet and looked around at the rest of her companions. Elrien and one of his apprentices had been the last to arrive, racing through a Veilgate together. The aged prophet's robes were singed, and he had blood on the side of his face. Aside from that he appeared fine. The young lady with him—Sheymi saw now it was Keymi—was clutching a broken arm against her chest with her other hand. Her face was bloodied as well.

The others sported a variety of wounds and burns, but nothing that appeared life-threatening. And everyone had survived, which was a miracle in and of itself considering they'd been outnumbered two to one.

"Well, that didn't go as expected," Erebius said, his tone bitter. "We lost Elliott and now we have demons outside the valley."

"At least we closed the gate," Keymi offered.

"That wasn't us," Elrien said, his eyes distant and his face thoughtful. "It was the Earthsoul. She has been strengthened." He pointed to the southwest. "Can't you feel it? A Blood Orb of Elsa is being wielded by a son of Fairimor."

Sheymi stiffened in surprise. Not at the announcement itself, but that she could feel the wielding Elrien spoke of. She'd been so fixated on the wieldings of the battle at hand that she missed it completely. It was akin to what she'd felt during the Night of Fire Jase had unleashed on Shadan's army, powerful yet distant.

"So what does that mean?" she asked, and Elrien smiled at her.

"It means there is still hope," he answered, then turned his attention back to the smoke rising in the distance. "The demons won't stay in one place for long," he said, changing the subject. "They are driven by their need to kill and destroy, and they will seek out the nearest town or village. I need you and Railen to return to the Great Wall and fetch reinforcements. The rest of us will stay behind to monitor the demons."

Railen felt him embrace *Ta'shaen*, and a Veilgate opened back to the top of the wall. He and Sheymi hurried through to the chaotic scene beyond.

Seth ducked beneath the glistening fangs of the giant spider-like demon, then spun around behind it and sliced off two of its legs. It let out a shriek and whirled toward him, but he dove beneath its massive abdomen and drove both of his swords deep into its chest.

Shrieking in pain, it spun first one way then another, unable to reach him, its frantic movements carving an even larger hole in its chest as Seth kept hold of his swords. Blood soaked him to his elbows before the creature finally teetered to the side and fell. With one final hissing shriek, its six remaining legs curled in against its body as it died.

Flicking the creature's dark blood from his swords, Seth moved to engage another demon, this one a bizarre blend of ape and scorpion. A group of *Bero'thai* had it surrounded, but it had taken three Elvan lives since cresting the wall.

And the scene was the same everywhere he looked: *Bero'thai* were dying and there simply weren't enough Dymas to help them defend the wall now that the first wave of demons had resumed their attack. They'd come as one, furious that their masters had been engaged by Elliott and the others, eager to take advantage of the shortage of Dymas.

Seth cast a quick look in the direction of the most recent lightning strike. Elliott was there somewhere, outnumbered and on the run, but obviously still alive. *Hold on, my friend,* he thought. *Help is coming.*

He just hoped it would arrive soon enough to save Elliott. The Great Wall... now that might be a different story all together. It was a terrifying thought, but a reality nonetheless. Especially considering that they were already being overrun and the bulk of the demon army—including those capable of wielding *Lo'shaen*—had yet to arrive.

One of the *Bero'thai* cried out as he was struck in the shoulder by the demon's scorpion-like stinger, and Seth caught him in his arms as he fell. He quickly dragged the man to safety only to find him already dead and his neck and face discolored by web-like threads of black which continued to spread outward from the wound.

Seth lowered the dead man's body to the stonework, then started for the demon once more. It was riddled with arrows and had the broken shaft of a spear lodged in its side, but it was still full of fight and had full use of its tail. Killing it wasn't going to be easy.

A Veilgate opened near the battlements and Sheymi and Railen rushed through from beyond. A split second later, the scorpion-tailed demon vanished in a flare of white as a bar of *Sei'shiin* channeled by Sheymi struck it in the chest.

Blinking against the spots of light the strike left in his vision, Seth hurried to greet the new arrivals. The help he'd been hoping for had arrived.

"Elrien sent us for reinforcements," Sheymi said, then glanced down the length of the wall and blew out her cheeks in frustration. "That isn't going to happen, is it?"

Seth shook his head. "Not if we want to hold the wall," he told her. "What happened out there?"

"A number of demons escaped the valley," Railen answered. "The area is remote, so they aren't a threat at the moment. Elrien just didn't want them getting too far away from where they are now. He and the others stayed behind to watch them and re-engage if necessary."

Seth felt like swearing. "Well, they are on their own for the moment. As you can see we are in need of reinforcements ourselves right now. Our forces are scattered from hell to breakfast."

He looked at the bursts and explosions of *Ta'shaen* happening far out in the valley. "We need to recall those Dymas. Can you two make contact with them and tell them to return? Their attack on the demons out there will mean nothing if we lose the wall."

"Yes, *shent ze'deyar*," Railen answered, and Seth waited anxiously while they did as requested, hopeful that the help they so desperately needed wouldn't be beyond the reach of their Awarenesses.

When Veilgates began opening along the top of the wall, he knew they'd been successful, and powerful strikes of Earthpower followed as the arriving Dymas attacked the demons, killing some and driving others back into the valley.

But they were still outnumbered, and the advantage gained by their sudden arrival was soon lost. Those demons still atop the wall plunged into the midst of the densest groups of Elvan soldiers, trusting in their thick hides and armored segments to protect them, wise enough to know that the close proximity would keep the Dymas from striking further for fear of killing their own.

"The bloody things are smart, I'll give them that," Seth muttered. Twirling his swords in frustration, he started for the nearest melee.

Sheymi's hand on his arm stopped him. "Wait. Where is the *Mith'elre Chon?*"

"Gone to Kunin after a Blood Orb," he told her. "As I said, our forces are scattered."

"And Elliott?" she asked.

Seth pointed to where he'd last spotted Elliott's lightning. "Somewhere out there."

"We'll find him," Railen said, and Seth nodded his thanks.

"God's speed, my friends," he said, then watched as a Veilgate opened to reveal the scarred landscape of Amnidia. Without another word, the two young Dymas raced through and were gone.

Seth turned back to the fight at hand.

The demons' decision to use the *Bero'thai* as human shields had deterred further attacks by the Dymas, but the Light-blasted creatures had underestimated the skill and determination of the Elvan soldiers. Where one *Bero'thai* fell, two more appeared to take his place, and demon blood fell like rain at their feet.

Seeing the nearest fight well in hand and unable to get past it to the next one, Seth sheathed his swords and moved to the battlements overlooking the valley. Directly below the wall, the nightmarish menagerie of the first wave was beginning to retreat as more and more strikes of Earthpower exploded in their midst, killing some and injuring others.

It would have been a welcome sight if those below represented the extent of the demon army, but Seth could only watch in frustration as the well-meaning Dymas played into their enemies' hands by expending precious strength they would desperately need once the main body of demons arrived.

Frowning, he raised a spyglass to inspect the main part of the demon army and found that it was again on the move. They'd lost less than a quarter of their number, and while it was impossible to say for sure, he was willing to bet that most of those killed by Elliott and the others had been lesser demons incapable of wielding Lo'shaen. The most dangerous demons were yet to arrive, and there were more than enough of them to overrun the Great Wall.

He lowered the spyglass, a cold knot of dread settling in his chest. And they would be here in less than an hour.

The wounds in Elliott's backside throbbed, but he didn't dare slow for fear of being overtaken by the demon which was still hunting him. Drawn by the smell of his blood, it was on him like a bloodhound tracking a wounded fox. He couldn't shake it so his only hope was to outrun it—a task being made increasingly more difficult by his wounds.

Trusting in his ability to bend Light to keep him hidden from enemy eyes, he stuck primarily to the more wide open spaces, avoiding large out-croppings of rock and ravines where the valley's inhabitants were likely to wait in ambush for prey. He moved as quietly as he could in his haste, but the crunch of shale and slag beneath his boots sounded loudly in his ears. Hopefully the valley's inhabitants were aware of the demon army and had vacated the—

A monstrous shape detached itself from a cluster of rocks a short distance ahead, and Elliott stopped, fear and frustration washing through him in turns. *Oh, for the love of Maeon, now what?*

He stood absolutely still and kept himself cloaked in bended Light. The shape materialized into a massive lizard-like creature, and it was apparent from its behavior that it had heard his approach. The only consolation: It wasn't a demon. At least he didn't think it was. Who knew with how many varieties of the bloody things there were? At the very least, it was a flaming big shadowspawn. Killing it would require lightning, and lightning would tell the demon hunting him exactly where he was.

Stilling his breathing, he remained where he was, hoping that by staying silent he could avoid a confrontation.

The creature cocked its head as if listening, then lifted its snout and tasted the air with a long, forked tongue. After a few flicks, it started forward, moving first one way then the other, pausing occasionally to taste the air. It was larger than a *Mrogin*, if somewhat slower and more deliberate in its movements.

*Not that it will matter*, Elliott thought disgustedly. Every step it took equaled five of his and it could obviously smell him. A few more flicks of its tongue and one or two more adjustments, and it would be right on top of him.

Elliott raised his sword and prepared to loose a killing barrage of lightning, but hesitated when the crunch of gravel sounded to the south and the lizard-creature whirled toward it.

*The demon*, Elliott thought, then nearly hissed aloud as Railen and Sheymi came into view atop a slight rise in the terrain. *It's about flaming time*, he thought, then flinched as the shadowcreature launched itself at them, pelting Elliott with a spray of gravel as it went.

Shielding his face against the sudden spray, he watched the creature go, then released the Power so his friends would see him.

The shadowspawn was faster than it looked, and it covered more than half the distance to Sheymi and Railen before Sheymi raised her hands and tore it apart with the Power. It was far more brutal than what he would have expected from her so he suspected she was either angry or tired. Considering all that had happened in the past few hours, it was probably a little of both.

He waved his thanks as he hurried toward them. Sheymi's use of the Power would have pinpointed their location to the demon trailing him, and he was eager to get out of range once and for all. Hopefully one of them was strong enough to open a Veilgate.

They started toward him as well, but vanished behind an explosion of superheated dirt and rock as Night Threads tore up the ground around them.

Elliott wrapped himself in bended Light as ear-splitting cracks of thunder shook the area, then held his breath as he waited for the explosion of dirt to settle. When it did, he found Railen and Sheymi safely crouched beneath a dust-laden shield of Spirit.

Breathing a sigh of relief, he cast about for the source of the attack and found a demon approaching from the north. It was the same one who'd been trailing him, but now it had a new target.

Scepter flaring brightly, it struck again, hammering the two Dymas with Night Thread after Night Thread, determined to collapse their shield, consumed by demonic rage.

*Oh no you don't*, Elliott thought. Raising his sword at the unsuspecting hellbeast, he struck with a bolt of lightning as thick as the demon itself. It vanished in an explosion that shook the ground for miles, and left a jagged white line lingering in Elliott's vision.

Like Sheymi's attack on the lizard-creature, it was excessive, but he didn't care. He was angry and tired and... well... angry. All of this was his fault. If he hadn't suggested they attack the demons before they reached the wall—

"You're injured," Sheymi said, stepping near and placing her hands on him.

He kept his face smooth even though he knew she was getting an up-close look at his injuries through her Awareness. After only a short pause, a rush of healing took his breath away.

"Thank you," he said, then smiled and added, "You didn't leave a scar this time did you?"

She arched an eyebrow at him, a mischievous smile on her face. "Who would see it if I did?"

Railen choked on a laugh, then smoothed his face and gestured to the Great Wall rising in the distance. "This fight isn't over," he said. "Perhaps we should get back to it."

When Elliott appeared through a Veilgate accompanied by Sheymi and Railen, Seth breathed a sigh of relief. Striding quickly forward, he took Elliott by the arm and looked him over. "Are you all right?"

"Nothing injured but my pride," Elliott answered, ignoring the smirk spreading across Sheymi's face. "What happened here?"

Seth pointed to the demons retreating amid explosive bursts of Earthpower. "We were nearly overrun in a second attack by the first wave of demons," Seth told him. "Obviously, they took exception to you killing one of their most powerful masters."

Elliott studied the retreating demons for a moment, then looked around at the carnage the creatures had left in their wake. Dozens of Bero'thai were dead. Scores more were wounded. And while no Dymas had been killed, they were weary from the extensive wielding of their Gifts.

Elliott shook his head in frustration. "So much for launching a preemptive strike."

Seth realized what Elliott was thinking and knew he needed to put a stop to it. "None of what happened here is your fault," he told his young friend. "To believe so is to suggest you alone gave the order to attack."

"It was my idea," Elliott countered.

"And it was embraced by the rest of us as the right course of action," Seth told him firmly. "We simply underestimated the abilities of some of our enemies."

Elliott's expression showed he wasn't convinced, but he did change the subject. "Where is Jase?"

"In Kunin. Endil was successful in recovering the Blood Orb, but Jase sensed he was in trouble and went to help."

Elliott nodded. "And Elrien?"

"Still in the Allister Highlands," Railen answered. "Some forty demons escaped the wastes, and Elrien and the rest of those who went with us initially are still there to monitor them."

"We can't allow demons to roam free," Elliott said.

"Nor can we allow our forces to be divided any more than they already are," Seth told him. "No one else leaves the wall until we hear from Captain Kium or Captain Alleilwin."

"Sorry, Captain," Elliott said. "Those demons are outside the wall because of me. It's my responsibility to make this right."

They locked eyes for a moment, and Seth could tell no amount of arguing would change the young man's mind. Finally he nodded. "Fine. But you'll go by way of General Eries' tent. He and the rest of the High Command need to know what is happening here and in the Allister Highlands. If Gideon is with them, tell him he is needed here."

"I will," Elliott said, then looked expectantly at Railen and Sheymi. A Veilgate opened in front of him, and he hurried through without another word. Railen and Sheymi, however, muttered irritably about being left behind.

"I need you here," Seth told them. "We're short-handed as it is."

The two continued to frown at him as they moved to the battlements to watch the approach of the demon army. Seth joined them, but remained silent. After a few minutes the tension between them began to lessen, and Railen broke the silence with a small laugh.

"I've been thinking about what you said earlier," he said. "About our forces being scattered from hell to breakfast. What exactly does that mean?"

Seth thought for a moment, then shrugged. "I don't know. It's just something my grandfather used to say. Usually in reference to my clothes or toys."

Railen smiled. "I like it. Do you mind if I file it away for future reference?"

"Be my guest," Seth told him, though in truth, he was starting to worry that there might not be a future. And he wasn't worried solely for those here at the wall, but for the entire human family. And rightfully so.

If the Veil could collapse so completely in Amnidia, it could collapse just as completely elsewhere. And that meant this wouldn't be the only demon army marching to battle against humanity.

He tried to picture what might be happening in Kunin with the Blood Orb and prayed it would be enough to balance the scales.

Scales, which at the moment, were so obviously tipped in Maeon's favor.

# CHAPTER 31

## *Awakened*

"THE LAST OF THE AGLA'CON are attempting to flee through Veilgates," Kelithor Dymas said, and Hulanekaefil Nid nodded.

He'd felt the use of the Power as well, but it was clear only a few of the cowards were strong enough to actually rend the Veil.

"Tell our Dymas to stop those they can," Hul said. "But I'm not overly concerned if a few escape. I want Shadan to know Melek is firmly back in the hands of its rightful king. I want him nervous about the need to watch his back as he advances on Kelsa."

"And those who are unable to escape?" Kelithor asked.

Hul looked at him. "I would like a few for questioning. Destroy the rest with *Sei'shiin*."

"Yes, my lord," Kelithor said and moved away across the courtyard.

Hul watched him go, then looked up at Nightingale Palace rising above the city. Smoke issued from several windows in one of the lower towers, and there were jagged holes in the stonework of two of the upper. The domed roof of the throne room was partially collapsed. It was relatively minor damage, all things considered. Elsewhere in the city, entire blocks had been destroyed, most of them set ablaze by the enemy as they retreated deeper into the city.

But like the retaking of Kamoth, the attack here had come from within as well as from without. By utilizing Veilgates and the passages leading into Nightingale Palace, his army had pinned the cultist soldiers against the very blazes they'd hoped would hold Hul's forces back. It had been a massacre.

But it wasn't entirely over as evidenced by the clash of steel sounding in the street beyond a row of buildings and the surges of Earthpower erupting in the direction of the palace. Motioning Captain Plat and his two squads of Crescent Guard in the direction of the more conventional fight, Hul started toward the nearest of the corrupted wieldings. It was several streets away, but a quick glimpse through his Awareness showed nine Agla'Con clustered together under a shield of Spirit held in place by the one in the middle. The others were launching attacks at a number of Dymas moving in to surround them.

It was a desperate move, and one which would only delay their inevitable demise. Had they been anything other than what they were, Hul would have felt sorry for them. But they deserved what was coming, and he wanted to be part of it.

Keeping the Agla'Con in view with his Awareness, he jogged across the courtyard, then made his way down a wide, tree-lined lane before cutting through a partially burned out building to the street beyond.

Bodies, most of them cultist, littered the street, but there were the arrow-riddled corpses of Shadowhounds and patches of scorched paving stones where K'rrosha had been burned from existence by Dymas. Hul picked his way through the carnage and was about to cut through the well-groomed garden of The Brass Ring Inn, when a sudden disturbance in *Ta'shaen* tickled his Awareness. It was distant but powerful. It was also familiar, a singularly destructive burst that felt very much like Jase's destruction of Shadan's camp all those days ago. And then he understood—a Blood Orb was being used somewhere very far to the west.

He was tempted to explore the point of wielding with his Awareness, but he knew right away he was too tired for such a precise viewing over such a distance. Besides, he would know soon enough if the Orb was being wielded by the enemy or someone friendly to the Earthsoul. Moving on, he kept his fingers crossed that the Veil would remain in place.

He'd only gone a short distance, when a second disturbance tickled his Awareness. Less a wielding and more a... a resonance, it flowed through the spiritual fabric of *Ta'shaen* like something alive and was marked by warm, pulsating tremors like those of a heartbeat. And it was pure.

Dismissing himself from the battle for a moment, he fastened his Awareness on the resonance of Power and traced it north toward its source. Like a bird, his spiritual view of the world sailed over Lake Kamasin and the peaks of the eastern arm of the Death's Chain Mountains, then skimmed the treetops of Velerem Forest until it reached the slopes of one of the forest's nameless mountains.

There Hul found a smattering of tenacious pines and colorful alpine flowers clinging to life in the midst of an extensive boulder field. Near the top edge of the boulder field where broken rock butted up against a sheer cliff face, he found a large pool of water. Fed by an underground spring, its icy cold waters flowed out of the pool, then down through the boulder field where they emerged as several small streams in the forest below.

Hul was impressed by the beauty of the place, but didn't pause to truly appreciate it. Drawn by the resonance of Power, he pressed his Awareness into the mountain and found a series of caves.

No, he corrected. Not caves. Passages. Passages carved by the hands of men. His pulse quickened at what it might mean.

He pressed his Awareness deeper into the mountain, following the resonance of Power from chamber to chamber via stairwells and passages lined with glowstone lamps and Old World markings.

He encountered the stream again, flowing in a perfectly cut channel in the floor of a wide passageway. A short distance further on, a vast chamber came into view. The stream of water stretched to an intricate fountain in the center of the room. Above the fountain a massive glowstone chandelier lit the room from end to end. More Old World writings were carved above an archway in the far wall, and he could read enough of it to know it was a dedication to the God of Creation.

He'd found a lost Temple of Elderon.

The resonance of Power was markedly stronger beyond the archway, and Hul eagerly pressed his Awareness onward into another large chamber. His luminescent view of the world brightened as he entered the room, and he marveled at the singularly powerful brightness of the source of the resonance which had drawn him here.

There, in an intricately carved candelabrum on top of an altar of grey-green crystal, an undefiled Blood Orb of Elsa shone pure and bright, awakened, he knew by the use of its sister Orb in Kunin.

*We're saved*, Hul thought, a wave of relief sweeping through him. This was it—everything he and the others had been fighting for was about to be realized. All he needed to do now was send word to Jase Fairimor.

He felt the Agla'Con's Awareness only a heartbeat before *Ta'shaen* trembled beneath a violent and corrupted rending of the Veil. Tendrils of red flashed through his spiritual vision like miniature lightning bolts as the Veil was torn open, and seven Shadan Cult priests strode into the large chamber where the fountain lay.

Hul pulled his Awareness back in time not to be felt by the men, but he picked up much of what they were thinking in the split second that his mind had touched theirs.

More of Lord Shup's cronies, they'd been here in Kamasin but had been preparing to flee now that the battle had turned in Hul's favor. They'd sensed the Blood Orb's awakening just as he had and had gone to claim it. Their intent—he'd felt it as strongly as if they'd spoken it aloud—was to present the Orb to Shadan as a means of obtaining forgiveness for their failure to hold Kamasin.

They'd come alone, desperate to capture the Orb ahead of any of their brethren who may have also sensed it. This was to be their prize, and they loathed the thought of sharing the glory with others.

Hul hoped their selfishness would prove to be their undoing.

Knowing there wasn't time to call for backup, Hul opened himself to *El'shaen te Sherah* and wove the necessary strands to part the Veil. He opened the gate directly beneath the archway leading to the inner sanctum and *Sei'shiin* burst from his fists before he was completely through the opening.

Lornishalin Pek, Lord Shup's second in command, vanished in a flare of white, as did the Agla'Con behind him. The others cast up hastily woven shields, but Hul managed to destroy a third Agla'Con before redirecting his flows to protect himself.

His Veilgate slid shut behind him, and he retreated down the corridor in the direction of the Blood Orb. Four to one odds weren't insurmountable. Not when the prize was the death or salvation of the entire world. He just wished he hadn't spent so much of his strength killing Agla'Con back in Kamasin. He was going to need everything he had left to kill these four.

They came after him as one, hurling thrusts of Fire that sprayed off of his shield into the stonework, obscuring the way before them and slowing their pursuit. The heat made stones crack, but in the tight confines of the passage it was their safest bet. Lightning or even a vicious thrust of Earth would have collapsed the ceiling and brought the mountain down on their heads.

It wasn't a bad thought if it meant it would keep the Orb out of their hands, but Hul wasn't ready to concede the fight yet. Opening a hole in his shield, he channeled another stream of *Sei'shiin* and sent the white-hot spear lancing toward them.

It struck one of the men's shields in a spray of white, and he dove to the side as it burned through, narrowly missing his head. The radiant spear punched a hole through the back of the man's shield as well, then burned a smouldering gash down the wall before disappearing into the chamber beyond.

Before Hul could close the hole he'd opened in his shield, a burst of heat from an attack of Fire drove him backward. Singed and coughing, he stumbled and went down, then rolled to his knees and faced his attackers once more.

He'd known opening his defenses in order to attack would be risky, but he didn't have many options right now. That he'd missed killing the Agla'Con added to his frustration.

Fortunately, each man still held a shield of his own making, proving they weren't willing to form a link to boost their abilities. Hul didn't know if it was their inherent mistrust of one another or an underlying hope to be the last man standing that kept them from linking, and he didn't care. As long as they fought individually, he had a chance to beat them.

*If my strength holds out, that is.*

The paving stones just outside the bottom edge of his shield exploded into shards as the nearest Agla'Con struck with a thrust of Earth, and the force of the blow knocked Hul back another step. Shards of rock pelted the sides of the passage, exploding into smaller shards and puffs of dust.

More strikes of corrupted Fire followed, and the air inside his shield grew uncomfortably warm, burning his lungs when he breathed. His hold on the Power wavered, but he fought through his weariness and strengthened his shield.

He retreated further, and the narrow passage gave way to the open expanse of the inner sanctum. Behind him, still glowing brightly atop the altar, sat the Orb of Elsa.

The resonance of Power he'd felt through his Awareness was even more pronounced now that he was here in person, and he let the radiance of the sacred talisman wash over him.

It filled his mind with light, warm and pure and alive—it was the most beautiful thing he'd ever seen. It was also completely vulnerable to the evil intentions of these men who had come here to violate it.

The very thought awakened a terrible, protective rage, and he struck with the last of his strength, opening a Veilgate in the midst of the Agla'Con. The razor-like edges of the gate sliced through the shields of the nearest two in an explosive detonation of Light and Spirit that tore them to pieces.

In the tight confines of the passage, the unraveling of their shields struck those of the other two Agla'Con with enough force to sever their hold on the Power. The Jexlair crystal in one of the talismans exploded, killing the man outright and knocking the other into the wall with such force that Hul heard his skull crack like an egg. He dropped lifeless next to the ruined corpses of his companions.

Bracing himself for what was to follow, Hul reined in his Awareness and released *Ta'shaen.*

It left him in such a rush that spots of light formed inside his head even as the world around him blurred into shadow. He fought to stay upright, but his exhaustion was too great and he collapsed next to the altar. Above him, the Blood Orb of Elsa dimmed, and Hul could only watch as everything vanished into darkness.

Throy Shadan watched from atop his K'sivik as Aethon and the other Agla'Con started Death's Third March moving again. It had taken most of the day just to round up those who'd fled or been scattered, and hours more to get them back into ranks and columns. More than a little destructive persuasion had been necessary to accomplish the feat, and several hundred cultists had perished because of it. But their deaths mattered little—this army was still more than sufficient to crush Kelsa and her allies and claim the city of Trian.

He allowed himself a smile. His enemies had to know how futile this war was. The prophecies—both the light and the dark—were clear that the final battle would be fought within the walls of the ancient city.

It made him wonder what they hoped to accomplish by coming out to meet him. Yes, they were hoping to delay Death's Third March long enough for Jase bloody Fairimor to find and use a Blood Orb in the Rejuvenation, but that could have been accomplished by simply fortifying Trian Plateau and waiting for him to come to them.

He shifted his scepter to his other hand, then nudged his K'sivik forward. It didn't matter to him where he met his enemies. Here or in Mendel Pass or within the walls of Trian—the end result would be the same: He would kill them all.

Then, when Con'Jithar finally claimed this miserable world, he would rule over those he'd conquered. Forever.

An amused chuckle escaped his lips, and his K'sivik lifted its head and turned a curious eye on him. "That wasn't for you, my pet," Shadan told it. "It was for the fools who think they can stand against me."

*And for the foolish hope they have in the Rejuvenation,* he added silently.

Blood Orbs there may well be, but the odds of finding one undefiled was *not* in Jase Fairimor's favor. Recent events were proof of that, first with the Orb Borilius had defiled in the Zekan temple, and now with the Orb in Kunin. He could feel that its reservoir of Power was nearly spent, but clearly its effect on the Earthsoul had been minimal, as far from a rejuvenation as removing a splinter was from a complete healing. Like Jase's use of the Orb in Melek, this recent wielding was a wonderful, extraordinary waste of incredible power that brought his enemies no closer to victory.

He was momentarily tempted to extend his Awareness to the point of the wielding, but decided against it. The events taking place in Kunin had nothing to do with him or his plans for Death's Third March. He could wait for the return of those Aethon had sent to investigate. It wouldn't be much longer now anyway. He could feel it.

As if summoned by his thoughts, a corrupted Veilgate opened in front of him. But it hadn't opened from the desolation of Kunin as he had expected—it had opened from the Pit. He quickly drew rein on his K'sivik as Shattuk Croast, the head of those tasked with refleshing Agla'Con, stepped near the fiery rimmed opening.

"My apologies for disturbing you, Great One," he said, eyeing the K'sivik nervously. "But my men and I are sensing a disturbance in *Ta'shaen* somewhere in the Velerem Forest. None of us are skilled enough to pinpoint its exact location, but we've narrowed the area to one of the northernmost mountains. We can't say for sure what is happening there, but it feels... uncorrupted."

Shadan reached down and scratched the neck of his agitated mount while he considered what he'd just heard. He knew Lord Nid was actively working to regain control of Melek, but there was nothing of interest in the Velerem Forest. Certainly nothing with any strategic or military value. This had to be something else, perhaps even something related to the use of the Blood Orb in Kunin.

The thought brought a sharp stab of panic. If another Blood Orb had somehow been awakened by the events in Kunin, he couldn't allow it to fall into the hands of the Fairimors.

Seizing *Ta'shaen*, he started to enlarge the rent in order to join Shattuk in the Pit but reconsidered when he realized his departure would draw the wrong kind of attention. From Aethon as well as from his enemies.

He looked across the columns of soldiers to where Aethon was riding alongside the Tamban commander at the head of a column of Tamban cavalry. There was no telling what the traitorous Fairimor would do if he got his hands on a Blood Orb of Elsa, and he wasn't willing to find out. Aethon had already challenged him once. What would keep him from doing it again? And this time with Power enough to emerge victorious.

"What are your orders, Great One?" Shattuk asked.

"You and your men are to leave the Pit immediately and find the source of the disturbance. If it is alive, kill it. If it is a talisman, bring it directly to me."

"Yes, Dreadlord," Shattuk said, and the rent snapped shut with a hiss.

Shadan started his K'sivik forward once more, excited about the sudden turn of events. If the unknown disturbance did indeed turn out to be a Blood Orb of Elsa, this laborious march would no longer be necessary. He would use the Orb's reservoir of Power to single-handedly claim Fairimor Palace, destroying all who dwelt therein and laying waste to the inner and outer cities.

He could accomplish the same thing by collapsing the Veil and ushering in the arrival of Con'Jithar, but the first scenario was much more appealing. He wanted the Fairimors—especially Jase—to look him in the eye as they died. He wanted them to know that he, Throy Shadan, the Destroyer of Amnidia, was the embodiment of Death's Third March.

Hulanekaefil Nid opened his eyes to find the Blood Orb of Elsa still glowing brightly atop the altar. The resonance of Power which had drawn him here had stilled, and *Ta'shaen* was quiet once more. Here and in Kunin. The reservoir of Power which had awakened this sister Orb had been exhausted. To what end, he couldn't say, but it was clear from the fact that the Veil was still in place that the wielder had been friendly to the Earthsoul.

Eyes still fixed on the Blood Orb, he tried to sit up and found that he was as weak as a newborn babe. His aching muscles screamed in protest as he pushed himself into a sitting position, and he had to wait several minutes before continuing up onto his knees.

He hadn't been this exhausted since he'd fought to keep Shadan's army from leaving Melek during Death's Second March. Not a comforting thought considering how he'd needed three days in a bed to regain strength enough just to light a candle with the Power.

He rose unsteadily to his feet and gazed down at the Blood Orb. Though quiet, it glowed brightly, awake and alive with the spirit of Elsa. Here was power enough to heal a dying world and he was helpless before it. Helpless to take it up lest it be defiled. Helpless to contact one whose birthright the Orb was.

Hul closed his eyes and opened his Awareness. *Ta'shaen* was there, but the Earthsoul was keeping it out of reach to protect him. As weak as he was, if he attempted to wield right now, he could burn the ability out of himself. Or worse, die of exhaustion.

He leaned his hands on the altar to steady himself. If he forced the issue, the Earthsoul would allow him to take hold of the Power in order to contact Jase or Endil

Fairimor. She was protective, but She wouldn't override his agency regarding something as important as this. She knew that he understood the consequences of his actions, and She would accept his sacrifice should he choose to make it. After all, what was death or the loss of the ability to wield in light of saving the world?

He was willing to accept either fate—he just didn't know if he was strong enough to actually accomplish what needed to be done. If he failed to make contact with the Fairimors, his sacrifice would be for naught.

It might be best to wait things out. There was still a chance that Jase or Gideon would sense the Orb's awakening and come looking for it. He just hoped they arrived before any more Agla'Con came sniffing around.

Hul took a deep breath and let it out, then opened his eyes and looked at the Blood Orb again. Now that the resonance of Power which had drawn him here was silent, it wasn't likely that anyone, be it friend or foe, would know to come looking.

He glanced around the altar room, then nodded. It really would be best to sit tight and wait for his strength to return. Once it did, he would open a Veilgate into Fairimor Palace. Jase would take possession of the Orb and the war would be over.

His decision made, he lowered himself into a sitting position and leaned back against the Altar of Elsa. He had just settled in when a powerful corrupted wielding announced the arrival of more Agla'Con through Veilgates. A quick thrust of his Awareness confirmed it.

Fifteen men in black and red robes were moving through a rent in the Veil, and behind them a literal army of K'rrosha waited to join them. Behind the ranks of the refleshed, stood the raised dais bearing Shadan's throne and the slab of black crystal his lackeys had used to reflesh him.

Hul was on his feet in an instant, his weariness vanishing beneath the sharpest rush of panic he'd ever experienced. An overwhelming sense of dread and remorse followed and for a moment he was paralyzed by indecision.

The brush of several corrupted Awarenesses jolted him into action.

"Forgive me," he whispered, and the world was swallowed by a storm of Fire and Light.

# CHAPTER 32

## Victory Through Loss

ELISON BREY LISTENED ATTENTIVELY AS Captain Tas gave his report, pleased with the progress he and those in his command had made thus far regarding the evacuation of Trian. Fairimor Palace had been cleared of everyone but *Bero'thai* and a handful of the most essential personnel. The inner city would be completely vacated in the next two or three days, and the northern half of the outer city should be emptied by the beginning of next week.

"None of the city's residents are happy about the evacuation," Medwin continued, "but the events of the past few weeks have convinced them it is the right course of action."

"Stalix Geshiann's failed coup did us a favor in that," Elison agreed. "Without it, our citizens would be relying on our word alone. I'm not sure it would have been enough. What else do you have to report?"

"That's it," the young captain replied. "Things are actually going well for a change."

"Thank Elderon for that," Elison said, then turned his attention to Lavin Dium. "What is your report?"

"Much the same as Captain Tas," the Elvan captain replied. "With one notable exception. Yes, the people are willing to comply with the evacuation order, but there are many who are trying to take too much with them as they leave. These unnecessary possessions are slowing them down and creating congestion in the narrower streets and at the city gates. I disagree with Medwin's assessment with how soon the inner city and the northern quadrants will be vacated."

"Your recommendation?"

"Tell the people to take only what they need to survive," Lavin said. "Food, clothing, tents, weapons—the essentials. What good is a piano going to be in the wild?"

"Point taken," Elison said. "You have my permission to restrict all but the essentials. In fact—" He was interrupted by a Veilgate opening in front of the fireplace.

Jase came through first and was followed by Endil. The latter held the limp form of a Chunin woman in his arms, and tears wet his face. Thorac came next, his face a mask of anger and grief. Thex Landoral followed with Dommoni Kia'kal and a handful of Dymas. The Dymas, Elison noted, consisted of Kelsans, Chunin, and Dainin, both male and female. When the last person was through, the gate slid shut.

Elison met Jase and Endil at the edge of the ring of couches. "I assume this means you were successful in recapturing the Blood Orb," he said, making way for Endil to lay the body of the Chunin woman on one of the sofas.

"Yes," Endil said, "but it wasn't without loss on our part." He ran a finger tenderly down the tiny woman's cheek. "Emma was but one of many Dymas lost during the battle."

Chieftain Kia'kal stepped near, his massive face like weathered tree bark. "And yet much good came as a result of their sacrifice," he said. "The Sons of Uri are all but destroyed, and their shrine is forever out of the reach of any who may have survived." He looked at Endil, his eyes filled with admiration. "But the most significant victory came as a result of Endil's use of the Orb to strengthen the Veil. It's hard to say for sure, but I believe he may have added weeks to her life."

Jase nodded as if he agreed with the Dainin's assessment, then looked at Lavin. "I don't know if you've heard, but the Great Wall is under attack by an army of demons."

"Since when?" Lavin asked.

"Since this morning," Jase answered. "I was there for the first part of the attack but left when I felt Endil access the Blood Orb. The *Bero'thai* were holding their own, but I fear they may be short-handed once the main body of demons arrives. If they haven't already."

"My *Nar'shein* will go to them," Dommoni said. "And if Captain Dium approves, we will fetch Captain Haslem and his *Bero'thai* from the rendezvous point along the way."

Lavin nodded. "Fetch them."

"Excellent," Jase said. "Instruct General Kennin and his men to join the rest of the Chunin army at the Kelsan camp."

"Yes, *Mith'elre Chon*," Dommoni said, then he and the rest of the Dainin moved back to the fireplace and disappeared through a Veilgate.

When they were gone, Jase glanced at the remaining Dymas before directing his comments to Elison. "Everyone else will stay here for the time being," he said. "They need time to rest and to mourn. Have Allisen bring them something to eat."

"I'll have baths drawn for them as well," Elison said. He glanced at Endil. "And I'll send word to Cassia that her son has safely returned."

"She will appreciate that," Jase said. Motioning for Elison and Thex to follow, Jase led them away from the ring of sofas, leaving Endil and Thorac and the others to grieve in peace. When they were safely out of earshot, Jase continued.

"Keep an eye on Endil and Thorac for me," he said, keeping his voice low. "They've both been through a lot. Endil especially. The use of that much Power can change a person." He cast a quick look in his cousin's direction, and Elison was impressed by the amount of concern he saw in Jase's eyes.

"I'm also concerned about the young woman, Jeymi Galaron. She doesn't know it, but during the battle at the Shrine of Uri, she overextended her Awareness and I discerned some of her thoughts. She loves Endil enough that she was prepared to kill him to keep him from falling into the hands of the Sons of Uri when they were in the warren. She's experiencing some guilt as a result."

Elison stiffened as a shiver of revulsion rushed through him. *How had they ended up in a bloody warren?* Instead, he glanced at Thex and said, "We will keep a close watch on them."

Thex nodded. "We will indeed."

"What word from the front lines?" Jase asked, changing the subject.

"Our last communication was shortly before you arrived," Elison told him. "Galiena and her people were successful in collapsing the Dragon Gates when their brethren attempted to open them. They also killed or captured all of those involved, including Krev."

"And Gideon?" Jase asked.

"Alive and well," Elison answered. "He is with General Eries in the Kelsan camp."

"I need to speak with them," Jase said. "Carry on with the evacuation. I'm leaving Thex here to help. He will oversee our Power-wielders until Beraline and Marithen return."

"Yes, *Mith'elre Chon*," Elison said, then watched as his young friend opened a Veilgate into the Kelsan camp.

"He's a remarkable young man, isn't he?" Thex said. "Hard as steel in regards to the enemy yet caring and compassionate toward everyone else."

Elison smiled. "For one tasked with saving the world from destruction, I'd say it is the perfect balance." He pointed Thex toward the ring of sofas. "Please, I'm eager to hear what happened in Kunin."

と

As the Veilgate closed behind him, Elliott took note of his location in the Kelsan camp and started in the direction of the command tent. Unless they'd moved it again, it should be just beyond the nearest row of tents.

The camp's occupants were bustling about in a flurry of movement that spoke of combat, but there was a look of excitement in nearly everyone's eyes that piqued

Elliott's curiosity. At the next opportunity, he stopped a passing Dymas. He'd seen the man before but couldn't put a name to him.

"I just arrived by Veilgate," he said. "Can you tell me what's going on?"

"We have two small armies from Death's Third March surrounded," he answered. "They were cut off from the rest of their filth when the Dragon Gates they were using failed. Dymas General Leda has ordered their complete destruction."

"God's speed, then," Elliott told him, "and thanks for the information."

"You're welcome, Lord Chellum. And if you are looking for the command tent, it's just ahead."

"Thank you," he said and let the Dymas continue on his way.

So, Galiena had been successful, had she? That was good news in a day filled thus far with nothing but disaster. It would make getting help for Elrien and those at the Great Wall a little easier.

When he reached the command tent, Teig Ole'ar rose to greet him.

"Is General Eries here?" he asked. "I bring word from the Great Wall."

"He is," Teig answered and, sensing Elliott's haste, threw open the tent flap so he could enter.

"I know that look," Gideon said as he entered. "What's wrong?"

"Take your pick," Elliott said, probably more sharply than he should have judging from General Eries' expression. "The demon army is about to overrun the Great Wall, and dozens more are running loose in the Allister Plains. And that's to say nothing of Jase flitting off to Kunin to do heaven knows what."

"I never flit," Jase said, and Elliott whirled to find him standing behind him, a tired smile on his face. "Sorry about leaving you stranded in Amnidia. I didn't have much choice."

"What were you doing in the valley?" Gideon asked, and Elliott couldn't tell if he was surprised or annoyed. Knowing Gideon, it was probably annoyed.

"Getting trounced by demons," Elliott said, then shot an irritated look at Jase. "No thanks to you."

"I said I was sorry," Jase said, then moved further into the tent. "So what is this about demons outside the valley?"

"They escaped through one of the Veilgates they commandeered," Elliott told him. "Elrien and the rest of those you sent with me are still there. And they are severely outnumbered."

Jase didn't hesitate. Turning his gaze on Idoman, he looked every inch the *Mith'elre Chon* as he issued orders. "Send every available Dymas to Elrien's aid," he said. "I want every last one of those demons destroyed."

"And the Great Wall?" Elliott asked. "They are facing even worse odds than Elrien."

"Not for long," Jase said, sounding pleased with himself. "I sent a small army of *Nar'shein* to their aid shortly before coming here. They were going to fetch a larger army of *Bero'thai* on their way."

"It still won't be enough," Elliott said, his frustration rising. "I know. I saw that demon army up close. Without more Dymas to counter the demons who can wield, the wall will be overrun."

"My people will go to them," Galiena said, and behind her Yavil nodded, his eyes eager. "They have experience combating demons and may have faced some of these same demons when our world was overrun by them."

Elliott stiffened in surprise at the comment, but Jase moved nearer Galiena and looked her in the eyes, his gaze searching. "I see your exhaustion," he told her. "Let Yavil rally your people in this effort while you rest."

"That is an excellent idea," Yavil said, stepping forward. "And since this time the suggestion to rest came from the *Mith'elre Chon* instead of me, perhaps it will be heeded." He kept his face completely smooth, but there was a glimmer in his eyes that hinted at amusement.

Galiena gave him a flat stare, then smiled at Jase. "It will be as you suggest."

Elliott stepped forward. "Well, what are we waiting for?" he said, ignoring the disapproving look Gideon directed at him due to his impatience. "Let's go."

Gesturing to the wall of the tent, Yavil opened a Veilgate just in front of the canvas. "After you, Lord Chellum," he said.

Elliott hurried through into the reddish light of Yucanter Forest and found himself in a large clearing surrounded by a dense line of trees. The greens and blues of the foliage were painted with dappled hues of purple and crimson from the upper canopy, but it was the dark splashes of real blood and the headless corpses of Dragons scattered about that truly caught his eye. Their massive, glittering forms lay sprawled among the grasses and shrubs like jeweled hills.

Dozens more Rhiven, most of them in human form, clustered around their slain brethren, a wide range of emotions evident on their faces. The most prevalent emotion he saw was anger, but there was a great deal of sadness and frustration as well. The faces of those still in their true form showed little beyond the fierceness of a Dragon, but their eyes were just as easy to read as the faces of the others. Killing their own kind was abhorrent to them, even if it was necessary.

"You might want to let me do the talking," Yavil said quietly. "Emotions are high right now, and I'd like to keep them from being redirected toward you."

Elliott tucked his thumbs behind his belt and nodded. "I'd like that as well," he whispered. Keeping his face smooth, he followed Yavil across the clearing.

Jase watched the Veilgate close behind Elliott and Yavil, then turned his attention to Gideon. His father's clothes were singed and sported a number of rips, all of which were stained dark with blood. That he'd been in need of healing was obvious.

"How is your strength at the moment?" he asked. "I can see from your appearance that you've been in the thick of things this morning."

"I have enough left for another fight or two," Gideon answered, but beside him, Galiena frowned, confirming what Jase had suspected.

"You need to learn how to lie better," he said. Gideon scowled at him, but Jase continued before he could speak. "Stay here and rest. There will be plenty for you to do tomorrow when Shadan reaches the western rim."

Gideon looked as if he might argue, but a look from Galiena stayed his tongue. "Where are you going?" she asked.

"To help Elrien," he answered. "I won't allow demons to roam freely outside of Amnidia. Not after what I witnessed last night in my dreams."

If Galiena was surprised by the announcement, it didn't show on her face. "God's speed, *Mith'elre Chon*," she said, smiling fondly. "And be careful."

He returned the smile. "I'm always care—"

A sudden shriek pierced his Awareness, a cry of grief and loss so terrible it tore at his soul and threatened to drive him to his knees. It struck with the force of an avalanche, and for a moment his physical perception of the world was swallowed by it. Reflexively, he wrapped his mind in *Jiu* to dampen the bombardment, but the rush of Spirit-sound punched through in a violent, desperate plea for help.

Somewhere to the east, a Blood Orb of Elsa had just been defiled.

The shriek vanished from Jase's Awareness as quickly as it had come, but Elsa's sorrow had become his. A chance to rejuvenate the Earthsoul had been irretrievably lost.

Sorrow turned to anger in an instant, and he reached toward the point of defilement with his mind, a quick narrow thrust that brought a lost Temple of Elderon into view in his mind's eye. It was hidden inside a mountain in the Velerem Forest. And it was teaming with Agla'Con.

He came back to himself in a rush to find Gideon wearing a mask of rage to match his own. As a firstborn son of Fairimor, he'd heard Elsa's cry as well, and he knew what it meant. His hands were knotted into fists, and he had embraced the Power.

Jase looked from Gideon to Galiena. She and the others were watching him and Gideon with a mixture of alarm and concern. General Eries was gripping his sword hilt. Idoman had embraced the Power.

"What is it?" Galiena asked. "What's wrong?"

"Our enemies just defiled a Blood Orb," Jase told her. Speaking the words made his chest tighten with renewed pain from the depth of the loss, but he fought through it, focusing instead on his anger. "I'm going to take it from them."

"Not alone, you're not," Idoman said, and Gideon was only a heartbeat behind him with a protest of his own.

"You are staying here," Jase told his father. "And you," he said to Idoman, "are in even worse shape than Gideon. Not this time."

"And yet Idoman is correct that you cannot go alone," Quintella Zakeya said, stepping forward. "I will accompany you."

Jase met her broad smile with one of his own, then, before Gideon could object further, he opened a Veilgate inside the mountain he'd glimpsed through his Awareness, and he and Quintella rushed through into the midst of the Agla'Con.

Elison Brey listened in amazement as Thex Landoral related the events which had transpired in Kunin. Considering all he and the others had faced, it was a miracle any of them had come home alive. It was an even bigger miracle that the small group led by Endil had survived long enough for Thex and his reinforcements to find them—a miracle that was due in large part to Emmarenziana Antilla.

Elison cast a quick look at her tiny, shrouded body lying on a nearby sofa, and a rush of admiration swept through him. He'd never met her in life, but he knew her kind—strong, courageous, and fiercely loyal to the Earthsoul. He had no doubt she would join the heroes of legend in the afterlife.

As Thex spoke of Emma, Elison watched Thorac and Endil for clues as to what they might be thinking. Grief still painted both men's faces, but their eyes were bright with admiration for their fallen friend. For a moment, it even looked like Endil might add to the conversation, but when he opened his mouth to speak, tears filled his eyes and he remained silent.

Thorac had remained equally quiet during Thex's account, a testament to how just how deeply the loss of Emma was affecting him. Normally, an adventure such as this would have resulted in enthusiastic tales of valor and manhood. Now, however, he seemed defeated. He seemed... lost. Jase had been right to suggest Elison keep an eye on him.

Before he could decide if he should attempt to draw Thorac into the conversation, a Veilgate opened in the middle of the Fairimor dining room and Lord Nid dove through from beyond. His white Meleki mane was singed brown at the back, and the back of his uniform trailed smoke from several smouldering burns.

Streamers of Fire pursued the Meleki King as he somersaulted across the floor, but he came quickly to one knee, and the killing tendrils were thrown back through the opening by a flare of white from Lord Nid's fist. Some distance beyond, two black-robed figures vanished in flashes of cleansing destruction, but Elison caught sight of others rushing in to fill the gap. They were lost from view as the Veilgate slid hastily shut in a shimmer of bluish-white.

Elison sprang to his feet and raced to Lord Nid's side. Still on one knee, the Meleki King held his glowing fist in front of him, watching the spot where the Veilgate had been as if expecting his enemies to follow.

The *Bero'thai* in the room were similarly concerned. Swords and bows at the ready, they closed in from all sides, taking up positions around Elison and the still-kneeling King. Thex and Thorac drew near as well, Thorac holding his axe, Thex likely holding the Power. The Dymas' eyes were fixed on the brilliant glow in Lord

Nid's fist.

"What—" Thex said, his eyes wide with horror, "what have you done?"

Lord Nid's face was anguished as he rose to his feet and lowered his arm. The brilliance in his fist dimmed but didn't fade completely, and Elison found himself staring at a small reddish-gold Orb that seemed lit from within. Thex's shock became his own.

"Is... is that a Blood Orb?" he asked.

The anguish in Lord Nid's eyes grew more pronounced. "It is," he answered, his voice filled with disgust. "I took it from a Temple of Elderon as it was being overrun by Agla'Con."

"Then you saved the world from destruction," Thex told him, his demeanor changing in an instant. Instead of horror, there was admiration in the Dymas' eyes.

Lord Nid shook his head. "I robbed the Fairimors of a sure chance to rejuvenate the Earthsoul," he countered. "What if this was the last viable Orb? I may have doomed us all."

"I refuse to believe that," Elison told him. "Thex is right. You saved us from certain and immediate destruction had our enemies taken it instead of you."

Lord Nid didn't seem convinced, but he nodded. "Where is Jase?" he asked. "I should turn this over to him."

"With General Eries in the Kelsan camp," Thex said. "I'll fetch him for you." Turning to the fireplace, he opened a Veilgate along the front of the mantle. A short distance beyond, Teig Ole'ar stood watch in front of a canvas tent.

The Elvan Master of Spies took one look at Lord Nid, then hurriedly pulled the tent flap aside and called for Gideon.

A few seconds passed, and Gideon emerged with Galiena at his side. The two moved directly into Fairimor Palace without a word to those on the other side, and Gideon motioned for Thex to let the Veilgate close. Gideon's eyes, fixed on the Blood Orb, shone with the same look of anguish present in Lord Nid's.

"Tell me what happened," Gideon said, staring at the Orb. "I felt the defiling, but I..." He looked Lord Nid in the eyes. "I hadn't expected it to come from you."

"I took it to keep it from our enemies," the Meleki King answered. "I..." He hesitated. "It might be best if I just show you," he said, and Gideon's and Thex's eyes grew more focused as Lord Nid opened his mind to them.

Elison watched their faces, frustrated at being left out of the conversation and jealous of their ability to communicate so clearly and completely in such little time.

After only a moment, Gideon nodded. "You did the right thing," he said. "Anything less and we would be facing our enemies in Con'Jithar."

"What about Jase and the Rosdan Dymas?" Lord Nid asked. "I saw from your thoughts that they went to investigate the defiling. Shouldn't we send help?"

"They are more than a match for a handful of Agla'Con," Gideon said, his words confident. "Even if Jase is more tired than he was letting on. Besides, none of us here have strength enough for another battle."

He looked pointedly at Thex. "Don't think I didn't sense your weariness through the mindlink. Even if you and I were at full strength, it would take longer to contact other Dymas to send than it will for Jase and Quintella to clear out the temple."

He looked at Endil and Thorac, and his face grew solemn. "It pleases me to see you both alive," he said. "And I would hear your tale if you would tell it. I can see in your eyes that it wasn't easy."

"That is the understatement of the century," Thorac muttered, and Elison was pleased to hear a little fire in his friend's voice. It meant he was coming back to himself—a necessity if he was to start healing.

"What would you like me to do with this?" Lord Nid asked, holding up the Blood Orb. It still glowed brightly from within, a reminder of the tremendous reservoir of Power it could access.

"Keep it for now," Gideon answered. "The *Mith'elre Chon* will decide how it is to be used."

⺘

Jase strengthened the shield he was holding around himself and Quintella, then watched through the eyes of *Ta'shaen* as the skilled Rosdan Dymas killed the three remaining Agla'Con with sizzling spears of *Sei'shiin*.

They vanished in flares of white, leaving behind bright, man-shaped after-images in Jase's mind's eye. After a moment, even those faded and there was nothing to show the men had ever been. Even better, Jase thought, was the fact that they would never be again. There was no refleshing for those destroyed by *Sei'shiin*. Which was as it should be.

Quintella released the Power, but Jase kept his shield in place. He was nearing exhaustion, but he wouldn't lower his defenses until he was certain the temple had been cleared of the enemy. The lack of corrupted disturbances in *Ta'shaen* hinted that the battle was over, but he wasn't going to risk that any of the Agla'Con had released the Power in an attempt to hide their presence. Only when he was sure they were dead or run off would he relax.

"Three or four escaped through a Veilgate," Quintella said, obviously upset with herself for allowing it to happen. "They were in the next chamber over, near what looks like an altar."

"I know," Jase told her. "But none of them had the Blood Orb. Whoever took it left just as we arrived."

"Did you see who it was?"

Jase shook his head. "No. But I have a way of finding out. First, let's make sure we are alone in this place."

Stretching out with his Awareness, he searched each of the passages and chambers on the current level, then did a broader search of the level above and the levels below. The temple was roughly the same size as the one in Trian but had a similar layout to the one in Kunin. When he was satisfied they were alone, he let his shield drop and released the Power.

Quintella did likewise, and they made their way into the altar room, passing the dead bodies of several Agla'Con along the way. Two had been so violently torn apart by the Power that they were barely recognizable as human.

"I didn't kill these men," Quintella said. "I was using *Sei'shiin*. This is someone else's doing."

Jase nodded as he stopped in front of the Altar of Elsa. "Let's find out whose."

Trusting Quintella to watch his back, Jase closed his eyes and immersed himself in *Ta'shaen*. Then, just as he'd done the night of Trian's liberation from Zeniff and his Agla'Con, he followed the threads of fate's fulfillment back in time. That he was so near the event he wished to see, both in time and in physical proximity, made the Viewing easier to accomplish. Luminescent images of the altar room took shape in his mind's eye, gradually coalescing into the vision he sought.

He found Lord Nid standing over the altar, his eyes on the Blood Orb, his face pinched with exhaustion and lined with pain. And with the image came a rush of agonized emotions. He felt the Meleki King's frustration, his desperation and sorrow and sense of failure. But he felt his determination as well, his willingness to do the unthinkable to keep an even more unthinkable event at bay.

Jase let the Viewing fade. There was no need to follow it through to the end—he knew what had happened. He knew, and he was grateful the Meleki King had acted as he did. The alternative would have been to surrender the world to Maeon without a fight.

"The Blood Orb is in good hands," he said to Quintella. "Come. I think I know where he has taken it." With that he opened a Veilgate into Fairimor Palace and left the defiled Temple of Elderon behind.

# CHAPTER 33

## Timeless Enemies

"Shouldn't they be back by now?"

The question pulled Elrien's attention from the demons moving across a hilltop some miles to the south, and he found Keymi frowning impatiently. Her broken arm had been healed and was now planted firmly on her hip as she waited for someone to answer her. It was the third time in the past hour she'd asked the same question and struck her impatient pose.

Elrien smiled in an attempt to calm her. "Patience," he said, watching her frown deepen. "They'll be here soon enough."

"But the demons—"

"Are in no position to do anyone any harm," Elrien said, cutting her off. The look he gave her silenced any further comment and made her bite her lip in frustration. As a member of Do'damia's ruling family, she was used to having her way. It was good to remind her that she was the apprentice and he the master.

He watched her a moment longer to ensure there would be no further outbursts, then turned his attention back to the demons. They were moving at an unnaturally quick pace and had covered some eight or nine miles since Elrien and the others had broken off their attack. They'd been forced to use Veilgates to keep pace with the tireless creatures.

He watched as they reached the south slope of the hill and began their descent. There was a small village some fifteen miles further on, and it appeared the demons were intent on reaching it.

Elrien wasn't sure if the vile creatures had searched it out with their Awarenesses or if they had picked up human scent, and right now it didn't matter—they were determined to reach the village and unleash their demonic rage. He wouldn't let that happen, and he would do it with or without reinforcements.

The next few minutes passed in silence as he and the others watched the demons reach the bottom of the hill and start across the grass-covered flat at the bottom. If they kept to their present course, they would pass out of sight of Elrien's natural vision behind the next of the highland's many swells. He would need to track them with his Awareness or use a Veilgate to move to a more southerly vantage point.

Before he could decide which it would be, a stirring in *Ta'shaen* alerted him to the opening of a Veilgate on the top of an adjacent hill. Two men stood framed within the opening, but neither came through. Instead, they took note of where he was, then let the gate close. A second one opened almost immediately a short distance to his left, and Elliott Chellum strode through with a sharp-faced man with bright red hair and yellow-gold eyes.

Elrien couldn't stop himself from staring. *So this is a Rhiven.*

"I brought help," Elliott said as he stopped before Elrien. "This is Yavil to al'Jagulair, Warder Advisor to Queen Morgranon. I see by your reaction that you know what he is."

Elrien dipped his head in greeting to Yavil. "I do," he answered. "My apologies if my reaction offended."

Yavil flashed his teeth in a grin. "No offense whatsoever," he said, offering his hand. "It is a pleasure to meet you, Elrien, Prophet and Protector of Aridan."

When Elrien again failed to keep his surprise from reaching his face, Elliott chuckled. "The Rhiven know a lot more about us than we do of them," he said, "but we can talk about that later. Right now we have demons to kill."

"With all due respect," Keymi said, stepping near. "We will need more than just the two of you if we are to succeed."

Elliott grinned at her. "Exactly," he said, then turned to Yavil. "Would you like to introduce the young lady to the rest of your group?"

"With pleasure," Yavil said, his golden eyes shining with eagerness. Elrien felt him embrace the Power, then watched through the eyes of *Ta'shaen* as the Rhiven deftly opened a larger than normal Veilgate.

Keymi and several other Dymas gasped in surprise as Rhiven in their true form raced through from beyond. Massive, glittering, and sinuous, they were surprisingly light on their feet as they spread out across the hilltop, encircling Elrien and the others in a wall of jewel-colored scales. By the time the last creature was through, Elrien had counted thirty.

"We would have brought more," Elliott said, "but the rest of the Rhiven went to the Great Wall to help combat the demons there."

"How many Rhiven are there?" Erebius asked. Unlike the younger Dymas, he'd kept his surprise in check. Which was understandable considering he and Tuari and the others had faced rogue Dragons in battle at the rim.

"That came to Kelsa to help," Elliott said, meeting Erebius' gaze, "sixty-seven. Of those, four were killed during the attack to bring down the Dragon Gates."

Erebius' eyes were sympathetic as he looked at Yavil. "I'm sorry about your loss."

"They died serving the Earthsoul," Yavil said. "Honor will be theirs in the afterlife." He turned his attention to the demons in the distance. "Unlike the demons, who will suffer the wrath of Maeon." His face hardened even as the eagerness evident in his eyes grew more pronounced. "It will be a pleasure sending them back to hell."

"How do you want to do this?" Elliott asked.

"Swiftly," Yavil answered. "The real fight is at the Great Wall." He looked at Elrien. "You and your Dymas can return to Aridan," he said. "Elliott, and I, and the Rhiven will take care of the demons here."

"Thank you," Elrien said. "I will pray for your safety and success." Motioning for Keymi and the others to follow, he opened a Veilgate back to the Great Wall and hurried through.

As the last of Elrien's Dymas moved through to the Great Wall, Elliott caught a glimpse of Seth standing at the battlements with Railen and Sheymi. Then all were lost from view as the gate slid shut.

"How well do you ride?" Yavil asked.

Elliott arched an eyebrow at him. "Well enough," he answered, unsure where the question was leading. "But I didn't bring a horse." He smiled inwardly and added, *Or a Myrscraw.*

"Horses are no good against demons," Yavil said. "You need a mount that can shield you from *Lo'shaen.* And you will need a saddle."

A small Veilgate opened inside what looked to be a finely furnished mansion, and two oddly shaped saddles lifted from a table and floated through on invisible currents of Air. The gate closed as Yavil took one of the saddles and motioned for Elliott to take the other.

"Any volunteers?" Yavil asked, and two slender females moved near. One, a blue-scaled beauty with a green mane, bellied down in front of Elliott much the same way a Myrscraw would. The other sported silver scales and a bright yellow mane and bellied down in front of Yavil.

"It's nearly the same as saddling a horse," Yavil said as he lifted the saddle into place behind the silver Dragon's front shoulders.

It took Elliott a moment to get over his shock at what was happening—at what was about to happen. *Ride a Dragon?* he thought in stupefied wonder. *How much stranger can my life get?*

"What are you waiting for?" the green-maned Dragon asked, and he glanced over to find her watching him, her serpentine neck forming a large curve, her golden eyes sparkling.

"Are you okay with this?" he asked. "I mean, I'm used to thinking of you as a person. And a lady person at that."

Her lips pulled back in a smile, revealing two rows of white, dagger-like teeth. "This is my true form," she reminded him. Her voice, though deeper and more resonant now that she was in Dragon form, still sounded like a woman's and was filled with amusement at Elliott's reluctance.

"Trust me," she continued. "You wouldn't be the first Power-wielder I've carried into battle. During the fall of our world, I bore many Rhayn and even some Rhiven against the demon armies of Maeon."

"Well, if you insist," Elliott said. Hoisting the saddle into place, he quickly tightened down the straps—it really was almost the same as saddling a horse—then climbed aboard. He found it difficult not to smile. *Riding a Dragon into battle—even Thorac would have a difficult time trumping this story.*

When he was settled, he asked, "What is your name?"

"Ayame'se to ol'Saviendra," she answered. "But you may call me Ayame."

"It is a pleasure to meet you, Ayame," he said, then tightened his grip on the lip of the saddle and looked over at Yavil.

"Ayame was instrumental in our survival when the armies of Con'Jithar laid siege to our capital city," Yavil said, his eyes sparkling with fondness. "She and her *sholin*—her rider—killed more than a dozen of the most powerful demons in Maeon's army." Shaking the thought away, he looked Elliott in the eyes.

"She has high expectations for you, Prince of Chellum, as you act as her *sholin* this day."

Elliott drew his sword. "I'll try not to disappoint."

"Just as I will try not to disappoint Shalish," Yavil said, running his fingers through her yellow mane. "It will be just like old times."

They started forward, and Elliott was amazed at how smooth the ride was. And how incredibly fast, at least twice that of the quickest racehorse he'd ever ridden. And where an equal number of horses would have sounded like a rumble of thunder rolling across the highlands, the Dragons ran in near silence, as light-footed as birds.

Shortly after they began running, the Dragons split into two groups. Yavil led one group north. Ayame took the other south. Their intent, Elliott suspected, was to surround the demons and come at them from all sides. Ayame confirmed it with what she said next.

"We will ring them in like sheep," she said. "And we will kill them where they stand."

"Sounds good," Elliott told her, but he had a hard time picturing demons as sheep. Not after experiencing their ferocity firsthand. Still, he liked Ayame's optimism. "Just tell me what you want me to do."

She chuckled deep in her throat. "I want you to kill demons."

Another mile passed in silence, then another. And with each step Ayame took, Elliott's anxiety increased. *Demons,* he thought. *How did it come to this?*

"Relax, my friend," Ayame said, and Elliott flinched.

"Did I think too loudly?" he asked, worried that he may have inadvertently let his thoughts slip outside his mindward.

"No," she answered, glancing back at him with a twist of her neck. "But you're squeezing the breath out of me with your legs."

Embarrassed, Elliott relaxed. "Sorry about that."

Ayame grunted, but said nothing. A short time later, she stopped on top of a large grassy swell to survey the scene before her. There, on top of another hill a short half-mile away, stood the cluster of demons. They'd spotted the approaching Dragons and were taking defensive positions around the hilltop's perimeter. The air around them grew dark with the power of the Void.

"They think to hold the high ground," Ayame commented, "but they've left themselves vulnerable to attack from within."

Elliott's anxiety intensified. "Why do I get the feeling you and I are the lucky ones who get to exploit that weakness?" *If it is a weakness*, he added.

"Yavil and Shalish will be there with us," Ayame said. "The rest of the Rhiven will ring the enemy in and attack from below. You and I will wait until the demons are fully engaged before we strike."

Elliott tightened his grip on his sword, and watched as the Rhiven who'd accompanied him and Ayame raced across the highland grasses toward the demon-covered hill. Further to the north, those who'd gone with Yavil were doing the same, slender ribbons of glittering death amid the lighter greens and yellows of the grasslands.

When those leading the Rhiven charge had closed to within a quarter of a mile, Night Threads lanced out of the sky to explode in bursts of red-black fire atop invisible shields. A heartbeat later, peals of freakish thunder reached Elliott's ears, rolling across the swell like the screams of the dying.

More Night Threads followed, but those too were deflected by Rhiven shields. Some of the demons switched to Fire, and a wall of flames sprang up around the base of the hill, a red-hot inferno that set the grasses ablaze and filled the air with columns of smoke.

The Rhiven didn't slow, their shields like bubbles as they pushed through the flames and smoke and started up the hill.

"I've faced some of these demons before," Ayame said, her neck snaking around so she could look at him. "I recognize the Power-signatures of their wieldings. They were present when the city of Laesh te'Cavrel fell."

"How is that possible?" Elliott asked. "That was nearly six thousand years ago."

"Time is not measured in Con'Jithar," Ayame answered. "There, only the eternities matter."

*Timeless enemies*, Elliott thought with a shudder, then hurriedly pushed the thought away. "But demons *can* be killed," he said. "They are mortal. Right?"

"Not mortal in the sense that you and I are mortal," Ayame said. "They can be killed, yes. But they have the potential to live forever unless acted upon by some external force."

"And once dead?"

"Their spirits join the rest of those consigned to an eternity in hell."

"All the more reason to heal the Earthsoul," he told her, giving an involuntary shudder. "I'd hate for all of us to be trapped there along with the demons. It's not hard to imagine how they would react to us being there."

"It happened to some of my people," she said, her voice bitter. "When our world fell, those who stayed behind to open the way for us to enter this world were swallowed by Con'Jithar. My father was among those lost."

Elliott felt sick inside. "I'm sorry for your loss," he told her, aware of just how inadequate it sounded.

"Thank you," she said, then turned her attention back to the chaos of battle.

The Rhiven had reached the top of the hill, and flashes of light mingled with stabs of darkness as the powers of heaven and hell exchanged blows. Smoke billowed skyward. Bursts of superheated earth exploded like fountains, filling the air with smouldering debris that rained across the battlefield in dusty sheets. Thunder roared down the steep slopes like an avalanche.

"It is time," Ayame said, and Elliott embraced the Power as Ayame opened a Veilgate in front of them and moved through into the mayhem beyond.

A vicious barrage of Night Threads exploded overhead the moment they were through, crackling down the edges of Ayame's shield like the demonic shrieks.

"You would think they aren't happy to see us," Elliott said, then drew in more Power than he'd ever held before and unleashed an attack of lightning so powerful everything vanished in a sheen of silvery-white. Like a volley of sizzling arrows, a rapid succession of killing stabs raced along the perimeter of the hill, punching through most of the weaker shields and vaporizing the demons beneath.

Several of the stronger shields wavered as the demons retaliated, and the Rhiven took advantage, hammering the dark auras with spears of El'shaen te Sherah. Five more demons died.

Those who remained drew in on themselves, and the air around them darkened as they seized more fully upon the power of the Void to protect themselves from the Rhiven. Surrounded, and fewer in number now than their attackers, they could only hunker in defense as the Rhiven closed in around them.

"No mercy!" Ayame shouted, and Elliott had to shield his eyes as the top of the hill went white with the brilliance of the Rhiven attack. Lightning, Sei'shiin, sizzling tendrils of greenish-blue Fire—it was a conflagration of cleansing annihilation that left spots in Elliott's vision long after it faded.

When he could somewhat see again, he cast about the hilltop, anxious to discover which, if any, demons remained. He found them to Ayame's left, six hellish monstrosities hunkered together beneath a seemingly impenetrable shield.

"They've linked their abilities," Yavil said as Shalish drew up alongside Ayame. "Not that it will matter now."

Sitting tall in the saddle, Yavil's face was alight with the excitement of battle. That, coupled with his bright red hair and goatee, really did make him look like a Riaki Flameburst. Elliott half expected him to break into song.

Instead, the Rhiven warder raised his arm and motioned for his people to advance. Heads raised and backs arched, the glittering army closed in on the demons from all sides.

The demons attacked, hurling Night Threads and bursts of corrupted Fire, but their frenzy was pathetically ineffective in light of the terrible majesty and power of the Dragons. It was easy for Elliott to look upon the demons as the sheep Ayame had named them to be.

"Would you like the honor of finishing them, *El'liott* of the house of Chellum?" Ayame asked, and Elliott stiffened in surprise at her use of the Old World pronunciation of his name. "My brothers and sisters feel it would be appropriate for the killing blow be delivered by the Sword of God."

"It's just a name," Elliott told her, suddenly uncomfortable by the emphasis she placed upon the title.

He felt her chuckle before he heard it. "Oh, it's much more than that, my young friend," she told him. "You have a magnificent destiny ahead of you."

"Assuming we don't lose the war with Maeon, you mean?"

"You can take the first step toward winning, right now," she replied. "As soon as their shield collapses."

"With pleasure," he said, and leveled his sword at the demons. As he did, the Dragon etchings on the slender blade caught the afternoon sunlight and cast a bright serpent-shaped reflection across Ayame's neck.

Elliott gazed in wonder at the image for a moment, and a sudden and overwhelming feeling of reverence washed over him when he considered the significance of the Old World etchings. This blade had been forged by these magnificent creatures in a time when they lived and worked and fought side by side with the First Race of Man. That he should be so fortunate to do the same now—there could be no greater honor in life.

He stared at the shimmering image a moment longer, then turned his attention to the demons. The ferocity of their attack had started to wane, and the dark aura sheltering them was decidedly less pronounced. It wouldn't be long now.

Opening himself more fully to the Gift of Light, he wove the strands necessary to channel lightning, then let the current build in the air directly above the demons. He could see it in his mind's eye, a sea of radiant energy waiting to be loosed.

Within moments, the rapidly accumulating strike became visible to the natural eye as well, and Rhiven and demon alike looked up at a crackling, pulsating, sphere of white-hot death.

Elliott continued to hold the strike in check even as he increased its potency, and thin thread-like feelers of energy sparked outward as if searching for a target.

Sensing their imminent demise, two of the demons tried to flee, and the shield above the entire group faltered, then failed completely. Elliott struck.

The resulting *boom* that followed the brilliant flash shook the hill to its core and was likely heard as far away as the Great Wall. It rolled away across the highlands like the voice of God, a final death knell for the timeless enemy. Only the sheltering bubble of the Rhiven's shields kept them upright.

When the titanic flash of the strike faded, the demons were gone. A smoking crater some ten paces across was all that remained.

"Well done, my *sholin*," Ayame told him, and around them the other Rhiven moved their heads in what he understood to be nods of agreement.

"Now," she continued. "Let's do the same to those approaching the wall."

# CHAPTER 34

## Second Wave

A PROFOUND SILENCE SETTLED OVER the Great Wall of Aridan as the first wave of demons fell back, retreating beyond the range of even the most Powerful Dymas watching from the battlements. Not that any of those here would expend what little energy they had left trying to strike from such a distance—they were just grateful for the respite, no matter how short-lived it might prove to be.

Seth studied the Dymas with concern. Most leaned wearily against the battlements or had flopped down in exhausted heaps wherever they'd been standing.

The *Bero'thai* didn't look much better. While all but the most seriously injured remained on their feet, their exhaustion was evident on their faces. But it was what Seth saw in their eyes that worried him the most. Elva's finest weren't just tired; they were losing hope. They'd survived, yes, but they'd taken a beating. He didn't think they could survive another. Himself included.

Sheathing his swords, he found a rag and did his best to clean the demon blood from his hands and arms. He'd need a mirror to properly clean the smelly gore from his face, so he didn't even try. It had started to dry now anyway, and wiping at it would only resurrect the stench. When his hands were mostly clean, he leaned his arms on the battlements and watched the demons in the distance.

Railen's voice interrupted the silence.

"Did you feel that?" the young Shizu asked, and Seth looked over to find him staring at Mount Tabor rising in the distance.

Sheymi, too, was staring in that direction and wore a look that seemed more curious than alarmed. "I did," she answered. "What do you make of it?"

Railen shook his head. "I won't know until I get a look at it."

Seth frowned at them, but neither seemed to notice. It wasn't the first time since joining him at the wall that they'd forgotten he couldn't sense things as they did, and it was starting to annoy. "Talk to me," he said, not caring that his frustration made it into his words.

"Something just happened in *Ta'shaen*," Sheymi said, glancing over at him apologetically. "It felt... well, pure. But it's hard to say for sure because of the curse. I think it was a sudden influx of Spirit." She looked north once more. "Railen is attempting to pinpoint the location of the largest disturbance. I'm searching for one a bit closer."

Seth followed her gaze. "How much closer?"

"Near the area where Captain Alleilwin and his men found the rent which allowed the Shadan'Ko to escape into the Fairholm Valley." She hesitated, her brow wrinkling in confusion. "Only I can't seem to find it. Even with the curse clouding my Awareness, I should be able to *feel* where it is."

"It's been closed," Railen said, his voice filled with wonder. "And so has the massive rent that let the demon army out of Con'Jithar. How is that possible?"

Seth smiled with relief. "My guess is that Endil or Jase accessed the Blood Orb," he answered. "The only way the Earthsoul could have closed the rents was if She had received a much-needed boost from the Orb's reservoir of Power."

"It might have been too little too late," Railen said. "There is a large group of demons some miles to the south of where the rent was. I can't see them, but I inadvertently touched their minds with my Awareness." He shivered with disgust. "There are hundreds of them, and they are moving fast. Much too fast to be like those marching in formation. I think they are more of those who came in the first wave."

"Great," Seth said. "Just what we need." *Just what we bloody need.*

He let his eyes move down the wall, and a knot of dread tightened in his stomach as he took a closer look at the weariness—not to mention the hopelessness—on the faces of Aridan's defenders. He knew they would continue to fight, but without time to rest or help from a significant number of reinforcements, they would fall. Hoping he'd kept his thoughts from reaching his face, he turned back to Railen.

"Do you have an estimate on when they might arrive?"

"If they maintain their current pace, I'd say within the hour."

Seth nodded, then turned his attention back to the demons. Hundreds remained, but thankfully none of them were able to scale the wall as so many of their dead companions had. If they'd possessed that ability, the wall would have already fallen.

Seth was still watching them when the sound of approaching horses reached his ears. He turned to find Captains Alleilwin and Kium coming from the east. Their uniforms were stained with demon blood, but they appeared unharmed. They drew rein as they neared and dismounted. Their horses stamped nervously and tossed their heads at the sight of the spider-like demon Seth had killed, and the captains were obliged to give the reins to nearby *Bero'thai* so they could join Seth at the wall.

"Calim Dymas informed us that more demons like those we just faced are approaching from the north." He cast a cursory glance at the dead spider-like creature lying a few paces away.

"Railen and Sheymi spotted them as well," Seth told him. "They will likely arrive about the same time as the main force."

Alleilwin's expression didn't change, but he nodded. "That was our estimation as well. We might need to make another call for help." He looked at the two Riaki Dymas. "Are either of you strong enough to open a Veilgate?"

"I'm so tired I couldn't light my own foot on fire," Railen answered.

Sheymi smiled at him, her eyes mischievous, then directed her answer to Alleilwin. "I could light Railen's foot on fire," she said, "but I don't have strength for much else."

Alleilwin nodded as if he had expected as much. "It's the same with the other Dymas I spoke with," he said, turning his attention back to Seth. "They're spent. If the demons attack again before help arrives...." He didn't need to finish the thought.

"Patience," Seth told him. "Jase and Elliott know the situation here. They won't leave us on our own." *I hope.*

He looked out at the amassing demons. The second wave of soldier-like beings was nearing the menagerie of beastly creatures which had retreated from the wall to wait for reinforcements, and an excited cacophony of cries and screeches and howls sprang up as the two groups caught sight of one another. Further to the north, the demons Railen had sensed through his Awareness came into view as well, a nightmarish stampede of scales and fur and leathery hide.

"And in the meantime?" Captain Kium asked.

Seth looked him in the eyes. "We wait."

Railen appreciated Seth's optimism regarding the arrival of reinforcements, but as the minutes wore on and the demon armies converged into one, he started to worry that the captain's trust in his friends might be misplaced. He could see in Sheymi's eyes that she was thinking the same thing.

"We were supposed to learn the new wieldings so we could teach them to the Dymas in Riak," he whispered to her. "But we may have delayed our return to Sagaris a bit too long."

Sheymi smiled at him. "We are where we are supposed to be, my love."

"Even if it means dying in a battle that is already lost?"

"If it is what the Earthsoul requires, then yes." She reached over and took his hand in hers. "But I do not believe this battle is lost, and neither do you. I can see it in your eyes." Her smile sent a rush of heat sweeping through him, and he had a sudden desire to kiss her.

"Okay, you two love birds," Seth said, moving up beside them, "save whatever you are thinking for the honeymoon. We've got a battle to fight."

Sheymi's face flushed red with embarrassment, and she hurriedly released Railen's hand.

"Then we are going to need weapons," Sheymi said. "Because we weren't lying when we said we have nothing left to give as Dymas."

"I know you weren't," Seth told her. "But you are too valuable to risk in a more conventional fight. We are going to evacuate our Power-wielders to the city of Aridan."

"No," Railen said. "Give me a sword. I was a Shizu long before I became a Dymas. It will be an honor to fight alongside *shent ze'deyar.*"

"And I will need a bow," Sheymi said. "I can handle one as well as any *Bero'thai* here."

Seth studied them both a moment before nodding. "If that is what you wish," he said, "then the honor will be mine. Good hunting." He turned to go, but stopped and looked back at them. "But stay near me in case I need to protect *you* for a change."

"Yes, Captain," they said, then watched him as he made his way to another group of Dymas.

"He means well," Sheymi commented. "But I don't think many Dymas are going to want to leave."

"Probably not," Railen agreed, then turned her so he could look her in the eyes. "I didn't know you had skill with a bow."

"I don't," she said. "But I wasn't going to let him send me away." She shrugged. "After all, how hard can it be?"

Railen stared at her. "Perhaps I better give you a quick lesson."

Moving to one of the wall's many weapons lockers, he strapped on a Shizu-style sword, then retrieved a bow with a draw weight he thought Sheymi could handle. After testing it, he grabbed a quiver of arrows and hurried back to her.

He had just handed her the bow when a chorus of demonic cries assaulted the air, rolling across the wasteland and breaking like an ocean wave upon the Great Wall.

Railen looked north to find scores of the more hideously shaped demons racing toward the wall. Like those from the first attack, these were big and fast and undoubtedly had the ability to scale the wall.

"Looks like I'll be learning on the job," Sheymi said. She slung the quiver over her shoulder and nocked an arrow.

Railen smiled at her. "Shavis would be proud."

"Yeah, well, Emperor Dromensai would be furious."

"It will be our little secret," he told her, then drew his sword and readied himself for whatever might appear over the edge of the battlements.

It arrived far sooner than expected, and the loud *thrump* of a spear-thrower being fired sounded to his left. It was followed instantly by a loud *crack* and a hissing scream. Railen turned to find an armored, insect-like demon toppling backward off the wall. It disappeared from view, but was replaced almost immediately by a creature that seemed half-spider, half-snake. Looking like a misshapen centipede, the demon came over the top of the wall in a flashing of legs and undulating, segmented scales.

Sheymi loosed an arrow, but it glanced harmlessly off the demon's back. The creature's eyes flared red as its head swivelled toward her, and it let out an angry hiss as it started forward.

"Well, that didn't do much," she muttered.

"At least you hit it," Railen said. He brought his sword up defensively but knew it would be about as effective against this creature as Sheymi's arrow had. "Aim for its eyes," he said. "If you can distract it enough, I might be able to remove a few of its legs." *If I don't get skewered by one of them first.*

"I was aiming for its eyes," she said, then quickly drew fletchings to cheek and released again.

This time her aim was better, but she still hit wide of the creature's head, and the arrow ricocheted off a bony plate.

"This would be *so* much easier with the Power," she hissed, then nocked another arrow and took aim.

"Keep shooting," Railen said as the creature skittered toward them. *Just don't shoot me in the back,* he added silently and stepped forward to meet it.

He ducked past the clicking, gaping mouth, and sliced a pair of legs free from the demon's right side. Hissing, it reared up, then looped in on itself, its mandibles stretching wide to grab him. He dove beneath it, somersaulting between another pair of legs and slashing them with a swipe of his blade.

He came to his feet to find the creature's tail whipping in from the left. He tried to dive out of the way, but an armored segment caught him across the back of the legs. The searing pain of breaking bones lanced through him as he was flung end over end toward the battlements. The world spun around him in a blur, and his sword slipped from his grasp.

Closing his eyes, he braced himself for the inevitable, abrupt, and likely fatal stop against the stoneworks. This wasn't how he had expected his life to end.

A number of powerful wieldings erupted along the top of the wall, and a cushioned grip of Air caught him just short of hitting the battlements. Stunned yet relieved, he opened his eyes to the sight of dozens of Dainin racing through Veilgates.

The unseen grip lowered him gently to the ground, and he watched in awe as the nearest of the *Nar'shein* engaged the demonic centipede with spears and clubs and hammers. Greenish-yellow blood misted the air as plated segments were pierced or crushed, and legs were ripped free of the creature's body.

Thrashing hysterically, it let out a final hiss of angry desperation, then the demonic light in its eyes dimmed as a vicious impact from a Dainin hammer crushed its head.

Elsewhere, the scene was the same. Demons, unable to stand toe to toe with the ferocious majesty of the *Nar'shein Yahl*, were killed or forced from the top of the wall. The relative silence that followed as they retreated northward once more was broken only by the loosing of thousands of arrows by an army of newly arrived *Bero'thai.*

Gritting his teeth against the pain of his broken leg, Railen forced himself into a sitting position and leaned back against the wall. His eyes fell on Sheymi, and he offered a silent prayer of thanks at finding her unharmed. She stood with Seth and a Dainin Chieftain beyond the centipede-demon's corpse, and her face was a mask of concern as she cast about, frantically searching for him. Their eyes met, and she relaxed visibly.

Excusing herself, she hurried past the segmented carnage and knelt at his side.

"You are lucky to be alive," she said, and he felt her open her Awareness so she could inspect his injury through the eyes of *Ta'shaen*.

"We all are," he whispered. He looked past her as Seth and the Dainin Chieftain drew near.

Sheymi followed his gaze, then hurriedly made room for the Dainin so he could inspect Railen's leg.

"That's quite an injury," the Dainin said, his eyes and voice gentle. It was a stark contrast to the killing rage present only moments earlier as the giant man engaged the demon. "But I've healed worse."

"I've had worse," Railen lied, then braced himself for the healing. As expected, it took his breath away, and he gasped at the sudden influx of warmth. The pain vanished in an instant. His strength returned.

Seth helped him to his feet. "This is Chieftain Dommoni Kia'Kal," he said. "He and his *Nar'shein* were sent by Jase. He and Endil were successful in recovering the Blood Orb."

"So, you were right," Railen said. "The influx of Spirit we felt *was* from the Orb."

"Yes," Dommoni said. "The Earthsoul has been strengthened." He hesitated, and his eyes moved to the army of demons. "For now. There is no telling how long it will last."

"Where is Jase now?" Railen asked.

"He was in Trian when we parted ways," Dommoni answered. "I do not know if he is still there. He seems to find it difficult to remain in one place for long." He smiled. "And I don't think we can attribute it solely to his calling as the *Mith'elre Chon*. The boy has ants in his pants."

Seth grunted. "Wait until you meet Elliott Chellum."

The *clop-clop* of approaching horses ended the conversation, and they turned as one to see Captain Alleilwin approaching with Captain Kium and another *Bero'thai* captain Railen didn't recognize.

"Captain Haslem and his men were with us in Kunin," Dommoni explained. "The *Mith'elre Chon* and I felt they might be needed here."

"You thought right," Seth told him. "But even these reinforcements won't be enough without more Dymas to assist them. As bad as the second wave of demons was, it is nothing compared to what is yet to arrive."

Dommoni nodded. "You are right, of course," he said, his eyes moving over the line of demons forming up in the distance. "But I do not think we will have to face them alone. There are stirrings in *Ta'shaen* that suggest something big is about to happen."

Railen hesitated, unsure if he should press the matter, but his curiosity got the better of him. "Any idea what that might be?"

Dommoni chuckled. "No. But I imagine it will be magnificent."

# CHAPTER 35

## *Wrath of the Rhiven*

"HERE THEY COME AGAIN," Seth said, pointing to a line of demons pulling away from the main formation to race on ahead. "It's the same tactic as before," he added. "The demon masters felt Chieftain Kia'Kal's arrival and are hoping to wear our Dymas down by throwing the more beastly creatures at us first."

"Well, it works," Railen muttered, and Seth cast a sideways glance at the young man to find him frowning.

"Yes," Seth agreed. "And this time those who can wield *Lo'shaen* are close enough to have a hand in things as well. The Dainin can't repel their attacks *and* engage those that make it atop the wall."

"We might not have to," Dommoni said, his eyes closed and his face pinched with concentration. "Help is coming." Eyes still closed, he raised an arm and pointed northward. "There."

Seth narrowed his eyes in that direction, but all he saw was the horde of charging demons. They'd already covered more than half the distance and, like a nightmarish ocean wave, were getting ready to break upon the wall.

"Are you—?" He cut off as numerous Veilgates opened behind the advancing horde and Rhiven in their true form flowed through from beyond.

Scales glittering brightly in the afternoon sun, they seemed alight with the Power, and brilliant stabs of lightning and swirling columns of Fire erupted in the midst of the demons. A third of the vile creatures died in the initial strikes, their formidable bodies flaring to ash or blowing apart in ruined chunks of sizzling flesh.

The line of Veilgates closed behind the Rhiven as they advanced and more stabs of lightning followed. More demons died.

Howling or hissing in anger and surprise, most of the surviving demons turned about to face their attackers while the rest continued on toward the wall.

"That will make our job easier," Captain Haslem commented as he nocked an arrow.

"That won't be necessary, Captain," a familiar voice said, and Seth turned to see Elrien and Erebius exiting a Veilgate. And they weren't alone. All along the top of the wall, flashes of blue announced the arrival of Dymas.

Night Threads crackled overhead but stopped short along the top of an invisible shield of Spirit. Invisible to Seth's eyes, anyway—he could see from the look of wonder on Railen's face that the sheltering dome was awe-inspiring.

Seth didn't know if the shield was the work of the Dainin or the newly arrived Dymas, and right now he didn't much care. The demons who could wield *Lo'shaen* had entered the battle—things were about to get ugly, even with the help of so many reinforcements.

A literal storm of Night Threads sought the lives of the Rhiven, but it, too, was turned aside. The resulting scream-like thunder echoed across the battlefield in ear-splitting accompaniment to the shrieks of the demons racing toward the wall.

"Destroy them," Elrien shouted, and threads of Air carried his words along the top of the wall.

The area immediately fronting the Great Wall erupted with Fire and lightning, and those were followed by explosions of Earth and thrusts of Air and Spirit. The rampaging demons vanished beneath the assault, and Seth was forced to shield his eyes against the intensity of the destruction. When the killing bursts faded a few moments later, the demons lay in ruin.

The demons who'd turned back to confront the Rhiven didn't fare much better, and Seth watched with grim satisfaction as the glittering, serpentine forms of legend ripped the hellish beasts apart with *El'shaen te sherah.*

As the last of the demons died, a profound silence descended upon the wall, and Seth glanced in each direction to find eyes wide and mouths hanging open in wonder. Only then did it occur to him that nearly everyone here was looking at the Rhiven for the first time.

Adding to their shock were the rumors they'd heard about Dragons fighting on the side of Throy Shadan on the battlefield of Death's Third March. For Dragons to come to their aid here at the Great Wall in the very moment they were about to be overrun was a lot for them to get their heads around.

Captain Haslem was proof. "What..." he began, then shook his head in disbelief. "How... how is this possible.?"

"The Rhiven nation is divided," Seth told him. "Some few may have sworn themselves to Maeon, but the rest follow Galiena'ei to ul'Morgranon, their Queen. Some of Galiena's people—specifically those you see before you—are servants of the Earthsoul."

"But the legends... the Festival of the Dragon...."

"Are false," Seth said. "But that is information for another time." He turned his attention back to the Rhiven.

With what had once been the second wave of demons destroyed, the Rhiven turned to face the main body of the demon army, but they didn't advance. They simply held their ground and watched as the columns of armored soldiers continued their march. They didn't look like much in relation to the monstrosities of the first and second waves, but they numbered in the thousands, and many of them could wield *Lo'shaen*.

"Do they intend to engage the demons on their own?" Railen asked, his concern for the Rhiven evident in his tone.

"This isn't all of them," Elrien said. "Some thirty more are with Elliott Chellum. He and the one called Yavil are leading them against the demons who escaped into the Allister Highlands."

"Of course he is," Seth muttered, shaking his head. "That fool boy doesn't know when he's in over his head."

As if speaking of Elliott had somehow summoned the young man, a massive Veilgate opened against the wall of the nearest tower and Elliott and Yavil came through on the backs of two Dragons.

This time Seth's surprise equaled that of those around him. He managed to cover it quickly, but Elliott's grin let him know it hadn't been quickly enough. The young man didn't say anything, content, it seemed to Seth, to enjoy the moment in silence. And why not, every man and woman within view was staring at him in stupefied wonder.

"You're here sooner than I expected," Elrien said. "I take it you destroyed the demons?"

"Yes," Elliott said, swinging down from the saddle. "Ayame and her people made quick work of them."

"He's being modest," the blue-scaled Dragon said. "Elliott destroyed as many as the rest of us combined."

Elliott shrugged as if it were no big deal, but Seth knew from the look in his eyes that he appreciated the compliment.

"That he did," Yavil said, grinning from ear to ear. "And became the first person since the destruction of the Old World to earn the title *Kel'sholin*."

"It means Dragonrider," Ayame said, her fondness for Elliott evident in her voice. "During the First Cleansing, we carried many Dymas into battle on our backs. It is a very efficient way to kill Agla'Con." She looked northward, her golden eyes shining with unbridled hatred, and added, "Or demons."

"We have saddles enough for twenty *sholin*," Yavil said, directing the comment to Elrien. "You are the Watchman of Aridan," he said. "You are welcome to join us if you have strength enough left to wield."

"I am honored by the invitation," Elrien told him, "but I am spent. There are others much more capable than I am at the moment." He smiled. "In the coming days perhaps."

"Of a certainty," Yavil said. "Many of my people will remain here at the wall until the war with Shadan is ended. They will be yours to command."

"Why would they do that?" one of Elrien's apprentices asked. Like the others, she was Elvan, but to Seth's eyes she looked too young to have experienced the manifestation of Gifts of Power. "After thousands of years of living apart from the other races, why now?" Ignoring the warning look from Elrien, she stepped nearer Yavil and looked him in the eyes.

"I mean no disrespect," she continued, "but Power such as the Rhiven possess could have been put into play long before now. Why didn't you act sooner?"

"That's enough, Keymi," Elrien scolded, but Yavil waved him off.

"It's quite all right," he said. "It's a fair question." Looking Keymi in the eyes, he offered her his hand. "But since I do not have time to answer it sufficiently at this moment, I promise to answer you in detail once the demons have been dealt with."

Keymi accepted his hand. "Promise accepted," she said. "On one condition."

Yavil smiled knowingly. "And what is that?"

"I want to go with you."

"As do I," another of Elrien's apprentices said. His face was bright with excitement as he pressed forward through the crowd.

Behind him, five others pressed forward also, and they were joined by still others. Within moments the Rhiven had their twenty *sholin*. And every one was as young or younger than Elliott.

Seth smiled appreciatively. The younger generations were always the first to lay aside fear and prejudice for the betterment of the world. He just hoped they survived to see the results of their labors.

"Let's do this," Elliott said, and Ayame bellied down so he could climb into the saddle.

"Elliott and I will attack with the *sholin* from the north," Yavil told Elrien. "The Rhiven already in the valley will hold their position. We will squeeze the demons in the middle and annihilate them." He pointed to the tower wall where he'd arrived, and a Veilgate opened in the same spot. "Dragonriders," he said, addressing the twenty young Dymas, "your mounts await."

Faces bright with excitement, they followed Yavil through to the grassy area beyond and spread out to meet those who would carry them into battle.

Elliott was the last to pass through, and he looked back at Seth as he reached the blue-edged opening. "We'll be back before you know it," he said, then he and Ayame disappeared as the gate closed silently behind them.

"You better," Seth said quietly. *Because I don't want to be the one who has to tell your family that you got yourself killed.*

He moved to the battlements to watch the approaching demons, and Elrien and the others around him did likewise.

Time passed slowly as what had once been an indistinct line of distant black gradually took shape as neatly arranged columns of soldiers. Before long, individual demons became recognizable as well. The hellish figures were armored from head to foot and carried an assortment of weapons.

Time seemed to slow further as the distance between the demons and the Rhiven waiting to engage them continued to shrink, and Seth braced himself as sporadic strikes of Night Threads and volleys of Fire began to break over the heads of the Rhiven.

Safely sheltered in shields of Spirit, the Rhiven stood their ground, a wall of glittering color amid the darkness and desolation of the valley's ruined landscape.

"Do you think they have a chance?" Railen asked, and Seth glanced over to find him watching the scene unfolding to the north.

"The Rhiven or the demons?"

The young man opened his mouth to reply, then stiffened in surprise and glanced over. "Oh, so you do have a sense of humor?"

Seth arched an eyebrow at him. "About what?"

"I think Railen was asking if you think the Rhiven have a chance against so many demons," Sheymi said. "They are severely outnumbered."

Seth smiled. "I know what he meant," he told her. "But I'd say the demons are the ones who are outnumbered."

"I guess we'll find out," Railen said, pointing northward.

Seth followed the young man's gaze to find multiple Veilgates opening behind the demon ranks and Rhiven bearing *sholin* streaming through from beyond. A heartbeat later, the area erupted into fire and chaos.

Sheltered in an impregnable bubble of Spirit channeled by Ayame, Elliott gripped the saddle with one hand and leveled his sword at a cluster of demons rushing in to attack from the right. Lightning crackled earthward in bolts as thick as tree trunks, and grey, pitted skin and blackened armor blew apart in sizzling chunks and shards.

"Well done, my *sholin*," Ayame said, "but let's have you target those who can wield. I will deal with those who can't."

Then, true to her word, she charged into the midst of a column of demons numbering in the hundreds. Like an invisible plow blade, her shield cut a path through the midst of the hellish creatures, knocking them aside and slamming them violently into those behind them. Dozens went down in a tangle of arms and legs and weapons, and demon blood spattered the edge of the shield like muddy rain.

"I'm going to let a few inside the shield," Ayame said, and a handful of demons stumbled forward in surprise as resistance vanished. A heartbeat later their weapons exploded, severing fingers and hands and peppering demon flesh with glittering shards.

Stunned by Ayame's skillful strike, the demons had little time to react as Ayame seized the nearest two in her massive jaws and crushed the life out of them. The third, a leathery-faced abomination more hideous than any Darkling Elliott had ever seen, ducked beneath Ayame in an attempt to escape her killing bite, but Elliott sliced its head from its neck as it stood to flee.

Ayame spat the demon corpses to the earth in disgust, then charged into the midst of another cluster, buffeting all but a few with her invisible battering ram. Once again, those not knocked head over foot were surprised to find themselves inside the protective ward.

They raised swords defensively but dropped them as their hands burst apart in sprays of bloody flesh and shattered bone. Howling in pain, the creatures could do little more than brace themselves for Ayame's wolf-like pounce. The sound of crumpling armor and pierced flesh sounded loudly in Elliott's ears.

"There," Ayame shouted only a moment before Night Threads exploded overhead. They crackled along the edge of her shield in spider-webbed patterns of darkness that writhed like something alive. A second barrage followed, but Elliott had seen the demon Ayame had indicated.

Wrapped in a shroud of *Lo'shaen*, it sported armor made of steel and bone and carried a short, polished scepter. Its eyes, like the end of the scepter, burned with the fires of hell.

"I see him," Elliott told her, then drew in as much of the Power as he could safely hold. When he was ready, he loosed it in a single bolt so powerful it burned the demon from existence as completely as if he'd used *Sei'shiin*. But unlike *Sei'shiin*, which was as silent as it was brilliant, the resulting crack of thunder and release of energy from Elliott's strike killed every demon within twenty paces of their master. They dropped as if poleaxed, their bodies trailing wisps of smoke as they fell.

"Who's next?" he asked, and Ayame turned toward a pair of demons cresting a small swell to the south. Scepters blazing, they were hurling Fire at a yellow Rhiven with a black mane. The large male was holding firm, but the lack of a counterattack showed his *sholin* was having trouble.

Elliott raised his sword at the demons. "Oh, no you don't," he hissed, and lightning lit the wasteland once more.

When a second singularly large strike of lightning followed closely on the heels of the first, Seth was able to pinpoint Elliott's location on the battlefield. It was, of course, right in the thick of things.

"Burn that boy," he muttered, then raised the spyglass to try to catch a glimpse of his young friend. He found him sitting straight-backed atop Ayame, sword in hand, face bright with excitement. The two had just crested a small swell and were surrounded by an innumerable host of demons.

The empty space immediately surrounding Elliott and his blue-scaled mount showed that Ayame had them wrapped in a shield of Spirit, but as Seth watched, a handful of demons somehow made it inside the invisible barrier.

He tensed as the creatures raised their weapons to attack, but he needn't have worried. Ayame relieved them of their weapons with a skillful strike of *Ta'shaen*, then seized them one by one in her jaws and shook them so violently Seth imagined he could hear the breaking of bones in their backs and necks. It was over in moments, and demons littered the ground like rag dolls, their ruined bodies broken and crushed.

And through it all Elliott continued to target those who could wield *Lo'shaen*, killing some and forcing others to retreat into protective auras of corrupted Spirit.

Other *sholin* did likewise, and the demon army started to fragment as those who could wield *Lo'shaen* found themselves on the defensive and slowly lost control of the situation. They were unable to fully protect those demons who couldn't wield, and the Rhiven and their *sholin* took advantage.

Bars of *Sei'shiin* ripped through the demon ranks in blinding bursts of light, and scores of demons flared from existence in curt, white-hot flashes. Others burst apart in fountains of sticky gore, while others were burned to ash by swirling columns of Fire.

Seth lost sight of Elliott during the minutes that followed, but a series of colossal stabs of lightning and their resulting peals of thunder showed he was still alive and in the fight. No one else struck with such unbridled strength—it had to be him.

"Elliott just destroyed the last of their Power-wielders," Sheymi announced, and Seth glanced over to find her watching the battle with a great deal of wonder. Her voice, however, sounded envious. Likely she wished to be part of it as a *sholin*. And why not? Riding a Dragon into battle was the stuff of legends.

"Destroyed is an understatement," Railen said, a broad smile on his face. "A strike like that is the equivalent of killing a cockroach with a sledgehammer."

"Who cares?" Captain Haslem said. "As long as they are dead."

"It's a waste of his strength," Sheymi said disapprovingly. "There are still hundreds of demons left to destroy."

"That won't be a problem now," Elrien said. "Without the protection of those who can wield, the lesser demons will fall quickly. And I don't think the Power will be needed to accomplish that."

He was right. As Seth watched, the Rhiven moved in from all sides, pouncing on the remaining demons like leopards pouncing on rabbits. Some were trampled to death. Others were seized in massive jaws and crushed. Still others were snatched up in those same toothy maws and violently shaken until life left them.

It was one of the most brutally violent yet amazing things Seth had ever witnessed.

And it was over in minutes.

"Blood of Maeon," Captain Haslem whispered in awe. "Why aren't they at the front lines of Death's Third March?"

"They were," Seth told him. "But their role in that part of this war is over. I wish it were otherwise, but... it's complicated. Just be grateful they decided to come to our aid here."

Raising his spyglass, he returned his attention to the Rhiven. They were moving through the sea of demon corpses looking for any who might have survived. When they found one, they didn't hesitate to crush the creature's head. When they were satisfied that every enemy had been destroyed, they started for the wall.

Seth turned to Elrien. "This battle is over for now," he said. "All Dymas with sufficient strength should tend to the wounded."

"And the Rhiven?" Elrien asked.

Seth turned his gaze on them once more. "We give them a hero's welcome," he said. "They bloody well earned it."

Elrien nodded. "That they did. And praised be the Creator for their help."

# CHAPTER 36

## Fate's Tangled Web

AS JASE MOVED INTO THE FAIRIMOR home through the Veilgate Quintella opened from the Temple of Elderon, he had the sudden, unmistakable impression that prophecy was about to be fulfilled. He could feel the all-too-familiar tickle of fate's tangled web as it settled upon the room, heavy and ambiguous and filled with a multiplicity of possibilities. As always, it wasn't clear who would benefit from the fulfillment, Maeon or the Earthsoul. He would need to choose his words and actions carefully.

Those in the room turned toward him and Quintella as the Veilgate slid shut behind them, and Jase took note of who was present. Gideon and Galiena. Elison and his staff of *Bero'thai*. Endil and Jeymi. Thorac and Thex. And lastly, Lord Nid.

The Meleki King held the still-glowing Blood Orb, and his face was a mix of anger and sadness.

Jase smiled reassuringly at him as he started forward, then locked eyes with Gideon when he rose to welcome him. It was impossible to tell from his father's expression if he'd felt the stirrings of fate as well, but he hoped he had. It would be helpful in navigating whatever might be coming next.

"I told you they would make quick work of the Agla'Con in the Temple," Gideon said, a proud smile on his face.

"A few escaped through Veilgates," Quintella admitted. "By now they will have reported to Shadan that we possess a Blood Orb."

"Good," Gideon said. "I want that refleshed cur to worry about what we might do with it." He looked pointedly at Jase. "He's seen firsthand what a Son of Fairimor can do with such power."

"On that note," Hul said, moving out from among the sofas. "I think this belongs to you." Face still somewhat troubled by his perceived failure, he offered Jase the

Blood Orb.

The stirrings of fate tickling Jase's Awareness grew more pronounced, and he hesitated. This was the moment of prophetic fulfillment he'd sensed on arrival. What he did next would seal it as fate, for good or for evil.

And he had no bloody idea what he should do.

*A little help here*, he thought, opening his Awareness more fully to what he could feel and trusting the Earthsoul to guide him.

For a moment nothing happened, then the answer came in a rush of images he'd seen before in a dream. No, a nightmare. And one that left him cold inside at what it implied. He was as powerless before the images now as he'd been during the nightmare and could only watch as they burned themselves even more clearly into his mind:

*An army of demons swarming the courtyard fronting the Overlook—*

*The spirits of the damned nearing the entrance to the Dome—*

*A powerful surge of Earthpower lancing from the Dome's entrance as Gideon appears—*

*A Blood Orb of Elsa shining like a miniature sun in Gideon's hand—*

*Hundreds, then thousands of the enemy vanishing in flashes of cleansing destruction—*

*The fading of the Orb's reservoir of Power—*

*Gideon's fall at the hands of an unseen enemy—*

The rush of images vanished as quickly as they had come, and Jase found himself still staring at the Orb in Lord Nid's outstretched hand.

"It is not for me to wield," Jase told him. "Please give it to Gideon. As the Guardian of Kelsa, it shall be his to wield in Trian's defense." Speaking the words drove a dagger through his heart, and he had trouble watching as the Meleki King handed Gideon the Orb.

Gideon accepted it without argument, but the look in his eyes let Jase know he'd caught a glimpse of the future images as well. What exactly he'd seen or how much, Jase couldn't say, but it was clear Gideon knew his part in the upcoming battle had already been written. He tucked the Orb away in his uniform, then smiled. "I'll try not to disappoint."

Jase reached forward and gripped his father's arm. "You never do."

"Why do I get the feeling something significant just happened?" Elison asked, his eyes moving back and forth between Jase and Gideon.

Gideon grunted in amusement. "Jase is the *Mith'elre Chon*," he said simply. "Everything he does is significant." He looked Jase in the eyes and added, "Some are just more significant than others."

The imaginary dagger in Jase's heart sunk deeper as he heard the resignation in his father's voice.

"You still have a choice in this," he told him.

Gideon smiled. "I know. And I have chosen." He looked pointedly around the room. "We all have."

It was then that the full weight of what Jase had seen settled on him, and a knot tightened in his throat. Gideon wouldn't be alone in the palace when Death's Third March arrived—Brysia would be here as well. So would Elison and Lavin and thousands of men and women who were willing to fight until the end. What that end would be was obviously undecided as evidenced by the lack of prophetic glimpses beyond that of Gideon's fall at the hands of... of whatever the creature had been.

Jase looked at each of his friends in turn, then met Gideon's eyes once more. "Yes," he said. "But to what end?"

"Nothing about the future is ever certain," Gideon said. "Fate may yet weave a completely different web for us to navigate. All we can do is act on what we know right now. Even if we don't like it."

"So, you *did* see some of what I saw," Jase said. He should have expected as much. Gideon was both a prophet and a seer, and had been for nearly three hundred years. His nod confirmed it.

"Yes," he said, "but it changes nothing." He put his arm around Jase's shoulder and guided him toward the sofas. Quintella followed, her beaded braids clicking softly as she walked. All eyes were upon her as she took one of the high-backed wooden chairs from a reading table and pulled it close to the ring of sofas.

"I will do what needs to be done," Gideon continued. "Just as you will." He chuckled. "It's in our blood."

Elison scowled at them both. "Any chance of you letting the rest of us in on your irritatingly cryptic conversation?"

"There's always a chance," Gideon said, seating himself next to Galiena. "But that is for the *Mith'elre Chon* to decide."

Jase chose a spot opposite his father and the Rhiven Queen, and Galiena smiled warmly at him as their eyes met. In all likelihood, she had been privy to the future images as well. Jase returned the smile before turning his attention to Elison.

"You already heard everything that needs telling," Jase told him. "Gideon will keep the Orb and use it against Death's Third March when it arrives."

"And you?" Elison asked.

"I'll be where the Earthsoul needs me most," he answered and left it at that. They didn't need to know that he had no bloody idea where that would be.

Elison seemed satisfied. "Well, you certainly have a knack for it," he said. "Especially if what Endil and Thorac said about your involvement in Kunin is true."

"Highly exaggerated, I'm sure," Jase said, winking at Thorac.

The Chunin Ambassador General smiled, but the fire usually present in his expression was still missing. It worried Jase to see his friend this way, but he knew it wouldn't last. Eventually all of Thorac's grief and pain and sense of loss would turn to anger. When that happened, hell itself would have reason to fear. It would be wise to help speed the healing process.

"Thorac and Endil and those they commanded," Jase continued, his eyes still fastened on Thorac, "are the ones who need thanking for what happened in Kunin. Things were already well in hand when I arrived."

"*That* is the exaggeration," Thorac said, and beside him Endil nodded.

Jase waved them off. "Our differing interpretations aside, you two have earned the right to rest." He looked at the shrouded body of Emma Dymas. "And so has Emma. I know she would be honored if it were you two who bore her body to Chunin and laid her to rest there."

There was a short moment of silence, then Thorac nodded. "It will be as you suggest. And thank you for your thoughtfulness in this matter."

Rising from the sofa, Jase moved across the Blue Flame rug and went to one knee in front of Thorac. "No, my friend, thank *you*. None of what happened in Kunin would have been possible without your expertise, wisdom, and skill."

Thorac turned to stare at Emma's shrouded body and sighed. "It wasn't enough, obviously."

"When we give our all," Jase said, drawing Thorac's eyes back to his, "it is enough. There is nothing more you could have done."

"He's right," Endil said, and Jase turned to find him frowning thoughtfully. "Emma knew what was going to happen. She knew, and she went in anyway."

Thorac narrowed his eyes at the prince. "What are you talking about?"

It was Jeymi who answered. "Right before Loharg arrived," she said, "Emma told us that not all of us would make it out of Kunin alive. Considering how outnumbered our forces were, I thought she was speaking generally, referring to soldiers on the battlefield. I see now she was referring to herself."

"Yes," a female voice said from across the room, and Jase and the others turned to see Aierlin and the other Chunin Dymas entering the room. Their hair was still wet from bathing, and they had donned clean clothes. Faces solemn, they made their way toward the ring of sofas.

When they reached it, Aierlin continued, "Emma knew—or at least strongly suspected—she wouldn't survive the conflict inside the shrine. She shared her fear about the matter with me several times as we traveled through that Light-blasted land, but she never offered any specifics about the premonition."

Thorac shook his head, a glimmer of anger in his eyes. "If she suspected..." He stopped, his hands knotting into fists. "If she suspected... why did she choose to go in?"

Aierlin's eyes were sympathetic as she answered. "I think you already know that answer to that," she said simply. "She was a servant of the Earthsoul. Where else would she be?"

Thorac sighed, his anger fading. There was still a great deal of sadness in his eyes, but he smiled. "She certainly was," he agreed. "And one of the finest to ever walk the earth."

"Which is why she deserves to be laid to rest with the rest of Chunin's heroes," Jase said, bringing the conversation back to where it started. "Tarfin South is just a Veilgate away, my friend. All you have to do is say the word."

When Thorac nodded, Jase offered him his hand and helped him to his feet.

Endil and Jeymi stood as well and followed Thorac to the sofa where Emma's shrouded body lay. As everyone else looked on, Jeymi embraced the Power and lifted the tiny body with tendrils of Air, then carried it to the fireplace.

Aierlin and the rest of the Chunin Dymas joined her there, and Aierlin opened a Veilgate into the palace of Tarfin South. Without another word, Thorac led the way through, and the Veilgate slid shut behind them.

"You were right about Thorac and Endil," Elison said once they were gone. "Emma's death rattled them both."

"They'll recover," Jase told him. "And seeing to Emma's funeral will help speed their healing along. They'll be back here ready to fight before you know it."

Elison nodded, then changed the subject. "Did Endil really use the last of the Orb's reservoir of Power to flood the Kunin valley and bury the Shrine of Uri?"

"He filled the valley with water, all right," Jase said, impressed by his cousin's feat. "But he didn't use the Orb—its reservoir had already been expended. He used his Gift, and he did it on his own strength." He glanced at Gideon. "Endil might think he still had access to the Orb, but he is as strong with Water as Elliott is with Light. It was both amazing and a little bit frightening to watch. I don't think he realizes just how incredibly powerful he is."

Gideon laughed. "I said the same thing about you on several hundred occasions. Only it was more than a little frightening. It was downright terrifying. There were times I was fearful you might do Shadan's job for him."

Jase arched an eyebrow at him. "You want terrified? You should have been standing in my shoes." He looked at Thex. "Which leads me to the request I have for you. When Endil returns, I want you to mentor him in regard to his Gift. It is no accident that the Earthsoul increased it to such an extent. Endil has an important role to play in the battles yet to come, and I need to know he can control his abilities."

He paused and a smile found its way to his face. "As Daris Stodd used to tell me—and Gideon undoubtedly said many times behind my back: *A sword in the hands of one untrained is as dangerous to the wielder as it is the enemy.*"

Gideon gave another laugh. "That's *much* kinder than any phrase I used."

"Of that, I have no doubt," Jase said, dropping the smile. He turned back to Thex. "Will you mentor Endil?"

"It will be a privilege."

"Thank you," Jase said, then turned to Lord Nid. "And thank you for keeping the Blood Orb from being taken by our enemies. I used the eyes of *Ta'shaen* to view what you did in the temple. Considering how outnumbered you were, it was nothing short of miraculous. Tell me, how did you know the Orb was there?"

"I sensed its awakening when Endil used the Orb in Kunin. Apparently, the Orbs are linked in some way. The use of one awakens another somewhere else in the world. And there seems to be a pattern. When you used the Blood Orb taken from the Zekan temple to bring the Night of Fire to Melek, you awakened the Orb in

Chunin. That Orb's use then awakened the Blood Orb in Melek."

"Like crux points," Jase said. "Crux points for the Earthsoul Herself."

"That's one way to look at it, I suppose," Lord Nid said. "But metaphorical similarities aside, it's obvious that one release of Power triggers the next and then the next and so on."

Elison leaned forward eagerly. "Then that means all we need to do to find a viable Orb is use the one we have."

"If only it were that simple," Gideon said, and the look he directed at Jase spoke volumes. He knew when and where he was fated to use the Orb, and by then it would be too late. Even if the awakened Orb was near enough for them to sense, the Veil would have already collapsed.

"What Gideon means," Jase said, "is that whatever Orb is awakened by the use of the one he possesses may not even be on this continent. It could be anywhere in the world."

"And not only that," Gideon added, placing a hand on the pocket holding the Blood Orb, "by the time I use this, Death's Third March will be on our doorstep. *Literally.* We won't have time to go looking for another Orb, even if we could sense it."

The moment of frustrated silence that followed was broken by Jase. "Then we will continue the search for lost temples until we find one," he said. "And our best bet is the maps Talia and the High Queen are working on. If we can bridge the Old World with the new, we will find what we are looking for. In the meantime, we continue the fight with Death's Third March. I want to kill as many of the enemy as we can before they reach Trian."

"I can help with that," Lord Nid said. "Kamoth and Kamasin have been retaken, and the cultist armies which held them have been destroyed. Aside from the Pit and a few meaningless pockets of resistance, Melek is once again in my control. My people and I are most eager to come at Shadan from the rear."

Jase nodded. "And pin them against the western edge of the plateau. Without the rampways to aid in their descent, they will have a devil of a time getting their forces down to the Bottomlands."

"Have they already been collapsed?" Elison asked.

"No," Quintella answered. "General Eries wanted them intact as long as we have people fleeing ahead of Shadan's army."

"Take word to Idoman," Jase told her. "Tell him not to wait any longer. I want the rampway collapsed by nightfall. We don't have much time before Death's Third March reaches the western rim. When they do, I want them standing on the edge of a bloody long drop."

He stood. "In fact, you've been away from the Kelsan camp long enough. By now they will have finished destroying those who made it through the failed Dragon Gates. You should probably be there when your Dymas return from their raid."

He offered Quintella his hand. "God's speed, Dymas. And please continue to watch over Idoman for me. I know he is taking the loss of Joselyn personally."

Lord Nid was on his feet in an instant. "Joselyn is dead?" He sounded like he'd just been stabbed.

Jase looked at him sympathetically. "She was killed yesterday when the Kelsan camp was attacked by demonspawn. We nearly lost Idoman as well. Ohran Peregam brought him back from the brink of death."

Lord Nid joined Quintella as she started for the fireplace. "I will accompany you," the High King said. "I would like to see Idoman before I return to Melek." He forced a smile. "Like Joselyn, I had the opportunity to mentor that remarkable young man when he first came into his gifts."

"Remarkable is an understatement," Gideon said. "He is one of the most Gifted Dymas I've ever met."

As Lord Nid moved past, Jase caught him by the arm, and their eyes met. "Think no more that your taking the Orb was some sort of failure," Jase told him. "Like everything, it was simply another strand in fate's bloody web. You did what needed to be done."

"I know," Hul said. "But I don't have to like it."

Jase released his arm and watched as he and Quintella passed through to the Kelsan camp. When they were gone, he turned back to the others.

"I'm needed at the Great Wall," he said, then extended his hand to Galiena. "And I would like you to accompany me." She'd been unusually quiet—even distant—during the discussion, and he knew why. Like Thorac and Endil, she'd been wounded emotionally and needed time to heal. Being with Yavil and the rest of her people would help with that.

She smiled as she took his hand, and he knew from the look in her eyes that she had sensed his thoughts. "You never cease to amaze, do you?" she said.

"What's so amazing about looking after people you care for?" he asked, then looked back to the others.

"I'll be in touch," he said, then opened a Veilgate to the top of the Great Wall.

Squinting against the brightness of the late afternoon sun, Aethon Fairimor rode in silence as he contemplated what Shadan might be up to. The refleshed Dreadlord could pretend all he wanted that nothing out of the ordinary had happened, but a Veilgate opening from the Pit meant trouble. That Shadan had momentarily seized the Power as if he might widen the Veilgate and abandon Death's Third March confirmed it. Something was wrong. But what?

Something that would have benefitted Shadan personally, Aethon decided, or the fool wouldn't have considered leaving in the very moment order had been restored to his army and it was moving smoothly again.

He cast a sideways glance to where the Dreadlord was riding his K'sivik. It had been more than an hour since the unexpected rending, and in the meantime, Shadan had surrounded himself with an entourage of Deathriders and Agla'Con wearing the mark of Shadan Cult priests. For good or bad, he was preparing to act on whatever he'd learned from Shattuk.

Aethon squinted westward once more. The sun was directly ahead, a blinding yellow-gold orb that bathed the western edge of the plateau in shimmers of heat and light. Fortunately, it would be dropping below the edge of the plateau soon, throwing the area into a welcome shade.

He let his eyes move across the sea of marching bodies, then took a deep breath and slowly let it out. It had been a rough day for Death's Third March. The loss of Krev and the other Rhiven. The slaughter of tens of thousands of his troops here and on the outskirts of the Kelsan camp. A Blood Orb being accessed in Kunin—

Aethon stiffened. That last... Could it have something to do with the message from the Pit and the sudden change in Shadan's behavior? A cold, dark fury came to life within him. It most certainly had to do with an Orb. And the greedy, power-hungry fool was hoping to keep it to himself.

He looked across the heads of the marching troops once more, fixing Shadan with a stare that would have sent Shadowhounds scurrying for cover. If Shadan had jeopardized the war effort because of this, he would tear his refleshed body to shreds and leave him in a quivering heap. He would be incapacitated but cognizant of his stupidity during the days it would take him to bind himself back together.

"I know that look," Raelig Tiafin said, and Aethon looked over to find the man watching him with a calculating smile.

Formerly the Captain of Kashilka Spike, Aethon had promoted him to Supreme Commander of the Tamban army here in Kelsa as a way of rewarding him for his efforts in recruiting the vast army of men loyal to the Fist of Con'Jithar.

The promotion didn't sit well with Ibisar Naxis, *Frel'mola's* lackey and Supreme Commander of the Tamban military loyal to the Fist of the Dark Bride, but that was exactly the point. As long as there was tension between the two factions, it wasn't likely they would band together to lay claim to what would rightfully be Aethon's. He grinned inwardly. After Shadan was eliminated, of course.

"And what look is that?" Aethon asked.

Raelig's smile widened. "You're thinking of challenging Shadan again."

"You're very perceptive," Aethon said. "But there will be no challenge. At least not until I learn what the refleshed cur is up to."

He looked to the seven *Jeth'Jalda* Raelig had taken on as his warder-advisors. Each had the Old World symbol for Con'Jithar tattooed on his forehead and was among the most powerful and vicious Power-wielders Tamba had to offer. Together they'd sworn a Tamban Blood Oath to protect their new commander and had bound the oath with the Power.

"Send word to the *Jeth'Jalda* under your command," Aethon told them, "and inform them that we will be stopping here for the night."

"Yes, Master Fairimor," they said, and he felt them open their Awareness to set the chain of communication in motion.

Squinting against the sun's brightness once more, Aethon opened his Awareness and touched the minds of the phalanx of Deathriders at the head of Death's Third March and ordered them to stop for the night. The hundreds of Shadowhounds linked to the K'rrosha stopped as well, flopping down in the plateau's grasses like so many well-trained dogs.

"If only the bloody cultists were that obedient," Raelig said, and Aethon looked over at him to find him frowning. It was no secret he and his men were disgusted by those who worshiped Shadan as some kind of god—they'd made it clear by refusing to be within a half mile of them. Aethon suspected their hatred of *Frel'mola* was to blame. Their feelings for her and her cult had been transferred to Shadan and his.

"The cultists serve their purpose," Aethon told him. "Just as *Frel'mola te Ujen* will when we reach the Kelsan Army."

"My misguided countrymen might take exception to leading the charge," Raelig warned. "Just as they did when they refused to take point for the Dragon Gates. And now they feel justified because of how badly the gates failed." He looked over, his face unreadable. "There are rumors circulating among them that you see them as expendable."

"Then they aren't as stupid as I believed them to be," Aethon told him. "But the fact remains that they are here to give battle to the enemy. And they will give it where and when I say."

"And the Fist of Con'Jithar?" Raelig asked. "Are my men also expendable?"

Aethon locked eyes with him. "No more than you or I, my friend," he answered. "All of us are nothing more than pieces on a board set by Maeon."

Raelig grunted. "You do a fair job of manipulating those pieces once they are set."

"Not good enough, obviously," Aethon said, all his rage and frustration at the day's events returning. "Or we wouldn't have lost one of our greatest assets."

Fueled by that anger, he turned his horse toward Shadan. "Come, let's discover what the mighty Destroyer is plotting."

With Raelig and his tattooed bodyguards following in his wake, he rode through the midst of his army without looking down. They knew better than to impede his progress, having been trained by Dathan's quick temper during those weeks he and Kameron had headed the army. If nothing else, his brother had left his mark by establishing that the Fairimors were not to be trifled with.

Thoughts of his slain brothers made the rage in him burn all the hotter, and he heeled his horse into a trot. Dozens of men had to leap aside to avoid being trampled. Fortunately for them, word that Death's Third March was stopping for the night spread quickly through the ranks, and Aethon's route to Shadan opened rapidly as men and Darklings alike gathered around the supply wagons for food and bedding.

As he drew near the Dreadlord, Shadan turned his K'sivik to face him. His good eye burned with irritation, and he gripped his scepter as if he were contemplating using it. Raelig's *Jeth'Jalda* warders took note of the threatening posture, and three took defensive positions around him while the other four spread out to make it difficult for Shadan to watch all of them at once.

The move wasn't lost on Shadan's entourage of Deathriders, and lances were lowered as they ringed their master in.

Shaking his head in disgust, Aethon opened himself to *Lo'shaen* and swept the nearest three aside with a powerful thrust of Air. Their shadowspawned mounts screamed in surprise and pain as they and their riders went down in a tumble of legs and lances. The K'rrosha scrambled to their feet as their mounts raced away in a thundering of startled hooves, but Aethon rode past them as if nothing had happened.

Still coursing with the Power of the Void, he stopped just short of Shadan and his K'sivik. "Enough of this gaming," he said, putting an edge to his voice. "I'm well aware that Shattuk contacted you from the Pit. What is this all about?"

Shadan's scepter flared dangerously, but Aethon held his ground, a corrupted bar of *Sei'shiin* a hair's width away should he need it. One wrong move and he would send this refleshed idiot back to the world of spirits, Maeon's orders be damned.

"Don't take that tone with me, Fairimor," Shadan rasped, his good eye boring into Aethon as if it might channel its own bar of *Sei'shiin*.

Aethon was undeterred. "I'll take whatever tone is necessary to get to the bottom of your newest conspiracy," he said.

The fiery glow of Shadan's scepter brightened momentarily, then abruptly faded. Shadan leaned back in the saddle, forcing a laugh. "Conspiracy?" he said. "What idiocy is this?"

Before Aethon could answer, the Veil was torn open by a powerful, but decidedly desperate use of corrupted Earthpower and Shattuk and three other Agla'Con stumbled through from beyond.

Aethon glanced at them briefly, then turned a humorless smile on Shadan. "Perhaps we should ask the idiots?" he said. "It's plain to see they have much to tell."

Visibly shaken and perhaps even a bit stunned, Shattuk took note of his surroundings, then dropped to his knees in front of Shadan. The nervous look he shot Aethon's way showed he wasn't sure if he should speak in his presence.

"Out with it, you fool," Aethon snapped, and Shattuk flinched as if struck.

"Forgive us, my lord," he said, directing his words to Shadan. "We failed. The disturbance we went to investigate... it was... it was a Blood Orb of Elsa. Pure and undefiled. We would have taken it, but High King Nid got to it first. He fled through a Veilgate with it."

Aethon failed to keep his surprise in check. "Lord Nid defiled the Orb?"

"We weren't the first Agla'Con to arrive at the temple," Shattuk said. "We found the remains of several of our brethren plastered upon the walls. I can only assume that Lord Nid destroyed them and was left too weak by the encounter to call for help.

I think he took the Orb to keep it from us."

"I'm sure that's what he did," Aethon snapped. "The man isn't a fool."

"The Orb has been rendered useless to its true purpose," Shadan said. "The Fairimors are no closer to bringing about the Rejuvenation than they were before. High King Nid did us a favor."

"By delivering the most powerful weapon in the world to our enemies?" Aethon asked. "Have you forgotten what Jase did to this army in Melek with the last Orb he had?"

"You mean the Orb you lost to him when he took your hand?" Shadan hissed. "That loss is on you, first among the living."

"And this one is on you!" Aethon growled. In his mind's eye the bar of *Sei'shiin* that would rid the world of Shadan once and for all began to take shape. It would be so easy. All he had to do was loose it.

Fighting through his anger, he continued, "If you would have sent me instead of this fool, the Orb would be in our possession now instead of Jase's. This bloody war would be over!"

"Then you do not understand the prophecies," Shadan said, his tone condescending. "Or you would know that this war won't end until we are inside the walls of Trian."

"A prospect made that much more difficult now that the Fairimors have a Blood Orb at their disposal."

"You let me worry about that," Shadan said. "You get back to managing our troops."

"Yes, sir," Aethon said, then raised a fist toward Shattuk and his companions and burned them from existence with sizzling spears of corrupted *Sei'shiin*. Without another word, he turned his back on Shadan and walked away, leaving the Dreadlord to consider how close he had come to joining his failed messengers.

# CHAPTER 37

## *Tactical Considerations*

"QUINTELLA DYMAS HAS RETURNED, GENERAL," Teig Ole'ar said, and Joneam Eries lowered the spyglass he'd been using to monitor the final stages of the battle between his troops and the enemy forces who'd been stranded here by the failed Dragon Gates.

"And?" he asked.

"The Blood Orb she and Jase went to investigate is in good hands. Lord Nid recovered it. He is here now. He came to check on Idoman."

"And Jase?"

"At the Great Wall."

Joneam nodded, slightly frustrated. He had hoped to have Jase's input on his plans for the next few days, but dwelling on the frustration wouldn't do anyone any good. He sighed inwardly. *Take it as a sign that he trusts you,* he told himself. *He'd be here if he felt he was needed.*

"I'll be along shortly," he told Teig. "I want to finish checking the status of the battle. Have Idoman signal our captains. We need to discuss our next move."

"Yes, General," Teig said, then disappeared back the way he'd come.

Joneam put his eye to the spyglass once more, fixing it on the enemy who'd arrived northwest of the camp. Except for a handful of non-cultist Meleki who'd surrendered, it had been a massacre in every sense of the word. The Shadan Cultists, frenzied, zealous idiots that they were, had rushed headlong into the Elvan cavalry only to be cut down by blade and arrow or trampled by steel-shod hooves.

Not even the thousands of Darklings with them had been that stupid, but had fled north and west toward the plateau, thinking perhaps, to find an avenue of escape upward into the cliffs. Only when they realized how futile an ascent would be had they turned to fight. Their bodies littered the base of the cliffs like flotsam strung along a rocky shoreline. The *Bero'thai* who'd pursued them had killed every last one of the creatures.

He studied the scene a moment longer, then swung the spyglass to the west. The setting sun threw a glare across the lens, but he could still see well enough to make out what was happening. Bursts of Power-wrought Fire and an occasional bolt of lightning showed where the last of the *Jeth'Jalda* were being engaged by Dymas, but the rest of the battlefield was still save for a few squads of Krelltin-mounted Chunin searching for the living among the dead.

The remains of the most dangerous kinds of shadowspawn littered the ground in twisted, smoldering chunks of ruined flesh, while lesser creatures like Darklings were mostly intact, killed by the more traditional means of sword or spear or arrow. The Dymas of the united armies had engaged shadowspawn only when necessary, preferring to target the *Jeth'Jalda* instead.

As he watched, that part of the battle ended as well. There was one final crack of thunder following a sharp stab of lightning, and then silence fell across the Bottomlands.

Joneam lowered the spyglass and pursed his lips in grim satisfaction. Of the thousands of Tambans who'd raced through so eager to repeat what they'd done atop the plateau, not a single soldier remained alive, and their armored corpses reflected the evening sunlight like so many fallen beetles.

He didn't know if their tenacity in battle was a result of the same zealous adoration for Shadan that the cultists possessed, or if it was simply in the Tamban credo to fight to the death. Whatever the reason, they were significantly more skilled than the cultist army and had inflicted a bit more harm than Joneam would have liked. The only consolation came from knowing that without the aid of Galiena and her people in collapsing the Veilgates, the outcome would have been very different. The massacre would have been reversed.

And that had him thinking they needed to reevaluate the current tactical situation.

Mirrored by his warders, he moved to his horse and hoisted himself into the saddle. Then without another look at the waning battle, he started for the center of camp.

Idoman had raised the red and yellow banner to call the High Command into assembly, but Joneam knew he wouldn't be passing any of the men on his way to join Idoman at the flag pole. The silvery-blue flashes of Veilgates being opened here and there throughout the camp confirmed it. The members of the High Command had seen the signal banner and were answering the call according to the new protocol.

Gone were the days of meeting in or anywhere near the camp—the Veilgate his enemies had opened directly into the command tent had shown the foolishness of that. He'd lost Joselyn and Kalear and had nearly lost Idoman as well. Never again would he assemble so many of this army's leaders in a place where they could be so easily reached.

*Fool me once*, he thought, directing it toward his enemies. *Never again.*

He spotted Idoman and Quintella and Lord Nid waiting for him beneath the flag pole, and he raised his hand in greeting as he neared. Idoman looked as if he might fall on his face from exhaustion, but he returned the wave.

Joneam swung down from the saddle in front of Lord Nid. "It's good to see you again, my friend," he told the King. "I take it things are well in Melek."

"They are," Hul said, eyeing Joneam's warders as they dismounted and took up positions around the banner area. "But we will talk more about that later. I understand you have a war council to attend."

"Yes," Joneam answered. "And you are invited."

Hul exchanged a quick smile with Idoman. "I know. Your young Dymas General already invited me. He said it was because he values my opinion, but really it's because he is still too tired to open a Veilgate."

"Almost dying will do that to a person," Idoman said with a shrug.

Joneam smiled at his young friend. "Let's get to it then," he said. "Where are we going this time?"

"Somewhere quiet," Idoman answered, winking at Quintella. She returned the smile as Idoman turned to Lord Nid. "If you would be so kind..."

The Meleki King nodded, and a Veilgate opened next to the flag pole. "After you, General."

Joneam signaled his warders to hold their positions until he returned, then moved through to the well-groomed garden beyond. He was greeted by the smell of the ocean and a cool yet humid breeze. Birds were singing, and flashes of feathered color darted among the trees and bushes. A short distance in front of him, the rest of the High Command and their escorting Dymas stood on a gravel pathway and were staring in wonder at something beyond the edge of his Veilgate.

He discovered what it was when Idoman and the others joined him and the Power-wrought opening shrank in on itself, revealing a spectacular view of Tetrica's waterfront. Glittering brightly with the reds and oranges of the setting sun, it was dotted with boats small and large.

As magnificent as the sight was, however, Joneam realized it was a headstone which had so captivated the assembly. The center-point of the immaculate little garden, it bore the following inscription:

*In Memory of Norel Vorsila*
*Beloved friend and mentor*
*Hero of the Battle of Greendom*
*Protector of the* Mith'elre Chon
*Champion of the Earthsoul*

"It's *chorazin*," Idoman said loudly enough for everyone to hear. "I watched as it was wrought by the *Mith'elre Chon*."

"Is that why you chose this place for the assembly?" one of the escorting Dymas asked. A petite, green-eyed Elvan girl, she looked even younger than Idoman and bore a striking resemblance to the Elvan Captain she was escorting. Joneam thought she must be the man's daughter.

"It's one of the reasons," Idoman told her. "To me, this marker is a symbol of hope. That the Earthsoul would assist the *Mith'elre Chon* in resurrecting a wielding lost to us since before the Destruction of the Old World helps me believe we can and will win this war. If things were truly hopeless, I don't think She would bother with such things."

"And the other reasons?" one of the Chunin Dymas asked. He was the escort for General Kennin, but Joneam didn't know if he had been present in Kunin with the general or had recently been assigned to him. Aside from the fact that the mission to rescue the Blood Orb had been successful, Joneam didn't have many of the details.

"It smells good here," Idoman said, then looked out over the harbor. "And the view is spectacular. Why go out into the Bottomlands or up into the Death's Chain Mountains when we can come here? A journey of a mile or a journey of ten thousands miles—through a Veilgate it is the same."

He smiled. "Besides. I sent Quintella Dymas here earlier today to set things up. Norel has a very large dining table in her cottage that we've put to good use. We'll discuss our next move in there."

Idoman hung back with the Dymas as Joneam led the High Command into Norel's cottage. Fourteen men in all, they represented the three allied nations of Kelsa, Elva, and Chunin, and ranged in rank from captain to general. Not since the Battle of Greendom had there been such an assembly, and he was impressed by the feeling of unity he felt from the men.

The feeling of unity was even stronger among the Dymas, and he let his eyes move over the group with admiration. *Children of* Ta'shaen, he thought. *Children of Earthpower. Brothers and sisters regardless of birth or nationality.*

"I know some of you knew Norel Dymas," he told them. "She would be honored to have you here. Please, enjoy a moment of peace and quiet while I address the High Command."

"Would you like us to ward the cottage against intrusion?" Halithor Dymas asked. A veteran of the Battle of Greendom, he had been present as Croneam Eries had led the Final Stand.

"Yes," Idoman told him. "And if you should sense the touch of any probing Awarenesses, you have my permission to investigate. The *Mith'elre Chon* may have destroyed the Con'Kumen chapter house here in Tetrica, but it may very well be some of the Agla'Con survived. If they reveal themselves, kill them."

"Yes, Dymas General," Halithor said, and the look he exchanged with some of the others showed he hoped there would be Agla'Con to hunt.

Idoman nodded for Quintella and Lord Nid to join him, and together they entered Norel's cottage. They found Joneam and the rest of the allied military leaders gathered around the large table, looking over the maps and pewter figures Quintella had laid out earlier in the day. He moved to the head of the table to stand next to Joneam.

"What you see," he said, "is what things looked like this morning before Shadan's pet Rhiven attempted to open their Dragon Gates."

Using tendrils of Air, he moved the pewter pieces on the respective maps. "Here is where things stand now. Death's Third March is poised to reach the western rim first thing in the morning. As you know, our forces are positioned here." He pointed to the area on the map where the highway leading from Talin Plateau to Mendel Pass merged with the highway leading from the causeway.

Frowning, he shook his head. "But this area was never meant to be anything but a rendezvous point for Elva and Chunin to join us as we retreated before our enemies. Unfortunately, that retreat happened much sooner than any of us anticipated, and with far less damage to the enemy than we had hoped for."

"My father's plan," Joneam said, picking up where Idoman left off, "was to have *all* of Shadan's army lay siege to Fulrath instead of just one third of it. Imagine what the activation of the Seal would have done to enemy numbers had that been the case."

Idoman nodded. "They still would have outnumbered us, but not so much that we couldn't have engaged them in a number of places as we fell back. Instead, we were forced to launch a number of fairly meaningless attacks through Veilgates."

He pointed to the map. "The only reason we stayed where we are until now was to bait them into using the Dragon Gates again so Queen Morgranon could attack the Rhiven traitors. Thankfully, the risk paid off. However, I agree with Joselyn Rai's assessment that we cannot stand toe to toe with Death's Third March out in the open. Their numbers are simply too great."

Speaking her name hurt more than he'd imagined it would, and he fell silent as he wrestled with the sudden sadness.

Joneam noticed his struggle and came to his rescue. "I agree," he said. "We would eventually be forced to retreat, and Mendel Pass would become a bottleneck for us. Any who were unable to make it into the pass would be overrun and slaughtered."

Finding his voice again, Idoman continued. "I propose we move our troops to Trian Plateau and use Mendel Pass the same way we used Zedik Pass. Let's turn it into a bottleneck for Death's Third March and fill it up with their dead bodies." Around the room, the men nodded their agreement.

"The Chunin Dymas are relatively fresh," General Kennin said. "I will ask them to open Veilgates for all footmen and supply wagons. The various cavalries, Krelltin and horse-borne, can ride once our Dymas' strength gives out."

"My people will open gates as well," Quintella announced. "We should be able to move the rest of your troops in a relatively short amount of time."

"That would be most appreciated," one of the Elvan captains said. "My men are weary from our journey from Andlexces."

"What about the western rampway?" General Gefion asked. "I know there are still a number of the plateau's residents who are fleeing ahead of Shadan's army, but we cannot leave it intact any longer. Our enemies will reach it by morning."

"The *Mith'elre Chon* ordered its collapse," Idoman told them. "We will see to it the moment we return to camp."

"How much time will we gain by bringing it down?" General Kennin asked.

"A couple of days," General Gefion answered. "It depends on how many Veilgates their Power-wielders are able to open."

"Before the rampways were built," Joneam added, "a number of smaller paths were cut into the living rock of the cliff face. They are narrow and steep, but they are passable. I imagine they will be put to use."

"I certainly hope so," Idoman said, not even trying to hide his smile. "I plan to attack with *Ta'shaen* as they are descending."

"Why not just destroy the pathways now?" Captain Ieashar asked. He was older than the rest of the Elvan leaders in the room, with streaks of grey in his short hair and eyes that showed he'd seen many battles. That his age was so apparent made Idoman think the man must be well over a hundred years old. A good long life for any Elvan. A miracle for a man in his line of work.

"And miss an opportunity to kill more of the enemy?" Idoman said. "Not a chance."

"I like your enthusiasm," the older man replied. "But I would like to know the specifics of your plan before I sign off on it. Whoever remains behind to carry out the attacks will be exposed to the entire might of Shadan's army. Things could go badly for them in a very short amount of time."

Idoman nodded. "Yes, they could," he agreed. "Which is why our Dymas won't be anywhere near the plateau. We will launch our attacks through Veilgates."

"You can do that?" General Kennin asked. "You can actually wield the Power on the other side of the opening?"

"When you put it like that, no," Idoman told him. "We embrace *Ta'shaen* where we stand, but our wieldings can pass through a gate just as easily as we can."

"Or as easily as a volley of arrows," General Gefion added. "We launched hundreds of such attacks while the enemy was marching through Greendom."

"Then by all means," Captain Ieashar said. "Let's kill the enemy."

"If it's agreed," Idoman said, "I will assemble a team of Dymas and oversee the details of the attack. We will also collapse the rampway before nightfall. I will leave the details of our withdrawal to Mendel Pass and Trian Plateau to you gentlemen, but I will place Dymas at your disposal to provide Veilgates."

Around the table, every head nodded.

"It is decided," Joneam said. "God's speed, Dymas General Leda. The rest of us will return to camp as soon as we finish up here."

"See you shortly, then," Idoman said and motioned for Quintella to follow. He was grateful she had taken it upon herself to watch over him. Not just so she could open Veilgates for him during his recovery, but because her broad smile and optimistic nature helped soothe his nerves.

Outside, the escorting Dymas eyed him expectantly as he moved to stand by Norel's gravestone. "I need some of you to come with me," he told them. "We need to collapse the rampway. The rest of you will stay here to bring our military leaders home."

As if at some unseen signal, nine of the fourteen Dymas stepped forward. "We're with you," a hazel-eyed Chunin said. She was small even for a Chunin and young, but Idoman could sense through *Ta'shaen* that she was as strong in the Power as anyone in the group.

Idoman smiled at the little woman, then nodded to Quintella who opened a Veilgate back to the Kelsan camp.

Hulanekaefil Nid watched Idoman and Quintella depart, then shook his head in admiration. "That young man has changed considerably since the last time I saw him," he said. "He's stronger. More decisive. No wonder you put him in charge of your Dymas."

Joneam grunted. "If even half of what I heard about his efforts at Zedik Pass are true," he said, "the only person who did more to disrupt and destroy the enemy was the *Mith'elre Chon*."

"I believe it," Hul said. "Idoman was a remarkable young man even before he reached his full potential as a Dymas." Still smiling, he turned his attention to the map.

"With Melek back in my control," he said, "I am prepared to send an army to assist you. I was thinking of coming at Death's Third March from the rear to pin them against the western rim."

"Can you get enough men through Veilgates quickly enough to have any real effect?" Captain Ieashar asked, and Hul smiled confidently at the grey-haired Elvan soldier.

"I'm willing to find out," he said. "Even if we aren't able to fully engage them in battle because of numbers, my arrival will force them to divide their attention between our two armies. Any disruption will slow them down. Remember, we don't need to destroy them all—we just need to delay them until the *Mith'elre Chon* can rejuvenate the Earthsoul."

"Any help you can give us is appreciated," Joneam told him. "It is your people who have suffered the most because of Throy Shadan. It would be understandable if they preferred to stay in Melek and fight the battle there."

"Oh, we will definitely being doing that," Hul told him. "I won't rest until every last member of his cult has been eradicated." He paused as a previously unconsidered notion began to take shape in his mind. It sent chills of excitement up his spine. *Of course! Why didn't I think of this sooner?*

"In fact," he said, deciding to act on the sudden thought. "I have something extra special planned for Throy Shadan. Something that will certainly distract him in his efforts to descend the plateau."

"Then God's speed, my friend," Joneam said. "Let us know if you need anything from us."

"I will," Hul replied, offering his hand in farewell. Joneam's grip was strong, and he offered a bow of respect. Hul returned the bow, then stepped back and nodded to the rest of the men as he started for the door.

"And good luck to you, gentlemen," he said. "Until we meet again."

Outside, he stopped briefly to inspect the *chorazin* headstone Jase had created. It was as flawless as any *chorazin* wrought by the Creator, and he ran his hand over it in appreciation. He liked Idoman's reasoning that it was proof the Earthsoul still had hope for the future, and he was determined to do his part to see that She wouldn't be disappointed.

He cast a farewell glance at the remaining Dymas as he embraced all Seven Gifts and opened the way back to Kamasin. It was time to take his offensive against the enemy to the next level. A level even Throy Bloody Shadan wouldn't expect.

Standing on a grassy swell some distance out in the Bottomlands, Idoman watched the rampway collapse in a rumble of breaking stone and snapping timbers. The magnificent structure had become the latest victim in Shadan's war on Kelsa, and necessary or not, its destruction made him angry. Like Greendom and the eastern rampways, like Fulrath and its magnificent tunnel, this marvel of human architecture which had taken years to build, vanished in a matter of seconds. The pattern didn't bode well for Trian, the next and assuredly final target of Death's Third March.

"Too bad there weren't thousands of cultists on those platforms," Teig said, and Idoman looked over to find the Elvan scout frowning.

"I considered waiting until the enemy put the rampway to use," Idoman said. "But I was worried Shadan or his Agla'Con would find a way to shield it. Trying to bring it down at that point would have been next to impossible. And it would have cost us many lives. It was better to do it now, before they even arrive."

Teig nodded. "Yes. I suppose it is," he said. "I guess I'm just angry that we had to collapse it at all."

"You and me both, my friend," he said. "You and me both."

A Veilgate opened nearby, and Quintella came through with three other Dymas. One was the green-eyed Elvan girl who'd been with him and the others in Tetrica. He'd learned from Teig that her name was Reyshella and that she was indeed the daughter of the captain she'd been escorting. She was as feisty as she was pretty, and he could tell by the look in her eyes that the inner fire was very near the surface.

"What a waste," she said, looking back in the direction of the ruined rampway.

A cloud of dust was billowing up from the base of the plateau and rocks and other debris were still cascading down the newly scarred cliff face.

"Mourning for something which has no life is the waste," Quintella told her. "Steel and stone and wood can be replaced. Not so with the life of a soldier." She pointed south toward the united armies. "And we just saved the lives of many by buying them the time they need to move to a more tactically sound location."

Reyshella blew out her cheeks in frustration. "I know," she said. "But it still makes me sad. My great-grandfather helped build that rampway."

"Perhaps when this war is over," Idoman said, drawing her beautiful gaze to his, "you could be among those who help rebuild it." Good heavens, but the girl was pretty.

She smiled at him. "I would like that."

He noticed the quizzical stare Teig was directing his way and cleared his throat. "We best be getting back to camp. It will be dark soon and I'd rather not be out in the open should the enemy come looking for those who just slowed them down."

# CHAPTER 38

## A Lull in the Chaos

WHILE CHIEFTAIN KIA'KAL AND HIS *Nar'shein* tended to the wounded, Seth stood in contemplative silence as he watched the approaching Rhiven. Their prowess on the battlefield was unlike anything he had ever seen. They had accomplished in under an hour what would have taken the soldiers defending the wall days to do—if they'd been able to do it at all. He didn't want to think about what would have happened if the demon masters had been able to attack the wall in earnest.

He picked out the blue-scaled Dragon carrying Elliott and wondered what it had been like for her and the rest of the Rhiven as their world fell.

It was easy to imagine how terribly outnumbered they must have been in those final hours when the full strength of Con'Jithar was marching to battle against them. Especially after witnessing just how easily they had obliterated the demons outnumbering them here today. It proved that this demon army—formidable as it had been—wasn't much more than a gust of wind compared to the storm yet to come. Not a comforting thought.

Even less comforting was the fact that out of the millions of Rhiven who'd inhabited their former world, less than three hundred had survived long enough to escape to this world. If creatures like the Rhiven could be slaughtered to the brink of extinction, what chance did the people here have if more demon armies were loosed by a collapsing Veil?

Not much, he decided. Which was why finding a viable Orb was so critical.

He was still watching the Rhiven approach when a chorus of excited shouts announced the arrival of the *Mith'elre Chon*. Turning toward the sound, he found Jase and Queen Morgranon exiting a Veilgate. Jase took note of his surroundings, then made straight for Seth.

"Is it over?" he asked, sounding as if he'd expected otherwise.

"Yes," Seth answered, then gave a bow of respect to Galiena. "Thanks to the Rhiven." He pointed over the edge of the battlements. "They are returning just now."

Jase's eyes moved in that direction, then went wide with surprise. "Is that Elliott?"

Seth grunted. "Quite a sight, isn't it?"

"If you think that is amazing," Railen said as he and Sheymi pushed past a squad of *Bero'thai* who'd stopped to stare at the Rhiven Queen, "you should have seen him and Ayame in battle. It was spectacular."

"I'll bet it was," Jase said, his eyes still on Elliott riding high on Ayame's back. Finally, he shook himself free of the sight and looked back at Seth. "Where is Elrien? We need to decide on our next move here at the wall."

Seth pointed to the east. "He's tending to the wounded somewhere beyond that next tower. But I suspect he will be returning shortly. News of your arrival races through the troops as if urged along with the Power."

He caught sight of Chieftain Kia'Kal towering above the *Bero'thai* and spotted Elrien walking beside him. "Here he comes now."

When Elrien arrived, Jase greeted him with a smile but his voice was all business. "Gather your captains," said. "And contact those we sent to Fairholm Valley. I want a report of all of today's happenings. It will help us decide how to proceed."

"Yes, *Mith'elre Chon*," Elrien said. "But may I suggest we meet somewhere a little more quiet? My study, perhaps?"

Jase looked around at the carnage and chaos left behind by the battle. "I would like that."

He turned to Railen and Sheymi. "I would like you two to join us. Chieftain Kia'Kal, you are invited as well." He offered his arm to Galiena. "Queen Morgranon will contact Yavil and ask him and Elliott join us when they arrive."

As Ayame carried him south toward the wall, Elliott closed his eyes and let the gentle sway of her long strides soothe his tired and tattered nerves. It had been a long and bloody day, and he was fortunate to have survived unscathed. Well, mostly unscathed. He still wasn't entirely certain Sheymi hadn't left a scar on his rump when she'd healed him. Still, it could have been worse. Without the help of the Rhiven, it would have been.

"Our presence is requested at the wall," Yavil said, and Elliott looked over at him in surprise. The Rhiven's yellow eyes were bright with excitement, and he was smiling as if he had a secret. Beneath him, Shalish's eyes glimmered with a similar light, even though her Dragon face was unreadable.

When Yavil offered nothing more, Elliott glanced down at Ayame. "Do you know what he is talking about?"

She twisted her long neck around so she could look at him before she answered. "The *Mith'elre Chon* is here with our Queen," she said. "They wish to speak with us."

"Sure," Elliott said, not even trying to control his sarcasm. "He arrives *after* the battle is over."

Yavil laughed. "But if had he arrived sooner, your time as Ayame's *sholin* may have been cut short."

Elliott smiled. "That's a fair point," he said. Leaning forward in the saddle, he ran a hand along Ayame's neck. "And I wouldn't trade those few extra minutes for anything."

"I'm not a horse to be stroked like some pet," she said, feigning irritation. Then she twisted her head around to look at him once more. "But the honor has been mine, young prince."

When they reached the base of the wall, a small door of Power-wrought steel opened, and a squad of *Bero'thai* came out to meet them. If they were nervous to be in such close proximity to Dragons, it didn't show.

"Welcome back, Lord Chellum," the one wearing the mark of captain said. "The *Mith'elre Chon* awaits you in Elrien's study. We will escort you to him."

Elliott nodded, and he and Yavil swung down from the saddles. "I would like you and Shalish to come, too," Elliott told Ayame. "Do you need me to remove the saddle before you change to human form?"

"That would be most helpful," she said, then hunkered down so he could undo the straps and lift the saddle free of her shoulders. "In the saddle bag there," she continued once he had it free, "you will find a robe I can wear."

Then without waiting for him to fetch it, she transformed into a tall slender woman with greenish-black hair. Shalish transformed as well, and Elliott found himself staring at two strikingly beautiful women. And both were as naked as the day they were born.

Face flushing with embarrassment, he hurriedly turned his back and busied himself with fetching Ayame's robe. When he had it, he held it behind him without looking.

"Thank you, my *sholin*," she said as she took it from him.

Her voice held far more amusement than it should have, and he kept his back turned while she donned the robe. From the corner of his eye, he saw Yavil grinning at him as he pulled Shalish's robe from her saddle. Then, still grinning, he unfolded the robe and moved out of Elliott's line of sight to help Shalish put it on.

When Ayame took him by the arm a moment later, he cast a quick sideways glance at her and was relieved to find her properly clothed. Shalish was as well, but it was clear from the smiles on their faces that they found the situation amusing.

"You do realize," Shalish said, her eyes sparkling with mirth, "that she was just as naked when she carried you into battle."

Elliott opened his mouth to reply, then closed it again when he realized there was nowhere this conversation could go that wouldn't end badly.

Ayame winked at Shalish, then offered Elliott her arm. "Shall we?" she asked.

Still speechless, Elliott took her arm, and they followed the *Bero'thai* inside.

Jase had just accepted a mug of chilled ale from one of Elrien's apprentices when the doors leading into the Elvan prophet's study opened and Elliott came in with a female Rhiven at his side. Yavil and another female Rhiven followed close on their heels.

Jase set the mug on a small table and rose to greet them. "You've been busy," he said. "And right in the thick of things if what Elrien says is true."

"That's Elliott's fault," Yavil said. "He has a knack for being where the fighting is at its worst."

"That he does," Jase agreed, ignoring the sour look Elliott directed at him. Instead, he locked eyes with the green-haired female at his friend's side.

"You must be Ayame," he said.

She nodded. "Yes. And it is a pleasure to meet you, *Mith'elre Chon*."

"Call me Jase," he told her. "We are all friends here." He turned to Elliott. "So, the first in a new generation of Dragonriders, huh? Your resume continues to grow."

Elliott arched an eyebrow at him. "My resume for what?"

Jase chuckled. "Whatever the Earthsoul has in store for you. My guess is it's going to be big." He gestured to the crescent-shaped row of chairs. "Come, my friends. We have much to discuss."

When everyone was seated, Jase looked at Dommoni. Even sitting cross-legged on the floor, he was eye level to those in the chairs, and as wide as three people combined. His broad, sun-darkened face was thoughtful as he studied the Rhiven.

"I've asked Chieftain Kia'Kal to speak first," Jase announced, and all eyes turned to Dommoni expectantly. "He has information that directly affects the Great Wall."

Dommoni looked from face to face before letting his eyes settle on Jase. "I've spoken with Chieftain Peregam regarding the rent which opened into Fairholm Valley," he began. "The *Nar'shein* sent to the area encountered a number of Shadan'Ko and other creatures which they promptly destroyed. Those not involved with hunting shadowspawn were working to close the rent when an influx of Spirit from Endil Fairimor's use of the Orb did it for them."

"The same thing happened to the commandeered Veilgate in the Allister Highlands," Railen said. "And a short while after that, the massive rent which allowed the demon army to enter this world closed as well."

Dommoni nodded. "Yes. And while it is comforting to know the Earthsoul had strength enough to heal those wounds, it will not last. Ohran sent a squad of *Nar'shein* to investigate the area, and they found it weak and unstable, much like a deep cut which has only recently been stitched. Put too much strain on it and the stitches will tear."

He shook his head sadly. "Even now, Con'Jithar presses heavily upon the area, and holes are once again opening. They are small and sporadic, akin to those of several weeks ago, but their size and rate of occurrence will increase until the Earthsoul can no longer fight them. When that happens..."

"Another demon army will march on the Great Wall," Railen finished for him. "So how much time do we have?"

"A few days, maybe," Dommoni said. "No one can say for sure."

"Then we must fortify," Captain Kium said. "I'll send a request to Andlexces for more troops. Lamshore and Do'hyleth should be able to send more as well."

Elrien shook his head. "Andlexces has none to spare," he said. "Every available man already left to assist Kelsa. The other cities might be able to send us a few, but it won't be enough to make a difference."

"If I may," Galiena said, and all eyes turned toward her. Sitting straight-backed and tall in spite of her weariness, she looked every inch the Queen she was. "My people will confront any demons that might arrive in the valley."

The announcement caught everyone by surprise, a welcome surprise if the smiles on the faces of Elrien and his captains meant anything, but Jase couldn't allow the Rhiven to risk themselves in what would obviously be a losing fight.

Galiena must have sensed the objection forming in his mind because she placed a hand on his arm to stop him from giving voice to it.

"Our part in the war with Shadan is over," she said. "My traitorous brethren are no more. Death's Third March will be forced to continue their advance without the aid of Dragon Gates. We accomplished what we set out to do. And we did it in spite of the reservations many of my people had.

"Remember, my young friend, that the majority of Rhiven want nothing to do with the races of men. They tolerated our involvement with Death's Third March only because our traitorous brethren were involved."

She smiled reassuringly. "They won't, however, remain idle when there is a chance to kill demons. And I don't mean just those who came with me initially—I mean *all* the Rhiven. Our race has a score to settle with the armies of Con'Jithar."

Yavil nodded with enthusiastic agreement. "Yes. Let us deal with any demons who escape Con'Jithar," he said. "Not only will we keep them from reaching the wall, we will ward the Soul Chamber until you arrive with a viable Orb."

As soon as the words were out of his mouth, Jase flinched as *Ta'shaen* came alive with a sudden tremor of Spirit energy. And clearly he wasn't alone in what he felt. Every person in the room, even those who weren't Dymas, sensed it as well. The Earthsoul, it seemed, had just seconded the motion.

"Well, that pretty much settles it," Elrien said, his voice filled with reverence and awe. "You obviously have the blessing of the Earthsoul. Just tell us what you need from us."

Yavil looked to Galiena, but she motioned for him to continue.

"Food and water, mainly," he answered. "And *sholin* for those of us who aren't opposed to working with the races of men."

"Done," Elrien said. "So long as I am one those *sholin*."

Yavil grinned at him. "I wouldn't have it any other way."

"What of the curse?" Jase asked. "I witnessed firsthand what it does to a person. Some of Captain Alleilwin's men succumbed to it while they were there waiting for me. In one last moment of sanity, some took their own lives to avoid becoming

Shadan'Ko."

Alleilwin nodded. "They were good men," he said, his voice heavy with sadness. "But it is those who were fully taken by the curse that deserve our pity. They are out there even now—Once-men who no longer remember anything of their former lives."

"We are aware of the curse," Yavil said. "And we are willing to risk it."

"But can *we* risk it?" Seth asked. His tone was civil, but there was a hardness to him that Jase knew all too well. The warder in him was troubled by the danger this situation posed—to the Great Wall, and to the nations beyond its protection.

"I mean no disrespect," Seth continued, "but the Rhiven are just as susceptible to the curse as any other living creature. If any of you were to succumb to the madness, we would be hard-pressed to stop you. Especially if you were in your true form."

"I agree," Galiena said, and Seth turned to regard her without a change of expression. "Which is why," she added, "the Rhiven will hunt the demons in rotations. No more than half of us will be in the valley at a given time. And never for longer than a day. Two at most." She looked to Jase and smiled. "If the *Mith'elre Chon* approves, of course."

"Who am I to question the Earthsoul?" he asked. "Or the generosity of the Rhiven people in helping where it is needed most."

"The dangers of Amnidia extend beyond the curse," Seth said. "There are creatures as formidable as any demon roaming that godforsaken place. And you'll have Mount Tabor to contend with as well. Its eruptions can be lethal in many ways. Magma, poisonous gases, falling rocks and fiery debris—any of them could cut off escape routes, preventing you from leaving the valley as soon as you might like."

"Then we will use Veilgates," Yavil told him. His smile had faded, and he seemed genuinely irritated that Seth kept arguing the point.

Jase would have shared the Rhiven's irritation if he hadn't realized what Seth was thinking. And it was a valid concern.

"Veilgates don't act right north of the Rift," Seth said, then turned a flat stare on Jase. "But don't take my word for it. Ask the *Mith'elre Chon.*"

Yavil's brow wrinkled with concern. "Is it true?"

Jase nodded. "It is. I attempted to open a Veilgate to escape the ruins of Cynthia, and it failed miserably. The curse somehow warped my abilities with *Ta'shaen.*" He looked from Yavil to Galiena and then back. "Seth is right. Tabor's volatility could leave you trapped against its slopes."

"Our people survived the Great Destruction," Galiena said. "I think we can deal with one volcanic mountain. With or without Veilgates."

"Tabor has quieted," Dommoni said. "Its eruptions were a result of the Earthsoul's weakness and pain. Endil's use of the Orb strengthened Her physically as well as spiritually. There is a lull in the chaos." He paused. "For now."

"Well, there you have it," Yavil said. "We're going." The look he directed at Seth said the debate was over.

Jase cringed inwardly. Seth had never responded well to such a look, and it didn't matter who it was from. Fearing an outburst, he opened his mouth to intervene, but Seth surprised him and everyone else in the room by offering a short bow of acceptance.

"This is your decision, of course," he said, directing the comment to Galiena. His steely gaze, however, showed he was far from pleased. "But be warned, should you or any of your people be overcome by the curse, they will be dealt with the same as any other kind of shadowspawn."

There was a nervous moment of silence as those in the room held their collective breath, waiting for the Rhiven Queen to respond.

"I would expect nothing less," Galiena said at last. "And I assure you, I will be watching my people closely. If it comes to it, I will end the life of any who turn. As their Queen, it is my responsibility."

"And we trust you to fulfill those responsibilities," Jase said, hoping to end the debate. He looked from Galiena to Seth, then let his eyes move over the rest of those gathered.

"There is danger in everything we do," he continued. "Seth's warnings are valid. I know—I've been to Tabor. It is truly a dark and awful place to be. But the Earthsoul has indicated that a Rhiven presence there will help the war effort. We will just have to trust that She will shelter and protect them as they work to protect us."

"Well said, my young friend," Elrien said, then looked to Galiena. "I can provide lodging for your people here at the wall, if you wish," he told her. "We have several stretches of apartments which are vacant at the moment. And they are far enough away from the apartments housing our *Bero'thai* to afford you some privacy."

"Some of us will stay here, perhaps," Galiena said. "I think most of my people, especially those who didn't come with us initially, would prefer their own homes. They will move in and out of the valley by way of Veilgates."

"A final word of warning on that," Jase told her. "The closer to Tabor you are, the more difficult it will be part the Veil safely—if you can part it at all. The curse is stronger in some places than it is in others. And, as happened to me, it can warp what you are trying to do. According to Gideon Dymas, Veilgates don't work at all within the walls of Shey'Avralier or inside Tabor itself."

"Thank you, *Mith'elre Chon*," Galiena said. "We will heed your warning."

Jase nodded, then turned his attention back to Elrien. "I'll leave the finer details of this plan to you and the Rhiven," he said as he stood. "I trust you will do what is necessary."

He motioned for Seth and Elliott to join him. "We are needed elsewhere," he said, then looked at Railen and Sheymi. "As are you two. You've been away from your duties on the Imperial Clave long enough."

If either of the two were surprised by the announcement, it didn't show. They simply stood and gave bows of farewell to those in the room.

He knew some of what they had done here and in the Kelsan camp, but the looks of gratitude on the faces of those bidding them farewell let Jase know he may have underestimated just how helpful they had been.

They would be sorely missed, but he suspected they had an even bigger role to play in Riak. He couldn't say for sure if one or both were *Ael'mion*, but like Elam Gaufin, fate seemed to shape itself around and according to their presence.

Jase led the way out of Elrien's study but stopped in a small anteroom at the end of the hallway. The room he'd stayed in after escaping the valley with Alleilwin and his men was just to his right, but the memory of being here seemed like it had happened years ago instead of a few weeks.

He had nearly died in that room, so weak from destroying the Reiker's scepter that he'd been unconscious for two days. Unconscious, but not untroubled. For two days he'd been tormented by dreams and visions so horrifying their images had been etched permanently into his mind.

Gideon ready to sacrifice him on the altar in the Soul Chamber. Seth killing Shadan'Ko and *Ba'trul* and other nameless shadowspawn while carrying Jase south to the Great Wall. Elrien meeting them when they arrived.

When he realized everyone was staring at him, he shrugged. "Sorry. I was just thinking about the last time I was here at the wall," he said. "Right after escaping the valley with Alleilwin and his men. I stayed in that room." He looked at Seth. "It wasn't the first time, was it?"

Seth shook his head. "No," he said, "it wasn't. After the mission to rejuvenate the Earthsoul failed, we were here for about a week while I recovered enough to return you to your mother."

Elliott stiffened as if he'd been stabbed. "Wait— What?" He was staring at Seth as if he'd never seen him before. "You were with Gideon and Areth? Why didn't I know this?"

Seth shrugged. "You were in Riak when it came up."

He frowned at Seth, then turned an even harder look on Jase. "How did *you* forget to mention that?"

Jase looked at Seth. "It wasn't for me to tell. But now that it's out in the open..." he trailed off, leaving it up to Seth to continue.

"This isn't the time or the place," Seth said. "Perhaps once we reach Chellum."

Elliott's expression turned suspicious. "Why Chellum?"

"Because I promised your father I would keep him updated on your foolishness," Seth snapped.

Jase kept his smile in check as he addressed Elliott. "We are going to move the Chellum army to Trian Plateau," he said, hoping to curtail whatever retort his friend was concocting. "Well, Seth is anyway. I'm going to check in with Idoman before going to Andlexces. I'll be spending the night there. I suggest you spend the night in Chellum. We all need some rest."

"What would you have me and Sheymi do?" Railen asked.

"Go to Chellum with Seth and Elliott," Jase said. "Get some rest. You can leave for Sagaris in the morning."

"And then... ?" Railen asked.

"Follow the whisperings of the Earthsoul," Jase answered. "She knows better than I what is needed in Riak."

He gestured at the wall. "I'll open the way. I have just enough strength left for a couple of Veilgates."

# CHAPTER 39

## *A Brief Respite*

ELAM HELPED HIS WIFE INTO a chair at the Chellum dining table, then seated himself next to her and took her hand in his. Jaina smiled at him before resting her other hand on her enlarged belly. Elam winked at her, then settled in as the rest of the dinner guests gathered at the table.

Decker and Rhea took their places at the head of the table, and Tana had joined them on the King's right. The two were already laughing softly about something Tana had said, and Rhea was smiling fondly at them, a motherly look in her eyes. It would be easy for anyone unfamiliar with the situation to mistake the young lady from Kindel's Grove as the King and Queen's own daughter, such was her comfort around them.

*Well, isn't she?* Elam thought. *All that's missing is the wedding ceremony to make it official.*

"I sure like her," Jaina whispered, and Elam glanced over to find her watching Tana with a smile. "Having her here in Chellum is good. For Decker especially."

"What do you mean?"

"Decker can pretend to be storm and thunder all he wants, but deep inside he's really a tender-hearted man who just wants to be a dad and grandpa."

"Don't let *him* hear you say that," Elam said. "He prides himself on the angry persona he's created for the Chellum Council."

"Those idiots need to see him that way," Jaina said. "He's their King. For those here tonight... it's good to see him like this."

Elam nodded his agreement. "I think you're right," he told her, then couldn't stop from smiling as Decker burst out laughing at another whispered comment from Tana. He watched the two a moment longer, then looked down the length of the table.

Raimen Adirhah stood some paces away, his face unreadable as he waited for others to select their seats first. Two of those he was waiting for were Tohquin and Kailei Nagaro. They had just entered from the dome and were leading Aimi to the table. As they neared, the little girl loudly announced that she would be sitting next to Tey.

Springing up from where she'd been teasing her cat, Tey seconded the announcement with a shout of her own, and the two little girls scrambled into seats at the end of the table opposite the King and Queen.

Elam smiled at the exchange, then watched as Cam and Hena took seats next to their little sister. Since arriving in Chellum, their emotional well-being had improved dramatically, but the news of their grandfather's death had set them both back again. They sat quietly, their eyes distant.

Alesha Eries and her son Garrick sat next to them, and Alesha's eyes were troubled as she looked at her niece and nephew. Elam's heart ached for the entire Eries family, but for Cam and Hena most of all. Witnessing the murder of their parents and grandmother at the hands of Shizu would affect them for the rest of their lives. Elam was just glad they had such a loving aunt to look after them.

From the Eries family, Elam turned his attention to Tohquin and Kailei. They had seated themselves next to Aimi opposite Alesha, and were watching the two little girls prattle on about every little thing that entered their minds.

Only when everyone else was seated, did Raimen finally select a seat, taking the chair next to Jaina. Like Tohquin, the Riaki wore his *komouri* uniform and had his sword strapped to his back, but his assassin-like appearance was overruled by the smile on his face and the look in his eyes as he watched Tey and Aimi talking.

It was the look a kindly uncle might have for his nieces, affectionate and adoring, yet fiercely protective. And like all Shizu, capable of unleashing death on any who might dare harm his precious little ones.

Elam appreciated the man's loyalty to those he'd sworn to protect, and the added strength of their swords was most welcome at a time when the enemy—Riaki or otherwise—could strike at any moment.

But not everyone saw Raimen and Tohquin as the loyal warders they'd come to be, and their presence in the Chellum home was causing a bit of a stir in the outer areas of the palace—especially among the more vocal politicians.

Which was strange since Seth Lydon's long history with Clan Gahara made it hard for Elam to imagine *not* having Shizu here. He pushed the thoughts aside and looked around the table once more.

Jonnil Dymas had arrived with Kallin and Eraline, two of the younger Dymas serving in the palace, and they had been joined by Captain Ebirin.

Per Rhea's request, additional places had been set should Elliott or Talia or Seth happen to arrive, but it had been a while since any of the extra settings had been used. Elam could tell by the way Rhea was staring at the empty chairs that she was worried about where her children might be.

Elam didn't think there was much to worry about where Talia was concerned. Not with Brysia to keep an eye on her. Elliott was a different story completely. The young man seemed to relish walking through the most intense parts of the chaos sweeping the Nine Lands. He had, in fact, made a habit of it. It made Elam wonder if the young man was right in the head.

He was still thinking about Elliott when Maisa and her kitchen staff arrived with trays of food and began placing them on the table. The smell of warm bread washed over him, and his stomach tightened with sudden hunger. Around the table, conversations fell into silence as Decker cleared his throat.

"I'd like to thank you all for joining us for dinner," he said. "With all the chaos sweeping the Nine Lands, it's nice to know we can still find small moments of normalcy. Dinner with family is one of those moments." He looked briefly in the direction of the empty plates, and a hint of tears gathered at the corners of his eyes. His voice was tight with emotion as he continued. "And you are family," he said. "As dear to us as our own blood kin."

His throat tightened and he was unable to continue.

A chorus of thank yous followed, and smiles were exchanged as everyone considered the King's words. The looks that passed between Alesha Eries and her Shizu warders further punctuated Decker's words. Though descended from completely different nations, the three had been bound together by ties even more powerful than blood or lineage—theirs was a family forged from the fires of adversity. A family created by the workings of fate and the will of the Earthsoul.

"Well," Decker said, his usual gruffness returning. "Let's eat."

The amused chuckling that followed was interrupted by a flash of blue light in front of the doors leading out to the gardens. A flurry of movement followed, and Elliott and Seth and two Riaki strode through from a dark-stone corridor beyond.

Jase Fairimor stood a short distance beyond, but made no move to join them. He simply waved a greeting then vanished as the Veilgate he'd opened slid closed.

"You mean you weren't going to wait for us?" Elliott asked as he approached the table.

His usual smile was in place, but he looked tired and very much the worse for wear. His uniform was scorched and burned and had blood spattered everywhere. Seth had been spared the scorch marks, but his uniform was no longer recognizable as being from Chellum, having literally been dyed in blood. The two Riaki—Elam realized they were Dymas—seemed unharmed, but he could see in their eyes that they were spent.

"Elliott!" Tana shouted at the same time Tey and Aimi shouted. "Railen!"

All three were out of their chairs and racing toward the new arrivals before anyone else could think to move.

Railen knelt and took the two little girls in his arms, but Elliott put up a hand to stop Tana short of embracing him.

"It would be a shame to soil that dress with demon blood," Elliott told her. "Let me change first."

"So you are planning on sticking around for a little while this time?" she asked, then reached up and touched his cheek tenderly. "You were hurt again, weren't you?"

"Nothing serious," Elliott said, looking at the female Riaki. "Sheymi Dymas healed me."

"My thanks to you," Tana told Sheymi. "And my apologies if he caused you too much trouble."

"Oh, he certainly did that," Seth said, then pointed to the tower stairs. "We will join you shortly. As you can see, we need to freshen up a bit."

"I'll say," Decker said, moving up next to Tana. "You smell like the dead."

"Don't let it ruin your appetite," Elliott told him. "And save something for me. I haven't eaten anything all day." He hurried up the stairs into the tower with Seth right behind him.

Decker motioned Railen and Sheymi to the table. "Please join us for dinner," he said. "And thank you for keeping my son alive."

"It went both ways," Railen said. Rising to his feet, he took each little girl by the hand and led them back to their chairs, then moved back around the table to sit next to Sheymi. Tana and Decker returned to their seats as well, and there was a moment of silence as everyone waited for instructions.

"Please," Decker said. "Eat. There will be plenty of food left for Elliott and Seth when they return."

Everyone did as they were told, but neither Tana nor Rhea ate much in the following minutes. Both watched the stairwell intently, eager for Elliott's return. Decker chewed slowly as he studied Railen and Sheymi, and it was clear he had many questions for the two. Out of respect for the children's sensitivities, however, he refrained from asking anything and simply ate in silence.

As always, Tey and Aimi ate quickly, then hopped down from their chairs and moved across the room to play with Tey's cat. The rest of the Eries children finished soon after and were excused to go play. Soon after that, Elliott and Seth returned.

Hair still damp, they sported clean clothes, and their sword hilts and sheaths had been wiped clean of blood. Seth's twin blades crossed the small of his back. Elliott wore his sword over his shoulder. Cleaning up had done nothing to remove the weariness from their faces, and that fact alone let Elam know just how fierce their fight had been.

Before they were even fully down the stairs, Tana was on her feet and hurrying across the room. She took Elliott in a tight hug, then kissed him before stepping back to look him over. "You will tell me everything that happened," she said, then stepped into Seth's path and hugged him as well.

The captain stiffened in surprise at the show of affection, then brought his arms up and hugged her back. *Decker was right,* Elam thought. *These people are family.*

"And you," Tana said when she stepped back, "will tell me if he leaves anything out."

Elliott pretended to be offended. "Would I do that?"

"Yes," Tana said, then took him by the hand and led him back to the table.

While Elliott and Seth helped themselves to the food, everyone else resumed eating as well. In truth, most everyone had finished and Elam knew they were just buying time for Elliott and Seth.

Elam took advantage of the moment to study Railen and Sheymi. The two were clearly in love with one another—the look in their eyes as they chatted was unmistakable. That look, he realized, hadn't been lost on Raimen or Tohquin, or even on Tohquin's wife. The three Riaki wore smiles of amusement as they watched their younger countrymen.

"Are you going to eat everything on the table?" Aimi asked, and Elam turned to find her standing at Elliott's elbow.

Elliott grinned at her. "You move as quietly as a Shizu," he told her, then scooted his chair sideways and hoisted her up onto his lap. "Did you learn that from your daddy?"

"Maybe," Aimi said. "But Mommy is pretty sneaky too."

Elliott looked down the length of the table at Kailei who was blushing at her daughter's comment. "Well, she is an honorary member of Deathsquad Alpha," Elliott said. "You would do well to listen to her and always do what she says."

"I will," Aimi said, then hopped off Elliott's lap and moved back to Tey and her cat as if nothing had happened.

"You're very good with children, Elliott," Jonnil Dymas complimented. "You'll make a good father."

Elliott seemed surprised by the comment, but Tana laughed. "There are a few things that need to happen first," she said. "Not the least of which is a wedding."

"Do you have a date in mind?" Seth asked.

Elliott and Tana locked gazes for a moment, then Elliott shrugged. "Just as soon as we end the war with Shadan," he said. "The people we would like to have in attendance are, as Seth would say, scattered from hell to breakfast."

"Assuming, of course," Tana began, a hint of warning in her voice, "that a certain someone doesn't get himself killed in the meantime."

Elliott grinned at her. "I'll be fine," he said. "I couldn't possibly face anything worse than I already have."

Decker leaned forward and looked his son in the eyes. "And just what, exactly, have you faced lately?"

Elliott didn't answer right away but looked down the length of the table instead. "I probably shouldn't say anything as long as there are children within earshot."

Alesha Eries pushed her chair back and rose. "I will take the children out to the dome," she said. "Come along, Garrick."

"I think I will join you," Jaina said, and Elam helped her up from her chair. She smiled at him as she squeezed his hand in parting. "Hearing about Death's Third March isn't good for me or the twins."

Elam kissed her on the cheek. "I'll be along when I can."

Both women looked at Kailei, but the Riaki woman shook her head. "Can Aimi tag along with you?" she asked. "I think I'd like to hear this."

Alesha smiled. "Of course she can," she said, then she and Jaina and the children made their way across the room and out into the dome.

When they were gone, Jonnil Dymas raised his hand to catch Decker's eye. "I've warded the immediate area against eavesdropping," he said. "Lord Elliott can begin anytime."

"Why me?" Elliott asked, shooting Jonnil an irritated glare. "Seth and the others were just as involved in this as I was."

"None of us rode a Dragon into battle," Seth said simply. "I think your dealings take precedence over ours."

Elam realized his jaw had dropped open in shock and hurriedly closed it.

Hoping no one had noticed, he glanced around at the others to measure their reactions.

Kailei Nagaro's reaction was similar to his own, but she recovered quickly. Tohquin and Raimen had kept their surprise in check, but both were staring at Elliott as if they'd never seen him before. So was Captain Ebirin.

Jonnil and the two younger Dymas seemed more curious than surprised, but Decker and Rhea and Tana were staring at Elliott with what could only be described as a sort of horrified astonishment.

"You... did... *what?*" Tana asked. Her eyes narrowed as her astonishment began to transition over to anger.

Seth leaned forward so he could look at her. "The battle was with an army of demons," he added. "Several thousand of them."

The scowl Elliott directed at Seth could have stripped the hide off a Shadowhound. "I've got this, Captain," he said through clenched teeth. "Thank you."

Seth grunted in amusement. "Just making sure you don't leave anything out," he said, then winked at Tana.

"And we appreciate that," Decker said. Like Tana, he suddenly seemed less amazed and more irritated that Elliott had been behaving like... like Elliott. "Why don't you start at the beginning, Son."

Aware of the stares of those around him, Elliott shifted uncomfortably in his chair as he searched for the words to begin. His hesitancy was a far cry from the spirited and boastful young man Elam remembered from a few months earlier. It seemed the days of animated and adventuresome storytelling had been replaced by the solemnities of reality. A reality that was dangerous and deadly.

"I was in the Kelsan camp with Seth and Gideon and Jase," Elliott began, "when word arrived from Aridan that a large area of the Veil had collapsed and a demon army was marching on the Great Wall." He shrugged. "When Jase said he was going to help, I knew I had to be there too. I didn't know why—I certainly didn't want to go fight demons—but I felt... compelled."

He shook his head. "I'm not a Dymas, so I don't know what the whisperings of the Earthsoul sounds or feels like. I only know that I needed to be at the Great Wall." He looked pointedly at Railen and Sheymi and Seth. "Just as you three needed to be there."

He spoke at length about all that had happened to him, and Seth and the two Riaki filled in the parts when Elliott had been separated from them. It seemed a miracle any of them had survived.

When at last Elliott fell silent, everyone at the table sat in overwhelmed silence, each contemplating what they had heard. Demons. Dragons. Elliott *riding* a Dragon. It was almost too much for Elam to take in.

It was Seth who finally broke the silence. "Now that we know the enemy has no intention of using Talin Pass," he said to Decker, "I've been asked by the *Mith'elre Chon* to move the Chellum army to Trian Plateau. I just need your approval."

Decker nodded. "You have it," he said. "I trust Jase's judgment." He looked at Elam briefly before turning back to Seth. "And the Home Guard?"

"They are to remain in Chellum," Seth said, and Elam breathed a silent sigh of relief. Not simply because he wanted to be with Jaina during the final weeks of her pregnancy, but because the threat of an attack by Elliott's enemies in Riak was still a very real possibility.

"Elam will remain in command," Seth continued. "Like Elliott, I am needed elsewhere."

"Elsewhere?" Decker asked.

Seth grunted. "Wherever the *Mith'elre Chon* is."

"Which is everywhere," Elliott muttered. "Today alone he hopped back and forth between four different nations."

"He assisted Endil in recovering the stolen Blood Orb from the Sons of Uri," Seth clarified. "And then went to investigate the defiling of an Orb in Melek. Turns out that Orb was taken by Lord Nid to keep it from our enemies. It's in Trian now, in Gideon's possession."

Decker shook his head. "The world has truly changed, hasn't it?" he said. "Veilgates have made it possible to do in a single day what would have taken weeks or months."

"Yes," Seth said. "And praised be the Creator that it has. Because we don't have weeks or months. We have days. And they aren't many."

"Which is why we will be leaving in the morning," Elliott said.

The announcement brought a frown to Tana's face, but Elliott ignored it. Standing, he offered her his hand and helped her from her chair. "Now, if you will excuse us, my fiancee and I need a moment to ourselves. We'll be out in the gardens if you need us for anything." He bowed to his father and mother. "Thank you for dinner. It was a much needed respite from the chaos of late."

With that, he led Tana to the small glass doors exiting into the gardens, and they disappeared out into the dusky light of evening.

"He's going to get an earful from her," Sheymi said, sounding oddly satisfied.

Seth chuckled. "Good. Maybe some of it will sink in this time." Still staring in the direction of the gardens, he rose from his chair and adjusted his swords. "I think I will make my rounds," he said. "For old times' sake. Care to join me, Elam?"

He smiled. "It would be a pleasure."

Seth nodded, then turned his attention to Railen and Sheymi. "There are extra rooms in the north tower," he told them. "Have the servants draw baths for you. You've earned a respite yourselves." He offered a Riaki style bow of respect. "Thank you for all you did today," he said. "If I don't see you before you leave, give my regards to Shavis Dakshar and Emperor Dromensai."

"We will," Railen told him.

Seth nodded one more time, then he and Elam started for the exit. As they went, Elam cast a quick look over his shoulder at the two Riaki Dymas. "Remarkable young friends you have there," he whispered.

"Remarkable is an understatement," Seth said with a smile. "Elliott and a great many others are alive because of their actions."

Elam studied his friend's chiseled profile for a moment as they walked. Finally he asked, "Why do I get the feeling that things were much worse than you or Elliott or the others were letting on?"

Seth grunted. "Because words are inadequate in describing such horrors. We can tell you *what* happened, sure. But the depth and breadth of those horrors can only be understood fully when experienced firsthand."

"I'm more than willing to take your word for it."

"Good," Seth said. "Because I need you here. There might not be a threat of demons upon the city, but the Chellum family is still in danger. I need you to keep them safe."

Elam nodded. *And so I shall*, he thought, doing his best to ignore the knot of foreboding tightening in his stomach.

# CHAPTER 40

## Elvan Archives

THE STUDY AREA IN THE CENTER of Elldrenei College's vast library was quiet save for the soft whisper of pages being turned. Brysia and those who'd come with her were silent and focused as they searched for information which might lead to the discovery of a Temple of Elderon. Beyond the study area itself, however, the aisles were alive with the sounds of books being opened and closed then stacked into piles or reshelved as scholars and professors of all ages assisted with the search. At the library's entrance an occasional murmur of disgruntled voices was heard as one dedicated student or another sought access to the library and was politely, yet firmly, turned away by the *Bero'thai* keeping watch.

Brysia felt bad about keeping the students from their studies, but finals weren't for another three weeks, and a day off wouldn't kill them. But the collapse of the Veil would if she and the others didn't find what they were looking for. Unfortunately, even with help from those who knew this library best, they hadn't discovered much.

With a sigh of frustration, she marked her place in the untitled manuscript she was reading, then looked up to see how the others were doing.

Talia and Xia had moved from the tables to cushioned chairs, and each held a large leather-bound book with gold lettering on the spine. They seemed oblivious to everything but the books in their laps, and their faces were concentrated as they read. Xia's lips moved slightly as she read, and Brysia smiled in amusement at her mother's unconscious habit. She knew this library as well as any of the professors and had been most eager to help in the search.

Brysia watched her mother for a moment longer, then turned her attention to the others. Beraline and Marithen sat at one of the long tables and were systematically moving through a stack of Old World anthologies of supposed scripture. That Marithen hadn't broken into one of her strange singsongs for some time meant she was reading something new. Only when a passage triggered some obscure memory was she prone to breaking her silence.

At an adjacent table, Andil and Cassia were looking over a collection of maps, but it was clear from the Sister Queen's expression that her mind was currently on something other than the maps. Endil, most likely. But Brysia suspected she was also concerned about the situation in Trian.

Sighing tiredly, she reached up to rub her eyes. They'd been at this all day, and they were no closer to solving the mystery of the lost temples than when they'd started. Elldrenei might have the most complete collection of Old and New World artifacts of any college in the Nine Lands, but she was starting to think there might be such a thing as *too* much knowledge.

That was proving true for the Old World maps as well. Elldrenei had hundreds of them, all so intricately detailed that looking them over was not only tiresome, it was frustrating. With so much detail available, they should have been able to make some kind of connection between Old World geography and the present locations of known T'rii Gates, but it simply hadn't been the case.

The Great Destruction had altered the world so completely that nothing recognizable remained. Cities and mountain ranges. Forests and roads and lakes. Oceans and continents. Nothing was as it had been. She may as well have been looking at maps of the Rhiven home world for all the good it had done.

Even Andil, who had a knack for cartography, was having trouble making sense of them. He'd moved to another large table at the far end of the study area but wore a frown as he studied a different set of maps unearthed from the archives. On a smaller table behind him lay a map of the Nine Lands. Newly sketched with only the most noticeable of landmarks, it had a handful of small red Xs to indicate the Veilgates they knew about. But that was it. Nothing new.

They were having the same kind of luck with the archive's collection of books.

Sure, they'd found dozens of tidbits regarding the arrival of the *Mith'elre Chon* and his role in the battles against Shadan's armies, but aside from one passage in an unabridged copy of the *Eved'terium*, they were things they already knew.

The one new bit of information spoke of an earth-shattering battle which would take place inside 'The Holy Mountain of The Second Creation.' Which mountain the prophecy referred to was unclear, but Brysia suspected Mount Tabor. Not only did it contain the Soul Chamber—the very place where Elsa's blood had sprung forth as talismans of rejuvenating power—but Jase was destined to return there one last time to invoke the Rejuvenation. Undoubtedly, the servants of Maeon would journey there to try to stop him—if they weren't there already—and the resulting battle would be... well, earth-shattering.

Thoughts of Tabor turned her attention to the stack of books she and the others had already gone through. Most were histories written during the first one hundred years after the Elvan people's arrival from the Elvan home world, and every single author had identified the slopes of Mount Tabor as the point of that arrival.

The claim was corroborated by the short, handwritten diary of a young Elvan girl who may have been a member of the first ruling family. Penned during the early days of the New World, sometime around A.S. 125, it was in the simplistic language of a child and described how Mount Tabor had been a much frequented place by Elderon in the days after he brought the Elvan race from their world to this one.

Clearly, in the young girl's eyes, as well as in the eyes of the Creator, Mount Tabor was hallowed ground. So much so that Throy Shadan had attempted to destroy it during Death's First March.

"Still thinking about the battle inside 'The Holy Mountain of the Second Creation?'" Talia asked, and Brysia looked over to find the young woman watching her. Talia's eyes were red, and she looked as tired as Brysia felt.

It was no wonder, considering that this section of the library alone contained dozens of shelves with thousands upon thousands of antiquated books—books which may as well have stretched a thousand miles for all the progress they had made today.

Brysia pushed the frustrating thought away and nodded in response to Talia's question. "Yes. And the words 'earth-shattering conflict' don't exactly fill me with confidence."

"The fact that we know there will be a conflict means Jase can prepare himself for it," Beraline said. "He won't enter blindly."

"But we don't even know what mountain the prophecy is referring to," Talia said. "It might not even be a mountain at all, but a metaphor for something else. Like a Temple of Elderon. It could even be Fairimor Palace and the Dome for all we know. Elderon did create them as an ensign to the nations. It is a literal mountain of *chorazin* wrought by Him as part of the Second Creation."

Brysia shook her head. "All possibilities, certainly. It's just that the bulk of the evidence points to Mount Tabor."

"Everything points to Tabor," Gideon said, and Brysia turned to find him striding down one of the aisles of books. He wore a smile and a freshly pressed dark blue uniform, but neither the smile nor the uniform could hide the fact that he was exhausted. Whatever battles he'd seen today had left him drained.

Brysia set the book aside and rose to meet him. After everything she'd heard about the day's events, it was difficult for her to hold back the tears, such was her relief to see him alive and unharmed.

Smiling as if he'd read her thoughts, he took her hand and kissed it. Tired he may be, but his grip was still as strong as a Dainin and as hard as steel. She winced beneath the strength of it.

"I missed you," he whispered before releasing her hand and stepping back to look her over. "You look tired."

"As do you," she said. "And the look in your eyes is one I've seen before. It speaks loudly of bloodshed."

Gideon nodded. "Today was certainly a day for the history books," he told her. "But we came out on top for a change. Galiena and her people were successful in eliminating their traitorous brethren, and Shadan's second attempt to use Dragon Gates failed. Thousands of his troops were destroyed."

"And the Great Wall?" Talia asked, moving forward. "We learned from Lord Reiekel that it came under attack by a demon army."

"I heard the same," Gideon told her, "but I wasn't there, so I do not know the outcome."

"We won," Jase said, and everyone turned as he appeared around the end of one of the bookshelves. The soft glow of bluish light in the area beyond the bookshelf vanished as the Veilgate Jase had wrought to come here closed.

"By the way," he said as he neared. "This is a library. Don't you know you are supposed to keep your voices down?" He shook his head in mock disappointment, then smiled at Xia. "Hello, Grandmother," he said. "I am pleased to find you here."

"Just helping out where I can," she said, setting her book aside. Talia did likewise and the two rose to hug Jase.

"I could feel that you were here before you spoke," Talia told him. "Just as I could feel you traveling the length and width of the Nine Lands. You went to Kunin and Melek today, didn't you?"

Jase shrugged as if it was of no concern. "I go where I'm needed," he said, then wrinkled his forehead in question. "Did you actually feel that through the *sei'vaiya*, or did you learn it when Elison sent word that Endil and I had returned?"

"Both," Talia told him. "And I could feel that you were using much more of *Ta'shaen* than is good for you."

"I do what is needed also," he told her. "As I said, we won. Right now, that's all that matters."

"Was it you who used the Blood Orb in Kunin?" Xia asked.

"No," Jase answered, turning his attention to Cassia and Andil. They'd remained at the maps but had stopped studying them to listen to Jase. "It was Endil. He destroyed the Sons of Uri, their bloody shrine, and the valley which held it. Kunin will no longer be a threat to us. In this war at least."

"Is Endil going to be all right?" Cassia asked. "Elison said he was devastated by the loss of Emmarenziana Antilla. I'm worried about him."

Jase smiled reassuringly. "He'll be fine. He just needs a moment to grieve. Which is why I sent him and Thorac to Chunin to lay Emma to rest."

"And then what?" Cassia asked. "Will he be joining you and the others on the front lines? Is he to become *El'Kali* like the rest of you?" Her worry was obvious, and there was a hint of accusation in the question. Almost as if she blamed Jase for Endil's involvement.

Brysia bristled at the comment and saw Xia do the same, but Jase's smile never faded as he answered.

"He earned that title the moment he went in search of the Blood Orb," Jase told her. What he said next showed he'd picked up on the implied accusation. "And as a Soldier of God, he answers directly to the Earthsoul. Even so, the path he takes in the days to come will be of his own choosing. Just as it was his choice to pursue the Blood Orb into Kunin."

"The details of which," Brysia said, looking at her son, "we are most eager to hear. Along with what transpired at the Great Wall and with the Rhiven."

"Then you will all need to take a break from searching the archives," Jase told her. "These are tales best told over a nice meal. Gideon and I haven't eaten much today, and I am starving."

Brysia smiled affectionately. "Aren't you always?"

Jase gave a noncommittal grunt, then turned his attention to the others. "You've all done enough for one day," he told them. "We can resume the search in the morning."

"We?" Talia asked. "Does that mean you will be sticking around for a while this time?"

Jase nodded. "For as long as the Earthsoul will allow," he said. "I haven't been in this library since I was a kid. I'm excited to see what we can find."

"Well, so far it hasn't been much," Cassia said, making an irritated gesture at the maps.

"Tomorrow's a new day," Jase replied. "I'm sure something will emerge. Come. Let's eat."

As Gideon and Brysia led the way toward one of the exits, Talia took Jase's hand in hers, so pleased to have him back she could barely breathe. He may have been half a continent away at times today, but the *sei'vaiya* had made her privy to much of what he'd been through. Fear and worry, anger and frustration, grief and remorse—a steady stream of impressions that let her know just how much danger he and the others had been in. It had her thinking she might never let go of his hand again.

"That will make eating difficult, don't you think?" he asked, and she turned to look him in the eyes. In the light of the glowstone chandeliers overhead, they were a piercing shade of grey and so filled with adoration for her that a rush of heat swept through her chest. Had they not been in the company of others, she would have taken his head in her hands and kissed him repeatedly. When he smiled, she knew he had sensed that thought as well.

"And that," he whispered, "would make it difficult to do anything."

She felt her cheeks turning red and pursed her lips to keep from smiling. "That is *not* what I was thinking," she lied.

"That's too bad," he told her. "Because I likely wouldn't resist."

"After dinner, then," she said, and was pleased when Jase's face turned as red as hers.

They stopped momentarily at the exit so Xia could speak with the two *Bero'thai* standing watch there.

"Let our scholars stay as long as they wish," she told them. "But continue to keep this area free of students. I don't want them interfering with our research. If anything significant is discovered in our absence, please send word to me immediately."

"Yes, my lady," came the reply, and Xia motioned for Gideon and Brysia to continue.

The hallway beyond the arched doorway was lined with a number of classrooms as well as the offices of some of the university's professors. Talia read the names on the plaques above some of the office doors as they passed and realized that many of them belonged to those Xia had summoned to help search the archives. After all the years of individual research and study and teaching it was appropriate that they were now working together on the most important academic project of their careers.

"I attended some classes in that room there," Jase said. "I was seven or eight at the time."

"What did you learn about?"

Jase shrugged. "I have no idea. It was during the summer, and I was really irritated that I wasn't fishing the Midion River with Daris instead of sitting at a bloody desk being lectured to by someone who looked old enough to have been born before the Great Destruction."

"Careful," Xia said from behind them. "Professor Ubadon still teaches here. He is, in fact, helping out in the archives right now."

"Great," Jase said. "Perhaps he will recognize some of what was written when he was a child..." he paused for emphasis and added, "two thousand years ago."

Another arched doorway waited at the end of the corridor and opened into a domed rotunda. A bronze statue of Galavan Elldrenei, the college's founder, stood in the middle of the room, and a number of benches lined the walls beneath dozens of paintings depicting the early days of the college. Doors to the right and left led to more classrooms as well as to student dormitories, but Brysia moved around the statue to the massive set of doors that was the college's entrance.

Gideon made a gesture with his hand as they approached, and the doors were opened by an invisible grip of *Ta'shaen*. Only then did Talia realize it was much later than she'd thought. The tops of the trees were painted in hues of reddish-gold, but beneath them everything had fallen into shadow.

Brysia took Gideon's arm as they descended the well-worn granite stairs fronting the building, and Jase turned to offer his other arm to his grandmother. She accepted it with a smile and they moved down the stairs and started along the wide stone path leading through the center of the college's main lawn.

A number of groundskeepers were moving from lamp post to lamp post to light the oil wicks, but they had started at the steps and hadn't gotten very far. The pathway ahead was darker than Talia would have liked, heart of the Elvan capital or not. If the last few weeks had proven anything, it was that no place was safe anymore, particularly a shadowed expanse of trees and shrubbery.

Gideon must have been thinking the same thing because he made another motion with his hand, and all the lamps ignited as one, brightly illuminating the way ahead.

The groundskeepers stopped and cast about in surprise, and it wasn't until they spotted Gideon that they relaxed and extinguished the wicks on their lighting poles. One even gave a wave of thanks, and shook his head in amusement.

"Gideon is a show-off sometimes, isn't he?" Jase said, and Xia laughed.

"You haven't seen the half of it," she replied, keeping her voice to a whisper. "You should have seen him when he was courting your mother."

They exited the college grounds through the main gate and found two armored coaches waiting for them in the street leading to Temifair Palace. Two squads of mounted *Bero'thai* accompanied each coach, and every last one of the men was armed with bow and sword.

Jase wrinkled his brow quizzically at his grandmother. "Are you expecting trouble?" he asked. "I would expect to see such an escort in Trian, but Andlexces?"

"Darklings escaping Amnidia coupled with the recent holes in the Veil have caused Lord Reiekel to rethink security measures within the city. Especially when it comes to the *Mith'elre Chon* and members of the royal family."

"Fair enough," Jase said as he opened the door for his grandmother and assisted her inside. "But if it's all the same to you, I'd like to ride on top. I can't stand being inside these blasted things."

"Doesn't that defeat the purpose of having an armored coach?" Xia asked.

"Not being able to see where I'm going is worse," Jase told her. "Besides, tired or not, *I* am the most dangerous thing in this city. Our enemies, if there are any loose in Andlexces—and I don't think there are—would do well to remember that."

Talia expected Xia to argue, but the Queen Mother simply smiled. "You really are like your father, aren't you?"

Jase grinned at her, then assisted Beraline and Marithen into the coach before closing the door. Talia stared at him in surprise.

"You aren't going to insist I ride inside where it is safe?"

"Do you want to ride inside?" he asked, reaching for the door handle.

She put a hand up to stop him. "Of course not. I'm just so used to Seth ordering me around that it caught me off guard."

Chuckling softly, Jase led her around to the front of the coach, and they climbed up to sit next to the coachman. The hatchet-faced man greeted them with a nod, then waited until they were settled in before snapping the reins and setting the coach into motion.

The escorting *Bero'thai* took up positions around them, and the *clop clop* of their horses' hooves on the paving stones echoed loudly in the streets. Most of Andlexces' residents had retired to their homes for the evening, so the usual din of voices was noticeably subdued. Of those who were still out and about, all but a few fell silent as the coaches moved past, and it was clear from their expressions as they spotted Jase that they knew who he was. Many of them had likely been present to greet him when he'd arrived from Aridan some weeks earlier.

Talia smiled at the wonder in their eyes, then locked her arm around Jase's and leaned her head on his shoulder, sighing deeply.

Just having him near was refreshing. Like a Power-wrought healing, it had strengthened her physically and emotionally and had erased all the dread and fear and anxiety she'd experienced in his absence.

And what was more, she could feel through the *sei'vaiya* that it had done the same for him. She took his hand in hers, interlocking their fingers. She wasn't joking when she'd said she might not let go of him ever again.

Jase turned and pressed his lips to the top of her head, and she felt a sudden rush of affection through the love-bond. She knew, too, that he'd sensed what she was thinking. "Seth will have something to say about it," he told her, "but it's an argument I'm willing to have."

She tilted her head so she could look him in the eyes. "What are you saying?"

"Your vision," he said. "Gideon's prophecy in Yucanter Forest. The time for its fulfillment is drawing near."

"*Without her we will fail,*" Talia whispered, then shivered as images of the horrific vision flickered through her memory, raw and vivid and very real. Jase approaching a pillar of light; eruptions of Fire and sizzling stabs of light and dark; cloaked, fiery-eyed figures swarming in from every side; blood and chaos and death—the end of the war, one way or the other.

"It certainly will be that," Jase said, and she realized too late that all of what she'd seen and felt had made it across the *sei'vaiya.*

"But," he continued, smiling reassuringly, "we will see that it ends in our favor. And we will do it together."

She arched an eyebrow at him. "Even if that means going into battle?"

"Especially then," he told her. "You're destined to keep me alive, remember?"

She laughed. "Something I've done multiple times already."

"True," he said, kissing her on the forehead. "But those were a bonus. The actual moment of Gideon's prophecy—of your vision—is yet to arrive."

A sudden thought struck her, and she knew through the *sei'vaiya* that Jase was thinking it as well. He had, in fact, been thinking it for some time.

He smiled at her. "It's interesting, isn't it?" he said. "We know from your vision that we will enter the Soul Chamber to attempt the Rejuvenation. And the only reason for being there—"

"Is if we have a viable Blood Orb," she finished, a wave of excitement rushing through her. "We're going to find one."

Jase nodded. "I've never doubted it," he said. A moment later, the feeling of confidence flowing through the *sei'vaiya* gave way to uncertainty, and he added, "It's what I'm supposed to do with it that scares me."

"You'll do fine," she said, but his doubt had become her own. Troubled, they rode on toward the palace in silence.

# CHAPTER 41

## Taking Leave

THE SUN HAD YET TO RISE when Elliott left his bedroom and started the long trek down the tower stairs to the Chellum dining room. The soft, grey light of early morning pressed against the windows but did little to illuminate the interior of the stairwell. He didn't mind. The soft light, the peace and stillness as the world gradually wakened around him, the promise of another day—he'd always found early morning to be the most soothing part of the day.

When he reached the next level, he paused at the door to Tana's room but didn't knock. As tempted as he was to wake her for one last kiss, they'd said their goodbyes last night. It had taken several hours.

He smiled at the memory, then started walking again. Tana understood he was needed elsewhere, and she accepted the fact that they couldn't really be together until the war was over. Besides, stopping to see her now would only make it that much more difficult to leave.

When he reached the Chellum dining room, he found Railen and Sheymi already there with Seth. He was moving to join them when the doors leading in from the dome opened and Raimen and Tohquin entered with two of *Ao tres'domei's* Dymas. Elliott didn't know the men's names, but he'd seen them on the battlefield in the moments shortly after the Tamban army had stormed through the Dragon Gates.

"I was hoping to see you before we left," Railen said when Elliott reached him. "And you two as well," he said to Raimen and Tohquin.

"Kailei and Aimi send their love," Tohquin told him. "But Aimi was still asleep and I didn't want to wake her."

"Kiss that little rascal for me," Railen said. "I'm glad she and her mother are here with you. Things in Riak are... complicated."

"And likely to become even more so," Sheymi added, "if Emperor Dromensai grants our request."

"Do you think he will?" Elliott asked.

Railen nodded. "I do. After all, what good will it do to spare Riak more grief if we lose the war with Shadan?"

"A good argument," Seth said. "Make sure Dai'shozen Dakshar is present when you make it. He will help the members of the Imperial Clave see the wisdom in it."

*Yeah*, Elliott thought. *With the sharp edge of his sword.*

Instead he said, "Thank you for your help the past few days. A lot of people might not be alive if it weren't for you. Myself included."

"You would have made it out of Amnidia without us," Railen said, shooting a quick look at Sheymi. She frowned a warning at him, but he ignored it and grinned at Elliott. "Your rear end may not have been intact, but you would have survived."

"And for that particular healing," Elliott said, meeting Sheymi's gaze, "you have my eternal gratitude. Even if you did deliberately leave a scar."

Sheymi stiffened with indignation. "I did not leave a scar. I—" She cut off when she realized he was grinning at her. Her lips pressed into a tight line and her eyes narrowed. "That was low, Elliott. Even for you."

"It was," he agreed, still smiling. "But now I won't need to use a mirror to find out."

Sheymi looked from face to face and found everyone trying not to smile. Her eyes narrowed further as they settled on Railen. "We should probably be on our way," she told him, and it was clear from her tone that she meant immediately.

Railen bowed respectfully to Seth. "It has been a pleasure fighting alongside you, *shent ze'deyar*," he said. "Until next time."

Seth returned the bow, then Railen turned to shake hands with Raimen and Tohquin. "Farewell, my friends. Don't forget to kiss Aimi for me." Stepping back, he turned to face Elliott. "You," he said, a smile moving over his face once more, "you be careful."

"I'm always careful," Elliott told him, offering his hand in farewell. Railen's grip was strong as he took it in his own, and they bowed formally to one another before releasing.

Elliott turned a smile on Sheymi, bowed deeply, then extended his hand. She hesitated, obviously surprised by the gesture. In Riak, shaking hands wasn't a widely accepted social convention to begin with—a man offering his hand to a woman was even more out of the norm. For a moment, he thought she might refuse, but then her expression softened, and she took his hand in hers.

Smiling, he pulled her forward and hugged her tightly. She stood stiffly for a moment, horrified that he'd just trampled another social norm, then slowly relaxed and hugged him back.

"I truly appreciate all you have done these past days and weeks," he whispered. "Thank you for being my friend."

She tightened her arms around him. "Thank you for being a friend to Riak." She leaned back and looked him in the eyes. "Now. Take good care of Tana, or I will come back and give you a scar that no Dymas on earth can heal."

Elliott chuckled as he released her. "Of that, I have no doubt." He looked from her to Railen. "You two be careful. The enemies I made in Riak know of our friendship. They may seek to target you as well."

"One might almost wish they would," Railen said. "For then I would have reason to destroy them."

"That sounded an awful lot like something Shavis would say," Elliott told him. "Are you sure he isn't a worse influence on you than I am?"

"It's a toss up," Sheymi said.

"Goodbye, Elliott," Railen said, then nodded at the others and offered his arm to Sheymi. Together they made their way to the glass doors fronting the Chellum Gardens and a Veilgate opened in front of them. They passed through without looking back.

Elliott tucked his thumbs in his belt and looked at Seth. "So, what's the plan for today?"

Seth grunted. "Same as yesterday. Survive."

Standing in the shadowed depths beneath the Dragon's Fangs, Taggert Enue took a slow, deep breath of the cold morning air, then let his eyes move down the steep, narrow slit of Talin Pass. With sunrise still more than an hour away, the canyon walls loomed tall and dark against the pale, greyish-blue of the brightening sky. Far below, shadowed grey lay like a blanket over the yellows and greens of the plateau's grasslands.

He blew out his cheeks in frustration and was rewarded with a cloud of frosted breath. It might be the middle of summer in the valleys below, but winter returned nearly every night at this altitude. It was surprisingly refreshing—to him at least. A good number of his men would say differently.

And they were starting to complain about being assigned to Talin Pass, believing that it was a waste of time. None had said it directly to his face, but he'd heard the rumblings. He agreed with them to some extent but would never say so publicly. This assignment had come from the *Mith'elre Chon*, and he would do his best to fulfill it.

*Even if it is nothing more than a farce to keep the men of Chellum safe.*

He knew Jase meant well by assigning him here, but it was frustrating to know the Chellum army could be of help elsewhere and was being kept from the fight.

He continued to watch as the sky lightened and the blanket of morning shadows gave way to the plateau's grasslands, content, for the moment, to breathe the cold air and listen to the sounds of the Chellum camp coming awake. Another hour and it would be business as usual as he looked for things for his men to do to keep them sharp.

A flash of blue light momentarily lit the canyon wall to his left, but it faded before he could get a look at who had arrived. He wasn't concerned—a corrupted Veilgate would have lit the area in red and sent a loud hiss echoing down the pass. But he was curious, and so he started toward the new arrivals.

Some twenty paces up the slope, Seth Lydon materialized out of the darkness with Elliott Chellum. Two male Dymas followed behind.

"Hello, Taggert," Seth said. He gave the Chellum camp a cursory glance and added, "I bring word from the *Mith'elre Chon*. He wants you and your men to join the rest of our forces in Trian."

Taggert felt a touch of panic. "So, it's come to that already, has it?"

"Not in the way you might be thinking," Elliott answered. "Death's Third March is still days away from Trian. But they have reached the western rim, and it won't be long before they flood the Bottomlands. Joneam and Idoman have decided to pull back to Mendel Pass where we can fight on a more equal footing."

"A wise move," he began, "considering how we fared last time we faced them in the open. What of the Dragon Gates?"

"No longer a threat," Seth answered. "Shadan's Rhiven have been removed from the equation."

"That's bloody good news," he said. "Bloody good news, indeed." He looked in the direction of the camp. More men were out of the tents and moving about, but a handful had stopped along the perimeter and were staring in his direction. Likely they had seen the flash of light from the Veilgate. "So, what does the *Mith'elre Chon* have in mind for us?"

Seth gestured to the two Dymas. "Kalin and Geb will assist your Dymas in moving the Chellum army to Trian. Elison Brey will decide how best to utilize you."

Taggert raised his fist to his chest. "I'm sure my men will appreciate the opportunity to do more than stare down the slopes of the pass."

The hint of a smile touched Seth's face. "As soon as you're ready then."

"We've been ready for days," he grunted.

He started up the slope toward camp but stopped when Seth and Elliott didn't follow. "You aren't coming?"

"Elliott and I are needed elsewhere," Seth said. "And our first stop is Trian. It's the last place Gideon was rumored to be, and I need to let Elison Brey know that you are coming." He turned his attention to Kalin Dymas. "Kalin, if you would please."

The darkness shrouding the pass was thrown back by a brilliant flash of blue, and the interior of Fairimor Palace was suddenly framed by the shimmering edges of a Veilgate.

"So long, General," Seth said, and he and Elliott strode through to the greenish-grey *chorazin* beyond. The Veilgate closed, and the area was thrown into darkness once more.

"Well," Taggert said, looking at the two Dymas, "there is work to be done. Let's get to it."

Jase finished buttoning up the shirt he'd found in his wardrobe, then pulled out a dark blue jacket and pulled it on as well. Like the shirt, it was a touch too big, but he didn't mind, preferring a looser fit over something snug. If he were forced to fight again today, he didn't want to have his movement restricted by clothes that were too tight.

He fingered the Elvan emblem for the Tree of Life embroidered above his heart, then turned and moved to the balcony doors. After pulling back the curtains, he pushed open the doors and stepped outside.

A cool breeze moving from the east greeted him and carried with it the smells of Geissler Woods and the Midion River. The sun had yet to crest the eastern horizon, but the sky was a bright, bluish white. It was so peaceful, so refreshing, that for a moment he could almost forget the world was dying. He closed his eyes and let the breeze wash over him, then opened them again and looked down at the city.

His room here in the eastern tower of Temifair Palace wasn't as lofty as his room in Trian, but it was still high, and the view of Andlexces was spectacular. The sprawling patchwork of blue- and green-tiled rooftops looked like ocean waves, rising and falling in outward succession from the palace walls. In the distance, the city wall loomed like a rocky shoreline beyond the swells of color.

To the south and east of the palace, the group of red-stone buildings comprising Elldrenei College rose from their forested grounds like an island amid the green. The bell tower was the most visible of the college's structures, and Jase knew it wouldn't be long before its magnificent bell sounded over the city, signaling the start of the day.

He sighed. Another day of what? Blood and death and chaos? Or a day of hope and salvation? Only time would tell. *And we don't have much left.*

He pushed that last thought away and gazed eastward once more. Beyond the edge of the city, Geissler Woods lay like a dark carpet, stretching away to the line of amber-colored light that was the horizon. And there, rising above the horizon like a sharp, stone dagger was Mount Augg. Its snow-capped peak blazed brightly in the morning sun and threw a wedge-shaped shadow across Geissler's canopy.

The sight conjured up thoughts of last night's conversations, and he shook his head in frustration at how little his mother and Talia and the others had found. There had to be *something* in Elldrenei's archives that would lead him to a Temple of Elderon. The scholars and prophets of the Old and New Worlds wouldn't have stayed silent on the matter. They would have written something down.

Another thought struck him, and he went cold inside. Or maybe they had compiled records and the servants of Maeon had found them and destroyed them to thwart the prophesied Rejuvenation.

No, he decided. If the enemy had possessed information regarding lost temples, they would have searched them out and taken the Blood Orbs they contained. They would have used the Orbs to bring down the Veil, and this war would have ended long before he was born.

They simply needed to keep searching. Something would turn up. It had to. If not....

He crushed the thought as if it were a Shadowhound, angry with himself for letting doubt creep in. They *would* find a viable Orb. The prophecies were clear on the matter. The *Mith'elre Chon* would enter Mount Tabor with one and the battle for the life of the world itself would be won or lost in that moment.

"No pressure," he muttered, then wrapped his mind in *Jiu* to calm his fears. As an added measure, he opened his Awareness and let the luminescence that was the Earthsoul wash over him. It had an immediate effect, and a sense of peace settled over him in what he could only describe as a spiritual hug.

*Thank you*, he thought, directing the sentiment to the Earthsoul.

The warm feeling intensified, and he smiled. He should do this more often. Especially if—

His smile vanished as a sudden stream of images flowed into his mind, images and a sense of fear and panic. Storm waves as tall as mountains striking the Zekan coastline. Forests withering into skeletal desolation. Tempests and lightnings laying waste to towns and villages. Demons slaughtering the inhabitants of the Nine Lands as rents opened and closed from Con'Jithar. Earthquakes in abundance—

The images cut off as a distant, almost inaudible *boom* sounded to the northeast. He felt it more than heard it and knew instinctively that it had originated somewhere deep inside the earth. *Another earthquake*, he thought and braced himself for what might follow. This one seemed different than all the others he'd felt, and he didn't know what to expect.

A heartbeat later, a rumbling like that of distant thunder reached his ears. It grew louder by the moment, and he watched as a visible shockwave raced across the leafy expanse of Geissler Wood. Like the first wave on a newly disturbed pond, it spread out in a widening ring as it moved toward the city.

The trees of the forest groaned in protest as the rapidly moving swell passed beneath them, momentarily lifting them and the earth they clung to several feet above where the forest floor had been. Branches and trunks and roots cracked or snapped completely. Leaves fell like green rain. Trees too many to count lost their grip in the loosened earth and toppled in every direction.

And still the shockwave continued on, a water-like ripple of solid earth that was unlike anything he'd ever seen. *How is that possible?* he thought, then braced himself as the swell reached Andlexces' outer wall and passed into the city.

The shockwave jarred homes and businesses alike, cracking walls and roofs and foundations, and shattering thousands of windows into crystalline shards. Trees swayed. Hanging plants and baskets swung violently. The bell in Elldrenei College's tower clanged loudly and sporadically.

Jase nearly lost his footing as the shockwave passed beneath the palace, and he had to take hold of the railing to steady himself as the tower swayed. The Power-wrought stone groaned and creaked but stood firm. A number of the tower's windows shattered, and tinklings of glass fell like waterfalls to the courtyards and balconies below.

Then, just like that, it was over. The tremblings and rumblings ceased. The earth became solid once more. The damage to the city, however, had likely been extensive.

The feeling in the back of his mind that was Talia suddenly grew more pronounced. She'd been awakened by the earthquake, and he could feel her fear and alarm through the *sei'vaiya*.

He focused his mind on the feeling and sent a rush of affection across the love-bond. Talia sensed the feeling, and the fear she'd been feeling melted away. A moment later, the rush of affection was reciprocated, and the words *I love you* sounded clearly in his mind.

It amazed him how keenly he could sense her emotions through the love-bond when he truly focused on it. He was even more amazed at how clearly he could sometimes hear her voice. Being in close proximity to her helped, but it wasn't the only contributing factor. Strong emotions, moments of internal contemplation centered upon the love-bond, the Gift of Spirit inherent in his and Talia's souls—all played a role in their ability to communicate with their minds. And thank the Light they did. Anything less and he would have lost her to Zeniff's—to Stalix Geshiann's—assassination attempt.

The sight of her lying in her own blood with an arrow through her neck was forever etched in his memory, but instead of letting it haunt him, he let it fuel his determination to keep her safe. It was why he would be keeping her by his side from now on.

He let the warmth of Talia's emotions wash over him for a moment longer, then pulled his Awareness back from the feeling that was his link to her mind and focused his attention outward once more.

Like Talia, the citizens of Andlexces had been awakened by the earthquake, and great numbers were rushing out into the streets, some fearful that their homes might collapse, others to inspect the damage or check on neighbors. The elevation of his room made it difficult to see how many people were injured, but he suspected there would be many. He just hoped no one had died.

He continued to watch the scene below until the sun crested the horizon, then turned and left his room. The *Bero'thai* stationed outside his door saluted as he exited, and he acknowledged them with a nod.

"Still on your feet?" he asked as he pulled the door shut behind him.

"That wasn't the first earthquake to shake Andlexces this week," the taller of the two said.

"No," the other agreed, "but it was by far the strongest."

Jase grunted. "That was nothing compared to what has happened elsewhere," he told them. "Andlexces is still being sheltered by the Earthsoul. In some areas of the world, entire mountains have split in two or fallen into rubble. Talin Plateau now has a rift to rival the one in Amnidia." He shook his head. "And it's going to get worse. Everywhere."

Leaving the two to stand in stunned silence, he started down the corridor.

He stopped at both his mother's and grandmother's apartments to check on them, then continued on when he found that all was well.

When he reached Talia's apartment, he was greeted by the pair of *Bero'thai* standing watch at her door. Their presence was more ceremonial than it was necessary, but they didn't need to know that. They may have even been offended to know he'd warded the area with threads of Spirit linked to powerful crux points. Any use of corrupted *Ta'shaen* or the arrival of any kind of shadowspawn would trigger the wards, alerting him to the situation and obliterating the enemy.

He nodded cordially to the two men, then rapped on Talia's door with his knuckles.

"Come in," she called, and the *sei'vaiya* trembled with a rush of emotion. She'd sensed it was him, and she was eager to see him.

*That makes two of us*, he thought as he turned the handle and moved inside. Her bedchamber lay at the end of a short hallway, and he found her there, standing in front of a mirror. She wore a simple blue dress that ended just below her knees and she was barefoot. The back of the dress was open, revealing a V-shaped portion of her beautiful and noticeably naked back.

He looked away, more than a little embarrassed.

"Will you button me up?" she asked, and he heard in her voice that she was trying not to laugh. The sense of amusement flowing through the love-bond confirmed it.

"Who puts buttons in the back?" he asked, wrapping his mind in *Jiu* in an attempt to subdue his embarrassment as he began fastening up her dress. Light of heaven, the girl had beautiful skin.

"Why, thank you," she said, then laughed. "And to answer your question about the buttons, obviously someone who's never had to fasten up their own dress."

"Or a man clever enough to realize his assistance would be required," Jase said as he finished with the last button.

She turned to face him. "How do I look?"

"Beautiful," he answered. "As always."

Smiling, she moved to sit on the edge of her bed, then pulled on a pair of white, knee-length stockings and a pair of black, ankle-high boots. When she stood, Jase looked her over, impressed with her choice of attire. A shorter dress for mobility and boots to navigate rough terrain—clearly she expected him to make good on his promise to take her with him into battle.

She nodded emphatically. "I do indeed."

"You do what? Look beautiful or expect to go into battle? Because I'm not sure if you are responding to what I said or what I was thinking."

"Both," she answered, then raised up on her toes and kissed him.

The kiss lengthened as he put his arms around her and pulled her close, but the rush of emotion was interrupted by a Veilgate opening out in the corridor. His lips left hers as he opened his Awareness to search out who had arrived. The corridor came into focus in his mind's eye, and he found Seth and Elliott framed with fiery-edged blue. Behind them, Elison Brey stood with his back toward the doors of the Overlook and the brilliant bar of sunlight streaming into the Dome.

Jase reined in his Awareness as the Veilgate closed, then looked Talia in the eyes. "Prepare yourself for an argument about staying by my side," he told her. "Seth and Elliott are here."

She arched an eyebrow at him. "You told me *you* would be willing to make that argument," she said. "Remember?"

He kissed her on the forehead. "And so I will." He took her by the hand and led her to the door. "Just be prepared to heal me if Seth's objections come by way of his swords."

Taking a deep breath to calm herself, Talia put a smile on her face, then tightened her grip on Jase's hand as they moved out into the corridor to greet Seth and Elliott. They seemed surprised to see her, and it was in that instant that she realized how exiting her bedroom with Jase so early in the morning must look to them. Her fears were confirmed when Elliott scowled at Jase.

"Did you spend the night in my sister's room?"

Jase grunted in amusement. "No. But I did help her get dressed. Why?"

Elliott stared at Jase as if he didn't quite believe what he was hearing, but the door to Brysia's room opened before he could say more, and Gideon came out with Brysia's hand in his.

Talia greeted them with a wave, then looked back to Seth. "Jase came to check on me only moments before you arrived," she told him. "He wanted to make sure I had chosen the proper footwear for today's activities."

Seth glanced at her feet. "You don't need hiking shoes for a day in the archives."

"I'm not going to the archives," she told him, pleased with how calm she kept her voice. "I'm spending the day with Jase at the front."

"Are you out of your mind?" Seth snapped at the same time Gideon said, "I think that is a great idea."

The two turned to stare at one another, and Talia braced herself for whatever might happen next. Sensing her anxiety, Jase gave her hand a reassuring squeeze and winked at her.

"You know the prophecies, Seth," Gideon said. "And we've had this discussion before. Jase is her warder now. Just as she is his. Any hope we have for the Rejuvenation lies in them being together. And since that time is rapidly approaching—since it could literally come at any moment—it might be a good idea if they are together when it happens."

"But why the front lines?" Seth asked, directing the question to Jase. "Why not Trian? Why don't you just stay here in Andlexces?"

"Because I am the *Mith'elre Chon*," Jase answered. "I go where I'm needed most."

Seth's eyes narrowed as he frowned. "So you keep saying." He tucked his thumbs in his sword belt and nodded. "Fine. Elliott and I will join you."

Talia felt Jase's amusement through the *sei'vaiya*. "I thought you might say that," he said. "And we welcome your company. We'll leave as soon as we finish breakfast."

# CHAPTER 42

## On the Earthsoul's Errand

RAILEN RELEASED THE POWER, and the Veilgate he'd opened into Sagaris Keep slid closed behind him. As it did, the swath of light spilling across the paving stones from the Chellum dining room narrowed, then vanished, and the open-aired courtyard where he'd spent so many hours teaching Elliott Chellum to use his Gift was thrown into shadow once more.

He'd chosen this courtyard for their arrival not just because it was such a fixed image in his mind, but because of its proximity to the Imperial Clave Chamber. It was near enough to be convenient, but not so near that it would send those tasked with warding the Emperor into a panic. Even more important, it acted as a nerve center for the keep—a stress index, so to speak, for the current political and military climate.

As his eyes adjusted to the soft morning light, he looked around, and the hair on the back of his neck prickled in alarm. Even at such an early hour, the courtyard should have been a hive of activity. Glowstone lamps should have lit the place from end to end, and he should have found large numbers of Shizu and Sarui practicing forms and Dymas or *Dalae* honing their skills with *Ta'shaen*. At the very least, Leiflords or other nobles should have been gathered in groups to conspire against one another.

Instead, the courtyard could have doubled as a graveyard.

"What do you make of the quiet?" Sheymi asked, glancing around guardedly.

Railen tightened his hold on her hand. "I'm not sure," he told her. "But it can't be good."

They started across the courtyard toward the archway leading into the keep, and Railen opened his Awareness and embraced *Ta'shaen* once more. He felt Sheymi do the same, but neither of them did anything with the Power. It was just a precaution should they find themselves in an unfriendly situation and needed to react quickly.

He felt the brush of a familiar Awareness and opened his mind to it, allowing a Communal link to form. Sheymi was only a heartbeat behind, and Jyosei Ikkai's voice sounded in their thoughts. *I wondered when you two would be returning,* Jyosei said. *Praise the Creator it is now instead of later. Emperor Dromensai has called the Imperial Clave into assembly.*

*What's wrong?* Railen asked. *The absence of practicing soldiers suggests they were needed elsewhere for the real thing. Has clan warfare broken out somewhere?*

*No,* Jyosei answered, *but Gizo and Kyoai are mobilizing. Apparently they think to capitalize on the situation along our southern border by staging a coup while the bulk of our forces are away. Here, let me show you.*

She opened her mind further, and all that she knew flowed through the link in a rush of images and sounds and emotions that would have taken hours to explain but came in an instant instead. Her knowledge became his.

The Arkanian armies streaming across the border were being led by more than just Power-wielding tribal priests. Many were under the control and direction of Con'Droth—demons from Con'Jithar. All across Riak, every clan loyal to Dromensai—and even some who had opposed him—had sent every available soldier to help turn back the invasion.

That had opened the way for Gizo and Kyoai, who had withheld their support, to attempt to seize control of Sagaris. They were at that very instant mobilizing outside of the keep's main gate. They didn't have any real chance of overthrowing Dromensai or his newly established government, but their stupidity would cost many men their lives here in the city and along the Arkanian border. That they allowed their own selfish interests to blind them to the real enemy—an enemy and a war that was so much larger than any one nation or group of nations—was infuriating.

When the barrage of information stopped and Jyosei's mind pulled back to a simpler Communal link, Railen nodded his understanding. *Ask Tereus to wait for us,* he told her. *We'll join you all in a few minutes.* He severed the link and looked at Sheymi.

The look in her eyes showed she'd sensed what he was thinking but that she had her doubts. "Do you think he will be able to help?" she asked. "He's likely to be otherwise occupied today."

"It never hurts to ask," he said, then embraced all Seven Gifts and opened a Veilgate into the courtyard fronting Temifair Palace. If the *Mith'elre Chon* couldn't help them, it wasn't likely anyone could.

With Seth and the others following closely on his and Talia's heels, Jase led the way through Temifair Palace toward the private dining room of the Elvan King. Over the years, Jase had shared a number of meals with his grandmother's brother, but had always had a difficult time thinking of him as family, great-uncle or not.

"Why is that?" Talia whispered, and Jase cast a sideways look at her.

"You heard that did you?"

"Heard isn't the right word," she told him. "It was more of a feeling. But I got the gist of what you were thinking. So, to repeat, why is that?"

Jase shrugged. "I don't know exactly," he told her. "He's never been unkind to me. It's just that our interactions were always so... well, businesslike. I never really felt the same kind of warmth or fondness from him that I felt from Randle. Or from Daris or Breiter or even your father, for that matter. Once, when I was five or six years old, I called him Uncle, and he corrected me. He told me he was my great-uncle and that I was to call him Lord Reiekel."

He shrugged again. "It put a bit of a damper on our relationship from that point forward, and I've never allowed myself to call him anything else. It doesn't help that he insists on calling me Lord Fairimor and has since the day he corrected me."

"But he *is* family," Talia said. "And I know from my interactions with him the past few days that he is very proud of who you have become."

Jase nodded. "I felt his approval when I arrived here from Aridan with Elrien's pupils," he told her. "But even that reunion was kingly and formal and... businesslike."

Talia squeezed his hand reassuringly. "Maybe that's just who he is," she suggested. "He wouldn't be the first person in your life to have difficulty expressing his feelings. Take Seth. He clearly loves you like his own son, but has he ever said it? No. I'm sure the same is true for Lord Reiekel."

Jase smiled at her. "Thank you," he said. "I've never thought about it like that before."

"What are you two whispering about?" Elliott asked from behind them.

"Nothing that concerns you," Talia said. Looking over her shoulder, she smiled sweetly. "If it did, we would have spoken loudly enough for you to hear."

"Secrets are rude," he told her.

She dropped her smile. "So is interrupting a private conversation."

They continued down the corridor in silence, passing a number of smaller hallways and antechambers, then entered a broad spiraling stairwell that wound its way down to the next level. There, they moved into a vaulted, hexagonal room with corridors branching off into different areas of the palace, and Jase looked around to get his bearings. The King's dining hall was a short distance down the corridor to the left and Jase angled toward it.

He was just shy of reaching it, when a pair of *Bero'thai* raced into the chamber from the stairwell leading up from the palace entrance.

"Lord Fairimor," one of the men called, "I'm so glad we found you. Two Dymas arrived from Riak a short time ago. They are in the courtyard fronting the main entrance and say they have an urgent message for you."

Jase felt the brush of Gideon's Awareness as he stretched it forth to investigate, and he turned toward his father in time to see his face darken with concern. "It's

Railen and Sheymi," he said, "and they are clearly upset."

Seth's eyes narrowed as he glanced at the ornate clock on the chamber's far wall. "They left Chellum when we did," Seth said. "That was less than twenty minutes ago."

The *Bero'thai* started for the stairwell, motioning for Jase to follow. "We'll show you the way."

"That won't be necessary," Jase told them. Embracing the Power, he opened a Veilgate to the courtyard and strode through with Talia at his side. His stomach growled as he did, but if he was going to miss breakfast, he wasn't going to waste strength by taking the stairs.

Gideon and the others followed, and Jase let the Veilgate close behind them. But he didn't release the Power—the whisperings of the Earthsoul were telling him he would need it again soon enough.

"What's wrong?" he asked as he moved up to Railen and Sheymi. "You two are supposed to be in Sagaris."

"We were," Railen said, "for all of five minutes. But with the Imperial Clave gathering to discuss an impending coup, we thought it wise to inform you of the situation. That, and the news coming from our southern border. Apparently, Amnidia isn't the only place where a demon army has broken free."

"And this demon army," Sheymi added, "is being strengthened by an army of Power-wielding Arkanian priests."

Jase blew out his cheeks in exasperation. "Of course it is," he said. "Maeon knows what he is about. If he can get us to spread our forces thinly over multiple fronts, Death's Third March will have a much easier time reaching Trian."

"Does that mean you won't be coming to our aid?" Railen asked. He sounded as if he'd just been punched in the gut.

"Of course I'm coming," Jase told him, and the whisperings of the Earthsoul intensified, confirming his decision. "You are an ally and a friend. To me and to the Earthsoul. Neither of us will abandon you in your hour of need."

Gideon stepped near. "This coup you mentioned. It's being staged by Kyoai and Gizo, isn't it?"

Railen nodded. "You don't sound surprised."

Gideon shook his head in disgust. "I'm not. I've wondered all along if they might try something stupid. How did Dai'shozen Dakshar respond to it?"

Railen shook his head. "We don't know. We didn't actually meet with the Imperial Clave. Jyosei Dymas filled us in via a Communal link. I told her to give us a few minutes to contact someone who might help."

"Then we'd best join the assembly," Jase said. He turned to his mother. "Have Beraline contact me if you find anything new in the archives," he told her. "It looks like it's going to be another busy day. On multiple fronts." He met Gideon's eyes briefly, then turned his gaze on Seth and Elliott. "I can see by your faces that you want to come along," he said. "And you are welcome to." He grinned at Elliott and added, "Just try not to get any more deathmarks levied against you."

Elliott stiffened, obviously offended. "It's not like I purposely sought out the first two. Things just... happened. It wasn't *my* fault."

Jase grinned at him. "It never is." Opening himself more fully to the Power, he wove the strands necessary to open a Veilgate into Sagaris Keep. Then, focusing more fully on the whisperings of the Earthsoul, he let Her guide the wielding. Going to Riak at this time was Her plan, and he trusted Her to pick an appropriate point of arrival.

Railen and Sheymi led the way, and as they passed Elliott, Railen raised an eyebrow at him. "Two deathmarks?" he asked. "Try six. Gizo and Kyoai aren't the only clans to put a price on your head."

"Like I said," Elliott began as he followed the Riaki through the opening, "that isn't my fault."

Jase motioned Gideon and Seth to go next, then escorted Talia through as well. Brysia followed them to the edge of the gate but stopped on the Elvan side.

"Be careful," she said, and Jase nodded.

"Always," he told her, then released the Power and looked around. They were in a high-domed rotunda fronting a set of tall, ornate doors. The room was empty but for two squads of Sarui. One squad wore the mark of Leif Iga. The other a mark Jase wasn't familiar with.

All the men's hands had gone to their weapons as the gate opened, but they relaxed their stances the moment they realized the new arrivals were friends.

"Welcome home, Dymas," the Iga captain said, directing the comment to Railen. "You are just in time. Emperor Dromensai is inside with the rest of the Imperial Clave." He eyed Jase and the others with curiosity but was far too disciplined to inquire about why they had come.

"Thank you, Kambei," Railen said, then gestured to the doors. "We won't keep him waiting any longer."

Kambei and one of his men moved to the tall doors and pulled them open, but Railen and Sheymi paused and motioned Jase and Talia to take the lead.

"After you, *Mith'elre Chon*," Railen said.

The whisperings in *Ta'shaen* intensified, then suddenly stilled, leaving Jase with a feeling of peace and an overwhelming sense of purpose. He was here to save Riak. Hopefully it would put Riak in a position to return the favor.

Taking Talia by the hand, he smiled at her. "Let's go meet the Emperor."

"He is here," Jyosei Dymas said, and Tereus Dromensai broke off the conversation he was having with Representative Jarrasei. Like the rest of the members of the Imperial Clave, the former Highseat of Clan Vakala sat a little taller at Jyosei's announcement and his eyes moved to the doors of the Clave Chamber.

A moment later, those doors opened and a tall, broad-shouldered lad strode in with a young woman at his side. She was exquisitely beautiful and bore a strong resemblance to Elliott Chellum. Railen and Sheymi came next, and behind them came Gideon and Elliott and a silver-haired Chellum captain that could only be Seth Lydon. Tereus took them all in with a glance, not at all surprised that they, too, had come. Then he focused on the young man once more.

*So this is the* Mith'elre Chon, he thought, studying the young man intently.

Strong and well-muscled, he moved with the grace of a leopard and the primed, explosive readiness of a Shizu. His uniform was of Elvan make and had the Tree of Life embroidered over the left breast—appropriate since he alone could save mankind from certain death.

He bore no weapons save those which could be wrought with *Ta'shaen*, but Tereus knew a warrior when he saw one. If even half of what he'd heard about this young man was true, he was an army unto himself, carrying death in one hand and salvation in the other.

A sense of wonder came over him as he watched Jase approach, and he couldn't stop himself from rising from the throne-like chair of the Emperor and moving down the steps of the dais. Doing so violated the expectations and decorum associated with his role as Emperor—even kings and queens were expected to kneel at the foot of the dais—but he didn't care. Jase Fairimor was more than a monarch of some nation whose borders were subject to change. He was the *Mith'elre Chon*—his kingdom was somewhat larger.

Tereus stopped near the Circle of Reckoning and continued to study Jase as he made his way toward him. He looked to be about the same age as Elliott or Railen but there was something in his eyes that belied youth. A deep, greyish blue, they sparkled with such fierceness and authority they would have been right at home on the face of Shavis Dakshar. Or Gideon, for that matter.

Jase and his female counterpart stopped before him, and Tereus was taken aback when Jase offered a deep bow of respect. "Emperor Dromensai," he said, "it is a pleasure to meet you."

"The pleasure is mine," Tereus told him, deeply impressed. "But I should be bowing to you. Not the other way around."

Jase smiled. "You are the Voice of Riak," he said. "And we are in your throne room. It seemed the honorable thing to do."

Tereus returned the smile. "You are the *Mith'elre Chon*," he said. "Unless I am mistaken, the entire world is your throne room."

"I have no desire to rule the world," Jase said. "I'm just trying to save it." He let his eyes move over the other members of the Imperial Clave before looking back to Tereus. "I understand you have a couple of problems that need to be dealt with," he said. "Here and along your southern border. What can I do to help?"

Jase listened intently while Tereus explained the situation in Sagaris and what he and his newly formed government hoped to do about it. To their credit, they'd been discussing a course of action which lent itself to a minimal amount of bloodshed but

one that would keep them holed up here in the fortress until sufficient forces could
be brought back from the southern border. The problem lay in the fact that those
fighting the Arkanians and their demon masters were already shorthanded and none
could afford to leave the battle.

"I have a better idea," Jase said when Tereus finished. "One that will solve the
problem here and alleviate some of the strain on your forces at the border." He
gestured at the doors. "If someone will please show me the way to the outer wall of
the fortress, I will see it done."

Sheymi edged forward, her eyes suspicious. "Why do I get the feeling this won't
end well for Kyoai and Gizo?"

"Because it won't," Jase told her. "But we don't have time to reason with people
who are obviously beyond reason. It's time they see things as they really are. They'll
either have a change of heart and move to support those at the front or they will die
in the streets of Sagaris. Either way, it's time to put an end to this senseless rebellion."

Tereus was silent as he considered. Finally he nodded. "Do whatever you feel is
necessary, Mith'elre Chon," he said. "The Imperial Clave will support you."

"I'll show you the way to the fortress gates," Railen said, and he and Sheymi took
the lead as Jase and Talia followed.

Out in the rotunda, Jase glanced over his shoulder and found Tereus walking
beside Gideon and Seth. Elliott walked closely on their heels, his head cocked
forward so he could listen to whatever they might say. The remaining members of the
Imperial Clave were bringing up the rear and had been joined by several squads of
Sarui acting as escort.

They moved down the first corridor without speaking, but Gideon's voice finally
broke the silence.

"Aside from the situation which brought us here," he said, addressing Tereus,
"what else is new in Riak?"

When the Emperor didn't answer immediately, Jase wondered if the question
had offended him. Then he felt Jyosei Dymas embrace the Power and weave a ward
against eavesdropping, and he knew Tereus was just being cautious.

"We've been using a Con'Kumen book of names to root out the rest of those
who've sold themselves to Maeon," he said. "Highseat Unosei's wife turned out to be
an Agla'Con and the mastermind behind her husband's ascension. She and several
others from Clan Maridan have been dealt with. The hunt continues for others, but
most of those we've gone after have disappeared. Apparently word got out that we
were hunting them."

"Or they were called up by Shadan," Gideon said. "Death's Third March has
suffered a few setbacks of its own. I wouldn't be surprised if the Agla'Con you seek
were given new assignments in his army."

"Then may they meet a speedy death at the hands of those who fight for the
Mith'elre Chon in Kelsa," Tereus said. "But just the same, we will continue to hunt
them here. Unless they have knowledge of Veilgates or access to K'rresh, they will be

leaving Riak on foot."

Jase glanced over his shoulder to see Gideon raise an eyebrow in question. "What do you mean?"

Tereus smiled. "Dai'shozen Dakshar has taken control of every Myrscraw in Riak. They've been gathered to the Imperial Aviary here in Sagaris or to the Aviary on Myrdyn. All travel between clans is being facilitated by Veilgates wrought by Dymas. I know the movements of every highseat and leiflord in the country. Even better, no striketeam, group of striketeams, or army can move upon another clan or leif unaware. In essence, we've crippled all aggressive movement until this threat is past."

"Brilliant," Gideon said. "Was that Shavis' idea?"

"It was," Tereus answered. "And, as you might imagine, it wasn't very popular with many of the clans."

"Who cares," Elliott said, then cleared his throat in embarrassment when Jase and Gideon and Tereus turned to look at him. Gideon looked as if he might say something about Elliott butting into the conversation, but the opportunity to do so was cut short by Railen.

"We're here," the young Dymas announced, and Jase faced forward once more as Sarui pushed open a pair of doors and led the way out into a large courtyard.

Jase looked around in surprise. He'd expected the harsh, sterile look of a military staging area. Instead, more than a dozen ornamental cherry trees in manicured circles of earth dotted the smooth expanse, and a multi-tiered fountain of polished stone rose in their midst.

The fountain's sparkling waters were surrounded by raised flowerbeds sporting a variety of exotic flowers, and from that splash of color, thirteen flag poles rose tall and straight.

Jase looked up to see the red sunburst of Riak rippling gently atop the tallest. Each of the other twelve poles were topped with a unique banner he supposed were the flags of the clans holding seats on the Imperial Clave.

"Quite a sight, isn't it?" Seth said as they walked among the trees, and Jase looked over to find his friend looking up at the flags as well. "Never in the history of Riak," he continued, "has the Imperial Clave been comprised of twelve different clans."

"The past few weeks," Tereus said, sounding more than a little bewildered, "have brought a lot of *never-in-history* events to this nation." He locked eyes with Seth for a moment, then looked at Jase. "Our current situation included. It makes me wonder what else fate has in store for us today."

Jase shook his head. "If it's anything like what I've dealt with the past few days..." he said, pausing for emphasis, "it won't be good."

A trickle of anxiety reached him through the *sei'vaiya*, and he glanced at Talia to find her frowning worriedly. *Well, it's true*, he told her silently, confident that she would get the sentiment even if the actual words didn't come through. She narrowed her eyes at him but said nothing.

As they passed beneath the last of the cherry trees, Seth held up his hand for them to stop. "If the *Mith'elre Chon* and the Emperor of Riak are going to make themselves visible atop the wall, it might be wise to have a shield in place around them."

"I'll take care of it," Sheymi said, and Jase felt her embrace the Power and wrap the entire group in a warding bubble of Spirit.

When it was in place, Seth led the way to a narrow set of stairs just beyond the needle gate and started up. Jase moved Talia to his other arm to keep her away from the exposed edge of the stairs, and together they made the climb to the top of the wall.

As Gideon and Elliott and the others moved to the edge of the wall and looked down at the assembling armies of Gizo and Kyoai, Tereus moved to stand next to Jase. He'd only been there for a few seconds, when an arrow thumped hollowly against Sheymi's invisible shield.

"I guess we know how someone feels about you as Emperor," Jase told him, and Tereus chuckled darkly.

"Actually," Elliott said from behind them, "I think they were aiming for me."

"Then go stand over there," Talia told him. "So we'll know the difference."

Elliott scowled at his sister, but he did move further down the wall. A string of arrows thumping against the shield followed him as he moved.

"He was right," Jase said. "They were aiming for him."

"Not all of them," Tereus said as another arrow meant for him was stopped short by Sheymi's shield.

"Isn't it a capital offense to threaten the life of the Emperor?" Talia asked.

"It is," Tereus answered. "Thus the storm of arrows being loosed at your brother. He did kill Emperor Samal, after all."

"Even so," Jase said as he scanned the throng of soldiers below. He was looking for those brazen enough to point arrows at his friends. When he found them, he opened himself to the Power and used a quick thrust of Air and Spirit to shatter the bows in their hands. They staggered backward in surprise, their hands and arms riddled with splinters.

"That got their attention," Seth said, sounding amused.

"If it didn't," Jase said, "this will." Opening himself more fully to the Power, he addressed those below. "Leaders and soldiers of Gizo and Kyoai," he began, magnifying his voice with tendrils of Air and sending it to the far reaches of the assembly, "my name is Jase Fairimor. I am the one the prophecies call the *Mith'elre Chon*, and I have come to Riak at this time on the Earthsoul's errand."

He paused to let the introduction sink in, then continued.

"Your country is being overrun by a horde of demons which have been freed from Con'Jithar by the collapsing of the Veil. They are being assisted by an army of Arkanians, some of whom can wield corrupted *Ta'shaen*. But you know this, don't you? You know, and you decided to use it to your advantage to lay siege to your capital in the hopes of overthrowing your rightfully appointed Emperor."

He glanced at Tereus before continuing. "I am here to make sure that doesn't happen." He looked back down at those gathered below and his contempt for their rebellion intensified.

"Since you refused to go to the aid of your countrymen, I have decided to bring the fight to you. This is the *real* enemy, not Tereus Dromensai or his cabinet."

The spiritual whisperings he'd felt earlier that morning returned, and he let them guide his Awareness as he extended it in a narrow, probing thrust toward the Riaki-Arkanian border. A forested area came into view and there, in the shadowed depths beneath, the enemy he was looking for.

With a grim smile on his face, he opened a Veilgate in their midst.

In the street below, the opposite side of that same Veilgate opened along the edge of the wall, and five hulking shapes plunged through into the midst of this foolish rebellion.

Seth pulled thoughtfully at his moustache as he watched the scene unfolding below. A number of Shizu and Sarui from both clans had fallen in the opening moments of the demons' unexpected arrival, but the rest quickly formed ranks to contain the chaos, pinning the horrific creatures against the wall.

Swords and spears flashed. Arrows and bladestars hissed like locust. Black, foul-smelling blood spattered the paving stones as the largest of the demons, a multi-limbed monster the size of a horse, fell into a quivering heap.

A second ape-like demon went down a moment later, but continued to slash at a squad of Sarui even as they drove their spears through its head.

The final three were more reminiscent of the soldier-like demons he had seen in the Valley of Amnidia. Wrapped in heavy armor from head to foot, they each held a shield in one hand and a long, slender-bladed sword in the other. Backs against the wall and fueled by frenetic desperation, they lunged forward into the midst of the surrounding Shizu, dark blades flashing.

The cries of the wounded echoed up the wall, and Seth glanced at Jase and Tereus to find them watching the chaos without emotion. Faces set and eyes hard, they were here to send a message to the rebellious clans: Fight for your country at the border or fight for your lives here. Either way, the end result was the same.

Seth returned his attention to the demons and watched as they inflicted a dozen more injuries, some fatal, before finally being brought down by a few well-placed arrows.

The entire skirmish had lasted less than a minute, but those who'd been caught up in it looked as if they'd faced an army the size of Leif Iga.

"Soldiers of Gizo and Kyoai," Jase said, his voice echoing across the multitude and down the streets stretching into the city proper, "that is but a single drop of rain from the storm your countrymen are facing at your southern border. Cease this foolish attempt to overthrow your Emperor and agree to join the fight against Soulbiter's minions or suffer more of my wrath. I await your answer. You have five minutes."

From the area immediately surrounding the banner of Gizo's Highseat, a volley of arrows hissed forward to thump like feathered hailstones against the shield directly in front of Jase.

Seth shook his head in disgust. "There's your answer. Now what?"

Jase made a motion with his hand, and the soldiers surrounding the Gizo banner were forcefully parted by an invisible thrust of Power. A gap several paces wide and a dozen paces long formed in their midst, exposing the smooth paving stones beneath. A heartbeat later two Veilgates opened back to back, each blue-edged opening casting its light upon the faces of the startled soldiers of Gizo. Surprise turned to horror in an instant as demons led by Power-wielding Arkanian priests rushed through from beyond.

"Kill the Power-wielders," Jase said, looking at Gideon and the other Dymas. "Leave the demons for Gizo and Kyoai."

The area fronting Sagaris Palace went white as stabs of lightning and streamers of *Sei'shiin* obliterated the Arkanian priests, but the use of *Ta'shaen* drew the attention of the demons accompanying them. Almost as one, they turned toward the wall and tried to fight their way through the ranks of Riaki soldiers, enraged by the pureness of the Power-wrought strikes.

But the army standing between them and the palace wall stiffened as the soldiers in it saw an enemy as vicious and vile as any they'd ever faced. They fell upon the demons with sword and spear and arrow, and ruthlessly and methodically brought them down. And yet there was a price for victory, and dozens of Shizu and Sarui went down in sprays of blood and shattered armor.

When it was finally over, the soldiers who'd engaged the demons pulled back a few steps and went to one knee as a horrified silence fell across the entire multitude. Then, one by one, Shizu and Sarui alike took their weapons in their hands and raised them toward the wall as an offering of allegiance.

A moment later, both Gizo and Kyoai raised the Flag of Negotiation.

Jase turned to Tereus. "They are yours to command once more," he said. "Have your Dymas facilitate their relocation to your southern border." He glanced at Railen and Sheymi and added, "Railen and Sheymi are eager to share their knowledge of all the new wieldings."

"Thank you, *Mith'elre Chon*," Tereus said, a look of admiration in his eyes.

"Thank the Earthsoul," Jase said. "This was Her idea." His eyes moved to Seth for a moment, then passed over Elliott and landed on Gideon. "And She isn't done with us yet."

He turned as a Veilgate opened just beyond the group, and Seth found himself looking at the soft, wind-rippled green of a rice field. A hundred paces or so beyond the field, sat the small Riaki city of Maisen.

"Come," Jase said, "we're needed at the front."

# CHAPTER 43

## A Change of Heart

PRIDE FILLED GIDEON AS HE FOLLOWED his son into Maisen. What Jase had just done in Sagaris had been hard-nosed and brutal but had been exactly what was needed. It would be some time before Gizo or Kyoai troubled Tereus Dromensai again. If ever. When the ally of your enemy was the *Mith'elre Chon*, you tended to step lightly. Gideon smiled. Jase truly was the Son of Thunder spoken of in the prophecies.

"Where is everyone?" Elliott asked, and Gideon turned to find the Chellum Prince glancing curiously about. The street they were on led directly through the center of town and was lined on both sides by businesses and homes. All were empty, the residents long since fled. It was easy to see why.

Bodies, both Arkanian and demon, lay scattered about. Some were riddled with arrows. Others bore gruesome sword wounds or the much more obvious signs of having been killed with the Power. Here and there scorched patches of earth, ruined sections of boardwalk, and shattered windows and storefronts further marred what had once been a peaceful farming community.

Gideon noted that no Shizu or Sarui lay among the dead, but that didn't mean there hadn't been casualties—any fallen Riaki would have been removed for proper burial after the fight was over.

"The schoolhouse just ahead," Jase said in answer to Elliott's question. "They are using it as a command post."

Gideon didn't need to ask how Jase knew. He'd felt his son probe the way ahead as soon as they were through the Veilgate. Before today, he would have done the same, but his trust in his son was so complete he no longer felt the need. Instead, he focused on what he could see around him, trying to measure just how serious the fight in Maisen had been. He'd counted some thirty-five demon corpses so far, most of them the armored, human-shaped monsters which had marched on Aridan, but that number steadily increased the nearer they came to the command post. Gideon frowned. This battle had been as bad as the one in Amnidia. And the Riaki soldiers hadn't enjoyed the added strength of Dragons.

They walked on, passing the rubble of a partially collapsed pottery shop and skirting the smoldering remains of another building. Finally, the wide open stretch of hard-packed earth that was the play area for Maisen's school children came into view. There, the demon corpses numbered in the hundreds and had been heaped into piles around the perimeter to make way for the army of Shizu and Sarui stationed outside the schoolhouse.

Several thousand strong, they clustered together by clan, weapons in hand, ready for the next encounter.

A number of them turned to watch him and the others approach, and a look of astonishment moved over their faces when they spotted Seth. The words *shent ze'deyar* spread through their ranks like a gust of wind moving through a forest. Within moments, the entire assembly had turned its attention to the new arrivals, and an aisle formed in their midst, allowing passage into the schoolhouse. The Shizu at the front of the aisle brought fists to chests in salute as Seth passed, and he acknowledged them with a nod.

"You really are a big deal in this country, aren't you?" Elliott whispered.

Seth narrowed his eyes at him but didn't reply, and they moved up the steps and into the schoolhouse.

Inside, they found Shavis Dakshar looking over a map with the Dai'shozen from Clans Hasho, Chisei, and Sekigaroga. Their conversation was being warded against eavesdropping by a young female Dymas in bright red *kitara* robes, and they were so engrossed in what they were discussing that they didn't immediately realize they had visitors.

Then Shavis looked up, and his surprise mirrored that of the men outside. He motioned for the Dymas to drop the ward as he hurriedly moved out from behind the table and strode forward to greet them.

"*Mith'elre Chon,*" he said, offering a bow. "What brings you to Riak?"

"The whisperings of the Earthsoul," Jase told him. Smiling, he added, "And Railen and Sheymi said you needed help."

Shavis looked beyond Jase as if expecting to see the two Dymas. "Where are they?"

"Teaching the Dymas in Sagaris the new wieldings you sent them to Kelsa to learn," Jase answered. "That, and they are preparing to move the armies of Gizo and Kyoai to your southern border."

"You mean their idiotic attempt at a coup is over?"

Jase nodded. "It is."

When he said nothing more, Gideon stepped up next to him. "The *Mith'elre Chon* is being modest," he told Shavis. "He single-handedly showed Gizo and Kyoai the error of their ways. It left them with no doubts about who the real enemy is."

Shavis stared at Jase, a look of understanding in his eyes. "That was you who opened Veilgates in the midst of the enemy. You used them against the rebel clans."

"Yes," Jase said. "And it woke them to the seriousness of the situation."

Shavis grunted in amusement. "I bet it did," he said. "But it also saved the lives of several dozen Shizu from Clan Hasho. They were about to be overrun when one of your gates opened in front of the enemy and they vanished from the battlefield."

"I'm glad it served more than one purpose, then," Jase said. He looked at Talia then back to Shavis. "This is Talia Chellum," he said by way of introduction. "Talia, this is Shavis Dakshar, Dai'shozen of Riak."

"It's a pleasure to meet you, Lady Talia," Shavis said, bowing deeply. He looked pointedly at Elliott and added, "Please tell me your resemblance to your brother is strictly physical."

Elliott scowled but held his tongue.

Talia, however, laughed openly. "You needn't worry about me," she said. "The only mischief I ever create is directed at my brother."

Shavis smiled at her. "Then we are allies indeed." Giving Elliott one last hard look, he moved around Talia to face Seth. The two stared at one another for a moment, then offered simultaneous bows of respect.

"It's good to see you again, my friend," Shavis said. "Your arrival means every clan in Riak will be represented at this battle. And for the first time in history we are all fighting on the same side. Too bad it took the end of the world to bring us all together."

Seth nodded, then gestured at the map. "What exactly are we facing?"

"Come and see," Shavis said, and the other Dai'shozen moved aside to make way for them. The map was a close-up of Riak's southern border and stretched some fifty miles into Arkania and as far north as Jai. The Riaki side was highly detailed and showed the area's roads and trails, as well as towns and villages and terrain. The Arkanian side was an unartistic blob labeled *Jungle*, but there were several short lines inked in red a few miles south of the border and a much larger one some thirty miles further south. There were also a number of small red Xs.

"Those are the breaches in the Veil," Shavis said, pointing to the red lines. "Each X is the location of an Arkanian village that possesses a *droth'del*—the bloody doors their priests use to free demons from Con'Jithar."

"I witnessed one being opened," Talia said, and Gideon smiled inwardly as Shavis and the other Dai'shozen turned to stare at her in disbelief. Oblivious to their stares, Talia shuddered and added, "It was horrifying."

Shavis studied her a moment longer, then looked to Seth for clarification.

"It is a long story," the Chellum captain said, then pointed back to the map. "Please continue."

Shavis hesitated, then shook his head and looked back at the map. "We thought the large breach would present the most trouble for us," he said, "but after the initial rush of demon soldiers—some three or four thousand—the area has been relatively quiet, with only an occasional monstrosity coming through."

"As with the rents which have opened here in the living world," Gideon said, "not all rents open in populated areas within Con'Jithar. It is just as random on Maeon's side as it is here. And his realm is much more vast than we would like to believe. Any demon not in the vicinity of the rent wouldn't know it was there."

"Good to know," Shavis said. "However, the *droth'del* are known to the demons on the other side, and their damned priests are calling them through by the hundreds. They are using them to unite the Arkanian tribes and encourage them to march to war against us."

"Actually," a voice said from behind them, "it is the other way around."

Before Gideon could turn to see who had spoken, Seth whirled as if he'd been stabbed. Swords bared, he stepped in front of Talia, his eyes flashing fire as he stared at the new arrival.

Gideon followed Seth's gaze and found a one-armed Riaki standing in the doorway. Clad in *komouri* black, he was greying at the temples and wore the mark of Vakala on his right shoulder. The left sleeve of his uniform had been sewn shut and ended just below the shoulder. It bore the mark of Shozen.

*Gwuler Hom*, he realized, and *Ta'shaen* filled him as he prepared to strike the man where he stood.

No, he corrected, rage surging through his chest, Hom wasn't a man. He was the black-hearted cur who had abducted Brysia and all but destroyed Seston. Crimes such as those deserved a swift and permanent death.

Taking hold of the Gifts of Fire and Light, he wove them together into *Sei'shiin* and prepared to strike.

"Stand down," Jase said as he moved forward to face the Riaki. When Gideon didn't comply, Jase turned and looked at him. "I said stand down." He looked at Seth to show he meant him as well.

Seth's eyes never left Hom as he slid his swords back into their sheaths.

Gideon released the Power, but kept his Awareness open should a cleansing strike still be needed. He didn't trust Hom any more than he would trust a Shadowhound, and he would kill him just as readily if the man so much as thought about seizing the Power.

Shavis moved around the table to stand next to him, and the look on the Dai'shozen's face as he studied Hom mirrored Seth's.

The tension in the room increased as Jase crossed the room and stopped within arm's length of the Agla'Con. For a moment, he simply studied Hom the way Gideon might study a scorpion he intended to crush beneath his boot.

"Give me one reason why I shouldn't kill you where you stand," Jase said at last. He spoke softly, but it only made the question that much more chilling. Gwuler Hom might still meet the end he deserved. Gideon would have smiled but for the rage still coursing through him.

Raising his palm toward Jase to show that it was empty, he reached slowly into the front of his uniform and withdrew a silver medallion with Riaki characters around the edge and what was obviously a Jexlair crystal set in the center. Holding it by the chain, he offered it to Jase, lowering it into the young man's outstretched hand.

"Thus begins my Reckoning," Gwuler said. "To House Fairimor, to Riak, and to the Earthsoul."

The words hit Gideon like a hammer, and his rage dissipated in an instant. And with it went his eagerness to condemn Gwuler. Change Riak to Kelsa, and he'd spoken those exact words more than two centuries ago after finally coming to his senses. And unlike Gwuler, who'd merely corrupted *Ta'shaen* as an Agla'Con, Gideon had given himself over to *Lo'shaen*. Holding onto his disdain for this man reeked of hypocrisy.

One glance at Seth showed the Chellum Captain was entertaining similar thoughts. About himself as well as about Gideon.

Elliott, however, stepped forward, his face hard and his hand on his sword. He looked on the verge of embracing the Power. "What makes you think you deserve a Reckoning? You sold your soul to Maeon decades ago. You are nothing but a—"

"That's enough, Elliott," Seth said. His tone wasn't so much irritated as it was resigned.

Gwuler dipped his head at Seth to show his thanks, then his eyes returned to Jase. "What say you, *Mith'elre Chon*? Will you hear my account?"

Jase studied Gwuler as if he were looking into the man's soul. Finally, he nodded. "I will hear you."

Gwuler went to one knee in front of Jase. "After I parted ways with your mother and the others..." He paused and looked meaningfully at Talia and Seth. "I was hunted for a time by a number of Arkanians from the village who had taken us prisoner." He looked at the talisman Jase held, and added, "I eluded them of course, and I did it without the aid of *Ta'shaen*."

"And why would you do that?" Elliott asked. "You had no qualms about using it on the Waypost in Seston or on Jase's mother."

Gwuler shot an irritated glance at Elliott which was mirrored by Seth and Shavis. Elliott of all people should know interrupting a Reckoning was the gravest of insults. Agla'Con or not, Gwuler had the floor. Gideon caught the young man's eye and shook his head at him.

Elliott's jaw tightened, and he tucked his thumbs in his belt. "My apologies for the interruption, Shozen Hom," he said. "Please, continue."

"I will by answering your question," Gwuler said, then he looked back to Jase. "My skills as a Shizu were sufficient to avoid detection. I wrapped myself in *Jiu* and let my training take over. But I did more than simply survive. I had a change of heart. Completely immersing myself in *Jiu* forced me to look inward, to think about the choices I've made in my life. I sold my soul to Maeon, and I will make my Reckoning for that foolish decision in the world to come. I could, however, lessen the seriousness of that Reckoning by corrupting *Ta'shaen* no more. The last time I used my talisman was when I fought alongside the Sister Queen and Captain Lydon and Lady Chellum."

He took a long slow breath before continuing. "It was that experience as much as my meditation that changed me. Your mother is an honorable and courageous woman, *Mith'elre Chon*. Please tell her that for me when next you see her." He looked at Talia. "And you, young lady, are every bit as much a warrior as Brysia Fairimor. Your actions in that godforsaken village saved the Sister Queen's life, which in turn saved mine."

Talia nodded her acceptance of the compliment, but anger and resentment still smoldered in her eyes. Gideon suspected it would be some time before she would see Gwuler as anything other than an Agla'Con.

*And what about you?* Gideon asked himself. *How do you see him?*

He looked from Gwuler to the talisman in Jase's hand, then back to Gwuler. The jury was still out, he decided. Yes, the man deserved a chance to repent of his crimes, but Gideon would need more than just Gwuler's word that he had changed. He would need confirmation from the Earthsoul. This man had been an Agla'Con for more than thirty years—this Reckoning would take time.

"The temptation to seize *Ta'shaen* was strong in those first few weeks," Gwuler continued. "But the more I resisted, the easier it became to resist Maeon's pull. Even when I was overtaken by four demons similar to those lying dead out in the schoolyard, I used sword and blowtube to defeat them."

He shook his head, a contemplative smile on his face. "Oddly, I've never felt more powerful than in that moment. Killing them with *Ta'shaen* would have been easy—not doing so tested me in ways too many to name. But it felt good. It felt...right."

He smiled. "I will spare you the details of crossing Illiarensei and making my way through the eastern jungle. Those weeks were the worst kind of hell and there are many moments I prefer not to relive. But know this: My nation is under siege and I wish to help defend it. I make an end of my report."

Lowering his head, he waited for Jase to speak.

A long silence followed, during which Shavis and Seth exchanged looks, and Elliott shifted his feet irritably. It was impossible to tell what they or Jase were thinking, and he gave up trying to figure it out. Gwuler had given his report to the *Mith'elre Chon*. It was up to Jase to respond to it.

Finally, Jase spoke. "I judge your words to be true," he said, then extended his hand, bidding Gwuler to rise. "Let the next part of your Reckoning begin."

"So that's it?" Elliott asked. "He's forgiven just like that?"

The stare Jase leveled at Elliott could have stopped a Shadowhound in its tracks. "Shozen Hom isn't the only one in this room to cross into the realm of Agla'Con," he said. "Or have you forgotten what I did to the chapter house in Tetrica?"

Elliott opened his mouth to reply, then shut it again without speaking, his eyes troubled.

Jase stared at Elliott for a moment longer, then glanced at Gideon. It was only for a second, but he knew Jase was thinking of his guilt as well. Not as Gideon the Dymas, but as Dunkin Fairimor, fallen king of Kelsa and wielder of *Lo'shaen*.

His son's meaning was clear: If Dunkin Fairimor could find redemption, anyone could.

"The *Mith'elre Chon* is right," Gideon said. "Shozen Hom deserves a chance to reconcile himself to his clan and country and to the Earthsoul."

"His reconciliation with the Earthsoul is already complete," Jase said, looking Gwuler in the eyes. "But you don't know that yet, do you?"

Gwuler stood straight-backed as he met Jase's gaze. "My debt to the Earthsoul can never be paid in full," he said. "Even if it could, what I did in corrupting Her power for so many years will take the same number of years to atone for. My honor demands it."

"Then make amends by using the Gifts She has restored to you," Jase told him. "I can feel them, even if you yourself have not yet recognized they are there."

Gideon felt Gwuler open himself to *Ta'shaen*, and a look of wonder came over the man as he embraced the Gifts of Light and Fire. He did nothing with them; he simply reveled in their pureness and power.

And he was powerful, Gideon realized. At least as powerful as Railen or Sheymi. But with only two Gifts—neither of them Spirit—he wasn't a Dymas. He was *Dalae*.

There was no way of knowing short of asking, but Gideon suspected the Gwuler of thirty years ago had reached a point in his life when he'd considered the absence of the other five Gifts a limitation. Like so many of those who became Agla'Con, he may have allowed his lust for power to blind him to what he enjoyed. *Like I did*, he thought. *Thank the Creator for second chances.*

Gwuler held the Power for a moment longer before releasing it. When he looked back to Jase, his eyes were wet with tears.

Gideon wasn't surprised by the show of emotion, though it was the first time in his life that he'd seen a Shizu cry.

"Welcome back," Jase said as he offered Gwuler his hand. As he did so, the whisperings tickling his Awareness suddenly stilled, confirming that he had done the right thing. Strange that only a few moments before he'd seriously contemplated killing this man. Without the Earthsoul's influence he would have. He would have burned him from existence without a second thought.

"Thank you, *Mith'elre Chon*," Gwuler said, his grip like steel as he accepted Jase's hand. "I'd lost hope that redemption was possible for me."

"It's what Maeon would have us believe," Gideon told him, and Jase glanced over to find a mix of emotions on his father's face. Undoubtedly, this encounter had painfully and pointedly reminded him of his own fall and redemption.

"But there is always hope," Gideon continued. "Hope for redemption from evil.

Hope for victory over our enemies. Hope for the Rejuvenation of the Earthsoul. To believe otherwise is to concede the battle without loosing an arrow."

"Well spoken," Shavis said as he moved forward to look Gwuler in the eyes. "And we have many arrows yet to loose. Especially now that Shozen Hom has arrived with important information regarding who is leading the Arkanian army."

Jase nodded. "Yes. What did you mean when you said 'it is the other way around?'"

"The village priests aren't calling demons through *droth'del*," Gwuler said. "Power-wielding demons are. They've killed or taken control of the Agla'Con who freed them."

"Taken control of?" Elliott asked. "How?"

"*Del'ah broma*," Talia said, and a rush of revulsion reached Jase through the love-bond.

"*Shar'tei broma*," Gwuler corrected. "And it serves a completely different purpose than its sister drug. The Arkanian priestesses made Brysia drink *del'ah broma* because it robs a Power-wielder of their abilities. It also has a stupefying effect, stripping the victim of free will even as it opens her mind to visions of Con'Jithar. What's more, it intensifies a demon's bloodlust and incites the desire to feed."

"Like soaking a lamb in blood and turning it loose in a lion's den," Talia said. "That's the way you said it in Arkania."

"You have a good memory," Gwuler said, sounding as if he wished it were otherwise. Likely his description to Talia then had been more to terrorize than to inform.

"The purpose of *shar'tei broma*," he said, "is to instill a demon-like bloodlust into those who drink it. Not only does it increase strength and stamina, it removes the awareness of pain. It does rob a person of freewill like *del'ah broma*, but it doesn't negate a Power-wielder's ability to wield. It enhances it by giving the demons control of the wielder's Awareness. It's Thought Intrusion and Coercion combined. Demons with the ability to wield *Lo'shaen* are in charge of the Arkanian army, my friends. Not the foolish priests who loosed them."

"How many of these particular demons are we talking about?" Shavis asked and Gwuler shook his head.

"I don't know," he answered. "Enough to control an army of Arkanians tens of thousands strong."

"The Arkanians won't be a problem once we eliminate their demon masters," Gideon said. "They have neither the skill nor the armor to stand against Shizu or Sarui."

"I agree," Jase said. "Our first priority should be the destruction of those demons who have control over the Arkanian Power-wielders."

"It would be wise to destroy the *droth'del* as well," Gwuler added. "As long as they remain, more demons can be summoned."

Jase looked at Shavis. "This is a job for *tres'dia*," he said. "As soon as they are assembled, I will teach them the wieldings they will need to counter *Lo'shaen* and defeat the demons. And then I will join them on their hunt."

Shavis turned to the young Dymas who'd been warding the command post when Jase arrived. "Send word," he told her. "I want every available Dymas on this."

"Yes, Dai'shozen," she said, and Jase felt her extend her Awareness. She would contact one or two Dymas who would then contact others. It would only take a few minutes, he knew, and every member of the Deathsquad of the Gifted would know about the upcoming mission.

Gideon stepped near. "Are you sure about this?" he whispered. "Going into battle here instead of in Kelsa isn't exactly what any of us had in mind."

"It's all the same war," Jase told him. "And right now, this is where the Earthsoul would have me be."

# CHAPTER 44

## *The Western Rim*

"WHERE IS THE *MITH'ELRE CHON?*" Joneam asked.

It was the fifth time in as many minutes, and the level of frustration in the general's voice had risen with each asking. And each time, he'd leaned that much closer to the window Idoman had opened in the sky west of the rampway's ruins. If he leaned any more, he was likely to slice his nose off on one of the tiny Veilgate's shimmering edges. Idoman was tempted to let him, if for no other reason than that it would give the general something new to complain about.

He eyed Joneam a moment longer, then returned his attention to the window.

A mere two feet wide, it looked down on the enemy at an angle and was high enough that he and Joneam could see the top of the plateau and what lay beneath it. The small window-gate would be invisible to all but the keenest eyes or probing Awareness.

Add the fact that he and Joneam and the six Dymas who'd come with them stood on the causeway several miles inside the Bottomlands, and there wasn't much chance they would be discovered.

The stillness cloaking the Bottomlands was broken a moment later by Joneam. Leaning even closer to the window, he grunted his displeasure at the *Mith'elre Chon's* absence and muttered another, "Where is he?"

Idoman shared some of Joneam's frustration, but he knew better than to question Jase's actions. At least not out loud. Joneam, however, had no such reservations.

"He needs to be here for this," he muttered. "Our men need to know he will stand with them."

Sensing its master's agitation, Joneam's horse stomped its feet a couple of times and tossed its head, snorting. Joneam's eyes never left the dark wall of bodies massing at the edge of the western rim as he unconsciously reached up and rubbed the animal's neck to soothe it.

*If only it were that easy to calm a general,* Idoman thought, then smiled, inwardly amused by the image the thought conjured up.

"Most of our men will never see this stage of the battle," Idoman told him. "Even those who do won't know who the wielder is. It could be me or Quintella or any number of Dymas from our striketeams."

"The Dymas will know," Joneam said. "And word will spread that Jase wasn't here."

"Jase goes where he is needed most," he insisted. "We just have to trust him."

Joneam's face pinched into an even deeper frown as he met Idoman's stare. "What could be more important than helping us slow Shadan's descent from the plateau?"

Idoman shrugged. "Oh, I don't know," he said. "Finding a Blood Orb, perhaps." His tone was more flippant than he intended, but Joneam's lack of faith in Jase was starting to wear on his patience.

Joneam stiffened, obviously offended by the remark, but he quickly got control of his emotions and nodded. "Wouldn't that be nice."

Idoman studied his friend a moment before speaking. "You sound as if you don't think it will happen."

"I don't know what to think anymore," Joneam said. He fell into a brooding silence as he watched the foremost troops of Death's Third March begin their descent.

Idoman sighed, then returned his attention to the plateau. With the rampway destroyed, the soldiers of Death's Third March had no choice but to use the steep, narrow trails carved into the cliff face. Not only did it string them out into single-file lines, leaving them exposed and vulnerable, it drastically slowed their march as they were forced to carefully pick their footing. For once, the enemy was having a difficult time of it. And they were playing right into his hands.

Aware of the compromising position Shadan's troops were in, several dozen K'rresh took flight, and *Ta'shaen* resonated with corrupted wieldings as the Agla'Con atop the beasts channeled shields and held them in front of those making their way down the trails. At the base of the cliffs, the Earthsoul reeled in pain as more than twenty rents were opened in the Veil and *Jeth'Jalda* streamed through from beyond. Fists blazing with corrupted Earthpower, they set up a perimeter at the base of the trails, some holding shields, some probing the area for the Dymas they had expected to find. A handful of the strongest Power-wielders held the rents open and were ushering large numbers of troops through.

"I told you they would come through Veilgates," Joneam grumbled.

"Yes you did," Idoman said. "And I said it wouldn't matter since none of our men are within striking distance." He grinned. "Let the *Jeth'Jalda* waste their strength moving troops off the plateau. Their need to recover later will slow Death's Third

March as surely as the loss of the rampway will."

"And your plan for those descending the trails?" Joneam asked.

"Nothing has changed," Idoman assured him. "I'm just waiting until those trails are filled. It will lessen the number of strikes we will need to make, and it will maximize casualties."

Joneam grunted, then raised a spyglass to get a better look at those descending the cliff face. He didn't speak for several minutes.

"Most of those making the descent are Darklings and other shadowspawn," he said at last. "Apparently, the bulk of the Meleki and Tamban forces are afraid of heights."

"Or they are waiting to see what our next move is," Idoman said. "We'll give those on the trails another half hour and then we will show them."

Joneam grunted. "Great, maybe by then the *Mith'elre Chon* will have decided to join us."

Perched on a large outcropping of rock on the northern slopes of the Kelsan mountain range, Quintella Zakeya watched through a small Power-wrought window as Shadan's troops continued their precarious descent down the western cliff face of Talin Plateau. Her window in the sky was directly south of the main part of the Dreadlord's army, and she thought she could see Shadan near the center. He looked no different than any other Greyling, but the large shadowspawned creature he rode was so different from the mounts his K'rrosha used that it gave him away. For a moment, she was tempted to open a Veilgate to see if she could burn him from existence with a spear of *El'shaen*.

"There are a lot of Agla'Con warding the trails," Fremia Dymas said, interrupting Quintella's thoughts. She glanced over to find the young woman watching the K'rresh that were hovering in front of the cliffs. The nervousness in her voice became even more obvious as she added, "And there are even more *Jeth'Jalda* taking up positions below."

Quintella placed a hand on the young woman's shoulder, and Fremia's beaded braids clicked softly as she turned to look at her. "Not to worry," Quintella told her. "Idoman's plan will work."

"Is that part of the plan?" Captain Dennison asked, pointing to the area just east of Death's Third March.

Quintella had to lean around her Power-wrought window to see what he was pointing it, and when she did, she found small wedges of black spreading outward from several dozen points in the midst of the trampled grasslands. Curious more than alarmed, she let her window slide closed, then immediately opened another in the air above the new arrivals. A rush of excitement swept through her as her eyes lighted on the banners of the Crescent Moon and the silver breastplates of Kamoth's Crescent

Guard.

"It's the Meleki army," she said. "Lord Nid made good on his promise."

As she watched, more Veilgates opened, and hundreds, then thousands, of Meleki troops rushed through to form ranks. By the time the final Veilgate closed behind them a few minutes later, Quintella estimated that some thirty thousand soldiers now stood behind Death's Third March.

Almost as one, the rear of Shadan's army turned to face the new arrivals, and *Ta'shaen* came alive with corrupted wieldings as Agla'Con and K'rrosha prepared to defend themselves. The Meleki army, however, had arrived out of range of all but the most powerful of Shadan's minions, and Quintella knew from the stirrings of Power resonating among Lord Nid's men that they were capable of deflecting anything which might be hurled their way.

"They're a little outnumbered, don't you think?" Captain Dennison said, his face lined with concern as he watched the new arrivals.

"That depends on what they decide to do," Quintella told him. "If they attack, yes. Shadan can move soldiers from the north and south once they are engaged to try to flank or even surround them. If Lord Nid waits for the enemy to come to him, he has room to maneuver."

Fremia Dymas nodded. "If he waits for most of the enemy to make their descent," she said, her eyes thoughtful, "he can press whoever remains behind and kill them before they make their escape."

"This is good timing for us," Quintella said, letting the window close. "We should use it to our advantage." Redirecting the Power, she opened a window into the Bottomlands to speak with Idoman.

He smiled at her as he moved up to the window. "I take it you saw the new arrivals?"

"Yes," she answered. "I believe the time has come to make our move."

"So do I," he told her. "Let's contact the others." Turning, he opened a window, and Mishi Dymas' face came into view through the shimmering opening. She and her team stood on the shore of Mirror Lake, and Mount Augg was visible behind them.

Mishi in turn opened a window on her left, directly in line with those Idoman and Quintella had opened, and Yaeger Dymas came into view. He stood atop the battlements of Fulrath's inner wall and behind him the towers of the fortress proper stood like sentinels over the silent city. Yaeger then contacted Wensin Dymas who opened a window to Carlis Dymas and so on until all ten striketeams were linked by Power-wrought windows.

Quintella marveled at the end result. Ten groups of Dymas separated by hundreds of miles essentially stood side by side as they prepared to attack the same target.

"You all know what to do," Idoman told them. "On my signal, hit them with everything you have." He raised his hand, and Quintella drew in as much of the Power as she could hold. She felt the other Dymas do the same and a rush of excitement filled her at what would follow.

"Now," Idoman shouted, bringing his arm down sharply.

Quintella let the window slide closed and immediately opened a much larger Veilgate in front of her and her striketeam. The Power-wrought hole sliced through the wing of a K'rresh, and the creature plummeted from view, taking its rider with it. The man's screams faded away as he dropped out of sight.

A split second later a second K'rresh passed in front of her Veilgate, tumbling earthward in a leathery-winged blur. It had been sliced nearly in two and unlike the first, it was riderless.

Quintella smiled. Idoman had been right—the Agla'Con were expending so much energy on the shields they were holding in front of those making their way down the trails that their own shields had been compromised. The Veilgates had sliced through them as if they'd been made of glass.

Another K'rresh appeared to the right of her Veilgate, sailing toward her on stiff wings. Its Agla'Con master sat high in the saddle, corruption blazing in his fist. The strength of the shield he held around him and his mount told Quintella the man had withdrawn his protection of the troops on the cliff face. It was an act of selfish preservation typical of these black-hearted vermin, and it would do nothing to change the end result of this fight.

"Kill him," Quintella said, and Julis Dymas opened a small horizontal window in front of her.

The other side of that small window opened inside the Agla'Con's shield, directly in front of his chest, and the razor-like opening sliced the man's heart in two as the forward momentum of his K'rresh carried him into it. The red glow of his talisman winked out, and his shield vanished. A moment later, he toppled backward out of the saddle and dropped from view.

Julis let the window close, then raised her hands and sent a tight spiral of Flesh and Fire spinning through Quintella's Veilgate. The thrust of Power struck the K'rresh in the head, and fur and bone and brains burst outward like a grotesque firework. The creature folded and went down, leaving Quintella with a clear view of the cliff face. It was less than thirty yards away—and it was now completely defenseless.

Reaching deeper into the Power, she enlarged her Veilgate to give the Dymas in her striketeam a wider angle. "Tear them up," she said, and watched with a feeling of righteous anger as the cleansing light of El'shaen te sherah streaked into the enemy's midst.

Opening such a large Veilgate at such a height did two things for Idoman: It filled him with a triumphant sense of absolute power over his enemies even as it weakened his knees with feelings of vertigo. Peering through a tiny Power-wrought window was one thing—standing on the edge of something he could easily fall through was something else altogether. He tapped his foot on the hard-packed dirt of the causeway to reassure himself that he was still on solid ground.

The rest of the Dymas in his striketeam, however, weren't bothered by the strange Power-wrought precipice and moved right up to the edge to strike down two K'rresh riding the winds a short distance beyond. Idoman took a step to the left to make way for them. He told himself it was so his team could get a better look at the enemy and not because he was afraid of the long drop.

Still, being able to look around the edge of the gate and see the causeway stretching away to the east lessened the sense of vertigo.

Feeling steady now, he fastened his attention on the thousands of Darklings painstakingly winding their way down the steep trails a short distance beyond where the last of the K'rresh and their Agla'Con riders had just been obliterated by striketeams from the other Veilgates. The Light-blasted creatures stared in stupefied surprise at the men and women standing, as it were, in the air before them. Surprise turned to horror an instant later when streamers of *El'shaen* spiraled through the opening and into their midst.

Armor and flesh were incinerated in bursts of heat. Rock exploded into hailstorms of grit and clouds of dust as the cliff face burst outward, pelting Darklings with killing fragments and hurling them from the trail. Directly across from him, an entire section of the zigzagging trail broke loose in a titanic *crack*, and an avalanche of stone thundered downward, crushing those beneath and scouring the cliff face free of their filth.

Corrupted lightning crackled upward from the *Jeth'Jalda* on the valley floor, but it did little more than heat the air in front of his Veilgate as they passed by. The *Jeth'Jalda* simply didn't have an angle on him or the others. Even so, he wouldn't risk one of them getting lucky, so he ordered Havishim Dymas to ward the bottom edge of the gate.

No sooner had the aging Dymas gotten the shield into place than it was struck by a sizzling bolt of red. The view through the gate was momentarily obscured by the flash, and a booming crack of thunder reverberated up the cliffs, dislodging rocks and gravel and even a few Darklings. Howling in terror, they flailed uselessly with their arms as they fell to their deaths. Idoman smiled as he watched them pass out of sight.

This was going even better than he'd imagined, but it wouldn't be long before the Agla'Con atop the plateau took action to try to stop it. In the meantime...

"Hit them again," he said, reveling in the moment.

"I told you they would attack," Aethon growled.

He wasn't looking at Shadan as he spoke, but every Agla'Con within earshot knew his words were directed at the Dreadlord. Shifting nervously, they cast worried looks in that direction. Shadan, however, seemed not to have heard. His attention was firmly fixed on the Meleki army massing behind them. They'd arrived through Veilgates moments earlier, but they were nowhere near large enough to mount an attack. Likely they would employ hit and run tactics through Veilgates. No matter. Whatever Lord Nid had in mind, it wouldn't end well for him or his men. The real threat—the most immediate threat—involved Kelsa's attack on those descending the Plateau.

Shooting an irritated look at Shadan, Aethon ripped a hole in the Veil and heeled his horse through to the edge of the plateau. What he found surprised him, and he didn't like being surprised.

Several hundred feet below, ten shimmering Veilgates stood suspended in the air like the windows and balconies of some invisible fortress. The Dymas standing within them were striking with impunity, killing those exposed on the cliffs before them.

The *Jeth'Jalda* who'd moved to the valley through Veilgates had launched a counterattack, but they were too far out of range to have any real effect, and their errant strikes were doing more harm than good.

Aethon turned to Asherim. "Tell those idiots to cease their attack," he ordered. Asherim nodded, then rent the Veil and moved to the valley below. The errant strikes ceased a moment later.

Giving himself over to the power of the Void, Aethon moved nearer the edge of the plateau and channeled Night Threads at the nearest of the Veilgates. Most stopped short in bursts of reddish black fire when they struck a Dymas' shield, but one of the sizzling spears of darkness made it through to the solid ground visible within the Power-wrought opening. Dirt and rock exploded upward in superheated sprays of death, tossing men and horses aside like toys. The Veilgate snapped shut in a flash of blue.

Along the edge of the rim, *Ta'shaen* came alive with dozens of corrupted wieldings as more Agla'Con joined the fight. Aethon left them to it. He'd shown them what to do, and there were more than enough of them to accomplish the task now that they were working together. He had more pressing matters to attend to.

Tearing another rent in the Veil, he moved back to where Shadan was still focused on the Meleki army. He could feel the intense scrutiny of the Dreadlord's Awareness as he surveyed the quickly growing mass of bodies, but Shadan didn't seem overly concerned by the sight. If anything, the tight smile on his grey-fleshed face hinted at amusement.

"An interesting move," he rasped, his good eye shining brightly. "Melek thinks to use the western rim against us now that Kelsa has destroyed the rampway and trails." He laughed, a gravelly sound that drew the eyes of every Agla'Con within earshot. "They should have brought a larger army."

"They just might," Aethon told him. He let the Veilgate hiss shut in a sputtering of angry sparks, and Shadan turned to regard him in irritation.

"But even what they have is sufficient to cause us trouble," he continued, meeting Shadan's one-eyed stare without blinking. "Without the rampway or trails, we are going to have to rely on Veilgates to move our troops off the plateau. I don't know if our Power-wielders have strength enough for that *and* for defending against whatever Melek has planned."

"You assume I don't have a plan of my own," Shadan sneered. "I've know for days that Lord Nid would be coming. Those I left behind in Melek have been keeping a close eye on things there." He looked back to the army massing in the distance. "This isn't all of Lord Nid's army. More will be arriving shortly."

"Then we really will have a problem descending the plateau," Aethon growled. "This is another fine mess you've gotten us into."

Shadan chuckled. "Where is your faith, Fairimor? I am the Destroyer of Amnidia. What comes next has been part of the plan all along." Turning his K'sivik about, he urged it toward the rim of the plateau.

Aethon scowled suspiciously at the Dreadlord's back as he rode away, then heeled his horse forward and hurried to catch up.

"Shadan is on the move," Idoman said, then stepped back from his Power-wrought window so Joneam could have a look for himself.

As Joneam moved to the window and peered through, Idoman let his eyes move over the members of his striketeam. He'd nearly lost some of them when a Night Thread channeled by Aethon Fairimor had exploded in their midst, and he knew it was a miracle the damage hadn't been worse.

The scorch mark across the front of Keilin Dymas *kitara*-style jacket showed how close he'd come to dying. Meishi and Ellin Dymas were equally lucky to be alive. Both had suffered broken legs and burns so severe the flesh of their calves and feet had been charred black.

Only the collapse of the gate and Haeli Dymas' skill as a healer had saved the three Dymas. Meishi and Ellin were shoeless now, and they'd cut their skirts off below the knees and discarded the burned remnants. Neither they nor Keilin would be fighting again today—their injuries and subsequent healings had left them drained of strength.

Idoman smiled at each of them, then turned his attention back to Joneam.

"What do you think?" he asked. He still had a ringing in his ears, and his shoulder ached from striking the ground after being tossed head over foot by the Night Thread, but they weren't anything that needed a Healer's touch. At least not right now. He wanted to make sure Haeli had strength enough to heal others if she was needed elsewhere.

Joneam pursed his lips tightly as he considered. He was leaning so close to the window shimmering in front of his face that Idoman was once again worried he'd injure himself on it. Finally, he stepped back and met Idoman's gaze.

"I think we're done here," he said. "No sense risking another attack on whatever trails *might* remain intact. As it stands now, Throy bloody Shadan is going to have a devil of a time getting his army off the plateau. We may have delayed them by several days."

"I agree," Idoman said. "And I think we can delay them further if we were to send men and Dymas to assist Lord Nid's army in pressing the enemy from the rear."

A Veilgate opened along the edge of the causeway and Quintella Zakeya moved through with her striketeam. All were present, but Idoman saw by the state of their clothing and the tired looks on some of their faces that they'd fared about as well as his striketeam during Aethon's counterattack.

"The Dreadlord is preparing to use the Power," Quintella said as she neared. "He's formed a mindlink with nearly every Agla'Con on the plateau and has taken control of their Jexlair crystals."

Alarmed, Idoman turned to the window he'd opened above the plateau and peered through at the scene beneath. Shadan had stopped about a half mile from the edge of the rim, and the soldiers and Darklings who'd been massing in front of him were hurriedly moving to the north and south to open the way for their refleshed leader. The end of Shadan's scepter burned a brilliant red, and it continued to increase in brightness as more and more Agla'Con talismans flared to life and joined the link.

Idoman let the window close but immediately opened another above the *Jeth'Jalda* in the shadows beneath the plateau. They had halted the use of Veilgates, and they and those they'd brought from the plateau were hurrying away from the cliff face. With a quick thrust of his Awareness, he found that they had also given themselves over to Shadan.

He felt the brush of a tremendously powerful Awareness and recoiled as if he'd been struck, fear and revulsion rushing through him in turns. The Awareness—Shadan's Awareness—pursued him as he pulled back, and he hurriedly released *Ta'shaen*. The window closed without incident, but Idoman found little comfort in his escape.

He'd seen what was coming. He'd glimpsed it firsthand when his mind had touched Shadan's and the Dreadlord tried to seize control of his Awareness, thinking perhaps, that he was just another Agla'Con.

"Idoman, what's wrong?"

It was Quintella's voice, and he looked over to find her watching him with concern.

"Shadan—"

He choked on the dead man's name, horrified at what was soon to come. He had to force himself to continue. "He's going to collapse the western rim."

Quintella stared at Idoman in disbelief. Collapse the rim? How was such a thing possible? She shook her head. It wasn't. Even with the aid of hundreds of Agla'Con and *Jeth'Jalda*, Throy Shadan was nowhere near strong enough to collapse so much stone. Carve out a few trails, maybe. But nothing which would be of any use to his troops. Idoman must have misunderstood what he had glimpsed of the Dreadlord's intent.

She was about to voice her opinion when a singularly powerful thrust of corruption jarred her Awareness. The entire spiritual fabric of the Earthsoul reeled in response to the wielding, and the luminescent world visible in her mind's eye dimmed as light was assaulted by darkness.

Atop the plateau, Shadan's scepter burned red with the powers of hell as he sent a spiral of *Lo'shaen* boring deep into the plateau. And yet it wasn't just *Lo'shaen*. Quintella sensed corrupted *Ta'shaen* as well—Fire and Earth and Spirit—all tightly woven together and bound with *Lo'shaen*. She went rigid in surprise—she hadn't known it was possible to wield both at the same time.

The view through her Awareness continued to dim as Shadan bored deeper into the plateau, cutting through layers of earth and rock as if slicing through living flesh. The tremors of pain resonating through the Earthsoul grew more intense, and cracks appeared in the cliff face where the rampway had been. The cracks turned to fissures, and the plateau shook as those fissures split the cliff face from rim to base. Crumbling rock fell in stony cascades and plumes of dust.

A sudden release of corrupted Power followed a moment later, and the base of the cliffs exploded outward in a titanic burst of shattered stone a half a mile wide and several hundred feet high. The once solid bedrock, now a roaring, grinding tidal wave of destruction, swallowed the ruins of the collapsed rampway and the abandoned waypost as if they'd never been.

The massive explosion left behind a cavern that stretched deep into the plateau, weakening the stone above. Shadan channeled again, and again a sudden release of corruption followed. A thousand feet of stone broke loose, crashing down into the cavern below it and sloughing forward in clouds of dust and grit.

Another burst of released energy followed almost immediately, and the upper third of the plateau's cliffs broke free, crumbling into ruin and spilling across the mountainous piles of rubble beneath. The area was lost in billowing clouds of dust, but Quintella didn't dare extend her Awareness for a look at what lay within. Shadan still had control of the Agla'Con and *Jeth'Jalda*, and she didn't want to risk touching his or anyone else's Awareness with her mind.

The billowing clouds of dust turned red as corrupted Fire lit them from within, but a sudden rush of Power-wrought wind swept them away to reveal a maelstrom of Fire hot enough to melt stone. Channeled by the armies of Agla'Con and *Jeth'Jalda* and guided by Shadan, the storm of corrupted Fire carved a wide, winding path down the center of the newly formed slope.

As smooth as any paved street from any of the world's great cities, it stretched from the feet of Shadan down through the artificial canyon he'd created and along the top of the slope until it reached the grasslands below.

His task complete, Shadan released the Agla'Con and *Jeth'Jalda* from the mindlink, and *Ta'shaen* began to quiet as they released the Power. Scepter still glowing with the terrible mix of power he'd been wielding, Shadan started down the newly wrought roadway. His army filed in behind him, cheering loudly and waving their weapons in the air. The Dreadlord had just shaved days off his march to Trian.

Quintella couldn't believe what she'd just witnessed. "How?" was all she could muster.

"Crux points," Idoman answered. "I don't know when he put them there but..." He shook his head. "I guess it doesn't really matter now, does it? He's gained the Bottomlands. The best we can do now is try to hold Mendel Pass."

必

"That was a nice trick," Aethon said as he followed Shadan onto the roadway he'd wrought to the Bottomlands. "Why don't you start with that next time?" He hoped his tone made it clear to the Dreadlord that the statement wasn't a compliment. "Do you have any other previously wrought crux points you would like to tell me about?"

Shadan laughed—or at least gave what passed for a laugh considering his damaged throat. As always, it sounded more like a wheezing cough. "And take all the mystery out of our march to Trian?" he asked. He looked over, his good eye flaring brightly. "No. But I will tell you when I wrought those used to carve out this magnificent roadway."

He gestured to the walls of stone rising to the north and south. "I put them here shortly after my first refleshing," he rasped. "I had intended to use them during our march twenty years ago, but the events which transpired on the day of the Battle of Greendom made it a moot point."

"You mean the event where you went to the Soul Chamber and were destroyed by Gideon?" He intended the comment as a jab, but Shadan grunted with amusement.

"Simply another fulfillment of prophecy," he said. "There couldn't very well be a Death's Third March unless the second march failed, now could there?"

Aethon scowled at the Dreadlord for a moment, then decided to change the subject. Instead of needling Shadan, he should be thanking him for speeding their march. He wouldn't, of course. His hatred of the refleshed idiot outweighed his gratitude. Now and always.

"We need to address the Meleki army moving in behind us," he said. "They *will* attack. Probably once the rear of our army is bottled up in here."

"I'm more concerned with the part of the Meleki army that hasn't arrived yet," Shadan said, his tone contemplative. "The one on the plateau is nothing more than a token force. The real threat is yet to arrive."

"And you think Lord Nid commands that one," Aethon asked.

"I'm sure of it," Shadan answered. He looked over at Aethon, and his eye narrowed to a slit. "But it isn't like Nid to separate his forces. He's planning something. I just don't know what it is."

Aethon opened his Awareness and extended it back toward the Meleki army, letting the sea of bodies come into view in his mind's eye. They had picked up their pace and were forming into columns in preparation of attacking the rear of Death's Third March. But they were far too small to do any real damage.

Shadan was right. This was a token show of force only. A feint.

*What are you up to?* He thought, then frowned as he tried to picture where Lord Nid might be.

# CHAPTER 45

## Arkanian Frenzy

THE ARMORED DEMON COLLAPSED in a lifeless heap, and the smoldering hole Doroku Atasei had burned through its chest plate left a trail of smoke as it fell.

He watched the fiery light in the creature's eyes wink out, then released *Ta'shaen* and drew his sword to meet the Arkanians rushing in on the demon's heels. He wouldn't waste his strength killing them with the Power. Not when his blade would do.

*Koro* mask in place, he spun into their midst, fluid, methodical, and deadly as he turned aside each clumsy attempt to reach him with sword or spear. Stroke after stroke, his blade found its mark, and fat, glistening drops of crimson fell like rain around him.

He was Shizu, and this frenzied riffraff had the sword skills of a goat. And they were frenzied, perhaps even possessed. He could see it in their eyes. The glimmer of humanity once present there had been stripped away. By the demons, certainly. But he suspected there was something else at work here. Something that had instilled a demon-like madness upon these people. And with it a demon-like strength.

For even as his blade continued to spill their blood, opening wounds that should have killed them or sent them staggering away in agony, they fought on, ignorant of the pain, refusing to die. Only when he began removing their heads did they fall. Even then, some continued to thrash about for much longer than was normal for a dead man. If he didn't already know better, he would have sworn he was doing battle with Greylings.

"What's gotten into them?" Honto Bishi yelled, his voice strained with the effort of battle.

Doroku glanced at Honto as the Shizu strikecaptain of Lief Posai sliced his opponent's head from his shoulders. A short sword gripped in each hand, the

Arkanian corpse staggered away, arms flailing blindly about. It ran into another fatally wounded Arkanian, and the two went down in a twitching heap.

"I don't know," Doroku answered, then embraced the Power and struck the five remaining Arkanians with a fist of Air so powerful it launched the five men head over heel back the way they'd come. They landed fifty paces away, their bodies so badly broken that even their demonic strength couldn't help them.

"Do that sooner next time," Honto said, moving to stand beside him. The rest of Honto's striketeam formed up around them, and Doroku could see by the look in their eyes that they shared the sentiment.

"I would if I didn't need to conserve my strength for demons," Doroku told him.

Honto's eyes narrowed inside the slit of his mask. "Then why this time?"

Doroku shrugged. "My arms were getting tired."

He sheathed his sword and bid Honto and his men to do the same. Across the now trampled rice fields, the rest of his small army stilled. For the second time in as many hours, they'd destroyed an enemy twice their size. But they'd lost a number of men doing it, both Shizu and Sarui, and had given up nearly a half mile more of Riaki territory.

It was the demons that had forced them into a fighting retreat. Without their help, his army would have held the Arkanian forces at the border. The same was happening elsewhere, he knew. Shozen Hakala and his army had lost ground to the east. Shozen Kyotei to the west. He hadn't heard from Shozens Jisho or Kamishi—their Dymas had failed to check in at the scheduled time. That meant they were either dead or still engaged with the enemy.

"What now, Shozen?" Honto asked.

Doroku scanned the sky. "We wait," he answered. "Our scouts should be visible any moment."

A few minutes passed in silence, then a nearby Shizu pointed to the southwest. "There."

Doroku followed the angle of the man's arm and spotted a pair of Myrscraw soaring high above the wall of green that was the Arkanian Jungle. Both birds weren't much more than specks against the vast blue of the sky, but there was no mistaking what they were. Nothing else moved like that. Nothing else had the speed.

As he watched, they quickly became recognizable as birds, but their altitude concealed their true nature and size. Anyone not Shizu or Sarui would have dismissed them as a pair of songbirds. When they were directly above him and Honto's men, they folded into a dive, two arrowhead-shaped wedges of black knifing earthward. Within a matter of seconds, the illusion of diminutive songbirds morphed into the reality of powerful, battle-tested creatures twice the size of a horse.

Just shy of the ground, both Myrscraw opened their wings to stop their dive, and the sky was momentarily darkened as they landed gently in front of Doroku.

Both Myrscraw bellied down to allow their Shizu riders to dismount, and Doroku stepped forward as they did. The two female Dymas stayed mounted, but bowed their heads in greeting as he approached. Doroku nodded in return then looked back to the Shizu.

"What did you discover?" he asked, and they shook their heads in disgust.

"Nothing good," one of the men answered. He wore the mark of Avalam and had a white scar running from ear to chin on the right side of his face. "An army of Arkanians six or seven thousand strong is five miles to the south and west of here. Another army of similar size has already crossed the border eight miles to the east. Shozen Rasokei is moving to intercept them, but he will be outnumbered when he does."

Doroku nodded. "How many demons are with them?"

"Five or six hundred," the Shizu replied. "Most are the lesser demons which wear armor." He glanced at the Darkling-like creatures Doroku had killed just minutes earlier. "The rest are monstrous."

"There are twenty or thirty," the other rider added, "who can wield *Lo'shaen*."

Doroku frowned. "Are you sure it was *Lo'shaen*?"

The man nodded. "Keishel Dymas confirmed it," he said, gesturing at the Dymas who'd accompanied him on his flight. "She also said the demons were using the Power on the Arkanians. Urging them on. Controlling them."

"That explains what we've seen here," Doroku said. "The Arkanians have been fighting like they are possessed."

"There's more to report," the Shizu from Avalam said. "We spoke with scouts sent out by Dai'shozen Dakshar. He has retaken Maisen, but the country to the east of there is being overrun. Dozens of smaller villages and countless farms are in imminent danger."

"How big is the enemy force?"

"Several thousand Arkanians and at least two hundred demons, three of which can wield *Lo'shaen*."

"We're needed in Maisen," Doroku told them. "The other Dymas and I will open Veilgates for our troops. "You two fly to Shozen Rasokei and inform him of the change. When you are finished—"

He was interrupted by an unearthly howl from the south. It echoed across the rice fields like the rolling of thunder, startling the men and women of his army and drawing all eyes toward the sound.

A moment later and less than a hundred yards distant, a demon materialized as if stepping from thin air. Roughly man-shaped, it stood taller than a Dainin and was very heavily muscled. The thick leather armor it wore looked to be made of the skins of other demons and sported plates of black metal to guard its vitals. The heads of several Arkanian priests adorned the spikes jutting upward from the creature's shoulder plating.

It held a long staff tipped with a large chunk of what looked like obsidian and which glowed with an inner fire. Doroku knew if he reached out and touched the talisman with his Awareness he would feel the darkness of *Lo'shaen*. The glow within the talisman suddenly lessened and fifty or sixty lesser demons materialized behind their leader.

"What the hell?" one of Honto's Shizu whispered, and Doroku glanced at him briefly before looking back to the demons.

"Bended Light," he told the man. "The largest demon is wielding Lo'shaen. It stopped there because it knew if it came any closer our Dymas would have felt the wielding."

"That, or it has a flair for the dramatic," Honto said dryly. "Can the other demons wield the Power?"

"I don't think so," Doroku answered. "They were wrapped in bended Light wrought by the big one." He glanced across the battlefield and found his army of Shizu and Sarui forming into defensive ranks, spears and swords in front, archers in back. The Dymas stationed with each group were casting up shields of Spirit.

"Why are they just standing there?" Honto asked. "Do they expect us to rush them?"

The hair on the back of Doroku's neck prickled in alarm as the answer came to him. "They are a distraction." He opened his Awareness to search the rice fields to the east. A quarter of a mile away, he felt the dark tremors of Lo'shaen being wielded and encountered an Awareness that was as ancient as it was evil.

At the touch of his mind, the demon dropped its cloak of bended Light. It and those it commanded came instantly into view of Doroku and his army. The creature was identical to the one to the south and commanded a similar number of lesser demons. Their feral cries pierced the air when they realized they'd been discovered, and they started forward as one, weapons at the ready.

"There is another army to the west," Keishel Dymas said. "And judging by the tremors of corruption I feel, it's as large as the other two." She winced as if she'd been stabbed, then rubbed her temples as she shook her head. "That was an Awareness I never want to encounter again."

As she spoke, the demon she'd come in contact with let its ward drop, and the army it commanded materialized. Like the one to the east, they broke into a run when they realized they'd been discovered.

"They are hoping to flank us," Honto said.

"That," Keishel Dymas said, her eyes widening with fear, "is the least of our worries."

Doroku followed her gaze to the north and found a fourth army of demons stepping from a cloak of bended Light a hundred paces away. How they had managed to get behind his army without being detected was a mystery for later. His first priority was to find a way to save his army from being destroyed.

"Get the Myrscraw in the air," he ordered, then looked at Honto. "And signal our men to engage the demons to the north. If we can cut our way through them, we will retreat into Nakasa Woods."

As the Myrscraw winged skyward wrapped in sheltering bubbles of Spirit, Doroku opened himself to the Power. He wove the strands necessary for *Sei'shiin*, then sent a dozen white-hot bars lancing toward the demon ranks.

They exploded well short of their intended targets as streamers of *Lo'shaen* from the demon master's scepter intercepted them, snuffing them in bursts of red and black fire. The glow emanating from the obsidian-like crystal on the end of the creature's staff intensified, and Night Threads crackled overhead, hammering the shields of the Dymas and driving many of them to their knees. Terrible, scream-like thunder rolled across the battlefield, and though there had been no casualties, Doroku knew it was only a matter of time.

He glanced at Honto and knew he was thinking the same thing. He could see it in the man's eyes.

"Should we fail to meet again at the end of this battle," Honto said, "it has been an honor, Shozen Atasei." He drew his sword and brought the blade up in front of his face in salute.

Doroku drew his sword and returned the salute, then motioned for his army to advance. "For Riak!" he shouted, urging the words along with tendrils of Air. "And for the Earthsoul."

A second barrage of Night Threads hammered his shield as his army advanced, but he and the other Dymas held firm. For now. That was sure to change once the other demon masters and their armies joined the fight. The only chance for surviving this—and it was a slim chance at best—would be to kill this nearest demon master and scatter his troops before the other three armies closed the gap.

Fixing the creature in his mind's eye, Doroku continued his advance, opening himself more fully to the Power and drawing in a literal river of Fire and Light. When he was ready, he channeled a thick, white-hot bar of *Sei'shiin* and sent it lancing at the creature.

The demon's scepter flared brightly, and the air around it darkened with the power of hell, a visible aura of darkness spider-webbed with red. It intercepted the killing spear of cleansing destruction, and Doroku watched in disbelief as his wielding was snuffed like a candle.

The aura surrounding the creature darkened further, and a fist of darkness slammed Doroku's Awareness, driving him to his knees and causing his link to *Ta'shaen* to waver. His shield wavered as well, and a Night Thread crackled into the midst of Honto's striketeam, hurling *komouri*-clad bodies into the air like rag dolls.

The dark explosion and instantaneous crack of thunder overwhelmed Doroku's senses, and the world vanished behind a haze of shadow and flickering points of light. The only distinguishable sound was a high-pitched ringing so intense he thought his head might burst.

In desperation, he wrapped himself in *Jiu* and opened his Awareness to view the battle through the eyes of *Ta'shaen*. Dark streamers of *Lo'shaen* marred the luminescent landscape in all directions as the demon continued to strike with violent precision, hurling Night Threads and spiraling stabs of counterfeit Flesh and Fire.

Dozens of Riaki lay dead, including a number of his fellow Dymas.

To his right, Honto was pushing himself to his feet, but the back of his *komouri* uniform was burned clear through. His exposed skin was blistered from shoulder to waist. He seemed disoriented and was weak on his feet as he staggered forward. Clearly, he was unaware of the host of armored demons rushing toward him with swords drawn.

Focusing on *Ta'shaen* once more, Doroku channeled blades of Fire and Flesh, and the nearest of the Darkling-like monsters blew apart in smoking chunks of rent flesh and sizzling gore. His attack was violent and largely uncontrolled, but it did the job. Unfortunately, it also attracted the attention of the demon master.

The massive hellbeast redirected its flows of *Lo'shaen*, and Doroku's view of the radiant world darkened as snake-like currents streamed in from all sides. They struck his shield with the force of an avalanche, and pain lanced through his Awareness, a white-hot knife of agony that nearly severed his connection to the Power. His shield held, but the amount of *Ta'shaen* flowing through him lessened dramatically. Another strike like that and he would lose his hold completely.

A powerful tremor of purely wrought *Ta'shaen* rocked his Awareness, and the dark power assaulting him cut off as the demon redirected it toward this newest wielding. Fighting through the pain still lancing through his mind, Doroku extended his Awareness to the point of origin and found Gideon Dymas coming through a Veilgate on the heels of a younger Dymas.

The young man's hands blazed with Power more pure and powerful than anything Doroku had ever seen. Eyes shining with righteous fury, the young Dymas loosed that Power in a brilliant stream that burst the snaking tendrils of *Lo'shaen* into motes of dust then burned them from existence like sawdust cast into a furnace.

The stream of potent, silvery energy—Doroku realized it was *Ta'shaen* but woven together in a manner unlike any he'd ever seen—struck the dark aura shrouding the demon, and the creature cringed visibly beneath it. Eyes glowing red with demonic rage, it retreated further into its power, channeling so much *Lo'shaen* into its protective shield that it vanished from sight. For a moment Doroku wondered it if had retreated back into the realm of Con'Jithar.

The young Dymas advanced on the demon, and, like an auger, the Power he channeled bored into the creature's dark aura, stripping it away, burning ever nearer the monster within. Darkness gradually gave way to light, and the demon took shape once more. A heartbeat later, the flow of energy burned through the last of the void-like shield, and the creature vanished in a flash of silvery-blue light.

An explosive boom followed, and the release of energy sent a shockwave northward through the ranks of lesser demons, upending some, sending others staggering.

They recovered quickly, and howls of rage at the loss of their master filled the air as they charged forward, driven by vengeance, eager for blood. They'd only gone a few steps when the forward ranks blew apart in fountains of gore, and blood-soaked armor clattered noisily to the ground amid the ruined bodies.

Startled by the ferocity of the killing thrust—it was the singularly most powerful wielding of Flesh he'd ever felt—Doroku traced the wielding to its source with his Awareness and found that it had come from a Kelsan lass standing inside a protective bubble of Spirit with Gideon.

Gideon felt the brush of his mind and opened himself to it, forming a Communal link. *Stay there*, he said, turning and making eye contact. *We'll come to you.* The link vanished, and Doroku reined in his Awareness.

Taking the young lady by the arm, Gideon ushered her forward as other Dymas moved ahead to engage the rest of the advancing demons. As he neared, the shield of Spirit he held around him and the young lady expanded to take in Doroku and Honto and Honto's men. The sounds of battle faded to a dull and distant rumble.

The young woman knelt and took his head in her hands. Then, in one powerful channeling of Flesh, she healed him of his wounds. Her bright green eyes sparkled with satisfaction as she released the Power and lowered her hands.

"You are a master with your Gift," he told her. "At both ends of the spectrum." He glanced pointedly at the demons she had killed.

"This isn't Lady Chellum's first battle," Gideon said. He offered her his hand and helped her to her feet.

Doroku rose with her. "I can see that," he said. "I see also that you bear a strong resemblance to Elliott Chellum. Are you related?"

"He's my brother," Talia said. "And my apologies for whatever he may have done to you when he was in Riak." She glanced at Honto and the other wounded members of Deathsquad Taro. "If you will excuse me, I need to tend to these men."

Doroku watched as she moved to kneel next to Honto, then turned his attention back to the battle. The other demon masters had closed the distance between their armies and the men and women of Riak, but they had stalled when they were met by Dymas coming through Veilgates.

They were channeling *Ta'shaen* in the same manner as the young man who'd destroyed the first demon master, and their *Lo'shaen*-wielding targets had retreated into the protective darkness of Con'Jithar. Not that it would matter. They were outnumbered and surrounded, and the spiraling spears of pure, white-hot energy being directed at them were burning away the sheltering auras.

One by one, the spheres of darkness vanished, and the demons within exploded in bursts of silvery-blue light, leaving the lesser demons they commanded undefended.

"It's called *El'shaen te sherah* in the Old Tongue," Gideon said with a smile. "The Power and Light of the Creator. All Seven Gifts woven together and bound with Spirit. And as you can see, it has the ability to defeat the Void."

His eyes moved to the young man who'd come with him, and he smiled fondly. "Lord Fairimor rediscovered the wielding," he said. "We've been teaching it to every Dymas strong enough to do it. Railen Nogeru and Sheymi Oroshi came to Kelsa a few days ago to learn it and several other new wieldings, but they got caught up in a war with demons there. I'm sorry that they didn't return to teach it to you and your Dymas sooner. If they had, many lives could have been spared here today."

Doroku nodded but remained silent as he studied Lord Fairimor. With the demon masters destroyed, the young man had turned his attention to the lesser demons. *El'shaen* flowed through him in fiery currents of cleansing destruction as he cut the demons down without hesitation or mercy. The rest of the Dymas who'd come with him were doing likewise, and creatures that had seemed so formidable only moments earlier fell like stalks of rice beneath the reaper's sickle.

"You are here now," he said at last, then looked Gideon in the eyes. "This Lord Fairimor... he is the *Mith'elre Chon?*"

Gideon nodded. "He is. And he has come to help you save Riak from this invasion."

# CHAPTER 46

## *Closing Doors*

STANDING IN A STEEP, NARROW CANYON overlooking the K'zzaum Pit, Hulanekaefil Nid gazed down at the wind-whipped clouds of midnight-colored sands as they were driven to and fro by unnaturally hot winds. The storm of black grit was fierce enough to strip the flesh off a Shadowhound, but its true purpose wasn't for defense; it was for concealment, a swirling shroud to hide Shadan's Fortress nestled in the center of this godforsaken valley.

He'd stood in this exact spot a few short months earlier, though in truth, it felt more like years. Especially when he considered all that had transpired since he'd freed Gideon Dymas and they'd fled this awful place ahead of an army of K'rrosha. Back then, when he'd stood here with his sons and the others who'd come with him to attempt the impossible, his heart had been filled with fear and trepidation at all the things that could go wrong.

Now... now he was bursting with excitement—a vengeance-driven eagerness to deliver a blow that would cripple Shadan's ability to reflesh Agla'Con. *And it will avenge my sons*, he thought, the feelings of vengeance intensifying. They'd died in this hellhole so that he and Gideon could escape. He would honor their memory by cutting the heart out of the bloody fortress. He would send a message to Shadan that Melek belonged to the Meleki people.

He watched the driving sands a moment longer, then turned to his team of Dymas. They stood silently, their eyes on the swirling maelstrom below. Twenty in all, they were some of the most powerful wielders he'd ever met, and they came from nearly every major city in Melek. All had seen more than their fair share of fighting the past few weeks, but they had jumped at the chance to join him on this raid. They'd lost friends and family to the war and were driven by similar feelings of vengeance.

A narrow Veilgate opened a short distance away, and Captain Plat hurried through with a pair of Dymas at his heels. Vol's eyes were bright with excitement.

"Our troops are moving to engage the enemy," he announced. "We had to move sooner than expected. Shadan collapsed a stretch of the western rim to form a massive stone rampway. He is moving down it as we speak."

He glanced at one of the Dymas who joined the conversation. "The good news is most of their Power-wielders are spent. Shadan drained them during the collapse of the rim."

"Take word to General Tok," Hul told Vol. "Have him join you immediately. Hit Death's Third March with everything we've got."

"Yes, my lord," Vol said, then cast a wary eye at the K'zzaum Pit and its nightmarish sandstorm before looking back to Hul. "And be careful in there." With that, he and the two Dymas vanished through another narrow Veilgate.

Hul turned back to his team of Dymas. "It is time."

Embracing the Power, he wove the Seven Gifts of *Ta'shaen* into one and parted the Veil into Shadan's throne room. Then, hands blazing with the cleansing light of *El'shaen te sherah*, he and his team of Dymas stormed the Dreadlord's heart of darkness.

Seth kept close to Talia as she moved among the wounded of Doroku Atasei's army. Even here, surrounded by an army of Dymas and with Jase and Gideon only a few paces away, it was difficult for him to relax his warder instincts. In light of her ability to defend herself, it was foolish to be so paranoid about her safety, but old habits died hard. Besides, it was a pleasure watching her work.

The eyes of everyone in the immediate vicinity were on her, but if they were surprised to find a Kelsan Healer among them, it didn't show. Those she laid hands on, however—Shizu, Sarui, and Power-wielder alike—were awestruck at how easily and completely Talia healed them of their wounds.

*That's my girl*, he thought, smiling fondly. He was even more impressed by the lethality of her strike against the demons when they'd first arrived. At first he'd attributed the killing strike to Jase, but had changed his mind when he'd seen the look in her eyes as she'd watched the demons collapse into ruined heaps. It was the same look of satisfaction she wore now as she healed.

A blinding flash of lightning ripped through the last of the demons pressing Doroku's army from the south, and Seth looked toward it as thunder rolled across the rice fields in a deafening rumble. It was the fifth such strike in just the last minute, and like the four which had preceded it, it had been significantly sharper and stronger than the last, almost as if the wielder were trying to outdo himself.

He waited until the rumble subsided, then turned to Gideon. "Was that Elliott?"

Gideon shook his head. "No. That was Shozen Hom. But he's with Elliott, and they have been alternating strikes." He looked at Talia and shook his head. "Leave it to your brother to turn killing demons into a competition."

"It takes two to compete," Jase said. "And Shozen Hom wasn't shy about showing Elliott what he is capable of."

Seth's curiosity got the best of him. "So, who won?"

"Depends on what you judge them on," Jase said. "Elliott is definitely stronger, but Gwuler is focused and precise."

Seth watched as Elliott and Gwuler turned their backs on the carnage they had wrought and began making their way toward him and the others. They looked to be having a conversation, and he wished he could hear what was being said. Judging from Gwuler's posture, he was lecturing Elliott on the use of his Gifts.

"It never ceases to amaze me how quickly things can change," he said. "One minute the three of us are ready to kill Shozen Hom. The next minute he's tutoring Elliott."

Jase turned to study the two men, and a smile moved over his face. "Good. Maybe this time, he'll actually listen to the lesson." He turned as a Veilgate opened nearby and Shavis Dakshar came through with Yosei Shimura, the Dai'shozen of Clan Hasho. They were accompanied by a pair of female Dymas in green *kitara*.

Shavis spotted Jase and hurried forward as the Veilgate slid closed behind him. "The Dymas are ready, *Mith'elre Chon*," he said as he neared. "And moments ago, the armies of Gizo and Kyoai arrived from Sagaris. Railen and Sheymi ushered them through along with twenty-six more Dymas. They are in Maisen awaiting your orders."

"This is *your* army, Dai'shozen," Jase told him. "I'm here to support whatever you decide."

Seth thought Shavis looked relieved. He'd been willing to give Jase command of Riak's armies, but he was clearly pleased it hadn't come to that. He let his eyes move across the remains of the slain demons, and his eyes narrowed in thought as he considered. Finally, he nodded as if to himself and turned back to Jase.

"We've been going about this all wrong," he said. "We've spread our forces along the entire Riaki-Arkanian border in an attempt to stop this invasion. That may have worked in times past, when our enemy was a disorganized mob led by a handful of village priests, but the demons—especially those who can wield *Lo'shaen*—are game changers. We can't stand toe to toe with them in equal numbers—they're too strong. Too dangerous."

"I can attest to that," Doroku grumbled, and Seth looked over to find him frowning. "I was completely at the mercy of that demon master. Only the *Mith'elre Chon's* timely arrival saved me."

"If you'd had the knowledge of *El'shaen*," Jase said, "things would have been different."

"Perhaps," Doroku said, but he sounded doubtful. He turned his gaze on Shavis. "But I think I see where the Dai'shozen is headed with this. We don't want to do battle with the demons. We want to kill them. We want to bring them down the way a pack of wolves would bring down an elk. En masse. One coordinated strike to overwhelm and kill."

Shavis nodded. "And to do that, we need all our Dymas in one place, not spread for fifty miles along our southern border. We'll launch our attack from a single locale, sending those with the ability to use *El'shaen* through Veilgates in striketeams. Through surprise, speed, and superior numbers, we will eliminate the demons who can wield *Lo'shaen*. If we can break their hold on the Arkanians, we will have an easier time driving them back into their own land."

"We'll need to destroy the *droth'del* as well," Gideon said, nodding to Gwuler and Elliott as they stopped next to Jase. Elliott had his thumbs tucked behind his belt, and it was clear from his expression that he'd taken exception to something Gwuler had said.

"As long as the *droth'del* remain," Gideon continued, "village priests have the ability to summon more demons."

"I will coordinate the attacks on the demons here in Riak," Shavis said. "The small Veilgates—these 'windows,' as you called them—will facilitate that nicely. Much faster and safer than using Myrscraw. We will spy out the enemy armies and then crush them where they stand."

"We can do the same for the *droth'del*," Jase told him. "If you wish it, Gwuler and I will coordinate the attacks. We will need ten or twelve Dymas to assist us if you can spare them."

"Take as many as you need," Shavis said. "Closing those blasted doors is priority number one for this offensive."

He turned to the two Dymas who'd come with him. "I need you to go to Shozen Jisho and Shozen Kamishi," he told them. "Tell them they are to disengage the enemy and return to Maisen through Veilgates."

"Yes, Dai'shozen," the two said, then the air parted before them and they hurried through shimmering door-like squares to somewhere beyond.

Shavis turned to Doroku. "We need to send word to Hakala, Kyotei, and Rasokei to do the same," he said. "Will you see to it?"

Doroku nodded. "Yes, Dai'shozen." He turned and looked across the battlefield, and Seth could only assume he was contacting other Dymas with his Awareness. A moment later, thin flashes of blue-light some distance away announced the departure of those he'd sent on the errand.

"Now for your army," Shavis said, looking around at Doroku's men. "Raise the banner for assembly. We're going to Maisen."

ヒ

The looks of surprise on the faces of the Agla'Con was as rewarding as anything Hul had ever witnessed, and he took a moment to enjoy it before burning them from existence with sizzling tendrils of *Sei'shiin*. In the shadowed, fire-lit darkness of the throne room, the men became brief but brilliant points of light that left human-shaped afterimages in his vision.

His team of Dymas struck as well, and the line of K'rrosha standing watch along the far wall flared brightly, bursts of crimson-colored fire and flesh that filled the air with foul smelling smoke.

*Ta'shaen* jarred in pain as Agla'Con in an adjacent room attempted to counterattack, and lightning exploded overhead, crackling along the shields Iso and Kol held around themselves and the others. Several red-hued bolts ricocheted off the invisible barriers, and columns exploded into splintered fragments and powder. A section of the domed ceiling collapsed, blocking an arched entryway and crushing several Shadowhounds which had just entered the room.

Hul smiled. *Keep it up, you filthy vermin, and you'll do our job for us.*

The Agla'Con must have realized the foolishness of using lightning in such a tight space because the attack broke off. They still held the Power, though, and Hul could feel them rushing toward the throne room. And they weren't alone. All throughout the fortress dozens of Agla'Con and K'rrosha were seizing the Power and were rushing to repel the perceived invasion.

"Collapse the rest of the entryways," Hul ordered. "If they want to confront us, they'll have to come through Veilgates." He smiled again. *Too bad we'll be gone before they arrive.*

Striding down the center aisle to the dais and Shadan's throne, Hul climbed the steps and channeled a sword-like blade of *El'shaen*. With a swipe of his hand, he brought the white-hot blade down on the altar used for refleshing and sliced the massive block cleanly in two. Still not satisfied, he swung the sizzling blade to the left and Shadan's throne fell in pieces across the polished stone of the dais.

*One more to go*, Hul thought, opening himself more fully to the Power.

When he was near to bursting, he loosed it in a spiraling column strong enough to collapse a city wall. The fiery spear struck the crystal slab of refleshing—Shadan's version of a *droth'del*—and the smooth wall of polished black blew apart in millions of glittering shards. They rained across the dais with a sound like tinkling glass.

"It won't be so easy for you now," Hul said aloud, intending the words for Maeon as well as for Shadan.

With one final nod of satisfaction, he turned his back on the ruined gateway to hell and moved down the steps to his striketeam. Shields firmly in place, they were watching him with smiles of appreciation. Hul acknowledged their appreciation with a smile of his own.

"To the western rim," he said. "I want to be there when Shadan receives word of this."

Focusing on the river of Power flowing through him, he reorganized it into the order required for opening a Veilgate and channeled them into the spiritual fabric separating life from death. Sunlight streamed into the throne room as Talin Plateau came into view before him, and he strode through, still smiling.

火

Shavis watched Jase Fairimor and his striketeam move through a Veilgate into the jungles of Arkania, then turned his attention to the rest of the striketeams assembled across Maisen's schoolyard. Twenty in all, each had been assigned at least one *droth'del* to destroy. The more skilled teams and those with the most powerful Dymas had two or three targets. Jase Fairimor and Gideon had each selected five.

"God's speed, *Mith'elre Chon*," Shavis muttered, then watched as Veilgates began opening across the schoolyard and striketeams vanished to somewhere beyond.

When the last team was away, he turned to Railen and Sheymi. They'd been opening and closing the small window-like Veilgates for the past few minutes, and he could tell by their expressions that they didn't like what they had found. "Have you selected our first target?" he asked.

Railen nodded. "Yes. The most immediate threat to our people is fifteen miles to the east of here, just south of Hosen. Three demons are using *Lo'shaen* to drive approximately four thousand Arkanians toward the village. The women and children have evacuated, and an army of three hundred men are preparing to defend their homes."

"They'll be glad to see us then, won't they," Shavis said. "Your plan?"

"Sheymi and I and four of Clan Hasho's Dymas will kill the demons capable of wielding *Lo'shaen*," Railen answered. "Dymas from Sekigaroga will attack the lesser demons while the rest of our forces attack the Arkanians from the north. Fifteen hundred archers from Clans Vakala, Gahara, and Hattori are assembled and ready to rain arrows on the Arkanians from above."

Shavis nodded. "And the archers know not to move through the Veilgate?" He was worried about those unfamiliar with the concept of Veilgates. Especially the newer wieldings. The Veilgate might appear vertical in front of them, but the other side was horizontal. And it was a hundred feet above the ground.

Railen chuckled. "I tossed a demon corpse through one to show what would happen to them if they do," he said. "Watching it slam into the unsuspecting Arkanians beneath made my point nicely."

"If a bit more gruesomely than was necessary," Sheymi added, then smiled when Railen narrowed his eyes at her.

"Let's get to it," Shavis said, cutting off whatever Railen had been preparing to say. The sooner they destroyed the first group, the sooner they could be on to the next. He and Elliott had wagered twenty Riaki gold pieces that Shavis' army could have the invading forces destroyed or on the run before the Dymas in Arkania could destroy the *droth'del*.

He started for the staging area. Taking Elliott's money was going to be such a pleasure.

火

"This is taking too long!" Elliott shouted, then tore up another one of the village's many huts with a barrage of lightning. The Power-wielding priestess who'd tried to hide in the hut staggered out into the open, then tripped and fell as Vomil Dymas ripped up the ground at her feet with a thrust of Earth.

The woman pushed herself to her knees and crouched beneath a shield of corrupted Spirit, her eyes wide with feral rage or fear or both. Like the other priestesses they'd encountered, she was bare-breasted and tattooed from head to foot. Even without the fiery glow of corruption emanating from her spear-like talisman, she would have been the most hideous creature he'd ever seen. That she'd willingly given herself to Maeon and been working side by side with a demon master at the village's *droth'del* made it that much worse.

"We aren't leaving her alive to rebuild this place after we leave," Gwuler barked in return. "She'd simply construct another *droth'del*."

A sound like hail hitting glass sounded behind Elliott and he turned to find twenty plus villagers skulking in from the jungle. Most were men, but there were a number of women and children as well. Each held a blowtube and was sending a flurry of poisoned darts hissing his and Gwuler's way. The tiny projectiles deflected harmlessly off the shield Vomil Dymas held around them, but little spots of color marred the invisible barrier where the poison had splattered free of the dart.

Very likely it was *del'ah broma*. The villagers knew if they could remove his ability to wield the Power, it would even up the fight.

*Sorry to disappoint you*, he thought, then channeled the explosive balls of Light he'd used during the final stage of his trials. Now, like then, they detonated in the midst of his enemies with concussive *flash-bangs* that sent the people staggering. The explosive orbs were not lethal, as lightning strikes would have been, but he had no desire to kill children.

The Power-wielding priestess, however, was a target worthy of death, and he'd had just about enough of this blasted village. Turning his attention back to where she crouched beneath her shield, he drew in as much of the Power as he could safely hold and channeled one last explosive sphere of light. A hundred times greater than the ones he'd just used on the villagers, it detonated directly above the woman's shield, driving the invisible barrier down with such force that it smashed her the way Elliott might smash a gnat with a slap of his hand.

Vomil and Gwuler turned to stare at him. He couldn't tell if they were relieved that the battle was over or disgusted with *how* it had ended.

"She isn't any more dead than if you'd killed her with a lightning bolt," Elliott said, then sent a series of smaller *flash-bangs* through the midst of another group of villagers to show Gwuler he had full control over the potency of his attacks.

He started for the large pavilion containing the *droth'del* and the blood-blackened altar fronting it. One wall of the pavilion had vanished in a flash of white fire when the bar of *Sei'shiin* Vomil Dymas had used to destroy the demon master had passed through it. The thatched roof and shattered fragments from the wood planks of the floor lay across the area like leaves left behind by a violent gust of wind. Elliott wasn't sure if it was the Dymas or the priestesses who had caused the most damage.

Vomil moved up next to him, and his face twisted with disgust as he looked at the shimmering wall of darkness framed by the stone slabs of this open doorway to hell.

"Best to destroy this before any more demons arrive," he said, then raised his hand and send a blinding spiral of *El'shaen* lancing into the dark grey slab of Power-wrought stone on the right. It burst apart in a spray of rocky shards that pelted the jungle beyond, shredding greenery and causing a cascade of leaves and petals. The shimmering wall of darkness vanished in a curt flash of red and the jungle behind the pavilion came into view.

"We best be on our way," Vomil said, motioning for the rest of his team to join him. Still holding shields to ward off the darts and spears of the enraged villagers, they gathered at the foot of the pavilion's steps. When everyone was there, Vomil opened a Veilgate back to Maisen, and Elliott led the way through. He was eager to see if he'd won the bet with Shavis.

"One demon and two Agla'Con priestesses," Jase said, then let the small Veilgate window slide closed in front of him. "And just like in the last four villages, they are positioned at the foot of the pavilion holding the *droth'del*."

"Same approach as last time?" Seth asked and Jase smiled at him. Seth had insisted on coming along even though he was the only member of the striketeam who couldn't wield the Power. He knew Seth meant well, but considering the number of times he'd left Talia behind to keep her safe, it was an interesting reversal. Not to mention ironic and slightly hypocritical.

From the corner of his eye, he saw Talia bite her lip to keep from smiling, and he knew she had sensed what he was thinking. She turned away, pretending to shoo one of the jungle's many bugs away from her face.

"Yes," Jase answered. "And we'll be in and out before the villagers even know what happened." He cast a meaningful glance at Talia before looking back at Seth. "But you and Talia stay close to me just in case something goes wrong."

"That's why I'm here," Seth grunted. In addition to his swords, he wore a pouch of bladestars on his belt and a quiver of arrows on his back. The bow he carried was made of fine ash, and he hefted it for emphasis. "Even if you don't believe it, the *Mith'elre Chon* needs a warder."

"Oh, I believe it," Jase told him, then turned to the other members of his striketeam. All but two were as young as he and Talia, but they were powerful and skilled. They'd come of age during the battle to take Sagaris from Emperor Samal, and had shown just how capable they were today with how easily they'd destroyed the first four *droth'del*."

"One more to go," he told them. "Are you ready?"

They nodded and *Ta'shaen* came alive as each embraced it and drew in as much as they could hold. Jase embraced the Power as well, then took Talia by the hand and moved to stand in front on his striketeam. Bow in hand and arrow nocked, Seth joined them, sticking close to Talia out of warder habit.

Jase could feel Talia's nervous excitement through the *sei'vaiya*, and he smiled reassuringly at her. Then he opened a Veilgate into the Arkanian village.

Aethon Fairimor flinched in surprise as a rent opened nearby and several Agla'Con stumbled through from beyond. At first he thought they'd come from somewhere up on the plateau, but then he caught a glimpse of dark columns and smoke-filled air as the rent snapped shut and realized the men had come from Shadan's throne room. Their hasty arrival coupled with the looks of panic on their faces spoke volumes, and Aethon braced himself for even more bad news.

Shadan interrupted the stream of Fire he was channeling toward the Meleki loosing arrows from above, and his eye narrowed as he looked down at the new arrivals. His K'sivik hissed in irritation and snapped its jaws at the men.

"What is it?" Shadan snarled, his face twisting with contempt. "Can't you see I'm busy?"

Raising his scepter once more, he sent a jet of Fire sizzling into a section of the Meleki army lining the cliffs above them. It was the second half of Nid's army, and it had arrived through numerous Veilgates some minutes earlier and had claimed the high ground above the ramp-like canyon Shadan had created. Even worse, the Meleki army which had arrived earlier that morning had advanced and was pressing Death's Third March from the rear. The Crescent Guard in particular was inflicting heavy casualties among those still trying to exit the plateau.

*Burn you, Nid*, he thought, then sent a string of Night Threads to join Shadan's fire. They danced along the cliff top in explosive stabs of black, tossing Meleki soldiers aside like ants and filling the air with thunder.

"But, your excellency," one of the Agla'Con said, "the Pit was attacked. The slab used for refleshing has been destroyed." He had to shout to be heard above the din, but he kept his head down, unwilling or unable to meet the Dreadlord's gaze.

Aethon's anger reached a flashpoint, and he loosed another barrage of Night Threads into the Meleki army to keep himself from killing the man and his companions for their failure to defend the Pit.

Shadan, however, was far less restrained and sliced the man's head from his neck with a blade of corrupted Spirit. It thudded to the ground and rolled to a stop at the feet of the dead man's companions. Faces frozen with looks of terror, they likely would have tried to flee if Shadan hadn't seized them in grips of Air and yanked them off their feet. They hung in the air before him, their boots several feet off the ground.

"How did this happen?" he shouted, and all around him men and Darklings paused to watch what might happen next. For a moment the battle raging overhead was forgotten.

"It was High King Nid," one of the men rasped, his fingers pulling uselessly at the invisible cords of Air wrapped around his throat. "We tried to stop him, but—" The sound of his neck snapping made several nearby cultists flinch in surprise.

Without another word, Shadan rent the Veil and heeled his K'sivik through into the darkness beyond. Behind him, still hanging in the air with eyes bulging and faces turning blue, the remaining Agla'Con struggled against their invisible bonds. They dropped unceremoniously to the earth a moment later when the rent snapped shut and the flow of Power holding them was severed.

Aethon glared down at them as they pushed themselves to their knees. "On your feet," he ordered. "We are needed on the plateau."

"Shadan just left through a Veilgate," Idoman said, and Joneam Eries lowered the spyglass he was using to monitor the battle taking place atop the plateau. He looked over at the young Dymas general and found him frowning thoughtfully as he peered through the window he'd opened above Death's Third March.

He'd ordered Quintella and the other striketeam leaders to resume hit and run attacks using Veilgates, but the enemy was simply too large for them to have much of an effect. And not all the Agla'Con and *Jeth'Jalda* in Shadan's army had been part of the link to collapse the rim. There were more than enough to counter the attacks being launched by Kelsa and Melek.

Joneam inhaled deeply, then let it out slowly to try to curb his frustration. The arrival of Lord Nid's armies had forced Shadan's hand in collapsing the rim to speed his march, but that was about it. No significant damage had been done. And most of the Dreadlord's army was now off the plateau.

He raised the spyglass once more and moved it slowly across the chaotic scene. Night Threads continued to erupt among the Meleki forces, and flashes of reddish light and flares of Fire danced along the rim. If he listened carefully, the strange, high-pitched thunder and muffled booms of explosions were audible several moments after each release of Power.

"Where do you think the Dreadlord went?" Joneam asked at last. "He isn't on the plateau, is he? Those are some pretty powerful corrupted wieldings."

"That isn't Shadan," Idoman said, sounding envious. "It's Aethon Fairimor. His abilities with *Lo'shaen* have been strengthened. Probably by the weakening of the Veil."

As Joneam watched, the explosive attacks launched by Aethon began to take their toll. The Meleki forces stalled, then slowly began to pull back from the rim to regroup. The banner of the Crescent Moon held firm near the top of the newly formed canyon-rampway, but it was clear they were no longer advancing. Lightning bolts and shimmering threads of *Sei'shiin* streaked from their midst and into the stragglers of Death's Third March as they hurried toward the Bottomlands.

Joneam lowered the spyglass as Idoman let his Power-wrought window slide closed. They looked at each other for a moment without speaking, then Idoman blew out his cheeks in frustration as he moved to his horse and climbed into the saddle.

"We best regroup as well," he said. "If we're lucky, we've got two days before they reach Mendel Pass."

亡

Aethon sent one final stab of Night Threads into the retreating Meleki army, then motioned for Asherim and the other Agla'Con nearby to gather around him. "You are in charge until I return," he told Asherim. "The rest of you assist him. Set up camp at the base of the ramp and position forces to hold it should the Meleki army try to follow. They will have to go through us if they want to join with Kelsa. That, or they will have to wait until their Dymas are strong enough to move everyone through Veilgates. Either way, they are stuck atop the plateau for a while."

Without waiting for an answer, he opened himself to the power of the Void and tore a hole in the Veil. He moved through into Shadan's throne room and found the Dreadlord standing atop the dais. He was staring at the spot where the crystal slab had been. Behind him, pieces of his throne and the altar of refleshing lay scattered across the floor.

"This will slow the refleshing of Agla'Con," Shadan said as Aethon joined him on the dais. There was a new level of bitterness in his voice. Bitterness and a deep, smoldering rage. "Lord Nid did this," he continued. "I want him dead. Use the last of our K'tyr if you have to, but I want his head on a spear before the week is out."

"High King Nid's death is long overdue," Aethon agreed. Then, to remind Shadan that he could agree without being agreeable, he added, "I'll see to it just as soon as I return from Tamba."

Shadan turned a wary eye on him, but Aethon ignored it. "I'll give your regards to *Frel'mola*," he said, then tore a hole in the Veil and left the Dreadlord to brood in silence.

# CHAPTER 47

## *Wagers and Worries*

"THEY'RE FINALLY ON THE RUN."

Railen's statement penetrated the calming shroud of *Jiu* Shavis had wrapped himself in, and he glanced over at his young friend briefly before pulling his sword free of the Arkanian soldier's chest. Eyes still burning with a frenzied light, the man staggered to the side and fell, his lifeblood spattering droplets of red across the green of the trampled rice field.

Shavis cleared the blood from the slender blade with a sharp flick of his wrist, then cast about for another enemy. There were none. Railen had been right that the Arkanians had had enough. They were fleeing south in droves, their weapons forgotten, the dark power which had clouded their minds fading now that the last of the demon masters had been destroyed.

"Who killed the final demon?" Shavis asked, more to break the silence than out of any real curiosity.

"Doroku," Sheymi answered. Her face was pinched with disgust as she surveyed the carnage strewn across the battlefield. *A battlefield*, Shavis thought angrily, *which had once been the finest rice fields in this part of the country*.

Now it was a trampled mess, good for nothing but to be plowed under. Hopefully the adjacent farming areas had been spared enough that the villagers in the area wouldn't go hungry in the coming months.

Shavis nodded in response to Sheymi, then gestured to Ronan Habishi, the Sarui general of Clan Derga. "Raise the banner for assembly," he ordered. "We have one last army to turn back."

"Yes," Railen muttered unenthusiastically. "The largest one."

"Large if you are counting Arkanians," Shavis said. "Small if you number the demons."

Railen grunted. "Which is a bloody good thing now that most of our Dymas are nearing their breaking point. Opening so many Veilgates over such a short period of time *and* fighting demons is taking its toll."

"I know," Shavis said, "and I appreciate all that you and the others have done today. You have set a new standard in warfare. When in all of history have so many invading forces spread over such a wide area been turned back by a single force?"

"Probably never," Railen said, a slight smile of pride creeping over his face. It vanished almost as suddenly as it appeared. "But we aren't finished yet, and this final jump will be the toughest yet."

Shavis smiled at the use of the word *jump*. Railen and the other Dymas had begun using it earlier in the day in reference to moving the Riaki army to the next attack point. Shavis liked it—what better way to describe a full-scale, instantaneous relocation of an entire army.

"But jump we will," Shavis said, "and if necessary, our regular forces will destroy the demons and drive the Arkanians back into their own land."

Railen must have taken the statement as a challenge because his eyes narrowed in irritation. "We have strength enough to see this through to the end. He looked pointedly at Shavis' sword. "Besides, blades are all but useless against demons."

Shavis grinned at him. "So you've said. On multiple occasions."

Leaving Railen to scowl at his back, Shavis made his way toward the banner of assembly, weaving his way through the lifeless bodies of Arkanians and leaping over several small ditches used for irrigation earlier in the season. They were dry now, as was the fertile soil bearing the now trampled crop, a sign of just how close to harvest the rice had been. He stooped and plucked a sheath from one of the stalks. The head was heavy with grain, and he rolled some of them around with his fingers to strip away the soft husks hiding the small white treasures within. It gave him hope that some of it could be saved.

He reached the banner, and the Dai'shozen of each of the clans gathered around him to receive their instructions. Some showed signs of having been wounded and then healed. Their faces were lined with fatigue and their uniforms and armor sported an array of slashes and holes stained dark with dried blood. But they were Shizu and Sarui, warriors of Riak. And they still had one battle left to fight.

He spoke quickly and kept his instructions short. They knew what to do and he trusted them to do it. As they left, they brought fists to chest in salute, then joined their respective clans.

Shavis drew his sword and nodded to Railen. "Contact those who will be opening the gates. We go on my signal."

"Yes, Dai'shozen," Railen said, and Shavis knew he was relaying the message to the others via his Awareness—he recognized the peculiar expression that moved over the young man's face whenever he was immersed in the unseen world. *Unseen for me, anyway*, he thought. It was difficult not to be jealous of Railen's abilities.

A few minutes passed as the armies gathered and the Dymas moved into position in front of them. When everyone was finally in place, Railen nodded as if to himself, then looked to Shavis.

"The Dymas are ready," he said, shooting a quick look at Sheymi who smiled at him. "All of us."

Shavis motioned for a nearby Shizu, and the man handed him a longbow and an arrow tipped with a whistle. Pointing the arrow skyward, he loosed it, and the high-pitched squeal of the whistle sounded long and loud as it sailed up and out of sight.

Across the rice fields, forty-five Veilgates opened as one and his army charged through into the midst of the startled Arkanians.

Railen and Sheymi and a number of the most powerful Dymas led the way, shielding those who followed from the Night Threads that erupted almost as soon as they were through.

"There!" Railen shouted, and Shavis followed his gaze to see a hulking, ape-like demon loping toward them through the midst of the Arkanians it held under its dark spell.

Sheymi raised her hands, and streamers of El'shaen streaked forward in blinding swirls of light. They struck the dark aura the demon pulled around itself, and the resulting explosion rocked the battlefield, upending Arkanians and killing many of them outright.

The demon slowed, pulling in on itself in a visible shroud of darkness. To the east and west four more demons were doing the same as they came under attack from the advancing Dymas.

"The demons are contained," Railen said, then he and Sheymi and the other Dymas began to close in, some sweeping the Arkanians aside with violent thrusts of Air, others casting up shields to deflect the hail of arrows and spears being hurled their way.

A number of Power-wielding priests and priestesses took up the fight, but they were obliterated within seconds by a second wave of Dymas who outnumbered their Agla'Con enemies almost ten to one. As soon as the corrupted wieldings vanished, Shavis drew his sword and entered the fray with Deathsquad Alpha at his side.

The Arkanians were unskilled compared to Shizu and Sarui, but they outnumbered his men five to one. Even worse many were under the influence of the demon because they'd drunk shar'tei broma. The demons, though contained by the Dymas, could still affect the battle by using Lo'shaen to drive the partakers of the drug into a frenzy. Until the demons were destroyed, this would be the most dangerous part of the attack.

Spinning to avoid a spear thrust, he removed his opponent's arm only to have the enraged man come at him with his bare fist. A thrust through the heart sent him staggering away, but it took him a lot longer than normal to die. And that was the case everywhere he looked. Iga's Shizu and Sarui were inflicting wounds that would have been death strokes to any other enemy, but went largely unnoticed by the Arkanians who'd received them. In the time it took them to die, they were managing to inflict a great number of wounds of their own.

"We need those demons brought down now!" he shouted at Railen.

"Working on it," the young man shouted. "We're tired! They aren't."

A spear hissed past Shavis' head, and he heard a loud *crack* as it struck the chest plate of the Sarui behind him. The Sarui hissed in pain as the tip sunk deeply enough to pierce flesh, but he yanked the spear free and tossed it aside.

"Just a poke," he told Shavis, then drew fletchings to cheek and loosed an arrow into the head of the Arkanian who'd wounded him.

A thunderous *boom* sounded to the west, and Shavis glanced over to find chunks of demon flesh raining down on the battlefield. The Arkanians in the area paused as if in a daze, some blinking in confusion, others rubbing their heads as if in pain.

*It's about bloody time*, he thought, then opened another Arkanian throat with a form called Heron on the Wind.

Movement to his right caught his attention, and he found an Arkanian moving to stab one of Iga's Shizu in the back.

*No you don't*, he thought, hurling a bladestar. It struck the man in the neck, and he cried out, giving himself away. His intended target whirled, bringing his sword around in an arc that nearly sliced the man in two. He spotted the bladestar Shavis had hurled and gave a quick nod of thanks before returning to the battle.

Shavis did as well, wrapping himself in *Jiu* and meeting the Arkanian frenzy head on. As clumsy and untrained as the Arkanians were, he felt like a wolf moving among sheep, powerful, lethal, and merciless. If not for the fact that they'd given themselves over to a demon he might have been able to pity them.

Time seemed to slow as he fought, and the sounds of battle grew muted as he immersed himself even more deeply into *Jiu*. He was one with his blade. He was Shizu.

A flash of white brighter than the sun lit the battlefield from end to end, and was followed almost immediately by an explosion that shook the ground. A second flash came seconds later and was followed by another boom and shockwave that ripped across the area like a sudden gust of wind. The Arkanians nearest Shavis flinched as if struck, then stood motionless in a daze, their eyes unfocused, their expressions blank.

Keeping his sword at the ready, he took advantage of the moment to rejoin Railen and Sheymi. They were watching the stunned Arkanians warily.

"That won't last long," Railen said. "And when it fades, we will have our hands full."

"Best not to wait then," Sheymi said. Her face pinched with concentration, and a wide Veilgate opened behind the stunned Arkanians. A wall of jungle green lay beyond, and Shavis heard the eery cries of several unfamiliar birds. Sheymi made a motion with her hand, and a powerful thrust of Air knocked the Arkanians backwards into the lush green beyond the shimmering edges of her Veilgate. The opening slid shut as soon as the last one was through.

Shavis smiled at her. "Much easier than killing them," he said. "Thank you."

"The killing isn't over yet," Railen said, indicating the battles still raging all around them. "The demons might be dead, but the influence of that damned drug still holds many captive. They're going to fight to the death."

"Contact our Dymas and tell them to use Veilgates as Sheymi just did," Shavis ordered. "Target only the most frenzied, but send them deep enough into Arkania that they will no longer be a threat to us."

Railen did as he was told, and Veilgates began opening and closing wherever the fighting was the worst. As the most frenzied Arkanians began disappearing from the battlefield, those less effected by the *shar'tei broma* recognized they were on the losing end of things and threw down their weapons. Within moments the entire lot was fleeing south toward their homeland.

"Good riddance," Railen said, and Shavis nodded at the sentiment.

"Come," he said. "Let's collect our wounded and return to Maisen. I've got an appointment with an arrogant young Kelsan."

Elliott completed the last fold on the crane he was making, then set the delicate red bird on the ground next to the other creatures he'd made while waiting for Shavis to return. There had been time enough to make a cow, a pig, a Shadowhound, two Dragons, and five varieties of birds. If not for the calming effect *shobutsu* had on him, he would have lost patience a long time ago.

Sitting cross-legged on the ground a short distance away, Gwuler Hom nodded his appreciation at his latest creation.

"You are very skilled at *shobutsu*," he said. "The Dragons are my favorite. Did you learn that pattern in a book?"

Elliott pulled the blue and green Dragon from among the collection and handed it to Gwuler. "No. I learned it on my own. But I modified my original design after spending time as a *sholin*."

Gwuler cupped the paper Dragon in his hand and smiled admiringly. "What's a *sholin*?" he asked.

"A Dragonrider," Elliott answered, smiling as a look of scepticism moved over Gwuler's face. He looked pointedly at the paper Dragon. "My mount's name was Ayame. She was a blue-scaled beauty with a green mane."

Gwuler stared at him, still skeptical. Finally he laughed. "That's a good one," he said. "For a moment I almost believed you were telling the truth."

"He was," a familiar voice said, and Elliott looked over his shoulder to find Railen and Sheymi standing behind him. "The world changed more than you know while you were in Arkania," Railen continued. "Dragons—or Rhiven as they call themselves—are real."

Gwuler's eyes moved to the paper Dragon, and a look of wonder painted his face.

"And you... you *rode* one?"

"Into battle against demons," Railen offered, seemingly amused by Gwuler's reaction.

"A tale for later," Elliott told his one-armed friend. "Right now I want to ask Shavis what took him so long." He looked at Railen. "Any idea where he is?"

"In the schoolhouse, debriefing the other Dai'shozen."

Leaving Gwuler to sit in stunned silence, Elliott started for the schoolhouse. When Railen and Sheymi followed, he raised an eyebrow at them in question.

"Why do I get the feeling you are acting as my warders at the moment?"

"Because we are," Sheymi replied. "Every Shizu and Sarui from Clans Kyoai and Gizo are here in Maisen, and the deathmark they put on you hasn't been lifted."

"That," Railen added, "and we wanted to watch you make good on your bet with Shavis."

"You've got it backwards," Elliott told them. "I returned from Arkania two hours ago. Shavis owes *me* twenty gold pieces."

"*You* may have returned before us," Railen said. "But two striketeams have yet to arrive. Gideon's and Jase's. The bet, as I recall, was that the Dymas would close the *droth'del* before the Riaki army turned back the Arkanians."

A cold knot tightened in Elliott's stomach, and the bet with Shavis was suddenly the farthest thing from his mind. "And Jase's absence doesn't concern you?" he asked. "Because it concerns me. Come on, we need to find out where he is."

They hurried their pace, weaving their way around supply wagons and passing numerous squads of Shizu and Sarui squatting on their heels or sitting cross-legged on the hard-packed earth. Many greeted him with a nod or a raised hand, but there were a few groups that watched him pass in silence, their eyes hard, their hands on their weapons. He didn't need to look at the marks on their uniforms to know they were from Kyoai, Gizo, or Maridan.

He locked eyes with a few of them, daring them to act, but they remained where they were. Apparently, Jase's object lesson that morning was still fresh in their minds. That, or they didn't want to risk retaliation by the clans loyal to Shavis Dakshar, a known friend of Elliott's.

It wasn't until he glanced over his shoulder and found Sheymi and Railen staring the men down that he discovered the real reason for the show of restraint. None of the men were foolish enough to challenge Dymas, and members of the Imperial Clave at that.

"I'm glad you two are taking your job as my warders so seriously," he told them. "There's no telling what might have happened if you weren't here."

"Sure there is," Railen said, sounding less than amused. "You'd start another bloody war."

"Only with those who deserve it," Elliott told him.

He was just shy of the schoolhouse when a Veilgate opened and Gideon came striding through with his striketeam close on his heels. He spotted Elliott and waved as his gate closed behind him. He wore a smile, but it faded as he sensed Elliott's concern.

"What's wrong?"

"Jase hasn't returned yet," Elliott told him. "Something's not right."

Gideon motioned to the schoolhouse. "Inside," he said. "I need to look at the map to know where to start looking for him."

"I'll gather more Dymas," Railen said. "If something went so wrong that the *Mith'elre Chon* can't handle it, we are going to need all the help we can get."

"I'm sure he's fine," Gideon said, but Elliott had been around him long enough to know he didn't mean it. Gideon was worried. And that scared Elliott more than the fact that Jase was overdue and that Talia was with him.

If anything had happened to his sister.... He pushed the thought away and followed Gideon inside.

# CHAPTER 48

## The Old-Fashioned Way

"THAT WASN'T SO BAD," Jase said, pleased with his team's efforts in bringing down the final priestess. She'd been as powerful as any Agla'Con he'd ever faced, but once her companions were dead, the combined strength of the Riaki Dymas had broken through her shield in very little time. Joshomi Dymas had burned her from existence a heartbeat later with *Sei'shiin*.

Glancing at the horde of enraged villagers milling beyond the edges of their shields, Jase started for the pavilion containing the *droth'del*. It was fifty paces beyond the smouldering corpse of the demon master and the headless form of the other priestesses. Viewed through his Awareness, the structure was a dark, semi-shadowed area in the otherwise luminescent landscape.

It surprised him to find it so far away. He hadn't realized they'd given up so much ground during the battle with the final priestess.

"She was a fierce one," Talia said, aware of what he was thinking. "Worse even than the two Seth and I faced with Gwuler and your mother."

"Which is why we should destroy the *droth'del* and get out of here," Ibari Dymas said, moving up beside them. "The amount of Power exchanged during the fight was a signal fire to any other Agla'Con or demons in the area. And that's to say nothing of them." She looked pointedly at the Arkanians testing the shields for weakness. "You can tell by the look in their eyes that they are under the influence of *shar'tei broma*. They're frenzied enough to try to follow us through a Veilgate."

Jase covered his nose as he moved around the charred body of the demon, then looked again at the villagers. In addition to an assortment of swords and spears and clubs, a good number of them held blowtubes and were maneuvering into position to fire darts if given the chance. Darts, Jase knew, which were undoubtedly tipped with a lethal poison like pyfer. Or worse, the strange concoction which could rob a

Power-wielder of their abilities.

The jolt of fear that reached him through the love-bond told him Talia had sensed that last thought as well. She confirmed it with what she said next.

"It was awful," she whispered. "I've never felt so helpless in my life."

Jase nodded, his eyes still on the Arkanians. He bore no ill will toward any of the villagers—they were victims of Maeon as much as anyone—but Ibari was right: They would attack the moment an opportunity presented itself.

And that moment, he suspected, would come when he and the others dropped their shields to pass through a Veilgate, a necessity since attempting to do otherwise posed a danger to the wielder.

He didn't share Ibari's concern that the Arkanians would try to follow, but the poisonous darts were a danger he couldn't ignore.

Extending his Awareness outward across the village until he'd located every blowtube, he embraced the Gift of Air and channeled dozens of small but precise strikes, turning the bamboo weapons into useless splinters.

Ibari and the rest of the Dymas turned to stare at him in wonder. "That was amazing," Joshomi said, voicing what Jase could see in the eyes of the other Dymas. "How did you learn to strike so many targets simultaneously?"

"By accident," Jase told her. "The first time I did it was to Darklings. It took the palace staff days to clean up the mess."

"He isn't kidding," Seth grumbled. "I was in the midst of that explosion of blood, and it took *me* days to clean up."

Jase shrugged an apology as they made their way past a small hut. It had red symbols scrawled on the walls, and the skulls of dozens of unknown animals of varying size hung like decorations. One, a snake skull the size of a cow's head, made Jase shudder. He didn't want to imagine how long the snake must have been or what it might have chosen as its prey.

A moment later, he reached the pavilion and stopped at the step leading up to the polished wooden floor. The darkness seeping out of the hellish portal was visible in his mind's eye, murky tendrils that writhed and pulsated like something alive.

"I'll destroy this one," Jase said. "Ibari, you open the Veilgate out of here once I'm finished. I'll keep the nearest Arkanians from interfering."

"Yes, *Mith'elre Chon*," she said, motioning everyone closer together as Jase embraced all Seven Gifts and wove them into *El'shaen te sherah*.

*Last one*, he thought, then sent two spears of cleansing destruction lancing toward the open slabs of the *droth'del*. The white-hot bars vanished into nothingness just short of the dark stone, snuffed by some unseen power as readily as a gust of wind would snuff the flame of a candle.

Then, before he could even blink in surprise at what had just happened, a bubble of darkness expanded outward from the *droth'del*, washing over him and the others with the feeling of an icy wind.

As it passed over him, his Awareness—the shimmering, radiant world that was his spiritual vision—went dark. The river of *Ta'shaen* flowing through him vanished as well, and he went cold inside when he realized he had lost the ability to wield. He could no longer sense the Power at all. The *sei'vaiya*, too, had vanished, and he could no longer sense Talia.

Behind him, she and the Dymas gasped in horror as they, too, realized what had happened.

Movement at the *droth'del* caught his attention, and the cold knot of fear gripping his heart tightened. A demon stood on this side of the Veil.

Human in shape and size, it carried a long slender sword and a rectangular shield with letter-like markings on all four sides. Both sword and shield were encrusted with glowing crystals, and Jase knew without question that they were the source of the demon's power.

Taking Talia by the hand, Jase braced himself for the killing strike of *Lo'shaen* he was certain would come. Without the Power, he and the others were completely defenseless. And this creature knew it.

It started across the pavilion, a wicked smile moving over its all-too-human-looking face as it raised its sword.

"Kill it," Seth hissed. "What are you waiting for?"

"It's creating a void in *Ta'shaen*," Jase told him. "Run! We need to get out of its range of ability."

Tightening his grip on Talia's hand, he spun around and sprinted away from the pavilion. He angled away from the villagers who'd dropped to their knees to worship the new arrival, and he offered a silent prayer that the demon's abilities were limited to creating the void. Otherwise, it meant the bloody thing was toying with them.

The panicked breathing of Ibari and the others was loud in his ears, but he didn't dare look back for fear of running into something. Instead, he kept trying to extend his Awareness, horrified that the bubble of Power-voiding darkness was larger than he'd expected.

They were still encompassed by it when they rounded the corner of a large hut with a beaded curtain as one of its walls and came face to face with a dozen angry villagers.

Jase dug in his heels and skidded to a stop, spinning Talia around behind him in the same movement. The villagers seemed as surprised to see him as he was them, and for a moment no one moved. Then Seth spun into their midst, swords flashing, and Arkanian blood wet the ground in sprays of red. Cries of pain filled the air as the silver-haired captain deftly cut a path through the villagers' midst.

Keeping himself between Talia and the Arkanians, Jase retrieved a spear from one of the dead. It was nowhere near as nice as his quarterstaff back home, but it was essentially the same weapon, even if one end was tipped with a blade.

*It looks like we're back to the basics*, he thought, striking a wild-eyed Arkanian in the throat with the blunt end of the spear. The man dropped his sword and staggered away, gasping for air, injured but alive.

Talia retrieved a spear as well and moved to join him. She'd been trained by Seth, so even in a dress she was far more skilled than any of the Arkanians. She proved it a moment later by turning aside a sword thrust from a tattooed man in a loin cloth and then cracking him so hard on the side of the head that he dropped like a rock.

Seth flowed back through the midst of the enemy, felling each of his opponents with ease, killing only when their drug-induced frenzy made it necessary.

But even as the last villager staggered away trailing blood, a second group emerged from the wall of jungle green rising along the edge of the village. They seemed more curious than angry, which suggested they'd come from a neighboring village. A moment later an even larger group emerged a bit further to the east. Eight of them, Jase saw, held spear-like scepters glowing red with the fires of corrupted *Ta'shaen*.

The Agla'Con struck without hesitation, and tendrils of Fire sizzled toward Jase and his team. Instinctively, he wrapped his arms around Talia and turned his back toward the Fire. The killing burst vanished into nothingness just short of impact, and the startled priests looked at one another in confusion.

Jase grinned. *The edge of the void.*

Releasing Talia, he took advantage of the men's distraction and raced into the luminescent world of *Ta'shaen*, opening himself to the Power and burning the nearest of the Agla'Con to ash with a brilliant spear of *Sei'shiin*. The man's companions responded immediately, and two cast up shields while the others loosed torrents of Fire.

Jase deflected the Fire with a shield-like thrust of Spirit, sending it spiraling into a nearby hut. Bamboo ignited like paper and the entire structure vanished into an inferno of heat. He reshaped the thrust of Spirit into a blade and sliced another Agla'Con cleanly in two. His severed corpse toppled into a heap next to several horrified villagers.

Before Jase could strike again, his Awareness went dark once more, and his link to the Power vanished. A quick glance behind him revealed that the demon was still in pursuit. And it didn't seem to be in a hurry. Wicked smile still in place, it twirled its sword ostentatiously.

The village turned red with the light of corrupted Fire as the remaining Agla'Con struck again, but the flows of corrupted Power vanished as they came in contact with the demon-wrought void.

Jase smiled as an idea began to take shape.

"I'll deal with the demon," Seth said, starting forward, but Jase took him by the arm to stop him.

"No, Seth. You might be the best swordsman this world has to offer, but that bloody thing is ancient. It's had thousands of years to practice its forms." He looked pointedly at the Agla'Con. "Besides, they can't touch us as long as we remain within the void."

Seth's eyes narrowed and a tight smile of understanding formed on his lips. "You want to bring the Agla'Con inside the void."

"Yes," Jase said, hefting the spear, "and then we will kill them the old fashioned way. Once they're dead, we'll outrun the demon and leave through Veilgates."

Seth kept close watch on the demon as he and Jase led Talia and the others across the village toward one of the larger openings bordering the jungle. It appeared to be a garden, with cultivated earth and neat rows of crops nearing harvest.

The demon followed, but it didn't hurry. Still, there was a hunger in its gaze that belied its seeming patience.

The Agla'Con outside the bubble of voiding followed as well, but they stayed well beyond the demon's reach. They'd seen what had happened to their wieldings, and they knew what had caused it.

"It isn't going to work," Seth said. "The Agla'Con know they'll be powerless if they enter the void." He pointed to the small army of Arkanians forming in the Agla'Con's wake. They were armed and angry. "And it is only a matter of time before they get involved. The void means nothing to them."

Jase studied the Arkanians for a moment, then frowned. "You're right. Recommendation?"

"You and the others get beyond the void and get out of here," he said. "I'll distract the demon."

Talia was immediately at his side. "No. We aren't leaving you behind."

Seth sheathed one of his swords and reached up to touch her on the cheek. "*Atanami en kojyo*," he said, then nodded to Jase. "Go."

"No," Talia said again, tears welling up in her eyes.

Grim-faced, and clearly unhappy with the turn of events, Jase took Talia by the hand and led her away. The rest of the Dymas followed, and Seth watched them until they vanished behind a nearby hut.

Drawing his second sword once more, he turned to face the demon. It had slowed its pace and was studying him the way a butcher might study a side of beef.

Seth stood his ground. *It won't be as easy as you think.*

The demon might be ancient as Jase said, but Seth didn't imagine Con'Jithar afforded the creature many opportunities to engage in swordplay. And certainly not against an opponent armed with swords forged by Dragons.

Settling even more deeply into *Jiu*, he waited calmly as the demon continued its advance. When he was satisfied that he had its complete attention, he attacked.

"I can't believe we are leaving Seth behind," Talia said, her words so filled with anger and disgust that Jase was glad the void had nullified the *sei'vaiya* when it had severed them both from the Power. He didn't want to feel what she was feeling at the moment any more than he wanted the distraction of hearing her thoughts. Especially since her anger was directed at him.

"We aren't leaving him behind," Jase told her. "But I want the demon and the

Agla'Con to think we are."

"But you—"

"Never said anything about leaving," Jase said. "But arguing about it with Seth would have been pointless."

A sword-wielding Arkanian rounded the corner of a hut, and Jase stepped into his path before he could react. Spear tip flashing, he opened the man's throat to silence any attempt to call others to the area. The man's lips moved without sound as he dropped his sword and clutched at his ruined throat, and blood welled from between his fingers as he toppled to the earth and died.

Jase felt bad about killing him, but he couldn't let the man ruin what he had planned. Casting back the way he and the others had come, he found that he'd put enough huts between them and the army of villagers to cut off their line of sight.

He pointed at the entrance to a particularly large hut. It was decorated with the feathered skins of dozens of brightly colored birds, and like the smaller red one they'd passed earlier, it sported an assortment of skulls. He had no idea what the strange lettering over the beaded door might mean, but he suspected the hut belonged to either the village priest or its medicine man.

"Everyone inside," he ordered. "We're out of sight of the villagers and their Agla'Con."

They did as they were told while Jase kept a look out for any who might see them enter. Then he joined them inside.

"The Agla'Con's Awareness are useless to them right now," he whispered. "They are blind to what is happening inside this bloody void." He paused as a mumble of voices sounded outside the hut, moving in the direction of the demon. When they had receded into silence, he continued. "So they are likely probing the edge of the void with their Awareness to try to catch us when we leave. If you stay put, they won't be able to find you."

"Wait a minute," Talia said, her eyes narrowing. "Where are *you* going?"

"To help Seth kill the demon," he answered. He looked at Joshomi. "As soon as the void vanishes, open a gate out of here. Seth and I will be right behind you."

"I'm coming with you," Talia said, but Jase put up a hand to silence her.

"Not this time. I don't think either of us would be comfortable with you impersonating one of their priestesses."

When he took off his shirt and handed it to her, her eyes went wide at what he'd just implied. He suddenly wished for the *sei'vaiya* so he could get a sense of what she might be thinking.

He hurriedly kicked off his boots as well, then stripped off his pants. Ignoring everyone's surprised stares, he moved to the far wall in nothing but his small clothes, where he donned one of the strange skirts made of strips of leather and long, brightly colored feathers. He secured it around his waist with leather ties, then grabbed one of the shoulder coverings and pulled it over his head. It, too, was made of strips of leather and bright feathers and felt strange against his skin.

Moving quickly to the other side of the room, he searched through an assortment of feathered helmet-masks until he found one he thought might fit. He pulled it on and moved back to the door where he retrieved his spear.

"As soon as you feel your connection to Ta'shaen return," he told them, "get out of here. Don't wait for me and Seth. We'll meet you in Maisen."

Winking at Talia through the mask, he turned and slipped out the door.

Seth turned the demon's blade aside with one of his own, then stepped lightly away as it swung its shield at him. The blasted thing had very little in the way of actual form, but it was faster than it looked. Faster than any human he'd ever faced, anyway, and the lack of form coupled with its speed made it unpredictable. Unpredictable meant dangerous.

He angled to the left and the demon followed, shield leveled before it and sword raised. The hideous smile had faded from its face when it realized Seth was a legitimate opponent. Now, fangs bared in a low continuous growl, it looked more like an animal than its human form would suggest.

Seth feinted with his left sword, and the demon went for it, swinging with enough force to slice through a stone pillar. The blackened blade hissed through empty air as Seth sidestepped the swing and spun around to slash the creature across the shoulder.

It wasn't a deep cut, but greenish-grey blood wet the Dragon-etched silver of his blade. Howling, the demon whipped around and swung at Seth with its shield. The rush of wind from the swing bore the foul stench of demon blood, and Seth forced a smile.

"Hurts, doesn't it," he taunted, meeting the demon's fiery gaze.

The creature lunged, bringing its blade around in an upward arc that left its right flank momentarily exposed. Seth opened a five inch gash in its side before ducking beneath a swipe of its shield.

Stepping lightly away once more, he bid the creature to follow by taking the form known as Bird Taking Flight. It was an open stance which invited attack.

"Krosen ta fala pessei," the demon said, bringing its shield in tight against its body and raising its sword in the air behind it. The stance was similar to Stork Among Reeds, but the demon's footing was off enough to make the form all but useless. Scoring the next hit would be almost too easy.

Movement to the right caught Seth's attention and he flicked his eyes in that direction to see several Arkanians moving toward him with swords in hand. They'd realized their god was faltering and had decided to help. Their eyes, he noted, were alight with drug-induced madness.

Leaving the demon standing in its flawed sword form, Seth moved to meet the Arkanian charge. They came at him as one, swinging wildly with the wide, single-edged blades used for hacking through jungle foliage. He killed them with barely any effort at all, then turned back to the demon to find it almost directly on top of him.

Bringing his *kamui* blades up in an X, he stopped a downward stroke that would have split his skull, then dove away as the demon swung at him with its shield. Pain lanced up his spine as the corner of the shield clipped him across the lower back.

He somersaulted to a stop among the neatly planted rows of crops and came up on one knee, swords raised before him. The demon followed, dark blade swinging, and Seth leapt away as it sliced into the ground where he'd been kneeling.

Back on his feet, he angled away from the demon, his eyes darting back and forth between it and the angry mob of Arkanians working up the courage to join the fight. Fifteen or sixteen were edging forward with swords and spears while the six Agla'Con shouted at them, urging them forward with talismans blazing.

Seth frowned in disgust. If not for the Agla'Con, this battle could be won. But killing the demon—something he fully intended to do—would only open the way for the Agla'Con to kill him with the Power.

He'd known that would be the case as soon as he sent Jase and the others away. But such was the duty and the life of a warder. As long as Talia and Jase were safe, it was worth it.

He glanced back at the demon to find it circling slowly to the right, hoping, Seth knew, to put him in between it and the advancing mob. It would attack as soon as he turned his back to engage. Best not to give it the chance.

Whirling, he sprinted toward the villagers to meet them head on. If he could kill them before the demon caught up, he would have a chance.

Some moved to meet him while others, surprised by the sudden attack, stood frozen, unsure how to respond. He deflected or ducked beneath the swords of those who tried to engage him, then fell upon those who'd let their surprise overpower their wits. They died where they stood, their blood wetting the ground around them.

Turning back to face those who remained, he found that the demon hadn't moved. Perhaps it thought ten to one odds were sufficient.

*Not in this or any other life*, Seth thought darkly.

Immersing himself even more fully in *Jiu*, he moved effortlessly from form to form, cutting his enemies down without hesitation or mercy. Deer in Rushes flowed into Panther Among Grasses flowed into Wading Heron flowed into Sparrow Darting Through Thorns. Slice after slice, thrust after thrust, Arkanians fell around him, their lives cut short by his Dragon-etched blades. And through it all, he kept the demon in sight, prepared to act should it think to join the fight.

It didn't. It simply stood motionless and watched Seth slaughter the Arkanian mob, its fiery eyes shining with what Seth could only describe as amusement.

"I can do this all day, you filthy cur," Seth said, flicking the blood from his swords and meeting the demon's gaze with a smile of his own. The longer this fight lasted, the more time Jase and the others would have to escape.

The *hiss-pop* of a dart striking him in the back sounded loudly in his ears, and there was a moment of sharp pain followed by a rush of numbness. His legs dropped from beneath him and his swords slipped from his grasp as he fell. The world rotated at an odd angle around him, and he came to rest on his side, his cheek against the bloodied ground.

He had a clear view of a collection of huts and an Arkanian priest making his way across the clearing toward him. The man held a blowtube in one hand and a long ornate spear in the other. The bottom of the spearhead, Seth noted, sported a large red crystal and was decorated with black feathers. Tiny skulls on strings rattled and clicked as the priest walked.

Something dark moved along the edge of his vision, but he was powerless to turn his head toward it. A moment later the demon moved into view, sword and shield lowered as it waited to receive the Arkanian priest.

"*Gromsal ickt fala,*" it hissed, and the priest bowed his head in a show of reverence as he stopped and went to one knee in front of the demon.

The demon made a sound that might have been a laugh or chuckle but really just sounded like the grunting of a pig. Turning, it looked down at Seth with triumph in its eyes as it raised its sword.

Seth stared straight ahead, bracing himself for what would come next. This wasn't where or how he had expected his life to end. But end it would. And it would end in failure since he had no way of knowing if Jase and Talia had been able to escape.

*Forgive me,* he thought and waited to die.

The grotesque sound of pierced flesh and bone echoed loudly across the area, and Seth marveled at how painless it had been. Strange that the poison responsible for his death should also shield him from the pain of that death.

Then, as he watched, the demon dropped to its knees in front of him, a long spear blade protruding from the center of its face. The light in its eyes slowly dimmed, and with it the fiery glow of the crystals on its sword and shield. Both slipped from the creature's grasp as it toppled to the side and lay still.

Standing over the creature, the village priest held the spear in place a moment longer, then pulled it free and tossed it aside. As he did, the sky came alive with Fire, spiraling columns of red that slammed into an invisible barrier a few feet overhead.

Ignoring the fiery torrent, the priest knelt next to Seth and removed the mask. The hideous carving gave way to reveal grey eyes and an apologetic smile. Seth didn't know if he should be furious or relieved.

"Sorry that I shot you," Jase said. "I needed the demon to believe I was its ally, and that was the only way I could think of to make that happen."

Seth tried to respond, but the power of the Arkanian drug Jase had used on him still held sway. It was probably just as well—the young man might not like what he had to say.

Stabs of corrupted lightning followed the Fire, and Jase flinched in pain. "We need to get out of here," he said, and Seth felt himself being lifted by a grip of Air. Jase set him upright on his feet and held his head up so he could see what Jase saw, but even so, he'd never felt so bloody helpless in all his life.

"This is going to be tricky," Jase said, his eyes on the Agla'Con. "I don't think I can hold the shield in place, carry you, *and* open a Veilgate out of here. Our best bet might be to wait them out."

A particularly large bolt of crimson lightning struck Jase's shield, and he flinched. "Actually," he said, reaching up to rub the side of his head. "Our best bet might be to make a break for the jungle. If we—if I—can outrun them, I'll have time to open a gate."

Seth would have glared at him if he'd been able to turn his head. He didn't know what was worse: dying at the hands of the Agla'Con or being carried unceremoniously through the jungle like a sack of grain. Fuming, he stared at the nearest Agla'Con as if that act alone could send the man fleeing into the jungle.

He was still looking at him when he vanished in a flash of white that left spots of white in his vision. A second Agla'Con flared from existence a heartbeat later and a third a split second after that.

The Fire and lightning hammering Jase's shield broke off as the remaining Agla'Con cast up shields to defend themselves, and Jase laughed aloud as sizzling tendrils of *Sei'shiin* streaked out of the jungle to explode against the corrupted bubbles of Spirit.

"Joshomi," he said, shaking his head in admiration. "She decided to ignore my orders."

*Just like you decided to ignore mine*, Seth thought, then scanned the area until he found the young Dymas moving out of the jungle. Talia was with her, and together they were clearing a path through the midst of the enraged Arkanians.

Ibari and the rest of the Dymas emerged a moment later, and burst after burst of *Sei'shiin* struck the shields of the Agla'Con in blinding flashes of white. One by one the protective bubbles collapsed, and the black-hearted men within joined Maeon in the afterlife. Horrified at the loss of the Agla'Con, the remaining villagers threw down their weapons and fled the scene, vanishing into the safety of the jungle.

Talia ran ahead of Joshomi and the others and stopped to look Seth over. "I saw what happened," she said, shooting Jase a look that could have sent a Darkling scampering for cover. "And I want you to know, I had nothing to do with it." She placed a hand on his forehead and closed her eyes. "But fortunately I can fix it," she added, and a moment later the feeling of powerlessness vanished as she healed him.

Seth took her in his arms and hugged her, then turned to scowl at Jase. "You and I will discuss all this later," he said. "First we need to finish what we came here to do." Without another word, he bent to pick up his swords and started in the direction of the *droth'del*.

He'd only gone a few paces when a Veilgate opened in front of him and Gideon and Elliott and Shavis rushed through with a small army of Dymas and Shizu on their heels. They slowed when they saw him, and looks of relief moved over each of their faces.

"Thank the Light," Gideon said. "What the blazes happened here?"

Seth grunted. "Ask Jase," he said. "I'm too angry to talk about it."

Gideon blinked in surprise at the remark, then turned to Jase, eyeing his clothes with morbid curiosity. "What did you do?"

"What was necessary to keep everyone alive," Jase told hm, his tone unapologetic. Taking Talia's hand in his, he led her in the direction of the pavilion. "Come. We have one last *droth'del* to destroy."

# CHAPTER 49

## "Where One Door Closes...

"I CAN'T BELIEVE YOU SHOT SETH with a poisoned dart," Elliott grumbled, and Jase glanced over at his friend to find him frowning. Walking next to Elliott, Shavis Dakshar wore a similar expression, his eyes and face hard. The squad of Shizu flowing silently in his wake were watching Jase as if he'd said something derogatory about their mothers.

Jase raised an eyebrow at all of them. "Would you rather I let him kill the demon so the Agla'Con could tear him apart with the Power? And it wasn't poisoned—it was drugged."

Talia squeezed his hand, and a ripple of amusement reached him through the love-bond. He smiled at her, pleased that the anger he'd felt from her earlier hadn't lasted—he needed to know he had her support even when he had to make a difficult choice. Her grip tightened again as she sensed the thought.

"Always," she whispered. "And I'll be there to heal you after Seth exacts whatever retribution he thinks he's entitled to."

"I appreciate that." Facing forward once more, he led everyone past the hut where he'd changed into the hideous costume he now wore, momentarily tempted to change back into his own clothes. This blasted getup itched to beat hell, and he was certain his exposed skin had become a feeding ground for every biting insect in the jungle. Unfortunately, he didn't think they had a lot of time before the villagers rallied or Power-wielders from another village arrived to investigate.

"There must have been something else you could have done," Elliott grumbled after a moment. "Using *poisoned* weapons is frowned upon by the Shizu code."

"Good thing I'm not a Shizu then, isn't it?" Jase told him. Judging by the way Elliott's eyes narrowed, it had been a bit more sharply than intended. "I didn't have a lot of time to come up with another plan," he added, softening his tone. "It was the only way I could get close enough without being recognized by the villagers, the demon, or the Agla'Con."

"How did you know the dart wouldn't just kill him outright?" Elliott asked, his anger subsiding slightly.

Jase grunted humorlessly. "I tested a couple of them on Arkanians."

"The lesson here," Talia said, directing a look at Elliott that was clearly a warning for him to let the matter drop, "is not to harass the victor about methodology, but to thank him for saving our friend's life." The look she gave Seth showed she was including him in the lesson.

Elliott looked like he might argue further, but their arrival at the *droth'del* silenced whatever he'd been about to say.

"Let's try this again," Jase said.

Opening himself to the Power, he wove the Seven Gifts together and loosed a white-hot stream of *El'shaen te sherah* into the dark stone of the doors. They burst into glowing fragments of molten rock, and the shimmering black void between them collapsed in on itself with a crackle of red.

He nodded in satisfaction, then looked at Shavis. "With your permission, I'd like to follow up with the other Dymas before I return to Kelsa. I want to make sure we closed all the *droth'del* threatening your nation."

Shavis nodded. "I would like to speak to them as well," he said. "And depending on what we learn, it might be time to send more of them to join *Ao tres'domei*."

"General Eries will appreciate that," Jase told him, then looked at Joshomi. "You can open the gate to Maisen now," he said. "Thank you for not opening it earlier, even though I ordered you to."

Joshomi smiled in embarrassment. "I fully intended to obey the order," she said, "but Talia convinced me otherwise. She said that since you disobeyed Captain Lydon, we were justified in disobeying you."

Jase laughed. "And so you were," he said. "So you were."

七

Amused by the startled looks of the group of scantily clad dancers waiting to be admitted into *Frel'mola's* throne room, Aethon stepped casually through the rent from the Pit, then let it snap shut in a crackling of sparks. Around him, the ten Deathwatch guards stationed in the large antechamber erupted into a flurry of movement, drawing swords and encircling him with a wall of blades before he could take another step.

"Well done," Aethon said. "Supreme Commander Naxis would be proud. Now, lower your weapons before I rip your arms off with the Power and use them to kill you with your own blades."

"No need to make a mess," a deep voice said from behind him, and he turned to see Ibisar Naxis framed in the doorway to the throne room. "*Frel'mola* was expecting you." He nodded to the Deathwatch. "Stand down," he ordered, and immediately swords were lowered and the men returned to their posts.

*Like well-trained dogs,* Aethon thought, surprised by how disappointed he was that a demonstration of his power hadn't been necessary. It made him realize he was starting to think more and more like Dathan. His brother would have killed the men on the spot.

Aethon locked eyes with Ibisar. "So, her excellency was expecting me, was she?"

Ibisar's smile was spiteful and condescending. "From the moment she learned the refleshing slab in K'zzaum had been destroyed."

Aethon kept his surprise in check, if barely. "That happened less than an hour ago," he said, eyeing Ibisar suspiciously. "Mind telling me how you learned of it so quickly?"

Ibisar's smile never changed. "As *Frel'mola* told you last time you were here, she knows *everything.*"

"So it would seem," Aethon grunted. Obviously she had spies in Death's Third March or in the Pit or both. It would make his eventual betrayal of her a bit more tricky unless he could find and eliminate them. Something he fully intended to look into once he returned to Kelsa.

Ibisar made a grand gesture of welcome with his arm. "Come, first among the living," he said, a hint of mockery in his voice, "the Bride of Maeon awaits."

Keeping his anger in check for the moment, Aethon moved into the throne room and strode down the aisle toward *Frel'mola.* As beautiful as ever in her stolen body, she sat seductively on her throne, framed by the fiery-edged rent into Con'Jithar. Her eyes glowed red with amusement as she watched him approach.

"Why, Aethon, my dear friend," she cooed. "What brings you to Berazzel?"

"You know what," Aethon told her flatly, and from the corner of his eye he saw Ibisar's hands tighten into fists. *Please,* he told the man silently, *do something stupid so I can kill you.*

*Frel'mola* saw the tightening of Ibisar's fists as well and frowned at him. "Leave us," she told him. "I wish to speak to Aethon alone."

Offering a deep bow, Ibisar turned to go, but the look he directed at Aethon as he turned was murderous. Aethon ignored him as he would any other servant who'd just been dismissed, but his pleasure at the man's anger ran deep.

"So," *Frel'mola* said as Ibisar strode away, "what would you like to talk about first? The loss of your refleshing slab? The need for more of my troops?" She stood, then put a finger on his chest and traced the Old World symbol for love. "Or maybe you've come to shift your allegiance to me. I promise I would only present a challenge to you in bed."

Aethon reached up and took her hand. It was icy cold, a powerful reminder that in spite of the radiantly beautiful facade of her stolen body, she was a K'rrosha.

"Tempting as that last might be," he said, forcing a smile, "you are the Bride of Maeon, and my allegiance is to your husband."

"As it should be," she said, her seductive smile vanishing. Keeping hold on his hand, she started down the steps of the dais.

"Come. I want to show you something." She led him to an arched doorway to the left of the dais, and two *Maa'tisis* hurriedly pulled the door open for her as she neared.

"Shadan may have lost the ability to quickly and easily reflesh our deceased brothers and sisters," *Frel'mola* continued, "but as they say, where one door closes..."

"Another opens," Aethon finished, and together they moved into a large, vaulted chamber. A refleshing room, he realized, but instead of a single slab of polished crystal, *Frel'mola* had three.

"Beautiful, aren't they?" she said. "I fashioned them myself. The one in the middle some six hundred years ago while I was yet in my own flesh. The other two I fashioned a bit more recently."

Aethon stared at the slabs, completely at the mercy of the rush of jealousy washing through him. Perhaps he had allied himself with the wrong Dreadlord after all.

"I never would have imagined so much kalamite existed in the world," he said at last. "Do you have a stockpile here in Tamba?"

"Not in Tamba, my naive young friend. Kalamite is not of this world any more than Jexlair is. I commandeered the kalamite for the newest slabs from a mine in Con'Jithar."

He stared at her, unsure if he was hearing the truth.

She narrowed her eyes at him. "You don't believe me. Well, suit yourself. It's the end result that matters, not your inherent mistrust of me or my abilities."

"And that end result is...?"

Her beautiful mouth curved into a smile. "I'll show you."

Turning him toward the glass doors of a balcony, she seized the Power and used a corrupted tendril of Air to pull the doors open. A cool breeze washed over him as he neared, but it felt warm compared to *Frel'mola's* icy grip.

The balcony overlooked a large interior courtyard, and Aethon's breath caught in his throat as the area below came into view. An army of *Maa'tisis* ten or twelve thousand strong stood at attention, their grey faces expressionless, their eyes glowing red with the fires of hell. At the appearance of their Dreadlord master, they raised jeweled scepters and shouted in unison. "*Frel'mola sem grazken! Frel'mola te Ujen kala seimei!*"

Aethon didn't speak Tamban well, but he understood enough of the shout to repeat it in the Common Tongue. "Long live the Bride of Maeon," he said. "The Fist of the Dark Bride stands ready."

"So, you're not just a pretty face after all," she said, eyeing him curiously. "I'm impressed. There aren't many in the Nine Lands willing to learn Tamban." She looked down at the *Maa'tisis* once more. "So what do you think?"

"I think you are planning to conquer Trian for yourself," he answered, watching her face for some sign of what she might be thinking.

"I thought you might say that," she told him, pursing her lips into a playful pout. "And it pains me that you don't trust me."

He grunted. "As you said: I'm not just another pretty face."

Squeezing his arm, she waved her other hand dismissively. "Nevertheless," she said, "they are yours to command. And another fifty thousand living troops stand ready to join you as soon as you desire."

"You're being awfully generous with your resources," he said. "What's the catch?"

"No catch, my pet," she said. "I'm simply demonstrating my love for my husband."

"Of course," he said, and let the matter drop. Twelve thousand Deathmen and fifty thousand soldiers would make a nice addition to his army regardless of where their allegiance might truly lie. He would simply need to keep an eye out for anything suspicious. Because despite *Frel'mola's* seemingly innocent generosity, she was up to something. Only a fool would believe otherwise.

Turning her back on the courtyard, she hooked her arm in his and led him back into the refleshing chamber. "Now that we've taken care of business," she said, "would you care to join me for a little pleasure?"

"If it involves your earlier offer of challenging me in bed, I'm afraid I'll have to pass. Refleshed Dreadlords aren't my type."

Her laugh was without humor. "Then perhaps you'll settle for a dance performance. Commander Naxis assures me they are the finest in all of Tamba."

"It would be my pleasure," he told her, as much out of curiosity for what passed for dance in this country as from a desire to further irritate Commander Naxis. The man was obviously jealous of how much attention *Frel'mola* was giving to an outsider. He might even be worried that *Frel'mola* was considering replacing him.

Aethon cast a sideways glance at the Dreadlord's exquisitely beautiful face and, for the briefest of moments, entertained the thought of becoming first among the living in Tamba.

Kneeling in the corridor leading to the grand throne room of Berazzel, Kaiden Kado kept his forehead pressed to the floor as *Frel'mola* passed with Aethon Fairimor at her side. To do otherwise was death, for looking upon *Frel'mola* without express permission was forbidden.

Kaiden smiled. But a good spy didn't need eyes when his ears could tell him all he needed to know. Like how neither *Frel'mola* nor her Kelsan companion so much as looked down at him or the other servants as they passed. To them, he was of no more significance than an insect, so far beneath their notice that he may as well not have existed at all. It made being a spy in this Light-blasted place that much easier.

He listened to them pass down the corridor and out of earshot, then rose and hurried in the opposite direction. As always, the entire palace was alive with corrupted wieldings, and *Ta'shaen* reeled and trembled in pain because of it.

He kept his Awareness safely inside his mindward out of necessity, but it pained him to do so. He was a servant of the Earthsoul, and he desperately wanted to do something to alleviate her pain.

*In time*, he told himself. *All in good time. Remember why you are here.*

It was difficult to resist the urge to lash out, but his resolve continued to tighten the farther away he moved from the refleshed Dreadlord. He could have destroyed her with a burst of Fire so easily, but revealing himself as *Shomei* would serve no purpose but to get him killed. His cover would be blown, and he would suffer a horrible death at the hands of the *Jeth'Jalda*. Or worse, *Frel'mola* once she was refleshed.

The thought sent a shiver through him and he quickened his pace. When no one was looking, he tied a strip of green cloth around his arm and kept his eyes on the floor as he walked, careful not to make eye contact with those he passed. The armband would tell anyone who saw him that he was on an errand and should not be interrupted.

It wasn't long before he reached the high-domed chamber of the palace's main entrance, and he crossed the tiled expanse with the same sense of purpose. He could feel the eyes of a pair of Deathwatch guards upon him as he approached the doors leading to the outside world, but they didn't question his reason for leaving the palace.

*Your mistake*, he thought as he passed between them and moved out into the daylight. *For now my people will know your Empress has created a refleshed army.*

He passed through the gate of the palace's outer wall without incident, and continued on into the bustling city. *Just another Tamban face in the crowd*, he thought smugly. Too bad for *Frel'mola* and her lackeys that he'd been born in Rosda, and it was to Rosda that he owed his allegiance. Rosda and the Earthsoul.

He waited until he was several blocks away from the palace before removing the arm band. Then, when he was certain no one was paying him any mind, he moved into the seclusion of a narrow, cluttered alleyway and made his way through the maze of back streets and alleys frequented by Berazzel's less fortunate—and occasionally less reputable—residents.

A half hour later, he reached the back door of the White Stag Tavern and slipped inside. Raucous laughter sounded loudly from the common room at the far end of the hallway, but he ignored it as he moved to the first door on his right and hurried inside, locking the door behind him.

The White Stag might be popular among the wealthier members of Berazzel's merchant class, but it was really just a front for Rosdan espionage, a safe house for spies like himself.

A single, curtained window let a small amount of light into the room, so he stood with his back to the door until his eyes adjusted to the near darkness. Everything was as he'd seen it last—five nondescript storage chests, an assortment of weapons on a lone table, several packs, and a box of dried foodstuffs.

He moved to the chest belonging to him, then stripped off the green and white livery of a palace servant and donned the soft greens and browns of a woodsman's clothing. It was much more comfortable than the livery, and he smiled in spite of the seriousness of the situation. Moving to the table of weapons, he strung a bow, then filled a quiver with arrows. With those on his back, he filled a small pack with a few food items, mostly dried meats and fruits.

Moving back to the door, he listened attentively for a moment to make sure the way was clear, then stepped out into the hallway and slipped out the back door and into the alley. With a little luck, he should be able to make it to his next destination by nightfall.

乇

Jase finished pulling on his own clothes, then stepped out from behind the bamboo screen and started for Maisen's schoolhouse. It was standing room only inside, but the way parted before him as he made his way to the podium at the front of the room and turned to face those who'd gathered. From the look of things, every Dai'shozen who'd been present with Shavis during his attack on the Arkanian armies was present. As were the Dymas who'd captained the striketeams against the demons holding the *droth'del*.

"Thank you for coming," he said. "And my condolences to all of you who lost friends and loved ones during the attacks."

"They died with honor," one of the Dai'shozen said. "Glory is theirs in the afterlife."

"So it is," Jase said, then let his eyes move over the congregation. "And glory is yours for conquering those who sought to overrun your nation. If the reports I've received are accurate—and I have no doubt that they are—the Arkanians have been chased back into their own lands, and the demons who led them have been destroyed."

"And the *droth'del?*" Clan Derga's Dai'shozen asked. "They've been destroyed?"

"Yes," Jase answered. "At least those Dai'shozen Dakshar had on his map. Short of searching every inch of that godforsaken jungle, there is no telling how many other villages may have access to the demons of Con'Jithar or where more rents might open."

"Which is why," Shavis said, drawing all eyes, "I will be sending striketeams to patrol the jungle on a line from the Inner Sea to the Storm Mountains. Ten miles south of the border should be sufficient to provide warning if another army seeks to enter Riak."

"And these striketeams," one of Avalam's Shozen began, "who will comprise them?"

"A small number of Shizu, Sarui, and Dymas from every clan who wishes to field one," Shavis answered. "I will assign the Myrscraw patrols who will be assisting in the effort."

"Still hoarding Shizu property, I see," a voice said, and Jase didn't need to look at the mark on the man's arm to know he was from Gizo or Kyoai. Even with the object lesson he'd delivered earlier in the day, the two clans seemed determined to incite rebellion whenever they could.

"Yes," Shavis said, his eyes boring into the man like augers. "And lest you forget, Shozen Imashi, the Shizu themselves are the property of the Emperor. So, unless you and the rest of Gizo's Shizu want to be assigned to the mile-wide rent thirty miles south of the border, you will hold your tongue."

"It still might not be a bad idea to send them there," Jase said, meeting Imashi's angry gaze. "There's no telling how many more demons might arrive from Con'Jithar." He looked at Shavis. "I can open the way for Gizo's Shizu right now if you wish."

Shavis looked as if he were taking the offer seriously, and the longer he deliberated, the more color drained from Imashi's face. Shavis finally shook his head. "That won't be necessary," he said. "I'm sure Clan Gizo would rather field teams along the line we just discussed."

Imashi's eyes smouldered with rage, but he dipped his head in acknowledgment.

"And the rest of our soldiers?" Doroku Dymas asked.

"Will remain here for the time being," Shavis answered. "As soon as I am satisfied the Arkanians won't be returning, they will be reassigned elsewhere. As you know, we have incurred a fairly significant debt to the *Mith'elre Chon*." He offered a bow of thanks to Jase. "And we will begin payment on that debt today as we send thirty more Dymas to join *Ao tres'domei*. It isn't as many as Kelsa deserves, but it is a start."

"And it is greatly appreciated," Jase told him. He let his eyes move over the faces of the men and women before him. "You won a great victory here today," he told them, "and you did it under the leadership of Dai'shozen Dakshar. Listen to his voice. Heed his council. If you do, Riak will ride out the rest of this storm relatively unscathed."

As soon as the words left his mouth, a powerful influx of *Ta'shaen* tickled his Awareness, affirming the words as prophecy. The light of wonder in Gideon's eyes showed he'd felt the Earthsoul's affirmation as well.

And it didn't stop there. Dozens of Dymas, including Railen and Sheymi, also showed signs of having felt the influx of Power. Faces bright with understanding, they whispered their thoughts about what they had felt. Railen put his arm around Sheymi as she wiped tears from her eyes. Doroku, Joshomi, and Ibari nodded to one another as if coming to an agreement, and the three stepped forward.

"We would like to be among those who are to join *Ao tres'domei* in Kelsa," Doroku said. A number of other Dymas gestured that they would like to be considered too.

"If I agree to that," Shavis said, directing his words to Doroku, "who would fill your role as Shozen of *tres'dia?*"

The short silence that followed was broken by Railen. "I will. With the Dai'shozen's permission, of course."

"You are a member of the Imperial Clave," Shavis told him. "Your responsibilities are political, not military."

"Really?" Sheymi asked. "Then why have Railen and I been on the front lines of two demon invasions these past few days?"

Jase chuckled before he could stop himself, and Shavis turned a flat stare on him. Jase met the look with a smile. "She has a point," he said. "They have more experience with demons than anyone else who could replace Doroku."

The muscles in Shavis' jaw tightened, and he looked as if he might refuse. Finally, he nodded. "It is proposed that Railen Nogeru act as the head of *tres'dia* until things quiet down here. At which time, we will reevaluate the appointment and the deployment of *tres'dia*. All in favor?"

Across the room, hands were raised in support, and Jase saw that it was nearly unanimous. Shavis took it all in with a glance, then nodded. "Any objections?"

He leveled a stare at the Shozen of Clans Gizo and Kyoai, but they kept their hands firmly at their sides.

"It is decided," Shavis said. "Railen and I will meet with our Dai'shozen to discuss our next moves. The rest of you get something to eat and get some rest. You are dismissed."

As people began filing out of the schoolhouse, Gideon and Seth stepped up to Jase. Doroku and the others who would be joining him moved near as well, and Jase smiled at them before turning his attention to Gideon.

"What now, *Mith'elre Chon?*" his father asked. "It's clear from the whisperings of the Earthsoul that you are no longer needed here."

"What whisperings?" Seth asked.

"Jase's words that Riak will ride out this storm unscathed were prophetic," Gideon told him. "All the Dymas here felt it."

"He said, *relatively* unscathed," Railen corrected. "That's why I volunteered to lead *tres'dia*. I plan to minimize whatever harm is yet to come."

"And I have complete faith in your abilities," Gideon told him with a smile. He looked back to Jase. "So, where are we needed?"

"Kelsa," he answered. "I want Idoman to know I haven't abandoned him."

と

Idoman finished reading the hastily written report he'd received from Captain Dennison, then scanned through a bulleted list Captain Tarn had written. As expected, Shadan's collapse of the western rim had necessitated some changes to their plans for moving the Kelsan army to Trian Plateau, and the two captains were doing what they could to accelerate the retreat.

"Tell Captain Dennison to move the supply wagons and other heavy equipment through Veilgates," Idoman told the lieutenant who'd delivered the messages. "I'll send him the Dymas he will need to open the gates. And Tarn is correct that our cavalry should move to the staging area on the plateau as well. But they can ride. I don't want to put any more strain on our Dymas than we have to."

"Yes, Dymas General," the other replied, then hefted himself back into the saddle and rode back the way he had come.

Idoman watched him go, then let his eyes move over the organized chaos that was men breaking camp. Most of the tents were down and were being rolled up and tossed into wagons, but there was a good deal more to do before he could give the order to march. He was grateful Death's Third March had decided to rest at the bottom of the newly formed ramp. Otherwise, most of this would need to be left behind to be used or destroyed by the enemy.

He was still watching the lowering of the command tent when a Veilgate opened and Jase Fairimor came through with Talia Chellum at his side. A number of others followed, including Gideon and Seth and Elliott and what looked to be about thirty Riaki Dymas.

Jase moved right up to Idoman as the Veilgate closed behind the last of the Dymas. "I was going to ask how things went," Jase said, "but the fact you are breaking camp would suggest that it did not go well."

Idoman pointed north toward the newly arranged cliff face. Ten miles distant, the changes weren't readily visible to the naked eye, so he embraced the Power and opened a window in the air above Shadan's army. "See for yourself," he said.

"Blood of Maeon," Elliott hissed, and Idoman nodded.

"Those were my thoughts exactly."

Jase studied the scene without speaking. Finally, he motioned for Idoman to close the window. "How did Shadan manage that?" he asked.

"Crux points," Idoman answered. "Hundreds of them. Heaven only knows when they were put there, but they bloody well served their purpose. Shadan just accelerated Death's Third March by two or three days."

"Then we'll just have to slow him down again," Jase said.

Elliott let out a hiss of frustration. "How?"

Jase looked at Idoman and smiled. "Crux points," he answered. "Just like we did in Zedik Pass."

"There is a possibility," Gideon said, sounding worried, "that Shadan may have placed crux points in other locations as well. Mendel Pass, for instance. Think what could happen to our army if that is the case."

"If they are there," Jase said, "we'll find them. But I don't think Shadan would risk collapsing the walls of the pass the way he did the plateau. He still needs to move an army through it, after all. Crux points inside the western rim make sense because they were a benefit. He won't negate the time he has gained just to kill a few more of Kelsa's soldiers. His objective is to reach Kelsa as quickly as possible."

"I agree," a familiar female voice said, and Idoman turned to find Quintella standing next to several other Rosdan Dymas. She wore a smile as always, but she looked tired. She moved toward Jase in a clicking of beads.

"I felt your arrival, *Mith'elre Chon*," she said. "And I can see in your eyes that your day has been even more eventful than ours."

"Nothing the combined might of Riak's clans couldn't handle," he said but didn't elaborate. Instead, he looked around as if expecting to see someone. "I caught a glimpse of the Meleki army there atop the plateau. Have we heard from Lord Nid?"

Idoman nodded. "Yes. He is with General Eries and the rest of the High Command on the south edge of camp. They're trying to decide what Melek's next move should be: join us through Veilgates or hang back so they can harass Shadan from the rear."

"I like the Meleki army where it is," Gideon said. "What better way to slow Shadan than by making him look over his shoulder."

"Funny you should say that," Idoman said, unable to hold back the smile that sprang to his face every time he thought about what Hul had done in the Pit. "Because Throy bloody Shadan is definitely looking over his shoulder now that his refleshing slab has been destroyed." His smile broadened as he continued. "Lord Nid and a team of Dymas attacked the Pit this morning and tore the place apart."

Gideon laughed aloud. "Praised be the Creator," he said. "That will cripple Shadan's ability to create more K'rrosha. It's still possible, I suppose, but it will be significantly more difficult without the slab."

Jase seemed amused by Gideon's enthusiasm. "It looks like we weren't the only ones closing doors to Con'Jithar," he said, then motioned everyone to follow. "Come with me. I want to congratulate Lord Nid on his accomplishment." He looked at the Riaki Dymas who'd arrived with him. "And then I will put you to work in Mendel Pass. I want Shadan to worry about what's in front of him as well as behind."

# CHAPTER 50

## *What Friends Do*

"WITH JASE'S HAND STILL GRASPED tightly in hers, Talia remained quiet as she and Jase led the way through the Kelsan camp in search of Lord Nid and General Eries. She took a long, slow breath and smiled. After so many days away, it felt good to finally be back in Kelsa, even if she was currently in the middle of a war zone. Home was home, after all, regardless of the circumstances.

"I couldn't agree more," Jase said softly. "Now we just need to defend it from those who would do it harm."

"Does that mean you are back on the front lines against Death's Third March?" she asked.

He shrugged. "I guess we'll find out. Every time I think I will be involved here, the Earthsoul calls me away on some other errand." He tried to laugh it off, but Talia knew from the feelings of helplessness reaching her through the *sei'vaiya* that Jase was being overwhelmed by all of it. "First it was Aridan," he continued. "Then Kunin. And then Riak and Arkania."

"You forgot Melek and Dainin," Gideon said, startling Talia so badly she tightened her grip on Jase's hand, popping some of his knuckles. She hadn't noticed the big Dymas edging near to listen in on the conversation, and she scowled at him to show her disapproval.

"I didn't forget," Jase said, meeting his father's gaze. "But welcoming Quintella and her people was a pleasure. And besides, I *chose* to go to Melek and Dainin."

Gideon laughed. "If you say so."

"You're not helping," Talia said, shaking her head at him when Jase wasn't looking.

"No he's not," Jase said. "The last thing I need right now is a thought exercise regarding fate versus agency."

Still smiling, Gideon shrugged, and they continued on in silence. A few minutes later, they spotted General Eries and Lord Nid. They were standing in a semi-circle with the rest of the High Command, and it was obvious they'd been alerted to Jase's arrival. A wide range of emotions painted their faces as they watched him approach, the most common being frustration.

"There you are," General Eries said as Jase neared. "We missed you today."

"You did fine without me," Jase said. "But I am sorry I wasn't here to help. I was needed in Riak."

"Riak?" General Gefion said. "Why on earth would you go there?"

Talia cringed inwardly, unable to decide if he sounded disbelieving or disapproving. From the corner of her eye, she saw several members of *Ao tres'domei* bristle at the general's tone.

"To put a stop to a full-scale Arkanian invasion," Seth snapped, giving Gefion a look so withering the man actually took an unconscious step backward. "An invasion that was led by thousands of demons loosed from Con'Jithar. So before any of you think about judging the *Mith'elre Chon* for his actions..." he let his eyes move down the line to let them know he meant all of them, "you might want to remember he represents all nations, not just Kelsa."

Talia struggled not to smile as she watched the silver-haired captain stare down the High Command. Seth's Riaki citizenship wasn't a secret to any of the men, but Talia suspected the outburst was less about patriotism and more about defending Jase. Even as angry as Seth was about Jase shooting him with a drugged dart, he hadn't hesitated in acting as the young man's warder.

"The war has many fronts," Jase told them. "And while some of you might find it frustrating, I go where I'm needed the most." He shook his head in frustration and turned to look north. "The problem is I feel like I'm standing in front of leaky dam. I put my finger in one hole only to have another leak spring up elsewhere."

"What's done is done," Gideon said, and it was clear from the way he was looking at the members of the High Command that he shared Seth's protective instincts. And not just those of a warder, but of a father. "I'm not sure the end result would be any different if the *Mith'elre Chon* had been here," he added. "If anything, things could have been a whole lot worse."

"I don't follow," General Eries said, frowning skeptically.

A sudden rush of understanding reached Talia through the *sei'vaiya*. "I would have tried to stop Shadan," Jase said, his eyes still on the western rim. "And I would have failed." He shook himself free of the thoughts Talia could sense warring inside him, then reached up and ran his fingers through his hair. "The Earthsoul called me away to keep me from getting myself and a lot of good men and women killed."

"And instead," Seth added, his face still hard as he watched the High Command, "he saved tens of thousands of lives in Riak."

Doroku Atasei stepped forward and dipped his head in greeting to the High Command. "And now *Ao tres'domei* stands ready to return the favor," he said. "Our lives were among those the *Mith'elre Chon* saved."

Leaving General Eries and the rest of the High Command standing in contemplative silence, Lord Nid moved forward to offer Jase his hand. "You're here now, my friend," he said. "That is all that matters."

Stepping back, he smiled at Talia. "It's good to see you again, young lady. I take it you're staying close by should the *Mith'elre Chon* need healing."

"It seems to be my lot in life," she said, then smiled at Jase.

"What is your plan for the Meleki army?" Jase asked.

"We are going to keep harassing Death's Third March from the rear," he answered, and Gideon nodded.

"I think that is wise," the big Dymas said. "But after what you did in the Pit, I think you should keep a low profile. Shadan is a vengeful cur. He's going to want you dead."

"He's been trying to kill me since he returned," Lord Nid said. "And yet here I am, alive and well and pleased to be an ever-deepening thorn in his refleshed side."

Jase reached up and clapped him on the arm affectionately. "Then keep sticking him," he said. "And thank you for coming to our aid."

"It's what friends do," the Meleki King said. "Now, if you will excuse me, I need to meet with the Meleki High Command to plan our next move. I'll keep in touch."

With that, he turned and opened a Veilgate into the midst of his army and moved through to join his men.

As the Veilgate slid silently closed, Jase looked back to the High Command. "Continue the relocation of our armies," he told them. "*Ao tres'domei* and I will inspect the pass for corrupted crux points. Once we determine all is clear, we will begin laying traps of our own."

He turned to Idoman. "If you can spare a minute away from your duties here, I would like you to join us."

"With pleasure," Idoman said, then motioned for Quintella to come as well.

Jase looked at Gideon. "Are you coming?"

Gideon shook his head. "I think I should check on the Queen," he said. "I want to know if she and the others learned anything else from the archives."

Jase nodded. "After I finish in the pass, I'll check in with Elison. He's going to need to accelerate the evacuation of Trian and its surrounding areas."

"What would you like me to do?" Seth asked.

"Come with me," Jase said. "We can talk about what happened in Arkania."

Elison Brey swung down from his horse and handed the reins to Jaleb, the last of the palace's livery boys. The young man took the reins with a smile, then led Elison's horse in the direction of the palace stables, rubbing the horse's neck affectionately and whispering words of encouragement.

Elison smiled, once again impressed with the young man's strength of spirit. Like many others who'd been present the day of Stalix Geshiann's coup, Jaleb had lost people who were dear to him, including his mother and father, an older sibling, and a number of friends. All had been killed by Darklings when the palace was overrun. Jaleb had survived by hiding in the straw in one of the stalls.

After Trian's liberation, and with no other family in the city, Jaleb had taken up residence in one of the small apartments near the stables, working to earn his keep, and, more recently, ignoring the order for all civilian staff to evacuate.

Elison was concerned for the boy's safety, of course, but he couldn't find it in his heart to make Jaleb leave. The horses and the *Bero'thai* who rode them had become his family, and he had no desire to leave that family after having already lost so much. Besides, the *Bero'thai* might not let Jaleb leave even if Elison gave the order. All of them looked upon the boy kindly, and many had started referring to him as "little brother."

Elison watched Jaleb disappear into the stables, then turned toward the palace entrance—

And flinched in surprise when he found Ammorin and Pattalla standing a few feet away, watching.

"Geeze," he hissed. "Don't sneak up on me like that."

"We weren't sneaking," Ammorin said, a broad smile moving over his face. "You were simply lost in thought."

"Then make more noise next time," Elison told them. "Otherwise it's sneaking."

"How proceeds the evacuation?" Pattalla asked, changing the subject.

"Slower than I would like," he answered. "And now we have a new problem."

"Looting," Ammorin said. "We heard of it from Captain Dium."

"It isn't just looting," Elison said. "Some people are claiming homes vacated by others. They aren't taking a few valuables as looters would, they're taking possession of the entire house." He shook his head in frustration. "What good will that do if the enemy burns it down around them?"

"What are the City Guardsmen doing about it?" Ammorin asked.

"Arresting those who are guilty," he answered, aware of the frustration rising in his voice. "But since we can't very well throw all of them into prison, the best we can do is escort them out of the city and hope they don't come back."

"But some of them are coming back," Lavin Dium said, and for the second time in under a minute, Elison jumped.

"Don't any of you people make noise when you walk?" he asked. "You could at least scuff your boots or something when you draw near."

"Wouldn't that undermine our abilities as warders?" Lavin asked, exchanging amused looks with the Dainin.

"It would certainly undermine the entertainment value of startling our dear captain," Ammorin said with a smile. He sobered almost immediately and knelt to look Elison in the eye. "You've been awful jumpy the past few days. Is there something we should know about?"

"What more do you need?" Elison asked. "The Veil is collapsing all across the world, the Earthsoul is in Her death throes, and Death's Third March is already to the western rim."

"Actually," Lavin said, "they've made it to the Bottomlands. Idoman Leda sent word by way of some of our Dymas that Shadan collapsed the western rim into a massive rampway."

Elison stared at him for a moment, then looked back to Ammorin. "And you wonder why I'm so jumpy."

Ammorin smiled knowingly. "You're worried about the people who have yet to evacuate," he said. "And your preoccupation with their safety has become a distraction. You weren't always this easy to sneak up on."

"So, you *have* been sneaking up on me."

"Not any more than was necessary to keep you safe," Ammorin admitted, "or to keep me and Pattalla entertained."

"You should tell him," Pattalla urged, and Elison narrowed his eyes at them both. "Tell me what?"

"We were with you for most of the afternoon," Ammorin said. "Wrapped in bended Light so as not to alert you or your enemies that we were warding you."

"And you are lucky we did," Pattalla added. "We stopped three different attempts on your life."

"Two were by people who appear to have ties to the Con'Kumen," Ammorin said. "The other was by an assassin hired by someone in House Geshiann. He gave his confession shortly before we turned him and the others over to the City Guardsmen."

Elison wasn't surprised to learn there were still Con'Kumen in the city. Nor was he surprised that someone in House Geshiann would hire an assassin to kill him. He was surprised—and more than a little irritated with himself—that he had been completely oblivious to the attempts on his life. "Thanks for watching out for me," he said. "And you were right that I'm preoccupied. I didn't notice a thing out of the ordinary today."

"Arrows pointed at your back aren't easy to see," Ammorin said. "But you should be thanking Captain Tas. He's the one who suggested we shadow you today. And he was spot on about where in the city the attempts would take place."

Elison smiled. "Medwin's a crafty one," he said. "I'm glad he's on our side."

"My apologies for changing the subject," Lavin said, his sharp Elvan features lined with curiosity, "but how did you get the assassin to confess it was House Geshiann that hired him?"

"Ammorin threatened to bite his arms and legs off and leave him in the middle of the street for the *Bero'thai* to find," Pattalla said, giving Ammorin a wide grin.

Elison stared at the Dainin Chieftain in disbelief. "That's a bit much, don't you think?"

Ammorin shrugged his massive shoulders uncomfortably, his face darkening with embarrassment. "It's the only thing I could think of in the heat of the moment."

"Well, it worked," Elison said. "So, thank you."

Ammorin shrugged again. "If you are going up to the Fairimor home," he said, obviously eager to change the subject, "we can save you the trouble of climbing all the stairs."

"I would like that," Elison told him, then watched as Ammorin made a small gesture with his hand and opened a Veilgate in front of them.

"After you, Captain," the Dainin said, and Elison moved through to find that Endil Fairimor had returned from Chunin. He sat at the dining table with Jeymi and Thorac and a number of Chunin wearing the mark of Dymas. Some Elison recognized—they'd been with Thorac and Endil in Kunin—but the rest had the appearance of new recruits.

The Veilgate closed with Lavin and the Dainin still at the stables, but Elison didn't have time to consider why they didn't join him in the palace. Endil and the others were staring at him, waiting.

"Lord Fairimor," he said, "you are back sooner than I expected."

Endil gave a tired smile. "We did what we went there to do," he said, his voice as tired as his smile. "Emma has been laid to rest in the Garden of Heroes, and we spent some time with her family." He looked at Thorac and smiled. "Well, the rest of her family, anyway."

Thorac smiled, but there wasn't a hint of what he might be thinking. Elison hadn't learned until after Endil and the others had left for Chunin that Emma was Thorac's sister-in-law.

"How is your wife holding up?" Elison asked as he moved to the table and took an empty chair across from Thorac. "I imagine her sister's death was hard for her."

Thorac's smile widened. "My wife is stronger than I will ever be," he said. "In fact, it was she who sent us back to Kelsa. She said Emma would expect us to stop moping around and get back in the fight. She is very much like her sister when it comes to things like that."

When he said nothing more, Elison let his eyes move down the table to the Dymas. "Were you friends of Emma as well?" he asked.

"She was our mentor," a green-eyed gal answered. Her hair was the brightest shade of red Elison had ever seen, and her face was covered with freckles. She looked younger than Jeymi, but there was a fierceness in her eyes that overshadowed her apparent youth.

"When we learned she'd been killed," another one of the younglings said, "we felt the need to pick up where she left off. We have come to stand with Kelsa against the Dark One."

"And your help is very much appreciated," he told them. "On behalf of High Queen Fairimor and her son, the *Mith'elre Chon*, I welcome you to Trian."

"Is he here?" the freckle-faced girl asked. "Will we get to meet the *Mith'elre Chon?*"

Elison was amused by her enthusiasm. "Hard to say," he answered. "I never know when he might drop in." He noted the sudden look of disappointment, then turned his attention back at Thorac. "Have you eaten? If not, I'll have Allisen bring something up."

"We already placed our orders," Thorac said, grinning more like his old self. "I hope you don't mind."

"Not at all," Elison said. "I'm glad you have your appetite back."

They made small talk while they waited for their food, and Elison learned the names of the young Dymas who'd been mentored by Emma. The bright-haired one was Haeley. The other three girls were Olisia, Bryston, and Annika. Mishka and Jardis were the two young men. Kelby, Gwenin, Aierlin, and Lizette, he already knew.

When the food arrived, the conversation tapered off as everyone ate, then gradually started up again as plates were emptied and pushed aside.

"So what did we miss?" Thorac asked, leaning back in his chair.

"Plenty," Elison told him. "Shadan and his—" He cut off as a Veilgate opened in front of the fireplace and Jase came through with Talia and Seth and Elliott.

Jase smiled as his eyes lighted on Thorac. "Hello, my friend," he said, striding forward to shake his hand. As he did, Elison caught a glimpse of Mendel Pass through the Veilgate as it closed. Idoman was there with a large number of Riaki Dymas.

"I was just asking Elison what we missed," Thorac said as he released Jase's hand. "So, what happened while we were away?"

Jase grunted a laugh. "More than I ever would have imagined possible, but stories will need to wait. Will a list suffice?"

Thorac grinned. "As long as we get all the details eventually."

"You have my word," Jase said, then frowned thoughtfully. "You already know about the demon invasion in Amnidia and the recovery of the Blood Orb from Melek," he began. "So that leaves Shadan's collapsing of the western rim to move his army into the Bottomlands. A second demon invasion into southern Riak—we put a stop to it, by the way. The Meleki army arriving on Talin Plateau to press Shadan from the rear." He paused and cast a quick look at Elliott. "Oh, and Elliott became the first of a new generation of Dragonriders."

Thorac's jaw literally dropped as he turned to stare at the Chellum Prince. "You *rode* a Dragon?" he asked, then shook himself free of the surprise and motioned Elliott to take a seat. "That is a story which cannot wait. Tell."

When Jase smiled at his friend's enthusiasm and motioned for Elliott to sit, Elison realized this had been his plan all along. What better way to get Thorac's mind off of Emma's death than to tease him with news of events and then drop a tidbit so tantalizing there would be no way he could pass it up?

Endil and Jeymi were equally intrigued and leaned forward eagerly. So did Aierlin and the older Chunin Dymas. The younglings, though curious about Elliott's adventures, were clearly more interested in the *Mith'elre Chon*. Eyes wide with awe and admiration, every one of them was watching Jase the way a young child might watch a heroic older brother.

Jase waited until Elliott had begun his tale, then motioned for everyone else to join him in the other half of the room.

"Nicely done," Elison whispered as they moved away from the table. "Thorac is back to being himself."

Jase shrugged. "Just doing what I can to help my friend."

They moved into the ring of sofas surrounding the Blue Flame rug, and Jase gestured for everyone to sit. When all were settled, he had the Chunin introduce themselves.

"Welcome to Trian," Jase told them when they finished, and Elison was impressed by how easily the young man put them all at ease. "If you will open your Awareness to me, I will quickly bring you up to speed on what we face."

As Elison watched, Chunin eyes narrowed in concentration, then widened again as images from Jase's mind reached the young Power-wielders through the Communal link. A few mouths dropped open. Every back stiffened in surprise or horror or both.

The Communal moment was short lived, but Elison knew it was over when a collective sigh of relief broke the silence.

"My apologies for the gruesome brutality of some of what you witnessed," Jase told them. "But you deserve the truth about what will be required of you if you choose to join this fight. It will be brutal and bloody, and not all of you will make it through unharmed. Physically or emotionally."

Elison cringed. *So much for putting them at ease,* he thought, then waited without breathing for someone to respond. It was Haeley who broke the silence, her bright green eyes shining with conviction.

"We are with you, *Mith'elre Chon,*" she said. "No matter what."

Jase smiled at her. "Knowing you were trained by Emma lets me know I can trust that statement," he told her, then looked at the others. "That goes for all of you."

"What would you have us do?" Olisia asked.

"We need to finish preparing the city for Shadan's arrival," he told them. "How skilled are you at creating traps and setting crux points?"

A few nervous glances were exchanged, then Haeley cleared her throat. "We have no experience with such things," she admitted.

Jase leaned forward and looked her in the eyes. "Then let me teach you."

Haeley Dromm felt like she couldn't breathe. She was in the presence of the *Mith'elre Chon.* The *Mith'elre Chon!* And he had just offered to teach her! This was not how she had expected things to turn out. Help Kelsa fight Maeon, yes. But learning from the *Mith'elre Chon* himself—she never would have dreamed of such a thing.

When she realized he was waiting for an answer, she swallowed hard and found her voice. "It would be an honor, *Mith'elre Chon.*"

"Please," he said, "call me Jase."

He turned his attention to Captain Brey. "I understand you are having trouble with looting and with people moving in to claim homes vacated by others."

Elison furrowed his brow at him. "How do you know that?" he asked. "You just got here."

Haeley watched the *Mith'el*— watched Jase laugh. "Ammorin told me," he said. "Just now, through his Awareness." His face sobered as he continued. "He also said three different people tried to kill you today. Do you remember how I reacted the last time someone tried to do that? The promise I made to the assassin you so freely forgave and sent on his way?"

"I do," Elison said, "but you know my reason for sparing that man's life."

"Yes," Jase said. "And I respect what you did that day. But I won't tolerate looting or people claiming homes which don't belong to them any more than I will overlook the fact that members of one of the prominent Houses hired an assassin to kill you."

Elison waved Jase off. "You have more important things to worry about. Let me deal with these lesser problems."

"I'll let you deal with the looters," Jase said. "But an assassination attempt on the Captain of the Home Guard is not a *lesser* problem. House Geshiann will learn firsthand the foolishness of trying to kill one of my friends."

He rose and Lady Talia rose with him. "Can I assume they've moved to their estates outside the city?" Jase asked, and Elison nodded.

"Good. This won't take long."

Striding to the fireplace, he embraced the Power and deftly—almost effortlessly, it seemed to Haeley—opened a Veilgate into a large, lavishly furnished room in the Geshiann estates. With Talia at his side, he moved through, and the startled cries of those in the room beyond vanished into silence as the gate slid shut.

"I would not want to be in that room right now," Elison said, and Haeley smiled.

"I would. I want to see what he does to them."

"Are you sure?" Olisia asked. "After seeing what he did to the demons and Agla'Con in Arkania, I don't know if I could stomach much more."

"Demons and servants of Maeon deserve a brutal demise," Elison said. "But the *Mith'elre Chon* won't harm defenseless civilians, no matter how misguided they might be. He'll send a powerful message, but it won't involve physical harm."

He sounded confident, but Haeley could tell by his smile that he wasn't so sure. And if Captain Brey was worried, maybe she should be too.

The looks on the faces of Eminor and Clevin Geshiann were better than Talia could have imagined, but she kept her face smooth as she watched Jase stare them and everyone else in the room into silence. She could feel Jase's anger through the love-bond, and while it was hot and mingled with contempt and a great deal of disgust, it was controlled.

The blood draining from the faces of Eminor and Clevin showed they believed otherwise. Clinging to one another in fear, they dropped to their knees and waited for Jase to destroy them with a burst of *Ta'shaen*. Talia would have pitied them if not for the fact they'd tried to have Elison killed.

Jase stared at the two until they looked at the floor to avoid his gaze, then turned to regard the rest of those in the room. Clevin and Eminor might be the senior members of House Geshiann, but Kalix and Jamisin were the most active politically. Cousins to Stalix, both held law degrees and had worked in Trian's court system as criminal defense attorneys. Talia suspected that if she looked into court records she would discover that the majority of those they'd represented over the years had turned out to be members of the Con'Kumen. Fortunately, Jase's destruction of the Con'Kumen organization had eliminated most of their clientele.

From Kalix and Jamisin, she turned her attention to the four women huddled together on a sofa. Two had the look of a Geshiann and were likely daughters or nieces of Clevin and Eminor. The other two had likely married into the family. A fifth woman occupied a nearby chair, and Talia blinked in surprise when she recognized her as Whillipel Volmara, one of those Stalix Geshiann had nominated for appointment to the Kelsan High Tribunal.

"You know why I'm here," Jase said, and the sharpness of his tone made Eminor and the others flinch. "The assassin you hired to kill Captain Brey gave you up shortly after he failed."

"This is outrageous," Kalix said, finding his voice. "The word of a hired thug holds no weight in a court of law."

Jase made a slight motion with his hand, and Kalix's eyes went wide as he reached to his throat

"I didn't give you permission to speak," Jase told him. "And this isn't a court of law. This is a warning from the *Mith'elre Chon* to you and to all those who would do harm to my friends or to this city." He hesitated while Kalix continued to struggle for air, then finally released him before turning to Clevin and Eminor.

"In light of everything House Geshiann has done over the years—and I'm only partly referring to your black-hearted cousin, the former Chief Judge—I'm dissolving House Geshiann as a member of the ruling class and stripping you of all the rights and privileges that came with your title. Neither you, nor any member of your family, will ever set foot inside Fairimor Palace again."

He turned to Whillipel Volmara. "The same goes for House Volmara."

Whillipel's face twisted into a mask of rage. "But I've done nothing!" she hissed. "These people ordered the assassination of your friend. Not me. I'm innocent."

"That's a lie," Kalix shouted, "she—" He cut off again, his eyes bulging.

Jase turned a hard eye on him for a moment then looked back to Whillipel.

"Wrong," he told her, and Talia was impressed with how calm he remained. "As you said: You did nothing. You knew of the plot to kill Captain Brey and you kept it to yourself. You are just as guilty as House Geshiann."

"Are you going to kill us?" one of the women on the couch asked. Her face was white and she was shaking.

Jase's expression never changed as he looked at her. "No. I'm not going to kill you. I need you alive to help spread the message about what happens to those who live and work in darkness."

Even without the *sei'vaiya* to help her sense Jase's thoughts and feelings, she would have known he was drawing in more of the Power—the look in his eyes gave it away. She'd witnessed it enough times to know something big was coming. Something destructive.

Hooking her arm through his, she braced herself just as the entire estate exploded outward in a burst of shattered debris. The bubble-like wall of ruined timber and plaster and glass rained down on the surrounding property with a tremendous, grinding roar that tore down outbuildings and ripped up well-manicured gardens.

Of the room she and Jase and the others had occupied, only the floor remained, a square patch of polished hardwood now exposed to the full light of day and surrounded by a field of rubble.

Clevin and Eminor and the rest of House Geshiann stared at the destruction in silence, unwilling or unable to speak.

"You would do well to leave Trian and never return," Jase told them. "If ever we meet again, I won't be this merciful." He turned and looked at Whillipel. "I wouldn't bother returning to your estate," he told her, making a small gesture with his hand and parting the Veil. Then, without another word, he led Talia through into the room beyond.

乇

Elison watched the Veilgate close behind Jase and Talia, then rose to greet them as they made their way to the ring of sofas.

"That didn't take very long," he said, then added a hesitant, "You didn't kill anyone did you?"

"No, he didn't," Jeymi answered, leaving the dining table to join him and the others at the sofas. Endil came with her, but Elliott and Thorac were still engrossed in swapping stories. Elison smiled, pleased to see Thorac truly enjoying himself once again.

"But," Jeymi added, "he certainly made a mess."

Elison raised an eyebrow at Jase in question. "What did you do?"

"Let's just say Houses Geshiann and Volmara are no more and leave it at that." The look he directed at Jeymi told her to let the matter drop, but she obviously didn't see it.

"Literally," she continued, shaking her head in disbelief and making an explosive sound accompanied by hand gestures. "Ka boom. No more house." She looked at Endil. "And you thought I was the destructive one."

"Every Dymas in the city felt what you did," Aierlin piped in. "Lucky for you we could feel the pureness of the strike. Otherwise we might have believed the city was under attack by Death's Third March."

"It will be soon enough," Jase told her. "Thus the need to clear out more of the riffraff."

"Volmara too, huh?" Elison asked.

Jase nodded. "Whillipel was part of the plot."

Turning his attention to the Chunin Dymas, Jase motioned for them to stand.

"So," he began, sounding like nothing out of the ordinary had just happened, "who's ready to learn how to lay traps to kill shadowspawn?"

# CHAPTER 51

## *Prophetic Possibilities*

BRYSIA PLACED THE BOOK ON top of the stack to be reshelved, then sighed tiredly as she picked up another and began thumbing through its pages. *Two days,* she thought, more frustrated with the lack of progress than she was willing to admit. *Two bloody days of cryptic nonsense and dead ends.*

And yet, what else could she and the others do but keep searching? There had to be something of value in Elva's vast storehouse of knowledge. Even a single passage of meaningful scripture could make all the difference. They just had to find it.

Movement to her right brought her out of her thoughts, and she looked up as one of Professor Neaman's graduate students picked up her stack of discards and scurried away. Brysia watched her go, then took a moment to watch the rest of Neaman's students.

Ranging in age from seventeen to forty, they'd come to Elldrenei to study Old World History, and all had jumped at the chance to help in the search. Most were Elvan, but there were several from Kelsa, two from Zeka, and one petite, yet feisty little woman from Chunin. Brysia smiled when she spotted her climbing a ladder to reach books on the top shelf. Like the rest of those in the program, her enthusiasm made up for her lack of knowledge. Brysia was just grateful for the extra help.

She spotted Professor Neaman exiting one of the rows with a stack of books in his hands and watched him join some of his students at a large table. They greeted him with smiles and made room for his stack of books. He'd cancelled classes so his students could help with the search, telling them it was a real-world application of their studies.

"Listen to this," Beraline said excitedly, and Brysia turned toward her as she started to read.

*And the voice of Her spirit said unto me: Look!*

*And I looked and beheld a tall mountain, even The Holy Mountain of The Second Creation. And I beheld also that it was dark within, such that I could not see. Not with the eyes of my body nor with the eyes of my spirit.*

*And the voice spake unto me again, saying: Knowest thou the meaning of this thing which I have shown thee? And I said, I know not.*

*And then the voice said: Herein lies the Blood Seed of the Rejuvenation. And none shall enter but by the Power of the Blue Flame. For without the Flame there can be no light, neither breath of life nor hope for salvation. Guard ye, therefore, the Flame, lest the way to salvation remain closed and the world perish in darkness.*

Brysia could barely contain her excitement as she considered what she'd just heard. Finally! Something that sounded—something that *felt* like prophecy. And not a dark prophecy either, but one sent from the Light.

The smile on Xia's face and the excited whispers coming from Cassia and Andil showed they thought so as well. Marithen was watching Beraline with such intensity that Brysia thought she might break into one of her singsongs. But the normally distant and distracted look so often present in her eyes was gone. She seemed clear-minded for a change; she seemed focused.

"What book is that?" she asked, and even Beraline seemed taken aback by the old woman's lucidity.

"I don't know," Beraline answered. "The title is written in Old World script, which is strange because the entries are in the Common Tongue, and the dates of those entries show they were written between A.S. 181 and A.S. 257. "

"May I see it?" Brysia asked.

"Of course," Beraline said, then marked the page with a slip of paper and handed the book over. It wasn't very thick, less than a hundred pages, and one of the corners looked like it had been chewed on by rats.

Brysia traced the raised gold symbols on the leather-bound cover with her finger, and her heart skipped a beat as she read. "*Isatsu Teisho en Robishar, Halleson mi Fairimor te Lisk.*" Then she translated: "The First Book of Robishar, Great-grandson of Fairimor the First."

She looked up. "Where did you find this?"

Beraline shrugged. "I didn't. One of Professor Neaman's students brought it to me."

"Do you remember which one? I want to know if there are more like this."

Beraline scanned the area for a moment, then pointed. "There. The young lady in the green and gold dress at that table there."

"I'll fetch her for you, my lady," a nearby *Bero'thai* said, then quickly made his way across the room to the table. The young woman looked up in surprise, then rose and hurried across the room.

"You wanted to see me, Queen Fairimor," she said. Her face was bright with excitement and she wore a friendly, eager smile.

"Yes, dear. What is your name?"

"Felicia, my lady. I'm one of Professor Neaman's students."

Brysia held up the book. "Where did you find this?"

Felicia looked at the Old World script on the cover, and her face grew even more excited. "I found it in the old wing of the Dremick Building," she said, then stiffened as if she'd said something reprehensible and cast about in embarrassment. Her cheeks turned red as she glanced at Xia then looked back to Brysia.

"I know I'm not supposed to go in there," she admitted, lowering her voice, "but hardly anyone uses the old wing anymore, so it's a nice place to study because it's so quiet. Anyway, a number of professors used to have offices there, and not everything they borrowed from the archives got put back where it belongs. When I heard we would be assisting you in your search for prophecies regarding the Rejuvenation, I brought it with me from the office I've been using for my studies. I've read parts of it before and knew it might be what you were looking for." Her face turned a deeper shade of red and she swallowed hard.

"Did I do something wrong, my lady?"

Brysia smiled reassuringly. "No, child," she said. "Thank you for bringing it to our attention. Perhaps it is time for me to find a quieter place to study as well." She let her eyes move around the room meaningfully.

"It is rather noisy in here of late," Felicia agreed. "Would you like me to show you the office where I found it?"

"That won't be necessary," she said. "I'm familiar with the Dremick Building." With the book still in hand, she gave Felicia a conspiratorial smile. "Besides, if you were to come with us, Professor Neaman would learn that you've been sneaking into the old wing and you would lose your quiet place to study."

The young woman seemed shocked. "You would keep this secret for me?"

"We all have secrets," Brysia said. "And without yours, we never would have learned of this book. Again, thank you for bringing it to us."

"You are most welcome," Felicia said, then curtsied to her and Xia and moved back to her stack of books.

Brysia watched her go, amused by the young woman's enthusiasm for academics and her willingness to bend the rules to find a little peace and quiet. Still smiling, she turned her attention back to Xia and Beraline. Marithen, bless her heart, had gone back to mumbling incoherently to herself and was absorbed in her reading.

"We need to speak to the head archivist," she told them. "Perhaps he will know if the *First Book of Robishar* has any sequels and, if so, where they might be."

Beraline nodded. "Agreed. And we should search the old wing as well. It's possible that whoever borrowed that book borrowed others with similar content." She looked as if she would say more but her eyes grew distant as she turned toward the doors at the far end of the room. When Marithen did likewise, Brysia knew they'd sensed a use of the Power.

"Gideon has returned," Beraline said. "But he arrived alone." Her eyes became focused once more, and she turned to look at Brysia. "He must be tired because someone else opened the Veilgate for him."

Brysia sighed. "Things must have been worse in Riak than we imagined," she said, then added a silent, *And Gideon likely flung himself into the middle of it.*

Which meant Jase probably had as well. Hopefully everyone had made it through the conflict unscathed. Gideon coming back alone didn't bode well for that, though, and fear tightened her stomach into a cold knot.

She rose as Gideon strode through the door, and the knot of fear vanished as he smiled at her. He was tired, yes—she could see his weariness on his face and in his eyes—but his smile was reassuring.

Dozens of pairs of eyes followed him as he moved across the room, but he paid them no mind as he wound his way through the tables and sofas of the study area. He'd come to report to his Queen, and the wide-eyed stares and awe-filled whispers of the graduate students would not slow that reunion.

Brysia rose to greet him as he neared, offering her hand as his Queen instead of his wife. He took it in his and kissed it, then bowed deeply. "My lady," he said. "I bring news from Riak and from the front."

She smiled to complete the charade, but inwardly she wanted to scream. She was so weary of acting like he was nothing more than her warder and advisor when they were around strangers that for a moment she considered ending the pretense by taking him in her arms and kissing him squarely on the mouth.

He must have seen something of her thoughts in her expression, because he squeezed her hand before releasing it with a smile. "Would you like to hear my report here or somewhere a little more private?"

She felt her cheeks flush with a sudden rush of heat. So he *had* sensed what she was thinking. She should have known he would. They might not share a *sei'vaiya* as Jase and Talia did, but there was something to be said for twenty-seven years of marriage when it came to reading one another's thoughts.

"Here will suffice for now," she told him, then glanced around at Professor Neaman's awestruck students. "Though we could do with a ward against eavesdropping."

"I'll take care of it," Beraline said, and the din of voices surrounding them was suddenly muted.

Motioning for Cassia and Andil to join them, Brysia returned to her seat and gestured for Gideon to sit in the chair opposite her. When everyone was settled, she turned to Gideon.

"We found something that might help," she said, patting the book in her lap.

"But first, I want to hear about your visit to Riak."

"It was quite a day," he began, rubbing at his beard as if not sure where to start. "Jase put an end to the coup with barely any effort at all. Gizo and Kyoai just needed a reminder on who the real enemy is, and Jase's use of Veilgates to allow demons into their midst did the trick. It was bloody brilliant."

Then, as Brysia warred with a wide range of emotions at what she was hearing, Gideon quickly summarized the rest of the day.

The shock of learning Gwuler Hom was alive and was once again a servant of the Earthsoul gave way to horror at the sheer size of the demon-led Arkanian army. The drug-induced frenzy of the Arkanians dredged up the utter helplessness and revulsion and fear she'd felt while being held captive in the jungle village, but those gave way to relief that the Arkanian invasion had been turned back and the demons and the *droth'del* which allowed them into the living world had been destroyed.

In the end, though, all the fear and anger and remorse was swallowed up in an overwhelming sense of pride for her son. Jase's decision to go to Riak had saved countless Riaki lives and had once again determined the fate of nations and possibly the Earthsoul. He proved that the war against Maeon could be won.

She had a number of follow-up questions, mostly regarding Gwuler's return and Seth's reaction to being drugged by Jase, but they were superfluous in light of the more serious matters still needing to be discussed. Not the least of which was the book she held in her hands.

"From Riak," Gideon continued, "we went to the front. I assume you heard what happened there today."

"Yes," she said. "Lord Reiekel has been sending us regular updates. At first we thought the report on Shadan collapsing the western rim was an exaggeration."

"If only," Gideon said. "But it happened, and now Death's Third March is in the Bottomlands. They will start for Mendel Pass tomorrow morning." His hands knotted into fists for a moment, then he took a deep breath and forced himself to relax.

"But it's not all bad news," he added. "Lord Nid moved the Meleki armies in behind Death's Third March. Even more significant, Lord Nid himself attacked the Pit and destroyed Shadan's means for refleshing Agla'Con."

Brysia was impressed but also shocked that the High King would risk himself in such a way, regardless of how significantly it would affect Shadan's abilities to wage war. "That *is* good news," she said. "This might be as well." She handed the *First Book of Robishar* to him and watched his eyes widen in surprise as he read the title.

"Where did you find this?" he asked, opening the book and leafing through its pages.

"One of the graduate students found it in the old wing of the Dremick Building," she answered, watching as Gideon looked up in surprise.

"I thought the old wing was off limits to students," he said. "Dean Bellistor will tan that young person's hide if she finds out."

Brysia felt a rush of sympathy that her husband still didn't know so much of what had happened in the world while he'd been locked away in Shadan's dungeon.

"Dean Bellistor was killed during the Battle of Greendom," she told him. "As were most of the rest of Elldrenei's Dymas-Professors. Those few who did survive didn't return to Elldrenei to resume teaching. Their offices have sat silent these past twenty years. It's become a kind of unspoken memorial to those who died, and no one but custodial staff enters the old wing anymore." She looked at Felicia and smiled. "No one but that young lady, anyway. And praised be the Creator she did. Please, read what's on the page Beraline marked."

Gideon turned to the bookmark, and his face took on a look of wonder as he read. When he finished, he sat quietly, his eyes narrow with thought as he considered what the passages might mean.

"The Blood Seed of the Rejuvenation," he said at last. "Blood Seed." He fell silent again as he scratched his cheek. "It's a term I've never encountered before, but I believe it's referring to a Blood Orb of Elsa."

"That's what I thought too," she told him. "And I still think the Holy Mountain of the Second Creation refers to Mount Tabor. This is the second time an Elvan author from the first two centuries has used that exact wording."

Her husband's face creased with thought as he read the passage again. When he finished, he looked up, and there was a glimmer of understanding in his eyes. "*I beheld also that it was dark within,*" he quoted, "*such that I could not see. Not with the eyes of my body nor with the eyes of my spirit.*"

"*The eyes of my spirit,*" Beraline began, "is a reference to Robishar's Awareness. He was a Dymas."

Gideon nodded. "When I was inside Tabor with Jase, not only were many of the passages and chambers devoid of visible light, my Awareness was useless to me. The luminescent view of the world available through *Ta'shaen* was lost in darkness. I could still wield the Power to light the way, but I could see nothing more than my natural eyes allowed."

"Shadan's Curse," Xia muttered, and Gideon nodded.

"Yes. Fortunately, the Soul Chamber is unaffected by the curse so I had a point I could focus on as we made our way into the mountain."

"So it is possible," Brysia said, a sudden hope sweeping through her as she followed her earlier thoughts about the Holy Mountain, "that you only saw part of what Tabor might contain. And if so, could there possibly be a Temple of Elderon somewhere inside as well? After all, in its day it was hallowed ground. Only the priests of the early church and the descendants of Elsa were allowed to enter. Some of those who entered are said to have heard the voice of Elsa. Robishar's words prove that much at least."

"It couldn't be that easy," Beraline said. "Could it? I mean, all this time, the means for the Rejuvenation has been right there in direct proximity to the Soul Chamber."

Gideon's face was a mask of seriousness. "There's only one way to find out," he said. "I go back to Tabor. And this time I take the Blue Flame Scepter with me. According to Robishar's vision, it's the only way the Blood Seed can be retrieved."

"What about Jase?" Brysia asked. "Are you taking him with you?"

Gideon's answer was immediate. "No. I won't risk him in this. If we're wrong about a temple being there, it will be nothing more than a dangerous waste of time."

"But if we're right," Brysia said, "then you will have to leave the Blood Orb behind while you fetch Jase."

Gideon smiled reassuringly. "But I won't leave it unprotected," he said. "We have some very powerful allies in Amnidia, remember? If a Blood Orb is there, the Rhiven will watch over it until I can return with Jase."

Brysia sighed resignedly. "When will you be leaving?" She'd just gotten him back and had hoped to spend more than a few minutes with him. In private, where they wouldn't have to pretend to be something other than husband and wife.

"Well," Gideon said smiling perceptively, "I am tired from battling demons all day. I suppose I could leave in the morning. It will give me a chance to rest, to read the rest of Robishar's book..." he hesitated and his smile widened, "and to do other important things."

Beraline cleared her throat, and Brysia looked over to find her smiling. "The ward I wove against eavesdropping doesn't obscure vision," she said. "If your husband is going to smile like that, you might want to go somewhere a little more private." Rising, she smoothed her skirts, then took Marithen by the arm to help her up. "We are going over to the Dremick Building to see what else we can find."

As Marithen stood, her eyes fell on Gideon and she smiled. "Why, Gideon," she said, moving forward to clasp his hand. "I didn't know you know were here. When did you arrive?"

Gideon smiled, his eyes sympathetic. "Just now," he told her. "It's good to see you again, Lady Korishal."

She reached up and patted him on the cheek. "It's good to see you again, too. Did you hear? We found a prophecy from Robishar Fairimor." Then as she was so apt to do, she recited the verses verbatim before digressing into a nonsensical singsong.

"On second thought," Beraline said, watching Marithen with concern, "I think we should return to the palace. Clearly, Lady Korishal needs some rest. I'll keep the ward against eavesdropping in place as we walk."

Gideon's nod showed he thought that would be a good idea, and they started for the exit.

"How are you going to get to Mount Tabor?" Brysia asked. "You certainly can't use a Veilgate to get there."

"Why not?" Beraline asked, but Brysia deferred to Gideon for the answer.

He frowned his frustration. "We aren't entirely sure," he admitted. "We know only that the taint left behind by Shadan's destruction warps the wielding somehow. Gates don't open where you intend or simply don't open at all." He looked at Brysia and smiled. "But I don't intend to ride a horse, if that's what you mean."

She narrowed her eyes at him. "Then how? Don't tell me you're thinking of riding there on a Dragon."

He shook his head. "Dragons aren't nearly fast enough," he said. "And there are too many bloody shadowspawn prowling the landscape for me to reach Tabor unnoticed."

Suddenly she understood. "Myrscraw."

Gideon nodded. "After what I've done for Riak recently, Emperor Dromensai owes me a favor."

Felicia watched as High Queen Fairimor and those with her made their way out of the room. It had been a pleasure to speak to her face to face, and she was still buzzing from the experience. And she was extremely relieved that the Queen was willing to keep her secret about the Dremick Building. She wondered if that's where the Queen was going right now.

"So, you're all chummy with the High Queen of Kelsa, are you?"

Felicia's smiled faded instantly at the sound of Trake's voice, but she forced it back into place before turning to face him. He stood with his arms folded and his usual condescending smile on his face. It was a look he'd perfected in the year since arriving at Elldrenei, and it ruined any chance he had at being handsome, not that she'd ever found Kelsan men handsome.

"She simply had questions about one of the books I found," she said, keeping her smile in place in spite of how much she disliked Trake.

His smile slipped momentarily before springing back into place. "What book?"

"I'm not sure," she said. "The title was in Old World script."

"Where did you find it?"

She looked around at the library meaningfully. "Where do you think I found it?" she asked. "We're in a library." Her tone was more flippant than she'd intended, but it had the desired effect. Trake's smile dropped into a frown, and he turned and walked away in a huff.

Realizing how tense the exchange had made her, she forced herself to relax by taking a long slow breath. She didn't like being deceptive, even with a moron like Trake, but she had no desire to lose her place of refuge. If the High Queen thought it was a secret worth keeping, who was she to give it away?

She watched Trake return to the table where he'd been working, and he scowled at her one last time as he sat.

*I really hate that young man,* she thought, then sighed and returned to her research.

But as she read, her mind kept returning to the book she'd found in the Dremick Building. She was pretty sure which passage of scripture had caught the High Queen's attention—how could it not with references like *Blood Seed* and *Holy Mountain* and the *Blue Flame?* What she didn't know was what any of it meant. Hopefully, the High Queen could make sense of it. Especially now that Gideon, the Guardian of the Blue Flame, had arrived to help.

She glanced over at Trake and found him watching her, and he hurriedly looked away, his face darkening with anger or embarrassment or both at having been caught watching her.

She shook her head in disgust, then opened another book and began scanning its pages, determined to find something else which might help the Fairimors keep the world from being destroyed.

# CHAPTER 52

## *Returning Favors*

IT WAS STILL DARK OUTSIDE when Gideon stepped into the corridor and quietly pulled the door to his and Brysia's room closed behind him. She had stirred from her sleep long enough to kiss him and to wish him well, but had dozed off again almost immediately. She was exhausted from her long hours in the archives, and he was content to let her sleep.

He glanced in each direction to find *Bero'thai* stationed at intervals along the corridor, then nodded in satisfaction that Brysia was so well-guarded. And with Beraline and Marithen in the next room over and Jase in the room beyond that, he knew his wife would be safe until he returned from Tabor. God send that it would be soon.

With one last look at Brysia through his Awareness, he started for the stairs. He wouldn't open a Veilgate until he was sure Jase wouldn't feel it, and that meant he'd need to go at least as far as the outer courtyard. He had no desire to enter into an argument about why the *Mith'elre Chon* should sit this one out. Particularly because he knew he would lose that argument.

He was passing the door to Seth's room when it opened and the Chellum captain appeared wearing his swords and a *komouri* uniform. He fell in beside him without a word, and Gideon frowned inwardly at what it meant.

"Who told you I was leaving?" he asked softly.

"Lady Hadershi," Seth answered. "She came out to greet us when we arrived from Trian. And don't worry. She spoke to me in private about your intentions."

Gideon cast a sideways glance at him. "And when was that? I felt your arrival, but it was too dark in my room to see the clock." That and Brysia had been asleep in his arms and he hadn't wanted to wake her.

"About midnight," the captain answered. "Jase spent most of the evening teaching a group of Chunin Dymas how to create crux points and use them to set Power-wrought traps into place along the evacuation boundaries in Trian."

"Chunin Dymas, you say?"

"Friends and students of Emmarenziana Antilla," Seth said. "They came to Trian with Endil and Thorac. Jase thought putting them to work would help take their minds off their loss."

"He's a wise man,"Gideon said with a smile. "Did Thorac and Endil come with you?"

"Endil did. He thought it would do Cassia's heart good to see him. Thorac and Elliott were still swapping stories. They will be joining the army at Mendel Pass. Thorac very much wants to kill a few hundred Darklings."

Gideon laughed softly. "I have no doubt he will find a way to do just that." He studied Seth's chiseled profile for a minute. "Did Beraline tell you how I plan to get where I'm going?"

"Why do you think I'm dressed like this? If Emperor Dromensai refuses your request for Myrscraw, I have the authority to grant it."

"And then?"

Seth turned a hard-eyed stare on him. "We go to Tabor together."

Elison Brey moved down the last of the south tower steps and stopped at the edge of the Fairimor dining room. It was dark save for a handful of glowstone lamps the *Bero'thai* left on for security purposes and so quiet he could hear the soft ticking of the grandfather clock on the far wall. Dawn was still an hour away, but he had too much to do to wait for the sun to rise.

Moving to the table, he found that Allisen had already laid out breakfast for him. Today it was a sandwich with two eggs, three strips of bacon, and a slice of cheese between two thick pieces of bread. And it was still warm.

Taking the cloth napkin from beside the plate, he wrapped it around the sandwich so he could eat while he walked, then started for the doors to the dome. He was nearly there when a flash of blue from a Veilgate chased the darkness from the room and Gideon and Seth stepped through from Temifair Palace. Seth, he noted with surprise, was dressed like a Shizu.

"Oh, good," Gideon said, when he saw him. "I was hoping you would be here. I need the Blue Flame Scepter, and I didn't want you thinking it had been stolen while you were out."

Without waiting for an answer, he made his way to the cabinet housing the talisman and took it out. The flame-like gem glittered brightly as it caught the light of a nearby lamp, matching the fiery light of determination shining in Gideon's eyes.

"Can you tell me why you need it?" Elison asked.

"It might be the key to finding a Blood Orb," Gideon answered. "Inside Mount

Tabor."

Elison stared at him, completely at a loss for words.

Gideon smiled at him. "That was my reaction last night," he said. "But we can't ignore the possibility." He hefted the scepter. "I'll have it back before you know it."

Elison nodded. "Please tell me it won't be just you two going," he said. "That mountain is likely to be full of Shadan'Ko and other shadowspawn."

"We'll be fine," Gideon said, then opened another Veilgate and moved through to a shadowed courtyard beyond. Seth followed without a word, and the Veilgate slid shut behind him.

*A Blood Orb in Mount Tabor?* Elison thought. *Could one have been there all this time? Could it really be that easy?*

乇

The sharp rap of knuckles on his chamber door brought Tereus Dromensai awake with a start. He sat up, his hand straying out of habit to the sword he kept propped next to his bed. It had been more than ten years since he'd traded his *komouri* for the *kitara* robes of a politician, but old habits died hard.

Setting the sword back in its place, he rose from the bed and moved across the room, stopping well short of the door. "Who is it?"

"Shavis Dakshar, my Lord," the familiar voice said. "Gideon Dymas and Seth Lydon are here to see you. They say it is of utmost importance."

Tereus grunted inwardly. *I didn't think it was so we could take breakfast together,* he thought, then pulled open the door, squinting as the brightness of the corridor flooded over him.

Shavis stepped aside so Tereus could address his unexpected visitors. Gideon, tall and formidable as ever in his dark grey uniform, held a jeweled scepter in his right hand. Seth Lydon wore his Power-wrought *kamui* swords and a *komouri* uniform and had a bow and a quiver of black-fletched arrows slung over his shoulder.

"Sorry to wake you, Emperor," Gideon said. "But I have need of a couple of Myrscraw."

Tereus blinked, then tried to cover his surprise by motioning everyone inside. "Come in," he said. "And please weave a ward against eavesdropping before saying anything else."

Gideon smiled. "Already in place, my friend."

"Then speak," he said. "Tell me what brings you here with such a request."

"We have a possible location for a Blood Orb of Elsa," Gideon answered. "But it isn't accessible by Veilgate."

Tereus did little to hide his confusion. "I thought everywhere was accessible by Veilgate."

"Not Mount Tabor," Seth said. "Shadan's destruction of Cynthia warped the Veil in and around the mountain. The only way of reaching it quickly is by Myrscraw."

"They are yours to use," Tereus said without hesitation. "But on one condition: I want you to take a couple of striketeams with you. If this is our chance to retrieve a viable Orb, we can't risk the two of you being overrun by whatever dark creatures might be lurking inside the mountain."

"I'll oversee the striketeams," Shavis said, and Tereus frowned at him.

"Considering the current situation here," he said, "a scouting mission into the Amnidian Wastes is hardly the place for the Dai'shozen of Riak."

"It's exactly the place," Shavis replied, and Tereus knew from the set of his friend's face that arguing this further would be pointless.

He looked at Gideon. "Does *shent ze'deyar* give you as much trouble as Shavis does me?" he asked.

Gideon glanced at Seth and chuckled. "You have no idea." His face grew serious once more and he nodded to Shavis. "And we would be honored if you were to join us."

"I'll meet you in the aviary in twenty minutes," the Dai'shozen said, then slipped out the door.

Tereus offered Gideon his hand. "God's speed, my friend. And good luck."

"Thank you," Gideon said. Turning toward a Veilgate that opened inside the doorway, he moved through to the Imperial Aviary. Seth followed, but not before he brought his fist to his chest in salute.

"*Nagaso kei Heian*," he said in the Riaki tongue. *Long live the Emperor.*

"Long live the Flame of Kelsa," Tereus whispered in return, then the Veilgate closed, and the room fell once more into darkness.

壬

"I'm glad he took Seth with him," Jase said, and Brysia stared at him as if she weren't quite sure it was her son who had spoken. Talia was equally surprised. Jase hadn't batted an eye when he'd learned where Gideon and Seth were going, and she could feel through the love-bond that he wasn't upset that they'd left without telling him. If anything, he felt relieved.

"I wouldn't say he *took* Seth," Beraline said. "Seth invited himself."

"Because you tipped him off that Gideon was leaving," Jase said, shaking his head with mock sadness. "And you didn't tell me. I'm hurt." He winked at Talia, and she sent a rush of affection through the *sei'vaiya*.

"I must say," Brysia said at last, "that you are taking this better than I expected."

"What did you expect?" he asked. "For me to be angry about being left behind?" He shook his head. "Trust me. I have no desire to go to Tabor unless I've got a viable Blood Orb in my hand. If Gideon finds one in Tabor, great, I'll go. Until then, this is his errand. Not mine."

He looked at the *Book of Robishar* sitting in his mother's lap. "What else did you find in there?" he asked, and Talia could feel the strength of his curiosity. Truth be told, she was curious too, and only slightly irritated that they had found their first meaningful passages while she was away.

"Three more references to the Holy Mountain of the Second Creation," Brysia answered, patting the book. "And four more uses of the words Blood Seed. Robishar seemed to prefer it over Blood Orb." She picked up the book as if she might open it, then set it down again, frowning.

"But none of the passages gave us any more insight than what we've already guessed at."

"Then we will just have to keep looking," Jase said, and Talia was amazed by the amount of hope and optimism present in his voice and in the love-bond. He rose and took her by the hand before smiling at his mother.

"Now, if you will excuse us, I'm needed in Mendel Pass."

Gideon finished lashing the Blue Flame Scepter to Rishi's saddle, then patted the giant bird on the neck. "Okay, girl," he said, "let's go."

As Rishi started toward the entrance with her half-walking half-hopping gait, Gideon cast about for Seth. He found him already atop his bird near the entrance speaking with Shavis Dakshar. If not for the distinctness of his silver hair, he could have been mistaken for just another one of Dakshar's Shizu, as comfortable on the back of a Myrscraw as a Rove Rider was on a horse.

Seth saw him coming, and gently urged his mount to make room for Gideon's in between his and Dakshar's.

"Shavis just filled me in on the plan to enter Amnidia," Seth told him. "I like it. Minimal use of the Power for a Veilgate. Minimal exposure to eyes on the ground here and in Amnidia. And no risk of the birds losing a foot or a wing as we pass through the gate."

Gideon nodded his understanding. "We're passing through a horizontal gate while in a dive," he said, and Shavis nodded.

"It's time to put the new wieldings you shared with us to the test," he said, then looked out the entrance into the pale light of early morning as he continued. "I had my Dymas open a couple of windows in the skies above Amnidia to see how far north we can go before the taint affects the wielding. It isn't very far. Just over a third of the way from the Great Wall."

"It's close enough," Gideon said. "Especially with Myrscraw to take us the rest of the way. The last time Seth and I went to that Light-blasted place we did it on horseback."

Seth grunted. "Yeah, but I came back out on foot. It was the hardest thing I've ever had to do in my life. There were times I didn't think I would survive."

Shavis studied Seth as if seeing him for the first time. Undoubtedly, he'd heard stories about the ruined valley, so learning Seth had crossed it on foot was sure to deepen his appreciation of his skills as a Shizu—feelings that were likely to increase even more once Shavis got a firsthand look at the place.

The loud clicking of Myrscraw talons on stone sounded behind them, and Gideon looked over his shoulder as the rest of Shavis' striketeam moved their birds into position. Twenty in all, the giant birds each bore two riders and supplies enough for three days. Most of the striketeam was comprised of Shizu, but Gideon counted eight Dymas in the group, five of them women.

Facing forward once more, he took a deep breath to settle his nerves. A moment later, Shavis signaled that it was time, and his bird hopped forward to the opening and dove straight over the edge, vanishing from sight.

Seth went next, and Gideon followed closely behind, bracing himself for the stomach-lurching rush to come. The rooftops of Sagaris came into view as Rishi neared the opening, then the sky rotated up and out of sight as the bird folded into a dive and knifed straight down the outside of the tower.

Ten floors below, the shimmering edges of a large Veilgate were visible against the dark roof tiles of the shorter buildings, and within those edges a seemingly endless drop to a shadowed landscape several thousand feet below.

Shavis's bird passed through without incident, and Seth was only a heartbeat behind. Then as the shimmering edges rushed up to meet him, Gideon's stomach knotted and he leaned a little lower in the saddle.

Then the wall of stone rushing past his peripheral vanished and he found himself knifing earthward in the midst of open sky. Instinctively, Rishi spread her massive wings, and Gideon's vision blurred as the sudden deceleration made his blood rush to his head.

When it cleared, he found himself gliding behind Seth and Shavis. The two had turned in their saddles to watch the rest of the striketeam arrive, and Gideon did likewise. The sight sent a rush of excitement washing through him as, one by one, Myrscraw appeared as if from thin air, feathery wedges of black that broke off in different directions to make way for those who were to follow. Then, as the last bird passed through, the hole in the sky slid closed as the Dymas in Sagaris released the Power.

Gideon watched the birds form a V behind him, then turned his attention to the earth below. The Great Wall of Aridan formed a straight line to the south, and its towers and battlements twinkled with the light of glowstone lamps and torches. To the north, the Rift lay like a scar across the broken landscape, deep and dark and full of evils best left undisturbed. How glad he was that he could simply fly over it this time instead of descending into its hellish depths. The very memory of the place sent a shiver up his spine.

From the Rift, he let his eyes move north, up the slopes of Tabor to its shattered peak. From this altitude its fiery mouth looked like a cauldron, and the churning, belching lake of molten rock writhed like something alive, spewing its contents down the eastern slopes in glowing rivers of red.

No one spoke as they winged their way toward the ruined mountain, but Gideon could guess at what they were thinking: This place was worse than any of them had imagined. *And why not?* he thought. *It's the closet place to hell there is in this world.*

As they passed over the Rift and the ruins of Cynthia began to take shape, Shavis edged his bird near. "Take point," he said. "We'll follow you in."

Nodding, Gideon nudged Rishi to move to the head of the V. Seth formed up on his left, Shavis on his right.

A few miles further on, a familiar Awareness brushed his mind, and he opened himself to it.

*Hello, Galiena,* he said. *I wondered if there might be Rhiven in the area, but I must say I am surprised to find you here.*

*Where should I be if not with my people?* she asked, and Gideon felt a rush of excitement as she continued. *Is it time?* she asked. *Is the Mith'elre Chon coming with a Blood Orb?*

*No,* Gideon told her. *We haven't obtained an Orb yet. But we found a prophecy that suggests there might be a Temple of Elderon and an Orb somewhere inside Mount Tabor.*

He felt Galiena's excitement intensify. *That's how it was on my world,* she said. *The temple housing the Blood Orb and the Soul Chamber was one and the same.* The excitement turned to assassin-like seriousness in an instant. *What can we do to help? Several of my people are a few miles south of the ruins of Cynthia right now. They are moving to intercept a small band of demons that appeared through a rent to the west of the city.*

*Have them engage the demons,* he told her. *Their use of the Power will distract any shadowspawn currently in the ruins. It may even draw some of them out. Either way, they will be focused on you and not us.*

*It will be our pleasure,* Galiena said, and the link to her Awareness vanished.

"We've got help on the ground," he told the others. "Several Rhiven are to the south and west of the city. They are going to attack a group of demons. It should distract whatever shadowspawn might be in Cynthia."

Seth and Shavis both nodded to show their approval, then turned their attention to the valley below. A few minutes passed, and then bursts of Fire chased the gloom from an area to the north and west of where they were.

Gideon nodded in satisfaction before looking back to the ruins of Elva's long-dead capital. He was near enough now that he could see the towers of Shey'Avralier rising like daggers above the sprawling mass of crumbling buildings.

The way to the Soul Chamber was on the ground floor of the largest tower, and Gideon supposed that would be the best place to start looking. If there was a Temple of Elderon somewhere inside the mountain, it was likely to be near the Soul Chamber. It might even share the entrance with it.

*Wouldn't that be nice,* he thought, then directed Rishi toward the tower with a gentle touch of his hand. As the finer details of the Power-wrought structure took place, he spotted a cluster of balconies on the southern exterior that could be used as perches for the Myrscraw.

"There," he said, pointing at the balconies. "Easy access in and out of the tower and much easier to defend than if the birds were on the ground."

"Will the balconies hold the weight of the birds?" Shavis asked.

"It's Power-wrought stone," Gideon told him. "That's why it's still standing."

Shavis nodded, and he and Seth led the way in.

A few minutes later, and with glowstone lamp in hand, he and Seth were making their way through what used to be the luxurious apartment of one of Cynthia's ruling families. All of the furniture had crumbled to dust, but there were pieces of hardware here and there—hinges and handles made of gold that had resisted the long years of decay. An unbroken mirror in an ornate golden frame hung on one wall, and Gideon caught a glimpse of himself as he passed, his reflection dulled by eight hundred years of grime.

They reached the apartment's entrance and stepped over a pile of rotting wood that used to be the door. Shavis and several members of his striketeam were waiting for them in the corridor beyond.

"Six Myrscraw landed on the level above," he said, "eight on the level below. One Shizu and one Dymas will remain on each level with the birds. If anything unsavory shows up, they will put the birds in the air but will keep them near for our departure. The rest of my men will join us on the stairs." He pointed to the shadowed archway at the end of the corridor.

Seth pulled the bow from his shoulder and nocked an arrow. "The rest of you do the same," he told the other Shizu. "Our Dymas are blind in this place. They can still use the Power, but they are unable to search the way ahead for enemies. We could be set upon at any time."

"And," Gideon added, hefting the glowstone lamp for emphasis, "I've instructed our Dymas not to use the Power unless it's absolutely necessary. I'd prefer not to alert any nearby shadowspawn to our presence. Not all of them will have been drawn away by the Rhiven."

"So it's back to the good old days," one of the men said, testing his bow. He noticed Gideon's stare and added a hasty, "I mean no disrespect, but when you are around, the rest of us feel obsolete."

Seth chuckled darkly. "I'd prefer not to be needed at all in this hellhole."

"Yes, *shent ze'deyar*," the other replied, his tone suddenly neutral.

"That being said," Seth said, his face a mask of Shizu calm, "be ready. Because we *will* encounter something unpleasant." Leveling the razored arrowhead down the corridor, he started forward.

The absence of windows made the corridor dark, so Gideon held the lamp high to light the way. It wasn't as bright as he would have liked, but it would do. Too much light—even that not wrought of *Ta'shaen*—would draw the wrong kind of attention.

They reached the stairwell and were met by those who'd landed on the level above. The two Dymas in the group also held small glowstone lamps so the Shizu would have their hands free for their weapons.

"Any trouble?" Shavis asked.

"Eight Shadan'Ko," one of the Shizu answered. "But they were no trouble."

"Shadan'Ko are a good sign," Seth said. "They tend to congregate in places where they can avoid being hunted for food by larger shadowspawn. Cross your fingers that this is the case here."

"What hunts Shadan'Ko for food?" Shavis asked. He seemed both intrigued and disgusted.

"Everything," Seth answered. "Shadan'Ko are at the bottom of Amnidia's food chain."

"Good to know," the Dai'shozen said, a hint of revulsion in his voice.

They continued to the level below and were joined by the rest of the striketeam. They had nothing to report, but Gideon could tell by the horrified looks on the faces of the Dymas that they didn't like having their Awareness blinded by the curse. He smiled reassuringly, then followed Seth down the stairs.

Several flights later, they reached the ground floor and the massive, cathedral-like chamber that was the entrance to the palace. The sickly yellow light of Amnidia's morning filled the doorway and the glassless windows high overhead, but it wasn't enough to chase the deepest shadows from the room, and Gideon looked around warily as he and the others entered.

Seth took a quick look around, then angled toward an arched opening directly across from the one leading outside.

Gideon nodded, impressed with Seth's uncanny sense of direction. The way to the Soul Chamber didn't look any different than it had twenty years ago, but Gideon didn't think he could have found it as quickly as Seth had. Especially without the use of his Awareness.

There was a sudden flash of movement to the left, and four Shadan'Ko sprang up from where they'd been sleeping among the rubble. A hiss of arrows followed, and the startled creatures collapsed into pin-cushioned heaps.

A second arrow already nocked and ready to loose, Seth moved forward to check that the Shadan'Ko were dead. He prodded one with his foot, then motioned everyone toward the corridor leading to the Soul Chamber.

Ten paces in, Seth loosed an arrow into the darkness ahead, and Gideon heard the sickening *thunk* of it striking flesh. The sound of a body thudding to the floor followed.

Gideon strained into the darkness, but it wasn't until they reached the far end of the corridor that he finally saw the Shadan'Ko. Seth's arrow had taken it squarely in the head.

"How did you see that?" he asked.

Seth shrugged. "It moved."

Gideon cast a glance at Shavis, but the Dai'shozen shook his head. He hadn't seen it either.

They passed into another cavernous chamber where several columns and part of the ceiling had collapsed, and Gideon frowned at the sight. For Power-wrought stone to have broken in such a manner meant significant shaking from an earthquake. A recent quake, which was a huge concern. And not simply because he was inside all that stone—he was afraid of what kind of damage they might find inside the mountain. What if the way to the Soul Chamber was no longer passable?

He squashed the thought as soon as it came, refusing to give up hope. Neither the Earthsoul nor the Creator would let such a thing happen. A Blood Orb would be found and Jase would take it to Earth's Heart.

Holding the lantern a little higher in an attempt to brighten his mood, he followed Seth through the darkness of the next windowless corridor. It was an odd thought, but he couldn't decide which was worse—the all-encompassing darkness of the windowless areas or the sickly light filtering in through long-dead windows and doors.

Two vaulted chambers, three corridors, and fifteen or so startled Shadan'Ko later, they entered the large dome Gideon remembered from his last visit here. Known as Temifair Dome in its glory days, it was reminiscent of the Dome in Trian except that it was made of Power-wrought stone instead of *chorazin*. That, and its ballroom, library, and tiered council area had been decimated by Throy Shadan more than eight hundred years earlier.

All that remained of the once glorious room was a rubble-strewn floor and a massive hole where the doors marking the entrance to Earth's Heart once stood. Anciently, the seemingly endless tunnel stretching away into the living rock of Mount Tabor would have been bright with the light of glowstone chandeliers and alive with the spirit of Elsa and of the Earthsoul. Now it was as dark as the depths of hell.

Fortunately, the most profound darkness lasted only as far as the first chamber and the stairs winding up into the mountain. There, part of a glowstone chandelier had survived the devastation and a few stones cast the chamber in a faint white light.

Seth signaled for Gideon and the others to darken their lamps.

"There are similar pockets of light in each of the landings for the next six levels," he told Shavis and the Shizu. "At least there were the last time Gideon and I were here."

Gideon nodded. "And the entrance to the Soul Chamber is on that last level," he added. "If there is a Temple of Elderon here, it will likely be found there."

"For the sake of the world," Shavis said, "let us hope that is the case."

They moved up the stairs in silence, leaving the light of the glowstones behind and climbing into ever-increasing darkness. Then, just as it was becoming impossible to see where to put their feet, the stairwell began to brighten once more as they neared the next level.

Seth moved ahead to peer into the second-level chamber, then signaled that all was clear, and they passed the opening and continued their climb. Not only did the air begin to grow warmer, it grew more and more foul-smelling as well.

They were passing the entrance of the fifth level when Seth held up his fist to signal a stop. Glancing over his shoulder, he whispered. "I smell smoke."

Gideon tested the air and realized Seth was right. There was a faint smell of smoke in the air. And it smelled like burning flesh.

"I'll check it out," Seth whispered, then disappeared around the bend and up into the darkness.

When he returned a minute or so later, he wore a frown. "*Ba'trul*," he whispered. "Five of them in the chamber on the next level. They're roasting a Shadan'Ko on a spit."

"Well," Gideon whispered, "there goes your theory about Shadan'Ko hiding inside the palace to avoid being hunted."

Seth frowned. "On the contrary," he said, "if Shadan'Ko are willing to risk being hunted by *Ba'trul* inside the palace, it proves that something worse is lurking outside."

"What's a *Ba'trul?*" Shavis asked. He sounded more irritated than worried, but Gideon knew that would change once he got a look at the creatures.

"You're about to find out," Seth answered. "Because they'll spot us the moment we try to pass."

Shavis drew his sword. "Then what are we waiting for? Let's get to it."

# CHAPTER 53

## *Bonus Killings*

STANDING IN THE MOUTH OF MENDEL PASS, Idoman Leda closed his eyes for a moment and let the cool breeze flowing down from the Kelsan Mountains wash over him. It smelled strongly of horses and men, but there were hints of pine and sage interspersed with the scents of dung and sweat.

"Shadan isn't wasting any time, is he?" Joneam grumbled, and Idoman opened his eyes to find his friend frowning through his spyglass.

Behind Joneam, the walls of Mendel Pass stretched up and away into the distance, a narrow lifeline for the united armies of Kelsa, Elva, and Chunin when the time came for the remainder of them to retreat in earnest.

*Which won't be long at the rate Death's Third March is advancing,* he thought, clenching his teeth in anger. He'd hoped to have several days to prepare to meet the enemy here in the pass. Instead, he would have hours.

"No," he agreed. "At this pace, his army will reach the mouth of the pass by this afternoon."

"That was our estimate as well," General Kennin said, and beside him Captain Ieashar nodded. They'd insisted on remaining on this side of the Kelsan Mountains with several thousand of their cavalry, Krelltin- and horse-borne alike.

The rest of the soldiers of the Chunin and Elvan armies, mostly foot soldiers, had been moved to Trian Plateau through Veilgates along with the supply wagons, and the bulk of Kelsa's forces. It had taken most of the night, but the *Shomei* and *Valhan* of Rosda and Glenda had facilitated the relocation under the direction of Quintella Zakeya and Keenan Nolan.

Idoman was truly grateful for everything the two had done for the cause the past few days. Without them or those they led, the situation here would have been a whole lot worse.

He felt a stirring in *Ta'shaen*, and a heartbeat later a Veilgate opened nearby.

Jase Fairimor came through with Talia Chellum's hand in his. Another couple followed closely on their heels, and they, too, were holding hands. The young woman wore the *kitara*-style jacket of a Dymas and had short, curly hair and freckles. Her companion had the look of a Fairimor.

"It's good to see you, Idoman," Jase said as he moved near. Then he gestured at his companions. "I'd like you to meet my cousin, Endil, and his friend Jeymi Galaron."

Idoman shook each of their hands. "It's a pleasure to meet you."

"Likewise," Endil said. "We've heard a lot about you."

Jase turned to gaze thoughtfully up into the pass. "Endil's experience in Kunin," he continued, "gave me an idea on how we can slow Death's Third March once it nears the summit. And I learned a couple of new wieldings that might help too."

"And in the meantime?" Joneam asked, lowering his spyglass.

"Our tactics haven't changed," Jase told him. "We harass the enemy through Veilgates while we set Power-wrought traps in the pass." He looked back to Idoman. "How is that going, anyway?"

"Good," Idoman said. "Dozens of traps have already been wrought and crux points are in place. They are virtually invisible to all but those who set them in place, but they will have a suitably devastating effect when triggered."

Jase nodded in satisfaction. "And the relocation of our troops?"

"Most are already at the southern mouth of Mendel Pass," Idoman said. "Our Power-wielders moved them through last night. Those who remained here will engage the enemy briefly and then withdraw, luring them into the traps we've set."

Jeymi Galaron stepped forward. "And what is the plan when Agla'Con or *Jeth'Jalda* enter the upper parts of the pass through Veilgates?" she asked. "You know they will. They will want to put troops behind you as you withdraw."

Idoman grinned at her. "They can try," he told her. "We set numerous wards higher in the pass. Each is linked to a crux point which will warn us of an enemy's arrival. We also have squads of *Bero'thai* and teams of Dymas interspersed along the roadway to intercept anyone foolish enough to come through."

"Seems like you have it all worked out," Endil said.

"Sure," Idoman told him, "except the part where we don't get killed."

"What took you so long?" Shadan rasped as Aethon moved through the rent into the Dreadlord's ruined throne room. Eye glowing red with frustration, Shadan looked past Aethon to the marbled courtyard inside the palace of Berazzel, and his grey face twisted with suspicion.

Aethon ignored the look and let the Veilgate snap shut. He wasn't surprised to find Shadan still here in the Pit. He had, in fact, anticipated it. It was the reason he hadn't returned to Death's Third March but had come here instead. He knew from experience that Shadan was prone to brooding over his losses. If he didn't do something to jar him back into action, the refleshed cur would sit here and stare at the shattered refleshing stone for days.

"*Frel'mola* is quite the hostess," Aethon answered without humor. "And she was most insistent that I join her for some entertainment." Let Throy Bloody Shadan decide what *that* meant.

"Lord Nid is still alive," Shadan hissed. "I want him dead."

Aethon almost laughed aloud at how childish the comment sounded, but he refrained. He was here to get Shadan back into the fight, not pick a fight with him. Besides, Aethon wanted Lord Nid dead as well.

"Then you are in luck," Aethon told him, moving up onto the dais to look at the shattered slab. "Because I acquired four K'tyr from Commander Naxis."

Shadan narrowed his eye at him. "Who?"

"Supreme Commander Ibisar Naxis, head of the Tamban military," he answered, pleased with how Shadan's suspicion regarding his contacts in Tamba kept deepening. Let the one-eyed idiot worry about what kind of power he might be able to bring to bear should he decide to challenge him again. Shadan didn't need to know he was just as suspicious of *Frel'mola's* motives as he was.

"He's first among the living in Tamba," Aethon added, then waved a hand dismissively. "The important thing is the K'tyr have already been dispatched. We should know within the next few hours if they were successful in eliminating Lord Nid."

Shadan's entire persona changed in an instant. The childish brooding vanished, and his eye flared brightly with the blood-lust Aethon had come here to awaken. "You know where he is," the Dreadlord rasped. It wasn't a question.

"No," Aethon admitted. "But there are really only two possibilities. He is either with the Meleki army still atop the plateau or he is in Mendel Pass. I will know as soon as I return to Death's Third March."

A hint of suspicion returned to Shadan's one-eyed gaze. "How will you know?"

"Because *Frel'mola* and her idiot commander aren't the only resources I have to fight this war," he said, smiling.

The hint of suspicion turned to all-out distrust. "What are you up to, Fairimor?" he hissed, and for the briefest moment, the end of his scepter glowed red with the power of the Void.

"Nothing that isn't good for Death's Third March," Aethon told him. "Come," he said, opening a rent into the midst of his army. "We have a King to kill."

乇

"Shadan has returned to his army," Captain Plat said, and Hulanekaefil Nid turned to find the Captain of the Crescent Guard frowning as he squinted through one of the large spyglasses positioned near the edge of the rim.

Hul turned back to the Dymas he'd been speaking with. "Continue healing those who won't survive without your help," he told her. "If our Dymas have strength enough after that, allow them to tend to the more superficial wounds."

"Yes, my lord," the Dymas said, then she and her companions left to do as instructed.

Moving to stand next to Vol at the edge of the plateau, Hul looked down at the Bottomlands. Two thousand feet below, Death's Third March was a massive patch of black moving away from the rampway Shadan had wrought the day before.

When he didn't immediately spot the Dreadlord, he looked at Vol. "Where is he?"

The captain stepped back from the spyglass, but held it in position. "See for yourself."

Hul put his eye up to the spyglass, and Throy Shadan came into view. Sitting straight-backed in the saddle of a shadowspawned horse, he could have been mistaken for just another K'rrosha if not for the fact that every creature in the area was giving him a wide berth. Everyone but the Kelsan riding next to him, anyway.

"Aethon Fairimor is with him," Hul said. "Think of how this war would change if we could destroy those two."

Vol grunted. "I think about it every other thought," he said. "I just don't think it's possible."

Hul continued to watch the two leaders of Death's Third March ride south toward Mendel Pass. "Why do you think he swapped his K'sivik for a horse?"

"Maybe he's hoping to keep a low profile."

Hul pulled his eye from the spyglass to stare at his friend. "Throy arrogant Shadan?"

Vol shrugged. "It was just a guess." He looked back down at the massive stain on the grasslands below. "What's our next move, my lord?"

Hul looked back to the army below, then lifted his gaze to Mendel Pass. "We'll hold here until Shadan's forces vacate the area below. Then we'll follow them to the pass and attack once the bottleneck forms." He offered the spyglass back to Vol. "In the meantime, I need to speak with Idoman and the rest of the United High Command. I want to know what they have planned."

"Hold the attack!" Aethon shouted, and the Agla'Con preparing to open the rents into Lord Nid's camp released the Power.

The four K'tyrs at the head of the procession hissed in frustration, but Aethon soothed their minds with a quick thrust of his Awareness. He soothed the handful of Quathas and Wohlvin and Hellhounds next, then glanced at the small army of Darklings marching behind them. Weapons in hand, they never even broke stride, oblivious, or perhaps just too stupid to be upset that the plan had changed.

Aethon turned to look at Shadan. "Lord Nid just left the plateau," he told the Dreadlord. "My spotters say he moved to Mendel Pass."

"Good," Shadan said. "Killing members of the Kelsan High Command along with Nid will be a bonus."

"I need to find them first," Aethon told him, irritated that he'd been so close to eliminating the Meleki King only to have him slip away.

"Why don't you call upon the other resources you mentioned?" Shadan taunted. "Or was that simply another one of your lies?"

"My eyes are in place," he said. "It won't be but a moment."

Opening his Awareness, he stretched it forth to one of the bladehawks he had perched in the cliffs high above Mendel Pass. Seizing the creature's tiny mind, he let what it saw come into view in his mind's eye. And there, clearly visible because of the bird's incredible eyesight, was Lord Nid. He stood in the mouth of the pass with several members of the High Command and a small number of Dymas. And—

Aethon smiled. And Jase Fairimor was with them. This would indeed be a bonus.

He released the bladehawk's mind and reined in his Awareness. "Open your minds to me," he told the Agla'Con. "I'm opening the rents for this attack."

Idoman listened as Lord Nid gave a report of what had transpired atop the plateau during last night's attack on the rear of Shadan's army. More than five hundred Meleki had lost their lives during the battle, but they'd killed five times that number of cultists and Tamban soldiers.

With Aethon Fairimor and Shadan away, and the Agla'Con and Jeth'Jalda weary from their part in the collapse of the rim, Hul's men had been able to rain arrows on the enemy from higher up on the rampway. They'd retreated back to the top of the rim in the wee hours of the morning.

"That will keep them looking over their shoulder," Jase said when Lord Nid finished. "Thank you for what you are doing."

"It was truly a pleasure," the Meleki King replied. "But one we will need to be more careful about next time. Both Shadan and Aethon have returned to Death's Third March."

"As we knew they would," Jase said, looking at the sea of darkness moving slowly but inexorably toward them from the north. "As they near Trian, both will start playing larger roles in each of the battles. They will seek to make a name for themselves and gain favor in the eyes of Maeon."

"The word from some of the Agla'Con we interrogated," Lord Nid said, "is that Aethon challenged Shadan for control of Death's Third March. He failed, but Shadan obviously didn't win convincingly enough to do away with your traitorous uncle. There seems to be an uneasy truce between them."

Jase nodded as he continued to stare at the approaching army. "Perhaps we can find a way to disrupt that truce."

"Wouldn't that be nice," Idoman said, then flinched as four Veilgates opened to surround him and the others and a K'tyr darted through each of the fiery openings. Instinctively, he opened himself to the Power, but his Awareness went dark and his link to Ta'shaen vanished.

Not again, he thought as memories of his fight with the Power-voiding demon that had killed Kalear and Joselyn swept through him, momentarily rooting him in place.

The four Veilgates snapped shut, but a dozen more opened beyond them. They faced away from the first four, shimmering squares that blocked much of the view of the Darklings and shadowspawn swarming through to engage those rushing to defend the Mith'elre Chon and the High Command.

The clash of steel rang out as Chunin soldiers and Bero'thai engaged the dark creatures, and the sound spurred Idoman into action. Drawing his sword, he stepped into the path of one of the K'tyrs, slicing one of its four arms free of its body and spinning away from the others. But he wasn't fast enough, and one of the scythe-like blades caught him across the ribs, opening a bloody gash.

Clenching his teeth against the white-hot pain, he engaged the creature again, slowing its advance even as he continued to give ground. Eyes glowing red with corruption, the K'tyr mewed demonically as it pressed him, eager for more blood.

Sword streaked black with the blood of the K'tyr slashing at him with its three remaining arms, Joneam Eries kept himself between the cat-faced creature and the Mith'elre Chon. Jase in turn kept himself in front of Talia, though how he intended to protect her, Joneam didn't know.

A short distance away, General Gefion went down in a spray of blood as a K'tyr's blade found his throat, and Joneam's heart burned with rage at the loss of his friend. But Gefion wasn't finished. With the last of his strength, he pushed himself to his knees and tossed his sword to Jase. The young man caught it by the hilt and spun into the path of the K'tyr who'd killed Gefion, removing one of the creature's arms with barely any effort.

Joneam was impressed with the boy's sword skills, but he didn't have time to dwell on it—the K'tyr seeking his life was pressing hard, its blades drawing closer with each swipe.

Tendrils of Sei'shiin streaked down the pass as nearby Dymas came to the rescue, and two Quathas and one Wohlvin vanished in explosive flares of white. A heartbeat later a knot of Darklings burst apart in sizzling fountains of gore, and a second knot was ripped apart by several stabs of lightning. The pass shook with the resulting thunder.

But the attacking Dymas couldn't strike the K'tyrs for fear of hitting their own, so Joneam and those around him were forced to fight on without the aid of Ta'shaen.

Joneam's blade found another one of the K'tyr's arms, and it hissed in pain as the blade the arm clutched clattered noisily to the ground. It barely slowed, continuing to lash at him with its remaining arms.

An arrow hissed in from the side to take the K'tyr in the head, and the creature dropped as if poleaxed. Joneam shot a quick look back along the arrow's trajectory and found Teig nocking another arrow and taking aim at the K'tyr attacking Jase. Before he could loose it, a Quatha raced in from the right, and Teig was forced to shoot it instead. The arrow took the creature in the chest, but its forward momentum carried it into Teig, and the two went down in a tangle of limbs.

Joneam started toward his Elvan friend to help, but the way was suddenly blocked by the hulking wolf-like shapes of two Wohlvin. Fangs bared, they crouched, preparing to leap.

He raised his father's sword before him, determined to kill whichever one leapt first. He knew there wouldn't be time to kill them both.

As soon as the rents opened around him and the others, Endil pulled the dartbow from its holster and shot the nearest K'tyr squarely in the chest. The creature hissed in irritation, but never even broke stride as it fell on General Kennin and sent the Chunin's blood spraying across the stony ground in a brilliant swath of crimson.

The murder complete, the K'tyr turned its gaze on Lord Nid and Captain Ieashar, and its eyes flared red with hellish hunger. Endil leveled the dartbow at the creature's face, and the light in one of the demonic eyes went dark as the second dart found its mark.

Howling in rage and pain, the K'tyr pulled the dart free, then started for Endil, scythe-like blades flashing.

"This is where we run!" Jeymi shouted, taking him by the hand and pulling. "I need to get outside the void the K'tyr are creating."

Endil followed, loosing darts at Darklings as he went, but they'd only gone a few paces when another, larger rent opened a short distance up the pass.

A man who bore a strong resemblance to Gideon stood within the massive hole, and Night Threads erupted from his hands, filling the air with screams of thunder. A squad of *Bero'thai* was ripped apart by the strike, and the tendrils of *Sei'shiin* streaking into the midst of the surrounding shadowspawn cut off as the wielder was killed.

More Night Threads followed, and Endil had just enough time to take Jeymi in his arms before the world exploded around them.

"Aethon," Quintella said, then deftly sliced a Quatha's head from its shoulders with a blade of Spirit. For a moment she had a clear view of the K'tyr attacking the *Mith'elre Chon*, but Lord Nid and Captain Ieashar stumbled into view and the avenue closed before she could strike.

Fighting beside her, Keenan took hold of a knot of Darklings with a grip of Air and hurled them into the wall of the canyon so violently the impact left bloody silhouettes of the creatures on the stone.

"I'm going after Aethon," Keenan said as he sent tendrils of Fire streaking into the midst of a pack of Wohlvin. "As long as the K'tyr live, the *Mith'elre Chon* and the others are powerless against him."

Before Quintella could object, Keenan opened a small Veilgate and rushed through into the midst of Death's Third March. A heartbeat later, Aethon's barrage of Night Threads cut off, and the rent framing him snapped shut in an explosive shower of sparks.

"Goodbye, my friend," Quintella whispered, sorrow warring with admiration at Keenan's selfless yet undeniably fatal decision.

Turning back to the battle, she burned another Wohlvin from existence with *Sei'shiin*, then swept a knot of Darklings aside with a powerful thrust of Air before setting her sights once again on the nearest K'tyr. She would save the *Mith'elre Chon*. Keenan's sacrifice wouldn't be in vain.

The inside of her head went white with pain as something slammed into her from behind, driving her to the ground and rending the flesh on her shoulders and back. Fighting through the pain, she blinked the dust from her eyes and squinted through the braids draped across her face.

A few inches away the reddish-yellow eye of a Quatha stared back, cold and unblinking. The creature hissed in satisfaction, then bared its teeth to finish her off.

"You shouldn't have hesitated," she told it, then blew it apart with a vicious thrust of Flesh, wetting the area around her with foul-smelling gore.

She tried to rise, but her limbs were already numb from the Quatha's poison and refused to respond.

*Shadowwound*, she thought as darkness claimed her.

Blinking against the points of light flashing sporadically in his vision, Endil rolled onto his side and looked over to find Jeymi lying next to him. The side of her head was streaked with blood, and her eyes were closed. His heart went cold as he thought his worst fears had been realized, but when he placed a hand on her neck he could feel a pulse.

*Thank the Creator*, he thought, then pushed himself up onto his knees and looked around.

The massive Veilgate opened by Aethon Fairimor was gone, but Darklings and other shadowspawn still swarmed the area like locust, outnumbering the Elvan and Chunin soldiers more than two to one. And at the center of the chaos, Jase and Idoman and the others were still doing battle with the three remaining K'tyr, cut off from those trying to reach them.

A nearby knot of Darklings noticed him and started forward, animal faces frenzied. Endil rose to meet them, loosing darts as quickly as he could pull the trigger. Unlike K'tyr and the rest of their more dangerous counterparts, Darklings weren't immune to the deadly poison and dropped dead whenever a dart struck flesh. He killed all but three before the last dart left the tiny weapon and the flashes of Power-wrought Light of the weapon's mechanism ceased.

"Of course," he muttered in frustration. Dropping the dartbow next to Jeymi, he raced to a fallen *Bero'thai* and took up the man's sword. He would have preferred a spear or a staff, but the sword would have to do. Hopefully, his minimal sword skills would be enough to kill the three that remained.

"Come and get me," he said, edging away from Jeymi, hoping to keep the Darklings' attention fastened solely on him.

A flash of bluish-green appeared at the edge of his vision, and a Krelltin raced past him to engage the Darklings.

"*Dromar Chunin!*" the rider shouted, and Darkling blood sprayed the air as a vicious swipe of a heavy, double-bladed axe removed the head of the nearest creature. Leaping from the saddle, the Chunin chopped the legs from beneath the second Darkling, then cleaved its head in two. The remaining Darkling snarled in rage as it approached, but the Chunin drew a long dagger from his belt and sent it flying into the creature's throat with a casual flick of his wrist. Then he turned, a broad smile on his face.

"I thought I might find you here," Thorac said, then turned his attention to another knot of Darklings. "Get Jeymi to safety," he ordered, climbing back into the saddle of his Krelltin. "I'll cover your escape." With that, he gave another Chunin battle cry and raced back into the chaos.

Jase removed the last of the K'tyr's arms, then buried his sword deep into the creature's chest. It hissed in surprise as the light in its cat-like eyes winked out. As it did, Jase's spiritual perception of the world returned, and he embraced the Power, drawing in as much as he could hold. Raising his hand at the K'tyr slashing away at Lord Nid, he burned the creature to ash with a spear of *Sei'shiin*.

Lord Nid nodded his thanks, then hurriedly embraced the Power as well and destroyed the final K'tyr with a thrust of Fire. And just in time, too. Another few seconds and Idoman would have fallen. Slashed and bleeding from multiple wounds, the young Dymas General was unsteady on his feet and dropped to his knees in exhaustion.

Jase looked around at the remaining hordes of shadowspawn, and a rush of anger filled him at how many lives they'd taken in this attack. Opening his Awareness to take them all in, he fixed their dark auras in his mind's eye, then struck them as one, tearing their corrupted flesh to shreds with a brutal thrust reminiscent of his strike in the Dome all those weeks ago. For a moment, the very air seemed to turn to blood, then all was silence. The attack was over.

He turned to Talia, then glanced at Lord Nid. "Let's tend to the wounded," he told them. "Tell our Dymas to heal the shadowwounds first. The longer they fester, the harder they will be to heal."

The two moved away to heal those they could, and Jase returned his attention to those who were beyond any healing. General Gefion, General Kennin, and Captain Ieashar were among the dead. As were numerous *Bero'thai* and Chunin.

Endil and Jeymi were injured but alive. So were Teig and Idoman and Joneam. Jase shook his head. Only he, Talia, and Lord Nid had made it through the encounter without injury.

Turning his attention further up the canyon, he spotted Elliott standing with Haeley Dromm and the other Chunin Dymas, though when they had arrived, he couldn't say. Then his eyes fell on Quintella lying on her side in the midst of tremendous carnage, and his heart tightened with dread as he hurried toward her. When he reached her, he found her face ashen and her skin cold to the touch. There were discolored wounds on her shoulders and back.

*Quatha*, he thought grimly, then gently probed her with his Awareness to determine if she still lived. He nearly shouted for joy when he discovered a faint pulse.

Opening himself more fully to the Power, he wove Flesh and Spirit together into a tight spiral, then directed it at the darkness that was the shadowwound. Quintella's body jerked as the healing weave touched the darkness, and Jase flinched, momentarily afraid to continue. He was far more skilled at killing than healing, but in this case, that might be to his advantage. Focusing more intently on the darkness, he attacked it with the luminescent, life-giving energy of the healing weave.

The shadowwound resisted, momentarily growing darker, then began to recede as it was consumed by the healing. A moment later it vanished from his mind's eye in a flash of bluish white.

Quintella inhaled sharply, and her eyes snapped open. "*Mith'elre Chon*," she whispered. "I—"

"Don't talk," he said softly. "I'm not finished yet." Releasing the Gift of Spirit, he channeled threads of Flesh into her wounds to close them and remove the pain. When he finished, he looked up to find Talia standing over him. She was smiling.

"You're getting better at healing," she said. "With a little more practice, you will be nearly as good as Gideon."

Jase grunted. "I've got a long way to go before I'm anywhere near as good as him," he said. "Or you." Talia smiled at the compliment, then moved off to heal others.

Looking back to Quintella, he took her by the arm and helped her sit up. Her eyes were filled with sadness as she looked around at those who'd been killed. Then she met Jase's eyes, and the sadness deepened.

"Keenan," she said. "He went after Aethon to stop his attack."

"I know," Jase said. "I saw him as the rent was collapsing." He reached up and brushed one of her beaded braids behind her ear. "And by now he will have been welcomed as a hero into Eliara."

Taking her by the hand, he helped her to her feet. With a smile, he added, "And I'm confident his selfless sacrifice has Aethon questioning the wisdom of launching this attack."

She frowned tiredly. "Do you really think so?"

"I'd bet my life on it."

Still holding her by the arm to steady her, he led her through the carnage to Joneam. He'd been healed of his wounds and sat on a large rock, his father's sword in hand. The look on his face as he watched the Dymas tending to the wounded was worrisome. If Jase had to guess, he'd say Joneam blamed himself for what had happened here. That, or he was starting to lose hope that the war could be won.

Jase reached the general at the same time as Talia and Lord Nid. Talia smiled at him, but he could feel her weariness through the love-bond. Healing so many wounded had taken it out of her. Lord Nid's face, however, was a mask of rage.

"This attack was meant for me," he said, shaking his head in disgust. "Retaliation for destroying the Pit. And now a lot of good men are dead. Because of me."

"They're dead because of Aethon," Jase told him. "You cannot—you *will* not—take this upon yourself. Guilt isn't an emotion any of us can afford to indulge in right now." He looked pointedly at Joneam to show he meant him as well.

"So what can we indulge in?" Thorac asked as he rode up on his Krelltin.

"Righteous anger," Jase told them. "We are going to make Aethon pay for what he did here today."

Thorac grinned. "When do we start?"

"Well, that certainly didn't go as planned," Shadan rasped, and Aethon turned to find the Dreadlord pushing himself back up onto his feet. He'd lost hold of his scepter, and his shadowspawned mount—or what was left of it—was strewn across the grasses of the Bottomlands like the unwanted scraps of a butcher shop.

Aethon was impressed. Whoever the Glendan Dymas had been, he'd nearly sent Shadan back into the realm of spirits. Of course it would have only been temporary, since the man had attacked with Flesh instead of *Sei'shiin*, but having to reflesh the Destroyer of Amnidia with Death's Third March already underway could have weakened the morale of the troops.

He frowned thoughtfully. And would it still be Death's *Third* March at that point or would it technically become the fourth? An interesting question, but one for later.

"On the contrary," he said, watching as Shadan channeled Air and retrieved his fallen scepter with an irritated flick of his wrist. "General Gefion is dead. As are General Kennin of Chunin and Captain Ieashar of Elva. The High Command will be reeling from this loss for days to come."

"But Lord Nid still lives!" Shadan shouted. Or at least as much of a shout as he could muster with his ruined throat. His scepter flared brightly, and he tore a hole in the Veil, allowing a K'sivik to lumber through from beyond.

"Giving up on blending in with the other K'rrosha?" Aethon asked.

Shadan ignored him as he climbed into the K'sivik's saddle. He let the rent snap shut, but his scepter continued to burn brightly. He pointed it at Aethon's chest.

"Your carelessness nearly ended us both," he growled. "I suggest you make amends by finishing Nid once and for all." He turned his K'sivik and rode deeper into the midst of the troops.

Aethon watched him go, more than a little disappointed that the Glendan's aim had been off. The march to Trian would have been so much more pleasant with Throy Shadan on the other side of the Veil.

# CHAPTER 54

## A Flame in the Dark

WITH THE BLUE FLAME SCEPTER tucked in his belt, Gideon hefted his sword and followed Seth and Shavis into the smokey chamber where the *Ba'tul* were crouching around their macabre meal. The five creatures looked up as one, and surprise quickly transformed into hatred, vicious and feral. Scorpion-like tails flaring upright, each monster snatched up a massive club and leapt to their feet.

Two died instantly as a storm of arrows loosed by Shavis' men took the beasts in the head and neck, splitting bone and spraying dark blood across the smooth stone of the floor. A third *Ba'trul* staggered as several arrows struck it in the chest, but it continued forward, howling in pain and rage.

More arrows followed, slowing it further, and Shavis moved forward to engage it, slender blade flashing in the light of the glowstones overhead. The Dai'shozen sidestepped a thrust of the scorpion-like tail, then sliced it free of the creature's body. The severed tail continued to thrash about on the floor, its dagger-length stinger glistening with poison, still dangerous, still deadly.

Shavis danced away, dodging repeated swings of the *Ba'trul's* heavy club as the creature pursued him.

The two remaining *Ba'trul* closed the gap before more arrows could be loosed, and the Shizu archers were forced to abandon their bows and draw their swords. But the slender blades were no match for the mass of the monstrous clubs, and several swords were sent skittering across the ground as the Shizu lost hold of them. One young Shizu cried out as a stinger pierced his chest, injecting him with shadow-tainted poison. He dropped to his knees as the stinger pulled free, then toppled onto his face and died.

And then Seth was there, twin blades flashing, and the *Ba'trul's* tail thudded to the floor in two severed chunks. Ducking beneath the creature's club, he slashed it across the back of its arm, then buried one of his swords in its side before stepping lightly away to engage the other monster.

Howling, the *Ba'trul* turned to follow, but three of Shavis' men rushed in and planted their swords in its back, burying them clear to the hilt. The creature stiffened, and its club slipped from its ape-like hand. It tried to take another step, but its legs buckled and it collapsed with one last heavy breath.

Gideon started for the final *Ba'trul*, anxious to help Seth, but Shavis beat him to it, and Gideon could only watch as the two Dai'shozen systematically cut the creature down.

"That wasn't so bad," one of the Shizu said as the final *Ba'trul* fell, and Shavis scowled at him as he moved to kneel next to the Shizu who'd been killed.

"Tell that to Jomin," he said, placing his hand over the young man's eyes and gently closing them. Then he stood and looked at the Shizu who'd spoken. "When we leave, you will carry Jomin out of here. I won't leave him behind to become food for these godforsaken things."

"Yes, Dai'shozen," the man said, bowing his head as if to apologize.

"We need to keep moving," Seth said. "*Ba'trul* can hear the cries of other *Ba'trul* from ten miles away."

"But we're inside a bloody mountain," one of the Shizu said.

"Exactly," Seth told him, frowning. "There's not a lot of room to hide." Swords in hand, he led the way back to the stairs and started up to the next level.

"If other *Ba'trul* were alerted anyway," one of the Dymas said, moving next to Gideon, "why didn't we just kill them with the Power? We could have spared Jomin's life."

"And awakened an army of other shadowspawn in the process," Gideon told him. "*Ba'trul* aren't the only dangerous creatures in this hellhole. I'd prefer not to draw their attention."

They continued up to the next level in silence, and Gideon joined Seth in the center of the large chamber at the top. It was exactly as he remembered. To the left, a section of the ceiling had collapsed and a massive pile of stone lay beneath the dark cavern left behind by the collapse. He glanced briefly at it, then turned his attention to the right side of the chamber.

There, a large, intricately carved archway marked the entrance to Earth's Heart, and the corridor stretching away into the mountain was bright with the light of glowstones set in the stonework of the walls and ceiling. Numerous candelabra in the shape of a beautiful, long-haired woman—Gideon thought they must be representations of Elsa—lined the walls at intervals, each holding a singularly large glowstone in her outstretched hands.

But it was more than just visible light that made the corridor so remarkable, it was the spiritual radiance Gideon could feel emanating within that took his breath away. The place was alive with the power of the Earthsoul. It was alive with the spirit of Elsa.

One of Shavis' Dymas gasped at the sight of the corridor, and Gideon smiled at her astonishment. Apparently, she hadn't believed light such as this could exist in such darkness, especially after experiencing the Awareness-voiding darkness of Shadan's curse.

"How... how is that possible?" she asked, her eyes fixed on the light stretching away into the mountain.

"Earth's Heart lies at the end of that corridor," Gideon told her. "You didn't think the entity holding the Veil in place would be a thing of darkness, did you?"

"What's to keep shadowspawn from entering?" Shavis asked. "I would think they would be driven to try to destroy what lies within."

"Wards," Gideon answered. "Set by the Earthsoul Herself. As long as She has strength enough to sustain them, any shadowservant, human or otherwise, who crosses the threshold or attempts to wield corrupted *Ta'shaen* will be immediately destroyed."

"It looks like that's happened recently," Seth said, moving to kneel next to the tattered remains of several obliterated corpses. Moving a scrap of cloth aside, he picked up a silver bracelet and held it up for everyone to see. The Jexlair crystal set in the talisman shone red in the light of the glowstones. He pointed to the other remains. "At least four Agla'Con died here," he continued. "And two K'rrosha. It's hard to say how many Darklings there were, but I'd say at least a dozen."

"Shadan sent them to test the strength of the wards," Gideon said. "He knows if he can destroy the Soul Chamber before we find a Blood Orb then it's game over for us."

"Question," Shavis said, his eyes on the brightly lit hallway. "If the wards prevent shadowservants from entering, how did Shadan gain access when he confronted you twenty years ago?"

"He didn't," Gideon told him. "I came out to meet him."

The admission brought the pain and anger and frustration of that day back in a flood, and images of those final moments flashed through his thoughts. His infant son lying on the altar next to the dagger meant to spill his blood. Shadan and an army of Agla'Con and K'rrosha standing in this very spot, striking relentlessly at the wards. The entire mountain shaking as a result of their attempt to enter the Soul Chamber.

"I...." He faltered, unable to find the words. He felt as if a dagger had just plunged through his heart.

Seth came to his rescue. "Gideon used the Blood Orb to destroy Shadan and strengthen the Veil," he said. "He sacrificed himself so that I might bear the *Mith'elre Chon* safely home to his mother."

"Wait," Shavis said, a look of wonder in his eyes. "Jase Fairimor was here as an infant? Why?"

"Because his is the prophesied Blood of the Rejuvenation," Gideon answered, and the imaginary dagger piercing his heart gave a sudden, sharp twist. "Only he can use an Orb for its true purpose. I was a fool to think otherwise."

"Then let's go find him one," Shavis said. "Where do we start?"

Gideon looked at the mountain of stone filling the left side of the room. He hadn't given it much thought the last time he was here because he'd already possessed a Blood Orb and had taken it and Jase directly into the Soul Chamber. Now, however, he suspected it hid what they'd come here to find.

"My guess is there," he said, starting forward. "Spread out. Let's see if we can get around this mess."

The Shizu did as they were told, skirting the edge of the pile and moving around to either side. When they found the pile stacked up against the wall, they began to climb, stepping lightly so as not to send stones tumbling onto those who followed. Those leading the way reached the top, and one moved down the other side, disappearing from view. He reappeared almost at once, motioning excitedly for Gideon.

"Old World writings," he called. "Carved into what looks like the top of an arch."

Sheathing his sword, Gideon scrambled up the pile and peered over the edge at the symbols on the wall. Some were chipped and broken, but enough remained for him to make out what it said.

"*Kadeidria en mei Eliazar*," he read, then translated, "Holiness to the Lord of Creation." A rush of excitement swept through him at what it meant. "We've found a lost Temple of Elderon."

Seth kept his excitement in check as he joined Gideon at the top of the rock pile. He frowned as he looked down at the inscription visible just above the sloping chunks of stone. "Not to trample on your enthusiasm," he said, "but how exactly are we going to get inside? You can't open the way with the Power."

"No," Gideon agreed, "but we should be able to move enough rocks out of the way to squeeze under the arch. This pile couldn't extend that far into the passage beyond."

"There's only one way to find out," Shavis said, then nodded to his Shizu who began rolling rocks away from the front of the arch.

It took them several minutes, but they managed to clear enough stones away to expose the bottom of the arch. As Gideon had predicted, the pile within dropped away at a sharp angle toward the floor of the corridor. But it was darker than the bowels of hell beyond the reach of the glowstones the Shizu held up to the opening. Only the first few feet of the corridor were visible.

"I'll tell you what I find," Seth said.

Moving to the opening, he took off his swords to keep them from snagging on the rocks, then squeezed under the edge of the archway and eased his way carefully down the slope. When he reached the bottom, he quickly belted his swords back on and produced a pair of glowstones. The way ahead looked as if it stretched away forever, a dark, seemingly endless abyss that was as silent as it was dark.

Holding the glowstones before him, he moved cautiously down the corridor. He'd only gone a few steps when he noticed that the light emanating from the glowstones had begun to dim. He kept going, watching in alarm as the light in his fist grew fainter with every step.

This wasn't natural, he knew. Even where Shadan's curse was strongest, physical light was visible. The taint only affected spiritual light. *Until now*, he corrected, turning back the way he'd come. He watched the light of the glowstones return to their former luster as he reached the bottom of the rocks.

"What did you find?" Gideon called from above, his face visible beneath the top of the arch.

"Darkness," Seth answered. "Unnatural darkness. It absorbed the light of my glowstones."

"Robishar mentioned such a darkness in his prophecy," Gideon said, squeezing through the opening, and moving down the slope on his backside. "Which, believe it or not, gives me hope that we are in the right place."

"Perhaps," Seth agreed, "but it also means we can't go any further unless you and the other Dymas use the Power."

"And once you do," Shavis said as he climbed down to join them, "every shadowcreature in the area will know we are here. And they will come to investigate."

Gideon nodded, then locked eyes with Seth. "Just like the last time we were here."

Seth grunted. "And let me remind you how much fun *that* was."

"Have the rest of your people join us," Gideon told Shavis. "It will be easier to defend ourselves in here. Unless they are willing to claw their way through all that rubble, the only creatures small enough to enter are Shadan'Ko. And I doubt they will come anywhere near here for fear of being eaten by whatever else comes calling."

Shavis called his people, then looked back to Gideon as the first of the Shizu began squeezing through the opening. "I suggest we leave the Dymas here to destroy anything that tries to enter the temple," he said. "The Shizu and I will accompany you and Seth."

"Agreed," Gideon said. Looking into the darkness of the corridor, he made a small gesture with his hand, and a brilliant sphere of light appeared to light the way. It threw back the darkness much more effectively than the glowstones and revealed the finer details of the corridor. It was wide. And like the rest of Shey'Avralier, it was constructed of Power-wrought stone, as smooth and perfect as the day it had been created.

Gideon nodded. "Let's go."

They started forward, but the Power-wrought sphere began to dim as soon as they did, its brilliance fading with each and every step. It wasn't long before the sides of the corridor were no longer visible, and they were surrounded by a seemingly endless darkness. Only the Power-wrought stone visible beneath Seth's feet gave any indication that they weren't simply floating in some endless abyss. He could no longer see the accompanying Shizu at all, though he knew they were but a few feet away.

"Can't you make it brighter?" he asked.

Gideon shook his head. "I've already done that," he said. "I'm channeling enough Light into that sphere to light an area the size of Fairimor Dome. This darkness is unlike any I've ever encountered before." His face, etched with shadows in the dimming light, pinched into a frown. "It isn't a taint or curse—it's *real* darkness, the kind I would expect to find in Con'Jithar, malicious, combative, aware. I can feel it fighting back."

Seth nearly cursed aloud. "So, now what?"

Gideon removed the Blue Flame Scepter from where it was tucked into his sword belt. "We test the rest of Robishar's prophecy."

As Gideon harnessed the river of Light he was channeling to create the sphere, the area around him and the others was momentarily lost in total darkness. Then he redirected it into the scepter, and the Blue Flame crystal flared to life with bluish-white light so bright he and the others had to squint against the brilliance.

Holding it aloft, he looked around, pleased with the result. The sides of the corridor were visible once more, as were the Shizu and the Dymas clustered back at the entrance. They were, he noted, much closer than he would have imagined.

"It felt like we walked farther than that," Shavis said, echoing the thought.

Gideon grunted, then led the way to the end of the corridor where they entered a large, high-domed chamber. Glowstone chandeliers hung from the ceiling and there were a dozen glowstone lamps lining the walls. All appeared to be shining brightly, but Gideon knew if not for the light of the scepter, the chamber would have remained in darkness.

On the far side of the room, beyond a beautifully ornate fountain that had long since gone dry, a wide set of stairs ascended higher into the mountain. He gestured toward it with the scepter.

"The Blood Orb will be in one of the upper chambers," he told them, then added a silent, *If it's still here.*

He didn't like dwelling on the negative, but he was starting to have his doubts. Not that this was a Temple of Elderon—he knew with a certainty from the dedication on the entrance that it was. He was worried that something had happened to the Orb in the eight hundred years since the destruction of Cynthia.

Quickening his pace, he led the way up the stairs, throwing back the darkness with the Blue Flame Scepter as he went. But the higher he ascended into the temple, the more concerned he became. The darkness... it was growing stronger. And not just in how it was shrinking the reach of the scepter's light—he could feel it attacking his link to *Ta'shaen*, weakening his abilities.

He realized he was sweating and reached up to wipe his brow with his sleeve. At first he thought it was due to the amount of *Ta'shaen* he was being forced to wield coupled with the exertion of climbing all the stairs, but he soon realized the air was indeed getting hot. And it continued to grow hotter the higher they went.

As they neared the antechamber fronting the sixth level of the temple, it suddenly became difficult to breathe and Gideon was forced to wrap them all in a sheltering bubble of Spirit. Only then, safe in the pure Air he was channeling into the sheltering bubble, did the stream of noxious gases beyond the ward become noticeable. They flowed out of the entryway like faintly colored smoke, swirling up the stairs to the level above, drawn upward, he realized, by a powerful updraft.

"That can't be good," Seth muttered, then extended his arm toward the stairs and added, "After you, my friend."

Channeling even more Light into the scepter to fight off the darkness, Gideon started up the stairs, determined to see this through in spite of how his fear and doubt grew stronger with every step.

Doubt changed to hope when he reached the seventh level and found light coming from the room at the end of a long corridor. *The altar room*, he thought, smiling with relief so profound it nearly brought tears to his eyes. They'd found what they were looking for.

He lessened the amount of Power he was channeling into the scepter, and was pleased when the light at the end of the corridor remained visible. It wasn't, however, the brilliant white of a Blood Orb or even that of glowstones but had a reddish tint to it. It danced and flickered like something alive.

His earlier doubt returned, and with it came a cold knot of fear that settled in his stomach like a sharp rock. Holding the scepter before him like the weapon it was, he moved toward the light.

As he neared, a deep, distant roar grew slowly audible. Like waves crashing on a rocky shoreline, it boomed loudly then ebbed, then boomed again, rising and falling in continuous but sporadic procession.

The air outside his shield grew instantly hotter as they reached the doorway and passed through into the chamber beyond.

Or what was left of the chamber, he thought, staring at where the opposite wall had been. Now, a massive, fire-lit cavern was visible, its glassy smooth sides rising toward the smoke-filled sky just visible beyond the top of Tabor's ruined summit. It was like looking up from the bottom of a well, albeit one that had been ripped apart from the inside.

He knew if he approached the edge and looked down, he would see a lake of molten rock, the fire and brimstone left behind by Shadan's wrath.

"Do you think the most recent eruption did this?" Seth asked. "Or is this a result of the battle from the Second Cleansing?"

"I don't know," Gideon answered, shaking his head as he moved forward to what remained of the Altar of Elsa. Like the others he'd seen, it had been constructed from a single block of polished crystal, though this one now lay in pieces. It was impossible to tell if it had been shattered during the eruption that had ripped Tabor open and obliterated the top third of the mountain or if the damage was the result of a more ancient cataclysm. All he knew for certain was that the Blood Orb was gone.

"It doesn't matter now anyway," he continued. "The Blood Orb isn't here." He went to one knee next to the ruined altar and picked up one of the pieces.

No sooner had his fingers closed on it than his Awareness came alive with a stream of images. They washed over and through him in a barrage of sights and sounds and emotions that took his breath away and left him unable to move or speak. Like all Viewings, he witnessed things as if he were there as they happened, but he was powerless to intervene and could only watch in horror as they played out.

*Throy Shadan, still in his own flesh, entering this very room after having killed everyone in the chambers below. Siamon Fairimor arriving to confront him with the Blood Orb he'd taken from the temple in Andlexces. Shadan retaliating with the Blood Orb he took from the altar here. Lightning and Fire. Blood and Death. Destruction on a scale not known to men since the final days of the Old World. And all of it the result of Elsa doing battle with Herself as the Orbs that bore Her name bound themselves to their wielders and the reservoirs of Power were unleashed.*

The Viewing continued.

*Shadan attempting to destroy the Soul Chamber and collapse the Veil. Siamon standing as the last line of defense for the sacred chamber. Both men lost in the immensity of the Power they were wielding, unaware of the collateral destruction of their battle. Out in the city of Cynthia, hundreds, then thousands, of Elvan and Kelsan soldiers died as Tabor was ripped apart from the inside and fire and stone rained from the sky.*

*And then the final, critical moment arrived when the two men reached one another and attempted to wrest the Orbs from one another's grip. As free hands closed over the fists clutching the Blood Orbs, the Orbs bound themselves to a second wielder, forming a paradoxical link of friend and foe. The reservoirs of Power merged, then retaliated against the wielders, detonating with enough force to blow off the top of the mountain and open a rent deep into the fiery bowels of the earth.*

*As the sudden release of Power burned itself from existence, the darkness of Con'Jithar rushed in to fill the void, tainting Ta'shaen, warping the Veil, and changing the valley forever.*

The Viewing ended, but Gideon remained where he was, sick inside at what it meant. Throy Shadan may have gone down in history as the Destroyer of Amnidia, but he hadn't wrought the destruction alone. Siamon Fairimor's ignorance regarding the properties of a Blood Orb had helped, and in equal measure.

Seth appeared at his side, his face lined with concern. "Gideon," he said, putting a hand on his shoulder. "What's wrong?"

Gideon struggled to find his voice. "A Viewing," he answered at last, still reeling from the barrage of images. "I know how Shadan destroyed the valley."

He set the chunk of crystal back with the rest of the ruined altar. "He used the Blood Orb we came here to find. He was met by Siamon Fairimor in an area deeper inside the mountain, in a passage linking this room with the Soul Chamber." He pointed to the fiery cavern of Tabor's active volcano. "They left that behind as they were destroyed."

Pushing himself to his feet, he lifted the Blue Flame Scepter before him and started back the way they had come. "Let's get out of here."

He moved quickly, keeping the protective bubble of Air around them until they were past the toxic gases streaming out of the level below. Then he strengthened the flow of Light he was channeling into the scepter, and the gem-like crystal flared brightly, throwing back the darkness pressing heavily upon them.

They reached the lowest level and started across the rubble-strewn expanse of the high-domed chamber, skirting the ruined fountain and making straight for the final corridor. They were just about there when *Ta'shaen* came alive with several pure, but powerful wieldings.

Instinctively, Gideon stretched his Awareness forward to investigate, but his spiritual vision remained dark. A moment later, a tumult of mingled sounds reached his ears—the grating of stone on stone and the howl of a *Mrogin* mingled with the sickening, explosive wetness of rent flesh. The panicked voices of the Dymas followed, echoing down the darkened corridor, loud and shrill.

Gideon broke into a run and Seth and the others followed, leveling arrows and raising swords as they ran. The darkness gave way before the brilliance of the scepter, and the Dymas came into view at the far end of the corridor. They were holding their position at the base of the sloping pile of stone, and the forelegs of a *Mrogin* were visible where the creature had clawed its way through the narrow opening beneath the arch. The remains of its head and neck were splattered across the stones in a steaming, blood-slicked mess that smelled as bad as it looked.

At his approach, the Dymas cast quick looks over their shoulders, then moved to the sides of the corridor to make way for him. Each of them still held the Power, and while he couldn't see it with his Awareness, he could feel it coursing through them—Fire and Flesh and Light. All of it ready to be unleashed at whatever might come on the heels of the *Mrogin*.

The grating of boulders sounded loudly from the archway, and the headless corpse of the *Mrogin* was pulled back through the opening by an incredibly powerful creature. Gideon didn't know if it was another *Mrogin* or something worse, and he wasn't going to wait around to find out.

Drawing in as much as he could safely hold, he wove the Seven Gifts into *El'shaen te sherah* and channeled it into the scepter. The Blue Flame talisman reacted to the wielding by releasing a burst of cleansing destruction so powerful it punched through the rocky barrier as if it were made of paper, exploding stone into molten fragments and pummeling the creatures gathering beyond.

Many were killed outright, including a hulking, plated creature reminiscent of a K'sivik. The creature died with the headless *Mrogin* still clutched tightly in its jaws. A number of *Ba'trul* and a second *Mrogin* scrambled to their feet, injured but very much alive. Gideon incinerated them with a stream of crackling blue Fire.

It was far more powerful than necessary, but Gideon didn't care. Every creature in Amnidia already knew he was here. He wanted them to think twice about coming to investigate.

"Let's go," he said, leading the way into the chamber beyond.

The arched corridor leading to Earth's Heart was still intact, but Gideon inspected the wards protecting it to make sure they were still in effect. They were, so he angled toward the exit, burning two more *Ba'trul* from existence when they rushed into the room with clubs raised.

With Seth and the others close on his heels, he raced down the flights of stairs as fast as he could, ignoring the creatures that fled into the side chambers to evade him but destroying all who stood their ground to attack. There weren't many foolish enough to do so—two *Mrogin*, a half dozen *Ba'trul*, and another K'sivik-looking monstrosity were all they encountered. The rest took one look at the Power blazing from the Blue Flame Scepter and fled for their lives into the darkness.

That changed when he reached the ruins of Temifair Dome and found a literal army of shadowspawn pouring into the room from the chamber beyond. It wasn't the size of the army that gave Gideon pause so much as it was the army's makeup. Once-men walked side by side with *Ba'trul* who loped alongside *Mrogin,* and all of them were being directed by a cloaked figure wrapped in an aura of *Lo'shaen.*

"I thought the Rhiven were going to create a distraction," Seth said, eyeing the demon.

"They did," Gideon told him. "Why do you think there's only one demon?"

Seth arched an eyebrow at him. "So, you can handle this?"

"No," he admitted. "But this can."

Raising the scepter, he continued to draw on *Ta'shaen* until spots began forming in his vision. Not since his use of the Blood Orb twenty years ago had he held so much Earthpower at once, but now, like then, he was being assisted by a talisman far more powerful than he'd imagined. Robishar had been right to prophesy it would be of use here in this godforsaken darkness.

The demon slowed as the Blue Flame Scepter grew in brightness, and the aura of *Lo'shaen* surrounding the creature intensified. The army it commanded charged forward, Once-men hefting swords and spears while *Ba'trul* raised clubs. The howls of *Mrogin* reverberated loudly off the walls and ceiling.

Gideon watched them come, with his natural eyes and through his Awareness now that the scepter had thrown back the curse. The normally luminescent view was still shadowed and murky, but it was visible. *Just as Robishar prophesied,* Gideon thought with a smile.

From the corner of his eye he saw Seth and Shavis and the others raising bow and sword to meet the demonic onslaught, but he knew their assistance wouldn't be necessary. He was the Guardian of Kelsa and Keeper of the Blue Flame. In deed as well as in name. This battle was his to win or lose. And he had no intention of losing.

Ignoring the army of shadowspawn bearing down on him, he fixed the demon in his mind's eye, inspecting its link to the power of the Void, measuring its strength.

He felt the brush of the demon's mind and seized it with his Awareness. He sensed the creature's rage and hatred and its loathing for everything alive, but the river of blue-white energy flowing through him into the scepter sheltered him from the soul-crushing foulness of those emotions. And there, coursing through the demon in waves, was an emotion he hadn't expected to find in a creature of the Void: Fear. The demon was afraid. As it should be.

*You should have brought a larger army,* Gideon told it.

Then he struck, sending a torrent of blue flame spiraling into the demon's protective black aura. Hotter than the bowels of Tabor, the fire bored through the protective darkness in a flash of white, dispelling the Void and incinerating the creature within. The explosion that followed leveled the shadowspawn within a thirty foot radius, thrusting them outward from the detonation with such force that bones shattered and blood misted the air.

Gideon struck again, slicing through the forward ranks of shadowspawn with a sweep of blue that turned them to ash and sent those behind them staggering away, blistered and smoldering. Howls of agony echoed loudly as the injured creatures sought cover, but there was nowhere for them to hide, and a second sweep of blue silenced their cries.

Those shadowspawn still beyond the reach of the killing fire—and there were a number of them—turned and fled back the way they had come, clawing and tearing at one another in their haste to flee the room.

Grudgingly, Gideon let them go. He would have loved to rid the world of their filth, but getting Seth and the others out of Shey'Avralier was a higher priority. Besides, even with the aid of this magnificent talisman, he was growing tired. He didn't think he could keep this up for much longer. Hopefully, without the demon here to keep them in check, the *Ba'trul* and *Mrogin* would seek easier prey and return to hunting the Shadan'Ko.

Sending a few sizzling bursts down the corridor ahead of him, Gideon led the way once more, eager to reach the Myrscraw, aware of his waning strength. He was nearing his breaking point, he knew. A few more minutes at most and he would need to release the Power to keep from injuring himself.

Doing his best to ignore the points of light flickering along the edge of his vision, he pressed on, leading the way into the cathedral-like entrance of the palace. He was relieved when he found it empty. No Once-men. No *Ba'trul*. Nothing.

With a sigh of relief, he eased back on the amount of Earthpower he was channeling into the scepter, and the radiant glow lighting the chamber lessened noticeably. As it did, bars of sickly yellow sunlight became visible once more. Streaming through the windows above, they cut through the shadows to form pools of light amid the rubble. Gideon knew from the sharp angle of those bars that he and the others had been inside the mountain longer than he'd thought. No wonder the demon had been able to gather an army.

He started forward once more, but Seth's hand on his arm stopped him.

"Gideon," the captain said, pointing to the door with one of his swords.

A robed figure stood in the opening, a dark silhouette against the framing brightness.

"That's quite a talisman," the silhouette said, and Gideon smiled. Beside him, Seth lowered his swords, relaxing visibly.

"It did the trick today," Gideon replied, then released the Power and let the light of the Blue Flame fade so Shavis and his men would know Yavil wasn't a threat.

Like Seth, they relaxed their stances, but their eyes were wary as they watched Yavil approach. Suspicion turned to wonder when he stopped before them and they looked into his yellow-gold eyes. Shizu they might well be, but even they weren't immune to the awe of looking upon a Dragon.

"Are you alone?" Gideon asked.

"For now," Yavil answered. "Others will be joining me shortly."

"And then what?" Seth asked. He sounded skeptical, but for good reason. Lingering in this horrible place any longer than a day or two was asking to be overcome by the curse.

Yavil smiled. "We will see that you exit the palace safely," he said. "Then we will do what we can to clear Shey'Avralier of the shadowspawn you drew here with your use of the scepter." He pointed at the tower where the Myrscraw were waiting. "Come. Your feathered mounts await."

# CHAPTER 55

## As Darkness Falls

JASE CHANNELED ONE FINAL BARRAGE of lightning through his Veilgate, then released *Ta'shaen* and watched the Power-wrought opening collapse inward with a flash of blue light. A short time later, the rumble of distant thunder reached his ears, moving up the northern slopes of the Kelsan Mountains in a long, deep peal he and the others could feel in their chests.

"So that's what righteous anger sounds like," Thorac said, and beside him, Idoman chuckled.

Jase cast a sideways glance at the two and found them smiling as they stared at the army sprawling below. Thorac's eyes were bright with excitement, but Idoman looked as tired as Jase had ever seen him. An entire day of wielding the Power as a weapon after being healed of the wounds he'd received from the K'tyr had taken its toll. The young Dymas General would need to rest if he hoped to be of use tomorrow. So would the rest of Kelsa's Dymas.

A rush of emotion reached him through the *sei'vaiya* and he sensed Talia's thoughts as clearly as if she had spoken them. *And so do you,* she thought, watching him with concern.

He grinned at her, then returned his attention to Death's Third March. It had stopped a mile or so short of the mouth of Mendel Pass, and there seemed to be some confusion about who or what would be taking point for the long, narrow climb to come. Considering what had happened to those who'd led the way into Zedik Pass, their hesitation was understandable.

"What do you think?" Joneam asked, directing the question to Jase. "Will they wait for morning?"

He met the general's gaze briefly before looking back down the slope. "It's hard to say," he answered. "If not for the Meleki army breathing down their necks, waiting until morning would be the smart thing to do. But I don't think they'll wait for Lord Nid to catch up. It's too risky. I think they'll enter the pass as soon as Shadan decides which of his troops he feels he can sacrifice. My guess is they'll send shadowspawn ahead to engage us and to trigger the Power-wrought traps."

"I would if I were them," Idoman said. "Darklings are fierce but stupid. The loss of a few thousand will be nothing in light of how many intelligent soldiers will be spared. Once our traps have been triggered, the bulk of Shadan's army can proceed relatively unchallenged."

"No," Jase said. "Not unchallenged. We'll have something special for them as they near the summit." He glanced briefly at the sun hanging just above the western horizon before turning back to Idoman.

"Send word to those stationed in the pass. Have them withdraw to the summit. If Shadan's intent is to trigger our traps at the expense of his shadowspawn, then I say we let him. We'll use the detonations of Power to measure their progress. I think it will be minimal. Even the most dim-witted creatures among them will hesitate once a few thousand of their companions have been destroyed."

"And when Agla'Con arrive to remotivate them?" Joneam asked.

Jase locked eyes with the general as he answered. "We kill them."

Standing at the eastern edge of the Overlook, Elison Brey gazed out across the sprawling mass of the city's rooftops and listened to Medwin's report on the status of the evacuation.

Things were still moving too slowly for his liking, but the *Bero'thai* had put a stop to the looting and commandeering of homes in the evacuated areas. Sending the offending parties out of the city through Veilgates had proven to be a powerful deterrent, especially since he'd let it be known that the point of exile was the Chellum Highlands. The highlands were relatively safe, but they were remote enough to keep those who'd been exiled out of trouble for the two or three days it would take them to make it back to civilization.

"Everything north of the river has essentially been vacated," Medwin continued. "The neighborhoods between East Road and the river should be empty by tomorrow afternoon."

"That's good news," Elison told him. He looked down at the Trian River winding its way like a dark ribbon through shadowed city. It would be dark soon, and the evacuation efforts would stall as people took shelter for the night. "Have our Dymas begin laying Power-wrought traps along the river as soon as they are able. I assume they've already laid traps along the other major routes?"

Medwin nodded. "The northeast quadrant is done," he answered. "The northwest quadrant between North Road and the inner wall should be finished by this evening. The Riaki Dymas who arrived yesterday have been most helpful."

"*Ao tres'domei*," Elison said, smiling. "Servants of the Blue Flame."

He shook his head in wonder. "If someone would have told me a month ago that an army of Riaki Power-wielders would come to Trian's defense, I would have called them insane."

"It is pretty remarkable," Gideon said from behind him, and he turned to find the big Dymas moving down the cobbled pathway toward them. Seth was with him, and both men looked tired. Seth's uniform, he noted, was spattered with the dried, greenish-black blood of shadowspawn.

"Almost as remarkable," Gideon continued, "as Emperor Dromensai allowing Jase to put down an attempted coup in Riak. What's more, he gave Jase charge of Riak's Dymas during the Arkanian invasion."

"What's so remarkable about that?" Medwin asked. "Jase is the *Mith'elre Chon* after all."

"Yes," Seth said, "but Riaki politics are a bit more complicated than ours. Emperor Dromensai may have jeopardized his career by giving so much power to an outsider. His enemies will tout it as a weakness and seek to undermine his credibility."

Elison noticed the question forming in Medwin's eyes and changed the subject before the young man could speak. "What did you find?" he asked, though he had already guessed at the answer. Gideon wouldn't have returned to Trian if he'd found a Blood Orb—he would have sought out Jase.

"A lot of Shadan'Ko and shadowspawn," Gideon answered, confirming the assumption. "But no Blood Orb. It had long since been removed from what remains of the temple."

"So, there was a temple there," Elison said.

Gideon nodded, then moved to the edge of the Overlook and looked down at the city. "How goes the evacuation?"

"Almost there," Elison told him, then gave a quick summary of the progress thus far. "I am concerned, though," he continued, "about all the women and children and elderly still in the southern half of the city. They aren't deliberately ignoring the warning to leave, they simply don't have the means or the stamina to travel and they lack the supplies to support them if they do."

"Assign a number of Dymas to provide Veilgates," Gideon said without hesitation. "I won't allow women and children to be slaughtered by our enemies when this war spills over into the southern quadrants."

"Where would you have me send them?" Elison asked.

"Tri-fork, Kindel's Grove, and Cainel for starters," Gideon answered. "When those are filled, any town or village in that area will do. The people of Omer Forest are generous. They will care for Trian's refugees until this over."

Elison nodded. "I'll have our Dymas get started on it right away."

Gideon was silent for a moment as he let his eyes move over the city. Finally, he nodded as if to himself. "It's time for me to return to Trian," he said. "I need to be here when Death's Third March arrives."

"That is the best news I've heard all week," Elison said, surprised by just how deeply relieved he was. "Will Brysia be joining you?"

"I certainly hope not," Gideon said. "I'm hoping the allure of the archives will be greater than her desire to join me."

"Fat chance of that," Seth muttered. "Face it. She's going to want to be by your side as the end approaches. And we both know there is no stopping her once she sets her mind on something."

"True enough," Gideon said with a smile. "It's one of the things I love about her." He turned his attention back to Elison. "I've put the scepter back in its cabinet," he said. "And I placed a number of wards around it to protect it. If anyone other than me or Jase tries to remove it..."

"My staff will clean up the mess," Elison finished for him.

"There won't be a mess," Gideon said with a satisfied smile. "The wards trigger a release of *Sei'shiin*. Clean, deadly, and efficient."

He turned toward a hedge growing a short distance away, and a Veilgate opened into Temifair Palace. "I'll be back soon," he said, then he and Seth moved through to the vaulted chamber beyond.

"Yes," Elison whispered. "With your wife at your side."

He watched until the gate slid shut, then turned to Medwin. "Station *Bero'thai* in front of the Blue Flame Scepter," he said. "I don't want any of our people destroyed because they were curious. I'd rather Gideon's wards be a failsafe should something *truly* go wrong. Innocent curiosity doesn't warrant a death sentence."

"Yes, Captain," Medwin said. He started away, then stopped and looked back. "Something happened in Tabor he isn't telling us about, didn't it? Something involving the scepter. He wouldn't feel the need to ward it so strongly otherwise."

"That would be my guess," Elison told him. "But he'll let us in on the secret if it's something we need to know. Until then, we trust him to do what he thinks is best. He is the Guardian of Kelsa." He glanced meaningfully out at the darkening city. "His return to Trian will do much to strengthen the hope of our people."

火

Crouching on the edge of the Old World ruins surrounded by the dense foliage of Terishal Forest, Kaiden Kado listened carefully to the sounds of life around him. The soft warbling of songbirds and the playful chittering of squirrels filled the air, and twice he heard the high-pitched screeching bellow of a rutting stag. All good sounds, he thought. Nature's way of telling him that nothing was amiss. The area was free of shadowspawn and their Power-corrupting masters.

He smiled. He'd learned early in his career to listen to animals. Nature was the voice of the Earthsoul in places like this. Sometimes they gave warning through an unnatural or oppressive silence, sometimes through angry or frantic calls or chirps.

But warn they did, if one knew how to listen.

The screeching bellow of the stag sounded again, high-pitched and angry. Another stag responded almost immediately with a deep, resonant bugle that ended in a throaty growl. The challenge had been accepted. A battle for herd supremacy was coming.

As tempting as it was to watch the duel, Kaiden focused on the task at hand. Cautiously, he opened his Awareness and extended it beyond the mindward to investigate the Old World ruins. As the area came into view in his mind's eye, his spiritual vision confirmed what nature had already told him: The area was free of enemies, human or otherwise.

Rising from his place of concealment, he picked his way across the uneven ground toward the single, large structure rising in the center of the ruins. Pyramid in shape, it bore numerous scars of that long-ago destruction, gaping holes and crumbling walls that seemed as if they should have brought the entire building crashing down. Yet, somehow it remained upright, a testament to the architectural skills of its builders.

Even more impressive was the red gate on the far side of the structure. He had no idea what it was made of, but it was hard as steel and looked as if it had been erected yesterday. Perhaps when the war with *Frel'mola* was over, he could investigate the gate further, perhaps learn some of its secrets.

He reached the pyramid-like structure and moved inside, and the sounds emanating from the forest grew quieter. They continued to fade from hearing the deeper he went, and by the time he reached the central chamber, all was silent. And it was dark. So much so, that he embraced the Power and channeled a small sphere of light.

As *Ta'shaen* flowed into him, he sighed deeply, basking in the feeling. It had been weeks since he'd embraced the Power, and he'd almost forgotten how good wielding could feel. It was like a drink of ice cold water after weeks of wandering in the desert. A savory meal after days without food. Light after the darkest night.

Holding the glowing sphere before him, he crossed the chamber to a pile of stones heaped up against the far wall. He went to one knee and carefully unstacked the top third of the pile to reveal the stone box concealed within the rubble. Inside the box lay the Communicator Stone he'd brought with him from Rosda.

He removed the stone and set it on top of the box, then channeled the flows necessary to activate it. A moment later the face of Raisa Zakeya, his contact in Rosda, came into view before him.

"Kaiden," she said, her voice filled with alarm. "What's wrong? You aren't due to make contact for another week."

"I know," he told her, "but this couldn't wait. *Frel'mola* has created a refleshed army some twelve thousand strong, and more are being refleshed every hour. She means to send them to assist with Death's Third March. She gave command of them to Aethon Fairimor."

"I'll let Grandmother know," she said. "Now, release the Power before our enemies pinpoint your location." Her glowing image vanished as she heeded her own advice and severed the link.

Kaiden let the Communicator Stone wink out, then returned it to its box and began piling on stones to conceal it once more. He wasn't worried that the enemy would feel his use of the Power—the Old World ruins were two days journey from the nearest village and three days away from Berazzel. The biggest risk would come when he returned to the palace. A week-long absence wasn't likely to go unnoticed by the other servants. Especially since it was his third in as many months. He didn't think anyone would intentionally give him up, but loose tongues got people killed.

He finished stacking the stones, then rose, bringing the small, Power-wrought orb of light around in front of him to light the way. The shadows in the room changed angles around him as he moved, but it was the shadows moving near the chamber's entrance that stopped him cold. Far too large to be human, they moved silently, hulking shapes just beyond the reach of his light.

*Shadowspawn*, he thought, and a cold knot of fear tightened in his chest at what it meant. *Frel'mola's* lackeys had found him. Horrified, he opened himself more fully to the Power and prepared a killing strike.

The creatures stepped into the light.

Lost in her own thoughts, Brysia sat at the banquet table in Lord Reiekel's private dining room and absently sipped her tea while her uncle and the others conversed over their meals. Gideon had been gone all day, and she was worried sick that something may have happened to him.

*No*, she thought vehemently, *he is fine. He can take care of himself. And so can Seth. They will be back shortly.*

"Are you all right, my dear?" Xia asked, and Brysia looked up to find her mother watching her with concern.

Brysia smiled as she lowered the tea cup. "Just a little distracted," she answered. "It never gets any easier letting him go off like that."

"Well, you can stop worrying," Beraline said. "He and Seth just arrived through a Veilgate. They'll be walking through the door in just a moment."

A wave of relief flooded through Brysia as she rose and started for the door. Before she could reach it, the knob turned and Gideon and Seth moved inside. Both looked like they'd been mauled by a Shadowhound.

Gideon must have read her thoughts in her eyes because he smiled reassuringly. "You should see the enemy," he said, then took her in his arms and hugged her tightly. He smelled horrible, but she didn't pull away, content to feel the hardness and strength of his body.

After a moment he released her and stepped back to look her over. "I have a lot to tell you all," he said. "But first, I need something to eat."

He let his eyes move over the others at the table, and a frown moved over his face. "Where's Jase?"

"Mendel Pass," Brysia told him. "At least that's where he went this morning. There's no telling where he might be now." Taking him by the hand, she led him to the table, motioning for the servants to fetch him something to eat. "He did promise to be back in time for dinner. Though it looks like that might not happen."

"Actually," Gideon said, his eyes on something out in the corridor. "He and Talia just arrived." His eyes narrowed. "And they aren't alone."

Before Brysia could ask who was with them, the door opened and Jase and Talia entered hand in hand. A young Tamban in hunter's garb walked behind them, and behind him came Quintella and two Dainin Brysia didn't know. The giant men ducked as they passed through the doorway, then straightened once more, their eyes bright with excitement.

Jase moved right up to her and Gideon. "Mother," he said, "this is Kaiden Kado, Quintella's grandson. These two are Chieftain Yanaval Paddishor and Edakkin Palo'Gar of the *Nar'shein Yahl*. They brought Kaiden to us from Tamba. He has important information about *Frel'mola* and her dealings with Aethon Fairimor."

"I see you, *Nar'shein*," she said, then locked eyes with the young man. "Welcome, Kaiden," she said. "Please, sit and tell us what you know."

As Kaiden delivered his message to Brysia, Jase watched her and Gideon for some sign of what they might be thinking. He'd already heard the Tamban Dymas' report, of course, so he knew what the young man had risked to bring them the information. Eavesdropping on *Frel'mola* and Aethon Fairimor had to be one of the bravest, most insanely dangerous things he'd ever heard tale of. Then to risk detection by activating a Communicator Stone—Kaiden was lucky the Dainin had sensed his use of *Ta'shaen* at the lost temple instead of shadowspawn or *Jeth'Jalda*.

From the look of admiration in Brysia's eyes, it was clear she was thinking the same thing, but she remained quiet until Kaiden finished speaking.

"Thank you for bringing us this information, Kaiden," Brysia said. "And thank you for your service to the Earthsoul."

Kaiden smiled. "You are welcome, my lady."

Brysia turned to one of the *Bero'thai*. "Our newly arrived guests look famished," she said. "Please have Mistress Rochelle prepare something for them."

The *Bero'thai* dipped his head in a nod and disappeared into the narrow hallway leading to the kitchens.

"The Old World ruins Kaiden spoke of," Lord Reiekel said, addressing the Dainin, "they were a lost Temple of Elderon, weren't they?"

Chieftain Paddishor nodded. "Yes. But its Blood Orb, if ever one existed, was not to be found." He turned his eyes on Brysia. "After we parted ways with your son in Kavet de'Leflure," he continued, "my *Nar'shein* and I returned to the Jyndar continent to continue the search for lost temples, expanding our search into Tamba. That is when we found Kaiden Dymas."

"They scared me to death," the young man admitted, eyeing the Dainin with continued wonder. "I thought they were shadowspawn. Or worse, demons from Con'Jithar."

"We very easily could have been," Chieftain Paddishor said, directing the comment to Jase. "The Veil has collapsed in more than two dozen locations in the mountains north of Tel'Haalaf. Thousands of demons are moving north into Terishal Forest. There are similar collapses near Tirza and Messembari."

"That could work to our advantage," Seth said. "Especially if those demon armies move against Berazzel."

"Yes," Jase agreed. "*Frel'mola*'s alliance with Aethon might be put on hold."

"Or," Kaiden said, his face pinching with worry, "she could harness their strength and use them to her advantage. She is the Bride of Maeon, after all, and her relationship with the Dark One is a very real thing. I was in the Palace of Berazzel when he paid her a visit."

Brysia leaned forward, a look of disbelief on her face. "He actually came to her in the living world?"

Kaiden shook his head. "He spoke to her through a rent in the Veil. Even in Her weakness, the Earthsoul refuses to allow him access."

"That could change at any time," Jase said as glimpses of the fall of the Rhiven home world flickered through his thoughts. There, Maeon had been an active participant on the battlefield.

"Let's address the threats we know," Gideon said, then turned his attention to Kaiden. "This army of K'rrosha *Frel'mola* gifted to Aethon, you didn't happen to overhear where Aethon intends to use them, did you?"

The young Dymas shook his head. "No. Nor did I learn where he plans to deploy the fifty thousand Tamban troops *Frel'mola* promised him."

"Just knowing he has that many more troops at his disposal is a help," Jase assured him. "We know *what* we are up against even if we don't know where or when we might face them."

"If I were Aethon," Seth said, pulling thoughtfully at his moustache, "I'd have them arrive on Trian Plateau south of our armies. We'd be forced to fight our way through them to reach Trian."

Jase nodded. "That's what I think as well. That's why I ordered the bulk of the united armies to pull back to Trian. A few thousand will remain in Mendel Pass to confront the enemy, but it is a token force only. We'll delay them as long as we can, then evacuate through Veilgates."

"You said *we*," Brysia said. "I'm going to assume you used that word in the collective sense, and not that you will be there in person."

Jase shrugged. "I guess we'll find out." He kept his eyes off Talia, fully aware of what she was thinking.

"What's to keep the Tambans from arriving directly in Trian?" Xia asked, forestalling the protest forming on Brysia's lips. "They could take the city from within."

"Several things," Jase told her. "Not the least of which is the prophecy that Throy Shadan will be the one to lay siege to the city. Even if *Frel'mola* decided to try to claim Trian as her own, her forces would be caught between a sizable army of *Bero'thai* and Dymas, innumerable Power-wrought traps, and an angry Shadan. I don't imagine he would react well to *Frel'mola* trying to claim what he sees as his." He pursed his lips thoughtfully. "One might almost wish she would try—a war between her and Shadan would help our cause."

"And the twelve thousand K'rrosha?" Brysia asked.

Jase shook his head. "I don't know. But wherever Aethon sends them, they're going to be difficult to stop."

"We'll cross that bridge when it comes," Gideon said. "For now, we can only fight the battles we can see."

"Speaking of which," Jase said. "What did you find in Tabor? Was it as dark as you suspected?"

"It was worse," Gideon answered. "Robishar's prophecy was spot on. Without the Blue Flame Scepter, we would have been completely blind in there." Glancing briefly at Seth, he shook his head. "Without the scepter, we wouldn't have made it out of there alive." Then, as everyone listened in awe, he relayed what had happened to him and Seth and the others while they were in the valley. He finished with an update on the Rhiven.

"Yavil and several others are going to clear Shey'Avralier of Shadowspawn. They'll do it in Dragon form to avoid using the Power."

"And the wards on the entrance to the Soul Chamber?" Brysia asked.

"Still intact," Gideon answered. "But should they fail, the Rhiven will protect Earth's Heart until Jase arrives with a Blood Orb."

He locked eyes with Jase once more. "So," he continued, "what happened with you today? Something horrible, I see." He looked meaningfully at Quintella.

Jase glanced at Quintella, and the thought of how close he'd come to losing her chilled his heart. "Aethon," he said, "made an attempt on Lord Nid, and the High Command got in the way. We lost General Gefion, General Kennin, and Captain Ieashar. Joneam and Idoman were wounded but survived." He reached over and took Quintella's hand in his, and his sadness intensified. "We lost Keenan Nolan as well when he confronted Aethon to stop the attack. Word from our spotters is that he nearly destroyed Throy Shadan in the process."

Gideon looked at Quintella and bowed his head in a show of respect. "I'm sorry for your loss," he told her. "Keenan was a great man."

She returned the bow, smiling tiredly. "He will be missed."

Jase squeezed her hand, then looked back to Gideon. "Thorac Shurr has assumed command of the Chunin army. Dael Arishar now heads the Elvan forces. They will assist General Eries in pulling the united armies back to Trian. Idoman will command the select few who will remain in Mendel Pass to act as a stopgap."

"Where is Death's Third March now?" Xia asked.

"Poised to enter the pass," Jase answered. "But there seems to be a debate as to who will be taking point. I believe it will be shadowspawn. And I think they will begin the climb sometime after nightfall."

Rochelle entered from the kitchen with several servants bearing trays of food, and the conversation paused while those who hadn't eaten helped themselves to the feast. The Dainin, he noted with a smile, each took an entire tray—enough food to feed ten men.

A pleasant silence fell across the room, and Jase drank it in almost as eagerly as he did the glass of ale Rochelle poured for him. The day had been long and loud, and he was grateful for the respite. He sensed Talia thinking the same thing and winked at her. She smiled, sending a rush of affection through the *sei'vaiya*.

But the moment was short-lived as Seth spoke. "Where is Elliott?"

"He went to Chellum for the night," Talia answered. "He—" she cut off as a tremor came upon the room, rattling dishes and causing the ale in the glasses and pitchers to slosh back and forth. The tremor passed as quickly as it had come.

"Those are growing more frequent all across the world," Chieftain Paddishor said. His face pinched into a frown as he added, "In some places the earthquakes are constant. The world is very literally coming apart at the seams."

"She'll hold together a while yet," Jase said. "Long enough for us to find a Blood Orb."

"You really believe that, don't you," Chieftain Paddishor said.

Jase looked him squarely in the eyes as he answered. "I do."

Paddishor smiled. "Then so do I."

The door to the dining room opened and a *Bero'thai* rushed into the room with Captain Plat. The Meleki captain's hair and uniform were singed, and he wore a look of complete panic.

Jase rose to meet him, but the feeling of dread sweeping through him as he looked the captain in the eyes told him all he needed to know. What came next confirmed it.

"*Mith'elre Chon*," Plat said, moving straight to him, "the Meleki army is under attack. Ten thousand K'rrosha at least. All on horseback. They arrived through Veilgates almost as one."

The feeling of dread grew stronger, but Jase forced himself to speak. "Lord Nid?"

Vol shook his head. "I don't know," he answered, his hands knotting into fists. "We got separated. There was so much corrupted Fire..." He shook his head as if to snuff out the memory. "Our Dymas did what they could to hold them off and to open Veilgates for our escape, but we were overrun. Thousands are dead. Thousands more are stranded in the Bottomlands where they are being hunted by the K'rrosha."

Jase turned to Gideon. "We need Dymas," he told his father. "Pull them from wherever they are needed the least—Trian, Chellum, Aridan, it doesn't matter—and get them to the Bottomlands."

"And you?"

"I'm going to Mendel Pass. Shadan will undoubtedly take advantage of the situation to march on our people there."

Chieftain Paddishor and his companion rose. "We will accompany *El'Kali* to the Bottomlands."

"I'll go with Jase," Seth said, adjusting his swords as he stood.

*As will I.*

Talia's thoughts came through the *sei'vaiya* so strongly that for a moment Jase wondered if she'd spoken them aloud. The absence of an objection by Seth told him otherwise.

Jase took her by the hand. "We all know where we need to be," he said aloud. "God's speed to all of you. And good luck."

With that, he opened a Veilgate into the darkness of Mendel Pass.

# CHAPTER 56

## Under the Crescent Moon

HULANEKAEFIL NID AWOKE TO THE SIGHT of the moon shining brightly in the night sky. Like the emblem of his nation, it was in its early stages, a slender crescent of white surrounded by a sea of stars.

He stared at it in wonder, disoriented and confused as to why he was looking up at it from the ground. And when had night fallen? It had been light just moments ago... hadn't it? Yes. Yes, it had, he decided. But then—

He couldn't remember.

Frowning, he tried to rise, but excruciating pain lanced through his head, filling his vision with flashes of light. As the pain faded, he realized he'd done little more than roll over onto his side. Tufts of grass tickled his face, and he was powerless to do anything about them.

He could only lie there and stare at the moonlit bodies littering the ground in front of him. They stretched away into darkness, silent and immobile and... and dead.

The thought should have meant something to him, but he was having trouble deciding what it was. His head hurt so badly he was having trouble—

The smell of blood and the stench of burnt flesh moved over him, borne forward by an unusually warm breeze. Why the breeze was warm was a mystery. As were the bright flares and flashes disturbing the night somewhere beyond the field of bodies.

What had happened here? And why did his head hurt so badly?

He tried to move again, but the inside of his head went white with pain. His view of the world was lost in it, and for a moment he thought it might claim him completely.

Then, as the pain faded, bits and pieces of memories flickered through his mind once more. He'd been riding a fine black mare alongside Captain Plat. They'd been discussing—no, they'd been laughing—at something one of his men had said. Then the air had opened around them.... Horsemen, cloaked and hooded—bearing lances. Streamers of red. Streamers of... Fire.

He closed his eyes and reached inward, trying to understand what it meant. Slowly, as if his arm weren't truly attached to his body, he reached up and touched his head. His fingers came away sticky with clotted blood. He looked at it, smearing it between thumb and forefinger. The memories returned in full.

The Meleki army had come under attack by K'rrosha. Some ten thousand strong at least, they had completely overwhelmed his men, killing thousands and scattering the rest. He and the other Dymas had defended where they could, but it hadn't been enough. They'd been overrun, and he'd been thrown from his horse as Fire erupted all around him.

He tried to rise again, but his legs refused to respond. He glanced down the length of his body to where they lay amid the charred grasses. He couldn't feel them or the ground beneath them. And, try as he might, he couldn't move them.

He'd broken his back, he realized, then closed his eyes wearily and lay still. It was probably just as well, he decided. He suspected that much of what he could smell of burnt flesh was originating from himself. To confirm it, he opened his Awareness and gingerly stretched it toward his ruined legs. They came into view in his mind's eye, and his stomach tightened with revulsion at the sight.

His right leg was blistered and blackened, and strips of crisped flesh stuck out at odd angles above his knee. His left leg was even worse. Seared free of all muscle from the knee down, it was stick-like and grotesque. Some of the bones in his foot were missing.

He reined in his Awareness and lay still, too weak, too sick, and too overwhelmed to move. And he could feel that he was growing weaker, that life was leaving him. He knew if he opened his Awareness to view the fabric of the Veil he would find that it was growing thinner, drawing nearer. He felt himself slipping rapidly toward death.

He opened his eyes once more to view the moon overhead. A crescent moon, he thought with a smile. Fitting that the emblem of his kingdom—of his very life— should be here as he left this life behind.

*Ta'shaen* trembled from yet another corrupted wielding, and Fire erupted somewhere behind him, lighting the expanse of bodies stretching away before him. He listened to the flame's wind-like roar, felt the heat of it upon the back of his neck. The agonized screams of dying men followed, short-lived though they were.

The leisurely thudding of an approaching horse became audible somewhere beyond his range of vision, and he listened as horse and rider slowly drew nearer. Tremors of corruption tickled his Awareness, and a reddish glow appeared a moment later, moving over the bodies of the fallen like something alive, growing wider and brighter as the source of the light approached.

Then he saw them: two Shadowlancers making their way slowly through the carnage, the tips of their lances glowing red with corrupted Fire which flickered and danced like the flames on a torch. Deliberate in their movements, they were using the hellish light to view the faces of the dead, looking, he knew, for those who might still live.

*Looking for me*, he realized, and his heart nearly stopped beating in his chest.

One of the K'rrosha reached the body of a soldier lying face down a few paces away, and tendrils of smoke spiraled upward from pierced flesh as the Deathman used its lance to roll the corpse over. Lance tip flared briefly to light the dead man's face, then dimmed as the rider urged his mount forward to continue the search.

Opening his Awareness once more, Hul tried to embrace *Ta'shaen* to destroy the K'rrosha, but the incandescent rivers of Power remained beyond his reach. He was too weak to wield, and the Earthsoul knew it. Taking hold of the Power now would kill him as surely as would the K'rrosha.

He reached deeper into himself, desperate to wield. Better to die in a fiery burst of his own making, he thought, than at the hands of these Light-blasted abominations. Try as he might though, *Ta'shaen* remained distant and elusive.

Defeated, he reined in his Awareness and lay still, waiting to be found. A few seconds later the nearest K'rrosha loomed over him and their eyes met.

"Well, look who we have here," the refleshed being said. "Still alive but obviously unable to touch the Power. Shadan will be most pleased about that. Though it would have been better for you to have died here on the battlefield."

Eyes flaring with evil glee, the K'rrosha lowered its lance and thrust the fiery tip through Hul's shoulder, piercing him just below the collarbone.

He nearly lost consciousness at that point, his tortured body overwhelmed by the searing, white-hot pain of being stabbed. Only the smell of his own burning flesh and the feeling of being lifted free of the earth kept him from blacking out. And blacking out, he knew, would have been a mercy.

Instead, he found himself looking down the length of the lance, his ruined legs dangling several feet above the ground. The grey-fleshed face of his tormentor split wide with a smile. "You don't recognize me because of the face I wear now," the K'rrosha said. "But in life, I was one you knew well." He raised the lance a little higher, and Hul's agony spiked as he slid forward another foot. "You should have killed me with *Sei'shiin*."

"Panishern," Hul whispered through clenched teeth. He reached for the Power, but it remained out of reach.

"Yes," the K'rrosha nodded. "And it's going to be a pleasure handing you over to Shadan. Word is, he plans on healing you just so he can kill you slowly."

"If you're finished toying with him," the other K'rrosha said, "we should be on our way. It's a long ride to Mendel Pass, and we wouldn't want him dying along the way."

"Quite right," the refleshed Panishern said, then looked in the direction of a sudden conflagration of Power. There, some hundred yards distant, a Dymas had just engaged a phalanx of K'rrosha, and the conflict lit the night with bursts of bluish-white interspersed with flashes of retaliatory red.

The exchange was brief, and the bursts of blue vanished as quickly as they had come.

Panishern gave a malevolent chuckle. "A fitting end for—"

A streamer of *Sei'shiin* cut the statement short, and Panishern vanished in a flash of white that lit the area for a hundred yards. In the same instant, tendrils of Air took hold of Hul while additional tendrils steadied the lance piercing his shoulder.

Panishern's refleshed companion wheeled its horse about to confront the threat, but a second spear of *Sei'shiin* burned it from existence before it could bring its lance to bear.

As darkness fell once more, the gruesome sound of rending flesh followed as Dainin materialized from the moonlight and speared the two shadowspawned horses through the head. Both collapsed into quivering heaps, and the fiery light in their eyes winked out.

The *Nar'shein* pulled their spears free then turned toward a third figure just visible in the faint light. Hul nearly wept with joy when he discovered it was Gideon.

"One of you heal him," Gideon said. "I'll remove the lance and ward the area while you do."

Hul felt a shift in *Ta'shaen* as one of the Dainin took control of the grip of Air holding him aloft. Stepping near, the other Dainin planted his spear in the ground then placed his giant hands on Hul's head. They were warm. Warm and surprisingly gentle.

"Ready?" Gideon asked, and Hul knew it was as much for him as for the Dainin. He braced himself for what would follow. As weak and injured as he was, the healing could just as easily kill him as make him well. He closed his eyes.

The flows of Air channeled by Gideon grew stronger as he pulled the lance free and tossed it away, and Hul gasped as it left his body. A second, more powerful surge followed as the Dainin channeled a rush of healing.

The world vanished into darkness.

Standing in the dark confines of Mendel Pass, Jase held Talia's hand and watched as erratic bursts of Fire lit the Bottomlands to the north. Most were nothing more than flares of red whose corruption barely registered in his Awareness, such was the distance between him and the wielders. Occasionally, though, a burst of white made him squint, and *Ta'shaen* resonated with the powerful, cleansing destruction of *Sei'shiin*. Here and there amid the fiery exchanges, flashes of blue showed where Veilgates were being used to evacuate Meleki soldiers from the battlefield.

"Do you think they will find him alive?" Talia asked.

"I don't know," Jase answered. "Captain Plat's report was pretty bleak."

"They'll find him," Seth said, and Jase glanced over to find his friend watching something further down the pass. His hair was the color of moonlight in the near darkness, and his eyes peered out of his chiseled face like polished bits of glass. Clearly, he didn't like what he was looking at.

"Right now," he continued, "we should be more concerned with that." He raised an arm and pointed down into the darkness.

Jase looked in the direction indicated and waited for his eyes to adjust to what Seth had already seen. Slowly, a faint red glow became visible, a hellish halo of red that moved up the roadway and along the sides of the pass like something alive. As he watched, distinct points appeared within the glow, sets of eyes that smoldered like coals and lit the faces of the Darklings and other Power-wrought creatures making their way up the steep slope. There were thousands of them.

"Well, I guess we know who Aethon decided to sacrifice," Idoman said. "I wonder if they know what awaits them."

"Probably not," Joneam muttered. "Shadowspawn are stupid."

"Yes," Seth said, "but there are more than enough of them to serve Aethon's purpose in triggering your Power-wrought traps."

"I'm counting on it," Jase said. "Like I told General Eries earlier, we'll use the detonations to track their progress." He turned his back on the reddish glow of shadowspawned eyes and motioned the others to follow. "Come, we'll watch the detonations from the summit."

Embracing *Ta'shaen*, he parted the Veil and strode through into the midst of the small army waiting in the darkness above.

え

Brysia sipped quietly at her tea and tried unsuccessfully not to look at the clock on the dining room wall. It had been more than three hours since Gideon had left to help the Meleki army, and there had been no word from him since. The lack of information was beginning to wear on her nerves.

She set her cup down and glanced at the two *Bero'thai* standing watch at the door. Eyes forward, they stood as motionless as stone, silent observers to her agonizing wait. Everyone else who'd been present for dinner had long since retired for the evening—her mother and uncle to their apartments, Quintella and her grandson and Captain Plat to the rooms prepared for them by the palace staff. She assumed Beraline and Marithen had retired as well, but she wouldn't be at all surprised if they'd returned to the library or the Dremick building to continue their search.

She was about to pour herself another cup of tea when a Veilgate opened along the far wall, and Gideon rushed through from the darkness beyond. Yanaval Paddishor and Edakkin Palo'Gar followed closely on his heels, their massive frames hunched as they ducked through the shimmering opening. Yanaval cradled the body of Lord Nid in his arms the way an adult might cradle a sick child, and the agonized look on the Dainin Chieftain's face told Brysia that things had not gone as planned.

The relief she felt at her husband's return vanished, and a knot tightened in her stomach as she rose to meet him. "Lord Nid?" she asked, afraid of the answer.

"Alive," Gideon answered, then added a hesitant, "but we could still lose him." He glanced at his unconscious friend, and it was clear from the pain in his eyes that he believed losing him was likely.

"Lord Nid's wounds," Yanaval began, "were greater than any I've ever encountered in one still living. I do not know how he survived long enough for us to find him."

"He's a strong man," Brysia said, as much to comfort herself as the others. "He'll pull through." She gestured to the *Bero'thai* standing watch at the door. "Please fetch Captain Plat," she told them. "He will want to know his King is here."

"Yes, my lady," one of the men said, then hurriedly slipped out the door.

Brysia looked back to Gideon briefly, then let her eyes settle on Lord Nid. "Now what?" she asked. "He is welcome to stay here, of course, but...." She paused, searching for the right words. "But if we might still lose him, I think he would prefer to be in his own home when he passes. Under the banner of the Crescent Moon."

"We'll let Captain Plat make that call," Gideon said, then fell silent as he waited for the captain to arrive.

A moment later the door opened and Vol hurried into the room. He moved up to Yanaval and reverently placed a hand on his lord's chest.

"What are his chances?" he asked.

"Slim," Gideon answered. "So much so, that Queen Fairimor suggested that you take him home to Melek so he can pass away under the Crescent Moon."

Vol was quiet for a moment as he considered. Finally, he shook his head. "You are his family now," he told them. "I think he would prefer to stay here."

"You can use the room prepared for you," Brysia said. "And you are welcome to keep watch over him for as long as you wish."

"Until the end, then," Vol said. "Whenever that might be." He bowed to Brysia, then motioned for Yanaval to carry Lord Nid to his room. With one last look at Gideon, he followed the Dainin from the room.

When they were gone, Brysia turned her attention back to her husband. "What of the rest of the Meleki army?" she asked.

"Still in the process of being rescued," Gideon answered. He took a deep breath and exhaled in frustration. "But we lost a significant number of men tonight. Throy bloody Shadan won't need to look over his shoulder any longer."

Brysia pursed her lips in frustration. "Which means he can concentrate more fully on taking Mendel Pass."

Gideon took her hand in his and looked her in the eyes, a knowing smile on his face. "I will go check on our son," he said. "Perhaps knowing that his mother is worried about him will convince him to stay out of the conflict. Mendel Pass is as good as lost already anyway."

"So, what does it take to convince you to stay out of the conflict?" she asked. "Worrying about you obviously hasn't worked." She gave a mirthless grunt. "Any more than it will with Jase."

He leaned forward and kissed her on the forehead. "Get some rest," he said. "I'll be back as soon as I can."

"If I had a pebble for every time I've heard that..." she muttered.

"You'd have a mountain the size of Fairimor Dome," he finished, forcing a smile. "I know." He kissed her again, then turned as the Veil parted behind him. With one final smile, he strode through into the darkness beyond.

As Gideon arrived through a Veilgate, Idoman pulled his Awareness back from where he'd been studying the shadowspawned army, then turned to face the big Dymas. Like the others who hurriedly gathered near, he was eager for news about Lord Nid.

"Did you find him?" Jase asked, the concern on his face clearly visible in the light of the moon.

"We found him," Gideon answered. "But he was so badly injured that healing him nearly killed him. He might not survive the night. Captain Plat is with him now in Andlexces."

"And the Meleki army?" Jase asked.

"Scattered," Gideon answered. "Those who aren't still fleeing for their lives in the Bottomlands have been moved to Trian through Veilgates."

"So hitting Death's Third March from the rear is no longer an option," Joneam said, his frustration flowing out of the darkness like a gust of wind.

"No," Gideon said. "But that doesn't mean we can't make the enemy pay for what they did."

"My feelings exactly," Jase said. "In fact, you're here just in time to see the beginning of their reckoning. The forward ranks of shadowspawn are less than a hundred yards away from the first detonation."

"There are Shadowhounds well past the first crux points," Idoman said, "but I anticipated them scouting ahead and fashioned trip lines that will only respond to massive amounts of shadowspawned flesh. A few Shadowhounds aren't enough to trigger them."

Gideon seemed impressed. "That's a new one."

"Credit the Earthsoul," Jase said. "She's inspired a lot of new tricks the past few days." His teeth reflected the white of the moon when he smiled. "In fact, I am eager to see how the newest one performs. It came to me the other day when *Ao tres'domei* and I were here laying traps."

"This I have to see," Idoman said, then extended his Awareness back down the pass to watch the approaching shadowspawn. They came into view in his mind's eye, the reddish glow of their eyes illuminating the canyon some fifty yards below where his Awareness hung like a bird in flight.

He felt Gideon and Jase do likewise and opened his mind to theirs, forming a

Communal link. Their excitement was palpable.

*Almost there,* he told them, his eyes on the knot of Darklings taking point. *Another twenty feet.* He couldn't stop himself from counting down their final steps.

*Ten... Five...* He braced himself. *Right about... there.*

The bottom of Mendel Pass went brighter than the sun as Fire and lightning erupted seemingly out of nowhere, ripping into the forward most ranks of shadowspawn with sizzling, white-hot fury. Darklings and Sniffers alike exploded into smoking chunks of ruined flesh or were burned to ash in an instant. Those shielded from the initial strike by the bodies of those in front of them dove for cover or were knocked from their feet by the concussive blast.

A second burst of Fire and lightning followed almost immediately, and the release of Power triggered the crux points Jase had put into place. Threads of *El'shaen* spiraled down the walls of the pass on both sides of the enemy soldiers, opening a number of small Veilgates to several locations beyond. In turn, additional crux points beyond the shimmering squares detonated, and *Sei'shiin* streaked through like fiery arrows, erasing from existence every creature they struck.

*Better than putting archers in harm's way, isn't it?* Jase said, sounding so pleased with the result that Idoman thought he might burst into laughter.

The streamers of *Sei'shiin* cut off as suddenly as they'd appeared, and the row of Veilgates slid shut, plunging the bottom of the pass into darkness once more.

Stunned by the strangeness and ferocity of the attack, those who'd survived it stood rooted in place, seemingly unwilling to continue their march. A small number of Darklings even turned and began making their way down the canyon to escape.

Light the color of blood illuminated the area as streamers of Fire erupted from K'rrosha scepters. The sizzling bursts incinerated a number of those who were fleeing and turned the rest about, urging them onward once more.

*One could almost pity the Darklings,* Jase said. *They will either die at the hands of their masters for refusing to march or they will die later in one of our traps.*

*It's definitely going to be a long night for them,* Gideon said. *But it's a chance for us to rest. I suggest we take it.*

Jase turned and looked at him. *Why do I get the feeling that was directed toward me?*

*Because it was,* Gideon told him, then his Awareness withdrew from the Communal link.

Jase exchanged looks with Idoman, then shrugged and reined in his Awareness as well.

"If all goes as planned with our traps," he said to General Eries, "the enemy won't reach the summit until after sunrise. In the meantime, have your men get some rest. I'll be back in a few hours."

Taking Talia by the hand, he embraced the Power and opened a Veilgate into Temifair Palace. Gideon and Seth followed them through, and the gate slid silently shut.

"The other Dymas and I will take turns keeping watch," Idoman said, and

Joneam nodded.

"One hour shifts," he said. "You need your rest more than we do."

"Yes, General," Idoman said. He watched Joneam and the others move away into the darkness of the makeshift camp, then extended his Awareness back down the pass to watch the enemy. They were nearing the next set of crux points, and he was eager to see what other tricks Jase Fairimor may have learned from the Earthsoul. It promised to be spectacular.

He glanced up at the silvery crescent shining brightly in the night sky, and his thoughts turned to Lord Nid.

"This is for you, my friend," he whispered, then flinched as the crux points were triggered and lightning ripped into the forward ranks of Death's Third March.

# CHAPTER 57

## Mendel Pass

THE SUN HAD YET TO RISE on Idoman Leda's small army, and the chill of the summit was noticeable as he stood on the edge of camp and gazed down the pass. In the growing light of the awakening day, the narrow passage and the steep slopes lining it were varying shades of grey against the pale blue of the sky above.

He'd been there but a few moments, when a Veilgate opened on his left and Jase Fairimor strode through from a tiled floor beyond. Gideon and Seth and Elliott followed close behind, but Talia remained in Temifair Palace with the High Queen and watched the shimmering hole in the air close in front of her. She'd worn a smile, but the worry in her eyes had been unmistakable. It made Idoman wonder if she'd chosen to stay behind or had been pressured by Jase.

No, he decided. Jase had made it clear to all—well, clear to Seth, anyway—that Talia could do as she wished. If she'd stayed in Andlexces it was because she felt she had something more important to do.

Idoman moved forward to greet the new arrivals. "How is Lord Nid?" he asked, bracing himself for what could be very bad news.

"Alive," Jase answered. "But it was touch and go for most of the night." He let his eyes move over the men and women of Idoman's small army. "How did things go here last night?"

"Quiet here at the summit," Idoman said. "Less so down in the pass. That new wielding of yours has the enemy spooked. They stalled three miles downslope from here when the Darklings decided they'd rather take their chances with the K'rrosha than with whatever we might unleash on them next."

"Good," Jase said. "That means Agla'Con will be brought in to use Thought Intrusion to coerce them into marching again. We'll target them as soon as they expose themselves by using the Power. In the meantime, I'd like to speak with your men."

"Of course, *Mith'elre Chon*," Idoman said, then instructed a nearby *Bero'thai* to raise the banner for assembly.

As the man hurried away, Jase turned and gazed down the pass. "We received word from Zeka," he said. "Last night a strong earthquake collapsed a thirty-mile wide section of the sea cliffs west of Thion. The resulting tidal wave destroyed what was left of Zeka's already embattled western coastline. Every town and village within two miles of the ocean was essentially scoured from existence. The wave was so large that it will likely reach the Jyndar Continent sometime later today."

Idoman felt sick inside. "Casualties?" he asked.

"Fewer than expected considering the size of the wave," Jase answered. "Most of those who survived the waves of the first collapse had moved inland to higher ground."

"Well, there's some good news, at least," Idoman said.

Jase nodded. "For now. The days ahead will prove difficult for them—their homes are gone."

The way he said it told Idoman what was really going on here. "And you think it is your fault."

"How could it not be?" Jase asked. "The longer the Rejuvenation is delayed, the more cataclysms can be laid at my feet. I'm supposed to heal the world, remember? Not watch it crumble around me."

"But crumble it will," Gideon said. "As was prophesied. It might sound strange, but even the cataclysms are proof the battle can be won, if for no other reason than these events were foreseen by the ancient prophets. "'*The voice of earthquakes and of tempests*,' they called them, and they were spot on in their predictions." He smiled. "And since they were right about that, it follows that they were also right about the Rejuvenation. It will happen, Jase. I know it."

"Not soon enough for my liking," Jase said. "And in the meantime..." he shook his head, "thousands—maybe even tens of thousands—of people will die for lack of a viable Orb. I don't know how much more of these '*voices*' I can take. Prophesied or not."

"Did something else happen last night?" Idoman asked, then flinched beneath the scowl Gideon directed his way.

Jase laughed bitterly, oblivious to the scowl. "What didn't happen? A series of earthquakes rocked the Great Wall, collapsing two towers and opening a breach a small army could march through. Fortunately, the breach is on the far eastern end of the wall, away from where the most recent battles with demons have been fought.

"In Chunin a lightning storm north and east of Bethel started hundreds of fires, and now most of the Northern Forest is burning. Further to the west the residents of Jasher are dealing with five feet of snow and ice from a hellish storm that swept in from the ocean. It will melt quickly enough, but there will undoubtedly be severe flooding."

He closed his eyes and took a deep breath, then opened them again before continuing. "There is a new mountain in the middle of Cresdraline Forest. A volcano erupted there overnight, swallowing the villages of Iathel and Hamin and setting the surrounding forest on fire. Two more eruptions in Amnidia formed mountains where the ruined cities of Elamais and Nahum once stood."

He turned and looked at Idoman. "And similar things are happening all across the world on both continents. Not only are the events becoming increasingly more violent and destructive, they are happening with ever-increasing frequency."

"All part of the prophecies," Gideon said. "The voice of the Earthsoul that time is running out."

"If She can speak so loudly concerning Her death," Jase asked, "why not just tell us where to find a viable Orb? She's spoken directly to both you and me on numerous occasions, and about things far less significant. Why remain silent about the one thing can bring an end to Her suffering?"

"I've wondered that many times myself," Gideon told him. "And I have no answer. We can only assume that perhaps She is bound by some law we couldn't possibly understand. Something tied to the laws of opposition we've spoken about. It makes sense that if She were able to reveal the location of a Blood Orb, Maeon would be able to do the same for his servants. The competition between good and evil would be nullified, and the world would descend into chaos."

Jase grunted darkly. "I'm pretty sure we've already descended," he said. "But I think I see what you mean. This fight will be won or lost by those entrusted to fight it in behalf of their respective deity."

Gideon patted Jase on the shoulder. "I couldn't have said it better myself."

A moment later the *Bero'thai* Idoman had sent to gather the men hurried up to them. "Our people are assembled, Lord Fairimor."

"Excellent," Jase said, and just like that all the worry and doubt and guilt Idoman had witnessed on his friend's face vanished. He was the *Mith'elre Chon* once more, calm, composed, and confident. None of those he was about to address would know—nor did they need to know—that the man they saw as their savior had looked as if he were about to give up.

"Men and women of the united armies," Jase said, urging his voice to the far reaches of the assembly, "Thank you for your efforts in Kelsa's behalf. This group may be small, but the traps you've laid and the skirmishes you've fought have delayed and will continue to delay our enemies, buying us the time we need to fortify Trian against Shadan's arrival.

"That is our mission, and it has not changed. Today we will continue the fight. Today we will deliver a blow to Death's Third March that will have Shadan wishing he'd stayed in Con'Jithar."

A cheer erupted from the assembly, echoing along the walls of the pass like a crack of thunder. Smiling, Jase waited until it subsided.

"As I said before," Jase continued, "you may be small in number, but you are formidable. As our enemies are about to learn."

He paused to let another round of cheering run its course, then added, "And yet it would be foolish to think we can hold the summit indefinitely. We cannot. We will hit them and then we will fall back, leading them into more of what our Dymas have left for them to find.

"Make no mistake, my friends. It will be dangerous, and it will be bloody. But if you stick to the plan as outlined by Dymas General Leda, we will leave a trail of carnage to sicken even the most vile shadowspawn. For the Flame of Kelsa, the liberty of all our peoples, and for the Earthsoul, it will be done."

This time the cheering reverberated up the canyon walls with such energy that pebbles and dirt were dislodged from their perches and cascaded down the rocky slopes in a clattering of stone and dust. Jase brought his fist to his chest in salute.

"Dismissed," he said, then released the Power as he turned back to Idoman and others.

Gideon wore a broad smile as he nodded his approval. "That was a great speech," he said. "Who writes them for you?"

"Completely off the cuff," Jase answered. "Like everything else I've done the past few days."

Gideon grunted. "But you do have a plan for today, right?"

Jase nodded. "I got the idea from Endil."

His eyes moved back to the men and women of the united armies, and Idoman followed his gaze. They were busy packing up the few things a mobile camp needed, which wasn't much considering how quickly they would need to move once the fighting resumed. Bedding and foodstuffs were placed in wagons to be sent ahead of the army through Veilgates. Horses were saddled. Weapons were strapped into place.

"Once this starts," Jase said, his eyes still on those breaking camp, "they are going to catch the brunt of Aethon's or Shadan's retaliation."

He turned to look Idoman in the eyes. "My guess is Veilgates will be used to send troops through to disrupt my attack. I know you have wards in place and Dymas stationed about to intercept any arrivals, but you won't be able to stop them all. Hold as long as you can, then hightail it down to the next rendezvous point. Maybe once the enemy realizes they can't stop me from here, they will break off the attack and come looking for me."

Idoman frowned, confusion mingling with fear that Jase would not be here. "Where will you be?"

Jase smiled. "Somewhere Shadan will never expect."

"I hope he knows what he's doing," Elliott said as the Veilgate Jase had opened into Arkania slid closed. Gideon had gone with him, but Elliott couldn't decide if it would help or simply make things worse. Neither one of them knew when to quit, but Gideon was definitely the more pig-headed of the two.

"They'll be fine," Seth said. "I'm more worried about what might happen here.

You saw the look in Jase's eyes. Whatever he has planned is going to enrage Shadan. So much so that he may decide to take a hand in the battle."

"Shadan's a coward," Idoman said. "He won't risk himself in a battle he knows he's already won."

"Maybe not," Seth said. "But he has more than enough Agla'Con and *Jeth'Jalda* to overwhelm us. Jase is right. Veilgates will be used to counterattack, and they'll come at us en masse."

"Let them," Elliott said. "Jase isn't the only one who has been working behind the scenes." He grinned at them, pleased with their reactions.

Seth's eyes narrowed. "What are you talking about?"

"You didn't think I've been going to Chellum just to spend time with Tana, did you?" he asked. "I mean, that has certainly been nice, but it wasn't the only reason I've been spending time there. I've rallied a few more friends to come help. They are skilled and rested and spoiling for a fight."

He looked at Idoman. "But since my Gift is limited to Light, I need you to open the Veilgate to bring them here."

"With pleasure," Idoman said. "Where are they?"

"The Chellum Gardens," he said. "Open the gate along the edge of the moat."

Idoman nodded, and the air parted to reveal the green and white granite of the garden's paved walkway and the neatly trimmed rose bushes lining it. And there, standing three abreast were thirty members of *tres'dia*.

They started through as soon as the gate was open, moving from the clean, smooth surface of the granite to the dusty hard-packed dirt of Mendel Pass. Most wore the *kitara*-style jackets popular among the Gifted, but five wore the leather and metal armor of Sarui, while only two wore *komouri* black. Those two came through last and moved up to Elliott.

"Lord Chellum," Raimen said with a smile.

"Hello, Raimen," he said. "Hello, Tohquin." He nodded to each in turn, then looked back to Idoman. "They are yours to command, Dymas General," he said, then flinched as an explosion rocked Mendel Pass some miles below.

"And not a moment too soon," Seth added. "Our enemies are on the move." He stepped near and took Elliott by the arm as Idoman began issuing orders to the newly arrived members of *tres'dia*. His grip was like steel and his face was hard. "Tell me you didn't leave Chellum completely defenseless," he said.

"Relax," he said, pulling his arm free. "I checked with Railen first. Gizo and Kyoai are so busy warding Riak's southern border that they don't have time to worry about settling their score with me. The biggest danger in Chellum right now is the risk of dying from boredom. Besides, we'll send them back to Chellum as soon as the battle here is over."

Another explosion rocked the pass below and was followed by flashes of lightning and ear-splitting cracks of thunder. Plumes of black smoke billowed skyward in several locations.

"K'rrosha have taken the lead and are sacrificing themselves to trigger the traps," Idoman announced. His eyes, narrowed in the way that showed he was watching through his Awareness, were fixed on the rising smoke. He frowned worriedly. "That's something I never would have expected from those black-hearted curs."

"The dead feel no pain," Seth said, shaking his head in disgust. "Actually I'm surprised Shadan didn't think of this sooner. Why sacrifice thousands of Darklings when a few dozen K'rrosha can accomplish the same task?"

"Right," General Eries said, "and K'rrosha can be refleshed so long as it wasn't *Sei'shiin* that destroyed them."

Another series of explosions erupted and were followed by more columns of greasy smoke.

"They're moving more quickly now," Idoman said, coming back to himself as he reined in his Awareness. "At this rate, they'll be here within the hour."

Standing next to Jase on the banks of Illiarensei, Gideon watched the dark waters of the monstrous river flow past in an ever-changing pattern of swirls and swells and spinning currents. The opposite bank, some twenty miles to the east, was but a thin strip of green against the blue of the horizon.

A large biting insect buzzed near his face, and he killed it with a narrow thrust of Air. "I really hate this country," he said, and Jase chuckled.

"So do I," he said. "But it has what I need and is far enough away from the point of attack that it will take Shadan some time to locate us." He didn't look over as he spoke but kept his eyes fastened on the small shimmering ball of Earthpower cupped in his hand.

It was linked to a crux point back in Mendel Pass, though how Jase had managed to connect them over such a distance was mind boggling. Proof positive once again that his son was the *Mith'elre Chon*. No one else could have wrought such a neat trick, himself included.

"And you are sure there aren't any villages nearby?" he asked. "The last thing we need is an army of enraged priests coming to investigate your use of the Power."

"No, I'm not sure," Jase replied. "That's why I brought you along."

"Great," he muttered, then opened his Awareness even further and did a sweep of the area behind them. When he found nothing but birds and animals and insects, he relaxed somewhat, but he was still nervous about what kind of attention Jase's actions might draw. If he had more time, he could set wards to warn them should any Power-sensitive creatures—human or otherwise—approach. There was simply no telling what might be near enough to sense Jase's wieldings.

He looked again at the dark waters of Illiarensei and braced himself for what was to come. It was likely to be soon. He was right, and only a few minutes passed before the glowing sphere of Power in Jase's hand suddenly gave a loud *pop* then vanished.

Jase smiled. "Let's see if those vermin can swim," he said, then channeled a massive amount of *El'shaen* and opened a Veilgate deep inside the river.

Seth watched the Shadowlancers come into view around the curvature and slope of the pass, and his hands moved instinctively to his swords. Two short *kamui* blades wouldn't be of any use against mounted K'rrosha, of course. But where there were K'rrosha there were likely to be Shadowhounds and Darklings.

Beside him, Elliott drew his sword as well and leveled it at the enemy. The Power-wrought blade was more of a talisman to the young man now than a weapon, something physical to help him channel his Gift. And that Gift had a far more powerful effect on the enemy than any blade ever could.

"Wait for Jase," Seth said. "We don't want to interfere with whatever he has planned."

Elliott frowned. "It would be nice to know what that is."

Seth agreed, but didn't say so out loud. He simply watched the K'rrosha continue up the pass. Some fifty or sixty moved at the head of thousands of Darklings and other types of shadowspawn, and the *clop-clop* of horse hooves and the tread of feet echoed up the pass. Hellhounds moved on the flanks, some walking on the faces of the canyon's nearly vertical walls.

A short time later, Idoman moved up to stand next to Elliott, seemingly appearing out of nowhere—a result, Seth realized, of the Power-wrought cloak he wore.

"Any moment now," the young Dymas General whispered. He wore his excitement like a mask as he watched the approaching nightmare.

"I bloody well hope so," Elliott muttered. "Much further and we'll be in range of their lances."

"There," Idoman said. "They just tripped Jase's ward. A thread of Spirit just zipped away to the south."

*To Arkania*, Seth thought, still not completely sure if going there had been a good idea.

"It better hurry," Elliott said. "We're in range."

The nearest Shadowlancers thought so as well, as evidenced by the raising of their lances. Tips flared brightly as they prepared to strike.

A massive Veilgate opened in front of them, and the thunderous roar of rushing water filled the pass, drowning out all other sounds as the wall of dark water spewing from the Veilgate swallowed everything in its path.

Seth couldn't see much because of how the fogged nature of the back of the Veilgate blocked his view, but steam filled the air along the gate's fiery edges, and the ground trembled beneath the roaring weight of the flood.

"Genius," Idoman said, laughing aloud. "Here, look." He pointed to a spot in front of Seth, and a small window opened in the air in front of him, providing a bird's-eye view of the pass from above Jase's gate.

The K'rrosha were gone, swept away by a force more powerful than any they'd ever faced and from which there was no escape. They would survive, of course, since they couldn't drown, but their mounts would certainly perish. So would the Darklings and other shadowspawn. Those that didn't drown would be crushed against the terrain or against each other.

The wall of water roared down the roadway in an avalanche of frothy mud and debris, sweeping away everything in its path. A few Darklings managed to scramble to safety on the slopes lining the roadway, but they lost their weapons in the process. Injured, wet, and defenseless, they watched helplessly as the torrent raged below them, sweeping away their terrified comrades and leaving them stranded.

In a matter of seconds, Mendel Pass was transformed into a river as violent and powerful as the Shiblane, an unstoppable spear-thrust of water that killed hundreds, then thousands of the enemy. At this rate, Seth realized, a rush of hope filling him, all of Death's Third March would be consumed. Jase had delivered the blow he'd promised.

But it didn't go unchallenged for long, and a series of angry hisses filled the area behind Jase's Veilgate as thirty or so Agla'Con rushed through rents in the Veil. Some cast up shields to ward the area while others attacked the edges of Jase's gate with stabs of corrupted Spirit in an attempt to collapse it.

"That won't work," Idoman said, then raised his fist in the air to signal his men.

Lightning crackled into the midst of the Agla'Con as Kelsa's Dymas attacked, but most of the sizzling bolts were deflected harmlessly away by those holding shields. One or two found their mark and black-robed figures blew apart in sprays of smouldering, super-heated flesh.

More rents hissed open in the midst of Kelsa's forces, and Jeth'Jalda and K'rrosha charged through from beyond. Chaos erupted all across the summit as Power-wrought weapons were brought to bear by both sides. Seth flinched as a number of lightning bolts and several jets of Fire struck Idoman's shield, but he couldn't pull his eyes off the scene below Jase's Veilgate.

A half-mile long now, the churning flow continued to rip through the ranks of enemy soldiers, a merciless river of destruction that swallowed everything in its path. The bodies of the dead and the flailing shapes of the dying covered the frothy surface like the flotsam and jetsam of some massive shipwreck.

Then a fiery-edged rent opened in front of the flood, slicing a number of fleeing Darklings in two as it stretched from one side of the pass to the other. The rushing waters flowed through to the grasslands beyond where they lessened in strength as they spread outward, depositing the dead in tangled, muddy heaps—sparing those lower in the pass.

"Shadan," Idoman said. "That's his doing."

"Well, it worked," Elliott muttered angrily. "Can you and the other Dymas collapse it?"

"Not without going to the source," Idoman said. "You don't want to go with me, do you?"

"To face Shadan?" Elliott hissed. "I most certainly do not."

"Then we've reached an impasse. A stalemate between Jase and Shadan, to see who can hold their gate open the longest."

A cold pit settled in Seth's stomach. "Shadan won't risk it," he said. "He'll send someone to find Jase. An army most likely."

"Is that even possible?" Elliott asked. "We don't even know where he is. Not exactly, anyway."

"I guess we'll find out," Idoman said, turning toward the chaos still erupting across the summit. "Come, we have a number of Agla'Con to kill. I'll keep us shielded while we do."

Aethon reined in his Awareness, anger warring with a newfound sense of awe for what Jase Fairimor had just done. Not only was the complexity of the thread of Spirit he'd set in place to warn him impressive, the fact that it had stretched across half a continent was mind-boggling. It shouldn't have even been possible. Especially for one so young.

Tracing the thread to Arkania hadn't been easy, and there was always the possibility that it was a ruse meant to lure him into a trap, but he wasn't going to just stand by and let Jase Fairimor do as he wished with the waters of Illiarensei. He would stop him.

He turned to Shadan and found the Dreadlord's good eye burning with newfound fury as he maintained his hold on the rent he'd opened in Mendel Pass. Several hundred yards to the south of where they stood, the fiery-edged hole continued to vomit the lifeless bodies of thousands of Darklings and other shadowspawn across the grasses of the Bottomlands.

Shadan's quick thinking had likely saved Death's Third March from complete annihilation since their entire force was bottled up in the pass. Jase Fairimor, burn his bloody, clever hide, had known what he was about with this attack. And it wouldn't go unpunished.

"I'm going to Arkania," he told Shadan. "You'll know when I find them."

"Find them quickly," Shadan hissed. "A gate this size—I can't hold it forever."

"You saved our cause," Aethon told him. "My compliments on your quick thinking."

Shadan turned to look at him. "That must have been painful to say."

Aethon grunted. "You have no idea." With that, he motioned for a nearby squad of *Jeth'Jalda* to follow, then opened himself to the power of the Void and tore a rent into the Arkanian jungle.

廴

"Now, how did you do that?" Gideon asked, so impressed with what he'd just witnessed that he almost couldn't form the words. Crux points designed to hold a Veilgate open... it was... it was beyond anything he'd ever imagined.

"With Spirit, obviously," Jase answered, then smiled sheepishly and added, "But the method just sort of came to me in the moment."

Gideon shook his head. "And here I was feeling guilty about not being around to train you. Truth is, you've taught me more tricks the past few weeks than I would have thought possible."

"One of the advantages of being the *Mith'elre Chon*, I suppose," Jase said. "Too bad it comes with all the other... unpleasantries."

"Speaking of unpleasantries," he said. "I felt the brush of a distant Awareness a few moments ago. Only Aethon or Shadan could have traced your thread of Spirit over such a distance."

"I felt it too," Jase told him. "No doubt one or both will be here soon to try to close the gate from this side."

"Your recommendation?"

Jase laughed. "We leave," he said. "I have no desire to go toe to toe with an army of Agla'Con. Why do you think I used crux points to hold the gate open?"

He nodded, grateful for Jase's wisdom in avoiding what would be a very lopsided confrontation. "To Mendel Pass, then?"

"To Mendel Pass," he agreed. "But first I have a little surprise I want to leave for whoever shows up."

廴

Eager to strike Jase Fairimor down with a barrage of Night Threads, Aethon charged through the rent with *Lo'shaen* at the ready. His Awareness resonated with a powerful wielding of *El'shaen*, and he stretched his mind toward it just in time to see a Veilgate close behind Gideon and Jase.

"Blood of Maeon," he cursed, then released *Lo'shaen* and watched the squad of *Jeth'Jalda* he'd brought with him fan out through the jungle.

"Hold your positions," he ordered. "We're too late."

"But the Veilgate," one of the *Jeth'Jalda* said. "Someone holds it open still."

"Not someone," Aethon said, fighting the urge to swear again. "Crux points."

"But... that isn't possible."

Aethon ground his teeth, envy and frustration washing through him in turns. "Apparently, it is."

He started cautiously toward the resonance of Power. "Be careful," he warned. "There is no telling what else they left behind for us to find."

Opening his Awareness once more, he swept every inch of the area where Jase and Gideon had been, then expanded it outward by degrees, searching for any crux points beyond those holding open the Veilgate. When he was satisfied that there were none, he motioned everyone forward.

At the bank of Illiarensei, he took a moment to examine the crux points wrought by Jase. Four in all, they were linked to the four corners of the Veilgate suspended deep in the river's dark waters. Collapsing one should be enough to close the gate.

"Bring it down," he ordered, watching through his mind's eye as one of the more skilled *Jeth'Jalda* stabbed the nearest crux point with a needle-like thrust of corrupted Spirit.

As the Veilgate collapsed, the spiritual fabric of *Ta'shaen* jarred violently with a sudden release of Power.

Too late, Aethon realized the release was the springing of a trap, and a literal storm of *Sei'shiin* erupted across the area. He could only stand in stupefied anger as everything was swallowed up in blinding flashes of white.

Elliott sent a vicious stab of lightning into the midst of the enemy Agla'Con and watched with a smile as a number of them somersaulted through the air, their bodies broken, their cloaks trailing wisps of smoke.

"Nice," Idoman shouted. "We've got them on the run."

"On the run?" Elliott yelled back, channeling another bolt that obliterated two *Jeth'Jalda* and rocked the summit from one end to the other. "There's nowhere for them to run. We're in a bloody pass. They're trapped."

Idoman frowned at him. "It's a figure of speech." Raising his hands, he sent white-hot threads of *Sei'shiin* streaking into an Agla'Con shield. They exploded with a blinding flash, tearing a hole in the wall of corrupted Spirit that left the Agla'Con inside exposed. Elliott killed him with a stab of lightning that left an afterimage of the man momentarily suspended in everyone's vision.

All across the summit the scene was the same. Agla'Con and *Jeth'Jalda* were falling like flies. Shadan's attempt to disrupt Jase's Veilgate had failed miserably and had served no purpose but to get a good number of his Power-wielders killed. And the members of *tres'dia* were only too happy to kill them. And being rested from a long and boring stay in Chellum, they were more than a match for the cronies of Death's Third March.

A Veilgate opened a short distance away, and Jase and Gideon stepped through. Gideon took one look at a cluster of *Jeth'Jalda* banding together to make their final stand, and *Sei'shiin* shot from his fingertips in sizzling bursts as thick as any bolt of lightning Elliott had ever wielded. The *Jeth'Jalda* vanished in flashes of white.

After a few more explosive bursts elsewhere on the battlefield, the area grew quiet save for the roaring of the waters spewing from Jase's Veilgate. Only then, did Elliott realize the oddity. He looked from Jase to the Veilgate then back to Jase.

"How is that still open?"

"Crux points," Jase answered. "But not for much longer. Aethon arrived just as we were leaving."

Idoman stepped near, his face curious and eager. "Just when I think you couldn't possibly outdo yourself," he said. "You need to show me how you did that."

"You have my word," Jase said, then let his eyes move across the area. "I see we have reinforcements," he added, nodding to Raimen and Tohquin and the rest of those who'd come from Chellum.

"They are here at my request," Elliott told him. "I thought we could use the extra help." He glanced at Seth, expecting a harsh comment about leaving Chellum unprotected, but the captain remained silent.

Idoman turned the conversation back to the Veilgate. "How much longer can we expect that to stay open?"

"Depends on how long it takes Aethon to find the crux points," Jase answered. His smile and the tone of satisfaction in his voice was unmistakable. "I suspect we'll know shortly."

Idoman's eagerness intensified. "You booby trapped it, didn't you?"

Before Jase could answer, the Veilgate snapped shut in a hiss of steam and the torrent of water cut off. Without the immense force to drive it forward, the back edge of the waters flowed up the roadway for a brief spell, then stopped and started down the canyon once more, following the path of least resistance. The roaring sound of the river-like flow receded with it.

Elliott looked at the mud-slicked roadway left behind by the flood. "That will be fun for the enemy to slog through."

"Do you think your trap killed Aethon?" Idoman asked.

"He'd need the luck of Maeon himself to survive that," Gideon commented, shooting a proud, father-like grin at Jase.

Jase smiled at the implied compliment, then gestured at the summit. "Let's tend to the wounded," he said. "And then we can plan our next move."

⺼

Shadan waited until the flood pouring through his Veilgate had subsided to a trickle before he released *Lo'shaen* and let the gate snap shut. The muddy expanse it had left behind stretched for almost a mile, a waist-deep mess of mangled corpses and debris that could have doubled for the landscape of Con'Jithar. Here and there, the wriggling of arms and legs was visible as survivors, most of them K'rrosha, fought their way free of the muck.

He glanced up at Mendel Pass, his heart burning with rage toward Jase Fairimor. Aethon bloody well better have found him and killed him. If not—

A rent hissed open to his left and he turned as Aethon strode through. He was alone.

"Where are the others?"

"Dead," Aethon answered, his voice so tight with anger Shadan worried he might lash out with the Power the way his idiot brother Dathan used to. He turned and stared up at the pass. "It's time to utilize all our resources," he continued. "The boy has grown too dangerous for us to stop on our own."

"So he still lives?" Shadan asked. He should have known Aethon would fail in killing the boy. It was a recurring theme for the fool.

Aethon turned a hard stare on him, one so filled with malice that, for a moment, Shadan worried Aethon may have sensed his thoughts. He opened his Awareness and prepared to seize the Power to defend himself.

"Not for much longer," Aethon growled. Turning, he tore open a rent and strode through without another word.

# CHAPTER 58

## The Holy Mountain

"ARE YOU SURE WE SHOULD be in here?" Shaelie asked, and Felicia smiled inwardly at her friend's nervousness. Apparently, she thought the round-about way they'd entered the Dremick Building was the equivalent of sneaking. It was, sort of. Just not in the way Shaelie thought.

The convoluted path they'd taken had been necessary to elude Trake. For some reason, the pretentious idiot seemed determined to attach himself to her research efforts in spite of multiple warnings that she neither wanted nor needed his help. She didn't know if Trake was jealous of her interactions with Brysia Fairimor or if he was simply trying to score points with Professor Neaman, and she didn't really care. He creeped her out and she had no desire to spend any kind of time with him. And she certainly didn't need him ruining her one true place of refuge in the Dremick Building.

"I have permission to be here from Brysia Fairimor herself," she replied. "She knows I like to come here to study, and she said she would keep it a secret."

"Because you found a prophecy she found interesting?"

"I guess so," Felicia answered. "I didn't really ask."

"So what are we here for today?" Shaelie sighed, trying to sound put upon. "Actual study time for our upcoming finals, or are we going to waste another day reading through cryptical, prophetic nonsense?"

"It's not nonsense," Felicia told her. "It could literally save the world from dying."

"So you've said," Shaelie mumbled. "A thousand times."

They continued down the long empty hallway in silence, passing the long-vacated offices of the Power-wielding scholars and professors lost during the Battle of Greendom. When they passed the office she'd claimed as her own private study, Shaelie frowned at her.

"So, we are skipping our studies. Again."

"You can study," Felicia told her. "I want to see what's in there." She pointed to a set of double doors near the end of the hallway. They'd been locked up until yesterday when the sweet, but obviously distracted, Lady Korishal had sliced the lock off with a blade of Fire so she and Lady Hadershi could inspect the room's contents. They hadn't found anything useful, but she was willing to bet they hadn't looked through everything yet either.

Once inside, Shaelie plopped down on a crate and pulled a stack of notes from one of her leather folders. Felicia watched her for a moment, then let her eyes move over the room. Obviously, it hadn't been used in decades, and a thick layer of dust covered most everything. And there seemed to be a little bit of everything—statues cast in bronze, pottery, rolls of parchment stacked in square, cubby-like shelves, paintings, and, of course, numerous books on shelves of varying heights. Three of the book shelves were free of dust, having likely been swept clean with the Power by Marithen or Beraline in their search yesterday.

"It's just a junk room," Shaelie muttered, and Felicia looked over to find her friend wrinkling her nose at all the dust.

Ignoring Shaelie's disgust, she moved to the wrought-iron book shelf at the far wall and pulled one of the books free of its resting place. The amount of dust on the top of its pages showed it hadn't been disturbed.

She blew the dust clear, then took a seat on another crate and began thumbing through the pages. It didn't take long to realize it contained nothing of importance, and she returned it to its spot on the shelf.

And so it went for the next hour. Book after book, page after page, passage after passage... of nothing.

She tried not to let her impatience get to her, but she shoved the most recent book to the back of the shelf a little more firmly than she'd intended. Instead of the sharp sound of the book striking the wall, however, she heard a soft, hollow-sounding thump.

Curious, she pulled the book free and reached through the slot to the back of the shelf, where she felt some kind of cloth. It was thin and smooth, but her fingers found what might be a tear. Yes, she decided, she could feel the edges distinctly.

She slid her fingers through the hole and found the smooth, slightly textured surface of what could only be a painting. And canvas, too, considering how it gave slightly when she pushed on it. She frowned. But who would hang a painting only to cover it with a book shelf? Did those who'd stored all these artifacts value this painting so little that they'd cover it with a shelf of books? Or had it just been an oversight because the painting was covered? Whatever the reason, she wanted a look at the painting.

Pulling several more books out of the way, she peered through the gap. A patch of red paint was visible through the tear in the grey cloth she'd felt. It *was* a painting. And she'd been right that it was on canvas.

"Come help me with this," she said, and Shaelie gave a dramatic sigh as she stood.

"Help you with what?"

"There's a painting behind this book shelf," she said. "I want to see it."

"Of course you do," Shaelie said as she pulled books from the shelf and began stacking them on a nearby desk. "But why stop there? Let's look in the closet as well."

"Painting first," Felicia said, ignoring her friend's sarcasm.

They had the shelf emptied in minutes, but the shelves prevented them from removing the covering, so she and Shaelie worked together to slide one end out away from the wall.

"Would you like to do the honors," she asked, but Shaelie shook her head.

"This is your project."

Carefully, her heart racing with excitement, Felicia reached up and undid the covering. It slid away, and she found herself staring at an exquisite-looking painting of a tall, snow-capped mountain. She took a step back, and her eyes fell on the splash of red at the mountain's base.

Her eyes went wide as she recognized it for what it was.

"I need you to go fetch High Queen Fairimor," she said. "Hurry, Shae. I think we just found what we've been looking for."

Trake Noevom spotted Shaelie exiting the Dremick Building and watched her hurry across the courtyard toward the library. She wasn't looking his way, but he stepped behind the trunk of a large tree just to be safe. When she had passed out of sight behind one of the courtyard's neatly trimmed hedgerows, he moved back out into the open and looked at the Dremick Building.

So, that was where Felicia had been running off to these past few days. It was probably where she'd found the book of prophecy the Kelsan Queen found so interesting. No wonder she'd been evasive in her answers when he'd inquired about it—she had no business in the Dremick Building. None of the students did.

He glanced again in the direction Shaelie had taken to make sure she wasn't doubling back, then started for the doors she'd exited. There was a good chance Felicia was still inside, and if so, he wanted to know what all the excitement was about. That, and he didn't like the way she'd been brushing him off lately. He was even more irritated with how easily she'd evaded him earlier, leaving him to wander the campus grounds like some lost dog, and he had several choice words for her regarding her snobbery.

He'd never admit to following her, of course, but it rankled just the same. Another thing he would never admit, to her or anyone else, was that he found her attractive and just wanted her to notice him. And he was determined to do whatever that might require.

With one last look over his shoulder, he moved up the steps of the Dremick Building and slipped inside.

Felicia stood before the painting with a tremendous feeling of triumph. After all the searching—after all the books and diaries, the maps and sketches and artifacts—after days and days of dead ends, here it was: The Holy Mountain of the Second Creation. Perfectly and simply captured in oil on canvas.

Her eyes moved to the artist's signature in the bottom corner of the painting, and her excitement increased. Temifair, it said, written in Elvan.

Temifair, she thought, so overcome with emotion that tears formed at the corners of her eyes. Temifair. The first Elvan Queen and mother of the Fairimor bloodline. How appropriate that she should give them the clue that would save the life of the Earthsoul.

She stared at the signature a moment longer then looked back at the T'rii Gate at the base of the mountain. And it wasn't just any T'rii Gate as evidenced by the fair-haired people exiting it—it was the gate Elderon had used to bring the Elvan people into this world. And that meant this was the mountain Robishar had seen in his vision. This was *the* Temple of Elderon. And in it the Blood Seed of the Rejuvenation. Lady Fairimor would weep with joy when she saw this.

"Is that what I think it is?" a familiar voice asked, and Felicia jumped at the sound of Trake's voice, balling her hands into fists to keep from letting out a squawk.

She forced herself to relax, then turned a frown on him as he moved up beside her. His grin showed he knew how badly he'd startled her.

"Sneaking up on people is rude," she told him, watching his smile fade.

"So is keeping secrets," he said flatly. "You haven't been finding prophecies in the library. You've been finding them here." He pointed at the painting. "So, answer my question. Is that what I think it is? The arrival of the Elvan people?"

His tone sent a rush of anger through her, but she nodded. "Yes."

Trake grunted. "Huh. So, the Blood Orb everyone has been looking for all these years has been right under our noses the entire time."

"It would seem so," she said, moving away from him slightly. Something in his tone put her on edge, and she was suddenly uncomfortable with the fact that the two of them were alone.

"Then I'm sorry," Trake said, moving so quickly that she didn't even have time to blink before his fist slammed hard into her face.

The blow sent a sudden flash of white lancing through her vision and she felt herself falling. A second flash followed as her head hit the floor, and she blinked against the lingering spots of light as Trake loomed over her. She put up her arms to ward him off, but he slapped them away, then his hands closed around her throat.

"I wish things could have been different," he said. "I really did find you attractive." He smiled as he added, "But my master will pay handsomely for this information."

Panicked, she flailed at him with her fists, but his grip tightened and her lungs began to burn for lack of air. In desperation she arched her back and flailed with her legs to try to throw him off, but her movements succeeded only in dislodging the medallion he'd been wearing beneath his shirt. The silver disk stopped just short of her face and swung violently back and forth as she struggled.

Tears leaked from her eyes as her vision dimmed, and she felt herself slipping toward unconsciousness. As darkness closed in around her, the swaying of Trake's medallion slowed, and the image of a black hand rotated into view.

Looking up into his eyes, she knew him for what he was.

"This is the room," Shaelie said, stopping in front of the storage room Beraline and Marithen had searched yesterday. She still sounded winded from hurrying, and Talia thought she seemed nervous about being in Brysia's presence. She had to hide her smile as she followed Shaelie and Brysia into the room.

"That's funny," Shaelie said as they entered, "Felicia must have tired of waiting for us. She probably went to look for you as well, hoping to speed things up."

"Then we will just have to thank her later," Brysia said. "Let's see the painting."

"It's there," Shaelie said, pointing, "on the wall behind the shelf."

Talia followed Brysia across the room, and a sudden rush of excitement swept through her as she moved around the end of the shelf and her eyes lighted on the painting.

A single, dagger-like mountain rose from a shimmering expanse of bluish-green waters. Its snow-capped peak, tinted with the red and gold hues of the rising sun, seemed to touch the sky. It was the most beautiful rendition of Mount Augg she'd ever seen. And there, nestled at the base, was a depiction of the Elvan arrival during the Second Creation.

Talia was stunned, momentarily at a loss for words. She could only stare at the painting in wonder, curious as to why... why out of the thousands upon thousands of books and maps and artifacts about the Second Creation, why this painting alone pointed to Mount Augg.

"The Holy Mountain," Brysia breathed, her tone reverent. Moving forward, she ran her fingers gently over the signature. "And painted by Temifair herself." She shook her head. "I simply can't fathom how we didn't find evidence of this sooner."

"Maybe we weren't supposed to," Talia whispered, then realized what she'd said, and shook herself free of the sudden string of thoughts the comment inspired. "I'll explain later. Right now, we need to get in touch with Jase and let him know what we found." She glanced at Shaelie. "What Felicia found."

"So," Shaelie said hesitantly, "this really is the clue you've all been looking for?"

Brysia nodded. "Yes," Brysia said, her eyes still on the painting. "Remember this moment, my dear young friend. For you were here when hope was restored to the world."

She turned and started for the door. "Come, we need to contact the *Mith'elre Chon*."

乇

Jase was helping a recently healed soldier to his feet when a Veilgate opened nearby. Brysia and Talia stood framed within, and he knew instantly that they finally had good news for him. Both women were literally trembling with excitement.

Gideon saw it as well and hurried forward. Jase joined him, and they moved through the gate to the courtyard fronting the Dremick Building. As soon as they were through, Beraline released the Power and let the Veilgate close behind them.

"You found something," Gideon said.

"Yes," Brysia said, but before she could elaborate, a Veilgate opened and Seth and Elliott hurried through. Elliott wore a frown.

"Thanks for waiting," he said, sounding truly offended. "If Idoman hadn't been nearby, we'd still be stuck in Mendel Pass wondering why you ran off on us."

"Not now, Elliott," Talia said, but the momentary irritation Jase felt through the *sei'vaiya* was lost in the literal waves of excitement washing through her.

"The clue we've been searching for," Brysia said, offering her arm to Gideon. "We've got the area cordoned off," she continued, "and Beraline set wards against eavesdropping, for viewing as well as for listening."

"It's that good, huh?" Elliott asked, and Talia nodded.

"The means to our salvation," she said, but beneath her excitement, Jase caught the first real traces of dread. She knew what finding a viable Blood Orb meant for him, and she was afraid to lose him.

*You won't lose me*, he thought, and knew from her smile that she'd heard it. He took her hand as they climbed the steps into the Dremick Building, and she squeezed his hand affectionately.

"I felt you travel very far to the south," she said. "Care to explain why you felt it necessary to go to Arkania again?"

"I needed water," he answered, then grinned at her when she furrowed her brow in question. "I'll explain later. Right now, this is more important."

As they neared the end of the hallway, the line of *Bero'thai* cordoning off the area parted to let them through. A few paces later, Jase felt the warding Beraline had put into place. Still holding Talia's hand, he entered the room.

As his eyes fell on the painting, *Ta'shaen* came alive with a powerful surge of Spirit, prickling the hair on his neck and arms and sending a rush of warmth through his chest. Prophecy, he knew, had just been fulfilled.

"I felt it, too," Talia whispered. "Through you."

"Felt what?" Elliott asked, peering over his sister's shoulder.

Without a word, Gideon walked to the painting and went to one knee to inspect the T'rii Gate. Then he reached out as if to touch the artist's signature but stopped short, seemingly uncertain. When he looked back, there were tears in his eyes.

"Temifair painted this?" he asked, and Brysia nodded.

"It would seem so," she answered. "And the style matches the other pieces we know were painted by her."

Gideon looked back at the painting. "She would have painted this more than two thousand years ago. How did it go undiscovered for so long?"

"Talia has a theory about that," Brysia said, turning to look at her.

"I do?"she asked, then stiffened as if remembering something and nodded. "I do." She approached the painting.

"What if we didn't find this until now because we weren't supposed to? What if, under the direction of the Earthsoul, it was hidden and preserved so our enemies wouldn't learn about it? What if Temifair or Imor foresaw this day and took action?"

She turned to look at them. "Consider all the books of prophecy," she continued, "both light and dark. Innumerable copies were printed so that everyone might have access to them. And look what happened to Mount Tabor as a result of Throy Shadan having access to those writings—he tried to destroy the Soul Chamber to prevent the Rejuvenation, and Tabor was left in ruin. If he believed—if he even suspected—that Mount Augg was the Holy Mountain of the Second Creation and that it contained the Blood Seed foreseen by Robishar, he would have attacked it as well."

Gideon looked at Brysia. "Who else knows of the painting?" he asked.

"Just Felicia and one of her friends," Brysia answered. She frowned. "Though we don't know where Felicia is at the moment. She left here to go look for me shortly after she found this but hasn't yet returned."

"And her friend?" Gideon asked.

"Out in the corridor with the *Bero'thai*. She's waiting for Felicia."

Gideon stood, his face thoughtful as he continued to study the painting. "Talia's theory rings true," he said. "But the Dremick Building was built less than five hundred years ago. How did this end up here, and where was it during the eighteen centuries prior?"

"We might never know," Jase said. "Let's just be grateful we have it now, and that it remained safely out of reach of our enemies."

Elliott moved forward to get a closer look at the painting, and Gideon moved aside to give him room. The prince's face was pinched with a frown. "I'm not trying to cast doubt on my sister's ideas," he said. "But are we sure this painting is authentic? It's in surprisingly good condition for something so ancient."

"It's authentic," Gideon told him. "I felt the stirrings of prophecy when I first arrived."

"I felt it, too," Jase said. "And I know one surefire way to confirm it." Turning to face the far wall, he embraced the Power and opened a Veilgate to the area depicted on the painting.

At least that was his intent, but something strange happened. The Veilgate opened, but the view beyond seemed to rotate back on itself, ending in a flash of white that collapsed the Veilgate as surely as if Jase had been severed from the Power.

Everyone stared at the spot in surprise. "Uh, what was that?" Elliott asked.

"A warding," Gideon answered, moving to stand next to Jase. "And one unlike any I've ever encountered." He embraced the Power, and Jase felt him weave the Seven Gifts together to open a Veilgate. The air parted before them, but with the same result. The view beyond rotated back on itself, and the hole in the air collapsed in a flash of white.

"There are stories," Brysia said softly. "Told by fishermen and sailors who call Mirror Lake home. I used to think they were just some kind of local mythology, but now I'm not so sure. They speak of Augg as being so tall it brushes against heaven. They say that the forest of thorns ringing the mountain's base was placed there by Elderon to keep people from defiling its slopes. The legend is that no living person has ever set foot on the mountain."

Elliott grunted. "Not since the Second Creation, anyway," he said, gesturing at the painting.

"Well," Gideon said, "the warding Jase and I just encountered is all the proof I need that the stories are true. Only Elderon could have fashioned such a ward."

"So, if we can't reach Augg by Veilgate..." Elliott began, looking meaningfully at Seth.

"We'll need to go by Myrscraw," Seth finished. "I'll speak with Emperor Dromensai. I'll need—" he cut off, and his hands moved to his swords.

"There," he whispered, starting forward, "in the closet."

Before he could reach it, the handle turned and the door opened. Felicia staggered out, and Seth caught her in his arms. The side of her face was bruised and her eye was swollen shut. She had dark bruises on her neck as well.

Talia rushed forward, embracing the Power as she went. She took Felicia's head in her hands, then, after a quick inspection of her injuries through her Awareness, sent a rush of healing washing through her.

Felicia's eyes went wide and she gasped. Pulling free of Seth, she moved to Brysia who took the young woman in her arms.

"Trake Noevom," she said, her words tumbling out in a rush, "the boy from my classes. He's a member of the Con'Kumen. He tried to kill me. He... he saw the painting. He knows what it means." Tears welled up in her eyes. "He means to report to his master."

As Brysia smoothed Felicia's hair, Jase moved to the doorway and called to the *Bero'thai* in the hallway. "Seal off the city," he said. "No one leaves. We are looking for a young man named Trake Noevom. No need to take him alive."

"Yes, *Mith'elre Chon*," the man said, hurrying away to raise the alarm.

Jase turned back to face Seth. "Contact Emperor Dromensai," he said. "Tell him the *Mith'elre Chon* has need of Myrscraw."

"You can leave from Trian," Gideon said. "You'll need the Blue Flame Scepter. It's the key to unlocking the mountain. And Endil should go, too. His is the only other hand that can touch the Blood Orb without defiling it."

Jase nodded. "Agreed." He looked at the T'rii Gate on the painting and added. "We should contact Ohran Peregam and tell him to recall the *Nar'shein* out searching for lost temples. They will be needed elsewhere now."

Elliott cleared his throat. "So, who else is going with you?" He tried to sound as if he didn't care one way or the other, but Jase wasn't fooled by the facade.

"If you've nothing better to do," Jase said, "I suppose you could tag along."

Elliott smiled, obviously relieved. "*El'kali* and *El'liott* together one last time, huh?"

"It won't be the last," he told him. "I plan on ending this once and for all." He turned his attention to Seth. "So, are you up for a third trip to Tabor?"

The captain grunted. "As if you even had to ask." Face unreadable, he looked at Talia. "Besides, she can't very well leave her warder behind."

Talia blinked at what he'd just implied, then a smile moved over her face as she reached over and took his hand. "No, I can't," she agreed.

Gideon looked at Felicia who was still crying softly into Brysia's shoulder. "I want you to take a number of our most powerful Dymas with you as well," he said. "Just in case Trake manages to elude capture. If our enemies learn the truth about Augg, they will come for you."

A sharp stab of panic lanced across the *sei'vaiya*, and the words *earth-shattering conflict* reached his mind as clearly as if Talia had shouted them.

He caught her eyes with his and smiled reassuringly. "A contingent of Dymas would be most welcome," he said.

"It would be wise to bring Shizu along also," Seth suggested. "If the inside of Augg is to be anything like what we experienced inside Tabor, your Awareness will be blind. You will need skilled sets of eyes."

"We'll take both," Jase told him. "Emperor Dromensai might feel better about letting us borrow Myrscraw if Shizu are flying them."

"I'll meet you at the Trian Temple," Seth said, then nodded for Gideon to open a Veilgate for him. He passed through into Sagaris Keep without another word.

Jase looked at his mother briefly, then locked eyes with his father. "We should be on our way, too," he said. "Our work here in Andlexces is finished. Trian needs the Guardian of the Blue Flame. It needs her Queen."

# CHAPTER 59

## Organized Chaos

GRIPPING HIS REINS TIGHTLY in frustration, Taggert Enue watched the steady stream of people moving along East Road toward the eastern rim of Trian Plateau. Mostly women and children and the elderly, they moved slowly—Croneam might almost say leisurely—away from Trian and her outlying townships. He doubted if very many of them had any real destination in mind, but he suspected some would take refuge in Yucanter Forest once they were off the plateau.

Shaking his head, he turned and looked at Trian nestled against the Kelsan Mountains six miles to the west. Nearly every township and estate and farm between Trian's outer wall and where he now stood had received the order to evacuate, but he wasn't sure how many had actually heeded the directive. Some people simply refused to believe that anything bad could happen to them. That, or they were afraid their homes might be looted by the opportunistic riffraff that seemed to crawl out of the woodwork during moments like this.

Similar scenes were playing out all over the plateau as South and Southeast Roads, as well as every other thoroughfare of any size, turned into rivers of refugees fleeing ahead of what was sure to be a cataclysmic event for Trian and her surrounding areas. Hundreds of thousands of people were taking part in what had become a chaotic migration of epic proportions.

Turning his horse westward, he sighed as he made his way slowly along the edge of the roadway, offering encouragement to those he passed. He'd only gone a short distance when he spotted Kustin Landar moving along with the flow of people. Like the rest of those tasked with overseeing the evacuation, he was on horseback and wore a bright yellow arm band so people would know to come to him for advice or help.

He smiled as he drew rein in front of Taggert. "How goes the fight?" he asked.

Taggert grunted. "This isn't a fight. This is playing nursemaid. And in all likelihood another ploy by Jase Fairimor to keep the Chellum army out of the real fight."

"The real fight will come soon enough," Kustin said, then nodded to a young mother holding the hands of her two small children. One, a dark-haired boy in dingy overalls, held the leash to a dog nearly twice his size. Wolfish in appearance, it was obviously gentle, but Taggert suspected it would fight like a Shadowhound if it felt the children were in danger.

"All we can do," Kustin continued, his eyes still on the young mother, "is encourage our people to move further out of harm's way." He turned and met Taggert's gaze. "But, if you are feeling the urge to draw your sword, there is looting taking place in the village we just passed. Some of the residents are putting up a fight, but the brigands are better armed."

"Well, then," Taggert said, whistling for his men. "I think we have something to say about that." Putting his heels to his horse, he started for the village as a dozen of his men formed up around him.

乇

Bornis Pendir watched Zea as she wrapped little Kindel in a blanket, then smiled reassuringly at her when she turned to look at him. Fairimor Palace had been her home for the past eight years, and he could see in her eyes that she was nervous about leaving. But leave she must, if she wanted to keep little Kindel safe.

"Don't worry," he told her. "You will like it in Kindel's Grove. And Velerie and Jukstin and I will be there with you."

"My warders to the end?" she asked, forcing a smile.

"The end of Shadan," Bornis said. "Jase is going to win this." He was surprised by how strongly he believed it. "And when he does, we will return to Trian, together. Your warders for life, if you will have us."

Zea seemed reassured. "Well then," she said, "let's be on our way."

Bornis winked at his little sister, then nodded to Velerie. A heartbeat later a Veilgate opened along the edge of the forest bordering his and Wytni's home, and he took her hand as he led the way through. The air smelled of rain, and the ground was soft. Wytni looked around in awe, mesmerized by the sudden change in scenery. That, and she seemed relieved to be home.

"Our home is your home," Bornis told Zea. "You and Velerie and Wytni make yourselves comfortable. Jukstin and I are going to make a quick trip into town. I want to make sure Mayor Murra knows what's coming his way."

"What do you mean?" Zea asked.

"The population of Kindel's Grove and its neighboring villages is about to swell with refugees from Trian. Fadus and the town council will need to prepare to receive them."

そ

Aside from the *clop-clop* of horse hooves, East Road was eerily quiet as Lavin Dium and his accompanying squads of Dymas and *Bero'thai* rode into Central Plaza. He reined in next to the central fountain and looked around appreciatively. Finally, after days of playing sheepherder, the neighborhoods lining the south side of East Road and everything north of the road itself had been evacuated. Now, only the Children of *Ta'shaen*, a small army of trained military personnel, and a few battle-worthy citizen volunteers remained.

He looked in the direction of North Road and pursed his lips worriedly. But without reinforcements, there simply weren't enough of any of them to hold the city for long. Even the combined might of the united armies once they arrived wouldn't delay the inevitable for long. And it wasn't just that they were so hopelessly outnumbered—Jase had foreseen the fall of the city. It wasn't at all comforting.

The sound of an approaching horse grew quickly audible, and he turned to find one of his men riding down Southeast Road toward him. It was Erif, and his face was set with a frown.

"Captain Dium," Erif said as he brought his agitated horse to a halt next to the fountain. "There's trouble brewing along the edge of the established perimeter not far from here. Some rabble-rouser got a rumor circulating that all of this is just a ploy by Elva to seize control of Trian."

Lavin was stunned. "And people believed it?"

"A few," Erif answered. "But I think most of those involved are simply using it as an excuse to move back into the restricted area."

"I've had enough of this," Lavin said, nudging his horse forward. "If the fools insist on dying, let's send them on their way."

Erif's brows came up in surprise. "What are you going to do?"

"I'm going to give them all swords and have Camiele Dymas send them to the front lines through a Veilgate."

"Uh, begging your pardon, Captain," Erif said. "But is that within our jurisdiction?"

Lavin grunted. "It is now. Come, we're going to put a stop to this nonsense right now."

Skirting around the edge of the fountain, he headed in the direction Erif had indicated. They were just about to exit the plaza when a small Veilgate opened from Fairimor Palace and Medwin Tas and Javan Galatea hurried through accompanied by a Zekan Dymas. She was young, with hair was so blond it looked white. She wore it in a long braid over her front shoulder which she gripped tightly with one hand as she looked around.

"Good news, Captain," Medwin said. "Nekia Dymas here just arrived from Thesston. Lord Pryderi sends word that the Arkanian invasion into southern Zeka has been repelled. And with Riak no longer a threat, he feels he no longer needs to patrol the Inner Sea. Every soldier he can spare is prepared to come to our aid."

"That is good news," Lavin said. "Have you informed Captain Brey?"

Medwin shook his head. "Not yet. He's still out at the outer wall with Ammorin and Pattalla. But High Queen Fairimor and Gideon have returned. They arrived with the *Mith'elre Con* just moments before Nekia Dymas. They suggested that you be the one to welcome Zeka's troops into the city."

Lavin blinked in surprise. "Now?"

Medwin looked around the empty plaza meaningfully. "There's plenty of room here."

Lavin laughed softly. "That there is."

He turned to Erif. "Take Camiele Dymas and two squads of *Bero'thai* to the trouble spot," he said. "I was serious about giving the rabble-rousers something productive to do."

Medwin arched an eyebrow at him. "What's this now?"

"Nothing that can't be handled with a Veilgate," Lavin told him, then nodded for Erif to proceed. As he and Camiele and the *Bero'thai* rode away, Lavin turned back to Nekia Dymas.

"Let's bring your people into the city," he said.

With Ammorin and Pattalla walking behind him as his uninvited warders, Elison dismissed the messenger, then continued along the top of Trian's outer wall without speaking. Finally, some good news. He'd wondered if Lord Pryderi would be able to send troops—he'd never imagined that he could spare fifteen thousand.

He glanced toward Central Plaza even though there was little chance of seeing what was taking place there. Fifteen thousand! It was a much needed miracle. Hopefully things along Zeka's southern border remained quiet. If Arkania mounted a second invasion, Pryderi might not have the man-power needed to turn it back a second time.

Turning back to the task at hand, he continued walking, and the soldiers and guardsmen stationed along the way saluted as he passed. He acknowledged them with nods, but didn't stop to engage in conversation. Everything looked to be in order—a relief considering the chaos and confusion taking place elsewhere in the city and in the townships beyond her mighty walls.

He reached the towers framing Northeast Gate and quickly climbed the stairs to the tower's overlook. Some hundred feet below, the curved street fronting the outer wall was empty but for teams of Dymas laying Power-wrought traps to greet the enemy when they arrived.

He looked at the narrow slit of Mendel Pass, and a cold pit settled in his stomach at how soon that arrival would be. Yes, Jase had delivered a watery death blow to tens of thousands of the enemy, but it simply wasn't enough to stop a monster as large as

Death's Third March. The most recent report from Idoman said the enemy had regrouped and were slogging their way up the muddy slopes once more. They would be reaching the summit sometime in the next few minutes.

Realizing just how agitated the thought made him, he took a deep breath and turned his attention to the patchwork of rooftops and roadways spreading outward from Trian's walls. Densely packed nearer the city, the maze of roads and buildings gradually thinned the further out from the city one went. Four or five miles out, large patches of green marking farms and estates broke up the darker sections of the rooftops of villages and townships. And there, wide as rivers and running straight as arrows through the midst of it all, were North, Northeast, and East Roads.

Moving to the large spyglass mounted at the edge of the wall, he raised it to his eye, and a quick look at North Road showed it to be deserted for as far as he could see. Northeast Road was empty save for several squads of Highwaymen and Guardsmen on patrol. The people, it seemed, had no desire to be between Death's Third March and its intended target, and they had heeded their Queen's warning to evacuate.

*Thank the Light for that*, he thought. He could breathe a little easier knowing that most of those he was sworn to protect would be out of harm's way. At least as long as the Veil still stood. If it collapsed, nowhere in the world would be safe.

He pushed the thought away and swung the spyglass toward East Road. The first two-mile stretch out from the city was empty, but the further out he looked, the more choked with people it became. Yes, they were heeding the warning to evacuate, but he was worried that they may have waited too long to do so. Hopefully, Taggert and the men of the Chellum army could speed things along.

He watched the exodus a moment longer, then turned his attention back to Northeast Road, following it until the townships gave way to the sloping grasslands rising toward Mendel Pass. He couldn't make out much in the way of detail, but he knew the dark mass spread across the plateau south of the pass was the bulk of the united armies of Kelsa, Elva, and Chunin. They were following the *Mith'elre Chon's* order to fall back to Trian by way of Northeast Road.

"For the final stand," he whispered, lowering the spyglass.

"Yes," Ammorin said, "the final stand."

Elison turned toward him, and the giant man went to one knee and looked him in the eyes, smiling. "You whisper more loudly than you think," he said, then chuckled and added. "But as evidenced by the arrival of the Zekan army, Kelsa won't be making the stand alone. All the righteous nations of the world will be here with you." He leaned forward for emphasis and added, "*All* the nations."

Before Elison could speak, a large Veilgate opened atop the wall below the tower, and Ohran Peregam strode through with nets and spears in hand. More Dainin followed, and Elison watched in wonder as they just kept coming, moving along the top of the wall to make way for more to follow. He tried to keep count, but it was impossible, and he gave up.

When the gate finally slid shut a few minutes later, Elison turned to Ammorin. "How many?" was all he could muster.

"One thousand, three hundred and two," his friend said. "But the two were already here." He winked at Pattalla before looking back to Elison.

"I'm not complaining," he said. "But... but why now? Why not earlier?"

"Because, as you said, this is the final stand." Ammorin showed his teeth in a grin. "And it is no longer necessary for the *Nar'shein* to search for lost temples of Elderon."

Elison stiffened at what the statement implied. "You mean—"

"Yes," Ammorin nodded. "Jase knows the location of a Blood Orb."

Jase felt the stirrings in *Ta'shaen* only moments before the Veilgate opened and Elison Brey strode through from the outer wall. Ohran Peregam ducked through next and was followed by Ammorin and Pattalla.

"I see you, *Nar'shein*," Jase said, and Ohran smiled.

"I see you, *Mith'elre Chon*," he replied. "My people are in place along the outer wall. They will act as a shield against Death's Third March for as long as lifeblood flows through their veins."

"I watched your arrival," Jase told him. "And you have my heartfelt thanks for bringing so many."

"I would have brought more," Ohran said, "but the rest of my people are working to preserve what's left of the Veil by destroying the demons trying to bring it down."

"And God's speed to all of them for their efforts," Jase said.

Ohran went to one knee in front of him and looked him in the eyes. "God's speed to you, young one, for what you must do in the coming hours."

A sharp stab of fear and worry reached him through the *sei'vaiya*, and he glanced over to find Talia biting her lip. He smiled at her before looking back to Ohran.

"Thank you, my friend," he said, then turned to face his parents.

"It's time," he said, then faltered, suddenly at a loss for words. Finally, he forced a laugh. "I've been so desperate for this day to come that I haven't taken the time to think about what I would say to you once it was here."

"Then don't say anything," Brysia said. "We already know what's in your heart." With tears in her eyes, she hugged him, then kissed him on the cheek and stepped back.

Gideon hugged him next, squeezing him so tightly he thought his ribs might crack. "I love you, my boy," he whispered. "And I know you can do this."

Jase grunted. "Because I'm the *Mith'elre Chon?*"

Gideon shook his head. "Because you're my son."

Clapping his father on the arm, he moved to the cabinet holding the Blue Flame Scepter and channeled the threads of Spirit necessary to undo Gideon's ward. The intricately cut crystal glittered brightly as he removed the scepter from its resting place and held it before him.

Offering his arm to Talia, he started for the archway marking the passage out of the back of the palace. "If you don't mind," he whispered. "I would like to make the journey on foot."

The rush of affection flowing through the *sei'vaiya* grew stronger. "Not at all."

Endil adjusted the dartbow on his hip, then offered his arm to Jeymi. He'd already said his goodbyes to Cassia and Andil who, at Endil's request, had remained in Andlexces. He'd insisted it would make the journey to Augg easier if he didn't have to worry about their safety.

Jase understood the feeling completely but didn't have that luxury. His parents were destined to be here until the end. Whatever that end might be.

With Elliott and Endil and Jeymi in tow, Jase led Talia to the Power-wrought doors leading out of the back of the palace, where he channeled thin tendrils of Air to trip each of the levers, then pulled them open to reveal the narrow path leading up to the temple. A razor's edge of stone less than a dozen feet wide, it stretched up to the temple like the spine of some giant beast.

Jase glanced up at the temple shining brightly in the afternoon sun and smiled as he took Talia's hand and started up the path.

He'd only gone a few steps when he sensed her thoughts through the *sei'vaiya*. "You are thinking about the last time we made this climb."

She nodded. "I am. Specifically about when I learned I was a Healer." She glanced over, her green eyes intense. "And how Gideon left us alone together so you could practice embracing and releasing the Power. I could barely breathe because of how badly I wanted to kiss you." She giggled. "If you think about it, it was kind of like our first date."

"I guess it was," he said, unable to hold back his smile. "And for the record, I wanted to kiss you too."

She squeezed his hand affectionately, and they climbed the rest of the way to the temple in silence. Once there, Jase led her to the small enclave and the stone bench they'd sat on the last time they were here. "In honor of our first date," he whispered as they sat.

Endil and Jeymi moved to a second bench, but Elliott continued on to the temple's entrance. After a brief inspection of the polished hardwood doors, he ran his fingers over the smooth, green marble of the walls, then moved to the eastern edge of the small courtyard fronting the entrance. There he stopped at the short wall ringing the courtyard and looked over the edge at the nearly two thousand foot drop into the walled area behind the palace.

After a moment, he returned to the enclave where Jase and the others waited.

"I can see why Seth said he would meet us here," he said. "It's perfect for Myrscraw."

"You really like flying, don't you?" Talia said.

"Just wait," he said, grinning from ear to ear. "It's like nothing else you've ever done." Without waiting for a response, he returned to the edge of the balcony to watch the sky for Seth.

Smiling at his friend's enthusiasm, Jase let his eyes move out over the city and its surrounding areas. From this height nothing seemed amiss, but he knew if he stretched out with his Awareness he would find the inner city and the northern half of the outer city empty and abandoned. A probe of the southern half of the outer city or the villages and towns south of East Road, however, would reveal chaos. *Organized chaos*, his mother called it, though he didn't see how the two words could be used together.

As the minutes wore on, he grew impatient and moved to the balconied edge to join Elliott. He wasn't afraid of heights, but he put a hand on the railing to steady himself just the same.

No sooner had he touched the smooth stone than his vision blurred and the world seemed to shift around him.

*He stands in the exact same spot, but night has fallen. Below him, much of the outer city is in flames, and the wall of the inner city has been breached in a dozen places. Demons are pouring through the gaps by the thousands.*

*And they aren't alone.*

*Spectral shapes of greenish-white move with them, and he recognizes them for what they are. With the Veil no longer in place, the spirits of the damned are taking a hand in the battle.*

*Elvan archers line the top of the Overlook as the courtyard below is quickly overrun, and demons reach the palace entrance. The sounds of splintering wood and shattering steel echo across the courtyard as the gates are ripped from their hinges.*

*The dead, however, aren't bound by the laws of nature, and they swarm up the sides of the Overlook and into the midst of the Bero'thai. Elvan blood wets the rapidly wilting foliage of the gardens as living flesh is rent by apparitional frenzy.*

*Jase stretches out his hand to help, but Ta'shaen is out of reach. He can only watch as the Elvan soldiers are slaughtered by the ghostly figures.*

*Suddenly Jase's Awareness comes alive with a powerful surge of Earthpower, and brilliant light lances from the Dome's entrance, a radiant burst of energy that strikes the apparitions and hurls them from the Overlook. They vanish into nothingness as they plummet earthward.*

*Gideon appears from out of the Dome, face like a thunderhead as he strides through the gardens toward the eastern edge of the Overlook. When he reaches the eastern rim, he unleashes a firestorm of Sei'shiin, and for a moment it looks as if the palace might be spared.*

*But the Orb's reservoir of Power isn't endless, and the glow in Gideon's hand begins to dim, then winks out. Night Threads lance out of the sky as something monstrous swoops in on leathery wings and lands amid the carnage.*

*The robed figure atop the winged demon scans the gardens casually, triumphantly, and the air turns dark around it as it seizes Gideon in an invisible grip and pulls him close.*

Jase's eyes snapped open, and he staggered backward from the railing and into the arms of Elliott and Talia. The sound of their voices was suddenly audible, frantic and worried as they called to him.

"Jase, what is it? What's wrong?"

Only then did he realize that he held the Power, and he glanced down at the Blue Flame Scepter crackling with unreleased destruction in his left hand.

Horrified, he released *Ta'shaen* and put his arm around Talia as she continued to steady him. The concern in her eyes was matched by the panic flowing across the *sei'vaiya*.

"Jase," she said again. "What's wrong?"

"A vision," he answered. "One I've had before. I saw...." He swallowed hard. "I saw Trian being overrun." He pointed at the balcony railing with the scepter. "I was standing right there, in the vision, watching it happen."

"Then forget about it," Elliott said. "Because you'll be in the Soul Chamber long before Death's Third March arrives."

"You're right," Jase said, but now he wasn't so sure. This was the first time a vision—a nightmare vision—had repeated itself with such clarity. And while he was awake. It terrified him knowing that Trian *would* be overrun. And now he was afraid he might be here to see it happen. And that would only be possible if he failed.

"You're right," he said again, hoping his doubt didn't show. To Elliott at least—he knew Talia was aware of what he was feeling.

He smiled at her as he slipped free of her arms, then moved back to the railing. He didn't touch it again, fearful that it might trigger another vision, but instead stared down at the city, silent and brooding.

Talia and the others joined him, but no one spoke as they waited for Seth to arrive. It was a long twenty minutes as images of what he'd seen—of what he'd *foreseen*—flickered through his thoughts.

So, it came as a relief when *Ta'shaen* came alive in the sky above them and four Myrscraw knifed straight down through a horizontal Veilgate. They shot past the balcony in a rush of wind and feathers, then unfolded their massive wings and banked up and to the left, circling around to land in the courtyard fronting the temple.

Seth sat in the saddle of the nearest bird, while a lone Shizu sat atop the next two. The fourth bird's saddle was empty, and Elliott rushed forward excitedly.

"Kiaush," he said, extending his arms as the bird lowered its head to greet him. Elliott pressed his forehead against the bird's beak, then reached up to stroke the feathers above its eye.

"The rest are waiting for us in the sky above Mirror Lake," Seth said. "Talia rides with me. Jase, you ride with Elliott. Endil, Jeymi, you'll each ride with one of the Shizu." He pointed. "Derian Oronei and Oroi Heminsei, respectively."

Jase kissed Talia on the cheek, then joined Elliott where Kiaush was already bellying down for him. Elliott climbed into the front of the saddle then motioned for

Jase to mount as well.

"Strap yourself in using those," Elliott said, pointing to the crisscrossing strips of leather.

Jase did as he was told, then tensed as Kiaush rose to his feet.

Elliott laughed. "You'll get used to the movement," he said. "And once you do, you'll never want to ride anything else."

Encouraged by his friend's enthusiasm, Jase forced himself to relax, only to tense up again when Kiaush started toward Seth's bird. The odd up-and-down and side-to-side swaying made his stomach lurch.

"We'll need a horizontal Veilgate big enough for the birds to fit through," Seth told him. "Open it a hundred feet directly below the balcony."

Jase nodded. "And the exit point?"

"Midway between Tradeston and Augg," Seth answered. "Similar altitude as here if you can manage it."

"I'll do my best," Jase said, then embraced the Power and opened the gate.

Seth's bird tilted its head to look down at the shimmering hole in the air, then dove straight over the edge without warning. Talia gave a surprised squawk as she disappeared from view. Derian's bird went next and Jase grinned at how wide Endil's eyes went. He couldn't say for sure, but it sounded like his cousin was offering a mumbled prayer.

Jeymi squealed in delight as Oroi's bird dove over the edge, and Jase tightened his grip on the leather straps holding him in the saddle as Kiaush followed.

As the bird's giant wings folded in along its body, Jase's stomach knotted as they dropped toward the Veilgate, but the feeling was exhilarating, not frightening. Elliott was right—this was unlike anything he'd ever done.

The blur of the cliff face streaking past gave way to the vast blue of Mirror Lake as they soared through the Veilgate, then Jase's vision blurred momentarily as Kiaush spread his wings to break off the dive.

Jase released the Power and looked around. Seth and the others were already forming up around Kiaush, and the rest of those he'd selected—some thirty birds with two riders each—were angling in from the right. There was one Shizu and one Dymas per bird, but Jase suspected that many of those wearing *Komouri* black were also capable of wielding the Power. Seth would have made sure of it.

He watched them draw nearer, then turned his attention to Mount Augg rising a short five miles to the north.

"The beginning of the end," he whispered, but his words were lost in the rushing of wind.

# CHAPTER 60

## Of Wards and Crux Points

"THEY'RE AWAY,"GIDEON SAID, reining in his Awareness and turning to look at Brysia. As always, she was the essence of beauty—queenly, regal, perfect.

She must have sensed something of his thoughts because she smiled. "If you keep looking at me like that, you might give away our secret."

Gideon glanced around at Elison and the others. "Everyone here already knows," he said.

"Yes," she said, "but what about when others are here who don't know? Or when we are outside the wards against eavesdropping or intrusion?"

"About that," he said, preparing for the argument he knew would follow shortly. "The enemy has shown us that attacks directly into the palace are an option." He looked pointedly at the spot where the demons had arrived the night of Jamik Hedron's attack. "Therefore, I think the High Queen of Kelsa should stay within my wards from this point forward. I will extend them to include the Dome and Overlook to give you more room to conduct your duties, but it would help all of us rest a little easier knowing you were protected."

She studied him without blinking for a moment, and he held his breath as he waited for her answer. "You may do whatever you wish as long as I have access to the Overlook. I don't want to feel like a prisoner in my own home."

Gideon exhaled in relief. "Excellent. I've asked a number of those who were with me in Fulrath to help. Namely Erebius and Junteri. They asked that Hallie, Everis, and Krissen Dymas accompany them." He smiled. "I told you what those three young women did during Fulrath's final moments. They're young, but they are as skilled as any Dymas I've ever fought with."

Brysia's eyes narrowed. "So, this was already decided? Prior to you asking for permission."

Gideon grinned at her. "Pretty much."

"What else have you already decided in my behalf?"

"Nothing. You're the High Queen, my dear. I'm just your warder."

She gave a soft, unamused laugh. "Yes. A warder who makes an awful lot of executive decisions."

His grin widened. "Careful what you say," he warned. "Or *you* might give away our secret."

Elison cleared his throat to get their attention, then gestured at Gavin approaching from the Dome with a number of his men.

"Sorry to interrupt," Gavin said, "but those charged with preparing the city for Shadan's arrival are here to give their report."

"Show them in," Brysia said, then glanced briefly back at Gideon. "We'll finish discussing your abuse of executive power later."

Gideon lowered his head in a bow. "Of course, my Queen."

Brysia rose as Lavin Dium and the others entered the room. Gideon rose with her, moving to stand beside her as the men approached. Gideon met Lavin's eyes briefly, then took note of who the rest were. Lyndon Ryban, First Captain of the City Guardsman. Kustin Landar of the Merchant's Guild. Medwin Tas and Javan Galatea. And six female Dymas Gideon didn't have names for.

"Please, have a seat, gentlemen," Brysia told them, motioning to the semicircle of chairs just off the edge of the library half of the room. She took the high-backed chair facing the semicircle, and Gideon moved to stand beside her as Elison took a seat next to Lavin. Ohran Peregam and Ammorin and Pattalla seated themselves on the floor behind the semicircle and were still taller than those in front of them.

Brysia smiled at them, then looked to Elison. "Captain Brey," she began, "we will hear your report first."

Elison glanced over his shoulder at Ohran before looking back to Brysia. "You already heard the best news," he began. "The outer wall is under the protection of thirteen hundred *Nar'shein Yahl.*"

"Thirteen hundred and two," Ammorin said, "including those seated behind you."

Elison laughed softly. "Thirteen hundred and two," he repeated, then sobered as he continued. "Everything north of East Road has been evacuated, and the *Bero'thai* and the City Guardsmen are making regular patrols to keep it that way."

"Additionally," Captain Ryban said, "we've put up barricades—wagons, and carts and crates—pretty much everything heavy we could find—to block the more narrow streets. It should force the enemy to use the main thoroughfares or at least slow them if they choose to spread out."

Elison nodded. "If we can keep them bottled up on the three main roads, we have a better chance of standing our ground. The danger comes if they get troops behind us."

"Which is where the Dymas come in," Lavin said, motioning to the Elvan woman on his right. "Camiele, if you would please."

"Before Ladies Korishal and Hadershi left for Andlexces," she said, "they showed us the most likely places the enemy might attempt to insert troops through Veilgates. Our Dymas have placed Power-wrought traps in most of those locations and are working to complete the rest." She looked at Gideon and smiled as she continued. "Many of the traps are variations of those you created in Fulrath. Some will even reset themselves a number of times before the crux points unravel."

"You were there?" Gideon asked. "In Fulrath?"

Camiele shook her head. "No. I was among those who came with the *Mith'elre Chon* to liberate Trian. I've been here helping fortify the city ever since. Much of what I and the others have learned to do was taught to us by the *Mith'elre Chon* when last I saw him." She hesitated, a look of awe in her bright blue eyes.

"It was the day he destroyed Houses Geshiann and Volmara," she continued. "He had a number of Chunin Dymas with him and took us all over the city, showing us different ways to set crux points. He is an excellent teacher, but he made it quite clear that it was you who taught him the most intricate wieldings. He spoke very highly of you."

"Thank you, Camiele," he said, impressed by how genuine she was.

"Speaking of crux points," Elison said, "I've asked Camiele and the others to set them on all the bridges spanning the Trian River. If we lose the northern bank, we'll destroy the bridges."

"Bridges can be rebuilt," Brysia said. "Do what you feel is necessary."

"How are things in the southern half of the city?" Gideon asked. "Particularly along the evacuation border?"

A look of disgust washed over Lavin's face and he shook his head. "The southern quadrants are a deathtrap waiting to happen," he said. "Simply put, not enough people left the city. If the enemy desires slaughter, they will have it."

A cold pit settled in Gideon's stomach at how many people remained in harm's way, but there was nothing to be done about it now. They would just have to trust that what Jase had foreseen regarding Shadan's assault was accurate.

"They've been warned," Brysia said. "And wards are being placed along the boundary to encourage the enemy to stay north. There's nothing more we can do for them." Her tone wasn't so much harsh as it was resigned.

"On a bright note," Lavin continued, "the army sent by Lord Pryderi has been welcomed into the city. Their base of operations will be Central Plaza, but I've asked them to take positions along East Road as a reminder to those in the southern quadrants that the northern half of the city is off limits."

"That will help with the problems we were having earlier," Medwin said, shooting a meaningful look at Lavin.

Brysia arched an eyebrow at the young man. "What problems?"

"Nothing a couple of Veilgates couldn't handle," Lavin said, frowning at Medwin. "There were a number of people stirring up trouble along the evacuation boundary," Medwin continued, pointedly ignoring Lavin's frown. "Some even went so far as to accuse Elva of seizing control of Trian for their own purposes, and they were encouraging Trian's residents to take up arms against them."

"Oh, really," Brysia said, her face hardening with anger. "And how did Veilgates handle the situation?"

Medwin shrugged. "At Lavin's suggestion, we armed those trying to pick a fight with Elva and sent them to the front lines. I'm pretty sure it changed their perspective on things."

During the exchange, Gideon noticed how Camiele's cheeks reddened with embarrassment, and he realized she'd been the one to open the Veilgates.

"Exactly what I would have done," Gideon said, catching Camiele's eye and smiling reassuringly. "I have no tolerance for anyone who questions the integrity of the Elvan people."

Camiele relaxed, visibly relieved that she hadn't done something wrong.

The conversation turned to what was happening outside the city, and Gideon listened without comment while Kustin Landar updated them on the evacuation of the outlying townships and the Chellum army's part in it. When talk turned to the finer details of how the villages beyond Trian Plateau were going to deal with so many refugees, Gideon cleared his throat to pause the discussion.

"Not that this isn't interesting or important," he said. "But I need to set wards on the rest of the palace." He motioned for Camiele and the other Dymas to join him. "I could use your help, if you have strength."

"For a chance to learn from the master," Camiele said. "We'll find strength."

Gideon smiled at the compliment. "Excellent. Let's get to it, then."

Dipping his head in a bow of farewell to Brysia, he locked eyes with her briefly to convey how much he loved her, then made his way out into the Dome.

It was empty but for the handful of *Bero'thai* on duty, but that suited Gideon just fine. The fewer people around to distract them, the better. He moved to the center of the room and stopped on the Blue Flame rug. Setting the crux points here would allow the detonation to reach anywhere in the Dome—it wouldn't matter where a corrupted Veilgate opened.

"We'll start with a trap designed to obliterate anything that comes through a corrupt Veilgate," he told them. "But unlike the first ones I set in the palace, we'll create these to target the edges of the Veilgate as well. That way, if we miss killing the enemy, we at least shut the way for reinforcements."

"Sounds complicated," one of Camiele's companions said, but her grey eyes glittered with excitement.

"It is. If it weren't, it likely wouldn't be worth using as a ward. Now, open your Awareness, and I'll show you how it is done."

Opening himself to the Power, he formed a bubble of Spirit and channeled a stream of *El'shaen te sherah* into it. He followed that with several bursts of *Sei'shiin*, then compressed the entire thing with a with a fist of Air, squeezing it down to the size of a single mote of dust even as he visualized what it would do when it detonated. The pressure within was so great that a second bubble of Spirit was needed to keep it from unraveling and releasing the strands of Power back into the fabric of *Ta'shaen*.

The tiny point of compressed energy would be virtually undetectable to any but him and the young ladies with him unless one was actively searching for it. Even then it would take someone with Jase's abilities to find it.

He set it directly above the image of the Blue Flame beneath their feet, then strung dozens of thin lines of Spirit between the Power-wrought trap and dozens of small crux points around the perimeter of the Dome. He linked those threads with shorter ones in between and the entire thing took on the appearance of a spider-web-like net in his mind's eye. A net designed to kill instead of catch. Sever any one of the lines between any two points and the trap would detonate.

Now came the tricky part of rigging the trap to reset itself. It required more finesse than strength and if done incorrectly would cause the trap to unravel. It involved creating a sphere of pure Spirit energy—he liked to think of them as miniature reservoirs not all that different from those linked to a Blood Orb—and then attaching the sphere to the trap via a conduit of Spirit.

When he was finished, he released the Power and waited. The trap held. And there was enough Power in the reservoir to reset it a dozen times.

"That is incredible," Camiele said, her voice filled with awe. "All the traps we've created so far involve only a single mode of attack. Fire or Flesh or *Sei'shiin*—nothing this complicated. How do the different strands of Power know what to target? The strands of *El'shaen* for instance—how do they know to attack the edges of the Veilgate instead of demons or Darklings?"

Gideon smiled at her. "Because I willed them to with my Awareness," he told her. "Remember, your Awareness is part of the Earthsoul. She knows your thoughts and intentions when you wield. Visualize the outcome as you wield and the Earthsoul will bring it about."

"Is that why," one of the other Dymas began, "traps wrought by Agla'Con are powerful but clumsy?"

"Exactly," Gideon said. "They lack finesse because they've lost the privilege of communing with the Earthsoul. They can will things to happen all they want, but it isn't going to happen. In fact, She fights them every step of the way. Any traps or crux points they create will be linked to a single strand of Power only. Usually Fire."

"But there is an exception, isn't there?" Camiele said.

"Yes," Gideon told her. "Those with the ability to wield *Lo'shaen* can create traps as intricate as this one." He pointed to the mote-sized speck suspended in the air before them. Then he chuckled and added, "But even those vermin are limited with what they can do by way of Veilgates. It's nice to have at least one advantage over them."

"I'd say your expertise with crux points is to our advantage as well," Camiele said. "And know I speak for all of us when I say we would love to help you ward the rest of the palace."

"That would be wonderful," Gideon told them. "I'll see to the Overlook. You ladies see to the outer palace. Start at the doors leading into the Dome and work your way out from there."

"It will be a pleasure, Guardian of Kelsa," Camiele said, then led the way to the doors. From what Gideon had glimpsed of their abilities through the eyes of *Ta'shaen*, they would lay a series of traps sufficient to slow Maeon himself.

It was time for him to do the same.

兺

Beraline Hadershi thanked the *Bero'thai* for his report, then pursed her lips in frustration as the man hurried away. There was still no word on the whereabouts of Trake Noevom, and Beraline knew that the longer they went without finding him, the less likely it became that they would. Even the Viewing she'd attempted in order to get a look at his final moments here in the Dremick Building hadn't shown her anything she didn't already know. After attempting to strangle Felicia and shoving her body in the closet, the murderous little cur had simply walked out the front doors and disappeared into the city. And since proximity was the key to success in a Viewing, she'd been unable to follow him much further than that.

Giving an audible hiss of frustration, she turned her attention back to the wards she'd placed over this wing of the building. They weren't just a barrier against eavesdropping—they obliterated spiritual sight as well. Any prying Awareness would see nothing but brilliant white light. It masked the storage room completely.

And should the enemy somehow manage to get an actual physical look in the room—an event she didn't think likely with so many *Bero'thai* keeping watch—the painting was wrapped in a cloak of bended Light held in place with crux points. Aside from those who'd already seen it, the painting had, for all intents and purposes, ceased to exist.

She knotted her fists in anger. Except for Trake, of course. And since he intended to report it to his master, it was likely the enemy would learn of it shortly. Hopefully Jase was well on his way to the mountain and would retrieve it long before Trake could give his report.

She finished inspecting the warding, then reined in her Awareness and turned to study Marithen who was staring abstractedly out one of the windows. The elderly Dymas had been unusually silent since seeing the painting, and Beraline was starting to worry that seeing it had done something to disrupt what was going on inside that confused mind of hers.

"Marithen," she called. No response.

"Marithen," she called again, moving toward her. "It's time for us to return to Trian. Gideon Dymas will need us."

When Marithen still didn't respond, Beraline took her by the arm and stooped to look her in the eyes. They glittered with the kind of killing intensity reserved for Darklings or shadowspawn, and seemed focused on something only Marithen could see. She seemed oblivious to everything else around her.

Beraline reached up and touched her cheek. "Marithen, it's time to go. We need to help prepare Trian for Shadan's arrival."

Marithen's eyes suddenly met hers, and Beraline flinched in surprise. "It's not his arrival that worries me," she said, and for one fleeting moment she looked and sounded like the woman she'd been before the Battle of Greendom had scarred her mind. Her eyes narrowed and she added, "*She* is coming."

The certainty of her dear friend's words sent a stab of fear through Beraline's heart. "Who is coming?" she asked. "Marithen, whose arrival are you worried about?"

The intense look in Marithen's eyes vanished, and she blinked. With a simple smile she took Beraline by the hand. "We should be on our way to Trian," she said. "Gideon will need our help."

Beraline watched her for a moment without speaking. Yes, she experienced moments of lucidity from time to time, but this one had been different... sharper, more clear, focused. It seemed as if she were *prophesying* instead of reciting or recalling bits she'd read in the prophecies.

Beraline's skin prickled as the stab of fear she'd experienced earlier grew. Marithen, she realized, had caught a glimpse of the future. A glimpse of something so terrible it had momentarily broken through the web of madness and confusion plaguing her mind.

And there was nothing she could do to find out what it was.

Squeezing Marithen's hand affectionately, she embraced the Power and opened a Veilgate into the gardens of the Overlook. Maybe Gideon would know what it meant.

# CHAPTER 61

## The Fists of Tamba

IDOMAN WATCHED THROUGH HIS Awareness as the final line of Power-wrought traps at the summit ripped into the forward ranks of Death's Third March, incinerating some with bursts of Fire and erasing others with streamers of *Sei'shiin*. Those were followed by a barrage of lightning that hammered Darkling and cultist soldiers alike, and the crackling stabs of white-hot energy filled the air with thunder.

When the tumult ended, Idoman looked at Quintella and the rest of the Dymas who'd remained with him at the rear of his quickly retreating army. Representing every nation but Tamba, Kunin, and Arkania, they were some of the finest, strongest, and most skilled Power-wielders he'd ever had the privilege of working with.

The carnage they'd wrought upon the enemy at the summit was unmatched by anything his armies had done to date. If not for the fact that they were so terribly outnumbered, they may have been able to hold indefinitely. But Death's Third March had prevailed for no other reason than Shadan had a seemingly endless supply of troops to throw in the chopper.

"You did well," he told them. "But it's time for us to pull back."

Quintella nodded, a tight smile on her face. Like everyone else, she was exhausted but willing and determined to fight on. "To the next line of crux points?" she asked.

Idoman shook his head. "There aren't any more," he told her. "The rest of our Dymas had neither the time nor the strength to set them. But the enemy doesn't know that, so they'll proceed with caution. It should give us the time we need to join our army to Joneam's."

"So that's it?" Aomin Dymas said, his weathered Chunin face turning the color of his hair. "We're just going to concede the southern half of the pass?"

"Yes," Idoman said. "We've lost the high ground. And without more traps to aid our attack, we wouldn't stand a chance."

"I agree," Quintella said. "The smartest move is to see our people safely down to the plateau."

Wrapped in a sheltering bubble of corrupted Spirit to protect him from the stench of death all around him, Aethon Fairimor moved through the midst of the carnage spread across the summit of Mendel Pass. The Tamban soldiers following in his wake wore grimaces of disgust, every man stepping carefully so as not to soil his boots with something foul.

Aethon frowned. The utter lethality of the Power-wrought traps was as impressive as it was frustrating. No Agla'Con or *Jeth'Jalda* could create such a multifaceted release of energy—it angered him that Dymas could. That ability coupled with the obvious advantages Dymas had with Veilgates made him wonder if it were the Earthsoul's way of tipping things back in her favor.

*It won't be enough*, he told Her silently. *As your pathetic army is about to find out.*

Moving to the southern edge of the summit, he gazed down the pass with his natural eyes for a moment, then extended his Awareness until the rear of the Kelsan army came into view. Clearly they'd given up trying to hold the pass and wanted to join the rest of their army as quickly as possible. Disrupting that reunion was going to be a pleasure.

"Commander Tiafin," he said, turning his attention to where Raelig stood with his *Jeth'Jalda* warders, "contact your generals. It's time to even the score with these fools."

Gideon had just set the final crux points in place atop the Overlook when *Ta'shaen* came alive with a powerful wielding of *El'shaen* and a Veilgate opened a short distance away. Beraline led Marithen through from inside the Dremick Building, then released the Power and let the gate close behind her.

She spotted Gideon, then motioned for Marithen to have a seat on one of the stone benches before hurrying forward. Her expression, he noted, was painted with worry. Marithen, however, seemed as distant and preoccupied as always and broke into one of her strange singsongs as she looked around at the gardens.

Beraline's worried expression grew more pronounced at the sound of it.

"What is it?" Gideon asked as she drew near.

"Trake Noevom," she said, shaking her head in disgust. "The little cur is still at large."

"The *Bero'thai* will find him," Gideon assured her. Then he leaned closer and looked her in the eyes. She was really rattled, he realized. And it didn't have much to do with one insignificant member of the Con'Kumen. "What's this really about?"

"Am I that easy to read?" she asked, forcing a smile.

"Right now you are," he told her. "What's troubling you?"

"Marithen," she said, then shook her head. "Not Marithen personally," she amended, "but something she said. She... I think she caught a glimpse of the future."

The hair on the back of Gideon's neck prickled. "She prophesied?"

Beraline nodded. "I think so. But she only said three words: *She is coming.*"

Gideon frowned. "That's it? No context?"

"Well, maybe," she said, turning to look at Marithen. "I'd just finished telling her that we needed to come here to help you prepare for Shadan's arrival when she looked me in the eyes and said, *It's not his arrival that worries me.* And it wasn't the jumbled ramblings of a woman with a shattered mind, either. It was clear and to the point. She was lucid, Gideon. The Marithen you knew before the Battle of Greendom."

"She is coming," Gideon said, and the hair on the back of his neck prickled again, this time from a stirring in *Ta'shaen.* It confirmed Beraline's suspicion that Marithen had glimpsed the future.

"Any idea what it means?"

Gideon nodded, a knot of fear settling in his stomach like a sharp rock.

"*Frel'mola,*" he answered, but before he could say more, a Veilgate opened and one of Joneam Eries' Dymas hurried through from the front lines.

"Gideon Dymas," the woman said. "There's trouble at Mendel Pass. Joneam Eries requests your presence."

"Tell the High Queen I've gone to the front," Gideon said to the *Bero'thai* standing nearby. "And keep an eye on Lady Korishal." Then, leaving the aged Dymas in her singsong, he took Beraline by the arm and led her through to the Kelsan camp.

As soon as he was through, his Awareness was assaulted by numerous corrupted wieldings coming from the north. A quick thrust of his mind's eye in the direction of the disturbance revealed thousands of Tamban soldiers rushing through rents in the Veil. Some fifty in all, the rents had been torn open by a hundred or more *Jeth'Jalda,* and a line of fiery-edged holes stretched for half of a mile across the mouth of Mendel Pass. More rents had been opened higher in the pass, and thousands more soldiers were taking up defensive positions there. They were facing north.

Joneam appeared at his side, his face pinched with frustration and worry.

"Idoman's army is still in the pass," Joneam muttered. "Bloody Tambans have cut them off."

"Did these come from Shadan's army?" Beraline asked. Gideon could feel that her Awareness was still extended, and her eyes were narrow with concentration as she watched the arrival.

"No," Joneam said. "These are reinforcements from Tamba. *Con'Jithar te Ujen,* Kaiden Dymas called them. The Fist of Con'Jithar. Apparently, they are the Tamban equivalent of the Shadan Cult."

"They were at one time," Gideon said. "They shifted their loyalty to Aethon

Fairimor after *Frel'mola* replaced them with *Frel'mola te Ujen*—the Fist of the Dark Bride."

"Is this what Marithen foresaw?" Beraline asked, her voice a frightened whisper.

"I don't know," Gideon said, pressing his Awareness near enough the gates to catch a glimpse of their points of origin. A moonlit expanse of water stretched away from a rocky shoreline beyond one of the fiery holes. Another rent revealed Tamban warships moored along the towering walls of several sea forts. A third rent opened from a massive pier reminiscent of those in Tetrica.

"These are naval forces," he continued. "*Frel'mola's* throne is in Berazzel."

"Fine lot of difference that will make to Idoman and his men," Joneam grumbled. "Tambans are Tambans, and there are a bloody lot of them."

"Agreed," Gideon said. "What is your plan, General?"

"To get our men out of Mendel Pass," he answered. "I've already sent Dymas to open Veilgates for them."

Gideon nodded. "And the Tambans?"

"There isn't much we *can* do," Joneam said, his frustration evident. "They're too far away to attack with the Power. Not without using Veilgates. And I don't think I want our Dymas wasting their strength in a battle that's already lost." He shook his head, and his frustration turned to anger as he continued. "Mendel Pass is in the hands of Death's Third March. The best we can do now is rescue those trapped within and continue falling back to Trian."

"Beraline and I will assist with the rescue," Gideon told him. Embracing the Power, he opened a Veilgate into Mendel Pass, then flinched as the area beyond was ripped apart by stabs of corrupted lightning, sending dirt and bits of smoking rock blowing past him in a rush of heat.

"This ought to be fun," he muttered as he and Beraline rushed through into the chaos beyond.

乇

Supreme Commander Ibisar Naxis dismissed the messenger, then turned on his heel and strode down the corridor toward the throne room of Berazzel. The scowl on his face sent soldiers and servants alike scurrying for cover, and the way before him opened as if he were Maeon himself.

At the entrance to the throne room, however, one of the *Maa'tisis* standing guard failed to move as quickly as it should have to open the door for him, and Ibisar burned the refleshed fool from existence with a burst of Fire. As it crumbled to ash at his feet, the other *Maa'tisis* scrambled to get the door open, then stepped hastily aside. Ibisar didn't give it a second look as he entered the throne room.

Sitting on her throne, her jeweled scepter in her lap, *Frel'mola* watched him approach, a disapproving frown on her face. Obviously she disapproved of his destruction of the *Maa'tisis*, which was ironic and more than a little hypocritical of her considering her penchant for destroying those who displeased her.

"My apologies," he said as he went to one knee in front of her. "Both for the intrusion and for the destruction of the *Maa'tisis*. But I just received urgent news regarding the Fist of Con'Jithar."

The refleshed Dreadlord studied him without speaking, her fiery gaze intent, and for a moment he feared he may have overstepped his bounds with her. But finally she smiled and bid him to rise. "You are forgiven," she said, waving her hand to dismiss the matter. "What is your news?"

"The portion of our military allied with the Fist of Con'Jithar just left Tamba by Veilgate," he told her. "They were recruited by Aethon Fairimor and have become part of Death's Third March."

"As they have been doing all along," *Frel'mola* said, surprisingly calm considering the gravity of the situation. Apparently she didn't appreciate the threat this posed should Glenda decide to attack the southern or eastern coastal cities. If nothing else, she should have been furious that Aethon had been recruiting Tamban soldiers to his cause while feigning loyalty to her.

"But we are talking about *all* of them," he protested. "Some fifty thousand soldiers and several hundred *Jeth'Jalda*. Our southern and eastern borders are vulnerable to attack."

Her exquisitely beautiful lips curved upward in a smile. "There were fifty-three thousand," she said. "And all of them gone with my blessing."

"You mean you authorized their departure?"

"Of course not, my pet. But what better way to get rid of an obsolete religion than to throw them to the wolves. Let them die for Throy Shadan and his idiotic march on Trian." Her smile grew more satisfied as she leaned back in her throne. "And I wouldn't worry too much about our eastern or southern borders. The Earthsoul will fail long before Glenda or Rosda could mount an attack against us."

The way she said it sent a chill of exhilaration racing up his spine. "You've seen the end, haven't you? The end of the world, I mean."

"Yes, my love," she answered, her voice dropping to a seductive whisper. "And we will be there for it."

When he remained speechless, she offered her hand and allowed him to help her to her feet. "Come with me," she said. "And I will show you how I've been preparing for my husband's arrival."

こ

Night Threads erupted overhead once more, sizzling stabs of reddish black that crackled down the sides of Idoman's shield like something alive. The scream-like thunder that followed was muted somewhat by his shield, but his Awareness shrieked in pain as Kallie Dymas lost her hold on the Power and her mind disappeared from the Communal link. The amount of *El'shaen* coursing through him lessened to the degree of Kallie's strength, and the shield weakened.

*She's still alive,* Quintella told him through the same link. *But she'll need healing.*

*Have the next group of evacuees take her with them,* he told her, then flinched in pain as more Night Threads hammered the shield. He waited until the corruption faded from his mind's eye, then looked up the pass at the newly arrived enemy. Most were soldiers and *Jeth'Jalda* from Tamba, but there were a number of Kelsan Agla'Con among them, including Aethon Fairimor.

As soon as the first rent had opened and Tambans began pouring through, he and twenty of the most powerful Dymas in the group had linked their abilities, and he'd taken control of the shield. It was large enough to shelter the whole of his small army, and it was giving them the time they needed to evacuate through Veilgates. For now. That would change if even one more of the Dymas in the link fell to the enemy.

Even worse, more *Jeth'Jalda* were arriving by the second, and he and the other Dymas couldn't attack without weakening the shield. And they were surrounded—he could feel the rents being opened below them in the mouth of Mendel Pass.

The only bright spot in all of it came as a result of the men and women of his army fleeing through Veilgates. He was able to reduce the size of the shield as they left.

A particularly powerful surge of *Lo'shaen* fell across the area in a swirling vortex of red and black, and the shield wavered as Brynlin Dymas lost her hold on the Power. Tendrils of killing energy slipped through the momentary lapse, and a number of Chunin cavalry and their Krelltin were ripped to smoking shreds. The inside of Idoman's head went white with a searing pain.

*Brynlin is dead,* Quintella told him. *Everyone else is on the verge of collapse.* She sounded calm, but her fear was palpable through the link. He glanced over his shoulder and found her kneeling next to Brynlin further down the pass. A short distance beyond that, *Ta'shaen* came alive with a number of pure wieldings, and Dymas raced through from the Kelsan camp. Some held the gates open so Idoman's people could escape. Others attacked the *Jeth'Jalda* with spears of lightning and streamers of *Sei'shiin.*

The Power-wrought bombardment of his shield lessened dramatically, and the link he shared with the other Dymas solidified once more. Drawing even more deeply upon the Power, he strengthened the shield, then touched the minds of the other Dymas.

*Begin switching with the new arrivals,* he told them. *Let them take your place in the link. Then get yourselves out of the pass.*

*What about you?* Quintella asked. *Aren't you coming?*

*When everyone is away, I'll follow.*

Her disapproval swept through his Awareness like a hot gust of wind. *I won't be leaving you behind, Dymas General Leda. Not now, not ever.*

*You won't have to,* a familiar voice said, and Idoman looked over to find Gideon and Beraline moving toward him through the remains of the Krelltin cavalry. *He'll be joining you shortly.*

*Gideon Dymas*, Quintella said. *Thank the Light.*

Gideon's face was a mask of death as he stared up the pass at the source of the torrent of *Lo'shaen*.

*Thank the Light, indeed*, he said, then nodded to Beraline who opened a window in front of them. It looked straight down on Aethon and his accompanying *Jeth'Jalda* from a height of only a dozen feet, and before any of them could look up, Gideon unleashed a literal storm of *Sei'shiin* that swallowed the area in an avalanche of light. The streamers of darkness hammering Idoman's shield cut off.

"Let's get you all out of here," Gideon said. "I'll take the shield."

With a sigh of relief, Idoman transferred control of the shield to Gideon, then motioned for Quintella to join him. Together they left the chaos of the pass behind.

"Gideon!" Aethon snarled, then glanced around at the burn scars on the ground where the *Jeth'Jalda* had been. Not a single one of the fools had been fast enough to deflect the killing strike, and their ineptitude had cost them their lives. He cast a wary eye up at the spot where the Veilgate had opened, then stretched his Awareness down the pass to the one who'd opened it.

Gideon was markedly stronger than the last time they'd met, and it had nothing to do with the Communal link he held the reins to. He'd launched the strike of *Sei'shiin* on his own, without the aid of other Dymas. Somehow, his abilities had been increased, most likely by the Earthsoul. He'd never considered that such a thing might be possible.

"Continue to hit the shield with everything you've got," he told a second group of *Jeth'Jalda*. "I'm going to see what I can do from inside it." He lowered his voice and added, "I have a bone to pick with my uncle."

With his Awareness still extended toward the melee, he started down the pass toward the shimmering dome of Spirit. It wouldn't be too hard to open a rent inside the dome, but it needed to be done in the right place at the right time. If not, he'd be torn apart the moment he stepped through. Still, it was a risk worth taking if it meant he could end Gideon's life once and for all.

He'd only gone a few paces when a rent opened in front of him and Throy Shadan came into view, his scepter as well as his eye blazing red with corruption. *And fury*, Aethon realized. *Something's gone awry*. Still filled with the power of the Void, he prepared to defend himself should Shadan lash out.

"You've gone too far this time, Fairimor," Shadan snarled, and his scepter flared as if he might indeed launch an attack.

"What are you talking about?" Aethon growled back. "I did exactly what I said I would."

Shadan leaned forward menacingly. "Then why is there a second army of Tambans arriving in the townships just outside Trian's walls?"

"*Frel'mola*," Aethon hissed through clenched teeth. The vicious tramp was making her move to claim Trian. He'd suspected she might try eventually, but this was a bold move, even for her.

"I'll look into it," he told Shadan. Redirecting the dark flow of power coursing through him, he tore a rent in the Veil and moved through to confront her.

Supreme Commander Naxis watched through his Awareness as the soldiers and *Jeth'Jalda* of *Frel'mola te Ujen* arrived in Kelsa via Veilgates numbering nearly a hundred. Some forty thousand had arrived already with that many more yet to come. Of those, more than five hundred were *Jeth'Jalda*, and there were ten thousand *Maa'tisis* as well.

True, this army was less than half the size of Shadan's, but its ranks were comprised of experienced, disciplined men and women, not the frenzied rabble Shadan had managed to pull together. The Blood Guard alone was the equal of the Shadan Cult and their shadowspawned pets combined.

"I know that look," *Frel'mola* said, and Ibisar reined in his Awareness and turned to meet her gaze. She sat tall in the cushioned, high-backed seat of her ornate phaeton, and her fiery eyes glimmered with amusement. She held neither reins nor whip with which to control the two magnificent horses pulling the small carriage—their minds had long since been subjugated by hers. Her thoughts were their command, and they were strictly obedient.

"I'm not sure what my Empress means," he said.

"We aren't here to challenge Shadan for control of Trian," she told him, then smiled and added, "At least not yet."

When he remained silent, she looked at the walls of Trian rising tall and dark above the rooftops of the abandoned township she'd arrived in. "A war between our forces and Death's Third March would serve no purpose and would greatly displease my husband. We'll worry about claiming Trian *after* the city has fallen. It might be as simple as asking my husband for it once Shadan and Aethon have been destroyed."

A sudden rumbling deep in the earth shook the area, and Ibisar had to take hold of the side of the phaeton to maintain his balance. Opening himself to the Power, he wrapped the wheels of the small carriage with bands of air to stabilize them, while around him the buildings of the township swayed. Windows shattered into tinkling shards, and timbers groaned and creaked with the movement.

"It's the Veilgates," *Frel'mola* said, sounding pleased. "The Earthsoul writhes in pain at our arrival."

A powerful Awareness touched the warding bubble of Spirit *Frel'mola* had placed around them to keep their conversations private, and her beautiful, refleshed lips curled into a smile. "Apparently She isn't the only one who's troubled by it."

Before she could say more, the fabric of the Earthsoul reeled in agony as a rent opened a short distance away and Aethon strode through from Mendel Pass. His face was set and his eyes were hard. He didn't release *Lo'shaen* as he approached the bubble of Spirit, and Ibisar prepared to defend himself and his Empress should the traitorous Fairimor try something foolish. This might be the opportunity he'd been waiting for all along. At the first sign of aggression, he would send the arrogant cur to join his brothers in hell.

*Frel'mola*, on the other hand, seemed unconcerned and let the sheltering ward of Spirit dissipate.

"Aethon, my dear friend," she cooed. "So nice of you to join us."

Aethon's hard expression didn't change, and the river of dark power coursing into him intensified. "Care to explain what you are doing here?" he said. "I thought we agreed *Frel'mola te Ujen* would join us *after* Death's Third March reached Trian. You aren't thinking about altering your part in all of this, I hope."

"Mind your tongue, Fairimor," Ibisar snarled, so close to striking the man with the Power that it literally sparked from his fingertips.

Aethon turned to look at him, and *Ta'shaen* vanished from Ibisar's Awareness as something dark sliced through it, severing his connection. The Jexlair crystal set in the heavy ring on his finger winked out, and he was left to stare at his enemy in surprise, as powerless as the day he was born. Aethon was far more dangerous than he'd given him credit for. That, coupled with the realization that he could have just as easily killed him instead of severing him from the Power, sent a shiver up his spine. Blood of Maeon, but the man was almost as strong as *Frel'mola*.

"Speak to me like that again, Supreme Commander," Aethon said, "and I will cut off more than your connection to *Ta'shaen*." The darkness pulled back, and Ibisar's Awareness of the Power returned.

"Now, now," *Frel'mola* said, "there's no need for violence. We all serve the same master."

Aethon grunted. "I wonder."

Ibisar bristled at the comment, but *Frel'mola* simply laughed. "A simple thank you would suffice," she told him. "After all, my arrival at this time cut off the Kelsan army's retreat. They are now caught between the Fist of the Dark Bride and the Fist of Con'Jithar. Perhaps we should stop bickering and annihilate them."

"So, that's why you came?" he asked, his skepticism obvious. "To cut off Kelsa's retreat?"

"Of course, dear one," she said. "And I brought enough troops to do just that."

"Or to try to claim Trian as your own."

*Frel'mola* laughed, but Ibisar could tell her patience was starting to slip. In truth, he couldn't comprehend why she hadn't already killed him for his blatant disrespect. "What need have I of another throne?" she asked. "Especially considering that the entire world will be my throne once my husband arrives."

"I guess we'll find out," Aethon said, but Ibisar wasn't sure what he meant by it. Without another word, he turned his back on them, and the fabric of the Earthsoul reeled once more as he opened a rent back to Death's Third March.

"He's suspicious," Ibisar said, not caring how obvious the comment was.

"He has a right to be," *Frel'mola* said, her feigned congeniality vanishing. Her eyes, burning with murderous rage, were fastened on the spot where the rent had been. "His insolence has changed my mind about laying claim to this throne. And I'm going to do so this very night."

She gestured with her scepter as she looked over at him. "Gather the Blood Maidens," she ordered. "We are going to introduce ourselves to the High Queen of Kelsa."

# CHAPTER 62

## Illusion and Reality

WITH MOUNT AUGG RISING to the left like a spear-head chiseled of stone, Jase held tight to Kiaush's saddle where he sat behind Elliott, and scanned the narrow strip of thorn-infested land separating the mountain's rocky slopes from the blue-green waters of Mirror Lake. If Temifair's painting was accurate—and he believed it was—the T'rii Gate she'd depicted should be just below them. But this was their third pass over the area, and so far all that was visible was a forest of brambles.

He'd tried searching the area with his Awareness, but it didn't reveal anything more than what his natural eyes had told him. The brambles were dense and all but impenetrable. The mountain was a snow-capped spike of grey-white granite with patches of densely packed conifers on its higher slopes and a skirt of grasses and wild flowers on its lower. Delving into the mountain with his Awareness proved it was as solid as it looked. And yet something felt... wrong.

He suspected a warding of some kind, but it was impossible to say for sure.

He shot a quick look at the western horizon and frowned. Only an hour or so remained before sunset, and while he desperately wanted to find the T'rii Gate before nightfall, he knew it would be wise to prepare for the alternative.

"We need to find a place to set up camp for the night," he said at last. "Take us down to that spot there." He pointed to a series of rocky outcroppings fifty or so yards up slope from the edge of the thorny forest. A small stream snaked its way through the outcroppings, a ribbon of silvery-white against the darker stone. It was most likely from a spring and would provide them with drinking water. The flat tops of the outcroppings would be suitable for laying out bedrolls.

Elliott nodded, and a gentle touch of Kiaush's neck turned the bird toward the area. Seth and the others followed, and a few seconds later they were settling to earth in a rushing of wind from the Myrscraws' giant wings.

Jase climbed from the saddle as Kiaush bellied down for him, then moved a short distance across the slope to get a look at what lay beneath them. It wasn't much. The boulder field below where they'd landed ended abruptly at the wall of thorns even as the small stream continued onward, disappearing into the thorn's formidable depths.

"Don't tell me you want to go in there," Elliott said. "Those bloody things will cut you to ribbons."

Jase didn't answer. The feeling he'd experienced earlier that something wasn't right had returned, and he knew better than to ignore it. He stared at the thorns for a moment, then turned to study the sharply rising slope of the mountain. Wild flowers and grasses of varying colors dotted the rocky expanse, and birds and squirrels and other small rodents darted about in flashes of color and movement. The slopes were alive with their calls and chirps.

He listened to them for a moment longer, then turned his attention back to the thorny canopy stretching away to the shore of the lake. Just as on the slopes behind him, birds and squirrels darted about, moving among the twisting mass of brambles with ease. And yet something about their movements wasn't quite right. He couldn't decide what is was at first, but the longer he watched, the more troubled he became.

One small bird in particular, a golden-crested finch, caught his eye, and he followed it closely. It hopped along one thorny branch, pausing to look around from time to time, then flew a short distance to another branch where it preened its wings for a moment before hopping along that branch as well. Hop, hop, look. Hop, hop, preen. Hop, hop, look. Every movement measured and precise.

*Too precise*, he thought, watching as it flew a short distance to another branch and began the process anew. The pattern was identical in every way to the bird's previous movements and seemed... rehearsed. No, he corrected. Not rehearsed. It seemed... artificial.

Opening his Awareness once more, he stretched it to the little bird and watched through the eyes of *Ta'shaen* as it continued moving across the top of the canopy. Then suddenly it was gone, vanishing from view as if snuffed from existence by a burst of *Sei'shiin*. For a moment he thought it had dived deeper into the thorny canopy, but a quick search turned up nothing.

He pulled his Awareness back for a wider view of the area and found that the bird had returned to the branch where he'd first seen it. As he watched, it retraced its earlier path with exactness, moving from branch to branch until it suddenly disappeared from view.

But this time, because he was watching for it, he saw it reappear as if materializing from thin air back at the starting point.

"Wait here," he told the others, then started down the slope, picking his way toward the small stream and what looked like a game trail running alongside it.

Seth joined him as he reached the stream. "Do you want to tell me what you are thinking?" he asked. His eyes were wary as he looked at the thorny expanse.

"I think we are looking at an illusion," Jase told him. "A Power-wrought camouflage of Light and Spirit. Something similar to the warding on the catacombs inside the Overlook. Only this one is extremely more complicated." He pointed to the finch. "Watch that bird for a moment and tell me what you see."

Seth did as instructed, then reached up to pull thoughtfully at his moustache. "I'm impressed," he said, "with the illusion and with the fact that you noticed it."

"I only spotted it because I was looking for something out of the ordinary," Jase told him. "I doubt a casual observer would notice."

Seth grunted. "I don't think this island gets many visitors," he said. "The area below us might be a Power-wrought illusion, but the brambles along the shoreline are very real. Just ask any number of Elvan or Kelsan sailors who've run aground there."

"So the real brambles keep people from landing on the island by boat," Jase said, starting down the game trail once more. "The illusion is to ward against an aerial arrival."

"It would seem so," Seth agreed, as sure-footed and agile on the rocky path as a mountain ram. "And I don't think Elderon had only Myrscraw in mind when He set them. What are the chances that no Agla'Con ever landed here with a K'rresh?"

"I'd be willing to bet they have," Jase told him, "but if Elderon went to such great lengths to turn our attention from this place, I'm pretty sure He left wardings for the enemy. Something that would erase them and their knowledge of the island from existence."

They reached the edge of the thorns, and Jase stopped just short of entering. He glanced at Seth briefly, then reached out a hand to touch the thorns. It passed through them without feeling or resistance and disappeared from view. He drew his hand slowly back and watched as it reappeared.

He looked back at Seth. "Let's go see what Elderon has been hiding from the world."

"You stay put," Seth said, his warder tone in full effect. "I'll investigate." Without waiting for an answer, he vanished into the thorns.

A hiss of alarm sounded on the slopes behind him, and Jase turned to find Elliott scrambling down the rocks toward him. Several Shizu followed, but all of them stopped in surprise as Seth reappeared.

"Well?" Jase asked.

Seth gestured at the thorns. "See for yourself."

Jase cast a look up the slope. "Keep Elliott calm," he said. "He freaked out when you disappeared."

Seth chuckled. "Good. We'll call that payback for all the times he's made me worry."

Jase smiled at the comment, then stepped into the warding.

The illusion of thorns vanished in an instant, and Jase found himself looking down the last few feet of the boulder field at a vast, grassy meadow.

Painted in hues of orange and yellow from the setting sun, it sported a carpet of wild flowers and scattered groupings of trees—cottonwoods and silver oaks and stout blue-needled pines. It stretched away several miles on both his left and his right and nearly a mile to south, where it ended abruptly at the real forest of brambles.

He closed his eyes and opened his Awareness to investigate. Now that he was inside the warding, the luminescent world of the Earthsoul came into view, and he could see the intricately woven threads of Light comprising the illusion, tightly woven together and draped over the area like a giant blanket. It was the most complex wielding he'd ever seen, and it was being held in place by crux points wrought of *El'shaen te Sherah*. They dotted the area like stars in the night sky, glowing points of radiant energy visible in his mind's eye.

He reined in his Awareness and opened his eyes to look behind him. He could see out of the ward just fine—it really was like the wards on the catacombs in that sense—and he knew of a certainty that what he'd come here to find was somewhere in the area below.

Talia was watching the spot where he'd disappeared from her view, but he could feel through the *sei'vaiya* that she wasn't concerned. She could feel that he was all right, and he sent a rush of warmth across the love-bond to confirm it.

Elliott, however, wore a frown. He'd reached the game trail and was hurrying down it toward Seth. Once again, the Shizu followed, seemingly on edge due to Elliott's reaction.

Jase stepped back into view, and called to them. "It's a Power-wrought illusion," he said. "Bring the Myrscraw. There's plenty of room for everyone inside it."

While the Shizu guided the birds, Talia picked her way down through the rocks with Endil and Jeymi and the rest of the Dymas. When they reached him, Jase led the way back into the warding.

"Light of Heaven," Jeymi breathed as they passed inside. "How is such a thing possible?"

"You just answered your own question," Jase told her. "But it's more than just Light. The entire thing is being held in place by crux points wrought of *El'shaen.* Open your Awareness and you will see them."

She did as instructed, and Jase felt the brush of her mind as she stretched it down into the meadow. The rest of the Dymas opened their minds as well, and he watched their faces as they examined the warding.

"That...is... amazing," Jeymi said at last, and Jase nodded.

"Yes," he agreed. "And it proves we are in the right place." He offered his hand to Talia, and they made their way down the last of the boulders to the knee-high grasses spreading away before them.

"What now?" she asked.

He smiled. "I do a more detailed probing with my Awareness," he told her. "I don't want to walk any further than necessary." He looked at Jeymi and the other Dymas and added, "Feel free to search as well," he told them. "The more eyes we have on the area, the better."

Opening his Awareness once more, he stretched it forth into the luminescent world stretching away before him. The threads of Light and the myriad crux points holding them in place dominated the shimmering view, but he forced himself to look past them and through them, the way he would if he were peering through a screen or a picket fence. As they grew less pronounced, the island's landscape came into view, and he sent his spiritual eyes soaring over the area as if he were a bird.

Based on the size and shape of the warding, he had a general idea where the center point was, and he sent his Awareness toward the small forest of blue-needle pines almost directly ahead. They bordered the wall of brambles on the far side of the meadow, a bright splash of color in the fading sunlight.

As his bird's-eye view moved across the meadow, he encountered an abundance of wildlife—birds and rodents, butterflies and beetles, a red fox following the scent of a number of grey rabbits, a doe and her spotted fawn bedded down next to the stream.

His Awareness reached the pines and passed inside. They were dense at first but thinned the deeper in he pressed. Fifty paces further on, they suddenly gave way to a clearing. And there, brightly illuminated in the center of a carpet of flowers and grass, was the *chorazin* T'rii Gate of Temifair's painting. Only this gate was different from all the others he'd seen—it was bigger. Wider. And it bore the raised image of the Tree of Life on both of its posts.

But even the T'rii Gate couldn't keep his eyes off the grey-green block of *chorazin* fronting the gate. The size of an altar in a temple of Elderon, it bore the raised image of the Blue Flame of Kelsa on its front.

Gooseflesh rose on his arms and neck at the sight of it, and a shiver of excitement washed over him. A powerful influx of Spirit tickled the air around him in what he recognized as confirmation from the Earthsoul. This is what he'd come here to find. This was the reason for the two-thousand-year-old wardings.

"I found it," he said, reining in his Awareness and turning to look at the other Dymas. "In the stand of pines directly ahead."

One by one they reined in their Awareness and turned to stare at him in wonder.

It was Jeymi who gave voice to what they were thinking. "How could you see anything through all the crux points?" she asked. "They completely overwhelmed my vision."

"Mine too," Seibei Dymas said. A rice farmer turned Dymas, the man had been present in Maisen when it had been attacked by demons. And, according to Shavis, had been instrumental in keeping it from being overrun. "But even without the light blinding my vision," Seibei continued, "I could not have found anything so quickly. You are truly Gifted, young lord."

Jase accepted the compliment with a smile. "Thank you. But, you have to remember I've had some experience with this sort of thing."

Seibei grunted. "Apparently."

Jase offered his hand to Talia. "Let's go take a closer look at what I found."

火

Gideon watched the last of Idoman's troops pass through the Veilgate Beraline held open into the Kelsan camp, then cast a wary eye back up the pass to the forefront of Death's Third March. They seemed confused by Aethon Fairimor's sudden departure, and the vast majority of them—both Agla'Con and *Jeth'Jalda* alike—had momentarily broken off their attack. It was now or never.

"Go," he told Beraline. "I'll be right behind you."

She did as instructed, and Gideon followed, holding the shield in place until the last possible second before releasing the Power and diving through the opening. It slid shut as Night Threads erupted in the area where he'd been standing.

He was helped to his feet by Idoman and Quintella, and the latter looked him over with concern. "Are you all right?" she asked, and he felt her open her Awareness to check for wounds.

"Not a scratch," he said. "Though the reason for that is Aethon Fairimor's sudden departure. Things would have been different if he'd stayed. Something more pressing than killing me must have pulled him away."

"More pressing, indeed," Joneam Eries said, and Gideon turned to find the general approaching with the rest of the United High Command on his heels. Joneam's face was tight with fear and frustration, and similar emotions masked the faces of those with him.

"A second Tamban army arrived while you were in the pass. They are in the Promish Township just outside Trian's walls. North and Northeast Gates are no longer an option for us."

Gideon went cold inside at the news. "How many troops?"

"Some eighty thousand," Captain Dennison answered. "At least ten thousand of which are K'rrosha."

"And *Jeth'Jalda*?" Gideon asked, already afraid of the answer.

"At least five hundred," Joneam said. "And Ohran Peregam sent word that *Frel'mola* herself is among them."

Gideon locked eyes with Beraline. "Well, now we know why Aethon broke off his attack. He had a more dangerous enemy to confront."

"I thought Tamba was an ally of Death's Third March," Joneam said, his eyes narrowing with confusion.

"The Fist of Con'Jithar has allied itself with Aethon, certainly," Gideon said. "But *Frel'mola te Ujen* likely has its own agenda. Especially if the Dark Bride leads them. She's put herself in a position to lay claim to Trian before Shadan arrives."

"Well, whatever their intentions," Captain Dennison said disgustedly, "they've got us. We can't very well fight our way through them to reach Trian. Not with Death's Third March breathing down our necks. They'd catch us in between them and we'd be annihilated."

Gideon nodded. "I agree," he told them. "But neither can we remain where we are." He shook his head, anger and bitterness washing through him in turns. "We've lost Trian Plateau, my friends. Our only choice is to fall back to Trian."

"How?" Joneam asked. "There are eighty thousand Tambans between us and the northern gates. Short of using Veilgates to move our entire army—a highly unlikely prospect considering how exhausted our Dymas are—we are cut off from Trian. Sure, we could try marching around the outer townships to enter the city through the southern gates, but *Frel'mola te Ujen* could simply watch our movements and reposition troops as needed."

"Well, we can't just stand here," Captain Tarn said, and Gideon felt a tingling of excitement as an idea sprang fully formed into this mind. And he knew it could work because he'd done it before. He glanced at the setting sun, and his excitement intensified. It would be dark soon, and for once darkness would favor Kelsa.

"That's exactly what we're going to do," he told them, then opened himself to the Power and wove a shield to prevent eavesdropping. "At least that's what it will look like to our enemies," he continued. "As Joneam said, we don't have enough Dymas to move the entire army. And with *Frel'mola te Ujen* on Trian's doorstep, I won't risk pulling Dymas from their positions there until I know the Dark Bride's intentions."

He looked north to where the Fist of Con'Jithar was forming up. "We are out of range for the time being," he continued. "And their Power-wielders are likely just as tired as ours after opening so many Veilgates. They'll wait until morning to come against us."

He looked back at the High Command and smiled reassuringly. "But we'll have something for them when they do. Now, listen carefully, and I'll tell you what I have in mind."

忆

"They're digging in," Asherim said, and Aethon broke off the discussion he was having with Commander Tiafin to investigate the statement. Like Mendel Pass, Trian Plateau had been swallowed in evening shadow, and it was difficult to make out what was happening with his natural eyes. But where Asherim had chosen to use a spyglass to get a look at the Kelsan army, Aethon preferred to use his Awareness.

He stretched it downward in a quick narrow thrust that brought his enemies into view in his mind's eye. True to Asherim's claim, they were preparing to stand their ground.

Aethon scratched his chin thoughtfully at the sight. But why? They were hopelessly outnumbered. Why would they make their stand here instead of fleeing to Trian?

"It's got to be a ruse," he said at last. "They're up to something. Keep your eyes on them and contact me as soon as you figure out what it is."

"Yes, First," Asherim said, then raised the spyglass once more.

"They probably think to set more of their damned booby traps," Commander

Tiafin muttered. "My guess is they'll sneak away after dark or simply retreat through Veilgates once we press them."

Aethon studied the mass of bodies a moment longer, then reined in his Awareness. "And we will press them," he said. "First thing in the morning. For now, contact your generals and instruct them to have the Fist of Con'Jithar make camp where they are. Just leave room for Death's Third March to exit the pass or we will hear about it from Shadan."

He looked back down at the united armies and smiled at the thought of what the morrow would bring. If the united armies insisted on remaining where they were, he would kill them where they stood. And then he would move against *Frel'mola* if necessary.

She could pretend at being his ally all she wanted, but he knew why she was here, and he had no intention of letting her claim what was rightfully his.

Channeling a sphere of Light to throw back the darkness, Jase led the way out of the pines and into the clearing where the T'rii Gate stood. Night had fallen just before entering the small pine forest, and the world around them had darkened that much more as the trees obliterated what little light had remained. But now, as he exited the trees and moved into the clearing, he found that the moon and stars were casting their soft, white glow across the area.

And there in the center of the clearing were the T'rii Gate and the *chorazin* altar he'd glimpsed through his Awareness. Both shone brightly in the moonlight.

He felt Talia's wonder through the *sei'vaiya*, and he turned to smile at her. She wore a cloak now—the air had cooled considerably since sunset—and when he took her hand, her fingers were cold.

"We'll make camp there," he said, nodding at the T'rii Gate. "A fire and some warm food will do us all some good."

As he moved toward the gate, he heard the surprised whispers of the Dymas as they made their way out of the trees and caught sight of the two *chorazin* structures. For most of them, this was the first time they'd seen a T'rii Gate firsthand, and they marveled at its beauty.

"It's different than the one in Arkania, isn't it?" Talia asked.

"It is. And not just because of its size. The Veilgate in Arkania is linked to other gates in this world. This gate is linked to other worlds." He moved his sphere of Light forward to illuminate the raised image of the Tree of Life on the side of the gate. "*Eloth en ol'shazar to eryth*," he continued, and Talia nodded.

"Yes," she said. "The Paths of Life and Creation." She looked over at him. "We know the Elvan nation arrived through this gate. Do you think Galiena and her people did as well?"

Jase pursed his lips. "I wouldn't be surprised. How many of this kind of gate could there be?"

"My guess is one," Seth said from the darkness beside them, and Jase glanced over to find the captain studying the gate. "Thus the extreme measures Elderon took to keep it hidden from the world."

"Speaking of those measures," Jeymi said as she and Endil stepped near, "they were wrought here, weren't they? That altar is the center point of the illusion."

Jase nodded. "Yes. And I get the feeling it isn't the only thing which was wrought here." He studied the altar a moment longer without speaking, then turned to the rest of the group.

"We'll spend the night here," he said loudly enough for all to hear. "Feel free to build fires. There's no danger of them being seen. As soon as you're ready, you can retire for the night."

"I'll gather some firewood," Elliott said, and he and Seth moved off into the dark. Some of the Dymas did likewise while others began unpacking the few supplies they'd brought. The Shizu hurriedly secured the Myrscraw for the night, then joined the Dymas. Within moments a makeshift camp had started to take shape.

Jase channeled several more spheres of Light around the top of the T'rii Gate, then linked them to crux points to keep them alight. When he was finished, he moved to stand before the altar and traced the image of the Blue Flame with his eyes. It was identical to the *chorazin* flames in Fairimor Palace and the Overlook, but just beneath it on the smooth face of the altar were several deep grooves. They formed a strange, circular pattern and were of varying widths and depths.

He knew they couldn't be incisions—*chorazin* couldn't be cut, not even with the Power. These had been formed at the time the altar had been created. They looked like... he blinked as a sudden realization struck him. They looked like key holes.

"Now what?" Talia asked. She'd sensed his wonder through the *sei'vaiya* and was curious about what it meant.

Jase smiled at her as he pulled the Blue Flame Scepter from his belt. "Now we open it."

Talia held her breath as Jase took a knee and held the chiseled flame-like tip of the scepter's crystal near the incisions on the altar. Eyes narrowed with concentration, he rotated it to the right until the chiseled edges lined up with the different depths and widths of the slits. When he was satisfied he had it right, he slid the crystal into the *chorazin*.

A loud *shink* sounded as the scepter was pulled tight, and that was accompanied by a flash of blue light. Jase looked up, his eyes wide as he stared at the spot above the altar. There was nothing there that Talia could see, but Jase seemed mesmerized, and the *sei'vaiya* literally seethed with wonder and excitement.

"What is it?" Seth asked, stepping near. He held an armful of firewood and sounded more curious than concerned. "What's happening?"

"A vision," Talia answered.

Focusing on the wave of emotions streaming toward her through the love-bond, she tried unsuccessfully to catch a glimpse of it herself. "One meant only for him."

"So, what do we do?" Elliott asked, dropping his armload of firewood next to the T'rii Gate.

Talia looked from him to Seth then back to Jase. "We wait."

As the shimmering blue image came into being above the altar, Jase's first thoughts were that he'd activated a Communicator Stone and that the man standing before him could see him as readily as he could see him. But the threads of Spirit and Light creating the shimmering image were different than any he'd seen before. They weren't linking him to some far away stone—they were linking the Blue Flame Scepter to the altar. And they were being powered by crux points set within the altar itself. They reached no further than the top of the altar, and it was clear from Seth's and Talia's conversation that they weren't visible to any eyes but his.

Which meant this was a Viewing. One that had been created and set in place by the man standing above the altar. A man that bore an uncanny resemblance to him. It was, he realized with a profound sense of awe, like looking into a mirror at an older version of himself.

*Blood of my blood*, the image said, the words sounding directly into Jase's thoughts. *I am Fairimor. Son of Temifair and Imor. First High King of Kelsa.*

*I have seen you, my son. Through visions given me by the Earthsoul, I've seen glimpses of your trials and heartaches, your temptations and your strength of character, your victories and your defeats. And while those glimpses were ever-changing and fluid, there was one constant: I saw this very moment, when you would kneel at this altar to receive instructions from me. What happens after this moment was beyond my view and remains uncertain.*

*But know this, my son. The end of days is upon you. The threads of fate and prophecy are unraveling. The scales holding light and dark in balance are about to be tipped. And you, blood of my blood, are the pivot point for all of it. What you do in the coming hours will determine the fate of the world, bringing about the Rejuvenation of life or the everlasting darkness of destruction.*

*It is for this purpose, Son of Fairimor, that I spent the remainder of my days on this holy island. I wrought the altar before you and placed within it this Viewing. I created the wards that shielded this area from view of the outside world. And most important of all, my son, under the direction of Elderon Himself, I placed wards on the Holy Mountain of the Second Creation to protect the sanctity of the temple it houses and to preserve the Blood Seed of the Rejuvenation. There is a ward wrought of each of the Seven Gifts.*

*I wish I could show you the exact locations of the crux points sustaining the wards, but this Viewing is limited in its ability to communicate and does not afford me that option. But I believe the path you have walked as the Mith'elre Chon has prepared you for this moment. You have the strength of Awareness to find the crux points and unlock the mountain. I know it. God's speed, my son.*

The shimmering image vanished, and the currents of *Ta'shaen* flowing through the Blue Flame Scepter ceased. A loud click sounded as the chiseled crystal detached itself from the altar.

He turned to find everyone watching him expectantly.

"What did you see?" Elliott asked, once again failing to keep his impatience in check.

"A message from Fairimor," Jase answered. "He told me what I need to do to gain access to the Blood Orb." He turned and looked up at the snow-capped peak of Augg looming tall and bright in the night sky. "Better settle in," he said. "This might take a while."

# CHAPTER 63

## A Keeper's Oath

AS BRYSIA FAIRIMOR LISTENED to Ohran Peregam's report of *Frel'mola te Ujen's* arrival, Ammorin watched the Queen's face for some sign of what she might be thinking. Aside from the slight narrowing of her eyes, there really hadn't been much of a reaction. She could have been listening to a report on the ups and downs of wheat farming for all the emotion she was showing. And that, Ammorin knew, was proof of just how deeply worried she really was, a facade to keep the rest of those in the room from panicking.

"Thank you, Chieftain," she said when Ohran finished. "I will gather what Dymas we can spare in the city and have them join you at the wall."

"That won't be necessary," Ohran said, his eyes bright within his weathered face. "We faced greater numbers than this during the Tamban-Dainin War."

Ammorin blinked in surprise at the obvious lie and looked at Brysia to see if she had noticed the discrepancy. He knew from conversations he had with her that she'd read the Dainin Histories. She would most certainly know how many Tamban invaders Dainin had faced. He held his breath as he waited for the Queen to reply.

"I'm sure," she said and left it at that.

"If anything," Ohran said, "I can spare a few *Nar'shein* to help ward the palace." He turned and locked eyes with Ammorin. "If Chieftain Shad'dai approves, of course."

Ammorin nodded. "I welcome any and all help you might send."

"Are you sure that's necessary?" Camiele Dymas asked, seemingly offended. "The wards Gideon and I and the others placed on the palace could repel Shadan himself."

Ohran smiled at her. "No one doubts your abilities, youngling," he said. "This is just a precaution should those wards somehow be overwhelmed or compromised. If that happens, the *Nar'shein* will see the Queen safely out of the palace." He looked back to Brysia. "Now, if you will excuse me, I will go select those who will be joining Ammorin and Pattalla as your warders."

Offering a deep bow of respect, he turned away from the collection of sofas and opened a Veilgate back to the outer wall.

Ammorin watched him go, then looked back at Brysia. She was staring at the spot where Ohran had opened the gate, and she was frowning. A quick glance around at the others revealed similar emotions. Elison wore a scowl of determination fit for an executioner. Thex Landoral and Camiele and the rest of the Dymas assigned to the palace by Gideon wore steely masks of determination. If not for his ability to sense the Power, he would have believed some of them had embraced *Ta'shaen*—Erebius and his daughter Junteri especially.

Only Pattalla and Lady Korishal seemed unperturbed. Pattalla sat with his forearms resting on his knees, his dark eyes calm and contemplative. Lady Korishal actually wore a smile, her lips moving in a silent singsong, her mind obviously elsewhere.

When he looked back to Brysia, he found her watching him. "What are your thoughts on this, my friend?" she asked. "Did your Cleansing Hunt for *Frel'mola* give you insight into what her intentions might be?"

There was a collective gasp of astonishment at the question, and he shot a quick look at the others to find them staring at him in shock.

"You hunted the Bride of Maeon?" Thex asked. "When? What was the outcome?"

Ammorin sighed, the pain of the memory striking him like a hammer. "I hunted her while she was yet in her own flesh," he said, the feeling of bitterness increasing as he spoke. "And I failed. She was too powerful." His sense of failure deepened as he added. "And since her refleshing, her strength has increased tenfold."

He looked back to Brysia. "To answer your question," he continued, "she's come to exploit the chaos caused by Death's Third March. *Frel'mola* has no ties to Shadan—her loyalty is to Maeon. My guess is she's come to claim Trian as her own. A gift for her so-called husband."

"That's insane," Thex said. "Even if her army could take the city on its own, there is no way they could keep it once Shadan arrived. He would attack her as readily as he would us, and Trian would be caught in the middle of a civil war between Dreadlords."

"Maybe that's what Maeon wants," Ammorin said. "He cares nothing for the lives of men. Not even those sworn to him. His goal is to destroy. It matters little how it is accomplished."

He was about to say more, when he felt the ward against eavesdropping tremble beneath the touch of a powerful Awareness. Judging by the looks on the faces of the other Dymas, they'd felt it as well.

Brysia noticed the looks also. "What is it?" she asked, her brow furrowing with concern.

"One of our enemies just tried to listen in on our conversation," Ammorin told her. "But they were turned away by Gideon's ward."

"That's what it's there for," Brysia said. "And this isn't the first time it's happened." She made a dismissive gesture with her hand to change the subject.

"We'll need to contact Gideon and the High Command," she continued. "We need a plan for getting our armies inside the city now that *Frel'mola te Ujen* is between us and them."

"I can go to them if you want," Thex said. "I want to know if Idoman and his men made it out of Mendel Pass safely."

"I'll go with you," Marithen said, and everyone in the room turned to look at her in surprise, Ammorin included. Those were the first coherent words he'd heard from her in days. "I want to see what that young rascal Gideon is up to."

Before anyone could respond, she rose and offered her hand to Thex. "Come, Gideon is out on the Overlook with Beraline."

Brysia's surprise grew more pronounced, and she looked to Ammorin for confirmation.

He shook his head. "It's the last place she saw them."

Thex smiled sympathetically as he took the old woman's hand. "The Overlook it is." He caught Brysia's eye as he passed and added. "We'll leave from there."

As they moved away, Brysia shook her head sadly. "And here I was thinking she might actually be of sound mind for once."

"I'm afraid not," Ammorin said. He followed her with his eyes as she exited the room, then sighed. "Beraline and I have delved into her mind on several occasions to see if there is something we could do to heal or at least lessen the madness. But it is beyond both of us. I'm just grateful that whatever happened to her didn't taint her ability with the Power."

After a moment of uncomfortable silence, the conversation turned back to the united armies and how best to get them into Trian. Ammorin listened while several ideas were proposed, but unfortunately, that's all they were at this point, ideas. Until they heard back from Gideon, there wasn't much they could do.

Yes, there were probably enough Dainin under Ohran's command to open Veilgates, but with so many Tambans just outside the city walls, it would be risky. Even so, it was better than the alternatives. He was about to say as much when the ward against eavesdropping trembled again.

A hush fell over the room as he exchanged looks with the other Dymas.

"The warding?" Brysia asked, and Ammorin nodded.

"I'll check on it," he said, then opened his Awareness toward the disturbance, wary but curious as to who might be so determined to get a look inside the palace. He moved cautiously, ready to withdraw the moment he glimpsed the mind of whoever might be probing.

But as he extended his Awareness beyond the ward, he encountered not one mind but dozens. They sensed him immediately, but instead of pulling back, they lashed at him with unbridled hatred, sending their thoughts in a barrage of Spirit-sound, frenzied, high-pitched, and murderous. Their words—if they were words—were in the Tamban language, and he didn't understand them. But he didn't need to—the sentiment was abundantly clear.

Wrapping his mind more deeply in *Jiu*, he withstood the assault and pressed on. Something else was at work here, and he wanted to see what it was. The small army of corrupted Awarenesses continued to lash at him as he searched, and he felt the first stabs of pain as one or more of them tried to sever his connection to *Ta'shaen*.

*It won't work*, he told them, not caring if they understood the Common Tongue. *And when I'm finished here, I will come for you.*

The attack on his mind intensified, but he fought through it, focusing instead on what lay beyond those attacking him. He found it a moment later, and his heart nearly stopped in his chest. It lay like a blanket across the whole of Fairimor Palace, a singularly powerful Awareness that made the hatred of those assaulting him seem like lover's kisses.

*We meet again, Nar'shein, Frel'mola* said.

A heartbeat later thousands of tendrils of corrupted Spirit swept in, and the crux points on Gideon's wards shattered like so many balls of glass.

With Marithen muttering incoherently at his side, Thex gently held her by the arm as they made their way out of the Dome and into the gardens of the Overlook. He felt pressed for time but couldn't bring himself to hurry the old woman along. She seemed so frail at times, physically as well as mentally. Right now was no different. In fact, she seemed even more distracted than usual. It made him wonder if she even remembered where they were going. Maybe allowing her to come with him to the front wasn't such a good idea after all.

A sudden tremor tickled his Awareness, and he knew instinctively that the wards over the palace were once again being tested by the enemy.

Beside him Marithen stopped walking, and the prophetic ramblings died on her lips as she stared at something far off in the distance.

When she turned to look at him a moment later, her eyes were focused and intense. "She's here," she said, and Thex flinched as *Ta'shaen* came alive with threads of corruption.

They seemed to come from everywhere at once, and he had just enough time to channel a protective shield of Spirit before the Veil was rent in a dozen places and *Jeth'Jalda* stormed into Fairimor Palace.

Ammorin's shout of warning came too late to save Ailor Dymas, and corrupted tendrils of *Sei'shiin* snuffed her from existence as the Veilgate she'd tried to open unraveled before her.

The crimson-robed *Jeth'Jalda* rushing through rents in the Veil struck again, and Erebius Dymas was tossed head over heels toward the fireplace as the sofa he was seated on exploded. A similar thrust of corruption upended Camiele and her three young companions, blistering their skin as it hurled them across the room. They landed in heaps a dozen paces away and lay still. Brysia didn't know if they were unconscious or dead.

A cleansing bar of *Sei'shiin* left Junteri's outstretched hand and one of the *Jeth'Jalda* bearing down on Brysia vanished in a flash of white. The woman's companions retaliated with streamers of Fire, and Junteri retreated into a protective shield of Spirit to defend herself. Hallie Dymas cast up a shield as well, but Krissen Dymas attempted to open a Veilgate. She was killed by corrupted streamers of *Sei'shiin* as the Veilgate collapsed.

Arrows hissed in from all sides as the *Bero'thai* on duty entered the fight, and three *Jeth'Jalda* staggered and went down. More arrows followed, but the razored shafts burst into splinters well short of their intended targets. A split-second later, the *Bero'thai* who'd loosed them burst apart as well, painting the *chorazin* with bright red Elvan blood.

It all seemed to happen slowly, as if time itself were being strangled by the attack, but Brysia knew everything she'd just witnessed had taken place in an instant. She also knew she couldn't just stand there dumbfounded while everyone else acted.

Angry now, she embraced her Gift and channeled a stream of *Ta* into the fresh-cut roses in the vases on the end tables. They came alive in a whipping, growing frenzy that snared the two nearest *Jeth'Jalda*, wrapping around their throats and killing them with dagger-length thorns.

The roses spent, she turned to the small ornamental trees she'd nurtured over the years, and they exploded from their ceramic pots in a flurry of roots and branches. The writhing masses swallowed two more *Jeth'Jalda*, and their screams were punctuated by the sound of breaking bones and spattering blood.

Before she could strike again, an invisible grip seized her by the throat, cutting off her air. She locked eyes with the *Jeth'Jalda* who held her, and the woman smiled malevolently as she started forward, scepter flaring brightly. Still struggling for breath, Brysia braced herself for what might follow.

A table struck the approaching woman with the force of a battering ram, and the invisible grip choking Brysia vanished. Gasping for breath, she sagged to her knees as Ammorin appeared above her.

"I've got you," he said, and the sounds of the tumult raging across the room lessened as a shield sprang into place.

Ammorin helped her to her feet as the crimson-robed *Jeth'Jalda* who'd invaded her home quickly surrounded her and the rest of her household. Jeweled scepters blazing with corruption, they channeled tendrils of Fire which danced along the edges of the Dymas' shields like something alive, testing them for weakness, taunting those inside. Brysia was relieved to find Elison among those who'd survived. He stood next to Pattalla, a look of utter rage on his face.

"Any chance you can open a Veilgate?" Brysia whispered.

"Not if we want to live," Ammorin answered. "You saw what happened to Ailor and Krissen. They were killed by the wards Gideon wrought to protect us from just such an attack. *Frel'mola* corrupted them somehow."

"I didn't think that was possible," she said, a sick feeling washing through her. Ammorin grunted. "Neither did I."

Brysia stared at the spot where Ailor had died. Gideon would be devastated when he learned his wards had been twisted in such a way. And he would blame himself for letting it happen. *He'll be even more devastated by* your *death*, she told herself. *Now focus and find a way out of this.*

She returned her attention to the *Jeth'Jalda*. All had long, dark hair but had shaved one side of their head. They all looked to be about the same age, and all were— She blinked in surprise at the discovery.

"They're all women," she said.

"Blood Maidens," Ammorin muttered. "*Frel'mola's* personal entourage of assassins. And every one of them as soulless and vicious as their Empress."

Near the fireplace, the air parted in a flash of blue, but the corrupted wards unleashed streamers of *Sei'shiin* which destroyed the two Dainin who tried to come through. A second Veilgate opened a moment later with the same result. This time three Chunin Dymas vanished in flares of red.

"We need to warn our Dymas about the ward," Brysia said, her heart breaking for those they'd just lost.

"Already done," Ammorin said. "There will be no more attempts to enter by Veilgate."

"But help is coming, right?"

"Ohran heads some twenty *Nar'shein*," Ammorin answered. "They arrived outside the palace by Veilgate along with dozens of Dymas from elsewhere in the city. Together, they are fighting their way inside as we speak." He looked down at her, his face creased with worry. "But the Blood Maidens didn't come alone. An army of *Jeth'Jalda* stands between us and those coming to help."

He glanced at the tendrils of Fire moving along the edges of his shield, then went to one knee so he could look her in the eyes. "Have no fear, High Queen of Kelsa," he said. "I swore an oath to protect you. That oath will be fulfilled, one way or another."

Smiling, she reached up and touched his weathered cheek. "I know it will. You're a *Nar'shein*."

He smiled, but it did little to hide the sudden look of sadness in his eyes.

She would have asked the reason for the look, but a corrupted Veilgate opened a short distance away, and an exquisitely beautiful woman in a shimmering gold dress stepped through from beyond. Her eyes, like her scepter, burned with the fires of hell.

Brysia's stomach knotted with fear, but she met the female Dreadlord's stare without blinking. *So, this is the Bride of Maeon*, she thought, steeling herself for what would follow.

As *Frel'mola's* rent closed behind her, Ammorin increased the amount of Spirit he was channeling into his shield, then settled in to wait. He could feel the exchanges of Power, both pure and corrupted, raging in the outer parts of the palace, and he knew it was only a matter of time before help arrived. He simply needed to hold on until it did.

"You don't need that," *Frel'mola* said, gesturing with her scepter, and Ammorin's shield burst apart around him. The inside of his head flashed bright with pain as he lost his hold on the Power. He staggered and almost went down. Only the vice-like grip of corrupted Air that took him by the throat kept him from falling on his face. A second band of Air wrapped around him, pinning his arms to his sides and holding him fast. The steely grip drove him to his knees even as it loosened its hold enough for him to breathe.

When the spots of light flashing in his vision faded, he found himself face to face with *Frel'mola.*

"It's been a long time, *Nar'shein*," she said. "How does it feel to know you have once again failed to defeat me?" She touched her scepter to his lips. "No need to answer, my pet. I can see it in your eyes."

He jerked against the bands binding his arms, his hands knotting into fists. If he could only reach her, he would tear her refleshed head from her body with his bare hands, then use her scepter as a club to kill the others.

She noticed the tensing of his muscles, and her eyes flared brightly with contempt as she leaned close and whispered in his ear. "And that, my dear *Nar'shein*, is why you will *always* fail."

The grip of Air tightened its hold, and he was tossed aside as if he were made of feathers. His breath left him in a rush as he thudded to a stop against the wall, but he pushed himself to his knees and embraced the Power, so close to using it as a weapon that Fire and Light crackled across his open palm.

The scepters of the nearest Blood Maidens flared with corruption as they prepared to defend their Empress, but *Frel'mola* laughed. "Even if you were skilled enough to strike me down," she taunted, "what then, *Nar'shein?*" She turned to face him, her arms spreading wide, inviting him to attack.

"Oh, wait," she continued, her tone mocking. "You wouldn't be *Nar'shein* anymore, would you?"

Her words stung as deeply as if she'd stuck him with the Power, and the memory of his experience with the female Agla'Con on the Overlook invaded his thoughts. He'd nearly broken his oath that day as well and had only been spared doing so by Talia's intervention.

Mortified by just how close he'd once again come to violating his calling as a *Nar'shein*, he pulled his Awareness back from the potent river of energy ready to break free from his hands.

*Frel'mola* sniffed her disgust. "Bind him," she said, and five of the nearest Blood

Maidens seized him in grips of Air and held him fast. "If he resists or attempts to embrace *Ta'shaen* again, kill his companions. Starting with those two."

Ammorin followed her gaze across the room to where Pattalla and Elison were on their knees in the midst of seven more of the crimson-robed assassins. Pattalla seemed dazed, and the bloody gash on the side of his head was purple and swollen. Elison was weaponless but seemed unharmed.

He locked eyes with the captain for a moment, then scanned the room for the others. Brysia still stood where she'd been when *Frel'mola* arrived, but Ammorin could feel the dark currents of corrupted Spirit that had severed her connection to the Power. Junteri had been severed as well. Kneeling next to her unconscious father, she pressed her hands to the sides of her head, dazed but alive.

Camiele and the rest of her young companions still lay where they'd fallen, but numerous Maidens had taken up positions around them, scepters at the ready—proof that the fledgling Dymas were still alive. He just needed to figure out a way to keep them alive until reinforcements arrived to help.

As if sensing his thoughts, *Frel'mola* turned a smile on him. "You might want to tell your Chieftain to stand down," she said. "If he persists in his foolishness, I will start killing hostages."

Ammorin clenched his teeth in anger as he opened his Awareness and stretched it toward the exchanges of Power rocking the outer palace. He found Ohran crouched beneath a shield of Spirit, sheltering a number of Chunin Dymas who were exchanging Power-wrought blows with the *Jeth'Jalda*. Carefully, he touched his friend's mind with his own.

*Chieftain.*

Ohran opened his Awareness to the touch, and a Communal link formed between them. *I hear you, Nar'shein*, came the reply.

*Stand down*, Ammorin told him, then sent a mental picture of the situation, and added. *If you don't, she will start killing hostages.*

*She will anyway*, Ohran said. *We cannot—*

*I will not let it happen*, Ammorin interrupted, and Ohran's shock was palpable as images of what Ammorin was considering made it across the link.

*You swore an oath*, Ohran objected.

*I've sworn many*, Ammorin agreed, stung by his mentor's disappointment. In that instant, Ohran's sadness became his, but he buried it beneath a mountain of determination. *These two, at least, I can keep.*

*But you—*

He severed the link and waited to see if *Frel'mola* or any of her Maidens had eavesdropped on the conversation. That he was still breathing suggested they hadn't.

Locking eyes with *Frel'mola*, he nodded. "It is done," he said, then offered a prayer that Ohran would comply. A moment later *Ta'shaen* began to still as the exchanges of Power lessened, then ceased altogether. Ohran had given him the time he needed. Now all he needed was a distraction.

"They aren't here for us," Thex said, then hurriedly let his shield drop and released the Power. It was risky, but not as risky as continuing to hold up a signal fire for every *Jeth'Jalda* in the area. Fortunately, enough of the Power was being wielded elsewhere in the palace to hide what he'd done.

Marithen released the Power as well, but it was clear from her expression that she was still watching something through her Awareness. Watching with eyes that would have been right at home on a leopard about to pounce. He'd never seen her so focused.

"Brysia needs our help," she said, starting for the Dome.

Thex caught her arm. "We're a little outnumbered right now," he told her. "Shouldn't we wait for reinforcements?"

"We are the reinforcements," she said. Clearly, the Marithen he'd known twenty years ago had returned. He just hoped she would stick around long enough to be of help.

"Do you have a plan?" he asked.

"A plan for what, dear?" She smiled sweetly, her eyes distant once more as she reached up and patted him on the cheek.

He ground his teeth in frustration. "Nothing," he told her, then looked across the gardens of the Overlook to hide his disappointment. He should have known it wouldn't last.

Then again, maybe it was for the best. He didn't imagine the two of them alone could have made much of a difference anyway. Not against so many. And not with the High Queen as a hostage. Her captors would kill her at the first sign of trouble.

But Veilgates weren't the only way to get Dymas atop the Overlook or into the Dome. The problem was he'd only been into the catacombs twice, and both times had been with Elison as his escort. Still, it was worth a try.

"Come with me," he said, then led her through the gardens to the gazebo sheltering one of the catacomb's entrances. After a quick scan of the immediate area with his Awareness to make sure it was free of the enemy, both in the flesh and in the luminescent world, he tripped the lever on the seal and watched it slide silently open.

He helped Marithen to the small room at the bottom of the winding stairs, then looked her in the eyes, trying to gauge what she was thinking. She seemed intrigued by the small room, so he helped her sit on the edge of the steps where she could look around. Leaving her here on her own was risky, but he knew he would be able to move faster without her.

"I need you to wait for me here," he told her. "I'll be back in a few minutes."

She didn't seem to hear, having slipped into one of her strange singsongs at the sight of the Blue Flame on the seal above her head.

Thex hesitated, still not sure he should leave, but when she started humming contentedly, he slipped quietly into the passage leading to Elsa's Font and broke into a run.

He'd been running for less than two minutes when he was met by Lavin Dium and a host of Kelsan Dymas.

"Thank the Light," he breathed, skidding to a stop in front of them. "Marithen and I thought we might be on our own. She's waiting in the chamber below the gazebo."

Lavin nodded. "Good. That's where we were headed. Captain Tas and Javan Galatea are leading other Dymas to exit points in the Fairimor home. As soon as everyone is in position, we'll strike." He motioned for Thex to lead the way.

Turning on his heel, Thex hurried back the way he'd come, so relieved to have help he could have wept for joy. They *would* save the Queen. They would—

The thought died as he reached the chamber where he'd left Marithen and found it empty.

A moment later the Earthsoul trembled as if hell itself had just arrived in the palace above.

"What is it you want?" Brysia asked, pleased with how calm she sounded.

*Frel'mola* laughed. "Why, I want everything, my dear young Queen. Starting with the head of your son. He is the *Mith'elre Chon,* is he not?"

"He is," Brysia answered. "But he isn't here. If he were, you would have already been destroyed."

"My, my," *Frel'mola* said, putting a hand over her heart as if startled, "it's a good thing I came when he is away then, isn't it?"

She let her fiery gaze move around the room as if looking for something, then frowned. "No throne," she said at last. "What kind of a Queen doesn't have a throne?" She waved her hand dismissively. "No matter. I'll have one made."

"Why bother?" Elison asked. "You won't be here long enough to enjoy it."

*Frel'mola's* eyes narrowed as she turned to see who'd spoken. "Well, aren't you the brave captain?" she asked, then motioned to one of the Blood Maidens standing behind him. "Kill him," she said.

The hard-eyed woman nodded, and a blade of Fire sprang from the end of her scepter. It hissed like something alive as she raised it above her head and prepared to strike.

"Excuse me," a voice said, and everyone in the room turned as Marithen Korishal came in from the Dome. She looked as she always did—lost and confused, and so utterly feeble that it was a miracle she could get around on her own. "Excuse me," she repeated. "I'm looking for my daughter. Have any of you seen her?"

*Frel'mola* arched an eyebrow as if she couldn't quite believe the audacity of the new arrival, then motioned for Elison's executioner to hold. The woman frowned, clearly disappointed that the killing stroke would need to wait, and the blade of Fire vanished.

Brysia breathed a sigh of relief for the reprieve only to hold the next breath for fear of what would happen next.

"And who might you be?" *Frel'mola* asked, and it was clear from the utter disdain in her voice that she didn't consider Marithen to be a threat. Neither did the Blood Maidens, as evidenced by the ripple of laughter moving across the room.

Marithen smiled in response to the laughter, seemingly oblivious to the malice in it. Only then did Brysia notice how clear the old woman's eyes were. How focused.

"I'm Marithen Korishal," she answered, and streamers of *Sei'shiin* erupted from her fingertips.

Marithen's attack on *Frel'mola* was the distraction Ammorin had been waiting for, and he took full advantage of the moment. Embracing the Power, he shattered the bands of Air binding him with a thrust of Spirit, then channeled a grip of Air and yanked the scepter from the hands of the nearest Blood Maiden.

She whirled toward him in shock, then died in a spray of blood as he clubbed her with her own scepter, shattering her skull and sending her careening into three others. The collision knocked them off balance, and they stumbled forward, corrupted Fire spewing from their scepters as they turned to face him.

He turned the searing blasts away with a shield of Spirit, then hurled the scepter as if it were a dagger. It struck the closest Maiden in the chest, sinking clear to the jeweled end as she toppled backward into death. The remaining two vanished in flashes of white as bars of *Sei'shiin* channeled by Marithen took them in the back.

Wrapping himself in a sheltering bubble of Spirit, he started for Brysia, kicking over sofas and chairs in his haste to reach her. As expected, the Blood Maidens who'd been restraining her had turned their attention to Marithen, so enraged by the old woman's attack that they didn't see Ammorin until it was too late. They died as his massive hands closed over their heads and he snapped their necks.

He dropped them like the filth they were, then brought Brysia into his shield and knelt to look her in the eyes. "Are you hurt?"

"No," she said, then looked at the conflagration in the center of the room. "But Marithen..."

"Holding her own," he told her. "But she won't last much longer without help."

Channeling even more Spirit into his shield, he fastened a number of crux points and set them in place to maintain the protective barrier in his absence. He'd seen the weaves *Frel'mola* had used to break through his first shield so easily, and he wasn't going to let it happen again. Maeon himself couldn't break this one.

When the last crux point was in place, he checked the shield one last time and smiled in satisfaction. The Queen would be safe until reinforcements arrived. Regardless of what happened to him, his oath to Brysia would be fulfilled.

"I've tied off the shield," he told her. "Stay right where you are and you will be safe."

"Where are you going?" she asked, clearly alarmed.

He looked to where *Frel'mola* waited inside a corrupted shield of Spirit. Her eyes were filled with rage as she watched Marithen, but she seemed content to let her Blood Maidens do the fighting. The very sight of her tightened his resolve to see this through. He'd made many mistakes in his life—what came next wouldn't be one of them.

"I have unfinished business with the Bride of Maeon," he said, then opened a hole in the shield and started toward her. A second, less powerful shield sprang into place around him as he channeled the threads of Spirit necessary to protect himself from the Blood Maidens. Thrusts of killing Power struck it repeatedly as he moved.

He'd only gone a short distance when he felt the brush of Pattalla's Awareness. He glanced in his friend's direction, but he didn't open himself to a mind-link. He didn't want Pattalla to know what he had planned. He was just grateful his friend was alive and that Elison and the wounded Dymas were under his protection. It made it easier to accept what might come next.

*Frel'mola* sensed his use of the Power as he drew near and turned a disdainful eye on him. Her scepter flared brightly as she entered the conflict, and Marithen vanished beneath a barrage of Night Threads. Terrible, scream-like thunder shook the room, shattering everything made of glass and overturning the smaller pieces of furniture.

Marithen's attack cut off, but the tremor of uncorrupted Power resonating within the barrage told Ammorin the old woman's shield had held.

"Not as strong as you think, are you?" Ammorin said, using a tendril of Air to pull a scepter from the grasp of one of the fallen Maidens. Hefting it like a club, he continued his advance.

The smile that moved over *Frel'mola's* face held no humor. "Strong enough," she said, and a stab of darkness struck his shield, bursting it apart just as it had the last time.

The inside of his head exploded with pain, and the scepter slipped from his grasp as he dropped to his knees. He fought through the pain and looked up to find her watching him with disgust. In her arrogance, she'd dropped her shield. Just as he thought she would.

"You are a failure," she scoffed.

"Maybe," he said. "But unlike you, I learn from my mistakes."

The look of surprise on her face as he burned her from existence with a white-hot bar of *Sei'shiin* was even better than he'd imagined it would be, but he didn't stop there. Rising to his feet, he turned on the Blood Maidens, unleashing a barrage of cleansing destruction that would have made even Gideon proud.

His days of a *Nar'shein* were over.

His days as a Soldier of God had just begun.

# CHAPTER 64

## New Directions

GIDEON FINISHED SETTING THE FINAL crux points into place, then opened a Veilgate to a hill overlooking the Kelsan camp to inspect his handiwork. Idoman and Beraline followed him through, and their eyes went wide at what they found. There, clearly visible to the enemy army making camp near the mouth of Mendel Pass, was a Power-wrought illusion of the united armies preparing to stand their ground. And it didn't matter if they were looking with natural eyes or through the eyes of *Ta'shaen*. They would see exactly what he wanted them to. Only when the perimeter was breached in person would the truth be known.

"Where did you learn to do that?" Idoman asked.

"The Battle of Capena," Gideon answered. "How do you think Valinar Aigin and I and the others survived being outnumbered three to one? Trickery. We lured our enemies in by making ourselves look more vulnerable than we were."

He glanced at the moon making its trek across the night sky and added, "But that particular illusion didn't take nearly as long to create as this one. Come. Let's check the progress of the evacuation." He motioned them through the Veilgate, then followed, letting the gate slide closed behind him.

It didn't take them long to locate Joneam Eries—he was surrounded by a small army of warders and hadn't moved far from the command tent. Quintella Dymas and Captains Tarn and Dennison were with him.

"Well?" Joneam asked when they reached him. "How does it look?"

"It's perfect," Idoman said. "Even I couldn't tell it was an illusion, and I knew what I was looking at."

Joneam looked to the line of watchfires marking the front edge of Death's Third March. "And you are sure it will hold until morning?"

Gideon nodded. "It will hold until their forward ranks reach the perimeter and trigger the Power-wrought traps."

Idoman arched an eyebrow at him. "What traps?"

"The ones you and I and the others are going to set." He looked back to Joneam. "Where are we with the evacuation?"

"The cavalry—both horse and Krelltin—are away," he said. "The Dymas escorting them will maintain the wards of bended Light until they are out of view of Death's Third March. Then they plan to ride hard for the eastern townships. Once there, they should be able to make their way around to Trian's southern gates without drawing too much attention from *Frel'mola te Ujen*. Their attention seems to be on Ohran and his men, anyway, which isn't surprising considering the history between the two nations."

"Let's hope it stays that way," Gideon said. "What of our footmen?"

"Divided into manageable groups and waiting to leave through Veilgates."

"Good," Gideon said, pleased with the report. "Do our Dymas have strength enough to get them away safely?"

"They said they do," Joneam answered. "But if not, Ohran said he will send *Nar'shein* to assist." He looked around at the wagons and tents and other equipment. "Too bad we have to abandon all of this, though. It's a bloody waste."

"But not a total waste," Gideon said. "I was able to use it to add depth to the illusion."

"Well, that's good, I guess," Joneam said. "Now, if you will excuse me, I need to speak with Generals Shurr and Alishar."

He moved away with his warders, and Gideon turned to Idoman. "Are you up to the task of creating a few more traps?" he asked.

Idoman grunted as if offended. "As if you even had to ask."

Quintella and Beraline joined them, and together they headed back toward the northern edge of the illusion. They were nearly there when a Veilgate opened and a female *Nar'shein* hurried through from beyond. She released the Power, allowing the gate to close, but her face was masked with concern as she cast frantically about the area.

Gideon knew instinctively that she was looking for him and a knot of dread tightened in his stomach as he hurried forward to meet her.

She spotted him, and a look of relief washed over her face as she hurried forward to meet him. "*El'kali*," she said urgently, "there is trouble in Fairimor Palace." Then, as if sensing his intent to embrace the Power, she added, "Please, don't open a Veilgate into the inner palace. The wards were corrupted by *Frel'mola*."

The feeling of dread flashed into panic, and he suddenly found it difficult to breathe. If anything had happened to Brysia...

"The Queen?" he asked, forcing the words out even as he braced himself for the answer.

"We don't know," she said. "The ward against eavesdropping was also corrupted so we haven't been able to get a look inside."

Gideon realized his hands had knotted into fists, and he forced himself to relax. He looked at Idoman.

"Go," the young Dymas general said. "We've got things here."

"I'm coming with you," Beraline said. "Marithen—" She broke off, her throat tight with worry.

Gideon nodded his thanks to Idoman, then turned to the Dainin. "Get us as close as you can," he said, then he and Beraline followed her through into a firestorm of corrupted wieldings.

⺆

Accompanied by Lavin and the Dymas he'd met in the catacombs, Thex Landoral raced into the Fairimor home to find Marithen hunkered beneath a shield of Spirit near the splintered remains of the dining table. From across the room, one of the Jeth'Jalda continued to hammer the old woman with stabs of corrupted Spirit.

He'd felt the vicious attack of Night Threads channeled by Frel'mola, and he'd feared the worst. Finding her alive was nothing short of a miracle. Clearly Marithen was stronger than any of them had imagined. But she was injured, and she needed help.

Opening his Awareness to the attack, he traced the threads of corruption back to their source, then raised his hand and sent streamers of Sei'shiin lancing toward the culprit. The shimmering tendrils burst apart in flashes of white as the shield withstood them, but the impact sent the woman staggering.

She vanished in a flare of white a heartbeat later when a spear-like thrust of Sei'shiin punched through her shield and struck her in the back. Thex followed the path of the cleansing strike to its origin, and his eyes went wide when he saw it had come from Ammorin.

The Dainin Chieftain stood in a sheltering bubble of Spirit surrounded by a dozen or more Jeth'Jalda, his eyes bright with a killing fury as he continued to wield Ta'shaen as a weapon. Two more Jeth'Jalda flared from existence when Ammorin channeled a sword-like blade of Sei'shiin and sliced through shields and wielders alike.

Next to Thex, Evelyn Dymas gaped openly. "Did he just—"

"Yes," Thex answered. "Now let's help him out."

As Pattalla Tamar continued to shelter Elison and the wounded Dymas from the maelstrom engulfing the Fairimor home, a different storm was brewing inside him. Ammorin Shad'dai, Chief Captain of the Nar'shein Yahl, his beloved friend and mentor for the past five hundred years, had broken his oath. He'd betrayed the order to which he'd been called, smashing two thousand years of tradition and turning his back on his fellow Nar'shein.

Pattalla watched as his friend destroyed another one of the Blood Maidens with a thrust of Sei'shiin, and the storm raging in his heart intensified. Not because he was appalled by Ammorin's actions, but because he was starting to think he wanted to be part of them. He wanted to join the fight—not with net and spear, but with *Ta'shaen*.

*No*, he thought. *Using the Power to kill is wrong.*

It was a truth he'd been taught from birth. A truth he'd sworn an oath to live by. A truth he'd never doubted.

Until now.

Now, as he watched his dearest friend use the purest form of cleansing energy known to man, it seemed foolish not to use it in such a way. It seemed wrong not to.

He looked down at Camiele Dymas. She'd regained consciousness, and he'd healed her of her wounds. Her eyes were wide with wonder as she watched Ammorin engage the remaining Blood Maidens.

"Are you well enough to take control of the shield?" he asked her.

She looked up at him and nodded. "If it isn't for too long."

"It won't be," he said. "I'm going to help Ammorin end this."

Camiele smiled at him. "I was hoping you would. With the world coming apart like it is, a new direction might not be such a bad thing. Even for the *Nar'shein Yahl*."

"It isn't," he agreed, then gave her control of the shield and embraced the Gifts of Light and Spirit. When he was ready, he nodded to Camiele, and she opened a hole in the shield.

The war of conflicting emotions raging in his heart was swept away by a profound sense of peace as he wove the two Gifts together into a cleansing bar of *Sei'shiin* and erased the nearest Maiden from existence in one curt, white-hot flash.

*This*, he thought with a smile, *is what it means to be a Keeper of the Earth.*

With his shield firmly in place, Ohran Peregam watched in contemplative silence as Gideon destroyed yet another *Jeth'Jalda* with a fiery burst of *Sei'shiin*. The Chunin Dymas fighting alongside him cheered, their adoration for the big Dymas evident in their eyes and voices.

Since his arrival, Gideon had single-handedly turned the tide of the battle, ending the stalemate caused by the *Nar'shein's* oath against using the Power as a weapon. The Guardian of the Blue Flame had destroyed eight Tamban Power-wielders in the first few moments after arriving, and Beraline Hadershi had eliminated another two.

Inspired by the Kelsan hero and his companion, the Dymas who'd come with Ohran and his *Nar'shein* had doubled their efforts, and *Jeth'Jalda* were falling like flies. They were on the run now, and Gideon and the others were pressing them with even more vengeance.

And all Ohran could do at the moment was help shield those who were doing the killing. That, and heal those injured by enemy strikes.

Behind him, the rooms and hallways of Gideon's advance were littered with the smoking fragments of ruined furniture and shards of glass from shattered windows and mirrors, but the *chorazin* remained unscathed, an indestructible kill box which had amplified Gideon's strikes.

The chamber ahead was fairing similarly, and Fire and lightning danced along the smooth grey-green *chorazin* like something alive, an inferno of destruction that obliterated everything not wrapped in shields of Spirit.

As he watched, a marble statue of Siamon Fairimor exploded into superheated shards, and two *Jeth'Jalda* in the vicinity were knocked off their feet. Their corrupted shields wavered, then collapsed, and Gideon destroyed them with *Sei'shiin*.

Without breaking stride, Gideon continued his advance as the remaining *Jeth'Jalda* retreated into the next corridor, and spears of cleansing destruction lanced from his outstretched hands to explode against their shields. Another *Jeth'Jalda* died. Then another.

The way ahead was the shortest route to the inner palace, and Gideon was determined to clear a path through it, even if he had to kill every last one of those who stood between him and his Queen to do so.

From somewhere up in the Fairimor home, a powerful burst of uncorrupted *Ta'shaen* rippled the spiritual fabric of the Earthsoul, and Ohran knew with certainty it had come from Ammorin. He'd seen his friend's intent during their brief conversation through the mind-link.

He pursed his lips tightly with sadness. He'd been holding out hope Ammorin would find another way, but it wasn't to be. Ammorin had broken his oath as a *Nar'shein*.

More surges of cleansing Power followed in rapid succession, but the ward against eavesdropping prevented Ohran from viewing them through his Awareness. All he could do was measure the intensity of the strikes by the tremors they sent rippling through the spiritual fabric of the Earthsoul. Then suddenly the tremors ceased. The battle in the Fairimor home was over.

As if sensing their Empress had been defeated, the *Jeth'Jalda* fighting in the corridor ahead of Gideon gave up trying to stand their ground and began fleeing through Veilgates. Gideon continued to strike at them as they left, but they were gone within moments. The tremors of corruption rocking Ohran's Awareness stilled.

When he was certain the area was free of the enemy, he released the Power and moved forward to join Gideon. As he did, a number of *Nar'shein* channeled sprays of water to extinguish the fires burning here and there across the room, while others channeled currents of Air to move the smoke up and out through the glassless windows and skylights.

Gideon waited until Ohran joined him, then they started for the corridor leading to the inner palace together.

"You and I have something to discuss," Gideon said, his tone so matter of fact it caught Ohran by surprise.

"And what is that?" he asked, stooping to avoid hitting his head on the shattered and tangled remains of a glowstone chandelier.

"You know bloody-well what!" Gideon snapped, then clenched his jaw to regain his composure. After a long deep breath, he continued. "My apologies, Chieftain. My anger isn't for you but for the situation. And for myself. What happened here is my fault. I never should have left the palace." He looked over, his blue eyes troubled. "If I'd have been here, Ammorin wouldn't—"

"You don't know that," Ohran said, cutting him off. "And I will not allow you to blame yourself. This was *his* choice. Now he must face the consequences of his actions."

"And that," Gideon said, his expression hardening once more, "is what you and I need to discuss."

亡

When the doors leading in from the Dome opened and Gideon strode in with Ohran Peregam at his side, Brysia allowed herself to relax. But as her tension left her, the carefully constructed wall she'd built around her emotions crumbled, and tears wet her cheeks as she rushed forward to meet him. He took her in his arms and hugged her tightly for a moment, then pressed his lips to her ear.

"I'm sorry I wasn't here," he whispered. "Can you forgive me?"

"Don't I always?" she asked, then stepped back to look him in the eyes. As expected, they were troubled. It was a look she knew all too well. She'd seen it a thousand times during the early days of their marriage when he'd take the weight of the world on his shoulders as if he alone were responsible for bearing it.

"Nothing that happened here is your fault," she told him. "So put it out of your head right now."

"That's exactly what I told him not five minutes ago," Ohran mumbled, and Brysia looked over to find the Dainin scowling at Gideon. "Maybe he'll believe it now that he's heard it from you."

Gideon met Ohran's stare without blinking, then took Brysia's hand and led her across the room to where Ammorin and the others waited. They'd cleared an area in the middle of all the debris and had arranged the few surviving pieces of furniture into a small semicircle. Everyone rose as she approached, but she motioned for them to retake their seats.

Ammorin and Pattalla, however, moved forward to meet them and each took a knee in front of Ohran. Heads bowed, they waited for him to speak.

A long, uncomfortable silence followed as Ohran studied them, and everyone in the room held his or her breath as they waited for the Chieftain to speak. Everyone except Gideon. He didn't seem at all concerned about what was to follow. If anything, he looked excited. A moment later she found out why.

"I see you, *Nar'shein*," Ohran said, and both Ammorin and Pattalla snapped their heads up in surprise.

"Don't speak," Ohran told them. "I'm still not sure that I agree with *El'kali* on this matter. In light of the sacred charge given you by the Earthsoul, you are oath breakers, and your brothers and sisters in the order will see you as such. Many will say you no longer deserve to be called Keepers of the Earth."

"But they saved all of us," Camiele interrupted, and Brysia turned to see her pushing herself up from one of the sofas. She was unsteady on her feet as she started toward them, but anger glittered in her eyes. "Ammorin destroyed the Bride of Maeon," she continued. "How is that even remotely deserving of your contempt?"

"Easy, young lady," Gideon said, trying unsuccessfully to hold back a smile. "He's not finished yet. Besides, I said that very thing to him not five minutes ago." He turned to look at Ohran, and the Chieftain's face pinched into an even deeper frown that the words he'd spoken just minutes earlier to Gideon were being used against him. Brysia bit her lip to keep from smiling.

"However," Ohran continued as if nothing had happened, "it has become increasingly difficult to ignore the wisdom in Gideon's argument." He paused and leveled a flat stare at Gideon. "It is, by the way, an argument he's made numerous times over the past two hundred years."

"And what argument is that?" Camiele asked, her anger giving way to curiosity.

Ohran took a deep breath and let it out resignedly. "That the Keepers of the Earth and the Soldiers of God are one in purpose. Both are charged with protecting the Earthsoul and with keeping and sustaining life. And while our methods have differed over the years, an Agla'Con killed with a spear is—to quote Gideon—*just as dead as if he'd been killed with the Power.*"

He turned his attention back to Ammorin and Pattalla, then, with some effort, he forced a smile. "What you two did here tonight fulfilled the charge of both callings, and it fulfilled it in grand fashion. You preserved the lives of those in your charge and eliminated the most vile woman ever to walk the earth. But what's more, the destruction of the Bride of Maeon and her Maidens was not an act of personal vengeance—it was justice for the Earthsoul."

He smiled again, more genuinely this time. "Rise *Nar'shein*," he said. "And take your place in the army of *El'kali*. He is your Chieftain now. May the Earthsoul shelter and protect you in the Cleansing Hunts to come."

"Thank you, Chieftain," Ammorin said, but Ohran waved him off.

"Don't thank me," he said. "This is Gideon's doing. I'm still not convinced it's a good idea."

"It is," Gideon said, "because contrary to what I said earlier, the Agla'Con we kill *are* more dead than those you kill because *Sei'shiin* eliminates the chance of a refleshing."

"So *Frel'mola* is gone for good?" Camiele asked.

Gideon nodded. "And may she suffer the wrath of her so-called husband for the eternities to come. Now, let's undo the wards she so easily corrupted and refortify the palace. The real fight, I'm afraid, is still yet to come."

*Yes,* Brysia agreed silently, her eyes on Ammorin and Pattalla. *But it will be much easier now.* For contrary to Ohran's belief that Ammorin and Pattalla would be shunned as oath breakers by their brothers and sisters, she believed they would be received by many of them as heroes.

The future of the *Nar'shein Yahl* may have just been altered forever.

Supreme Commander Ibisar Naxis stood in stunned silence as the full weight of what he'd just learned settled upon him. *Frel'mola* destroyed? It... it didn't seem possible. The Dark Bride was the most powerful *Jeth'Jalda* to ever walk the earth. Much more powerful than Throy bloody Shadan and Aethon Fairimor. More powerful even than the one claiming to be the *Mith'elre Chon.*

And yet somehow she'd been destroyed. Really and truly destroyed. No chance of a Refleshing. Just... gone.

For as long as the Veil remained intact, anyway. Once Con'Jithar claimed the Earthsoul, she would return, even if it was only in spirit form. In the meantime, he was on his own to lead Tamba's forces.

He looked at Trian's outer wall rising tall and dark above the rooftops of the township his army occupied, and for a moment he was at a loss on how to proceed.

Bringing *Frel'mola te Ujen* here was part of Maeon's plan—a strict directive given to *Frel'mola* by the Dark Lord himself. But without *Frel'mola* here to lay claim to the throne, the invasion now seemed pointless.

And yet he couldn't ignore the Dark Lord's wishes. Not if he wanted a place of glory in the world soon to come. Maeon expected blood and death and chaos to fall upon this city, and he expected Tamba to lead the charge.

He knotted his hands into fists as he weighed his options. Return to Berazzel or stay and fight? There was really only one choice. His best bet for power and dominion in Con'Jithar would be to finish what *Frel'mola* had started.

First, though, he needed to deal with those who'd failed to protect her. Knowing what they were capable of made that failure all the more infuriating.

"You have some explaining to do," he said, his eyes boring into those of the Blood Maidens who'd brought him the news. The only three to have survived the failed attack, they knelt in the middle of the darkened street, surrounded by the rest of the *Jeth'Jalda* who'd returned alive. They seemed uncharacteristically nervous for women of their reputation.

"You said she was destroyed by *Sei'shiin,*" he continued. "Who dealt the blow? The Guardian of Kelsa? The *Mith'elre Chon?* Out with it, burn you! Who destroyed our Empress?"

"A Dainin," one of the women answered, and an audible murmur of surprise swept through those around her. Ibisar shared their surprise, but he kept his face smooth as he studied the woman. She had to be mistaken. The *Nar'shein* didn't use the Power as a weapon. Foolish as it seemed to him, it was in violation of their supposed charge as Keepers of the Earth.

He narrowed his eyes at her. "Are you certain?" he asked. "You didn't mistake another's wielding for his?"

"No, Supreme Commander," she answered. "I saw the strike through my Awareness. And it wasn't his only use of the Power as a weapon. He destroyed seven or eight of my sisters with *Sei'shiin* as well."

Ibisar looked back at the dark outline of Trian's wall rising against the starry backdrop of the night sky, and a cold pit settled in his stomach. Even with their foolish code the *Nar'shein* were a force to be reckoned with. The prospect of facing *Nar'shein* who'd forsaken their oath not to use the Power to kill caused him to question his decision to remain here as part of Death's Third March.

"What would you have us do, Supreme Commander?" the Maiden asked, and he turned to find her and the other two watching him expectantly.

"You know what is required," he told them. "See to it quickly."

Without another word the three women rose, and the crowd of *Jeth'Jalda* parted before them as they moved away down the street. They'd scarcely made it out of sight when a rent hissed open where they'd been kneeling and Aethon Fairimor strode through with Raelig Tiafin and a number of *Jeth'Jalda* loyal to the Fist of Con'Jithar.

Ibisar locked eyes with Tiafin for a moment, putting as much contempt for the man into the look as he could, then dismissed him as the maggot he was and faced Aethon Fairimor. The self-proclaimed 'first among the living' wore a tight smile that immediately put Ibisar on edge.

"My condolences on the loss of your Empress," Aethon said, sounding anything but sincere. His tone grated almost as much as the fact that he'd learned of her destruction so quickly. He must have spies among the *Jeth'Jalda* of *Frel'mola te Ujen*.

"What is it that you want?" Ibisar asked flatly.

Aethon spread his hands wide in a display of friendship. "Just a word with my allies in this cause," he said. "With *Frel'mola* destroyed, you are the head of this army now."

Ibisar nodded. "You may speak," he said, pleased with how condescending he made it sound. He was indeed the head of this army, and Aethon would do well to remember it.

Aethon cast a meaningful glance across the area. "Perhaps we should go somewhere a little more private," he suggested, then opened a rent into the throne room of Berazzel.

"I could have chosen a more neutral location," Aethon continued, "but I wanted to prove that I have no ill will toward you or *Frel'mola te Ujen*. We are, after all, small cogs in a much larger wheel."

Ibisar scowled at him. He had no desire to go anywhere with the man, but to refuse now would be to show weakness in front of his men. Especially since the supposedly neutral sight was Berazzel. He suspected Aethon had sent his own men ahead to secure the place.

"After you," Ibisar said, motioning Aethon forward.

"This won't take long," Aethon told Commander Tiafin. "Don't start a war with *te Ujen* while we are away. They are, as I said, our allies, not our rivals."

"Yes, Lord Fairimor," Tiafin said, and the look he shot Ibisar's way spoke volumes. He'd noticed the omission of *Frel'mola's* name in the title and found it amusing.

Ibisar's men, on the other hand, were furious. Several even seized the Power.

"It's *Frel'mola te Ujen*," one of the men said, and Aethon turned to regard him without blinking. Daring him, Ibisar knew, to try something with the Power. Catching the man's eye, Ibisar shook his head, ordering him to stand down.

Aethon stared at the man a moment longer, then moved through the rent into *Frel'mola's* throne room. *And it is* her *throne room*, Ibisar thought as he followed Aethon through. *Not mine. Not yours. Hers.*

As the rent snapped shut behind them, he cast about the room, searching for the ambush he was certain was waiting for him. When he found the room empty, he met Aethon's gaze, but he didn't relax, still expectant of treachery.

"We need to discuss your ascension," Aethon told him. "With *Frel'mola* destroyed, someone needs to assume command here in Tamba."

Ibisar narrowed his eyes at the man. *This* was Aethon's reason for bringing him here? To separate him from his men by having him lay claim to the throne? What kind of a fool did the man think he was? *Frel'mola* may have been barred from returning to this world as a *Maa'tisis*, but she would return with a vengeance once the Veil collapsed.

"I have no desire to rule my homeland," Ibisar told him. "Unlike you, I know where my allegiance lies. My place is with my men."

"I thought you might say that," Aethon told him, and the very air around him went dark as he embraced *Lo'shaen*.

Ibisar seized the Power to defend himself, but Aethon severed his connection as easily as he had the last time he'd confronted the man. Then a searing pain lanced through his mind as something dark forced its way into his thoughts. *Thought Intrusion*, he realized, and for the first time in a very long time, he felt true fear.

He tried to resist, but Aethon was too powerful, and the tendrils of darkness bored ever deeper. Like something alive, they snaked through every part of his Awareness, laying bare his thoughts and intentions, robbing him of free will. Only when the threads of darkness began to take root did he realize what was coming. Aethon wasn't content just to know his thoughts, he was taking control of them. This was Coercion.

*Yes*, Aethon said, his voice sounding loudly in Ibisar's thoughts. *But I will leave just enough of your mind intact for you to appreciate what it is that I am doing.*

乇

The rent back from Berazzel opened much sooner than Raelig Tiafin had expected, and he watched with curiosity as Aethon and Ibisar moved through from beyond. Both men were frowning, but it looked as if they'd come to some sort of agreement. The Veilgate hissed shut as Ibisar released the Power.

"That was fast," Raelig said as Aethon joined him. "What did you two talk about?"

"A change in leadership," Aethon answered. "Quiet now. This will be best coming from the Supreme Commander."

Even more curious now, Raelig watched as Ibisar moved to face the *Jeth'Jalda* commanders of *Frel'mola te Ujen*. His stride was as pompous and arrogant as ever as he approached them, and several of the men took unconscious steps backward as he neared. He narrowed his eyes at them, his lips curling with disgust.

"Word of our Empress' death has already reached our homeland," he told them. "And as you might imagine, there are a number of fools who think to lay claim to the throne. Some have already begun marshaling forces to do just that."

A ripple of angry murmurs moved through the crowd, and Ibisar nodded his agreement to the sentiment. "But rest assured: The Throne of Berazzel belongs to *Frel'mola*, and I will destroy all those who seek to take it."

He paused, and it looked to Raelig as if he were struggling to find the words. He turned and glanced briefly at Aethon, then got control of himself and continued. "In my absence, Commander Raelig Tiafin will take charge of *Frel'mola te Ujen*."

Raelig didn't know whose surprise was greater, his or the *Jeth'Jalda* of *Frel'mola's* cult. He managed to keep his surprise in check, but murmurs of disapproval sounded loudly from Ibisar's men.

"Enough!" Ibisar growled, and silence fell over the assembly as completely as if he'd used the Power. "I don't like it any more than you do, but I am needed in Tamba, and Commander Tiafin is Tamba's highest ranking officer in my absence. Therefore, you will put aside your differences with the Fist of Con'Jithar and follow Commander Tiafin until I return. Maeon send it will be soon."

With that, he seized the Power and opened a rent back to Berazzel. He took a step toward it, then stopped and looked at his men.

"Avenge our Empress," he told them. "Show the Fist of Con'Jithar why *Frel'mola* favored you over them." The rent snapped shut behind him.

Raelig was silent a moment as he studied his newly acquired troops. He could see their contempt for him etched in their faces, but he knew their fear of Commander Naxis would keep them from lashing out. For now.

"You heard the commander," he said at last. "We have an Empress to avenge. Let's show the Nine Lands what the Fists of Tamba are capable of."

When a cheer went up from the assembly, he looked at Aethon in surprise.

"They're all yours, Commander," Aethon told him. Then, smiling as if he knew some great secret, he tore a rent in the Veil and disappeared into the darkness of Shadan's camp.

Raelig turned to his warders. "Send word to our captains," he told them. "We have work to do."

と

Trapped inside the maze of darkness wrought upon his mind by Aethon Fairimor, Ibisar Naxis watched in horror as his outward self continued to obey the commands impressed upon him by Aethon. True to his word, Aethon had left just enough of his mind intact for him to appreciate what was happening, and that made the Coercion all the more agonizing.

But the real torture, even more than feeling so completely powerless, was how he had no idea what was to come until it happened. It reminded him of all the times he'd been tormented by nightmares as a child. Nightmares which seemed to spring fully formed into his subconscious mind.

This nightmare, however, was real. And he feared it was just beginning.

He'd arrived back in *Frel'mola's* throne room through a rent the Coercion had caused him to open, but this time the room was occupied. A number of *Maa'tisis* had sensed Aethon's use of *Lo'shaen* and had come to investigate, believing, perhaps, that *Frel'mola* had returned and that she would have need of them.

"You are dismissed," he heard himself say, and his mind screamed in frustration as the *Maa'tisis* offered quick bows and started away.

*Come back, you fools!* he shouted. *This isn't me!*

"And make sure I am not disturbed," he added, watching as they pulled the doors closed behind them.

*Come back.*

He turned toward *Frel'mola's* throne, and a wave of panic swept through him at what it implied. *No!* He shouted, willing his body to stop, lashing against the darkness controlling his actions. *I will not sit on her throne.*

He reached the dais and started up the steps.

*I will not!*

Enraged, he pressed against the shroud of Coercion with such force that he felt some of the darkness dissipate. The part of his mind that was his grew stronger, and a rush of excitement swept through him at what it meant.

The Coercion was wearing off—he was regaining control.

He struck the darkness again as he reached the top of the dais, and his stride carried him past *Frel'mola's* throne. *Yes!* he thought. *I will—*

The thought died as he stopped in front of the rent Maeon had opened into Con'Jithar. He seized the Power.

*No!* he shouted, then watched helplessly as he channeled threads of corrupted Spirit and collapsed the wards *Frel'mola* had placed over the rent to shield Berazzel from demons.

He willed himself to run, but his body refused to move, rooted in place by Aethon's dark wielding

A moment later the first of what was sure to be an army of demons stepped into the living world.

"*Krosen ta fala Jeth'Jalda,*" the creature hissed, and the world vanished into darkness as it struck.

"Well?" Shadan asked as Aethon's rent closed behind him.

"It's done," Aethon answered. "*Frel'mola te Ujen* is now under the direction of Commander Tiafin."

"What did *Frel'mola's* lapdog think of his new assignment?"

Aethon chuckled. "Exactly what I wanted him to think. And like his overly ambitious mistress, he will trouble us no more."

Shadan's eye narrowed. "What exactly did you do?"

"Something I should have done a long time ago." He dismissed the matter with a wave of his hand. "But that is neither here nor there. With both Tamban Fists under our control, Death's Third March can proceed as planned. Trian will be ours by the end of the week."

He turned and looked at the watchfires of the Kelsan army glittering in the darkness to the south. Not much had changed since they'd settled in, but an awful lot of the Power had been wielded there over the past few hours. And that meant their Dymas were laying Power-wrought traps as part of their preparations to meet Death's Third March. *As if it will even matter,* he thought. The fools didn't stand a chance.

"First though," he said, turning to meet Shadan's one-eyed stare once more. "I want to destroy the rest of those who think they can slow our advance."

# CHAPTER 65

## *Waiting Game*

DAWN BROKE OVER TRIAN bright and clear, but to the south and east, storms raged on the horizon, a menacing line of swirling grey-black clouds as dark as the recently departed night.

Elison watched the intermittent flashes of lightning for a few moments, then continued along the top of the wall toward his destination. Dainin greeted him as he passed, and he returned the greetings with a smile. Most had *arinseil* nets tucked in their belts and carried spears, but there were many who bore no weapons at all. Inspired by Ammorin's destruction of *Frel'mola*, they'd set aside the traditional weapons of the *Nar'shein* to join the ranks of The Soldiers of God. From now on, their weapons would be wrought of *Ta'shaen*.

Their decision to forsake the oath they'd taken as *Nar'shein* didn't sit well with many of the Chieftains, but none of the elders would voice it openly. Not after hearing that Ohran Peregam had, for all intents and purposes, given Ammorin and Pattalla his blessing, reluctant though it had been. He was just glad Ohran was wise enough not to interfere with the agency of those whose only desire was to serve the Earthsoul and protect life.

He'd learned this morning that most of those who'd chosen to follow Ammorin's lead—some three hundred or so—were younglings in the *Nar'shein* order. Young for a Dainin, anyway. What was two hundred years when one's life span could reach a thousand? He hadn't been surprised by the information—the younger generations were always the first to adapt to new situations.

As he neared the towers rising above North Gate, he spotted Ohran standing at the wall with Chieftains Hammishin and Paddishor. They were looking out across the rooftops of Promish Township and appeared to be having a fairly spirited conversation. He caught the tail end of the conversation as he passed through the ward one of them had channeled to prevent eavesdropping.

"That is a terrible idea," Chieftain Hammishin said. "Not to mention sacrilegious."

"I agree," Chieftain Paddishor said. "Moreover—" he cut off when he sensed Elison's approach.

"Captain Brey," Ohran said, the maze of wrinkles on his face rearranging themselves into a smile. "What word from the Fairimor home?"

"Gideon finished unraveling the corrupted crux points," Elison said. "And new wards are being set under the direction of Erebius. Gideon and Brysia and those who were injured are finally getting some much needed rest."

"And you?" Ohran said, leaning closer and looking him in the eyes. "Did you get some rest?"

"A little," he lied. "But there is too much to do and not enough men to do it."

He moved to the wall and looked down at the maze of streets and rooftops spreading away to the north. The streets directly below the wall were empty, but the Tamban army was visible several blocks away, just out of effective striking distance with the Power. Surprisingly, they'd made no attempt to engage those atop the wall, content, it seemed to him, to wait for Death's Third March to join them.

"I overheard the last part of your discussion," he told the three. "What's a terrible idea?"

"Allowing those who've taken the name of El'kali to launch a preemptive strike," Hammishin said, and beside him Paddishor nodded.

Elison looked at Ohran. "And what do you think about it?"

The Grand Chieftain shrugged his massive shoulders, his expression resigned. "It isn't my decision to make."

"But—" Hammishin started only to be cut off by Ohran.

"We've been over this," he said, his tone firm but patient. "They answer to Gideon now."

"Then perhaps I should speak with them," Gideon said from behind them, and they turned as one to find him standing inside the ward against eavesdropping.

"You are supposed to be resting," Elison told him.

Gideon grunted. "I was about to say the same thing to you." Moving up to the wall, he gazed out over the township for a moment then looked at Ohran. "I agree with your counterparts that a preemptive strike is a bad idea," he said. "Our Dymas attempted a preemptive strike on the demon army approaching Aridan, and it ended in disaster. We lost a lot of good men who otherwise would have remained alive."

He turned his attention back to the Tambans. "Tempting as it is to attack, our best bet is to stay put and to continue fortifying our defenses."

"Then you will speak to the younglings?" Hammishin asked.

Gideon nodded. "I will."

A short silence followed, then Ohran said, "Elison said you finished removing Frel'mola's corrupted wards."

"Yes," Gideon said, his voice filled with bitterness. "It wasn't overly difficult considering that I was the one who set them in place." He shook his head. "I still can't fathom how she managed to turn them against us."

"What I can't fathom," Elison said, hoping to keep Gideon from dwelling on his perceived failure, "is why *Frel'mola* tried to seize control of the palace in the first place. She had to know it would infuriate Throy Shadan. Why pick a fight with Kelsa *and* with Death's Third March?"

"Vanity," Ohran said. "She and Shadan have been rivals for centuries. On both sides of the Veil. This was likely just another attempt to one-up him—to elevate herself in the eyes of Maeon."

"Well, she's gone now," Elison said. "Thanks to Ammorin." The comment drew a frown from Chieftains Hammishin and Paddishor, but Ohran kept his face smooth.

Gideon, however, smiled openly. "Thanks indeed," he said, then glanced down the wall at some of those who'd forsaken their oath as Keepers. "Now, if you will excuse me, I will speak with your younglings about their role in the battles to come."

"I'll come with you," Elison said. Bidding the *Nar'shein* Chieftains farewell, he hurried to catch up.

亾

Talia woke to the smell of rabbit being roasted over a fire. It pulled her from sleep as thoroughly as if she'd been kicked, knotting her stomach with hunger and making her mouth water. The fact that she *hated* rabbit proved just how hungry she was.

Clutching the blankets of her bedroll against her for warmth, she sat up to find Elliott tending a spit where three perfectly browned rabbits were sizzling in the heat. Overhead, the sky was a cloudless blue, but the absence of color on the tops of the pines showed that the sun had yet to rise.

Jase sat cross-legged on the ground in front of the altar, his eyes closed, his hands resting on his knees. His face was smooth, but she could feel the depth of his concentration through the *sei'vaiya*. She wondered how long he'd been awake, if, indeed, he'd gotten any sleep at all. His bedroll didn't look like it had been used.

She let her eyes move over the rest of the camp to find most all of the Dymas still asleep. The Shizu, however, were up and preparing breakfast at a number of small cook fires. Seth and Derian Oronei were noticeably absent.

She watched the Shizu for a moment longer, then looked back to Elliott and his rabbits.

He noticed she was awake and grinned at her. "Smell good, don't they?"

"They actually do," she admitted. "I guess I'm hungrier than I thought."

His grin widened as he lifted a skewer free of a second spit to reveal three small game birds. "Chukars," he said. "I know how much you dislike rabbit."

"Thank you," she said, touched by the gesture. Pulling the blanket around her shoulders, she joined him at the fire. "Where did you find them?"

He gestured at Augg. "Up on the slopes. Seth and I made a sweep of the island just as it was getting light. We wanted to make sure we are still alone here." Reaching into his pack, he withdrew two thin metal plates and a pair of forks. "The chukars are ready when you are."

She accepted a plate, then used a fork to pull a bird free of the skewer. It smelled wonderful and tasted even better. She ate in silence for a few minutes, content to take the edge off her hunger, then shot a meaningful glance at Jase.

"How long as Jase been awake?"

Elliott shrugged. "I don't know. He was sitting there when I woke up."

"He slept," Seth said, moving up behind her. "I woke him shortly before Elliott and I left on patrol."

"Well, that's good," Talia said, then narrowed her eyes at Seth. "How much rest did you get?"

"Enough," Seth answered. "It's sitting around that makes me tired."

"Better get used to it," Elliott said, offering Seth one of the rabbits. "Something tells me we are going to be here for a while."

The ward of Earth draped over Mount Augg made it easy for Jase to picture it as a blanket. A thin, tightly woven blanket no more than a single crux point deep. The realization that it didn't actually extend into the mountain should have been a relief, but it wasn't. He'd located more than three dozen crux points thus far and knew from his attempts to shatter them that they were but a fraction of those Fairimor the First had set in place. And they were spread over an area larger than the city of Trian.

Fortunately, the hurricane-like storm of light and sound that had nearly overwhelmed him on so many other occasions—particularly when he'd attacked the Agla'Con wards on Fairimor Palace—was noticeably absent. Without the thoughts and emotions and sounds of people—without the chaos of life that was a populated area—*Ta'shaen* was quiet. There was no hornet-like buzzing. No blinding flashes of light. No pain. Just the soft, ambient murmur of nature in all its simplicity.

He sighed inwardly. *Yes, but there is an awful lot of it to search.*

Steeling himself for the hours to come, he focused on the crux points he'd discovered so far, fixing them in his mind. They stretched from peak to base, but there was no recognizable pattern to them or to the threads of Earth and Spirit linking them together. Some had huge distances in between. Others were strung together like beads on a necklace. It didn't make any sense.

This was going to be more difficult than he thought.

Sailing high above Death's Third March in the saddle of his K'rresh, Asherim Ije'kre watched the forward ranks of shadowspawn as they approached the united armies of Kelsa, Elva, and Chunin. Contrary to his belief that they would sneak away during the night, the fools had finished digging in, determined to stand their ground.

In the growing light of the quickly brightening day, they were clearly visible, standing in formation, ready to fight. Along the forefront of the army, soldiers bearing spears and swords stood side by side with archers. Cavalry, both horse and Krelltin, were clustered on the edges, ready to hit Death's Third March on the flanks. Dymas in their ridiculous *kitara*-style jackets were visible throughout. The deployment was nearly identical to that which Croneam Eries had used during the Final Stand at the Battle of Greendom.

*And just like then*, Asherim thought. *It's a foolish tactic. And this time they won't be saved by Gideon's use of a Blood Orb. This time, my master's army will destroy them.*

Marut Saroj and his K'rresh glided near, and Asherim looked over to find the Zekan's face pinched into a frown. Marut reminded him a lot of Borilius Constas. And not just because he was Zekan—the man had a lust for killing and an even bigger lust for power. Like Borilius, he was prone to putting himself above the cause if he thought it would elevate him in the eyes of Maeon.

"Why aren't they attacking?" Marut said, shouting to be heard above the rush of wind.

Before Asherim could answer, a surge of *Ta'shaen* rippled through his Awareness, and a powerful dome of Spirit sprang into place above the united armies.

"There's your answer," Asherim said. "They really do mean to stand their ground."

Marut's eyes narrowed with malice. "Then why aren't we attacking?"

"Patience," he said. "Aethon intends to trigger whatever booby traps they've set for us." He pointed to the line of Shadowhounds and K'rrosha separating themselves from the main body of Shadan's army to take point in the attack. "See. He's already given the order."

"I wonder how the K'rrosha feel about being sent to the slaughter."

Asherim's response was automatic. "The dead feel no pain." *They also have no choice.*

Marut grunted. "And the Shadowhounds?"

"Too stupid to know the difference."

Nudging his K'rresh with his heel, he banked to the right, then leveled into a glide so he could watch the proceedings without having to look through the flapping of the beast's leathery wings.

Marut followed, and together they watched the K'rrosha and their Sniffers close on the forward ranks of the united armies. Surprisingly, none of them moved, confident, it seemed to him, in the ability of their Dymas to protect them.

The K'rrosha lowered their lances, and the tips flared to life with corrupted Fire. In response, lightning erupted above their heads, silvery stabs of energy that obliterated a number of the refleshed horsemen, their mounts, and the Sniffers running alongside them. But it did little to slow the advance, and Shadan's refleshed cavalry continued to close the distance.

Fire erupted upward from the ground as trip-lines of Spirit were severed, and more K'rrosha tumbled into flaming ruin. The high-pitched screams of their injured mounts, and the howls of blistered Shadowhounds assailed the sky. And still the charge continued.

Fifty yards remained between the two armies.

The men and women of the united armies stood their ground.

Forty. No one moved.

Thirty. Fire erupted from the lances of the Deathriders, swirling torrents of red-hot death that burst apart on the Dymas' shield.

Twenty. Tendrils of *Sei'shiin* erupted from the sky like a miniature lightning storm, and a dozen more K'rrosha vanished in bursts of white light.

Ten. Asherim held his breath as lance tips continued to spew their fiery death at the enemy shield.

Five. A titanic thrust of *Lo'shaen* channeled by Throy Shadan struck the shield, and it vanished. A heartbeat later the thunderous charge of the K'rrosha and their hounds plunged into the midst of the soldiers of the united armies—

And disappeared from view.

The entire length of enemy soldiers stood as if nothing had happened, poised and patient and ready for battle. Then the illusion collapsed as the K'rrosha riding within triggered another trap and a single burst of killing energy exploded outward. Reminiscent of the one Gideon had used in the Chellum camp all those nights ago in Talin Pass, it erased the K'rrosha and their hounds in an instant, and Asherim was left to stare in amazement at the abandoned enemy camp.

Standing in front of a string of small shops in the township he'd selected as the rendezvous point for the united armies, Idoman let the small Power-wrought window close, then turned to grin at Joneam Eries. "That worked out better than I thought it would."

Joneam nodded begrudgingly. He still wasn't happy about leaving so many supplies behind to be used or destroyed by the enemy, but he couldn't ignore the fact that Gideon's plan had spared the lives of every man and woman in the united armies. Now they just needed to finish getting everyone inside the walls of Trian.

The foot soldiers and the bulk of their Dymas were already within the city, having been taken directly there through Veilgates during the night. Those on horseback—or on Krelltin if they were Chunin—had finally reached Southeast Road, but they were still a mile out from where he and Joneam waited.

The Chellum Army, however, had just now come into sight down the road. Like the united armies, General Enue and his men had given the army of *Frel'mola te Ujen* a wide berth as they made their way south and west through the townships.

He didn't know if the Tamban invaders had held their position along North and

Northeast Road because they were oblivious to the armies sneaking around them, or if they simply didn't care. Either way, Gideon's plan had worked.

And thank the Light it had. Meeting the Tamban army anywhere out here in the townships would have been a disaster. There were simply too many civilians who hadn't heeded the warning to leave, thinking perhaps that they were far enough away from the areas under siege to be out of danger.

He watched as a significant number of people, eager to start their day, moved in and out of the shops, buying and selling and essentially going about their lives as if nothing out of the ordinary were happening. He couldn't decide if he should praise them for their faith in the military to protect them or if he should shout at them for their idiocy in remaining in an area where all hell was very literally about to break loose.

He was still trying to decide if he should say something when a Veilgate opened and Elison Brey strode through with Gideon and an escort of Dainin. None of the Dainin, he noted, carried *arinseil* nets, which suggested they'd followed Ammorin Shad'dai's lead and now bore the title of *El'Kali*.

He smiled at the thought. He'd heard of Ammorin's destruction of *Frel'mola*, of course—the news had swept through the ranks of the Children of *Ta'shaen* like wildfire—but seeing the Dainin warriors firsthand was a huge boost to his morale. Judging from the smile on Joneam's face, he was encouraged by the sight as well.

And why not? The Bride of Maeon destroyed. An army of *Nar'shein* turned *El'kali*—victory really wasn't beyond reach.

"Dymas General Leda," Elison greeted as he and the others approached. "It's good to see you again." He nodded to Joneam. "You, too, General Eries."

"It's good to be seen," Idoman replied. "There were a couple of moments the past few days when I didn't think any of us would make it out alive. Last night included." He looked at Gideon and smiled. "Your wards worked brilliantly," he told his friend. "Shadan must be beside himself with rage at how thoroughly you duped him."

"I hope he is," Gideon said. "He's much more predicable when he's angry."

"So, what is his next move, do you think?" Joneam asked.

Gideon scratched his cheek thoughtfully. "My guess is he'll order *Frel'mola te Ujen* to move to East Gate to make way for the Fist of Con'Jithar at Northeast Gate. Death's Third March will lay siege to North Gate because Shadan will want the shortest route to the palace for himself."

"Why not move directly into the palace through a Veilgate?" Joneam asked.

Gideon chuckled darkly. "After what happened to *Frel'mola*... he won't risk it. He might be the most powerful Agla'Con to ever walk the earth, but he is a coward. And he knows I have the Blood Orb that Lord Nid rescued from the temple in Melek. He won't attempt to take the palace until he's sure I'm dead or the Orb's reservoir of Earthpower is spent."

Idoman nodded. "And our next move?"

Gideon looked down the road at the Chellum Army. "We get the rest of our forces inside the city before Shadan arrives," he answered. "At the rate Death's Third March is moving, they will reach North Gate by this evening. Knowing Shadan, they will attack shortly thereafter."

"Are you sure he won't wait until tomorrow morning so as to give his troops a chance to rest?" Joneam asked. "I would."

"That's because you care about the people you lead," Gideon said. "Shadan doesn't. He'll watch every last one of his people die if it means getting what he wants."

Ohran Peregam felt the stirrings in *Ta'shaen* just moments before the Veil parted and Gideon came through with Elison Brey. Several others followed, including Idoman Leda, Joneam Eries, Taggert Enue, and Quintella Zakeya. The gate slid shut before Ohran got a good look at where they'd come from, but he suspected it was somewhere outside the city. He would have heard if the Chellum Army had reached Trian.

"I see you, *El'kali*," Ohran said as they neared.

"And we see you, *Nar'shein*," Gideon replied. Moving directly to the wall, he looked over the edge at the rooftops spreading away to the north and east, and added, "They're moving, aren't they?"

"Yes," Ohran answered. "As of about an hour ago."

"You were right," Idoman said. "Shadan wants the most direct route for himself."

"Which is why," Ohran said, wishing it were otherwise, "I asked the *Ara'so Nar'shein* to join me and the other Chieftains at North Gate. We will confront Shadan when he arrives."

"The who?" Elison asked.

"The New Oath *Nar'shein*," Gideon answered, smiling appreciatively. "Or more appropriately, the Keepers of the New Oath." His smile widened and he gave a small laugh. "I like it. Who came up with it?"

Ohran shrugged uncomfortably. "I did. Just now."

Gideon stepped forward and looked up at him. His smile was still in place, but admiration glimmered in his eyes. "It will do much to mend the divide among your people," he said. "You are truly wise, Grand Chieftain of the *Nar'shein Yahl*."

Ohran bowed his head in acceptance of the compliment. "Thank you, *El'kali*."

Gideon clapped him on the arm, then looked back out at the northeastern townships. "*Frel'mola te Ujen* likely isn't happy about being ordered to relocate to East Gate," he said, "but without *Frel'mola* here to counter Shadan's order, they don't have much of a choice. They are part of Death's Third March now, whether they wanted to be or not."

He turned and met Ohran's gaze. "Continue to track their movements," he said. "If they attempt to move beyond East Gate to try to intercept the united armies, we might need to change our minds about your younglings—about *Ara'so*—launching a preemptive strike. I may even lead them into battle myself."

"They are yours to command, *El'kali*," Ohran said, the words bitter in his mouth. "Now if you will excuse me, I need to prepare the *Nar'shein* for Shadan's arrival."

Idoman watched Chieftain Peregam move away down the top of the wall, then turned to Gideon.

"He isn't happy about the New Oath *Nar'shein*, is he?" he asked. "Regardless of the name he gave them or his blessing of you leading them into battle."

"No," Gideon answered. "He isn't. But great leaders do what is necessary even when they don't like it." He glanced at Taggert, and a smile moved over his face.

"Take General Enue, for instance," Gideon continued. "He's been spoiling to get back in the fight for days but has, as he put it: *been playing nursemaid to refugees.*"

Taggert scowled at him. "Kustin talks too much. And for the record, I never used the word refugees."

Gideon chuckled. "Be that as it may, it's time to get you and your men back in the fight."

"It's about bloody time," Taggert muttered. "Where would you like us to deploy? And don't give us some out-of-the-way place to *keep us out of harm's way* as Jase would put it."

"Unfortunately," Gideon said, his entire demeanor sobering in an instant, "once this starts, nowhere in the world will be out of harm's way." He motioned them toward the tower stairs. "Come, we have much to do and not a lot of time to do it."

⼢

"This is bloody taking forever," Elliott muttered, and Talia glanced over to find her brother frowning over one of his paper animals.

"What is?" she asked, "Jase, or whatever it is that you are folding?"

He turned a flat stare on her, then finished his latest creation in a flurry of finger movement and set it on the ground in front of him. It was a bird of some kind, with a blue body and green wings. "You know what I'm talking about," he said. "He's been sitting there for eight hours. Without a hint that he's any closer to accomplishing... whatever it is he's trying to accomplish."

"It won't be much longer," she told him. "I can feel it."

Elliott pushed himself to his feet. "If you say so," he said, stretching his back and letting his eyes move across the makeshift camp. Talia followed his gaze, but not much had changed since Elliott's last round of complaints.

Dymas were chatting quietly in small groups or were lounging on their bedrolls. Some of the Shizu were practicing forms while the rest gathered firewood or prepared food or sharpened weapons. Seth, bless his ever-vigilant heart, hadn't moved from where he stood with his back against one of the T'rii Gate's posts. Endil and Jeymi sat with their backs against the other post and were so deeply immersed in their whispered conversation that a Shadowhound could have run through camp and they wouldn't have seen it.

Elliott must have thought they needed to be interrupted because he stepped near and cleared his throat to get their attention.

"Do either of you want to help me round up something to eat?"

Endil exchanged a quick look with Jeymi, then nodded. "I'll come with you," he said. "What do you have in mind?"

"Anything larger than a rabbit," Elliott answered, moving to his pack to retrieve his bow and a quiver of arrows.

"There are big horn sheep on Augg's higher slopes," Seth said. "I saw them on our patrol this morning."

Elliott arched an eyebrow at him. "And you are telling me this because..."

"It's time for another patrol," Seth answered. "And you won't need your bow. Myrscraw never miss."

The look of surprise on Elliott's face quickly gave way to a smile as he realized what Seth had just implied. "I'll ready Kiaush," he said and hurried across the clearing to where the Myrscraw waited.

"On second thought," Endil said. "I think I'll say here. Flying makes my stomach hurt."

"I'd like to come," Jeymi said. "I loved the feeling of flying. Besides, you need a Dymas with you in case you run into trouble."

"What about you?" Seth asked, and Talia blinked in surprise when she realized he was talking to her. "You have been sitting here all day. A change of scenery might be nice."

"No thank you," she said. "It really won't be much longer, and I want to be here for him when he comes back to himself."

Seth nodded. "Have him contact Jeymi if we haven't returned by the time that happens."

"I will," she said, then watched as he and Jeymi joined Elliott at the Myrscraw. Seth assisted Jeymi into the saddle, and a moment later the giant birds were lifting into the air.

She watched until they'd vanished beyond the tops of the pines, then turned her attention back to Jase. His face was pinched with concentration, but the *sei'vaiya* literally seethed with excitement and a profound sense of accomplishment. The wait, she knew, was almost over.

With the whole of Mount Augg visible in his mind's eye, Jase took a moment to appreciate what he'd done. It had taken much longer than anticipated, but he believed he'd just located the final crux point holding Fairimor's ward of Earth in place. Now there was only one way to find out.

First though, he wanted one last look at what his ancient forebearer had so magnificently wrought. Contrary to his first thought that Fairimor's ward was like a blanket, he'd learned several hours ago that it was more like a shell. A blanket implied a covering which was smooth and which would soften or even distort the true shape beneath. But this shell—he really couldn't think of it any other way—was an exact replica of the mountain's exterior. Stone for stone, seam for seam, and fissure for fissure, it was perfect. And it wasn't illusion—it was real. Threads of Earth channeled and then linked in such a way as to create actual stone. Stone which would vanish the moment he shattered the crux points, revealing whatever it was Fairimor had wished to keep hidden. And the time for the revealing was now.

Reaching even deeper into the vast luminescence that was the fabric of life itself, he readied a thousand individual threads of Spirit energy and took aim at the network of crux points. He would have one chance at this. If he missed, he would need to relocate each and every one of the minuscule points of energy and rebuild the framework in his mind's eye.

He struck, and his view of Augg vanished beneath a brilliant flash of white that momentarily swallowed the whole of his Awareness. Then, as the sea of white light faded and Mount Augg came back into view in his mind's eye, he saw that the crux points were gone. Aside from that, nothing else seemed to have changed.

Then he saw the entrance, a large arched doorway cut directly into the living rock of the mountain just up slope from the outcroppings where they'd landed with the Myrscraw last night. It was visible now, he knew, because the stone Fairimor had wrought to conceal it had dissolved. And it wasn't the only opening to have appeared. Higher up, a number of smaller, window-like holes were now visible on the cliff faces, and a search of the lower slopes revealed six more arched entrances at varying heights.

The sight reminded him of the vision he'd had of Galiena's mountain city on the Rhiven home world. Only this mountain had never been inhabited. It was first and foremost a Temple of Elderon, and like all temples it would be a multi-leveled maze of corridors and chambers, if significantly larger than all the others.

Letting his Awareness shrink to a more practical size, he focused on one of the window-like openings high on a cliff face. It was still large enough to allow a Myrscraw to perch, but a slight tremor of Earthpower alerted him to more crux points. Narrowing his Awareness even further, he zeroed in on one of the crux points and found it connected to a powerful warding of Flesh.

It was similar to the warding Gideon had placed on the Temple of Elderon in Trian to protect it from Shadowspawn, only this ward wouldn't discriminate between natural flesh and that wrought of corrupted *Ta'shaen*. Any living thing that attempted to enter the temple while the wards were in place would be obliterated.

He shifted his attention back to what he knew to be the main entrance. It, too, was warded by lethal bursts of *Sha*, and he studied the crux points for a moment before focusing on the small stream flowing out of the entrance via two small aqueducts. They disappeared into the depths of the boulder field, only to emerge a short distance later as the stream he'd discovered upon arrival. The aqueducts ran parallel to the sides of the corridor and stretched away into the depths of the mountain. He knew if he followed the water to its source he would find that it, too, was tied to crux points and a ward to prevent entry deeper into the mountain.

And that meant there would be one for Fire, Air, Light, and ultimately Spirit. Not only had Fairimor wrought a ward from each of the Seven Gifts, he'd placed them in ascending order.

He returned his attention to the wards wrought of Flesh. Fortunately, they were clustered around each entry point and not spread across the entire mountain like the warding of Earth had been. It should make them much easier to collapse.

First, though, he needed something to eat.

The *sei'vaiya* alerted Talia that Jase was coming out of his trance, and she moved to greet him as he did. She got to him just as his eyes opened, and a broad smile moved over his face at finding her so near.

"Where have you been all day?" he asked, taking her hand and pressing it to his lips.

"Where have you been?" she countered. "There were a couple of times during the day when I wondered if you would ever come back."

He looked up at the snow-capped dagger rising above the tops of the pines. "I wondered the same thing a couple of times," he said. "Augg's a bloody big mountain."

He pushed himself stiffly to his feet and let his eyes move over those in the camp. All talk had stopped at his return, and everyone was watching him expectantly. "The first of the wards is down," he told them. "But it was the largest. The other six should go much more quickly."

He cast a quick look at Talia and added a quiet, "I hope."

She squeezed his hand. "It will."

Stretching his back again, he looked around the camp. "Where are Seth and Elliott?" He noticed Endil sitting alone and added, "And Jeymi?"

"They got tired of waiting," Endil answered. "So they went hunting for big horn sheep. Seth said for you to contact them if they weren't back before you came out of your trance."

"No need," Derian said, pointing skyward. "Here they come."

Jase looked up to see two Myrscraw gliding in above the treetops, each with a large ram in their talons. Elliott waved excitedly as the birds settled to the ground, then leapt from the saddle as Kiaush bellied down.

"Per our long-standing agreement," he said, pulling a knife from his belt, "this is for you."

"What long-standing agreement?" Endil asked as he helped Jeymi from the saddle.

"That whoever doesn't make the kill," Jase said, taking the knife, "has the privilege of dressing the animal."

"Then return the knife," Seth said, "because Kiaush made the kill. Not Elliott."

Elliott opened his mouth to object, then closed it again and took the knife. "I knew I should have taken my bow," he grumbled, then took the ram by one of its horns and dragged it away into the trees.

Seth took the other ram by the horns, then looked at Jase. "Why don't you and Talia take a walk," he said, following Elliott. "After all that sitting, it would be good for you to stretch your legs."

"Yes it would," he agreed. He took Talia by the hand and led her in the opposite direction of Seth and Elliott. When they were out of earshot, he leaned close and whispered, "Do you think Seth did that to irritate Elliott or to reward you for your patience?"

"Probably a little of both," she whispered back. "But he's right that you need a break." A rush of affection flowed across the *sei'vaiya* and with it a glimpse of what Talia was thinking. The most solid image was of her wrapping her arms around his neck so she could kiss him.

"And that, my dear," he whispered, "is an even better idea than a walk."

# CHAPTER 66

## Siege of Nations

GIDEON BID THORAC FAREWELL, then opened a Veilgate back to the top of the wall midway between River Gate and East Gate. Lyndon Ryban, First Captain of the City Guardsmen, was there to meet him as he came through. Glowstone lamps lit the top of the wall in both directions, and the towers rising above the gates were pillars of light against the night.

"Those Krelltin are quick, aren't they," he said, looking over the edge of the wall to where the Chunin Cavalry was taking up positions below.

"Yes," Gideon said, following Lyndon's gaze. In the light of the glowstone lamps illuminating the empty streets, the birds were feathered splashes of color, fluid in their movements and far more sure-footed on paving stones than a horse would have been. "And small and agile enough to easily maneuver through the more narrow streets. They'll be a huge help to you and your men as we try to keep *Frel'mola te Ujen* bottled up between East Road and the Trian River."

"And if the servants of the Dark Bride decide to push south into the city in search of an easy slaughter?"

Gideon heard the worry in the captain's voice, and he admired him for it. Lyndon's highest concern was, and always had been, the safety and well-being of the people of Trian. It was, he knew, the reason Lyndon had volunteered for this spot at the wall. He felt obligated to be part of the first line of defense. Unfortunately, there were simply too many civilians who hadn't left for the City Guardsmen to protect them all.

"Hopefully the wards we set south of East Road will change the enemy's mind," Gideon told him. "But if not, and some do make their way south into the city, they won't have as easy a time as they think. When pressed, even the most peace-loving folk will fight with the strength of lions."

Lyndon nodded but still seemed doubtful. "We'll make sure it doesn't come to that."

Gideon put his hand on Lyndon's shoulder. "I know you will." He looked back down at the seemingly narrow swath of streets and rooftops between East Road and the river. "My guess is they'll make a push straight west and try to take the main avenue. If they take it, have your Dymas destroy the bridges. We'll use the river to separate their forces."

"Will do," Lyndon said, then offered Gideon his hand. "In case we don't meet again," he said. "It has been a pleasure serving the Blue Flame."

"The pleasure has been mine, Captain," he told him. "May the Creator shelter and protect you in the hours to come." Releasing Lyndon's hand, he turned and opened a Veilgate to the towers rising above Northeast Gate. Like the others, they were bright with the light of glowstone lamps.

Joneam and Taggert turned to face him as he arrived. A short distance away, Idoman and Quintella broke off the conversation they were having with some of the Dainin of *Ara'so* and hurried forward as well.

"Death's Third March is nearing North Gate," Taggert said, and Gideon nodded.

"I know. Ohran contacted me a few minutes ago." He looked down at Northeast Road and the curving avenues intersecting it. "Are your men in place?"

"Yes," Joneam answered. "And we have good news. Word just arrived from Agisthas. General Crompton is sending additional troops. Now that the Shadan Cult is no longer a threat in Melek, he was able to pull five thousand troops from the border. They'll be arriving in the next few minutes. And what's more, General Crompton is coming with them."

"That is good news," Gideon said. "The old wardog will want to be in the thick of it, which is fine considering that he and his men are well-rested. I trust you to deploy them as you see fit."

Joneam nodded, then moved to the outside edge of the wall and looked down at the maze of roads spreading outward through the townships. Like *Frel'mola te Ujen*, the army of the Fist of Con'Jithar had stopped several blocks short of the wall, and the area they inhabited was bright with the flickering oranges and yellows of torchlight and pockets of red from orbs wrought of corrupted Light.

"If I didn't believe the fight could be won," the general said, "I'd order our Dymas to set the township ablaze and incinerate those curs where they stand." He turned and locked eyes with Gideon. "But I want our people to have a place to come home to after we end this."

Gideon clapped Joneam on the shoulder. "It's that kind of hope that will get us through this. Good luck, General."

Joneam brought his fist to his chest in salute. "And to you, Guardian of the Blue Flame."

"Tonight," he said, looking from Joneam to the others, then back to Joneam, "we are all Guardians of the Blue Flame."

He turned to Idoman. "Is the communications network in place?" he asked.

The young Dymas General nodded. "Yes, with three Dymas per relay point should someone fall."

"Excellent. Make sure to send me regular reports. Once this starts, I won't be able to leave the palace."

Joneam frowned at him. "Why?"

He shrugged. "Prophecy," he answered and left it at that. Joneam didn't need to know what he and Jase had glimpsed of those final moments when the palace would be overrun. It would undermine the faith that might keep them alive. Just because he was fated to fall at the hands of whatever dark creature he and Jase had glimpsed, it didn't mean his friends had to.

"God's speed, my friends," he said, then opened yet another Veilgate and moved through to North Gate.

"I see you, *El'kali*," Ohran said as Gideon let the gate slide closed behind him.

"I see you, *Nar'shein*."

Joining his friend at the edge of the wall, he surveyed the scene below. North Road was bright with the hellish light of corrupted Power and stretched away into the distance like a bloody dagger. As he watched, the maze of smaller streets branching off of North Road also turned red with corrupted Light as the soldiers of Death's Third March began spreading out in preparation of attacking the wall.

"Any sign of Shadan?" he asked.

Ohran shook his head. "Nor of Aethon either."

"They'll surface soon enough," Gideon said. He watched the expanding threads of light a moment longer, then turned to Ohran. "Everyone else is in position," he said. "I'm returning to the palace. I'll be there for the duration."

Ohran went to one knee and looked him in the eyes. "God's speed, my friend. And may the Earthmother shelter and protect you should we fail to meet again at the end of this battle."

"God's speed, Grand Chieftain of the *Nar'shein Yahl*," Gideon said, then embraced the Power and opened the way into the Fairimor home.

As Gideon strode through from the darkness beyond the Veilgate, Brysia was so relieved to have him back home that she practically leapt from her chair to greet him. He took her in his arms and hugged her tightly, then kissed her on the top of her head and stood back to look her over. She took advantage of the moment to do the same with him.

His eyes told her all she needed to know. He was tired and worried but determined to do whatever was necessary to protect her, the palace, and the city of Trian from Death's Third March. It was, she knew, why he'd been gone all day.

"You need some rest," she told him. "Gavin told me you left before daybreak."

"I kissed you goodbye," he said in his own defense. "But you were sleeping too soundly for me to want to wake you."

"Wake me," she said. "I don't want your last words to me to be something I didn't hear."

"No more chance of that," he said. "I'm here for the remainder of the war."

She eyed him suspiciously, not sure if she was willing to believe it.

"It's true," he told her. "That little glimpse of the future I was telling you about.... It isn't far away now." He opened his mouth to say more but hesitated.

She stopped him before he could. "We've been over this," she said, her tone firm. "My place is here with you. We'll spit in Shadan's eye together if it comes to that, but I'm not leaving. And that's your wife talking, not your Queen. Don't make me get *her* involved in this."

He smiled in defeat and pulled her close for another hug, then lifted her chin and kissed her gently on the mouth. "It will be as you say, my wife."

"Good. Now that we have that settled, what have you been up to all day? Ammorin tells me you've been to practically every corner of the city."

"Don't forget his trip out to the southeastern township to welcome the Chellum Army," Ammorin said, and Brysia smiled as Gideon turned a flat stare on the Dainin. He sat in the middle of the floor in the library half of the room, his tree-trunk arms resting on his knees.

"And how do you know all this?" he asked. "Have you been spying on me?"

Ammorin met the stare without blinking. "I don't need to," Ammorin said. "The Children of *Ta'shaen* spread news faster than any village gossip could. The communication network you had Idoman set up just made it that much easier for them." A smile moved over his face as he continued. "They are energized by your presence, *El'kali*. You cannot fault them for that."

Gideon sighed, then gestured to the emptiness of the room. "I see you finished cleaning up the mess."

"The *Bero'thai* did," Ammorin told him. "Pattalla and I worked on strengthening the wards over the palace. I still don't know how *Frel'mola* was able to corrupt them, but I know what it felt like when she did. I won't let it happen again." He shrugged. "Or at the very least, we will have a warning if Shadan tries."

"He won't try," Gideon said, and Brysia sensed there was more to his confidence than the fact that he possessed a Blood Orb. Probably, it had something to do with that glimpse of the future he'd told her about.

He must have sensed what she was thinking because he changed the subject. "How is Marithen?"

"Surprisingly well," she said. "Physically, at least. Nothing about her damaged mind has changed. And oddly enough, she has no recollection of her encounter with *Frel'mola* but thinks we still need to search for prophecies in order to find a Blood Orb. She's out in the Dome with Beraline."

"I'll take that over the alternative," Gideon said, then let his eyes move over the room once more. "If I'm going to be stuck in here for the rest of the war, we should probably bring in a sofa or two. I'm too old to sit on the floor."

Ammorin chuckled. "Way ahead of you, my friend," he said. "The *Bero'thai* are fetching several pieces as we speak. I requested a dining table for you as well. It should be here soon, along with a hot meal from Mistress Allisen."

As if speaking it made it so, the doors leading in from the Dome opened and Gavin entered. He was followed by two more *Bero'thai* carrying a table and six who each carried a high-backed chair. A moment after that, Allisen came in from the kitchens with a tray of food.

Gideon took Brysia by the hand and led her to the table. Ammorin joined them, and they were just getting settled when a Veilgate opened along the wall, and Lord Nid came through with Captain Plat at his side. The captain's eyes were worried as he watched his King, and his hands were poised to catch him if he should fall. Considering how near death the Meleki King had been, Brysia decided it was a legitimate concern.

Lord Nid, however, seemed amused by Vol's attentiveness but moved straight to the table as Brysia and Gideon rose to greet him.

"It's nice to see you up and about," Gideon told him, then looked at the blue-edged hole in the air and added, "And strong enough to open a Veilgate."

"It's nice to be up and about," Lord Nid said. "And, yes, I've recovered enough to wield. Though it will still be some time before I'm back to full strength."

"He wanted to be here for the end," Captain Plat said. "Whatever that end might be."

Lord Nid cast an amused look at the captain. "I'm no longer incapacitated," he told his friend. "I *can* speak for myself."

Vol looked embarrassed. "Yes, of course."

Hul looked at Brysia and smiled. "Your mother and your uncle send their love. They also told me the good news regarding your son. Any word on how that is going?"

"No," she said. "And there won't be. He won't risk communicating with us for fear the enemy might learn of things."

"We'll know soon enough if he is successful," Lord Nid said. "One way or the other, we will know."

"Have you eaten?" Gideon asked, motioning the two to the table.

"Yes," Hul replied, "but please, you and Brysia proceed with your meal. We'll wait." He looked around the nearly empty room. "What the blazes happened here?"

"*Frel'mola*," Gideon answered, then shot a quick look at Ammorin. "Sit with us, and I'll bring you up to date."

His dinner forgotten, Gideon rehearsed all that Lord Nid had missed, pausing every now and then to let Brysia and Ammorin fill in the things he'd overlooked or hadn't been present for. When he finished, Lord Nid sat in contemplative silence.

"Things are accelerating," he said at last. "And I don't mean just with the arrival of Death's Third March on your doorstep. Word arrived from Melek that the Veil has collapsed completely in the Pit. An army of demons marches on Kamasin. A second collapse occurred along the southern edge of K'theg Forest. The demons are days away from the nearest major city, but there are dozens of smaller towns in the area. I fear for them."

Brysia understood the feeling completely. With so many civilians now trapped within Trian's walls, there would undoubtedly be casualties.

"Melek isn't the only place experiencing the acceleration you spoke of," Ammorin said. "And isn't limited to holes opening in the Veil. The boost the Earthsoul received from Endil Fairimor's use of the Blood Orb is waning. She's failing physically. The *Nar'shein Yahl* abroad in the Nine Lands have reported that in some areas the quaking of the earth is constant. Old mountains are collapsing into rubble. New mountains are heaving themselves skyward. Rivers are being rerouted. Lakes are draining into fissures. The world as we know it is literally coming apart at the seams."

"How long before Trian is affected?" Brysia asked, once again thinking of the civilian population. "Clearly, the Earthsoul has been sheltering us from the worst of it. When might that change?"

"It could change in the next minute," Ammorin said. "There's no way to know for sure."

"And since there is no way of knowing," Gideon said, "let's address the here and now." He locked eyes with Lord Nid. "Death's Third March is outside the city," he said. "But you already know that. It's why you are here."

The Meleki King nodded. "I promised I would be here with you at the end," he said. "Thanks to you I lived long enough to fulfill that promise. The Meleki Army—what's left of it—stands ready, my friend. Just say the word and I will have our Dymas bring them into the city."

"There's room in Central Plaza," Gideon said. "And thank you. After all your men—after all your nation has been through, I would understand if you wanted to sit out the remainder of this war."

Lord Nid gave a humorless laugh. "And miss the end of the world?"

"The Siege of Nations," Ammorin said, and Brysia turned to regard him curiously.

"What was that?"

"It's a line from the *Tei'shevisar*," Ammorin replied. "The Prophet Ominshea penned it in reference to Maeon's war on the Nine Lands." He rubbed the side of his face thoughtfully as he continued. "I always thought it was a general reference, but I think now Ominshea may have foreseen this moment. Trian isn't alone in this crisis—most of the nations of the world are here with you. Shadan is laying siege to all of them."

"Proof that the Meleki army should be here," Hul said. With some effort, he pushed himself to his feet. Vol rose with him, his concern for his King clearly visible in his eyes. Hul arched an eyebrow at him. "Do I really appear that frail to you?" he asked.

"Not at all," Vol answered at the same time Gideon said, "Yes."

Hul grunted. "Maybe a little fresh air, then. I'd like to watch from the Overlook as my men arrive."

As they started for the doors leading out of the Fairimor home, Gideon caught Vol's eye and smiled. A moment later the air parted in front of Lord Nid to reveal the gardens near the eastern edge of the Overlook.

Lord Nid cast a withering glance over his shoulder as he passed through, but he didn't object.

Still smiling, Gideon offered Brysia his arm and they followed the two Meleki out into the night. The air was cool and smelled of flowers, and Brysia inhaled deeply. Ammorin joined them, and the Veilgate slid closed, momentarily plunging the area into darkness. A sphere of Light sprang into existence a heartbeat later and moved with them as they approached the short wall.

A rustling of bushes and a series of soft grunts sounded to the right, and Ammorin went to one knee as Kino came loping out of the darkness. The wolverine moved right up to Ammorin and rubbed his muzzle affectionately against the Dainin's open palm. Then he swung his head from side to side for a moment as if searching for something. Or someone, she amended, realizing Kino was looking for Talia.

"She's still not here," Ammorin said, then stroked Kino's fur with his fingers before following once more. Grunting softly, Kino turned and slipped off into the darkness.

"Where has he been?" Brysia asked. "I haven't seen him since the day he saved me and Talia by attacking the Changeling. I was worried he'd been killed during the attack by Aethon's Power-voiding shadowspawn."

"He dug a burrow near the southern wall," Ammorin said. "I've been feeding him in Talia's absence. He doesn't like many people besides her."

"And you, obviously."

Ammorin shrugged. "As I said, I bring him food."

They reached the short wall, and Hul leaned on it for support as he looked out over the city. "Any minute now," he said, and Brysia followed his gaze to the scene below.

The southern half of the city looked as it always did, a sparkling expanse of lights from thousands of homes and businesses. The north half of the city, however, was a patch of darkness etched with the brightly lit lines of its roads and splotches of light that were groups of soldiers. The outer wall was a vast semicircle of light bordering the hellish glow of Shadan's army beyond.

Then flashes of bluish light appeared in the vicinity of Central Plaza and Brysia imagined she could see the Meleki Army racing through from beyond. Several minutes passed, then the points of blue light vanished.

"It is done," Lord Nid said, and a long silence followed as he and Gideon and Ammorin continued to stare out over the city. Brysia wasn't sure if they had reached out with their Awareness to communicate with other Dymas or if they were simply lost in thought, and right now it didn't matter. She was with her husband, the night was cool and refreshing, and things were quiet. She wanted to enjoy the moment.

As if sensing her thoughts, Gideon put his arm around her and pulled her near. She sighed contentedly and leaned her head on his shoulder. They stood like that for most of an hour.

Then all three Dymas turned as one as a Veilgate opened on the path behind them and Railen Nogeru and Sheymi Oroshi came through with two hard-faced Shizu on their heels.

A smile moved over Gideon's face as he raised a hand in greeting to the two young Dymas, then he froze in surprise as his eyes landed on the older of the two Shizu.

"Emperor Dromensai," he said, "to what do we owe the pleasure?"

Brysia blinked. The Riaki Emperor had come to Trian in person?

"It is we who owe you, my friend," Emperor Dromensai replied. "And we have come to repay the debt."

Gideon stared at Tereus in wonder. That he had come in person was the highest honor an Emperor could bestow on a neighboring nation. That he wore a *komouri* uniform and had a sword strapped to his back meant this was more than an ambassadorial visit—Tereus was here to participate in the battle.

"Don't look so surprised," Tereus said, an amused smile moving over his face. "I was a Shizu long before I put on the robes of highseat or Emperor. And for a lot longer."

Gideon shook himself free for speech. "Yes you were," he said, then gestured to Brysia. "Emperor Dromensai, this is Brysia Fairimor, High Queen of Kelsa."

Tereus offered a deep bow of respect. "Lady Fairimor."

"Emperor Dromensai," she said, returning the bow. "Welcome to Trian."

"Thank you," Tereus said, offering another bow. "With your permission, I will have Railen and Sheymi bring the Riaki army into the city. They will just need to know where you would like them deployed."

"I will defer that decision to Gideon," she said, turning to look at him. "He knows better than I what is needed."

"The inner wall," he said. "The *Bero'thai* are spread pretty thin and will appreciate the reinforcements. I'll have Captain Dium concentrate his forces at the main gate and at River Gate. Riak can take the northern gate."

"It will be done," Shavis said, nodding to the two young Dymas.

Sheymi embraced the Power, and a Veilgate opened to the top of the inner wall. She and Railen moved through, and Gideon led Brysia back to the edge of the Overlook. Tereus and Shavis and the others joined them, and Gideon watched through his Awareness as Veilgates opened all across the top of the inner wall and Shizu and Sarui hurried into position. It was impossible to say for sure, but he estimated the Riaki force at more than eight thousand.

"Things must have quieted in Riak," Gideon said.

"No," Tereus said. "But we decided to test the *Mith'elre Chon's* prophecy that Riak will, as he put it, *ride out the rest of this storm relatively unscathed* if we heeded the advice of Dai'shozen Dakshar."

Gideon looked at Shavis. "So, this was your doing? You gave the order to come to our aid?"

Shavis exchanged a quick look with Tereus. "Emperor Dromensai and I came to the decision together," the Dai'shozen said. "But it was Elliott who convinced us to act in faith." He frowned. "He's annoyingly persistent."

"Wait a minute," Gideon said. "Elliott's been coming to Riak?"

"We thought you knew," Tereus said. "He's come several times during the past week."

"Always at night?" Gideon asked, then sighed when Tereus nodded. "Well, now I know why he was so eager to return to Chellum whenever he could. I thought it was so he could spend time with his fiancee."

"She came with him on two occasions," Tereus said. "Lovely young woman."

"Yes," Gideon agreed, then looked back down at the inner wall. "How many members of *tres'dia* came with you?"

"Forty-eight," Shavis answered. "Including Railen and Sheymi. Like I said, Elliott was most persistent that Riak would be spared if we came to your aid."

A short silence followed which was broken by Tereus. "I trust that the Myrscraw I loaned to *shent ze'deyar* have been put to good use."

Gideon nodded. "He and the *Mith'elre Chon* are well on their way to recovering a viable Blood Orb. With any luck, Jase will bring about the Rejuvenation before Trian is overrun."

"Excellent," Tereus said. "Now if you wouldn't mind opening a Veilgate, Dai'shozen Dakshar and I will join our men."

Gideon did as requested, and the two passed through to join Railen and Sheymi.

"Remarkable men," Lord Nid said when they were gone.

"Yes," Gideon agreed. "In fact—" He flinched as *Ta'shaen* came alive with a multitude of corrupted wieldings and the sky beyond the outer wall went red with Fire.

"And so it begins," Ammorin said. "Just as Ominshea prophesied."

*Yes*, Gideon thought. *The final battle between light and dark.*

Putting his arm around his wife, he watched as Fire hammered the shields of the Dainin. And all the while, images of his future flashed unbidden through his mind.

# CHAPTER 67

## *Deadly Distractions*

OHRAN PEREGAM FROWNED THOUGHTFULLY as the Fires wrought by his enemies hammered the shields of the *Nar'shein* in rivers of heat, cascades of red that flowed down the invisible barrier and poured into the streets fronting Trian's outer wall. Some of the buildings below had caught fire, and dark smoke billowed upward, obscuring his view of the township beyond.

He momentarily considered extending his Awareness for a better look, but decided against it. He knew where the K'rrosha were located from the tremors they were creating in *Ta'shaen*. He also knew this was but a small part of what was yet to come. As of yet, none of the Agla'Con had seized the Power.

"What do you make of this?" Chieftain Paddishor said, his eyes calm as he watched the conflagration.

Ohran grunted. "They're trying to distract us," he answered. "The real attack will follow shortly." He looked down the wall at his people. Traditional *Nar'shein* stood side by side with those of the New Oath, their philosophical differences set aside. Defenders and Soldiers—flip sides of the same coin. All of them Keepers of the Earth. It would be interesting to see how they complimented one another in battle.

"The Agla'Con are on the move," Paddishor said, his Awareness fastened on the scene beyond the billowing wall of smoke. "They're urging Darklings and Shadowhounds ahead of them. They're going to sacrifice them to spring the Power-wrought traps."

"And use the detonations to cover their own wieldings," Ohran said. "Tell our people to prepare for incoming. We are about to experience our first true test."

As Paddishor relayed the message, Ohran hefted one of his *arinseil* nets, then embraced the Power and prepared a shield of Spirit.

Less than a minute later, the area directly below went bright as noonday as

*Sei'shiin* erupted from a line of crux points to destroy the forward ranks of shadowspawn. A series of horizontal lightning strikes followed, crackling tendrils of death that streaked down the smoke-filled streets in rumbles of thunder. Darklings and Shadowhounds alike blew apart in smoking chunks of ruined flesh.

More detonations of Power followed as the shadowspawned creatures charged mindlessly forward, but the purity of the strikes was suddenly marred by corruption as Agla'Con began rending the Veil.

Most stormed through into the streets of Trian some distance north of the wall, while a few opened rents inside the Dainin shield and arrived directly atop the wall. Fists blazing with corruption, they hurled lightning and Fire and spears of corrupted Flesh.

Ohran deflected one of those killing spears back into its wielder, and the man blew apart in a spray of blood and flesh. His partner slipped in the gore but managed to remain on his feet. He went down a heartbeat later as Paddishor's net enveloped him in a crackling of green fire. The man's talisman winked out, and he died a moment later as Paddishor crushed his head beneath his foot.

More Agla'Con arrived on the heels of the first, and Ohran pulled his shield tight about him as the immediate area vanished in a sea of red. Closing his eyes against the brightness, he watched through his Awareness as the men continued to hammer away at him, relentless, rage-filled, and reckless in their attempts to kill him.

They vanished in flashes of white a moment later, completely oblivious to the fact that not all of the *Nar'shein* were wielding the Power for defense.

The *Ara'so* who'd destroyed the Agla'Con moved near. "I see you Chieftain," she said. *Sei'shiin* erupted from her fingertips a second time, and another enemy vanished in flare of white.

Then she was gone, racing away down the wall to fight elsewhere.

Ohran watched her go, a strange mix of emotions warring within him. He was both impressed and saddened by her prowess as a Soldier of God. But what was done was done, and there was no going back now.

Hefting his net, he strengthened his shield and started in the direction of a cluster of Agla'Con, eager to join Paddishor in his hunt.

Idoman deflected the crimson-colored lightning bolt into a squad of Tamban soldiers racing toward him, and their ruined bodies somersaulted over the edge of the wall and vanished into the night. A moment later the sickening thuds of their armored corpses striking the courtyard below sounded loudly in his ears.

The *Jeth'Jalda* who'd hurled the bolt struck again, but Quintella turned that one aside as well. Idoman ended the man's life a moment later with a spiraling tendril of *Sei'shiin* that sliced through his shield as if it were made of cloth.

The afterimage of his demise was still visible in the air when two more *Jeth'Jalda* appeared to take his place. They were fighting in tandem, one holding the shield while the other channeled streamers of Fire and Flesh. Two of Taggert's men died in bursts of superheated gore before Idoman could protect them.

Outraged, he opened a Veilgate beneath the men's feet, then closed it as they fell through, slicing their heads from their necks in a razored flash of blue light. Their headless corpses landed amid the Tamban soldiers lying dead in the street fronting the city gate.

"That's a new one," Quintella shouted, her toothy smile bright in the light of the glowstone lamps lining the wall. "But you should kill them with *Sei'shiin*."

"I know," he told her, "but sometimes my creativity gets the best of me." He pointed to an area four streets west of the wall where flashes of red light marked the arrival of more *Jeth'Jalda*.

"There," he said, opening a Veilgate into the midst of the chaos. Four *Jeth'Jalda* in green and black uniforms whirled to face them only to vanish in flashes of white as Quintella struck with *Sei'shiin*. Behind them, the four squads of Tamban Deathwatch dove for cover as Quintella sent tendrils of green fire streaking toward them. They were set upon a moment later by a small army of City Guardsman that appeared seemingly out of nowhere, and the clash of steel rang out sharply. Idoman let the gate slide closed, confident of the outcome.

The situation atop the wall, however, was less certain, and he and Quintella started for the towers rising above Northeast Gate. Hundreds of Tamban soldiers had arrived through rents and were being engaged by the men of Chellum. Dymas and *Dalae* were assisting where they could, but they couldn't strike effectively for fear of hitting their own. And Taggert, he saw, was in the thick of it.

With a small shield of Spirit in one hand and a sword-like blade of Fire in the other, Idoman stepped into the melee. Beetle-armored Tambans moved to engage him, but his Power-wrought blade sliced through sword and armor and flesh alike, filling the air with the stench of seared flesh.

Quintella followed close behind, and *Ta'shaen* came alive with powerful but agile strikes of Flesh. He could see them in his mind's eye, radiant tendrils of killing energy that burst open the hearts of those they touched. Wide-eyed, the stricken men dropped their weapons, then staggered and fell, startling those around them because of the lack of any outward injury.

With his Awareness still extended, Idoman probed the way ahead, looking for the signature tendrils of red that indicated corrupted wieldings. He found some nearer the tower, emanating from a woman in crimson-colored robes. One side of her head was shorn, and her face was a mask of maniacal frenzy as she watched the battle raging around her.

She had seized enough of the Power to lay waste to an entire city block, and the Jexlair crystal on the end of her scepter burned with a fiery intensity unlike any he'd ever seen. He thought it odd that she'd done nothing more than weave a protective shield around herself.

Quintella spotted her as well, and Idoman heard the fear in her voice as she called to him. "Blood Maiden," she shouted. "One of *Frel'mola's* assassins."

"Why is she just standing there?"

When Quintella didn't respond, he redirected the flows of Spirit he was channeling for his shield, expanding it outward into a protective bubble and bringing Quintella inside.

The sounds of battle dropped to a dull roar, but Quintella's eyes never left the Blood Maiden. He took her by the arm to make her look at him. "Quintella, what is it? What's wrong?"

"Blood Atonement," she said. "For failing to protect *Frel'mola*. This is a suicide mission." Channeling a massive sweep of Air, she parted the way before her, knocking aside friend and foe alike. She raised her hand, and a white-hot bar of *Sei'shiin* streaked down the newly formed avenue to strike the Maiden's shield in an explosive burst of energy that shook the Power-wrought stone of the wall and sent soldiers staggering.

The Maiden's shield held, and Idoman watched in horror as she continued to seize *Ta'shaen* as if nothing had happened. To her, maybe nothing had. She seemed oblivious to everything but the ever-increasing brightness of the talisman in her hand.

The look of insane rapture on her face chilled Idoman's blood, and it suddenly occurred to him what Quintella meant by suicide mission.

A heartbeat later the Maiden's Jexlair crystal exploded.

With the last of the *Jeth'Jalda* pinned down by Chunin's Dymas, Thorac and his men were finally free to engage the Tamban soldiers who'd arrived in the city through Veilgates. Hefting his axe, he nodded to Captain Fraam who raised a curved horn to his lips and sounded the attack.

Thorac's Krelltin sprinted out of the dome of Spirit wrought to protect them, and the rest of the Chunin cavalry followed. The metallic rustling of the chain mail protecting the birds' necks kept rhythm with the soft padding of their feet as they ran, and the sound sent a rush of excitement washing through him.

Swords and shields were raised as the enemy prepared to meet the charge, but Krelltin were as unpredictable as they were fast, and enemy blades met empty air as the fleet-footed birds literally ran circles around them. Thorac and his men, however, knew their birds' next moves as surely as they knew their own, and Tamban blood wet the paving stones as Chunin steel struck true.

Overwhelmed by the unexpected lethality of their opponents, the forward ranks of Tambans broke, then began to pull back, pressing upon those behind them in their haste to retreat. The Chunin cavalry pursued them, striking without mercy, leaving a trail of Tamban bodies in the blood-slicked streets.

Then, just when it looked like the rout was complete, reinforcements arrived through Veilgates, twenty K'rrosha with scepters blazing red with corrupted Fire.

The Chunin Dymas met the attack with shields of Spirit and streamers of *Sei'shiin*, but they weren't fast enough to save all of Thorac's men, and seven Krelltin and their riders vanished in the inferno. Their agonized cries as they died seared

Thorac's heart, but he kept his grief in check by focusing on his rage. *Kill now, grieve later*, he told himself.

The conflagration of Power lasted but a moment, and when it faded, the K'rrosha were gone. So were the Tambans—they'd fled into the vast network of side streets and alleyways.

"Find them," Thorac shouted. "I don't want them getting behind us or moving into the southern quadrants."

"Yes, General Shurr," Captain Fraam said, then raised his horn to his lips once more and sounded the notes which let the cavalry know the hunt was on.

His men responded immediately, and Krelltin raced away into the maze of streets in pursuit. The ringing of steel on steel sounded a heartbeat later.

"Kill them all," Thorac whispered, then turned his Krelltin back toward the staging area. He'd gone less than half a block when Aierlin rode up next to him on her Krelltin. Gwenin was with her but was obviously preoccupied with something she was watching through her Awareness.

"Did that attack seem strange to you?" Aierlin asked. "It felt... small. Much smaller than it could have been considering they outnumber us more than four to one."

"They're feeling us out," he said. "Measuring our strength. Testing our tactics. They may even be trying to wear us down a bit before coming at us in full." He opened his mouth to say more, but a brilliant flash of red stayed his tongue. It came from the vicinity of Northeast Gate and illuminated the whole of the city for one colossal instant. A moment later, a sharp *boom* reached their ears, rattling the windows of the buildings as it passed over them.

"What the blazes was that?" he asked.

"I'm not sure," Aierlin said. Turning her Krelltin about, she looked in the direction of the explosion, and her eyes narrowed with concentration as she stretched out her Awareness to investigate.

She was still searching when a second titanic flash lit the night above River Gate. The thunderous *boom* that followed arrived much more quickly this time and with a lot more energy. It shook the ground and shattered windows and caused the Krelltin to shake their heads in irritation.

A split second later a third flash coupled with an instantaneous *boom* rocked the night above East Gate, and Thorac looked up in time to see dozens of bodies somersaulting through the air. Those not killed outright by the blast died moments later as they landed among the rooftops and roads beneath the wall. He was thankful he was far enough away not to have heard the impacts.

He watched Aierlin until her eyes became focused once more.

"Tamban Blood Maidens," she said. "Three of them. The explosions were a result of them deliberately seizing more of the Power than they could hold."

Thorac stared at her. "And...?"

Aierlin shook her head sadly. "It was devastatingly effective."

Taggert watched the last of the Tamban soldiers fall, then turned his attention to where the crazed *Jeth'Jalda* had been standing when her talisman had exploded. He still didn't know which of his Dymas had opened the Veilgate in front of the explosion to absorb the blast, but their quick thinking had saved the lives of hundreds of men, his included.

"Tend to the wounded," he ordered, then made his way to the point of the explosion and looked down at the burn marks etched into the Power-wrought stone, a sunburst-shaped testament to the destructive power of the strike.

He was still staring at it when Quintella moved up next to him.

"Are you hurt?" she asked.

He shook his head. "No. Thanks to whoever opened the Veilgate."

"It was Idoman," Quintella said. "He'll be along shortly. He went to check on those at the other gates. This wasn't the only attack of this kind."

"Who was that woman?"

"They call themselves Blood Maidens," she answered. "These attacks were penance for their failure to protect *Frel'mola*."

"I see," Taggert said, running the toe of his boot over the damaged area. "Will there be more attacks like this?"

Quintella's beaded braids clicked as she shook her head. "Hard to say. But if more do come, Idoman showed us how to minimize the destruction. For our troops anyway. Those on the opposite side of the gate paid dearly for this attack."

"Where did he open it?"

"In the middle of *Frel'mola te Ujen*," she answered, a smile on her face. "Appropriate since it was they who sent the woman to her death."

She turned toward the edge of the wall, and a split second later a Veilgate opened and Idoman moved through from East Gate. "Captain Ryban is dead," he announced. "No word yet on who might replace him."

He glanced briefly at the scar on the stone near Taggert's feet, then let his eyes move down the wall. "Toss the Tamban dead over the front of the wall," he said. "I don't want their filth tripping our men."

"And our dead?" Taggert asked.

"Put them in the tower for now," he said. "We'll give them a proper burial after all this is over. In the meantime, we need to prepare for the next wave."

Standing at the edge of the Overlook with Brysia at his side, Gideon watched as Power-wrought exchanges of killing energy continued to light the dark expanse of the city in dozens of locations. Thunder followed some of the flashes, rolling up the roadways and across the rooftops like the crashing of storm waves. As of yet, though, only corrupted *Ta'shaen* had been used in the attack, which meant neither Aethon nor Shadan were taking a hand in the battle. The scream-like thunder of Night Threads would have been unmistakable.

Brysia hadn't spoken a word since the attack began, but he knew what she was thinking in spite of her silence. She was worried for those in the southern half of the city, and her eyes hadn't left the maze of rooftops since the attack began. So far things there had remained quiet. Hopefully it would stay that way.

He felt the stirrings in *Ta'shaen* a moment before the Veil parted behind him, and he turned as Elison came through with Pattalla. Both wore frowns fit for a demon as they joined him and Brysia at the edge of the Overlook.

"The reports are coming in," Pattalla said, his dark eyes fastened on the city below. "And they aren't good."

"I didn't think they would be," Gideon grunted. "We heard about the Blood Maidens. What else do you have for me?"

"The attacks on those atop the wall have been repelled," Pattalla answered. "But we see now they may have been nothing more than a distraction—the equivalent of an ostentatious sword-twirl at the beginning of a duel."

"And to some extent we were taken in by it," Elison added. "Yes, we destroyed those who arrived in close proximity to our Dymas, but thousands more arrived deeper in the city after our Dymas revealed themselves by engaging the first wave of Agla'Con and *Jeth'Jalda*. There simply aren't enough Dymas to cover an area so vast."

He looked out at the city. "That second wave—mostly cultists from Death's Third March—came through in smaller groups and immediately went to ground, taking cover in homes and businesses. Short of going door to door to root them out, they're here to stay."

"Aierlin Dymas reported that a large number of Tamban Deathwatch did the same thing. Thorac's men are hunting them, but thousands are in hiding."

Gideon had to fight to keep his frustration in check. "Do we have an approximate location?"

"Both sides of First Avenue on the south of the Trian River."

"And the cultists?"

"Just north of the Trian River between North and Northeast Roads. My guess is they will make a play for the bridges once reinforcements arrive."

"I would if I were them," Gideon said. He realized his hands had knotted into fists, and he forced himself to relax. This would be so much easier if he were out on the battlefield instead of being cooped up here in the palace.

"Send word to Captain Dennison," he said. "Have him send Rove Riders to North River Lane. We need to hold those bridges at all costs."

"And the First Avenue Bridge?" Elison asked.

"I have faith in Thorac's ability to hold it for a while yet," he answered. "He'll know when the time comes to have our Dymas trigger the crux points to destroy it."

"Have there been any attempts by our enemies to enter the Palace?" Pattalla asked.

"Not yet," Gideon answered. "But Ammorin is keeping an eye on the wards should Aethon or Shadan attempt to bring them down. He's in the Dome with Lord

Nid and twenty more members of *Ara'so*."

"I would speak with him," Pattalla said, then offered a bow and strode away on the cobbled path.

When he was gone, Gideon turned to Elison. "I'm sorry to hear about Captain Ryban," he said. "He was a good man."

"And a good friend," Elison replied, then slammed his fist down on the top of the wall. "Bloody Blood Maidens and their bloody suicide mission," he cursed. "We lost a lot of good men to those hags."

Brysia turned to look at him, and he dipped his head in apology. "Sorry for the rough language, my lady."

"No need to apologize," she said. "I used nearly the same words myself when I learned of Lyndon's death." She placed a hand on Elison's arm. "Have you chosen someone to replace him?"

When Elison hesitated, Gideon knew what the captain had decided before he spoke. "I will be leading the City Guardsmen from this point forward," he answered. "And I ask for your blessing on my decision."

Brysia reached up and touched Elison's face. "You have it," she said. "Although it gives me one more person I need to worry about."

"Thank you, my lady," he said, then looked at Gideon. "If you wouldn't mind opening a Veilgate for me, I'll join my men at the wall."

Gideon did as requested, then turned to Brysia when Elison was gone.

"Well, at least we know what the enemy has planned," he said. "They'll continue to attack the wall as a diversion to move troops into the city. There's simply too much city and not enough Dymas to protect it."

He put his arm around her and turned her toward the Dome. "Come," he said. "Let's get you inside. There's nothing more either of us can do until the fight reaches the palace."

# CHAPTER 68

## *Through the Eyes of Ta'shaen*

WITH THE NET OF CRUX POINTS fixed in his mind's eye, Jase channeled the threads of Spirit necessary to shatter them, then watched the warding of Flesh over Augg's main entrance collapse. *Well, that was easier than expec–*

The thought died as the wards sprang back into place.

*Of bloody course,* he thought, then opened his eyes and turned to find everyone watching him expectantly.

"Well, I'm glad we had a good meal," he told them, "because this is going to be harder than I thought. The wards over each of the entry points are linked after all. Not to one another—but to a center point somewhere else in or on the mountain."

"It makes sense," Seibei Dymas said. "Otherwise any Power-wielder could gain access to the mountain. Your forebearer was wise to create such a failsafe."

Jase nodded, then looked around at the others. "You're welcome to retire for the evening," he told them. "No need for all of us to lose sleep."

"I'll take first watch," Seth announced.

"I'll join you," Seibei said, and motioned for several more Shizu to join them.

Jase watched them go, then closed his eyes and extended his Awareness once more. A single central crux point, he thought. The equivalent of searching for a particular grain of sand on a beach.

Jeymi waited until she was sure Jase had extended his Awareness over the whole of the mountain, then opened her Awareness as well and pressed it forward out of the Power-wrought illusion Fairimor had wrought over this part of the island. As soon as her spiritual eyes passed through the insanely bright web of crux points warding them, Mount Augg came into view, tall and menacing against the night sky.

*Beautiful isn't it,* Jase said, his thoughts coming directly into her mind.

*Yes,* she answered, then worried she might be a distraction to him and started to withdraw her Awareness.

*You can stay,* he told her. *It's actually nice to have company for a change.*

*It's strange, isn't it?* she said. *That we can see out of the illusion with our natural eyes but not with the eyes of Ta'shaen. Not without extending our Awareness beyond the edge of the ward, anyway.*

*There are a lot of strange things here,* Jase told her. *Not the least of which is how I can see into some areas inside the mountain with my Awareness but not into others. Hopefully what I am looking for isn't in one of those areas. Otherwise...* He left the rest of the thought unspoken, but she knew from the Communal link what it would be.

*So where are you looking now?* she asked. *I can sense your Awareness spread clear across the mountain, but I have no sense of where it is focused.*

*That's because it's focused everywhere,* he told her, sounding amused. *Well, sort of. I know we always refer to this as looking through the eyes of Ta'shaen, but when you are extended as far as I am, it's more like listening to music. I hear the whole of the symphony, but when I need to I can zero in on specific instruments playing the notes.*

*Interesting analogy,* she said. *So where are you zeroed in?*

*The main entrance,* he answered. *I just fixed the last of the crux points in my mind. I'm going to do the same with one of the other entrances on the lower slopes and one up in the cliffs. That way, when I collapse them and they reset themselves, I should be able to triangulate an approximate location for the central point sustaining the wards.*

*Sounds complicated.*

*You have no idea,* he said. *Makes me wish Fairimor would have just left a key under the doormat.*

He fell silent, and Jeymi sensed a sudden increase in concentration resonating through the vastness of his Awareness. Several minutes passed, and the feeling intensified, then all at once a massive influx of Spirit struck three spots on the mountain. The wards collapsed only to spring back into place a heartbeat later. Jeymi held her breath as she waited for Jase to speak.

*Well,* he said, sounding only partially pleased, *the good news is I found it. It's on the far side of the mountain, about a third of the way up.*

*And the bad news?* she asked.

*I need to collapse all the crux points at the wardings, then shatter the central point before it has a chance to reset.*

She bit her lip worriedly. *And you can do that, right?*

*I guess we'll find out,* he said, then the quiet intensity of concentration settled over his Awareness once more.

Jeymi waited patiently, but as the next hour passed in silence, the inside of her head started to ache with the strain of keeping her Awareness extended. Finally, she reined it in and opened her eyes to find most of the camp asleep.

Elliott and Endil were sitting around one of the campfires with Derian Oronei and three other Shizu, and Elliott was absently poking at it with a stick, sending little whirls of sparks up into the night. Talia lay curled up in her bedroll a few feet away, but her eyes were open and fastened on Jase. She noticed Jeymi looking at her and smiled.

"Welcome back," she whispered, then added, "You look tired."

"I don't know how he does it," she said, scooting near. "My head's killing me and I didn't do anything but *look* at the mountain."

Hearing her voice, Endil left the campfire and moved over to join them. He picked up a blanket along the way and wrapped it around Jeymi's shoulders before dropping down next to her.

"So, could you see what he was doing?" he asked.

She shook her head. "No. His ability to spread his Awareness over such a large area is beyond anything I could ever hope to achieve."

"I achieved it once," Endil said. "When I used the Blood Orb in Kunin. I thought it would crush me."

"I guess that's what makes Jase the *Mith'elre Chon*," she said, still impressed by what she'd witnessed of his abilities. She glanced over her shoulder to where he still sat, wrists on knees, face pinched with concentration. "After my head clears, I want to watch some more. I can't do anything to help, of course, but he said having company was nice."

"Then perhaps," Seibei Dymas said, moving up out of the darkness, "the rest of us should take turns as well."

"He would like that," Jeymi said, then flinched as Jase embraced the Power and sent threads of Spirit all across the mountain. That was followed in the very next instant by a single thrust of Spirit as powerful as all the rest combined.

She held her breath as she waited to find out what it meant.

"He did it," Talia whispered. "I can feel his sense of accomplishment through the *sei'vaiya*."

A moment later Jase opened his eyes and let out a long sigh of relief. "The warding of Flesh is down," he said. "Next up: Water."

He pushed himself to his feet and rolled his shoulders to loosen stiff muscles. He looked at Seibei. "I heard what you said about joining me," he told the Riaki. "And you are welcome to do so."

Jeymi arched an eyebrow at him. "You mean you can do what you are doing all across the mountain and still hear what we are talking about?"

He shrugged. "I hear bits and pieces," he said. "Mostly, it comes to me through the *sei'vaiya*." He winked at Talia who smiled as if she intended to kiss him all over his face.

"Give me a few minutes to stretch my legs," he told Seibei, "and we'll get back to it." He offered his hand to Talia. "Would you like to walk with me?" he asked, and she immediately climbed from her bedroll to join him, pulling a blanket around her shoulders as she did. Jeymi watched them move off into the darkness, then rose and offered her hand to Endil.

"A walk sounds nice," she said. "Will you join me?"

"Absolutely," he answered, and together they moved away from the firelight.

Seibei watched as the two young couples moved off into the darkness, then made his way over to the altar and took a seat next to it. Closing his eyes, he took a deep breath and immersed himself in the luminescent world of *Ta'shaen*. It was like stepping out of a dark room into the brilliant light of day, such was the network of crux points overhead.

He still couldn't fathom how Fairimor had wrought such a complex illusion, and he knew he probably never would. It was here to conceal them and that was all that mattered.

Shaping his Awareness into a narrow, more telescopic view, he extended it beyond the edge of the illusion and watched as Mount Augg appeared before him. It was tall and forbidding against the backdrop of stars, but knowing what it contained somewhere in its depths made it one of the most beautiful sights he'd ever seen.

He was still caught up in its beauty when he sensed Jase's Awareness.

*Thanks for being here,* Jase said.

Seibei smiled. *The pleasure is mine,* Mith'elre Chon.

*See the main entrance there?* Jase said. *The one with the aqueducts? There's a crux point set at the end of each. I found them after the warding of Flesh collapsed. There are more at the far end of the corridor near what looks like a hole in the Veil, but is really a thick wall of perfectly clear ice. The illusion of depth and darkness is due to the lake of water it's holding back.*

Seibei pressed his Awareness forward into the entrance. *Can you break the ice?*

*Easily,* Jase answered. *But like the rest of the wards, it would simply reset. Fortunately, it feels like there are far fewer crux points this time. My guess is Fairimor tapped into a series of natural springs instead of channeling the water into existence as he did with the first two wards.*

Seibei nodded his understanding. *So, the wall of ice is essentially a plug. Pull it—*

*And the water will drain from the temple. The only problem: The rest of the lower entrances are also capped. And like the wards of Flesh were, they are linked to a central point somewhere in the midst of the reservoir.*

*Do you want help finding it?*

*I think I just did,* Jase answered, and Seibei was so surprised he nearly lost control of his Awareness.

*That was fast.*

Jase's amusement was palpable. *I've had practice. And my suspicion that Fairimor used it to tap into a natural water source was correct. Follow the corridor with your Awareness. Like all the others, it leads to a cavern in the center of the mountain.*

Seibei felt him embrace the Gift of *shiin* and a small sphere of light appeared to guide him to the location. When his spiritual eyes reached the spot, he found a vast circular cavern filled with water. No, he thought, not a cavern. This had the perfectly round shape of a well and descended straight as an arrow into the depths of the earth. It stretched upward a great distance as well, but the top was hidden from view by a powerful warding of Spirit. It negated his spiritual vision as surely as if he'd been severed from the Power.

*That's the final ward,* Jase told him. *And it has more than one purpose. As you just noticed, it blocks the upper part of the mountain from view of our Awareness. It's also the ward that prevented us from arriving on the island by Veilgate.*

*How do you collapse a ward you can't see into?*

*I don't know,* Jase said. *But I'll worry about that once we get there. First, let's finish what we started here.*

*What you started, you mean,* Seibei said. *I haven't done anything.*

He felt another trace of amusement, then Jase's Awareness grew quiet as he concentrated on the task at hand.

The minutes stretched into hours, and the inside of Seibei's head started to ache from the strain of keeping his Awareness extended. He fought through it, determined to see what would happen when Jase collapsed the wards.

Another hour passed, and the stars began to fade as the sky lightened in the east. A short time later, he felt the brush of Jeymi's mind as she extended her Awareness toward the mountain.

*How's he doing?* she asked.

*I'm not sure,* he answered. *He said there were fewer crux points to find this time, but that was several hours ago.*

*I was wrong,* Jase said, his concentration wavering slightly. *There were nearly as many as with the warding of Earth. I didn't see them at first because they are strung at varying intervals for the full length of all the corridors. But I think I just about have them all. I won't try to shatter them until I know for sure. If I miss even one, I'll have to start over.*

*Take your time,* Seibei told him. *We aren't going anywhere.*

Another hour passed, and Jeymi withdrew her Awareness. Seibei, however, watched as the first rays of the morning sun painted the top of the mountain in hues of amber, then began their slow descent down the steep slopes. The full light of the sun cresting the horizon reached the main entrance a few minutes later.

Shortly after that, Jase embraced the Gift of Spirit, and the crux points maintaining the wards of Water shattered. So did the walls of ice holding back the underground lake, and the mountain trembled as the tremendous pressure behind those walls was released and the well inside Augg began to drain.

Water erupted from each of the lower entrances in jet-like bursts, and fragments of rainbows became visible in the rising sprays of mist. The powerful streams of frothy white roared down the slopes and across the boulder fields, turning rocks in sharp rumbles of stone.

The sound brought the camp awake in an instant, and Seibei opened his eyes to find Shizu and Dymas alike springing to their feet. Sword blades were bared and a number of the Dymas embraced the Power.

"It's all right," he told them. "Jase just collapsed the warding of Water."

He felt a number of the Dymas press their Awarenesses forward to investigate and watched their faces as they spotted the raging torrents of water.

"All that was inside the mountain?" Jeymi asked, clearly astonished by the sight.

"It filled the first four levels of the temple," Jase said, and Seibei turned to find that he had reined in his Awareness. He wore a smile as he listened to the distant roar of the water. "And that's only part of it. There is a spring in the center of the mountain which feeds the fountains and aqueducts inside the temple."

"So, you've seen the temple," Elliott asked, sheathing his sword and releasing the Power.

"The first five levels," Jase answered. "The upper two are still blocked from my view."

Seth strode through the midst of the Shizu and stopped in front of Jase. Seibei could tell by the way the captain was looking his young friend over that he was worried about how Jase was holding up.

Jase saw it, too, and smiled. "I'm fine," he said. "Immersing myself that deeply into *Ta'shaen* is almost as restful as real sleep." He looked at the dying campfire and added, "I could do with a little more of that ram meat, though. Living in the luminescent world of my Awareness doesn't get rid of hunger."

Seth nodded, then signaled the Shizu to stoke up the fire. As they hurried to do as ordered, Seth returned his eyes to Jase. "So what's next?"

"The wards of Fire," Jase answered.

Seth gave a small wave of his hand. "Let me rephrase that. What's next for this camp? You said you've seen into the first five levels. Do we enter the temple and have you collapse the wards from there or do we remain here?"

Jase turned and looked in the direction of the mountain, and Seibei knew he was probing it with his Awareness. The roaring of water was still audible as the inside of the mountain continued to drain, but it wouldn't last much longer. They should be able to enter if Jase thought it wise to do so.

Finally, Jase came back to himself and faced Seth once more.

"We stay here," he said. "I have no idea what releasing the wards of Fire might do, and I don't want to risk that it might be akin to what just happened with Water. I'm starting to think Fairimor put the altar so far from the wards because getting any closer is dangerous."

"It certainly would have been with the last ward," Jeymi said.

Seth nodded and turned to Elliott. "Let's you and I see if we can't fetch another big horn sheep or two while Jase enjoys some of what's left of the first two."

"Can I take my bow this time?" Elliott asked.

"Certainly," Seth answered. "But if you miss, you're dressing out both kills."

Elliott narrowed his eyes at him, and it looked for a moment that he might change his mind. Finally, he nodded. "Fine. But if I do make the kill with my bow, you'll dress them out."

Seth agreed and they moved to the Myrscraw. A moment later they were winging their way toward the mountain.

Jase watched Seth and Elliott disappear over the treetops, then turned to find Talia staring at him with a slight frown on her face. He'd already sensed what she was thinking through the *sei'vaiya*, so he wasn't surprised by what came next.

"You were lying about how tired you are," she said. "Why?"

He shrugged. "There's a lot to do yet and not a lot of time to do it." He took her hand and led her away from the others. Lowering his voice, he continued, "I didn't want to alarm him or anyone else with what I sensed while I was immersed in the spiritual view of the world."

"And what did you sense?" she asked, suddenly apprehensive.

"That the Veil is about to collapse in earnest. It will begin with an increase in the number of sporadic holes which have been opening across the Nine Lands. Only those to come are going to be much larger than what we've seen so far. And they're going to occur everywhere. The Earthsoul is no longer strong enough to keep them away from populated areas."

The blood drained from her face. "Chellum?"

He nodded. "Chellum. Trian. Andlexces. Nowhere will be safe. The beginning of the end is upon us."

# CHAPTER 69

## *The Beginning of the End*

STANDING AT THE EASTERN EDGE of the Overlook, Gideon shielded his eyes from the morning sun rising over Trian. He couldn't, however, shut his Awareness to the chaos raging in a dozen places across the city. The fabric of the Earthsoul seethed in agony as flashes of lightning and bursts of hellish fire erupted across entire quadrants in a bizarre, ground-level storm of Power-wrought destruction.

East Gate still held, but Elison and his army of City Guardsman had been separated from the Chunin army who'd fallen back to Second Avenue after destroying the First Avenue Bridge. He still hadn't learned how an army of Tambans and the *Jeth'Jalda* who led them had managed to take such a large area so quickly, but the quadrant between East Road and the Trian River was, for the moment, in their hands.

Elison and his Guardsmen had taken refuge in and atop the wall, but it was only a matter of time before they had to retreat or risk being overrun. Ohran had sent a number of *Ara'so* to the area through Veilgates, but Gideon wondered how much of an effect it would have now that the tide of battle had already turned there.

River Gate still held, but the number of Power-wrought attacks on the area had to be taking its toll on those trying to hold it.

Northeast Gate was faring better than her sisters to the south, and Gideon attributed it to Dymas General Leda and his uncanny ability to predict what the enemy would do next. Aside from the suicidal attack by the Blood Maiden, nothing else had taken him or his men by surprise. It was, he believed, why the Fist of Con'Jithar had pulled back on its attack there and was sending large numbers of troops into the city through Veilgates instead. All had arrived well out of range of Idoman or his men, and were working to fortify positions wherever they arrived. Hopefully, Captain Dennison and his Rove Riders could disrupt whatever the

Tambans had planned.

North Gate had fared better still, a result of the protection of Ohran and his Dainin. They might be outnumbered a thousand to one, but the scum of Death's Third March had learned firsthand that numbers weren't everything. Between the Keepers' unparalleled skill at using the Power for defense and the *Ara'so's* newfound freedom for unbridled slaughter, Shadan's minions found themselves facing the ultimate war machine.

It made him wonder how long it would be before Shadan or Aethon took a hand in things. That neither of the two had yet revealed themselves anywhere on the battle field was mystifying. He couldn't fathom what they might be waiting for.

The sound of footsteps on the path behind him pulled his attention away from the chaos out in the city, and he turned to find Brysia approaching with Elder Nesthius. The Queen held the aging High Priest by the arm and seemed to be the only thing keeping him upright. Gideon was shocked to see him. He'd been under the impression that Nesthius had left along with the rest of the palace's residents.

"Look who came for a visit," Brysia said when they reached him.

Gideon offered his hand to Nesthius and helped guide him to the wall. "How did you get back into the city?"

"I never left," he answered. "I've been in my office or in the chapel praying for us all." He looked at the explosions of Power breaking loose across the city and added, "I should have prayed harder."

"I'm afraid it will take more than prayer to save us now," Gideon said. "We need Jase to use the Blood Orb he went to retrieve."

"Brysia told me about that," Nesthius said. "And praised be the Creator for His wisdom in preserving one for Jase to use." He turned and looked Gideon in the eyes. "But he better use it quickly. Time is about to run out."

The hair on the back of Gideon's neck prickled in alarm. "You saw something in a vision." It wasn't a question.

Elder Nesthius nodded. "It is why I have come." He hesitated, his eyes bright with emotion. "I saw the end of days spoken of in the prophecies," he said. "I witnessed the complete collapse of the Veil as the Earthsoul took Her final breath. I watched as Con'Jithar arrived in Trian."

The feeling of alarm morphed into panic, and a cold fist took Gideon by the heart and began to squeeze. "Did you get a sense of when that might happen?"

Nesthius squinted out at the morning brightness. "No," he whispered. "But if Jase fails in his mission, I fear we may have just witnessed our final sunrise."

Before Gideon could respond, an audible *boom* sounded deep inside the earth. It was followed by a visible shockwave that moved across the city, shaking everything so violently that windows shattered and shingles sloughed off of roofs. Clouds of dust billowed skyward from the cascade of shingles. In a number of places, entire buildings collapsed into rubble. Gideon gripped the wall in front of him as even the Power-wrought solidity of the *chorazin* of the palace and Overlook trembled.

Elder Nesthius sighed. "And so it begins."

The shaking continued for several minutes as a number of strong aftershocks followed, and Gideon took Nesthius' arm to support him. Brysia held his other arm, and together they waited for the tremors to subside.

They were still waiting when a familiar Awareness touched Gideon's and he opened himself to it.

*I hear you, Chieftain,* Gideon said.

*We've got trouble,* Ohran told him. *That earthquake was the physical manifestation of a much more serious problem. Take a look at the base of the Kelsan Mountains west of Mendel Pass.*

Gideon did as instructed, pressing his Awareness toward the area in a narrow, bird's eye view that stopped a few miles short of the mountain. His heart nearly stopped at what he found. A section of the Veil a mile high and ten miles wide had collapsed, and the dark and blighted landscape of Con'Jithar was visible beyond. So was an army of demons rushing toward the opening with weapons in hand. Some of those weapons, he noted, blazed red with the insensate evil of *Lo'shaen*. As he watched, the entire lot—some six or seven thousand strong—passed through into the living world and angled straight for Trian.

*Another rent of similar size opened just beyond the eastern townships,* Ohran said. *Fortunately it opened away from us, so any demons will have to work their way around the edges before they can come at us.*

*Which they will,* Gideon said, shifting his Awareness until the wall where Ohran stood came into his mind's eye. *Let's hope neither group discriminates when it comes to killing. I'd love for them to thin our enemies for us.*

*Throy Shadan must be worried about it,* Ohran said, pointing to a spot out in the northern township. *He just revealed himself by taking control of more than a hundred Agla'Con and* Jeth'Jalda.

As the strength of the shield Ohran and his *Nar'shein* held over the wall increased in anticipation of an attack, Gideon pressed his Awareness toward Shadan and found a lightning storm of red and black corruption crackling toward the Dreadlord as he harnessed the abilities of his black-hearted servants.

*It looks like—*

Ohran's Awareness vanished from the link as a tremendous surge of *Lo'shaen* ripped across the already frayed fabric of the Earthsoul. It struck North Gate like a colossal battering ram, a vicious thrust of dark energy that knocked the gate from its hinges and sent the Power-wrought steel tumbling into the city in clanging shrieks of metal and showers of sparks. A second titanic thrust breached Northeast Gate, and a heartbeat after that East Gate was ripped free of the wall as well.

Gideon stared at the gaping holes in astonishment. Throy Shadan had just accomplished in a few seconds what his three armies had been unable to do over the course of an entire night. It came at price, though—the Agla'Con and *Jeth'Jalda* who'd lent Shadan their strength wouldn't be able to wield again for hours. So why had he taken a hand in the battle now? And in such an extreme way? Why weren't his armies storming into the city?

He felt the brush of Ohran's Awareness and breathed a sigh of relief that his friend was still alive. When the mindlink had been severed, he'd feared the worst.

*Our enemies are moving off the main roadways,* Ohran said. *They're giving the demons a clear path into the city.*

*Of course they are,* Gideon said, frustration and an utter sense of helplessness washing through him. *And not simply to avoid them in battle.*

He got a rein on his frustration, and added, *Send word to all our Dymas. Shadan is going to let the demons lead the charge. He'll wait for our Dymas to engage them, and then he'll undoubtedly launch an attack of his own.*

Brysia knew from the look on her husband's face that he'd extended his Awareness and was watching whatever was happening out at the wall.

She should be used to it by now, but it made her crazy that she had no idea what was going on beyond what she could perceive with her natural senses. First the earthquake, and then the ear-splitting explosions of some terrible impact—she took a steadying breath and tried to subdue her impatience at not knowing exactly what had happened.

Several more minutes passed in silence, then Gideon turned to look at her and Elder Nesthius.

"Your vision is proving accurate so far," he told the aging High Priest. "The Veil just failed in two locations on Trian Plateau. We now have armies of demons to contend with."

Brysia went cold inside. "Won't the demons attack Shadan's forces as readily as they would us?"

"To some extent," Gideon answered. "But Shadan has ordered his Power-wielders to clear the main roadways."

"He's creating a path of least resistance," Nesthius muttered.

"At least until the demons reach the wall," Brysia said.

"The gates have been breached," Gideon said, dread heavy in his voice. "Shadan tore them from their hinges as if they were made of rotting wood."

Brysia stared at the outer wall in disbelief. So, that's what she'd heard—the destruction of the gates. "How long before the demons arrive?"

Gideon's eyes narrowed as he looked to the north. "A couple of hours at most," he answered, then shook his head and turned to meet her gaze. "But I fear they won't be the worst of what we will be facing in the hours to come."

Elder Nesthius arched an eyebrow at him. "You fear or you know?"

Gideon grunted. "Both," he answered. "And it's that knowledge that makes me fearful." He turned Elder Nesthius toward the Dome. "Come. We best get you back inside where... where you can continue to pray for our safety."

His eyes briefly met Brysia's, and she understood what he'd stopped himself from saying. *Back inside where it is safe.*

Safe. The word had become obsolete.

Velerie Kivashey was listening to Bornis issue instructions to the most recent group of refugees from Trian Plateau when another earthquake shook Kindel's Grove, rattling the newly replaced windows of Zander's Mercantile and causing the hanging baskets of flowers and herbs to sway.

Everyone paused while the tremor ran its course, then returned to what they were doing as if nothing had happened. They were growing accustomed to the signs of the Earthsoul's failing, and she didn't know how she felt about it. On the one hand, it might be a manifestation of the tremendous amount of faith they had in Jase's ability save them. Or it could simply be a lack of understanding of just how serious the situation really was. It was hard to tell where they stood.

She watched Zander finish loading a bag of flour into Jaylin Daeblin's cart, then followed him with her eyes as he moved back into his store. Bornis finished speaking with the new arrivals—four families with children ranging in age from newborn up to twelve—then ruffled the hair of one of the little boys and nodded for Captain Nian to show them to their temporary homes.

With so many houses and businesses sitting empty because of Aethon Fairimor's massacre of its people, Kindel's Grove had become the perfect place for those fleeing ahead of Death's Third March. And, oddly enough, as the survivors of that horrific night welcomed people into their community, opening the homes of dear friends lost, it helped them to heal emotionally. Proof positive that generosity and service were always better then selfishness and isolation.

"That makes twenty-seven new families in three days," Bornis said as he joined her on the bench in front of the mercantile. "At this rate, we will run out of places to put them by tomorrow."

"The inn and tavern still have room," Fadus said as he exited the mercantile. Zea and Wytni were with him, and Wytni's broad smile as she carried little Kindel warmed Velerie's heart.

"And the Daeblins and a number of other families approached me with offers of opening their homes as well," Fadus continued. "The new arrivals might be sleeping in attics or on floors, or even in barns, but they will have a roof over their heads. And right now that's all that matters."

He looked as if he would say more, but a chorus of startled voices sounded further up the street, and he looked toward it. "Now what do you suppose..." he began but trailed off as Braelynn Dryssibyn and Jemmishin Baalishan came into view. Each carried an *arinseil* net and a spear, and they were running.

Velerie smiled appreciatively as she watched them hurry down the street. Like so many of the younger generation of Dainin, they'd followed Ammorin's and Pattalla's lead to become Soldiers of God—and she, for one, thought it was about bloody time.

As the crowded street parted before them, Velerie saw that the blades of their spears were streaked with greyish-black blood, and she went cold inside at what it meant.

"Mayor Murra," Braelynn said, going to one knee so she could look him in the eyes. "We intercepted a demon entering the outskirts of Kindel's Grove. It arrived through a hole in the Veil not far from the Fairimor property."

"Just one?" Fadus said, and Velerie couldn't decide if he was relieved or surprised. After what they'd heard of other collapses, it was probably a little of both. It could have just as easily been a thousand demons as one.

"For now," Braelynn answered. "Yorrindal and Naemmon are watching the rent in case more arrive. Together with the wards we put over the area, they will destroy anything else which might come through." She looked at her blood-slicked blades. "We killed the demon after the manner of the *Nar'shein* to keep our presence hidden in case others arrived before we reached the rent. When we were satisfied that none had, we came directly to you."

Fadus ran his hand over his mostly bald head in frustration. "This village just opened its doors to two dozen families fleeing monsters like this. They were supposed to be safe here."

"That's just it," Jemmishin said, his weathered face pinched with sadness, "nowhere in the Nine Lands is safe anymore."

"So what do we do?" Bornis asked, and Velerie could tell by the sound of his voice that he was just as frustrated as Fadus. He'd brought Wytni and Zea and little Kindel here to get them out of harm's way, not switch one type of danger for another. Yes, Trian was under siege by the armies of Throy Shadan, but Trian had the united armies to help combat the threat. Bornis had her and Jukstin, Braelynn and her team, and a handful of Highwaymen. What could they do against demons from Con'Jithar?

"We gather those who live in the outlying areas and bring them into the village proper," Braelynn said, then glanced pointedly at the axe Bornis wore on his hip. "And we prepare for war," she said. "We—"

She cut off as another earthquake rumbled across the area, causing the boardwalk beneath them to creak and the mercantile to sway. One of the newly replaced windows cracked, and a flock of recently perched doves fluttered back into the air.

It passed almost as quickly as it had come, but an uneasy silence fell over the village as everyone waited to see if it was truly over. A moment later something dark brushed her Awareness, a cold, rage-filled, hate-filled touch of an ancient mind that made her skin crawl.

"I felt it, too," Braelynn said, and the amount of dread in her voice turned every head within earshot.

"Felt what?" Bornis asked.

Braelynn looked in the direction of the highway and her hand tightened on her spear. "Demons."

乇

Elam Gaufin had just finished making his morning rounds and was passing through the Chellum Gardens when Raimen and Tohquin appeared as if from thin air, startling him so badly he reached for his sword.

"I thought we talked about you not doing that anymore," he said, scowling at both of them.

"You talked about it," Raimen said. "We listened."

"But we never agreed to anything," Tohquin added.

"Well, you bloody well better agree to it now or I'm sending you both back to Riak."

The two exchanged looks, then Tohquin changed the subject. "Jonnil Dymas wishes to speak with you. Apparently, three more homes and two businesses collapsed in Merchant's Quarter during the most recent earthquake. Five people were killed. Another four homes inside the city were damaged, but there were no casualties. However, a section of Festival Lane has buckled, and there is a large crack in the outer wall near the northern gate."

"Bloody earthquakes," Elam muttered. "What's next? A hurricane?"

"Don't tempt fate," Raimen said. "We just received word from Drusi Bridge. A thunderstorm swept down out of the Glacier Mountains overnight and hailstones the size of cabbages fell on the southern half of town. Dozens of homes damaged or destroyed. Fifteen people dead."

Elam closed his eyes for a moment to mourn the dead in both cities, then opened them and started for the glass doors leading into the Chellum home. "Any word from Trian?" he asked.

"The city is under siege," Tohquin answered. "North, Northeast, and East Gate have all been breached. River Gate still holds, but with the others destroyed, it's only a matter of time."

"And that isn't the worst of the news," Raimen added as he pulled the door open for Elam. "The Veil has collapsed in two locations on Trian Plateau. Thousands of demons are moving toward the city."

Elam shook his head in disgust. "This just keeps getting worse."

"You don't know the half of it," Jonnil Dymas said, rising from where he sat with Decker at the dining table. "A rent just opened in the foothills south of the Chellum River. Several hundred demons are moving our way as well."

"And here I was worried about an attack by Gizo or Kyoai," Raimen muttered.

"What do you recommend we do?" Elam asked, addressing the question to Jonnil. "Do we go out to meet them before they reach the city?"

"Yes," Jonnil said. "We can't allow them to reach a populated area. If they do, it will be a slaughter."

Elam nodded. "Take as many Dymas as you need," he said. "I'll have Captain Somish mobilize the Merchant Guard to intercept any demons that make it past you."

Jonnil arched an eyebrow at him. "Make it past us? Where's your faith?" Standing, he offered a bow to Decker, then started for the doors leading to the ballroom. He'd only gone a few steps when he whirled as if he'd been stabbed. His eyes, wide with alarm were fixed on the windows fronting the Chellum gardens.

"Demons!" he shouted. "A rent just opened near the moat."

Elam was on his feet in an instant. Sword in hand, he sprinted for the door leading to the gardens. As he neared it, he spotted a number of grotesque shapes lumbering toward him, massive, misshapen creatures that were more animal than man.

A bolt of silver lightning lanced out of the sky to strike the nearest creature in the head, and it burst apart in chunks of sizzling grey flesh as thunder rattled the glass of the windows. The strike enraged the rest of the demons, and they threw their heads back and released a chorus of bizarre snarls and howls as they continued to bear down on him. Another bolt of lightning followed, and then another, exploding demon and garden foliage alike.

And still they came, numbering twenty or more, their eyes burning with demonic fire.

He went cold inside when he saw this was a battle he could not win. Sheathing his sword, he pulled the lever sticking from the wall and released the large steel doors hidden inside the walls of the palace. They slid effortlessly along the rollers, and he listened to the series of metallic clicks as the heavy locks set in the walls snapped shut behind them.

The approaching demons vanished behind a wall of steel as the doors came together with a resonant *boom*. The muted sounds of shattering glass were followed by dull thuds and scrapes as the demons launched themselves at the doors.

Elam turned back to the others. "Sound the alarm," he told Jonnil. "We've got work to do."

七

Cassia Fairimor smiled at the two *Bero'thai* standing watch outside her bedroom door, then pulled the door closed behind her and started down the corridor toward Lord Reiekel's private dining room. The two Elvan soldiers followed silently, their hands on their swords, their faces serene.

Two more *Bero'thai* waited at the end of the corridor, and one pulled the door open for her as she approached.

She nodded her thanks as she moved through into the dining room.

Andil looked up as she entered, then rose to greet her. "Good morning, Mother," he said, kissing her on the cheek. "You just missed Lord Reiekel," he continued. "He left in a hurry after receiving a message from Aridan. He didn't say what it was, but he seemed upset as he left."

Cassia pursed her lips worriedly. "More bad news regarding the collapse of the Veil, most likely," she said, then shook her head and moved to the table. Andil held her chair for her before taking his own.

"I've been thinking," he said, and she knew what was coming before he said it. "My place is in Trian. I feel like a coward sitting here in Andlexces while my friends and family, while my countrymen, are fighting for their lives."

"We've been over this, my son," she said. "If Endil and Jase fail to return, you will be the last of the sons of Fairimor. Duty requires that you be ready to assume the throne should it come to that."

"If Jase doesn't return," he argued, "it means he failed to rejuvenate the Earthsoul—and that means there won't be a throne to return home to."

"We don't know that," she said. "There are no guarantees that success in his mission as the *Mith'elre Chon* will bring him home alive. There are, in fact, a number of prophecies that hint otherwise. The Rejuvenation requires sacrifice. *Blood* sacrifice."

"All the more reason for me to return to Trian," he said, his anger starting to show. "If Jase is willing to sacrifice himself for us, we should be willing to do the same for others."

"Foregoing your own desires in order to do what is necessary *is* sacrifice," she told him. "And this is yours."

She reached over and put her hand on his. "I don't like it either," she said. "Knowing that Brysia and Gideon are in Trian waiting to receive Death's Third March tears at my heart every time I think about it. But they asked me to stay here." She gave an unamused laugh. "Well, Brysia asked. Gideon ordered."

"And did he give the order to keep me locked away from danger like some pampered coward?"

"Your uncle doesn't doubt your mettle, Andil. He's simply preparing for the possibility that you might need to lead Kelsa if this ends in our favor."

He looked as if he might argue further, but the door opened and a *Bero'thai* stepped inside the room. "You need to come with me," he said, his tone urgent. "The city is under attack. We need to get you somewhere more secure."

"Under attack?" Andil said, rising to his feet and taking a protective stance next to Cassia. "By whom?"

"Demons," the *Bero'thai* answered. "And they're already inside the city walls."

Cassia took Andil's hand, and they followed the Elvan soldier out into the hallway where dozens more *Bero'thai* waited with weapons in hand.

As they started for the interior of the palace, the bell in Elldrenei College's tower clanged loudly, a clarion call to action.

Cassia caught a glimpse of the bell tower out of one of the windows as she hurried along, and beyond the tower, flashes of reddish black corruption. They crisscrossed the sky in sizzling stabs of death that filled the air with strange, scream-like peals of thunder.

Night Threads, she realized. The demons attacking Andlexces were wielders of *Lo'shaen.*

*God help us,* she thought, and she and Andil followed the *Bero'thai* deeper into the palace.

乇

Trake Noevom tightened his grip on the reins as another tremor rumbled across the abandoned township, breaking the glass in more of the empty houses and causing his horse to dance nervously.

"Easy girl," he said, patting her neck. "It will pass."

And it did. Just like all the ones before it. How many was that now? Seven? Eight? He'd lost count. And it wasn't that important anyway. What was important were the five K'rrosha riding toward him from the back edge of Death's Third March.

They held their lances erect, which meant he wasn't in danger of dying just yet, but he would need to tread carefully in the next few moments if he wanted to survive the encounter. He wore his Con'Kumen medallion on the outside of his shirt for them to see, but even that might not be enough if they felt he posed a threat. Or even if they were in a bad mood, which seemed to be the mood of choice for most Deathmen.

When they were near enough to see his hands clearly, he made the short series of finger motions identifying himself as a member of the Brotherhood.

"What is your name, *Mae'kishon?*" one of the K'rrosha asked, its red-eyed gaze narrowing menacingly.

"Trake Noevom," he answered. "I seek an audience with my master, the Agla'Con Marut Saroj."

The K'rrosha exchanged looks with one another, then the one who'd spoken lowered its lance at Trake's chest. "Why aren't you already with the rest of Death's Third March?"

"I've been on assignment in Andlexces," Trake answered. "And I have important information for my master regarding my time there."

The refleshed being's eyes narrowed further, and Trake held his breath that it would believe him.

"He's this way," the K'rrosha said at last. Raising his lance, he wheeled his shadowspawned horse about and started back the way he had come. Trake urged his horse to follow, then swallowed nervously as the remaining four K'rrosha took up positions around him and escorted him into the midst of Throy Shadan's army.

# CHAPTER 70

## *The Final Ward*

TALIA'S HAND ON HIS ARM brought Jase awake with a start. He sat up, embarrassment and alarm washing through him in turns.

"How long have I been asleep?" he asked, trying to shake away the last of the grogginess that had settled over his mind. He'd fully intended to immerse himself in *Jiu*, but had instead succumbed to his weariness. Obviously, he was more tired than he'd been willing to admit. Even to himself.

"Less than an hour," she said, and he could feel the warmth of her loving assurance through the *sei'vaiya*. "Which is about seven hours less than you deserve."

"I'll sleep after I rejuvenate the Earthsoul," he told her, pushing himself to his feet. Taking a deep breath, he looked around the camp. Elliott and Derian were carrying the second of the two rams toward the cookfire. Elliott had blood up to his elbows, and the look he directed at Seth spoke volumes.

"He missed the kill, didn't he?" he whispered, and Talia nodded.

"Serves him right for always turning everything into a competition."

Jase laughed. "I guess it does." He motioned for Seth to join them.

"The backstraps are more tender," Seth commented as he walked past where Elliott was cutting strips of meat from the ram's hind quarters.

Elliott scowled at him, but he rolled the ram onto its side and began removing one of the backstraps.

"Feeling a little more rested?" Seth asked when he reached them.

"Not really," Jase told him. "Whose idea was it to let me sleep, anyway?"

"Mine," Seth said. "Just as it was my idea to get some food in your belly. You can't save the world if you die of sleep deprivation or starvation or both."

"I'm fine," Jase said, but from the corner of his eye he saw Talia shaking her head.

"He's not fine," she told Seth. "Which is why I argued against waking him. He needs to rest."

Jase started to object, but she turned a hard eye on him. "And don't you dare say that you'll rest when you're dead. I know you just thought it."

"I did just think it," he said, then looked at Seth. "But I learned it from him."

Talia narrowed her eyes at him, but the *sei'vaiya* told him her irritation was feigned. Taking her hand, he led her to the fire and took one of the skewers of meat Elliott had prepared.

"I'll rest while I cook this," he said, sitting next to the fire and holding the skewer near the bed of coals. "But then it's back to collapsing the rest of the wards. As I said earlier, there's a lot to do and not a lot of time to do it."

Marut Saroj touched the minds of yet another knot of Darklings, then watched them scurry off the roadway like so many overgrown rats. Of all the shadowspawn in Shadan's army, he hated Darklings the most. They were bloodthirsty and unpredictable and just stupid enough to pick a fight with the quickly approaching army of demons. Shadan had been wise to order their removal from the roadways.

"Make sure all the Quathas and Wholvin are out of the way as well," Marut shouted to the Agla'Con under his command. "Then start cordoning off the sides of the roadway with wards of Fire. Nothing strong enough to kill—we want them to keep their sights set on Trian, not anger them to the point they attack us."

"Pardon the interruption, Master Saroj," a voice said, and Marut turned as a K'rrosha stepped near, "but this one claims to be a *Mae'kishon* in your service."

He stepped aside to reveal a young man wearing the Black Hand Medallion of the Con'Kumen.

Marut looked from the medallion to the young man's face and nodded. "He is what he claims," he told the K'rrosha. "You are dismissed."

As the K'rrosha moved away, Marut looked Trake in the eyes. "You are a long way from Andlexces," he said, watching the blood drain from his face. "I trust you have an explanation for this."

"I do," Trake said, then looked around guardedly. "But... you might want to hear it in private."

Marut looked around at the throng of soldiers moving about and nodded. "Walk with me," he said, and started down one of the nameless side streets.

When he was certain he was out of sight of any who might question his actions, he seized the Power and opened a rent to another nameless street well beyond the area occupied by Death's Third March. He let the rent snap shut, then channeled a ward against eavesdropping.

"Well, *Mae'kishon*," he said. "Let's hear it."

"It's the *Mith'elre Chon*," Trake said. "He's discovered the location of a Blood Orb of Elsa."

Marut's failure to keep his surprise in check sent the boy cowering to his knees. "When?" he hissed. "Where? Out with it, boy! The very success of Death's Third March is at stake."

"Mount Augg," Trake answered. "He learned of it two days ago."

*Two days!* Marut thought, a stab of fear lancing through his heart. *He could very well be on his way to the Soul Chamber by now.*

He realized he was clenching his hands into fists and forced himself to relax. He needed to think this through carefully.

He was tempted to make a play for the Orb himself—he could certainly rally enough support from Agla'Con loyal to him to do so. But then what? Use it to collapse the Veil and usher in the world of the dead?

Doing so would earn him a place of glory in the world to come, certainly. But if he failed to capture it, or if Jase Fairimor used if before he could locate him, there wouldn't be a place deep enough or dark enough in all Con'Jithar to hide him from Maeon's wrath.

No. Making a play for the Orb himself was too risky. He'd seen firsthand what had happened to the fools who'd tried to claim previous Orbs for themselves— Borilius and his lot with the Orb in Zeka and the morons from Kamasin and the Orb in Melek. Failure in life and in death, not an enticing prospect.

So, who to pass the information on to? Shadan or Aethon? Both? They alone were strong enough to go head to head with the *Mith'elre Chon*.

And even if they chose not to go in person, only they could authorize an army of Agla'Con to go in their stead. Either way, strength sufficient to challenge the *Mith'elre Chon's* could be gathered.

His decision made, he looked down at Trake. "On your feet," he said. "We need to get this information to the First."

七

Jeymi watched as Jase shattered the crux points sustaining the wards of Fire, then blinked in surprise when nothing out of the ordinary happened. The tightly woven threads of killing destruction simply vanished back into the fabric of the Earthsoul.

*Rather anticlimactic, wasn't it?* Jase said, sounding intrigued. *I was expecting something a little more... fiery.*

*Maybe it was for the best,* she said. *We wouldn't want you lighting a signal fire that might be seen by our enemies.*

*Still,* he said. *Those were some pretty impressive wards. I can't say for sure what they would have looked like had they detonated, but there was enough energy stored in them to melt stone.*

*So, is it on to the wards of Air?* she asked.

*Yes,* he answered. *But not in the way you might think. Robishar Fairimor's prophecy hinted at the answer even before I found some of the crux points linked to the wards of Air. He said, and I quote:*

> And none shall enter but by the Power of the Blue Flame. For without the Flame there can be no light, neither breath of life nor hope for salvation.

*Breath of life, he said. An Old World term for air to breathe. The crux points Fairimor set are keeping Air out of the mountain. If we tried to enter now, we would suffocate.*

*That's amazing,* Jeymi told him. *He really did set these up such that only you could release them.*

"In more ways than you know," he said, and she opened her eyes to find him looking at the *chorazin* altar. "He also said that none shall enter but by the Power of the Blue Flame."

"So what does that mean?" she asked, then glanced around at the others as they stopped what they were doing to listen.

"It means I can't collapse the rest of the wards on my own."

Rising to his feet, he retrieved the Blue Flame Scepter from his bedroll. "The wards of Fire have been removed," he announced. "All that remain are Air, Light, and Spirit."

He looked at Seibei. "Do you remember when you asked me how to collapse a ward I can't see into? Well, here's the answer." Hefting the scepter, he returned to the altar and sat down in front of it.

Then, as he'd done the night they arrived, he slid the chiseled edges of the flame into the keyhole slots in the front of the altar. The same loud *shink* sounded as the scepter was pulled tight against the *chorazin*, and the Blue Flame crystal flared to life with a sudden release of *Ta'shaen*.

At first Jeymi thought Jase had embraced the Power, but she quickly realized he hadn't. The stream of Power flowing out of the scepter was linked to a crux point set somewhere up on the mountain.

Eager to find out where, she opened her Awareness and extended it toward the mountain, following the glimmering thread of energy with her mind's eye. It passed into the mountain, then vanished into darkness so complete she momentarily wondered if she'd lost hold of the Power.

*Don't worry,* Jase told her. *I can see where it ends. There's a central crux point on the fifth level of the temple. It's linked to a number of others, and I can see them all as clearly as if I'd set them myself. They're all I can see, since the upper levels are still blocked to my Awareness, small points of light in a sea of darkness. But the scepter...* he added. *Somehow it's facilitating my spiritual eyes.*

*And?*

*Pull your Awareness back out of the mountain,* he said, and she felt his excitement as clearly as if it were her own.

She did, and Augg came into view once more. It was then that she felt the brush of Seibei's Awareness.

*Watch the trees on the higher slopes,* Jase told them, then opened himself to the Gift of Spirit and struck what he alone could see.

As the crux points collapsed, a sudden rush of wind moved up the slopes, causing the trees to sway. It increased in speed as it rose higher, picking up leaves and bits of grass and kicking up dust. The swirls of color allowed her to track the rushing of Air with even more precision, and she watched in amazement as it was sucked into the window-like openings high in the cliffs.

Several minutes passed while the rivers of Air poured into the mountain, filling all the corridors and chambers of the Temple of Elderon with Fairimor's metaphorical breath of life. Then all at once, the entrances on the mountain's lower slopes belched clouds of discolored mist, swirling tempests powerful enough to knock a horse off its feet.

Cocking her head toward the mountain, Jeymi listened with her natural ears and was surprised by just how noticeable the sound of the tempest was.

*You never cease to amaze,* Seibei said, and Jeymi nodded in agreement.

*Give credit to the scepter for this one,* Jase said. *There is no way I could have done that on my own.*

*There's no way we could have done it even with the scepter,* Jeymi told him.

*Maybe,* Jase said.

*Light next?* Jeymi asked.

*Yes,* Jase answered. *But....* He trailed off and remained silent for so long that Jeymi felt the need to say something.

*But what?*

She felt Jase rein in his Awareness, and she and Seibei did likewise.

"It's bended Light," he told them, his eyes still on the mountain. "And it's masking the crux points as well as whatever light source Fairimor thought needed to be hidden. And there are thousands of them."

"My guess is glowstones," Seth said as he moved up to stand next to Jase. He was pulling gently at his moustache, and his eyes were thoughtful as he stared up at the mountain.

Jase glanced at him curiously. "What makes you say that?"

Seth chuckled. "I've been to Earth's Heart, remember. It, and the temple Gideon and I explored earlier in the week, is lighted by glowstones, some unlike any I'd ever seen before. I would imagine that this temple, *the* temple of our Creator, would be likewise furnished. He's the God of Light, after all, not a god of darkness."

"So how do I pinpoint crux points I can't see?" Jase wondered aloud. "I can feel them, but it's an approximation. Unless I can fix them in my mind's eye with exactness, I have no chance of shattering them."

"Use the scepter," Seth said. "Not just to find the wards, but to shatter the crux points inside them. The scepter is a weapon, Jase. You know that—you've used it as one. You might need to use it as one again."

He glanced briefly at the scepter, then looked back to Jase. "When we were inside Tabor, Gideon used the Blue Flame to throw back the darkness, and that was *real* darkness. Not glowstones masked in bended Light. If it can defeat that kind of darkness, that kind of evil, it can most certainly collapse crux points set by one of your righteous ancestors."

Jase thought about it for a moment, then nodded. "I think you're right," he said. "And I know how it is to be done. I learned it when I used the scepter to liberate Trian." Moving to the front of the altar, he knelt in front of it and took a hold of the scepter with both hands.

A hush fell over the camp as everyone waited to see what would happen, and Jeymi found herself holding her breath as she waited for Jase to embrace the Power. She knew whatever came next would be spectacular.

With the eyes of everyone on him, Jase wrapped himself in *Jiu* to quiet his mind, then opened himself to the Power. All Seven Gifts flowed into him, but he kept them separate, still not quite sure what to do. In Trian, he'd woven Spirit and Fire and Light into one and channeled them into the crystal flame, and it had responded with spiraling tendrils of bluish-white cleansing destruction.

But he wasn't here to cleanse evil. He was here to unlock wards of protection *against* evil. He was here to reveal what couldn't be seen by either his natural eyes or through the eyes of *Ta'shaen*.

Physical light on the one hand, spiritual light on the other.

*Shiin* and *Sei*. The two most powerful forces in all of creation.

Reaching deeper into himself, he set aside the other five Gifts and embraced Light and Spirit, then wove them together in the opposite direction of the weaves used to create *Sei'shiin*. *Sei'shiin* was a weapon of cleansing. *Shiin'sei* would be the key to uncovering what was hidden.

He channeled the tightly woven stream of *Shiin'sei* into the crystal flame, and watched as the shimmering lake of Earthpower residing within the powerful talisman welcomed it, then redirected the flows into the altar.

The altar began to glow from within. A moment later so did the raised image of the Blue Flame on the side opposite of the scepter. The light emanating from the raised image continued to increase in brightness, forcing all who were watching with their natural eyes to look away.

All at once a powerful burst of *Shiin'sei* lanced forth from the center of the flame, a brilliant beam of light that streaked toward the mountain like an arrow. It struck a crux point he hadn't seen—one suspended in the air on the outside of the mountain—and the potent stream of energy split into a thousand smaller streams, all of which lanced into the mountain like a volley of arrows.

Every arrow found its mark, and crux point after crux point shattered in a flare of white. As they did, the wards of bended Light vanished and the light they'd been concealing appeared. Chandeliers of varying sizes hung from Power-wrought chains in many of the lower chambers. Lamps and candelabra lined the sides of the corridors connecting those chambers. In the higher levels, larger-than-life statues of a woman held glowstones the size of melons. The entire interior of the mountain was suddenly ablaze with brilliant, bluish-white light.

And there, atop an altar in the center of the highest level of the Temple of Elderon, was the Blood Orb he'd come here to retrieve. It rested in the hands of a golden candelabrum in the shape of a woman and shone brighter than the sun. Tears gathered at the corners of his eyes as he took it all in.

The stream of Power flowing out of the scepter cut off, and his view of the Blood Orb vanished as the wards of Spirit shielding the upper levels from view sprang back into place.

"Well?" Jeymi asked, and Jase turned to find her and everyone else watching him expectantly. "Did it work?"

He arched an eyebrow at her. "You didn't see what happened?"

"We saw only the brilliance of the scepter," Seibei said. "Followed by a tremendously bright flash and a release of Power. The entire thing happened in the blink of any eye." He narrowed his eyes at Jase. "What did you see?"

"Everything," Jase answered, "and it felt a lot longer than the blink of an eye."

Elliott stepped near, his eyes glittering with excitement. "When you say you saw everything..."

"The Blood Orb is there," Jase told him. "On the seventh level of the temple." He felt Jeymi and several other Dymas reach toward the area with their Awarenesses, but he knew what they would find before they spoke.

"I see only darkness," Jeymi said. "The wards shielding the area from view are still in place."

"Yes," he told them, "they are. But there is light inside the mountain now. The scepter triggered a crux point that removed the wards of bended Light. We'll be able to see just fine with our natural eyes."

"So are you going to remove the wards of Spirit?" Seth asked. "Or do we enter the temple now that we can see?"

A rush of conflicting emotions reached him through the *sei'vaiya*, and he looked at Talia to find her biting her lower lip. She knew what obtaining the Orb meant, and now that the possibility of doing so was here, she was both hopeful and scared.

Jase smiled reassuringly at her, then looked back to Seth. "I said we can see with our natural eyes," he told him. "But the rest of the Dymas and I will be blind. We won't be able to probe the way ahead for the shortest path to the Orb. I saw it yes, but I did not see how to get there. And from what I saw of the lower levels, there are a bloody lot of passages inside that mountain, not all of which lead to our destination."

He looked up at the mountain. "I'd prefer not to have to climb any further than necessary. If I collapse the final wards, not only will I be able to see the exact location of the Orb, I can take us there by Veilgate. We'll be in and out of the mountain before you can say Shadan's a filthy cur."

Taking hold of the scepter once more, he closed his eyes and wrapped himself in *Jiu* to clear his mind and focus his thoughts. When he was sufficiently calm, he extended his Awareness up into the mountain to fix the warded area in his mind's eye. It came into view as a dome-shaped void in the luminescent landscape.

But now that he really had a chance to study it, he realized it wasn't darkness, not in the way the Void or the taint in Amnidia or Kunin was darkness. It was more like a ward against eavesdropping, a curtain drawn over a window to keep light in and prying eyes out. He simply needed to find the strings to draw the curtain back open.

He continued to study it for a while, then, because of the increase of Awareness afforded him by the Blue Flame Scepter, he noticed what looked like a second dome of Spirit. Much larger than the one warding the temple inside Augg, this second ward had the appearance of slightly fogged glass and stretched outward from the top of the mountain for miles in every direction. Only when he traced its curvature did he realize it enveloped the entire island and extended well into Mirror Lake.

And it was set into the fabric of the Earthsoul itself. It was part of the Veil.

How Fairimor had managed such a thing, if indeed it had been him and not the Creator, was beyond anything Jase would have imagined possible. At least not without the aid of something as powerful as a Blood Orb or.... He smiled. Or the Blue Flame Scepter.

*None shall enter but by the Power of the Blue Flame*, Robishar had prophesied. It was time to put the prophecy to the test.

With his Awareness still pressed against the vastness of the sheltering bubble of Spirit, he opened himself to the Power and prepared to channel *El'shaen te Sherah* into the scepter. *El'shaen te Sherah*—the Power and Light of the Creator. Anything less wouldn't be strong enough to collapse wards such as these.

A tremor rippled across the shimmering dome, and Jase hesitated, unsure of what he'd felt. Frowning, he focused his attention on the spot where the tremor had originated, but there was nothing there.

Then the wall of Spirit trembled again, and this time Jase saw the reddish-black tendrils of corruption which had caused it. An Agla'Con had just attempted to reach the island by Veilgate. Another spot of corruption appeared, then vanished. Another followed, then another. And they just kept coming, doggedly persistent, desperate to reach the mountain. He went cold inside. His enemies knew he was here.

And not just any enemy, either. Some of the attempts had been wrought of *Lo'shaen*. Aethon Fairimor was among those trying to reach Mount Augg.

*Yes*, a familiar voice said, sounding directly into his mind. *And I will claim the Orb for myself.*

Jase reined in his Awareness and released the Power. Pulling the scepter free of the altar, he rose and turned to face the others. Confusion painted every face. Every face but Talia's—she'd sensed the encounter with Aethon and knew what was coming.

"Ready the Myrscraw," he ordered. "We're going in now."

"What about the wards of Spirit?" Jeymi asked.

"Keeping our enemies off the island," he told her. "Aethon knows we're here. If I collapse the wards now, he will open a rent directly into the mountain. He's already tried several times, and has an army of Agla'Con testing the wards every few seconds, not because there is any chance to break through but to keep us from entering the mountain by Veilgate. He wants to turn this into a footrace."

"I want the Myrscraw in the air in two minutes," Seth ordered. "Derian, your team will escort the *Mith'elre Chon* into the mountain. Oroi and his team will intercept the enemy when they arrive. They'll be coming by K'rresh. Move, people. We don't have much time."

火

The rent Aethon opened on the northern edge of Tradeston sent people and animals alike scurrying for cover. The initial shouts of surprise turned to screams of terror as the first K'rresh lumbered through the opening and Marut Saroj urged the massive bat-like creature into the air. More K'rresh followed in rapid succession, and the screams of the people faded to horrified silence as they watched more than fifty of the leathery hellbeasts take to the air.

Aethon watched as the airborne army disappeared into the distance above the shimmering expanse of Mirror Lake, then he took one last look at Mount Augg and severed his connection to *Lo'shaen*. Those cowering on the other side let out squawks of surprise as the rent snapped shut with a hiss.

He turned to Asherim who'd watched the entire thing without comment. The Meleki was irritated that Shadan hadn't been informed of the situation, but keeping the Dreadlord in the dark for the time being was in the best interest of Death's Third March.

With demons bearing down on them from two sides, Shadan's presence alone would keep things from descending into complete chaos. As it was, not all of the demons would take the path of least resistance and enter the city. Those that didn't would need to be dealt with.

"The demons will be here any minute," Aethon said, directing the comment to Asherim. "Make sure the Agla'Con and *Jeth'Jalda* are in position to guide them into the city."

"Yes, First," Asherim said, his tone cool.

"And someone fetch this lad a sword," he said, watching with amusement as the blood drained from Trake Noevom's face.

"Welcome to Death's Third March," Aethon told him, then opened a rent and moved through to where Commander Tiafin waited with his *Jeth'Jalda* warders. He didn't need to look back to know Trake was terrified by the prospect of joining the battle—the sounds of retching announced the boy's fear loud and clear.

# CHAPTER 71

## *Race Against Time*

"THAT ONE THERE," Jase said, pointing to a window-like opening high on Augg's eastern face. Elliott nodded, and Kiaush angled toward it.

He'd already done a probe of the mountain, and as far as he could tell, the window appeared to be part of the temple's seventh level. Now they just needed to pray that it actually went where they needed it to.

A look over his shoulder showed that the other Myrscraw and their riders were fanning out across the mountain, some to enter the temple through other openings, some to prepare to receive the enemy when they arrived.

He glanced at Seth and Talia riding the breeze to the right of Kiaush, and Talia gave a small wave. A nervous wave, Jase knew. He could feel her tension through the love-bond. He tried to send feelings of reassurance that all would be well, but he wasn't sure how well it worked. It was impossible to mask the sense of urgency he felt.

*It's okay,* came her thought. *I feel it too.*

He winked at her, then looked at the others. The Shizu guiding the birds bearing Jeymi and Endil were winging their way toward one of the higher openings—Jase believed it was part of the seventh level as well—and both would be there momentarily. Splitting up meant they would be able to cover more ground, and it didn't matter if it was him or Endil who retrieved the Orb so long as no one else touched it.

Kiaush came to rest in the cave-like entrance in a flurry of giant feathers, and Elliott and Jase hurriedly dismounted. As soon as they were off, Kiaush leapt back out into the open sky to make room for Seth's bird. Jase took Talia's hand and helped her out of the saddle, and Seth followed as soon as she was clear. His bird followed Kiaush back into the air.

"One of Derian's men will remain behind to keep our birds aloft and out of range of the enemy," Seth said. "They'll be ready to pick us up as soon as we have the Orb."

"And the Myrscraw of Oroi's team?" Elliott asked.

Seth's smile was that of an executioner. "They'll show those bloody K'rresh what flying really looks like." He pointed down the corridor. "Shall we?"

Holding the Blue Flame Scepter before him, Jase took the lead. There was enough daylight coming through the opening to get him to the end of the corridor where the natural stone of the mountain gave way to an ornate archway wrought of *chorazin*.

"Is that what I think it is?" Elliott asked, and Jase nodded.

"Yes. And it marks the boundary of the wards of Spirit. Once we enter, I won't be able to see a thing with my Awareness." Taking a deep breath to steady his nervousness, he stepped over the threshold into the Temple of Elderon.

His Awareness went dark in the same instant that he had to squint against the sudden brightness of numerous glowstone lamps set into the walls of a slightly rectangular chamber. The chamber, like its arched entrance, was *chorazin*, smooth and only slightly different in color than the greyish granite of the mountain.

At the far end of the chamber were two more archways. One was a passage that went deeper into the mountain. The other, a set of stairs that spiraled down and out of sight.

He made straight for the passage, moving as quickly as he dared, fighting the urge to run. Yes, he needed to reach the Orb before the enemy arrived, but running blindly from place to place would serve no purpose but to get him lost.

He needed to be smart about this—he needed to build a mental picture in his mind of his route so he could retrace his steps should they run into a dead end or find themselves leaving the warded area.

The corridor ended in a large domed oval with six more arched openings branching outward like spokes in a wheel, and Jase hesitated as he moved into the room, his sense of urgency spiking.

Behind him, Elliott embraced the Power and channeled a small sphere of Light, and Jase turned to find him smiling sheepishly. "I just wanted to make sure we could still touch the Power," he said, letting the sphere wink out.

"The ward over the temple only masks a Dymas' view of the spiritual world," Jase told him, then looked at the spot where Elliott's sphere of light had been. "And you just gave me an idea."

Embracing *Ta'shaen*, he channeled a small sphere of Light at the top of the archway they had just come through, then created crux points to keep the sphere alight. He might not be able to see the threads he was channeling, but he could still *feel* them. It was akin to tying his shoes in the dark or with his eyes closed—he'd done it so many times, he didn't need to see his fingers or the laces.

Elliott grinned. "Like marking a path in a forest by leaving twine on branches."

Jase nodded. "Exactly. We can move a lot more quickly without worrying if we're retracing our steps." He pointed to the nearest archway. "Let's go," he said, and this time he allowed himself to run.

With shields of Spirit firmly in place, Ohran Peregam and his army of *Nar'shein* waited to engage the demon horde approaching North Gate. As he had anticipated, the majority of the demons had taken the path offered them by Shadan, eager to storm Trian in search of what they assumed would be easy slaughter. The few who'd attacked Death's Third March—savage, misshapen monsters unable to control their bloodlust—had been destroyed.

*And thank the Light for that*, Ohran thought. The remaining demons were going to be difficult enough to face as it was.

"I sense *Lo'shaen* being wielded by as many as thirty of them," Chieftain Paddishor said, and Ohran looked over to find his friend's face pinched with disgust.

"I sense it too," he said. "Are the *Ara'so* ready?"

Paddishor nodded. "They're just waiting for the signal."

Ohran returned his eyes to the approaching demons. All were human in form but ranged in size from the smallest Kunin to nearly the size of a Dainin. All wore heavy plated armor of some unknown metal and carried an array of weapons. But it was those whose weapons glowed red with the power of the Void that were of the greatest concern. They alone possessed the kind of power to defeat a *Nar'shein* in battle. What they didn't know was the *Nar'shein* no longer had to fight this battle alone.

Weaving Light and Fire together into a narrow streamer, he sent it lancing into the sky. An instant later *Ta'shaen* came alive as Veilgates opened on both sides of the demons and the New Oath *Nar'shein* struck from beyond, targeting those who could wield *Lo'shaen* and destroying more than half of them with *Sei'shiin* before the creatures could cast up protective shields. Hundreds more died in the seconds that followed, but as the element of surprise vanished, the effectiveness of the strikes lessened.

Ohran sent a second streamer into the sky, and the Veilgates slid closed as the *Ara'so* broke off their attack. But it was only the first strike, and more Veilgates opened beneath the demons. They disappeared from view as they dropped away into empty air, clawing at one another in desperation as they fell several thousand feet to their deaths. Ohran smiled grimly as he watched the demons die, his earlier reservations about Dainin using the Power as a weapon vanishing once and for all.

His Awareness shrieked in alarm as a powerful thrust of *Lo'shaen* channeled by Shadan erupted across the sky. Instinctively, he and the other Dainin strengthened their shields in anticipation of being struck, but the river of dark energy arched over the Dainin shields and landed in the city several blocks south of the wall.

Ohran stretched his Awareness to the spot, and what he found chilled his heart worse than any scene of carnage he'd ever witnessed. Shadan had deliberately targeted an already frayed part of the Veil, and the strike had been sufficient to rip a significant number of holes into the realm of Con'Jithar. Holes that continued to expand even after Shadan's use of *Lo'shaen* vanished. Holes that merged with one another to form a rent a hundred paces wide.

That the Dreadlord was able to do such a thing meant the final collapse of the Veil was underway. It also meant that it was no longer a matter of days before it failed completely, but a matter of hours.

"Hurry, Jase," he whispered, then touched the minds of several *Ara'so* and bid them to join him in his hunt of the demons arriving through the newly opened rent.

亡

"Another dead end!" Elliott hissed. "How many bloody rooms can there be in this place?"

Jase shared the sentiment, but he managed to keep his frustration from his voice. Inside, however, he wanted to scream. He knew from the *sei'vaiya* that Talia did too.

"Well, at least we know where the Orb isn't," Seth said, turning on his heel and hurrying back the way they'd come.

When they reached the rotunda at the end of the corridor, Jase set a sphere of light on the floor beneath the archway to mark it as a dead end, then looked around. Only one entrance remained unmarked.

*Maybe this one*, he thought as he started for it.

Powerful exchanges of *Ta'shaen* being wielding outside the mountain brought him up short, and he cast a worried look at the others.

"They're here," he told them, then tightened his grip on the Scepter and moved through the archway.

The corridor turned into a spiral staircase almost at once, and he took the stairs two at a time as he climbed, listening to the rhythmic thudding of his feet on the *chorazin* and trying to ignore how much it sounded like the ticking of a clock.

亡

A stirring in *Ta'shaen* alerted Idoman to Quintella's return, and he turned to greet her as she hurried through a Veilgate.

"East Gate is in the hands of the enemy," she said, her beaded braids clicking as she shook her head in disgust. "The *Ara'so* and I assisted Elison and his men in their retreat to River Gate, but it is only a matter of time before that, too, is overrun." She turned and looked at the ribbon of blue winding its way through the city and added, "Elison plans to use the river as a barrier as his men retreat along North River Road. They will join us at Northeast Bridge."

"And the demon army?" Idoman asked, then flinched as a barrage of corrupted lightning crackled along the edge of the shield he and the other Dymas were holding over the area.

"Well on their way to First Avenue," she answered, raising her voice to be heard over the rumble of thunder. "But I sent Dymas ahead to warn General Shurr they were coming."

Idoman nodded, then flinched as another barrage of corrupted lightning struck the shield overhead. It was much stronger than the previous strikes had been and much more controlled.

Quintella noticed it as well. "The *Jeth'Jalda* who assisted Shadan in destroying the gates are regaining their strength," she said.

Idoman nodded. "They are. But we'll hold them off for a while yet. I'm more worried about what Shadan just did in the northwest quadrant."

Taggert, who'd been listening to the conversation with a frown on his face, narrowed his eyes at them. "What did Shadan do?"

"He attacked the Veil," Idoman answered. "And opened a hole into Con'Jithar."

Taggert's face pinched into an even deeper frown. "So what does that mean?"

"It means," Quintella said, looking the aging general in the eyes, "that we are almost out of time."

七

Standing just inside the warding of Spirit draped over the Temple of Elderon, Seibei Wasaki watched the light at the end of the corridor dim as a K'rresh landed in the opening. The silhouettes of two Agla'Con were visible atop the creature, their talismans blazing red with corrupted *Ta'shaen*.

He waited until they were in the act of dismounting, then took advantage of the momentary distraction to step out of the ward shielding him from their Awareness and killed them both with spears of *Sei'shiin*. The K'rresh tried to flee, but he burst its head open with a thrust of Flesh and watched it disappear from view.

He felt the brush of Amari Dymas' mind and opened himself to her thoughts.

*Nicely done,* she said. *But there is trouble on the far side of the mountain. Yasuri Dymas is dead, and those who killed her have entered the temple through the entrance she was guarding.*

*How many?*

*At least eight. I spotted four riderless K'rresh leaving the area.*

*Oroi and his men will kill the K'rresh,* he told her. *We need to get Dymas to Yasuri's entrance to hunt the Agla'Con.*

*I'll take Emami and Jorea Dymas with me,* she said.

*God's speed,* he told her, then reined in his Awareness and moved to the opening to scan the sky for more enemies.

Derian Oronei waited while the Agla'Con moved past the enclave he and Porea Dymas were hiding in, then slipped silently out of his hiding place and removed one man's head with a single swipe of his blade. His companion whirled, fist blazing red with corruption, only to vanish in a flash of white as Porea Dymas struck with *Sei'shiin.*

"You really should let me kill them both next time," she said, looking at the pool of blood spreading across the grey *chorazin.* "Your way is too messy."

"It is," he agreed. "But it's also very satisfying. I love the fact that they're blind in here. It levels the playing field."

"I'm blind in here, too. Remember?"

"I do remember," he said, stepping over the Agla'Con's body. "That's why I'm here."

Porea wrinkled her nose in disgust as she moved past the corpse, then Derian took her hand, and they continued on down the corridor to the next chamber.

As they entered, Derian slowed, momentarily unsure of what he was seeing. The opposite side of the chamber seemed to end in darkness, but he quickly realized it was because he was looking into a vast cavern.

"It's the center of the mountain," Porea whispered in awe. "The well, Jase called it. Come." Still holding Derian's hand, she started forward.

They stopped at the waist-high railing of what was obviously a balcony, and Derian glanced over the edge. The well—it was hard to see it as anything else—seemed to drop away forever. Its smooth curvature was ringed by hundreds more balconies, small points of bluish-white light that filled the cavern with a soft glow.

Derian looked up, and his heart skipped a beat at the sight. The seventh level of the temple was just overhead, a domed ring of arched doorways connected by narrow walkways and framed by statues holding large glowstones.

Two more walkways spanned the open expanse of the well, slightly arched catwalks that intersected one another in the center of the cavern. And there, at the intersection, was the Blood Orb of Elsa.

Porea gasped openly as she caught sight of it.

"What do we do now?" Derian asked her. "Try to make our way to the seventh level, or stay here and keep an eye on it?"

"We stay here," she said. "There might be Agla'Con above us in the temple. If any find their way onto the catwalk, I will destroy them."

乇

Ammorin stood at the edge of the Overlook in contemplative silence, watching with heavy heart as the chaos of war reached ever deeper into Trian. For every explosive exchange visible to his natural eyes, there were ten more visible in his mind's eye. At the moment, the fabric of *Ta'shaen* seethed with hundreds of wieldings, both pure and corrupted.

And that was just the Power-wrought part of the battle. He knew if he were to make a detailed inspection of the chaos, he would find the outer streets of Trian littered with the bodies of tens of thousands of soldiers who'd bled out their lives in a battle very few of them had fully understood.

The sound of someone approaching caught his ear, and he turned as Gideon joined him at the wall.

"Did you hear what Shadan did to the Veil?" Gideon asked.

"I watched it happen through my Awareness," he answered. "But he attacked an area that was about to collapse on its own anyway. Not even he has that kind of Power. Not yet, anyway."

Gideon gazed out across the city. "He has enough."

"And yet he remains outside the city," Ammorin said, then looked his friend in the eyes and added, "because he fears *you*."

An unamused grunt sounded in Gideon's throat. "He fears this," he said, holding up the Blood Orb of Elsa Jase had given him. "But he won't remain outside the city much longer. The time to use the Orb is rapidly approaching."

Ammorin eyed him quietly for a moment. "What exactly did you and Jase see in that vision of yours?"

Gideon's eyes didn't leave the city. "I saw the end," he answered but offered nothing more.

Ammorin looked back out at the growing number of fires. Most were located between First Avenue and the outer wall, but in just the past few minutes several had erupted along the Trian River near the Second Avenue Bridge.

*Where Thorac and his men are*, he thought.

He wasn't worried about the Chunin army alone—with more than forty thousand Tambans already through East Gate, the entire northeastern quadrant was in danger.

"Any word on Elison Brey?" Ammorin asked.

"The *Ara'so* I sent to ward Elison checked in with me just moments ago," Gideon answered. "River Gate just fell to the enemy. Elison is leading the City Guard deeper into the city. They're hoping to join the Zekan and Meleki armies at the Central Avenue Bridge and make their stand there." He shook his head in disgust. "If we fail to hold that bridge, Idoman and his men will be cut off. They'll be forced to work their way along the river to the bridge on North Road."

The comment sent a stab of fear knifing through Ammorin's chest. "Did the Chellum Army lose Northeast Gate?"

"No," Gideon answered. "But I'm worried the longer Idoman holds, the more precarious his situation becomes. If *Frel'mola te Ujen* gets a sizable force between Idoman and the river—" He cut off as another sizable earthquake rolled across the city.

The massive tremor temporarily halted the battle as every living creature had to fight to stay upright. The *chorazin* of the palace was slightly more immune to the shaking, but, even so, both he and Gideon took hold of the edge of the wall. The most intense part of the quake lasted only seconds, and the fighting down in the city resumed as soon as it passed.

The aftershocks, however, continued for so long this time that Ammorin put his hand back on the *chorazin* and opened his Awareness to the tremors. He may have traded in his *arinseil* nets for *Sei'shiin*, but he was still a Keeper of the Earth—he knew how to listen to the voice of the Earthmother.

"What is it?" Gideon asked.

"The tremors," Ammorin said, a cold pit settling in his stomach. "They aren't going to stop this time."

"It's worse than you think," Pattalla said, moving up beside them. "This most recent quake originated in the Kelsan Mountains directly west of the city. A section of the Veil several hundred yards wide collapsed across the face of the peak above the Temple of Elderon. A horde of demons is headed our way. They are unlike any I've ever seen. Some can fly. Others have a Shadowhound's ability to cling to stone. They'll be here in the next ten or twelve minutes."

Gideon turned to Gavin and the other *Bero'thai* who'd come with Pattalla. "Clear the Overlook," he said. "I want all of your men inside." As Gavin raced away to do as ordered, Gideon looked back at Ammorin. "Let's hope the wards we put over the palace work against demons."

"They will," he said. "Corruption is corruption, after all."

"Yes," Pattalla agreed. "But the wards will only reset themselves so many times before their crux points fail."

Gideon's face darkened with worry. "What are you saying?"

"We didn't set enough wards."

With Jeymi jogging beside him, Endil turned a corner and nearly ran headlong into a Zekan Agla'Con. The man seemed just as surprised to see them as they were him, but Endil recovered from the shock more quickly, and the green light of his dartbow flashed once as he shot the man in the chest. He dropped into a heap as his talisman clattered noisily across the floor.

"That's what you get for hunting alone, you worthless cur," he muttered as he turned his back on the Zekan's corpse and started back the way they had come. No need to retrace the Agla'Con's path. It wouldn't go anywhere but back outside.

"There," Jeymi said, pointing to a side corridor they'd run past just moments earlier. "I don't think we've tried that one yet."

"They all look the same to me," he grumbled. "We should have come up with a system."

"Agreed," she said. "Next time we are racing Agla'Con through the inside of a mountain, I'll bring a loaf of bread so we can leave crumbs."

He chuckled in spite of the stress he was feeling. "And that's why I love you."

"Because I'll bring bread?"

"Because you think there will be a next time."

They hurried on, passing a number of the largest statues Endil had seen yet. All were of women with hooded robes and veiled faces. *This has to be the right way*, he thought, offering what had to be his seven hundredth prayer. Ten paces later, he made a sharp right and found that his most recent prayer had been answered.

The Blood Orb of Elsa and the altar on which it sat was thirty paces away, the center point of two intersecting catwalks spanning a seemingly bottomless cavern.

Ignoring a sudden sense of vertigo, he left the safety of the corridor and started across the catwalk. Hopefully, Jase wouldn't be far behind, since he had absolutely no desire to hold onto the Orb any longer than was necessary.

He kept his eyes on the altar to avoid looking down, but the absence of a handrail was unnerving. Light of Heaven, but that was a long drop.

A flash of movement to his right caught his eye, and he glanced over as two Agla'Con stepped onto the other catwalk.

Their eyes met as the talisman in the man's fist went red, then an invisible fist of Air knocked him and Jeymi off the catwalk and into the abyss.

乇

Jase felt the burst of corruption just seconds before he turned the corner and found two Agla'Con approaching the Altar of Elsa from the far end of the catwalk stretching away before him. With their eyes fixed on the radiant glow of the Blood Orb, they hadn't seen him yet.

*Your mistake*, he thought, then sent them tumbling to their deaths with a vicious swipe of Air. Their screams sounded loud and long as they fell.

More Agla'Con arrived through the archway at the other end of the catwalk, and Jase prepared to meet them by channeling threads of Fire and Light and Spirit into the Blue Flame Scepter. The crystal facets responded with a burst of blue flame that burned through hastily woven shields and incinerated those within.

Then, before more enemies could arrive, he sprinted across the catwalk and took possession of the Blood Orb, lifting it from the raised hands of the golden candelabrum.

It welcomed his touch with a brilliant flash of light and a rush of warmth, and the now familiar voice of Elsa sounded directly into his thoughts.

*Run, my son*, she said. *Run. Earth's Heart is under attack. You must take me there before all is lost. Run!*

Jase ran. He held the scepter before him to clear the way should any of his enemies try to bar his way and he ran.

Talia and Seth and Elliott followed, their breathing loud in his ears as they worked to keep pace. He had no idea where he was going, only that he was going the right way. It could have been the Blood Orb or the scepter or just blind luck guiding his steps—all he knew was he needed to run.

Before he knew it, he reached an archway marking the threshold of the wards of Spirit, and his Awareness returned in all its luminescent glory. And there, shining in his fist like a miniature sun, was the salvation of the world.

But there were threads of corruption darkening the spiritual landscape of his mind's eye, and he sought them out with the precision he'd honed over these past few days, fixing them in his mind's eye the way he'd fixed hundreds upon hundreds of crux points. Only these weren't crux points, they were the hellish fires of Jexlair crystals, the godforsaken talismans of the enemies of Light.

Raising the Blue Flame Scepter before him, he stepped into the light of day and struck. A number of *booms* sounded simultaneously across the area as talismans exploded, killing the men and women who wore them. Fifteen died on Augg's steep slopes, another twelve plummeted earthward along with their shadowspawned mounts.

*Impressive*, Seibei said, his voice coming into Jase's thoughts. *I see your hunt was successful. Your Myrscraw are already on their way.*

*Thank you*, Jase said. *Please do what you can to get the rest of our people out of the mountain safely.*

*We'll clean up here*, Seibei said. *God's speed, my friend.* The touch of his mind withdrew, and Jase reined in his Awareness as the Myrscraw approached.

A rush of wind filled the opening as the two birds landed, and he and the others scrambled into the saddles. He tucked the scepter into his belt but kept hold of the Blood Orb, gripping it so tightly his knuckles turned white. It was warm and pulsating and alive, and filled with a sense of urgency.

The birds leapt free of the cliff face and angled north, moving with such speed that they passed through the wards preventing Veilgates after just a few minutes.

"I'll open the way to Amnidia," he shouted, then embraced the Power and opened a large horizontal Veilgate in front of and below Kiaush.

Elliott nodded, and a gentle touch on Kiaush's neck sent the bird into a dive. Seth's bird followed, and Jase held his breath as the two birds knifed toward the shimmering hole in the air. They passed through, and the bright blue of the sky and the shimmering waters of Mirror Lake turned to smoke-filled darkness and desolation in an instant.

The sudden deceleration of Kiaush breaking out of the dive momentarily darkened Jase's vision as blood rushed to his head. When it cleared, he found himself looking at the fiery wedge of Mount Tabor rising in the distance.

*The end of the journey*, he thought. *One way or another.*

# CHAPTER 72

## *Heroes of Light*

WITH THE BLOOD ORB GRIPPED tightly in his right fist, Gideon put his left arm around Brysia and held her close against him. She was trembling with fear, but her back was straight and her head high as she listened to the rage-filled cries of the demons swarming over the outside of Fairimor Palace. True to Pattalla's claim, they could walk on any stone surface—*chorazin* included—and they were pouring into the palace through every window or door they could find.

He'd given up trying to watch them through his Awareness—there were simply too many to follow. He'd also grown weary of being assaulted by their vile, hate-filled minds.

During the short time he'd watched them approach, he discovered that the majority of them were insect-like monstrosities, with multiple limbs and appendages and glistening, armored exoskeletons. The rest were a hodgepodge assortment of misshapen animals—what must pass for apes and pigs and wolves in Maeon's dark realm—and all were heavily muscled. Three or four of the ape-like creatures appeared to have the ability to wield *Lo'shaen*.

A detonation of Power tickled his Awareness, and he glanced at Ammorin who nodded. The foremost demons had just triggered wards in the outer ring of crux points higher in the towers and had been summarily destroyed. Closer, sharper releases of Power along the edges of the Overlook followed, and pain-filled shrieks echoed across the gardens.

*The gardens,* he thought. *Where I use the Orb.*

Images from the vision he'd had of that moment—what was very likely to be his final moment—flashed through his mind, and he watched them with the same kind of resignation a condemned man might watch his feet as he climbed the steps of the gallows. There was no escaping his fate, only the pride of meeting it with dignity.

And meet it he would. Once the Earthsoul collapsed.

*And that*, he realized grimly, *will be any minute now.*

Squeezing Brysia against him just a little tighter, he kept count of how many times the crux points reset the wards which were holding the demons at bay. It was shocking just how quickly he was being forced to count.

Standing next to her husband in the center of the Dome, Brysia listened to the shrieks and howls of the demons being obliterated by the wards Gideon and the others had placed over the inner palace. It sounded like they were getting closer, but she didn't ask for fear of the answer. A moment later the answer came anyway.

"The outermost sets of crux points have run their course," Ammorin announced. "The demons are almost to the Dome."

"How many are left?" she asked, pleased with how calm she sounded. She didn't want anyone to know how truly terrified she was.

"Enough to outlast the wards," Ammorin answered, then smiled reassuringly. "But we'll be ready for those that arrive." Around the room, Pattalla and the rest of the *Ara'so* nodded. Even Lord Nid looked confident, and he still hadn't returned to full strength.

Brysia smiled her thanks, then glanced briefly at Beraline and Marithen and the other Dymas before looking at the *Bero'thai*. With swords and spears and bows in hand, they stood ready to assist the Dymas, but in light of what was coming, it was difficult for her to look them in the eyes without feeling guilty. They were here to protect her from an enemy they had no chance of defeating.

She flinched as the shrieks and howls of dying demons suddenly seemed so much nearer, unearthly cries that rent the air and made the hair on her arms stand on end.

"The next set of wards are down," Gideon said, and Brysia fastened her eyes on the doors of the Overlook, bracing herself for what would follow.

The doors trembled as something heavy struck them from the outside, and a dull, thudding *boom* reverberated along the inside of the Dome. A second heavy impact sounded from the doors leading out to the palace, and third from the entrance to her home.

"We braced the doors with currents of Air," Gideon whispered. "It will take a lot more than a few bony heads to break through."

"And when they do break through?" she asked.

"They run into my finest wards yet."

She tilted her head to look at him, and he winked at her. "I'm the Guardian of the Blue Flame, remember?"

She knew intuitively that his confidence was feigned, and it scared her as badly as the demons pounding at the door. "What's wrong?" she asked. "Beyond the obvious, I mean."

"Isn't that enough?" he asked, and she knew better than to press the matter further. She already knew the answer anyway. He was worried this attack would force him to use the Blood Orb before it was time, and he was frustrated that he was being forced to sit out the fight for fear the Orb would respond of its own will. He wanted the full reservoir at his disposal when Shadan finally made his move.

Turning her attention back to the doors of the Overlook, she watched as a set of razor sharp claws punched through the thick wood then yanked the doors free of their casing.

Several monstrous shapes leapt forward but were stopped cold by the wall of Air which had braced the door from the inside. Hissing with rage, they continued to throw themselves at the invisible barrier until blood ran in black rivulets down the outside of it. Then all at once they withdrew.

"*Lo'shaen!*" Ammorin shouted, and Brysia flinched as something dark struck the entryway and the wall of Air burst apart with the sound of shattering glass.

A number of wolf-like demons raced through the opening and were obliterated by tendrils of *Sei'shiin* that materialized as if from thin air. More demons followed but with the same result as the final set of crux points responded to the presence of demonic corruption.

Behind her, the door to the inner palace was breached by another thrust of *Lo'shaen*, and a demon that may have been part scorpion scrambled through into the Dome. It, too, vanished in a flare of white as Gideon's wards destroyed it.

But they kept coming—mindless, bloodthirsty nightmares so eager to kill that they would throw away their own lives just for the chance. Twenty more died in a matter of a few seconds.

Then the wards failed to reset, and the stream of hellbeasts flowed into the room unchecked.

"*Bal'tei Nar'shein,*" Ammorin shouted, and the room went bright with the light of *Sei'shiin* as the Dainin attacked. More demons died. More kept coming, rivers of bristly fur and segmented armor too powerful to hold back for long.

The doors to the outer palace exploded inward in a spray of smoking fragments, and Night Threads streaked into the Dome, killing two Dainin and upending several others. A second strike of the dark, killing energy followed, but it was stopped short by invisible shields of Spirit. Ear-splitting cracks of thunder shook the Dome, then suddenly faded to a dull roar as Gideon wrapped them both in a protective bubble of Spirit.

The ape-like monster who'd channeled the Night Threads lumbered into the room, and Lord Nid stepped into its path, *El'shaen* streaking from his outstretched hand. It struck the demon in the chest, a white-hot blade of pure, potent energy that punched a hole clean through the monster. It blew apart in sizzling chunks of ruined flesh, and its scepter clattered across the floor.

Two more demons capable of wielding *Lo'shaen* moved in from the Overlook, and tendrils of darkness streaked across the room. Some exploded off of Dainin shields in bursts of reddish black, others tore up a section of bookshelves, filling the air with splintered wood and the smouldering pages of ruined books. Several *Bero'thai* fell wounded amid the destruction.

The Dainin retaliated with spears of *El'shaen*, and the demons retreated into sheltering auras of darkness. Pattalla strode toward them, fists blazing with light, and very literally punched a hole through the darkness to reach the nearest demon. The creature was so surprised by the attack that it never even moved as Pattalla's hand closed over its throat and he broke its neck.

"He just demonstrated both Dainin ideals with that move," Gideon whispered, his voice filled with admiration. Then he raised his hand at the other demon, and the aura of darkness trembled as tendrils of *Sei'shiin* struck it from three sides. The demon whirled to face Gideon, then died in a flash of white as Pattalla finished it with a stream of *Sei'shiin*.

"I thought you were going to sit this one out in favor of the battle to come," she said.

"I said I wouldn't risk using the Orb," he said. "That wasn't a risk."

The daylight streaming in through the ruined doorway to the Overlook suddenly cut off as a massive shape landed just outside. Pattalla whirled toward it, hands alight with *El'shaen*, but a flash of scaly black hissed through the opening and struck him in the chest. The force of the blow sent the giant man toppling head-over-foot, and the Power blazing in his fists winked out.

The square of light darkened further, and Brysia's breath caught in her throat as a demon squeezed through the opening. As soon as it was inside, it scrambled forward on a dozen spidery legs, its massive wedge-shaped body sprouting an array of spikes and quills and whip-like tentacles.

Brysia took an unconscious step backwards and looked up at Gideon. His face was a mask of rage, but the Blood Orb in his hand remained silent. It was then that she realized the ear-splitting sounds of battle had returned—the shield Gideon had been holding around them was gone!

When his connection to *Ta'shaen* suddenly vanished, Gideon's first thought was that it had something to do with the demon squeezing through the doorway—that, like some of the others he'd faced, the creature had the ability to create a Void in the Power. But then the luminescent world sprang back into place a heartbeat later, and he knew the situation for what it was.

The Veil had momentarily collapsed—the life-sustaining Power of the Earthsoul had faltered.

And it had been enough to give the demons the upper hand when the *Ara'so* had temporarily lost the ability to wield. Ten or more went down in sprays of blood as demons swarmed them from all sides, dragging them down the way a pack of wolves might fell a bison.

Shields replaced *Sei'shiin* as those who managed to re-embrace the Power before the demons could reach them suddenly found themselves on the defensive. Wrapping themselves and the surviving *Bero'thai* in protective bubbles of Spirit, they found themselves surrounded as the rest of the demon horde entered the Dome.

Less than thirty remained, but they were formidable—almost as formidable as the wedge-shaped behemoth blocking the doorway to the Overlook. Seven or eight of them were cloaked in auras of darkness, a visible manifestation that they could wield the Power of the Void.

Gideon sensed a shift in *Ta'shaen* as many of the Dainin linked their Awareness so they could fight in tandem, one wielding *Sei'shiin* while the other maintained the shield. The strategy worked, and five more demons vanished in flashes of white before those capable of wielding *Lo'shaen* came to their aid and turned the cleansing bursts aside.

Beraline and Marithen had retreated to the tiered seats of the council area along with Lord Nid and the other Dymas, and the entire group had formed a Communal link. Beraline had control of the link and was using the added strength to target the demons who could wield *Lo'shaen*. She killed three before the Earthsoul faltered a second time.

The collapse was just as brief as the first one, but the result was catastrophic. Two more Dainin and the squads of *Bero'thai* they protected died. Night Threads ripped up the tiered seats of the council area, tossing Beraline and the others into the air like so many ragdolls.

*Ta'shaen* returned, and shields sprang back into place as Gideon and the rest of the Dymas regained control of the Power.

"I can't wait any longer to use this," he said. "If I do, there won't be anyone left to protect." Turning toward the spidery behemoth skittering his way, he raised his fist and prepared to open the floodgates on the Orb's reservoir of Power.

The shield he held around himself and Brysia vanished as his Awareness went dark with yet another collapse of the Veil, but it wouldn't matter—the reservoir was still accessible through the Orb even if the Earthsoul itself had failed. He would end this now.

The *hiss-pop* of pierced flesh was accompanied by a searing pain in his right leg. He looked down at the spot and found a dagger-length quill sticking in his thigh. The circle of blood spreading outward across his pant leg was an unnatural color of red spider-webbed with black.

*Poison*, he thought as he yanked the quill free and tossed it to the ground. A sudden dizziness washed over him, but he fought through it and raised the Orb once more. He would destroy this creature, he would...

He had no sense of the Power. Not in his Awareness. Not through the Orb.

The flashes of *Sei'shiin* being wielded behind him proved the Earthsoul was back in place, and that he'd lost the ability to wield. His vision blurred and his dizziness brought him to his knees. Only Brysia's hand on his shoulder kept him from falling on his face.

"Run," he told her, but she shook her head.

He heard the hiss of steel as she pulled his sword from its scabbard and moved to stand in front of him.

The spidery-legged demon slowed slightly, and its massive wedge-shaped body sprouted an array of spikes and whip-like tentacles. One of the tentacles shot forward in a flash of black and knocked the sword from Brysia's hand. Then another one whipped forward to ensnare her, pinning her arms to her sides. A mouth opened inside of a mouth, and a proboscis tipped with barbed needles slid forth as the creature lifted Brysia into the air.

Gideon lurched to his feet and stumbled after her, but the demon ensnared him as well, pinning his arms to his sides and squeezing so tightly he felt ribs break. He tried to call for Brysia, but the wind had left his lungs. He struggled madly, desperate to reach his wife, desperate to save her.

A square of brilliant white light opened between Brysia and the demon, and a shining figure stepped from the opening. Fiery sword swinging, Daris Stodd, Brysia's warder in life and in death, severed the tentacle gripping Brysia, then brought his sword around and sliced the needle-tipped proboscis from the demon's mouth.

Hissing in pain as it retreated, the stricken creature released its hold on Gideon, and he landed with a painful grunt as a maelstrom of tentacles lashed at Daris.

Whirling and spinning with the skills he'd honed in life, Daris pursued the creature, severing every tentacle that whipped his way. Then, as the last tentacle dropped in a writhing heap at his feet, he stepped forward and drove his shimmering blade deep into one of the demon's eyes. There was a flash of silvery-blue as the sword sliced through flesh and bone and brain, then the demon blew apart into sparkling motes of dust that crackled from existence as they drifted to the floor.

Similar flashes of light were occurring elsewhere in the Dome, and Gideon winced in pain as he turned to investigate. What he found took his breath away.

Nine more Heroes of Light moved among the demons, striking them down with swords embued with the Power of Eliara. Randle fought alongside his brother Areth. Galadorian Stromsprey stood with Unnai Staniss—the warrior wielding a shining blade of steel, the Dymas wielding *El'shaen te sherah*.

And there in the thick of it all was Breiter Lyacon and the four young heroes of Kindel's Grove. Corom and Helem who'd died defending Zea Lyacon in the Church of Elderon. And Galam and Gillium who'd died defending Zea the night of Aethon's attack on the Overlook.

Ammorin's massive frame appeared above him, and Gideon looked up as the *Nar'shein* Chieftain knelt and placed his hands on his head.

"You have a shadowwound," he said. "I must heal it before the Earthsoul collapses for good."

Gideon hissed aloud as a rush of healing swept through him, partly in relief as the pain of his broken ribs vanished, but mostly from the sharp stab of pain in his leg as the shadowwound fought back. His vision blurred further and he felt as if he might pass out. Then the darkness of the demon poison vanished, and *Ta'shaen* returned.

He allowed Ammorin to help him to his feet, then took Brysia in his arms and hugged her so tightly she grunted for want of air. "I thought I'd lost you," he whispered, then stepped back to look her over. "You should have run," he scolded, forcing a smile.

She looked at Daris as he strode past them to engage one of the remaining demons. The hideous, insect-like monster saw him coming and turned to flee, only to run into the flaming point of Breiter Lyacon's sword. The demon burst apart in a flash of blue-white fire.

"Maybe it's a good thing I didn't," she said.

Gideon pulled her into his arms once more, and tears gathered in his eyes as he watched the Heroes of Light make quick work of the five remaining demons. As the last one fell, Daris made his way back toward them, a smile on his face as he looked them both in the eyes.

"It's good to see you both again," he said. "Now if you will excuse us, my friends and I are needed elsewhere."

Moving to the brilliant doorway of his arrival, he brought his sword blade up to his forehead in salute.

"*Keishun en 'liott krentis*," he said, then moved through into the light.

The doorway folded inward on itself, and the brilliant glow spilling across the floor vanished in a vertical flash of silver.

With tears of gratitude in her eyes, Brysia watched as the door of light closed behind Daris, then she turned to watch as the others departed in similar fashion. Two of the shining warriors, however, paused short of the rectangles of light and looked back at her.

"I think your brothers wish to speak to you," Gideon said, taking her hand and leading her toward them.

"Hello, little sister," Randle said.

"Big brother," she replied, her heart so filled with love that she gave up trying to hold back her tears. She looked at Areth. "Bigger brother," she said, laughing in spite of the sobs racking her from the inside.

Areth laughed as well, then brought his sword to his forehead in salute. "Long live the High Queen," he said. He looked at Gideon and nodded before looking at Brysia once more. "Until we meet again," he said and moved through the doorway of light. Randle followed, and the doorway folded inward in a flash of silvery-white.

"Until we meet again," she whispered.

Then, taking Gideon's hand, she steeled herself for the unpleasant task of numbering the dead.

"The Dainin have lost the wall."

Sheymi's announcement turned every head within earshot, and Railen turned to

Shavis to see how the Dai'shozen would respond.

"It was bound to happen," he said. "The enemy is simply too bloody large."

"It wasn't that so much as it was the sporadic collapses in the Veil," Sheymi told him. "The *Nar'shein* could have held for days otherwise."

"Where are they now?" Shavis asked.

"On the other side of the army of demons Shadan ushered in when he collapsed that section of the Veil."

"And the demons?" Tereus Dromensai asked.

Sheymi pointed to the wide curvature of First Avenue stretching away from the inner wall. "Coming into view any moment."

Railen fastened his eyes on the area and did his best to ignore the constant tremors shaking the stone beneath his feet. A few minutes later the front of the demon army came into view, a wall of black that flowed up the street like the surging of storm waves driven inland by high winds.

"Blood of Maeon!" Tereus hissed, and Railen nodded.

"Let's hope the Dainin catch them before they reach the wall," Sheymi said. "If they don't, we're going to have our hands full."

"Especially if we lose the ability to wield again," Railen said.

Tremors in *Ta'shaen* alerted him to multiple rents being opened in the Veil directly below the wall, and he leaned over the edge to investigate, ready to channel *Sei'shiin* at whoever or whatever might arrive.

"What is it?" Sheymi asked, looking down at the rents.

"I don't—"

A surge of *Lo'shaen* as powerful as those that destroyed the gates of the outer wall streaked through the fiery opening, and the entire length of the inner wall shook as it impacted, punching a hole the size of a house through the Power-wrought stone. The blast of shattered stone ripped through homes and businesses on the other side of the wall, and a plume of dust billowed upward. A second thrust streaked through a different gate with the same result, and that was followed by ten more in rapid succession, each as powerful as the last. When the rents snapped shut a moment later, entire sections of the wall lay in ruin.

Railen met Sheymi's horrified gaze for a moment, then looked to Shavis. "I think we're going to need a little help here."

With the ground trembling beneath her feet from the most recent earthquake, Velerie Kivashey burst another demon's head open with a thrust of Flesh, then took up a sword from one of the fallen Highwaymen with a tendril of Air and buried it in the chest of the demon that was pressing Jukstin. The young man shot a quick look of thanks in her direction before moving to engage another demon.

Like the last two she'd killed, most of the demons were human in form, with grey pitted skin and red and yellow eyes. They wore black metal armor and carried a variety of swords and clubs. And though they were relatively easy to kill with the Power, there were a bloody lot of them.

Even worse, *Ta'shaen* kept vanishing from her Awareness for moments at a time, leaving her and the *Nar'shein* without the ability to wield. The most recent lapse had resulted in the death of three Highwaymen when the tendrils of *Sei'shiin* she'd been channeling vanished just short of the demons she'd intended to kill.

"We've got demons behind us!" Bornis shouted as he buried his axe in the head of the wolf-like demon lunging at him. He pointed to the dark shapes emerging from the alley between the mercantile and another building, then yanked his axe free in a spray of blackish blood and turned to meet the new arrivals. One, a hulking human-shaped beast with four arms, hefted a pair of clubs and moved to engage him.

Velerie sliced its head from its neck with a blade of Spirit, then gritted her teeth in frustration as *Ta'shaen* vanished once more. The momentary lapse allowed the next few demons to reach Bornis, but he managed to kill the nearest one with a vicious swing of his axe before another slashed him across the ribs. He staggered backward, hissing in pain, and barely managed to bring his axe up in time to avoid having his head split open.

*Ta'shaen* returned, and Velerie ripped the demons apart with a powerful thrust of Flesh. Braelynn channeled as well, and a dome of Spirit sprang into place around them, stopping the demon advance.

Racing up to Bornis, Velerie placed her hand on his side and healed him of his wound.

"Thanks," he whispered, then hefted his axe and cast about the area. Velerie did as well, and her heart sank when she realized they were surrounded.

Fadus and Zea and the rest of those they were protecting were huddled together on the boardwalk fronting Zander's Mercantile. Wytni's face was a mask of terror. Little Kindel was crying while Zea tried unsuccessfully to soothe her.

Jemmishin had positioned himself in front of them, spear in hand, and *Ta'shaen* coursed through him as he ripped demons to shreds with stabs of lightning. Jeymi joined him in his attack, and thunder echoed loudly off the shield and rumbled away down the street.

Enraged by the attack, the remaining demons threw themselves at the shield, testing it for weakness, waiting for *Ta'shaen* to fail once more. *And it will*, Jeymi thought. *Any second now*. And when it did, they would be overrun.

*Ta'shaen* came alive with wieldings unlike any she'd ever felt, and she stretched her mind toward one of them to see a rectangle of light opening in the street behind the demons. A shining figure strode through the opening with a flaming sword in hand, and the demons in the air whirled to face him, howling with unbridled hatred.

The angelic figure strode into the midst of the demons with blade swinging and demons died in bursts of silvery-blue fire. Not far away, another shining soldier loosed arrow after white-hot arrow into the demon horde, and the gleaming shafts punched through armor and flesh alike.

"That's Helem," Bornis said, his voice filled with wonder. His eyes moved to a second angelic archer. "And Corom." He pointed to two others, and Velerie smiled when she recognized them.

"Galam and Gillium," she whispered, and Bornis nodded, his eyes wet with tears.

*Ta'shaen* faltered briefly, then sprang back into place, but the momentary lapse had no effect on the Heroes of Light as they continued to slaughter the demons. The few that made it inside Braelynn's shield during the Power's absence were immediately killed by Jemmishin who burned them from existence with streamers of *Sei'shiin*.

Had it not been for the arrival of Helem and Corom and the others, the most recent collapse would have been the end. Now it was the demons who were being annihilated, and Jeymi watched in wonder as the first swordsman who'd arrived cut a path through them as if they were made of straw.

"Breiter!" Zea gasped, and Velerie turned to find her friend's eyes wide with astonishment. Holding Kindel against her chest, she rose and started toward her husband. Jemmishin shadowed her, his eyes on the last of the demons should any more of them make it inside the shield.

They didn't, and the last one burst apart in a spray of fiery motes as Breiter buried his sword in the creature's chest.

Velerie released the Power as silence fell across the area. Braelynn and Jemmishin did as well.

All eyes followed Zea as she stopped in front of her husband. Sheathing his fiery sword, he smiled at her, then held out his hands for Kindel. Zea handed her over, and Velerie's heart ached with a strange mix of joy and grief as she watched Breiter kiss his baby girl.

At his touch, Kindel stopped crying and grew calm, her tiny eyes fixed on the face of her father. "Hello, beautiful," he said, then kissed her again and handed her back to her mother.

"I've got to go," he said, reaching up to touch Zea's cheek. "I love you."

Turning on his heel, he started back to the doorway of light, and the four young heroes of Kindel's Grove followed, each returning to the door through which he'd arrived. They passed through without looking back, and the shimmering holes folded in on themselves and vanished.

Overwhelmed by emotion, Zea dropped to her knees and sobbed openly. Little Kindel, however, continued to stare at the spot where her father had vanished back into the afterlife.

ㄼ

When the door blew inward in a spray of shattered wood, Andil Fairimor raised his sword and prepared to meet the demons pouring into the room. This was the end, he knew. The last of the *Bero'thai* who'd been charged with protecting him and his mother and grandmother had been overrun. He alone stood between the hellbeasts and his family now. And he had no illusions about what the outcome would be.

A sudden blinding light filled the room as four rectangles of light opened in front of the demons and shining figures wrapped in brilliant auras of light moved through from beyond. One struck the approaching demons with streams of potent, white-hot energy, while the other three met the charge with swords of fire.

The forward ranks of demons vanished in flares of white or bursts of sizzling flesh that crackled and sparked before swirling away as ash. Howling with rage, the second wave of demons pressed the new arrivals, but the result was the same. The third wave died as well. Then the fourth. Like rabbits running headlong into an approaching cavalry charge, they continued to be annihilated until none remained.

The shining warriors of light turned to face them, and Andil blinked in surprise as his eyes met those of his father.

Cassia gasped audibly and started forward, and, as she did, Andil looked at the others who'd arrived. The man standing next to Randle bore such a strong resemblance to him that Andil knew him for who he was. *Areth*, he thought, though he'd never met his uncle in the flesh. Beside Areth stood Unnai Dymas, and beside Unnai, Daris Stodd.

*Death isn't the end*, he thought.

Smiling through his tears, he watched his parents embrace, then dropped his sword and hurried forward to join them.

亡

Thorac's Krelltin collapsed as a Tamban arrow took it in the head, and Thorac watched the world rotate around him as he was thrown clear. He landed unceremoniously on his back in the middle of the street, and spots of light flashed through his vision from the impact. Scrambling to his feet, he brought his shield and axe up in front of him as more than a dozen Tamban soldiers closed in from all sides.

"*Dromar Chunin!*" he shouted, determined to kill as many as he could before they got him.

The air parted before him in a flash of silvery-white and a small, shining figure moved out of a rectangle of light.

*Emma*, he thought, then squinted against the brilliance of an attack so bright the day seemed to dim in comparison. Tendrils of shimmering Power erupted from her fingertips like a miniature lightning storm, and Thorac's enemies vanished from existence in curt flashes of white.

More shimmering tendrils followed, and the advancing column of Tamban soldiers dove for cover as those leading the way were destroyed.

"Fall back to Central Plaza," Emma ordered. "I'll hold them here while you do."

Thorac hesitated, momentarily tempted to argue, but the look in Emma's eyes stayed his tongue. She'd risked her eternal soul to return to the world of the living—the least he could do was obey her commands.

"Who am I to argue with a Hero of Light?"

"Exactly," she said, smiling fondly at him. "Now go."

He brought his fist to his chest in salute, then hurried away, shouting for his men to follow. He looked back only once, but what he found gave him hope that the battle was not yet lost. Emmarenziana Antilla, small as she was, shone brighter than the sun as she unleashed a firestorm of Light and Fire into the armies of darkness.

Pressing his hand on the arrow wound in his side, Elison fought through the pain as he and his men fled from the demons pursuing them. Northeast Bridge was in sight now, and if they could cross it before the demons caught them, they'd be joined by reinforcements. And so he ran, aware of how the blood leaking between his fingers increased with every step he took.

They were nearly to the bridge when an army of Tamban Deathwatch swarmed from the side streets to block their way.

"Burn it all," he hissed, then cast a quick look over his shoulder to find the horde of demons bearing down on them.

"How do you want to play this, Captain?" one of the Guardsmen asked.

Before he could answer, the front of the buildings went white with brilliant light, and seven radiant beings strode through what appeared to be doorways of light. Elison's astonishment deepened when he recognized the men for who they were.

Breiter and Daris and Unnai stepped into the path of the demons. Randle and Areth Fairimor started for the Tambans and were joined by Taka O'sei and a long-haired Kelsan that could only be Galadorian Stromsprey.

"For the Blue Flame," Elison shouted, then he and his men joined the Heroes of Light in battle.

Idoman watched in wonder as Joselyn Rai swept the top of the wall clear of the enemy with a thrust of *El'shaen te sherah* brighter and more powerful than anything she'd ever channeled in life.

"That's our cue," Taggert said, taking Idoman by the arm and pulling him in the other direction. "We need to go. Now. Before you lose the ability to wield again."

Idoman nodded, but he couldn't pull his eyes away from his beloved mentor, so mesmerized by her brilliance that he stumbled several times as Taggert pulled him along.

"Idoman," Taggert said. "Don't waste the gift she is giving us. She can't remain here for long, and neither should we."

Idoman shook himself free of the trance Joselyn's arrival had put him in, then met Taggert's gaze. "Yes," he said. "Of course. You are right."

Opening himself to the Power, he opened a Veilgate and prayed the Earthsoul wouldn't falter again while he and the others moved through. The men of Chellum were waiting for him on the other side, and all of them had their eyes fastened on the wall looming tall above Northeast Road.

"What was that?" one of the men asked, and Idoman smiled as the brilliance that was Joselyn wreaked havoc on the soldiers of Tamba swarming into the city below her.

"A friend," he answered. "Come. She's given us the time we need to reach Northeast Bridge ahead of the enemy."

The demons swarming over the top of the wall were reminiscent of those Sheymi had faced at the Great Wall of Aridan, and the memories of what had happened there chilled her heart. This was a fight she and the others could not win.

Her hold on the Power vanished as the Earthsoul faltered once again, and the squad of Shizu she was protecting were trampled by a spike-footed demon with patches of fur protruding from its armored segments. She burned it to ash a heartbeat later as *Ta'shaen* came back to her in a rush, but it was too late to save the Shizu.

Ten small demons with multiple legs and scorpion-like tails crested the edge of the wall a short distance beyond where Shavis and Tereus were fighting side by side, but when she tried to strike the demons with the Power, *Ta'shaen* slipped from her grasp once more. The lapses were growing more frequent, and they were growing longer.

By the time the Power returned, the Emperor and his warder were surrounded by the hideous little monsters, and she couldn't strike for fear of hitting her friends. Sword blades flashing, the two fought for their lives as more demons arrived over the top of the wall.

She heard Railen cry out, and turned to see him staggering backward from a boar-like demon covered in grey quills. She burned the monster to ash with a burst of *Sei'shiin*, then rushed to Railen's side as he stumbled and went down. Two of the demon's quills were lodged in his forearm.

"I can't sense the Power," he said, then his eyes went wide as three more monstrosities crested the wall right above them.

Sheymi brought her hand up to destroy them, but a bright square of light opened between her and the demons, and a shining Sarui in full armor strode through the opening.

*Kalear,* she thought, then watched in amazement as he destroyed the demons with white-hot spears of *El'shaen*. Turning toward Shavis and Tereus, he made a small gesture with his hand, and the frenetic little beasts attacking the two burst into sparkling clouds of ash.

Dozens more of the shimmering doorways opened along the top of the wall and in the streets below, and the slain members of *tres'dia* fell on the demons like the fiery sword of God.

乇

Teig Ole'ar loosed the last of his arrows into a knot of Darklings swarming down the street toward him and Joneam, then dropped his bow and drew his sword. The rest of Joneam's warders were out of arrows as well, and sword blades glittered brightly in the noonday sun as they formed a wall in front of their general.

Teig cast a quick look over his shoulder at the Dymas. That none of them were striking the Darklings with the Power meant they'd once again lost the ability to wield. Judging by the horrified looks in their eyes, it may have been permanent this time.

He looked back at the approaching enemy. *At least it keeps the Agla'Con and the chael'trom from wielding,* he thought, then prepared to meet the enemy charge.

A silvery-white rectangle of light opened a short distance away and a radiant figure strode through from beyond. His long white hair and the sword in his hand shone like the sun. His uniform and cape were the brightest white Teig had ever seen. The image of the Fighting Lion of Fulrath embroidered on the cape, however, burned a brilliant gold.

"Father," Joneam said, his eyes wide with wonder.

"Hello, Son," Croneam replied, then looked at the Darklings. "Shall we?"

Joneam hefted his father's Dragon-etched blade, and Teig watched in stupefied wonder as father and son fought side by side once more.

乇

Standing beneath the silver oak in the center of the Chellum Ballroom, Elam Gaufin listened to the horrific cries of the demons making their way toward him through the palace. The way ahead of the demons had been evacuated as much as was possible, but Elam's heart broke with how many people had ignored the warning to flee.

Those who had heeded the warning were holed up in the Chellum dining room and were under the protection of half of *tres'dia*. The other half of the Riaki Power-wielders were here with him, as was every member of the Home Guard who'd been able to get here ahead of the demons. The battle to save House Chellum from extinction would be won or lost beneath the branches of the silver oak.

"They're here," Jonnil Dymas said, and a heartbeat later the doors leading into the dome were knocked from their hinges as demons flowed into the room.

A hail of arrows hissed into those leading the charge, and a number of them staggered and went down and were trampled by those behind them. More arrows followed, and more demons fell. Those that tried to rise were finished by thrusts of Flesh and streamers of *Sei'shiin*.

The demons continued to spread out across the dome as they entered, and the archers resorted to targeting individual demons instead of loosing as one. The members of *tres'dia* continued their attack as well, but it cut off after only a few seconds.

"The Earthsoul collapsed again," Jonnil said, and hisses of frustration moved through the ranks of the Riaki Dymas.

Elam's men continued loosing arrows, but it did little to slow the advancing horde. He cast a quick look at Jonnil and found his face pinched with concentration. Concentration that turned to worry and then all out panic.

"It's not coming back," he said. "We can't touch the Power."

Elam crushed the sick feeling sweeping through him, then drew his sword and prepared to meet the demon charge. The hiss of steel echoed across the dome as the rest of the Home Guard joined him. Swords raised, they waited.

*Faithful to the end*, Elam thought, then turned his attention back to the demons and locked eyes with the one he intended to kill.

The interior of the dome went bright as noonday as a square of light opened in front of the demons. The shining figure of a woman stepped out of the light and raised her arms in the direction of the demons. A split second later the foremost among them thudded to a stop against an invisible barrier and were crushed from behind by others. Fat, wet drops of demon blood ran in streaks down what appeared to be empty air.

"She wields *El'shaen*," Jonnil said, his voice filled with awe. "She has a direct link to Eliara itself."

The demons continued to pile up against the barrier, further injuring or killing those in front of them in their frenzied haste to reach the glowing figure before them.

When the last of the demons had entered the dome, the shining soldier from Eliara let the barrier drop, and the interior of the dome vanished behind a flash of light so bright everyone in the room had to shield their eyes or risk blindness.

The crazed howls and shrieks of the demons cut off, but Elam didn't risk a peek until he realized the light was receding. When he could see clearly once more, he looked to the shining figure.

She turned toward him, a smile on her face. Her eyes, which in life had been milky-white with blindness, were bright and clear and as blue as a summer sky.

"Hello, Elam," she said, seemingly amused by his surprise. "You didn't think I would name you *Ael'mion* and then let you be slaughtered by demons, did you?"

"I..." he began, then fell silent, completely at a loss for words.

Still smiling, she moved back through the doorway of light, and it folded in on itself and vanished.

"Goodbye, Norel," he whispered, then looked at Jonnil. "Is *Ta'shaen* still out of reach?"

Jonnil nodded, his face pale. "The Earthsoul is spent," he answered. "This world is about to be swallowed by Con'Jithar."

# CHAPTER 73

## *End of Days*

As Kiaush passed over Cynthia's crumbling outer wall and glided over the scarred remains of its long-dead buildings and streets, Jase glanced down at the dome he and Captain Alleilwin and his men had spent the night in all those nights ago, and a shiver ran up his spine at the memory. The rest of the Power-wrought stone of the roof had collapsed, leaving a ring of stone filled with rubble.

A bit further on, two *Mrogin* were slinking along through the murky half-light of what passed for day this deep into Amnidia's wasteland.

"I hate those bloody things," Elliott muttered, but Jase didn't reply.

Instead, he looked up at Shey'Avralier towering above the ruined city. An occasional flash of light lit the base of the palace's main entrance, but the tremors rippling through *Ta'shaen* were pure. A moment later, he felt the brush of Yavil's mind.

*Welcome, Lord Fairimor,* he said, *and congratulations on finding a Blood Orb. We hold the courtyard fronting—*

The Communal link vanished, and Jase tensed, afraid something had just happened to the Rhiven. Then he realized he'd lost touch with more than just Yavil's mind. His Awareness of *Ta'shaen* had vanished—he could no longer sense the Power at all.

It came back to him a heartbeat later, and a moment after that, he felt the familiar touch of the Rhiven's mind once more.

*It seems you are arriving just in time,* Yavil told him, his fear and dread flowing across the link. *That was clearly a sign that the Earthsoul has reached her end—the equivalent of a dying man's last few faltering gasps for breath. Quickly, my friend, we hold the courtyard fronting the palace's main entrance.* His mind withdrew.

"There," Jase said, pointing to the cathedral-like dome at the base of two large towers. "Yavil and the Rhiven are waiting for us."

Elliott nodded, guiding Kiaush toward the spot. They cleared the last of the crumbling buildings, and the palace's front courtyard came into view.

Twenty Rhiven in their true form had cordoned off the main entrance, a semicircle of massive, glittering shapes that may as well have been the Great Wall of Aridan for all the hope the army of Shadan'Ko had of breaking through it. Snarling and growling like the animals they now were, the Shadan'Ko stayed back out of range of the Dragon's claws and their gleaming white teeth.

Only when a *Mrogin* or *Ba'trul* ventured too close did the Rhiven use the Power as a weapon, and then only as much as was necessary to kill it and nothing else. They were saving their strength should anything worse be drawn to the area.

Kiaush glided in over the heads of the Rhiven and settled to the ground in front of the entrance. Jase and Elliott leapt from the saddle as Kiaush bellied down for them, then Elliott urged the bird skyward as Seth's bird touched down.

"Rhiven ward the way ahead," Yavil said, his bright red mane only slightly dulled by Amnidia's sickly light. "Galiena is awaiting your arrival at the entrance to Earth's Heart."

"Thank you, my friend," Jase said, then took Talia by the hand and raced inside. *And may the Creator shelter you in the moments to come*, he added silently, a cold pit settling in his stomach.

Talia squeezed his hand reassuringly as they ran, and he tried to clear his thoughts to shelter her from the storm of anxiety brewing inside him.

*It's not working*, she told him, her own thoughts so filled with fear that he wondered how she managed to take her next breath.

True to Yavil's word, Rhiven stood watch along the way, glittering sentinels who not only showed him the path he needed to take, but who cheered him and the others on as they ran.

They passed into a particularly large dome and were forced to slow as they picked their way across the rubble-strewn floor. The corpses of *Ba'trul* and *Mrogin* and several creatures he didn't have names for were scattered about the room, and the stench of their blood filled his nostrils as he led the way past them.

"Temifair Dome," Seth said, then pointed to the jagged hole in the far wall. The Power-wrought stone of Elvan making had been blasted clear of the living rock of Mount Tabor, and the corridor beyond seemed to stretch away forever.

"This way, *Mith'elre Chon*," a blue-scaled Rhiven said, and Jase felt her embrace the Power. A line of small spheres of Light sprang into existence along the ceiling to light the way.

Jase and the others finished picking their way through the rubble, then ran once more. They were nearing the end of the corridor when *Ta'shaen* faltered again, and the illuminating spheres winked out. They sprang back to life an instant later, but the fact *Ta'shaen* had failed again so quickly sent a rush of fear sweeping through him.

They passed through into another cathedral-like chamber, and the Rhiven waiting inside directed them to a wide set of stairs ascending into the mountain. The bodies of more shadowspawn were scattered about, but Jase gave them only a cursory glance as he moved to the stairs.

More Power-wrought spheres of light lit the way, and the Rhiven channeling them watched from the arched entrances of each of the levels as Jase and the others climbed the stairs. They had just passed the third level when *Ta'shaen* flickered again, casting the stairwell into momentary darkness before springing back once more. Another sign of the Earthsoul's imminent demise, the faltering encouraged Jase to move faster, and the muscles in his legs burned as he raced up the stairs to the sixth level.

Galiena was there to greet him as he arrived, her raven-colored mane a sharp contrast to the glittering brilliance of her crimson scales. Her forearms and claws sported a fresh coat of grey-black blood, and Jase spotted a heap of shadowspawn corpses piled against the far wall.

The Rhiven Queen noticed his look and smiled, showing two rows of white, dagger-length teeth. "Killing them with the Power would have drawn the attention of those out in the city," she said simply, then turned and walked beside him as he approached the large, intricately carved archway marking the entrance to Earth's Heart.

"Magnificent, isn't it?"

Jase nodded, completely at a loss for words. The corridor beyond the archway stretched away into the mountain, its gradual slope rising up and out of sight. It was bright with the light of glowstones set in the stonework of the walls and ceiling, and candelabra and statues identical to those inside the temple in Mount Augg lined the walls at intervals. Each statue held a singularly large glowstone in its outstretched hands.

But it was more than just the abundance of visible light that took Jase's breath away, it was the spiritual radiance he could feel emanating within. The place was very literally alive with *Ta'shaen*, so potent and powerful that it remained in place even when the luminescent world outside the archway momentarily flickered from existence once more.

"Now you know why the ancients referred to this place as a heart," Galiena said. "It is the source of the spiritual life-blood of this world—a crux point that disseminates *Ta'shaen* to every fiber of the physical world, giving and sustaining life in the very same manner the heart in your chest circulates your blood."

"The falterings in *Ta'shaen* we've been experiencing," Jase said, his eyes still on the radiance of the corridor, "they had no effect on the Soul Chamber."

"For now," Galiena said. "The lapses in the Power elsewhere are a result of the Earthsoul closing in on Herself to conserve what's left of Her strength. She's withdrawn *Ta'shaen* from Her extremities to keep the heart beating. It won't be long before what you see before you falters as well."

"Then let's do this," he said, hoping he sounded more confident than he really felt. Tightening his grip on the Blood Orb, he crossed the threshold of the archway into Earth's Heart.

And tripped an invisible thread of corrupted Spirit that streaked away to the south, a Power-wrought alarm that had just alerted whoever had set the thread in place. It had been laid just outside the wards sheltering the corridor, and had reacted to the presence of the Blood Orb in his hand, an extremely sophisticated wielding that could have only been placed there by one of two people: Aethon Fairimor or Throy Shadan. Either way, they were about to have some very unpleasant company.

He hissed his frustration as he turned to meet Galiena's yellow-eyed gaze.

"Go," she said. "We'll hold them off as long as the Power remains."

"Uh, what just happened?" Elliott asked.

"Shadan will be here any moment," Jase told him, then opened himself to the oasis of *Ta'shaen* stretching away before him and tried to open a Veilgate into the Soul Chamber. It rotated back on itself and vanished in a flash of light just as those at Mount Augg had done.

"I guess we run," he said. "Quickly. We don't have much time."

With a river of *Lo'shaen* coursing through him, Throy Shadan channeled a banner of Fire into the air as he led three thousand K'rrosha through the ruins of North Gate and into the city of Trian.

*The Ancient City*, he thought. *My city.*

He felt *Ta'shaen* falter then spring back into place for what was likely to be the last time. When it failed next, his enemies would be powerless before him, and he would crush them all. Even Gideon and his precious Blood Orb would be no match for the power of the Void when it arrived in full.

A thread of *Lo'shaen* streaked in from the north to strike his scepter, and an audible clang, like the ringing of a bell, sounded loudly in his ears. The alarm he'd placed across the entrance to the Soul Chamber had just been triggered by the presence of a Blood Orb.

Somehow, in spite of all that was evil in the world, Jase bloody Fairimor had gotten his hands on a viable Orb.

Outraged, he redirected the flow of *Lo'shaen* into what remained of the fabric of the Veil and tore a rent into Shey'Avralier.

"Shadan just left through a Veilgate," Lord Nid said, and Gideon felt the Meleki King rein in his Awareness. He was too weak to wield after being healed of his injuries, so he'd taken it upon himself to keep watch on what was happening out in the city.

"He's going after Jase," Gideon said, offering a silent prayer for his son.

"Somehow he's learned of the Blood Orb."

Kneeling next to Beraline, he placed his hands on her head and healed her of her wounds. Like Marithen, she'd suffered a number of broken bones and had sustained serious internal injuries after being hurled through the air by Night Threads. Beraline would survive. Marithen probably wouldn't.

All across the Dome, the rest of the Dymas who'd survived the demon attack were also healing those they could, moving quickly from person to person before *Ta'shaen* vanished for good.

Gideon moved to Hallie Dymas, but when he reached into her with his Awareness, he found that she'd already passed. So had Erebius. Junteri lay next to her father, her face pale, her eyes filled with tears.

"He's gone," she said as Gideon knelt beside her. "I couldn't save him."

He placed his hands on her head and healed her, then helped her sit up. A moment later, *Ta'shaen* vanished and his Awareness went dark. When the darkness remained, he stood and started for the Overlook. The moment he'd been shown in visions and nightmares was upon them—the end of days had arrived.

"It's gone for good, isn't it?" Junteri called.

"Yes," he answered, his eyes on the doorway. The light streaming through it—light which only moments ago had been the brightness of noonday—was rapidly fading. Already it was as pale and sickly as the light in Amnidia, and it would continue to fade until darkness reigned supreme.

A moment later, a chorus of ghostly cries echoed across the city as the spirits of the damned arrived to take a hand in the battle. Gideon kept walking, determined to meet the threat.

He could feel Brysia's eyes on him as he walked, and he turned a smile on her. "I love you," he said.

Then, facing forward once more, he raised the Blood Orb before him and opened himself to its incredible reservoir of Power.

With Sheymi at his side, Railen Nogeru watched from the top of the inner wall as countless demons streamed through the breaches Throy Shadan had opened into the inner city. The most vicious creatures among the horde, including those who could wield *Lo'shaen*, had been destroyed by Kalear and the other Heroes of Light before they'd vanished back through the doorways of light to fight elsewhere.

Only lesser demons remained now, and without the ability to scale the walls after the manner of their more terrifying cousins, they were content to take the easiest path. Even so, it was a terrifying sight, a literal river of armored corruption flowing unchecked into the inner city.

The few Dymas who still had strength enough to strike were killing those they could, but even that abruptly ended a moment later when *Ta'shaen* vanished for the final time. Shortly after his Awareness went dark, Railen realized visible light was fading as well.

He looked up at the sun. It was still visible in the sky, but its brilliance was dimming rapidly. Within moments it had been reduced to a sickly-looking orb of red against a background of ever-darkening grey. The world, he realized in horror, was being swallowed by the Void.

A frenetic wailing of voices rent the air out in the city, and everyone on the wall turned as thousands of apparitional shapes materialized in the streets. They moved with the fluidity of the wind itself, ethereal figures of greenish-white that left a trail of bodies in their wake as they flowed toward the palace.

"The spirits of the damned," Sheymi whispered, her voice tight with fear.

At a loss for words, Railen put his arm around her, and together they watched the ghostly army swarm up the sides of the Overlook and disappear into the gardens.

As the Blood Orb bound itself to him as its wielder, Elsa's Awareness became his, and the luminescent world sprang into existence in his mind's eye. He saw the Dome, the Overlook and gardens, the inner and outer cities—he saw everything.

Hundreds of thousands of soldiers were bleeding out their lives in futility as the darkness of the Void continued to descend over the earth, blotting out the sun and turning day to night.

The air itself grew heavy, making breathing difficult for all, friend and foe alike. The trees and shrubs and flowers in the Overlook's lush gardens withered and turned black. The crystal clear waters of the stream turned murky and foul smelling.

In the outer city, entire neighborhoods were in flames, and thick black smoke billowed skyward, further darkening the sky. Thousands of demons marched through the streets of the inner city, and they weren't alone—spectral shapes of greenish-white moved with them, their ghostly cries riding the winds as they left death and injury at every turn.

More ethereal shapes appeared in his mind's eye as men and women died and their spirits left their bodies. Those who had been righteous while in life looked around in horror, immobilized by the discovery that they were trapped on the wrong side of the Veil. And they would remain trapped, Gideon knew, unless Jase rejuvenated the Earthsoul. Their fate would be the same as the wicked.

He beheld all of it in an instant, then focused his attention on the front of the Overlook. The *Bero'thai* who'd survived the battle in the Dome had taken positions there and were loosing a steady stream of arrows into the demons swarming into the courtyard fronting the palace.

The Light-blasted creatures fell dead or wounded, and were trampled by their own kind, but the river of armored bodies didn't slow. They reached the palace entrance, and the sound of splintering wood and shattering steel echoed across the courtyard.

Everything he had witnessed since embracing the Orb was almost exactly as it had been in the nightmarish visions he'd had of this moment, and that let him know what was coming next. And because he knew, he could change the course of the next few moments, at least enough to save the lives of the *Bero'thai* fighting to hold the Overlook.

Stepping out of the Dome, he raised his fist and sent a radiant burst of energy streaking over the heads of the *Bero'thai*. It reached the edge of the Overlook just as the frenzied apparitional soldiers arrived, catching them by surprise and burning them from existence like leaves thrown into a furnace.

The *Bero'thai* turned to stare at him with looks of wonder in their eyes, then made way for him as he moved to stand at the edge of the Overlook.

"All of you inside," he ordered. "There is nothing more you can do out here."

As they hurried away, he gave himself more fully to the Power coursing through him and let the voice of Elsa guide his actions as he unleashed a firestorm of *Sei'shiin* into the demons and shadowspawned creatures swarming in the courtyard below. They flared from existence in curt flashes of bluish green, little more than gnats in light of the awesome power of the Orb.

He stretched his Awareness across the inner city and marveled at the god-like omnipotence of the view. He saw every face, heard every sound, felt every emotion. He separated ally from enemy, fixing them in his mind's eye with a precision only possible with the aid of his long dead ancestral mother.

*Yes, my son*, she whispered. *Now finish what you started.*

He struck, channeling tens of thousands of individual strands of *Sei'shiin* that dropped out of the sky as one, a white-hot lightning storm of cleansing energy that threw back the growing darkness for a single titanic instant.

With the inner city cleansed, he stretched his Awareness past the ruined wall into the outer city, taking note of where the fighting was at its worst. He struck again, sparing the lives of thousands of Trian's defenders by destroying twice that number of demons.

He turned his attention to the army of Tambans moving along Northeast Road, then channeled Fire from the sky and burned a mile long stretch of the invaders to ash. But as he did, he sensed a lessening in the torrent of energy flowing toward him from the Blood Orb. The reservoir was nearing its end. One or two more Powerful strikes and it would be gone.

Opening himself more fully to the spirit of Elsa, he listened carefully to her promptings and let her guide him as he selected his next targets. A knot of Darklings on the verge of overpowering a Chunin soldier and the female Dymas he was protecting. Nine demons pursuing a Zekan captain down an alley. Four shadowhounds slinking along the outside edge of the wall in hopes of ambushing an injured Dainin. The targets were widespread and varied and seemingly random, but Gideon knew better than to ignore the promptings.

He simply did as directed, knowing that each and every strike brought him that much closer to the end of the flow of Power.

*You did well, my son,* Elsa said, then the brilliant glow in his hand began to dim as the flow of Power waned. It ceased completely a moment later, and his Awareness went dark as the Orb winked out.

Then, just as he'd foreseen, Night Threads streaked out of the darkness, and he was thrown to the ground as they exploded along the face of the Overlook. Scream-like cracks of thunder followed as the winged monster from the vision swooped in on massive wings and landed heavily in the gardens a few feet away.

He rose to face it, but an invisible thrust of *Lo'shaen* slammed him in the chest, knocking him backward through the withered landscape. Fighting to regain his breath, he pushed himself to his feet once more, unwilling to give his assailant the satisfaction of seeing him stay down.

The monster—he saw now that it was a bat-like demon from Con'Jithar—swivelled its head toward him, and the fire in its demonic gaze flared brightly.

"Still as proud as ever," the hooded figure atop the demon said, and Gideon's rage spiked as he recognized the voice.

"Aethon," he said, his contempt for the man turning the name into a curse.

Sliding down from the demon's back, Aethon pulled back the hood. His eyes were alight with his victory, and he was smiling.

"Uncle," he said, shaking his head with mock sadness. "That's no way to speak to family."

"You have no claim to the Fairimor name," Gideon sneered. "You lost your birthright when you sold yourself to Maeon."

"Maybe so," Aethon said. He made a seemingly insignificant motion with his hand, and Gideon's feet were knocked from beneath him with a sweep of *Lo'shaen*.

He hit the ground hard, and the wind blasted from his lungs as his vision momentarily blurred. When it cleared enough for him to see, he found Aethon standing over him with a blade of counterfeit Fire in his hand.

"But then so did you, didn't you...Dunkin?" He waited, an arrogant smirk on his face.

"So, you finally figured it out," he said, and a strange sense of peace washed over him. Peace not because the truth was out, but because that truth had shown him the way he might survive the next few moments.

Aethon shrugged. "No. It was just a guess. But thank you for confirming it. It will make killing you that much more rewarding."

Gideon gave a scornful laugh. "You're forgetting something," he said and watched Aethon's eyes narrow suspiciously.

"And what's that?" he asked. Raising the blade of hellfire, he prepared to strike.

"I lost my birthright long before you were born."

Opening himself to the Power of the Void, he sliced Aethon's head from his neck with a blade of counterfeit Fire.

Aethon's body dropped into a heap, and the fiery sword of corruption in his hand winked out. His head, eyes frozen wide with surprise, rolled to a stop a short distance away.

"You should have brushed up on your history," Gideon said. Pushing him to his feet, he stabbed Aethon's demon mount through the head, then released *Lo'shaen* and moved back to the edge of the Overlook.

He'd survived the events of the nightmarish vision. He'd know in the next few minutes if any of them would be surviving the end of everything.

*Hurry, Jase,* he thought. *Time is just about up.*

# CHAPTER 74

## *The Blood of Fairimor*

STANDING INSIDE THE WARDS PROTECTING the entrance to Earth's Heart, Galiena channeled a stream of *Sei'shiin* at Throy Shadan as he strode through the rent he'd opened into the chamber in front of her.

The Dreadlord, however, was quick, and a shield of counterfeit Spirit sprang into being to deflect the cleansing strike. Light and darkness collided in an explosive burst that shook the walls of the chamber and burned deep gashes across the floor.

The flare of red from Shadan's scepter intensified with the Power of the Void, and he retaliated with a barrage of Night Threads. The stabs of corruption struck Galiena's shield with the force of a battering ram, but they triggered a release of Power from the wards protecting the Soul Chamber as they crossed the threshold.

Streamers of *Sei'shiin* impacted the Dreadlord's protective shroud, driving him backward and forcing him to break off his attack. Eye burning with rage, he waited for them to pass, then strengthened his shield and moved toward her, stopping just outside the arch.

"You were wise to take shelter inside the wards," he rasped, his good eye glowing with the fires of hell. "But they won't last. I can feel them weakening." His grey lips curled into a smile. "And so can you."

He stepped across the threshold, and Galiena braced herself as another release of *Ta'shaen* hammered his shield. It was noticeably weaker than before and cut off much more quickly.

"See," he said smugly. "How many more of those do you think the Earthsoul has left?"

"Enough for Jase to bring about the Rejuvenation," she said, only now she wasn't so sure.

His scepter flared brightly. "Let's find out."

七

"Shadan is trying to collapse the wards," Jase said, and Talia felt his panic through the *sei'vaiya* as strongly as if it were her own. She tried to send feelings of reassurance, but it was impossible to share something she didn't feel herself.

And so she ran without speaking, as fearful of what lay ahead as she was about Throy Shadan.

The corridor began to level out, and, as it did, the top of an archway came into view. The sight urged them all to run faster, and a few seconds later they passed through into a vast, oval chamber constructed of white *chorazin*.

The sheer splendor of the room took Talia's breath away. A second arched corridor stood on the far side of the room. A massive chandelier hanging from a heavy gold chain graced the top of the domed ceiling. Seven gold statues of the now-familiar-looking woman lined the room at intervals and were interspersed by raised images of the Old World symbols for Eliara and *Ta'shaen*. And there, in the center of the room, shining as with some inner light, was the Altar of Elsa.

Jase made straight for it, a look of determination in his eyes and a storm of emotions in his heart. Talia followed, but Seth and Elliott stopped just inside the entrance. Elliott drew his sword, then vanished in a cloak of bended Light. Seth drew his swords as well and moved to one side of the archway where he settled in to wait for whoever or whatever might arrive behind them. Talia offered a quick prayer that it wouldn't come to that—the captain's *kamui* blades, Power-wrought though they were, would be no match for Shadan and the power of the Void.

She and Jase reached the altar, and he pulled the Blue Flame Scepter from his belt and handed it to her. "Hold it tightly," he said, then opened his right hand and pressed his palm against one of the crystal's sharper edges. With a quick sideways thrust, he opened a deep gash in the center of his palm.

Talia winced as she watched his blood well forth, a bright flow of red that formed a pool as he cupped his hand. Some of it leaked between his fingers and fell like crimson raindrops on the polished white of the floor.

"*And the ancient blood shall be awakened by the new,*" he said, quoting the prophecy from the *Dy'illium*. Smiling, he transferred the shining red-gold Orb from his left hand into the waiting pool of blood, then closed his fist around it. The storm of emotions reaching Talia through the *sei'vaiya* stilled as Jase turned to kneel at the Altar of Elsa.

With droplets of blood dripping from between his fingers, he closed his eyes and placed his hand on the altar. It reacted immediately to his touch, flaring so brightly from within that she had to shield her eyes. A pillar of light spiraled into existence a few steps beyond the altar, a brilliant conduit of silvery-white several feet in diameter. Stretching from floor to ceiling, it pulsed like something alive, regular and rhythmic, like the beating of a heart.

*Yes,* Jase agreed, his thoughts coming through the *sei'vaiya*. *Earth's Heart.*

Rising, he skirted the altar and stepped toward the light. He was just shy of entering when Seth shouted a warning.

Talia whirled as Throy Shadan strode into the room. Scepter blazing red with corruption, he swept Seth aside with a negligent flick of his wrist that sent the Chellum captain hurtling into the wall with a bone shattering thud. He dropped into a heap as his swords clattered to the floor next to him.

Shadan turned his one-eyed gaze on Jase, and a triumphant smile moved over his grey face as he raised his scepter to strike.

Talia knew what would follow because she'd seen it—both in vision and in the hundreds of nightmares she'd had since that prophetic moment. She knew, but she was no longer afraid. This was where she was supposed to be. This was her destiny.

At peace with her role in fate's tangled web, she stepped in front of the killing strike meant for Jase.

When the love-bond vanished from his mind, Jase knew Talia was gone, and the better part of who he was died with her. Anguish unlike any he'd ever known tore at him, a searing stab of grief that nearly brought him to his knees. And it wasn't just because she was gone, but because he could have saved her.

He'd felt Shadan's arrival. He'd felt the strike that nearly ended Seth's life. And he had watched through his Awareness as Shadan raised his scepter and channeled the spear of counterfeit Fire that killed Talia. She'd sacrificed herself to save him and by doing so, she had saved them all.

And he had let her.

He'd let her die because he knew that using even the smallest amount of the Orb's reservoir of Power for anything other than its intended purpose would negate the Rejuvenation. It was, in fact, the reason Shadan had struck at him—the Dreadlord knew the Orb had bound itself to its wielder and that it would react protectively. He would have survived, Shadan would have been destroyed, and Talia would have been spared.

And the world would have ended in ruin anyway.

Knowing it as truth didn't make it any less painful, and he watched her collapse next to the altar, a smouldering hole burned through her chest, her beautiful green eyes open but devoid of life.

*See you on the other side, my love,* he thought, then stepped into the light.

For Elliott, the events surrounding Shadan's arrival in the Soul Chamber were a blur. Seth being struck...Talia shielding Jase with her body...Jase vanishing into the pillar of light—everything seemed to happen in an instant.

What happened next seemed to take forever, and Elliott felt as if he were trapped in one of the bizarre nightmares he'd had as a kid. Nightmares where everything happened in slow motion and where he felt as if he were trying to run underwater.

Still cloaked in bended Light, he started for the Dreadlord with sword raised.

One step— Shadan raised his scepter toward the pillar of light.

Two steps, then three— The jeweled end of Shadan's scepter flared red as he prepared to strike.

Four steps— He tightened his grip on his sword.

Five steps— Shadan sensed his presence and turned to meet him.

Elliott brought his sword down, and time returned to normal as he sliced Shadan's hand off at the wrist.

The glow of hellfire winked out as hand and scepter fell, but Elliott wasn't finished. Whirling, he brought his sword around in a broad sweep and sliced Shadan's head free of his neck. It rolled off the Dreadlord's shoulder and landed with a sickening thud at Elliott's feet.

Dropping his cloak of bended Light, he met the severed head's fiery one-eyed gaze, then kicked it squarely in the face, launching it across the room. He knew K'rrosha could knit themselves back together if given time, and he wasn't going to give Shadan the chance.

The headless corpse lashed at him with its other arm, and Elliott sliced it free at the shoulder, then removed the rest of the first arm before chopping both legs from beneath it. Kicking the severed limbs away from one another, he watched them twitch and convulse as Shadan's spirit fought to regain control of his refleshed body.

"Good luck with that," Elliott muttered as he sheathed his sword.

His eyes moved to Talia, and the anguish he'd been suppressing with his rage threatened to break free. He fought it back down out of necessity, and hurried over to Seth to check for a pulse. He breathed a sigh of relief when he found one. It was weak, but Seth was a fighter. If Jase successfully healed the Earthsoul, Seth would make it. Physically, at least. He might not recover from what Talia's death would do to him.

The wall he'd built around his grief began to crumble again, and he knew he couldn't fight it any longer. With tears in his eyes and a massive void in his heart, he moved across the room and knelt next to his sister.

He gently placed a hand over her eyes to close them, then studied her beautiful, peaceful face. For all of their pretended sibling animosity, he'd never loved anyone as much as he loved her.

"I'm sorry," he whispered, running the backs of his fingers down her cheek. "I failed to protect you."

The dam holding back the full extent of his grief burst, and he took her limp body in his arms and hugged her tightly against him, weeping.

Suspended in a sea of white as endless as eternity itself, Jase stared at the pulsating Blood Orb in his hand and watched as the drops of blood leaking from between his fingers fell away into the light to be carried away as if by some invisible wind. Each drop, he realized, was synchronized with a single beat of his heart.

*Open yourself, Blood of my Blood,* Elsa said, her voice coming from all around him.

*Surrender.*

Jase cast about the endless light in confusion. Surrender? His Awareness was already open to the point of forming a Communal link—he couldn't open it any further than that. And the mingling of their blood had bound them physically as well as in spirit. What more was needed?

*Surrender.*

*I don't understand.*

*Surrender.*

He closed his eyes, and reached into himself, searching for whatever might be holding him back. If it was anger or grief over Talia's death, he was in trouble—there was no letting go of that. Not at the moment anyway. Maybe not ever.

He didn't think it was fear. At least not the fear of dying. He'd come to terms with that a long time ago. Besides, without Talia, there wasn't much to live for.

Thoughts of her final moments flashed through his mind's eye, and he clenched his teeth to keep from shouting curses at the top of his lungs. Bloody prophecies and their bloody threads of fate! Pulling him and those he loved every which way. Just once he would like to feel as if he were in control!

His frustration vanished beneath a sudden epiphany.

He was afraid of losing control. No, he was afraid of not being *in* control. Of himself. Of the situation. Of anything.

This flaw—this weakness—had manifested itself in the simple fear he had of riding inside a coach instead of holding the reins to the horses. And it had reared its ugly head by way of the blatant disregard he'd once had for rending the Veil. He hadn't done it because it was necessary, he'd done it to take control of the situation. Even during the times he'd claimed to be on the Earthsoul's errand, he'd harbored resentment for Her and the errands. Since day one, he'd walked the paths of fate begrudgingly.

Thoughts of Talia's final moments returned, and he embraced them with love and admiration instead of with anger and frustration. The *sei'vaiya* had revealed her final thoughts to him. She hadn't been afraid. She'd embraced her destiny willingly. She'd surrendered to it.

He must do the same.

A powerful rush of warmth filled him as Elsa spoke. *Yes, my son. You see the truth at last.*

*Forgive me for not seeing it sooner,* he said. *Let the Earthsoul's will be done.*

The sea of light vanished, and Jase found himself standing on top of an unbelievably tall mountain with an all-encompassing view of the world spreading away before him. He saw every continent and every body of water from the largest ocean to the smallest stream. He beheld every raindrop.

He saw every stone of every mountain and every needle and leaf on every tree in every forest. He beheld every blade of grass.

He saw every living creature from the largest whale to the smallest insect. He beheld the face of every living person. The world was beautiful and pristine. It was Elderon's perfect creation.

*Things as they were*, Elsa said. *Now behold things as they are.*

The scene morphed into one of horror. Darkness had descended over the entire world. The sun was a pale red sphere in a murky sky devoid of stars. The entire face of the earth trembled from earthquakes both great and small. Entire mountains were being shaken to pieces while others were vomited into existence by volcanic eruptions which further darkened the sky. Storms raged. Oceans heaved. Rivers and streams turned foul or dried up. Everything green had withered or decayed. The people of every nation were dying, some as the result of natural disasters, others at the hands of demons and the frenzied spirits of the damned. The entire world had descended into chaos.

*How do we stop this?* he asked.

*Look!* she said, and the scene changed again.

This time it was the luminescent landscape of Elsa's Awareness, a shimmering outline of the Earthsoul Herself. Brilliant points of light dotted that landscape and stretched to the far reaches of the physical world. Some were scattered about on the face of the land—most lay at the bottoms of the oceans or were buried deep inside the earth.

Blood Orbs, he realized in awe. And there were hundreds of them.

The brightest Orbs were linked to one another by threads of Spirit and pulsed in unison, steady and rhythmic.

Like a heartbeat, he thought, looking again at the Orb in his hand.

Its pulsating rhythm now matched his heart beat for beat, which in turn matched the pulsating throbs of the Orbs scattered across the world.

And that vascular network continued to grow as the drops of blood leaking from between his fingers were borne away on threads of Spirit to merge with the awaiting Orbs, awakening them, linking them—to one another and to the Soul Chamber—and opening the way for the Rejuvenation.

*Behold the blood of Fairimor reunited*, Elsa said. *Behold the salvation of the world.*

Cradling his sister's body in his arms, Elliott stared at the pillar of light beyond the altar and wondered what was happening within. Jase had been gone long enough that his grief had run its course. Now only anger remained, and it burned hotter than the bowels of Tabor.

He was angry at the loss of Talia. Angry at the disappearance of Jase. Angry that Seth was dying and that he was helpless to do anything to stop it.

But mostly he was angry at the Earthsoul for allowing all of it to happen. Why, after all they had been through, after all they had suffered in Her behalf, had She failed them now?

A scraping of claws on stone sounded from the entrance, and he leveled his sword at it, ready to loose a killing bolt of lightning should the new arrival prove to be a threat.

He relaxed as Galiena's glittering red form came into view, but his anger at the Earthsoul spiked anew when he saw that the Rhiven Queen was injured. She was pulling herself along with her forelegs because her back and both of her hind legs were broken.

*At least she's alive,* he thought, trying to rein the anger in. *Look for the good here.* Lowering Talia's body to the floor, he rose and hurried across the room to Galiena.

Her eyes, shining like Kelsan Marks, were on the pillar of light. "It's happening," she said. "The Rejuvenation is underway."

*A lot of good that does Talia,* Elliott thought, using his anger to keep his grief in check. He couldn't afford to break down again, not now that there might be a chance to save Seth.

"I know you're hurting," he told her. "But can you do something for Seth? I don't think I could stand to lose someone else I care for."

Galiena's eyes were sympathetic as she looked at Talia, then she met Elliott's gaze, and large tears formed at the corners of her eyes. "I'm so sorry for your loss," she said. "Yes. I will do what I can for Captain Lydon."

Dragging her broken body across the room, she placed one clawed finger gently on Seth's chest and closed her eyes. A moment later, Seth gasped mightily and sat up, his eyes darting about the room in alarm

"Easy," Elliott said. "Shadan is no longer a threat."

"Talia?" he asked.

Pushing himself weakly to his feet, he started toward her.

"She's gone, Seth," he said, and speaking the words aloud brought all of his grief back to the surface. Tears filled his eyes as he continued. "She died saving Jase from Shadan."

"And Jase?" Seth asked, sounding so empty and defeated that Elliott worried he might fall on his swords in shame.

"Bringing about the Rejuvenation," Galiena answered. She sagged to the ground in exhaustion and lay still, her eyes fixed on the pillar of light.

Seth nodded, then walked unsteadily toward Talia's body. Elliott moved with him, ready to catch his friend if he should fall.

When they reached the altar, Seth dropped to his knees next to Talia and bent to kiss her on the forehead.

"*Atanami en kojyo,*" he said. And then he wept as keenly as the day he'd lost his beloved Elisa.

As the last of the Blood Orbs were awakened by his blood, Jase Fairimor experienced a profound sense of peace. For the first time in his life, he'd truly surrendered his will to the Earthsoul. Now he sensed it was time to surrender his life as well.

*It's Yours,* he told her. *Do with me what You will.*

The vast network of Blood Orbs flared as one, and his view of the spiritual landscape of the world momentarily vanished beneath a sea of brilliant white light. When it faded, he found himself standing once again on top of the unbelievably tall mountain with the same all-encompassing view of the world. The world as it was at that very moment. The Veil had collapsed, and blood and death and chaos reigned supreme across the face of the entire world.

Maeon, the Lord of Darkness, had arrived.

And he'd arrived in Shey'Avralier at the entrance to the Soul Chamber. He'd come to stop the Rejuvenation.

*You're too late*, Jase thought. Smiling, he embraced all of the Orbs as one and unleashed a flood of Earthpower sufficient to heal a dying world.

# CHAPTER 75

## *Seeds of Opposition*

MOVEMENT ALONG THE EDGE of his vision caught Elliott's attention and he turned to find a man in crimson and black robes standing in the entrance to the Soul Chamber. A crown of fire flickered above his raven-colored hair, and his eyes glowed red with demonic fire.

*Maeon*, he thought, and his heart nearly stopped in his chest.

Seth, however, was on his feet in an instant, swords in hand.

Maeon laughed. "YOU THINK TO CHALLENGE ME, MORTAL? WHAT CHANCE DO YOU HAVE AGAINST THE LORD OF DARKNESS?"

He stretched out his hand as if to touch something, and the area in front of him sparked in protest as tendrils of red and black corruption spider-webbed out from his fingertips.

The Veil, Elliott realized. It was still in place inside the chamber. Encouraged, he raised his sword and unleashed a bolt of lightning as thick as a tree. It struck Maeon in the chest and drove him backward several feet.

Maeon laughed again, but his eyes flared brightly with anger, and the crown of fire turned a deeper shade of red. "HOW PATHETIC," he said. Raising his hands, he attacked the Veil again, striking it with a spiraling torrent of dark energy that punched through the spiritual barrier with an audible hiss and sent tendrils of red crackling through the air.

"ENOUGH!" a voice said, and Maeon's attack vanished like a snuffed candle. The interior of the chamber was suddenly awash in brilliant white light, and Elliott turned to find a shining figure standing a short distance from the altar. His hair and robes were as white as freshly fallen snow, and shone with a brilliance unlike anything on earth. Nothing, not even *Sei'shiin* could be as bright. And yet Elliott could look upon the new arrival without shielding his eyes.

But who was he? Jase returned from the pillar of fire? One of the famed Heroes of Light? The answer came when Seth knelt and lowered his head.

Elliott's eyes went wide with wonder, then he, too, knelt before his Creator.

"THOU HAST NO PLACE HERE!" Elderon said. "THE BLOOD SEEDS OF THE REJUVENATION HAVE BEEN AWAKENED. THE PROPHECY REGARDING THE SONS OF ELSA IS FULFILLED."

"I COME ONLY TO CLAIM THAT WHICH IS MINE," Maeon snarled.

He made a small gesture with his hand, and tendrils of darkness snaked forth to take hold of the dismembered parts of Shadan's refleshed body. With the Earthsoul snapping and crackling in protest to Maeon's dark touch, the tendrils pulled the still twitching parts beyond the edge of the Veil, where they were incinerated by a burst of counterfeit Fire.

As the fire faded, the spirit of Throy Shadan became visible, a ghostly figure of greenish white that stared in stupefied horror at his unforgiving master. He opened his mouth to speak, but tendrils of darkness shot from Maeon's hand to silence him. Shadan's spirit collapsed into a groveling heap at the demon god's feet.

Maeon turned his demonic gaze on Elderon once more. "THIS ISN'T OVER," he hissed. "EVEN NOW, MY SERVANTS ARE SOWING THE SEEDS OF THIS WORLD'S DESTRUCTION. MY BLOOD, MINGLED WITH DARK MATTER FROM ONE OF YOUR FORMER WORLDS, IS BEING CAST ACROSS THE FACE OF THIS PATHETIC REALM AND ARE SPRINGING FORTH AS TALISMANS OF GREAT POWER." He chuckled malevolently. "BLOOD SEEDS OF THE APOCALYPSE, I CALL THEM. DARKNESS TO COUNTER LIGHT. AN EQUAL OPPOSITION IN ALL THINGS."

Elderon made a dismissive gesture with his hand. "DEPART."

Maeon stiffened as if to refuse, then turned and strode into the abyss that opened in the air behind him. As he did, a whip-like tendril of counterfeit Fire wrapped around Throy Shadan and dragged him, kicking and screaming, into the depths of hell.

Elliott turned his attention back to Elderon and watched as he moved across the room and placed one hand on Galiena's glittering head. "RISE, *GALIENA'EI TO UL'MORGRANON*," he said, and her broken body was immediately healed. She stood, then lowered her head in reverence to her God.

Elderon smiled affectionately, then turned his gaze on Elliott.

Elliott lowered his eyes and kept them down as Elderon approached.

"EL'LIOTT CHELLUM," he said, and Elliott's heart burned within him at the sound of his name. "THE SWORD OF GOD IS STRENGTH." There was a slight pause as Elderon stopped in front of him. "RISE, MY YOUNG FRIEND, AND SHOW ME YOUR SWORD."

Elliott did as instructed, and his heart continued to burn as he looked his Creator in the eyes. They were the deepest blue Elliott had ever seen, full of infinite love and infinite wisdom. Elliott raised his sword in front of him, lengthwise, one hand on the hilt with the flat edge of the blade resting in his other hand. The Dragon etchings along the blade shone brightly in the light of Elderon's brilliance.

Elderon stretched out a finger and touched the blade, and everything was lost in white as the Power-wrought steel flared brighter than *Sei'shiin*. When the flash of light faded, Elderon was gone. The blade, still glowing as if with some inner light, bore the symbol for Eliara at each end of the Dragon etchings.

"An Infinity Blade," Galiena whispered, and Elliott turned to find her yellow eyes bright with wonder. "Very literally the Sword of God," she continued. "A fitting weapon for your namesake."

Elliott ran his finger over the symbols for Eliara, then returned the blade to its scabbard and turned his attention back to his sister.

"He didn't bring her back," he said, his grief returning in a rush. "Why? He's the Creator, the Giver of Life. He can heal any wound. Why didn't He heal my sister?"

"Elderon's workings are beyond mortal comprehension," Galiena answered. "All we can do is have faith that it is for the best. The best for Talia and the best for us."

"But—"

"Let her go, Elliott," Seth said. Grief still painted his face, but his voice was uncharacteristically soft. "She's in a better place."

Elliott looked at the pillar of light beyond the Altar of Elsa. "And Jase?" he asked, not even trying to hide the bitterness he felt. "Is he in a better place? Are we going to lose him, too?"

Seth shook his head. "I don't know. But I'm not leaving here until we find out."

With the spent Blood Orb still clutched in his hand, Gideon stood at the edge of the of the Overlook and watched as the world continued to darken beneath the arrival of Con'Jithar. The areas of the city he'd cleared of demons and the spirits of the damned were once again being overrun. The Heroes of Light had vanished—he hoped back into Eliara since he didn't want to believe they had been erased from the eternities by dying here with those they'd come to protect.

The ground quaked continually. The air had become suffocating and toxic, and his eyes and his lungs burned as he fought for breath. Swirling, horizontal columns of fire and lightning lit the darkness overhead, bizarre storms of corruption that raged alongside the last of Mother Nature's fury.

This was the end. Jase had obviously failed to reach the Soul Chamber.

Movement to his right caught his attention, and he turned as Brysia stepped up to the edge of the Overlook. Her face was pale, and she was having trouble breathing. Ammorin and Pattalla were behind her, and they, too, were pale.

Gideon took Brysia's hand in his, and they watched without speaking as the world continued to die.

The inside of his head flashed white as his Awareness sprang into being, and he watched as a tremendous surge of pure, potent energy ripped through the descending darkness, halting its advance.

A split second later the earth ceased to quake. The violent storms, both natural and unnatural, were dispelled. A hush fell over the world as all sound vanished and everything came to a stop. Time itself seemed to slow... then paused.

When it resumed, the disembodied spirits of the damned vanished. The K'rrosha exploded into flame and ash, brilliant bursts of bluish-white light that lit Trian from one end to the other. The Darklings and other shadowspawn were consumed by Fire a moment later. The demon armies howled their rage as the Veil coalesced around them and they were cast violently back into Con'Jithar.

With the shimmering fabric of the Veil back in place, the darkness began to lift and the sun gradually brightened once more, changing from a sickly, blood-red orb to orange, then to yellow, and finally to its original white luster.

The wilt and decay vanished, and the gardens of the Overlook turned green once more as trees and shrubs and flowers grew right before his eyes. The stream ran clear. The air was fresh and clean. All across the city, those who'd been injured in battle or by the calamities of nature were instantly healed.

"He did it," Brysia whispered, her voice filled with awe.

"Yes," Gideon said, his heart overflowing with pride for his son. "He did." Then he added a silent, *Now only time will tell what it cost him.*

Putting his arm around his wife, he watched through his Awareness as the rivers of Earthpower streaming through the spiritual landscape of his mind's eye continued to throw back the Void.

冘

Standing atop the Great Wall of Aridan, Elrien stared at the Valley of Amnidia in wonder. The curse was gone. The ruined landscape had been transformed from barren dirt and slag to grass-covered hills and groves of trees. Mount Tabor stood tall and proud once more, a spire of granite bathed in sunlight.

The Shadan'Ko had been transformed. Their Darkling-like appearance had been replaced by the traits of their ancestors, those who had first succumbed to the curse eight hundred years earlier. Most were Kelsan, but there were Elvan and Meleki among them as well. The madness which had corrupted their minds and spirits was gone, and they stared at one another in speechless amazement, their weapons forgotten.

"Praised be the *Mith'elre Chon!*" Elrien shouted, urging his words to the far reaches of the wall with channels of Air. "Praised be the Son of Thunder!"

The shout was taken up by the *Bero'thai*, and their voices rolled north across the green swells of the restored valley like thunder from a summer storm.

Elrien listened to the revelry for a moment longer, then turned to Keymi and the rest of the Dymas who'd survived. "The Shad— Those below us need to be welcomed back into the human family," he said. "Please see to it."

"Yes, Master Elrien," Keymi said. She bit her lip thoughtfully as she looked down at them. "What should we call them from now on?"

Elrien thought for a moment, then smiled as the whisperings of the Earthsoul gave him the answer. "Amnidians."

The sound of glass crunching underfoot couldn't take away from the splendor of the Chellum Gardens, and Elam smiled as he took Jaina's hand and helped her through the twisted metal frame of the now glassless door. Decker did the same for Rhea, then offered his hand to Tana. They made their way slowly through the gardens without speaking, marveling at the transformation brought about by the Rejuvenation.

The scent of freshly bloomed flowers hung heavy in the air, and the sounds of songbirds echoed along the palace walls. Life had returned to Chellum.

Thanks to Jase.

When they passed out of the gardens to the walkway lining the moat, Mauf slid from the water to block their way. With pink tongue extended, he chittered loudly at them.

"It's good to see you, too, pal," Elam smiled, bending to rub the lumtar's snout.

Jaina bent to do the same, then gasped. "My water just broke."

Elam stared at her, immobilized by the announcement. *The babies are coming... now?*

Jaina calmly took him by the hand and turned him toward the gardens. "Tana, dear," she said, "please run ahead and fetch Jonnil Dymas. My husband and I will be along shortly."

Elam shook himself free of his shock. "Are you sure you should be walking?"

"Would you prefer I give birth here in the gardens?" she asked, then giggled at him. "I'm fine, my love."

"If I act that stupid when it comes time for you to deliver," Decker said to Rhea, "have Seth slap me."

Elam scowled at him, then looked back to Jaina. Her face was calm, and she wore a pleasant smile.

"Just think," she whispered, "our babies might be the first to be born into the new world."

He squeezed her hand affectionately. "Wouldn't that be something."

Standing in the midst of the neatly planted rows of her garden, Maira Aulious listened to the sounds of life all about her. Omer Forest was alive again—alive and as green and vibrant as she'd ever seen it.

She turned and looked at her home. With its broken windows and missing shingles, it still bore the signs of the violent storm which had raged over Seston, but at least it still stood. Many of Seston's residents weren't so lucky.

*But we are alive*, she thought. *Thanks to the Fairimors.*

She wasn't even going to pretend to understand what had just happened. She knew only that the world had descended into darkness and had been pulled back from the brink of destruction by unfathomable, unseen powers. And she knew that Daris had been part of it because his sword was still missing from his headstone.

As if thinking of him had been a summons, a rectangle of light opened just beyond the short fence surrounding her family's private cemetery, and brilliant white flooded the area as Daris strode through from beyond.

He shone as bright as the newly restored sun in the sky, but even so, she could look upon him without shielding her eyes.

"Hello, Maira," he said, smiling.

He moved to his grave, and his sword blade flared brightly as he raised it, point down, above the headstone. An audible *sching* followed as he returned it to its final resting place. Still smiling, he left the small graveyard and joined her in her garden.

"My work here is finished," he said, then reached out and took her hand in his. His touch was warm and his grip gentle as he raised her hand to his lips and kissed it. "I'll be waiting for you," he said, then kissed her hand again before releasing it.

With tears of joy in her eyes, she watched him return to the doorway of light and vanish back into the eternities.

そ

"What are your orders, Dymas General Leda?" Quintella asked, and Idoman looked at Ohran before answering.

The Dainin Chieftain's face was unreadable, but he made a motion with his hand for Idoman to continue. "This is your call, my young friend. Not mine. But the *Nar'shein* will support you in whatever you decide."

Idoman looked in the direction of the outer wall where the fighting had resumed shortly after the Rejuvenation had taken effect. Aided by their Jexlair talismans, both the Agla'Con and the *Jeth'Jalda* had once again seized *Ta'shaen* and were using it in battle. Even with the destruction of the Refleshed and the rest of Shadan's shadowspawned soldiers, the bloody cultists had resumed fighting as well, too frenzied or simply too stupid to realize they couldn't win without the Dreadlord's aid.

Large numbers of Tamban soldiers, however, were pulling back or had taken a knee in the streets to show they no longer wished to fight. Some had even raised flags of truce.

"We kill the Power-wielders to the last man," he announced at last, and Ohran nodded his approval. "I want their filth cleansed from the earth. I want the cultists destroyed as well. They aren't likely to surrender anyway."

"And the Tambans?" Joneam asked.

"Kill all who insist on fighting," he said. "Those who surrender will be allowed to leave in peace. We'll send them home to Tamba through Veilgates."

"That's awfully generous considering what they did," Taggert grumbled.

"Maybe so," Idoman said. "But I won't kill them simply for the sake of vengeance. This war is over, and they lost."

"You are wise beyond your years, young Dymas General," Ohran said. "I will have the *Ara'so* deal with the *Jeth'Jalda*. My *Nar'shein* and I will attend to those who surrender."

He dipped his head in goodbye and hurried away down the street.

"This will be the second time he sends a defeated Tamban army away in peace," Quintella said. "He did the same thing at the end of the Tamban-Dainin War."

"I know," Idoman said. "What do you think influenced my decision?"

He let his eyes move across Central Plaza and the tens of thousands of survivors of the united armies, then glanced in the direction of the cultist army. They'd stalled at the river, but the fact that they were in the city at all disgusted him.

"Send word to all our Dymas," he said. "We're going to finish what Jase Fairimor started."

乇

With Jeymi's hand in his, Endil Fairimor stood in the temple entrance high on the slopes of Mount Augg and gazed in wonder at the newly reborn world. Mirror Lake shimmered brightly in the sun. The forest of thorns was gone, and in its place lay a patchwork of wild flowers and flowering shrubs, grasses of varying colors and groves of trees. Songbirds filled the air with music.

"He did it," Jeymi whispered. "He really did it."

"Yes, he did," he said, then turned a smile on Porea Dymas. She stood next to Derian, and tears of joy wet her cheeks as she studied the scene below. "And we are here to see it because of your quick action. Jase always said Air was the most useful of all the Gifts. Now I believe it."

Porea returned the smile. "I was in the right place at the right time, was all."

"Still," he said. "Thanks again for catching us. That was a bloody long drop."

"It was for the Agla'Con," Derian chuckled.

They fell silent for a time, content to enjoy the view of the newly restored world. Finally, Jeymi broke the silence. "We should return to Trian," she said. "The Rejuvenation might be complete, but the city is still under attack. They will need our help."

乇

"The Reservoirs of Power have run dry," Galiena announced, and Elliott looked from his sister's face to find the Rhiven Queen watching the pillar of light intently. She'd changed back into human form and wore a red robe tied at the waist with a strip of gold cloth. Yavil stood beside her, and wore robes of green.

Elliott was glad Yavil had the foresight to carry extra clothes in the bags of his *sholin's* saddle—having them standing around naked would have been awkward to say the least.

"What does that mean?" he asked.

"It means the pillar of light before us is about to disappear and Jase will return."

Elliott pushed himself to his feet, and moved to stand next to Galiena, eager yet apprehensive to meet Jase when he returned. He wasn't certain Jase knew that Talia had been killed, and he was afraid of how he would react. *Probably about as well as I did*, he thought, steeling himself for what might follow.

Seth joined him, and they waited in silence for the light to vanish.

When it finally did, Jase wasn't there.

"I... I don't understand," Elliott said, fighting to keep his emotions in check. "Where's Jase?"

Galiena shook her head, obviously as confused as he was. "I don't know. The Rejuvenation is complete. Jase should be right there."

"There is a prophecy," Seth said, his voice calm in spite of the anguish on his face. "Gideon told it to me the first time we were here. It is from a little-known manuscript called the *Esdraelon*. I didn't want to believe it—I wasn't fully convinced it was prophetic. It seems now that it was." With his eyes still on the spot where the pillar of light had been, he quoted:

> "And in that moment when the Seeds of Opposition are planted, the Firstborn Son of the Blood of Elsa will die in the Heart of the Holy Mountain. That by his blood the ancient blood may be awakened and the two be reunited into soul eternal."

Turning his back on the spot, he moved past the altar and picked up Talia's lifeless body. "Please open a Veilgate to Trian," he said. "We need to let Gideon know what happened here." He looked at the spot where Maeon had stood to confront Elderon. "He'll be especially interested to learn of the Blood Seeds of the Apocalypse. Whatever the blazes those are."

Galiena looked at Yavil. "Gather our people," she told him, "and have them join us in Trian."

"What of those who wish to return home?" he asked. "They came to fight demons, and now those demons are gone. They still oppose any and all interaction with the races of men."

"This isn't a request, my friend. It's an order. And it comes directly from Elderon."

Yavil's eyes went wide. "He spoke to you?"

"He put the words directly into my mind as he healed me of my wounds," she said, amused by his surprise. "Now go."

Yavil opened a Veilgate to Shey'Avralier's outer courtyard and strode through to the waiting Rhiven. As he did, Elliott caught sight of Ayame and breathed a sigh of relief that she had survived.

The air parted in front of Galiena, and the gardens of the Overlook came into view.

"After you," she said, and Elliott led the way to where Gideon and Brysia waited for news of their son.

# CHAPTER 76

## *New Beginnings*

"THE HEADS OF THE NATIONS are assembled," Elison said, and Brysia pulled her eyes from the city long enough to meet his gaze.

"Gideon and I will be along in a moment," she told him, then returned her attention to the city as Elison made his way back through the gardens of the Overlook toward the Dome.

The fires had been put out, but the northern half of the inner wall was in shambles. Hundreds of homes and businesses had been reduced to rubble by both the battle and by earthquakes. But somehow, miraculously, the majority of those in the southern half of the city had been spared.

Those in the northern half of the city, however, the brave men and women of the united armies, hadn't faired nearly as well, and tens of thousands lay dead. Their bodies had been gathered into parks and plazas and were awaiting cremation since there were simply too many to bury.

Outside the city, the scene was the same. Tens of thousands of Tambans had been killed, both by demons before the Rejuvenation and by the Dainin in the days after. The Shadan cultists had been killed to the last man, and their bodies lay scattered along North Road from the banks of the Trian River inside the city to the mouth of Mendel Pass. It was a scene of carnage unlike any since the Great Destruction.

She let her eyes move over the city once more, then looked at her husband.

"Three days," she said, aware of how weary she sounded. "Three days and nothing. Our boy isn't coming home, is he?"

"No," Gideon answered, his voice heavy with bitterness. "He isn't."

Brysia took a deep breath then let it slowly out, desperate to hold back her tears. She would be addressing the Kings and Queens of the other nations in a moment, and she couldn't afford to be a blubbering mess when she did. When she was sufficiently calm, she took Gideon by the hand, and they started for the Dome.

*Bero'thai* ghosted through the gardens on each side of the path, and Brysia appreciated their dedication in spite of the fact that she and Gideon were the most dangerous things on the Overlook should an enemy be foolish enough to move against them.

Gavin greeted them as they neared the doors, then he and another *Bero'thai* pulled them open. Hinges squeaked loudly, and Gavin offered an apology. "I'll have our craftsmen tend to that right away."

"That's not necessary," Brysia told him. "It's the sound of newness. I like it."

Gavin smiled. "As you wish, my lady."

As they moved into the Dome, a hush fell over those seated in the undamaged tiers of the council area. Rising almost as one, they watched with solemn faces as she and Gideon approached.

The area they occupied was half of what had once been. The rest of the tiers had been demolished by Night Threads and had been roped off until they could be repaired. The long, crescent-shaped table of the Kelsan High Tribunal had been destroyed as well, but a smaller table had been brought in as a temporary replacement.

She let her eyes move over the faces of those who'd answered the invitation, and a shiver of excitement swept through her. Not since the Second Creation had the rulers of so many nations sat together in council.

Lord Pryderi of Zeka sat next to Emperor Dromensai of Riak, who in turn sat beside Galiena. Lord Reiekel and High King Nid occupied the same row of seats as Lords Nanda, Olwen, and Moirai of Chunin. Chantera Zakeya, Queen of Rosda and the daughter of Quintella, sat next to Hallan Obodai, Lord of Glenda. Chieftain Peregam, bless his heart, sat on the floor in front of them all because the tiers were too small for his bulk. Only Kunin, Arkania, and Tamba were not represented.

Gideon must have sensed what she was thinking because he whispered, "Impressive sight, isn't it?"

"Yes," she replied, her eyes moving from the heads of state to the rest of those who'd answered the call to assemble. Kings and Queens and governors, they'd arrived from every major city in each of the representative nations, and they'd come with members of their cabinets, with family, or had come alone.

Most noticeable to all were Decker and Rhea Chellum. Everyone in the room had heard of Talia's sacrifice, and a good number of them had answered the summons not just to be part of this council but to pay their last respects to the Chellum Princess. Elliott and Tana and Seth were with them, as were a number of Fairimors. Xia and Alexa had arrived with Cassia and Andil. Endil and Jeymi had arrived three days ago directly from Mount Augg.

The Fairimors and the Chellums, she thought. Two families who would have been bound together by marriage were now bound instead by loss.

She made eye contact with each of her family members as she approached, then looked at the others, pleased that Shavis Dakshar and the twelve members of the Imperial Clave occupied an entire row behind Tereus Dromensai. If not for *Ao'tres Domei* and the Shizu, the mission to retrieve the Blood Orb from Mount Augg would have failed.

The last two tiers were occupied by the Kelsan High Command and the members of Trian's Core Council.

Brysia led Gideon past the table and stopped in front of her guests.

"Please," she said, offering a bow of thanks for the show of respect, "be seated." She and Gideon, however, remained standing. "And thank you for coming."

"Thank you," Lord Nanda said, "for bearing the brunt of Death's Third March." The other two Chunin Kings nodded their agreement, and a number of *here heres* were voiced by others, including Lord Pryderi and Lord Nid.

Brysia waited for them to quiet. "I appreciate the sentiment," she told them, "but I didn't request this assembly in order to lament the past but to make plans for the future. Are there people to mourn? Certainly. The *Mith'elre Chon*—my son—did not return from Earth's Heart. And, as you know, Talia Chellum lies in state in the Church of Elderon. Her burial is scheduled for this evening in the Fairimor Gardens next to my son's empty grave. All who wish to attend are invited."

Her throat tightened with emotion, but she fought through it. "But as I said, I am not here to lament. We have much to be grateful for and much that needs to be celebrated. The entire world has been given a second chance at life. We should commemorate that moment by recognizing the tremendous gift we have been given."

"What do you propose?" Emperor Dromensai asked.

"I propose that we keep the Ha'lel Calendar as it was given to us by the Creator, but that we shift our reckoning of time in honor of the Rejuvenation. If we do, then today would mark the third day of Fayu in the year A.R. 1."

Lord Pryderi raised his hand. "And A.R. would stand for...?"

"After Rejuvenation," she answered.

"I like it," Ohran Peregam said. "My people will support this proposal."

"As will Riak," Emperor Dromensai said, and behind him Shavis and the Imperial Clave nodded their agreement.

"The Southern Kingdom is in," Lord Nanda said, and Lords Olwen and Moirai echoed him with statements of their own.

That opened the flood gates, and the rest of the nations chimed in as well. Melek and Elva, Zeka and Glenda and Rosda—the vote was unanimous.

"Thank you, my friends," Brysia said. "And welcome to the New World."

"Welcome to the New World."

As soon as the words left Brysia's mouth, Gideon felt a sudden influx of Spirit wash across the room, and he knew instantly that it wasn't limited to just the Dymas—everyone in the room had felt it as evidenced by the rapture on their faces and the tears in their eyes.

"The blessing of the Earthsoul," Gideon told them. "She is pleased with our decision to alter our reckoning of time."

"Yes," Ohran agreed. "And not since the early days of the Old World have so many people felt Her presence so strongly all at once. This truly is a new beginning for Her and for us, but it is also a reminder of the early days of this world, when all men and women were privileged to hear Her voice, not just those Gifted with *Ta'shaen*."

A profound silence fell over the assembly and lasted for several minutes while everyone considered what they'd just felt.

It was Emperor Dromensai who finally broke the silence. "Forgive me for intruding on the moment," he said. "But I sense that you have more you wish to discuss."

"Yes," Gideon said. "And not all of it is pleasant. Yes, the world was given a second chance at life by way of the Rejuvenation. But Maeon was victorious in his own right."

A whispered murmuring of disbelief moved through the assembly.

"How so?" Lord Nanda asked.

"For the answer," Gideon said, "I will defer to those who were in the Soul Chamber when Shadan and Maeon each arrived to try to stop the Rejuvenation." The murmurs turned to gasps of disbelief, but Gideon spoke over the top of them. "Queen Morgranon, Lord Chellum, and Captain Lydon, if you would please." He motioned the three to come forward.

With the eyes of everyone on them, the three left their seats and joined Gideon and Brysia at the front of the tiers. Then as everyone listened with awestruck wonder, they described Elliott's defeat of Shadan, Maeon's arrival to claim the refleshed Dreadlord's soul, and the confrontation between the God of Light and the Lord of Darkness.

Galiena concluded with Maeon's promise that his war against the living world would be waged anew. "The Blood Seeds of the Apocalypse, he called them," she said. "They are after the manner of the Jexlair crystals he created when he mingled his blood with the dust of the Old World—Talismans of power to be used as weapons by his servants—but these are his blood mingled with dark matter from the realm of Con'Jithar. The remains of one of the worlds he's already destroyed."

"So what exactly does that mean?" Lord Pryderi asked.

"It means any shadowservants who get their hands on one," Gideon said, "will be able to tap directly into the Power of the Void."

"But weren't some of them already able to do that?" Chantera Zakeya asked. "*Frel'mola* and Shadan and Aethon, for example."

"Let's not forget the Rhiven who served Aethon," Idoman added. "Or the hundreds of demons capable of wielding *Lo'shaen*."

"*Frel'mola* and Shadan and many of the demons," Gideon said, "were able to wield *Lo'shaen* because they already possessed talismans such as those we are discussing. But they brought those with them from Con'Jithar when they arrived in the living world. Some of the demons had access to the Power of the Void simply by virtue of their demon blood."

"And Aethon and the Rhiven?" Queen Zakeya asked.

"By virtue of their strength." He looked at Idoman and Railen and Sheymi, and added, "There are many in this room strong enough to wield *Lo'shaen* without the aid of a talisman, but they value their souls enough not to. Maeon's so-called Blood Seeds of the Apocalypse will make it possible for any Power-wielder to embrace *Lo'shaen*."

"So instead of ending the war with Maeon," Tereus said, "the Rejuvenation opened the way for a new offensive by those who serve him."

"Yes," Gideon said. "But the Rejuvenation was never intended to end the war with Maeon—I don't think it is a war that *can* be ended. Light and darkness are eternal and will forever be in opposition to one another. The purpose of the Rejuvenation was to heal the Earthsoul and restore the Veil, and that purpose was accomplished."

He shook his head. "But with an increase in light came opposing darkness."

"So what do you recommend we do?" Lord Reiekel asked.

"What we've always done," he answered. "We fight the darkness."

Elliott kept his face smooth as he and Seth and Galiena answered a number of follow-up questions, but inside he was as agitated as a bag full of feral cats. He didn't like the way everyone was looking at him as if he were some kind of hero. A hero wouldn't have failed to save Talia. His hypocrisy made him want to scream.

So it was with great relief when the questions finally ended and Gideon excused him and the others to return to their seats.

Tana took his hand in hers as he sat, then leaned close and brushed his ear with her lips. "You didn't tell them about the Infinity Blade," she whispered.

"Not something they need to know about," he whispered back. "Especially since I don't even know what having it means."

"It means Elderon trusts you," she said, then kissed him on the cheek and sat back in her chair.

*Trusts me to do what?* he asked her silently. *To fail again?*

Retreating into a brooding silence, he listened with ever-increasing irritation as the leaders of each nation gave a report on how the collapse of the Veil had affected their people and how they planned to move forward. Even with all the claims of hope and optimism for the future, the reports painted such a picture of blood and death and loss that Elliott wondered if the apocalypse mentioned by Maeon hadn't already happened.

But then his father stood to give his report on the state of affairs in Chellum, and some of his agitation dissipated at the sound of his father's voice. It was surprisingly calm—an oddity in and of itself—but his father was actually smiling as he spoke.

"If it's all right with High Queen Fairimor," he said, "I'd prefer to skip the report on casualties and move to the part where we celebrate."

Brysia motioned for him to continue. "By all means."

Decker's smile deepened. "Three days ago, a young couple very dear to the Chellum family celebrated the birth of twin boys. They were healthy and strong and entered the world less than an hour after the Earthsoul was Rejuvenated."

Without another word, he sat, leaving the entire assembly to stare at him in surprise. A moment of silence followed as everyone in the room considered the beautiful simplicity of what they'd just heard.

Before he realized what he was doing, Elliott had risen to his feet. He felt a brief moment of complete and utter panic as all eyes turned toward him, then a profound sense of peace washed over him as he realized what he had to say. To them and to himself.

"I'd like to thank my father for bringing us back to the purpose of this assembly as stated by High Queen Fairimor," he said. "She told us that she'd called us all together that we might look to the future. That we might be grateful. That we might celebrate. I mean no disrespect, but the majority of what we've heard this past while has been nothing more than despair in the guise of thinly-veiled hope."

He looked around the room to show he meant all of them, then continued. "So, unless anyone has anything truly celebratory to say, I suggest we adjourn. The Chellums and the Fairimors have two very important lives to celebrate."

Sitting once more, he looked at Brysia and Gideon and found them watching him as if they'd never seen him before. For a moment no one spoke, then Tereus Dromensai broke the silence.

"I second Lord Chellum's motion to adjourn," the Riaki Emperor said. "I, too, would like to celebrate the lives of Talia Chellum and Jase Fairimor. I can think of no better way to show my gratitude for what they did in our behalf than by being present when they are laid to rest."

"All in favor?" Brysia asked, clearly moved by Tereus' words.

Every hand in the room went up.

Tears filled Brysia's eyes, and she was unable to continue.

Gideon came to her rescue. "This assembly is adjourned until tomorrow," he said. "All are welcome to stay in the palace, of course. Just speak to any of the *Bero'thai* and they will find rooms for you."

He offered his arm to Brysia, and they started for the Fairimor home as the din of voices gradually filled the room.

Standing, Elliott offered his arm to Tana. "Let's go see my sister," he said, still surprised by how completely at peace he felt.

*Which,* he thought with a smile, *is what she would want for me.*

え

The evening sun painted the Fairimor Gardens in varying hues of amber and gold. Here and there, bars of sunlight angled through the treetops to create spots of light on the foliage. The air was cool and smelled of lilac. Birds and butterflies darted about in flashes of color. A squirrel chittered somewhere in the distance.

Standing next to Brysia at the head of the grave meant for his son's empty casket, Gideon took it all in and tried to maintain his composure. It was beautiful in spite of how terribly his heart ached.

"Jase would have liked this," Brysia said, taking his hand in hers. "He used to sit out on the front porch just so he could watch the color of the light change over Omer Forest."

"Talia used to sit in the Chellum Gardens and do the same thing," Decker said, and Gideon cast a sideways glance at his friend. He stood at the head of the grave meant for Talia, and his face was wet with tears as he studied the gardens. Tears filled Rhea's eyes as well, but she kept them from falling with a small white handkerchief. To the Queen's right, Tana was doing likewise, her beautiful face lined with grief.

Gideon watched her until she looked his way, then he smiled at her. She returned the smile, but a new rush of tears made her look away. Decker put his arm around her and held her close until the carriages bearing Talia's and Jase's coffins came into view at the end of the lane running through the center of the gardens.

Those who'd attended the council of nations earlier in the day lined both sides of the lane, and all watched in respectful silence as the carriages rolled past where they stood. Most had never met Talia or Jase, but their admiration for what the two young people had done to bring about the Rejuvenation was strong. Gideon suspected it was the largest assembly of world leaders ever gathered to pay respect to fallen heroes.

Nearer the gravesite were the Dymas who'd fought alongside Jase during so many of the battles the past few weeks. Idoman and Quintella stood with Tuari and Railen and Sheymi. Thex stood next to Beraline, who was still mourning the passing of Marithen Korishal but had come to pay her respects in spite of her grief.

Elrien and a number of his apprentices stood alongside members of *Ao'tres Domei*, and Chieftain Peregam and his Dainin stood behind all of them.

The drivers brought the carriages to a stop a short distance beyond the mounds of freshly dug earth, and *Bero'thai* stepped forward to open the doors for the pallbearers waiting inside.

Elliott and Seth emerged from the first carriage along with Elam Gaufin and Taggert Enue. Endil and Andil exited the second carriage with Elison and Bornis. Faces somber, they moved to the rear of their respective carriages and reverently removed the caskets they'd been asked to bear to their final resting places.

Tears blurred Gideon's vision as they drew near, and he heard the muffled sobs of Brysia and Rhea and a number of others. Tears wet Decker's face as well, but he wore a smile as he watched his son and the others bearing his daughter's casket. They stopped at the foot of the grave and set the casket onto the gold cords they would use to lower it into the ground.

"Hold there for a moment," Decker said. "I wish to look upon my daughter one last time." Moving forward, he went to his knees and raised the lid of the coffin to peer inside.

"*Atanami en kojyo*," he said, then bent and kissed Talia on the forehead before standing once more.

Seth was reaching to close the lid when Gideon's Awareness came alive with a powerful wielding of *El'shaen te sherah*. A silver-edged doorway opened between the mounds of earth, and the entire area went bright with brilliant white light.

Squinting against the brilliance, Gideon watched as the silhouette of a man appeared within the doorway. He stepped through into the living world, but his identity was still obscured by the radiant glow pouring past him. He released the Power, and the doorway folded in on itself in a flash of silvery light, throwing the area into sudden darkness as the eyes of all were forced to readjust to the softer light of evening.

When he could see again, Gideon found himself looking at his son.

His first thought was that Jase had returned as a Hero of Light, but he soon realized his son was alive and in his own mortal flesh. Amazing since he had just arrived from somewhere beyond the Veil.

"Jase," Brysia gasped, rushing forward to meet him.

"Hello, Mother."

He took her in his arms and hugged her tightly, pressing his cheek against the top of her head. After a moment, he released her, and his eyes moved to Talia's coffin.

Without a word, he strode forward and went to one knee next to her lifeless body. When he embraced *El'shaen* again, Gideon opened his Awareness and watched through the eyes of *Ta'shaen* as Jase parted a section of the Veil within the luminescent world. It wasn't a Veilgate like those used for travel, but an actual part in the spiritual fabric separating this life from the next. And there, standing just inside the shimmering opening, was the spirit of Talia Chellum.

Only those with the ability to embrace the Power could see what he saw, and of those, only Jeymi and Ammorin had opened their minds to it. The rest of the Dymas watched with their natural eyes as Jase placed his hands on Talia's head and healed her of the wound which had taken her life. As he did, Gideon watched Talia's spirit reenter her body. Her eyes opened as she took her first renewed breath.

Gasps of disbelief mingled with shouts of joy moved through the crowd, and Elliott and Seth and Decker pressed near as Jase took Talia in his arms and lifted her from the coffin.

Elder Nesthius stepped near as well, his eyes bright with excitement.

"All hail the *Mith'elre Chon!*" he shouted. "All hail the Savior of the World!"

# Epilogue

## *Stalemate*

WITH TALIA'S HAND IN HIS, Jase Fairimor stood at the eastern edge of the Overlook and watched as the sun rose over Trian. Even with much of the city in shambles, it was beautiful, the kind of beauty that spoke of promises fulfilled and promises yet to come.

Talia smiled as the *sei'vaiya* conveyed to her what he was thinking. "I couldn't have thought it better myself."

Jase chuckled but said nothing, his eyes still on the city. In spite of the glory of the dawning day, he was beginning to feel overwhelmed by what lay ahead. There was a lot of work to do yet, and none of it would be pleasant. In addition to all the dead who needed to be laid to rest, there were families to notify that loved ones wouldn't be coming home. And that was to say nothing of all those who'd been displaced from their homes, some of which had been completely destroyed. It would be months, possibly even years, before things returned to normal. If they returned at all.

Sensing his agitation, Talia squeezed his hand reassuringly. "Why don't you think of something else," she suggested.

"Like what?"

"Tell me how you managed to restore my life. I thought only the Creator can heal death."

"Only the Creator can."

"But you—" She cut off, confused.

"Acted as His vessel in the wielding of *El'shaen*," he said. "Without His express permission, I could not have done what I did. It was His will that you be restored to life, though I pled for you while I was yet on the other side."

"You saw Him?"

"It was Elderon who opened the way for me to return."

She fell silent for a moment, unsure if she should voice the question which was troubling her. The *sei'vaiya* alerted Jase to it anyway.

"No," he answered. "It didn't feel like we were away for three days. Apparently time moves differently in the afterlife. To me, it felt like minutes."

"That's how it felt for me, too."

He smiled as he put his arm around her, and they continued to watch the sunrise without speaking. What need had they of words in light of the *sei'vaiya*? It conveyed emotion more clearly and deeply than speaking ever could.

"And yet, it's still nice to hear you say it," Talia whispered.

"Say what?" he asked even though he'd already caught part of her thoughts through the love-bond.

She craned her neck to look him in the eyes. "I love you."

"I love you, too," he said, and she poked him in the ribs with her knuckles.

"Not by way of reply," she told him. "You were supposed to initiate it."

Chuckling softly, he turned so he could look her in the eyes, then raised her hand to his lips and kissed it. "I love you, Talia Chellum."

"That's more like it," she said, then raised up on her tiptoes and kissed him.

"I thought we might find you out here," a familiar voice said, and they broke off the kiss to find Gideon and Brysia coming down the path next to the stream.

He'd expected to find smiles of amusement on their faces at having caught him and Talia kissing, but their faces were somber. His mother, he realized, had been crying.

"What is it?" he asked, suddenly on edge.

"Nothing that hasn't already been," Gideon answered. He and Brysia stopped at the edge of the Overlook and gazed out across the city. Gideon forced a smile. "It looks like it's going to be another beautiful day."

The silence that followed put Jase even more on edge, and he studied his parents faces carefully. Not only had his mother been crying, she looked tired. As if she'd been awake for most of the night. Gideon just looked... defeated.

"I'm serious," Jase said. "What's wrong? Whatever it is, we'll fix it."

"If it could be fixed," Gideon said, his voice resigned. "It would have happened during the Rejuvenation."

He took his father by the arm. "I'm the *Mith'elre Chon*," he said. "I'll find a way."

Gideon kept his eyes on the city, refusing to meet his gaze.

Jase looked to his mother for help.

"Gideon," she said, "he has a right to know."

Gideon continued to stare out at the city without speaking. Finally, he nodded.

"Come with me," he said. Turning, he embraced the Power and opened a Veilgate into a narrow corridor in the catacombs of the Overlook.

It was in the deepest part of the catacombs, and the sound of rushing water Jase knew to be the origin of the Trian River was loud in his ears. Gideon continued down the corridor without hesitation, and the Veilgate from the Overlook slid closed behind them as he released the Power.

Memories of the last time he was here flashed through his mind, and a knot tightened in his stomach as he followed his parents ever deeper into the catacombs. A moment later tremors of corruption tickled his Awareness, and the feeling grew stronger with every step. He knew what was waiting for them at the end of the corridor. He knew, but he followed anyway.

*I will find a way to fix this*, he vowed, and a sudden rush of love and support and sympathy reached him through the *sei'vaiya*.

*We'll do it together*, Talia thought.

They stopped in front of a door warded with Spirit, and Gideon used the signet ring on his right hand to release the crux points holding the warding in place. As the sheltering bubble of Spirit vanished, the tremors of corruption resonating in Jase's Awareness spiked. Gideon opened the door.

Even though he knew what he would find, seeing it firsthand chilled Jase to his core. The altar in the center of the room was still shrouded in an aura of darkness as powerful and tangible as any he'd ever faced. And there, frozen within the darkness, was that part of Gideon's soul that had been captured by Maeon.

"How..." he began. "The Rejuvenation is complete. The Veil and the Earthsoul have been restored. How is this possible?"

Gideon shook his head sadly. "I don't know. I was certain the Rejuvenation would dispel the darkness enough for me to reunite the broken dagger. But when your mother and I came down here last night, this is what we found. And it's stronger than it was before."

"But that shouldn't be possible," Jase said. "I—" He cut off as footsteps sounded out in the corridor. He turned as Seth and Elliott and Galiena entered the room.

Seth's expression was unapologetic as he locked eyes with Gideon. "I told them about Dunkin Fairimor," he said. "But it turns out that Queen Morgranon already knew. Just as she knew that you would be here at this time."

"Elderon spoke to me in the Soul Chamber," she said, looking from Gideon to the aura of darkness. "He told me what this is and how to defeat it."

"How?" Jase asked at the same time that Gideon asked, "What is it?"

Galiena's golden eyes were sympathetic as she answered Gideon.

"A stalemate between darkness and light," she answered. She looked pointedly at the wraithlike figure within the darkness. "When the dagger-talisman split and Maeon breached the Veil to seize that part of your soul, the Earthsoul fought back in your behalf. She did to Maeon what he had done to you, if on a much smaller scale. This darkness, this bubble of evil, is a sliver of the demon lord's soul."

Brysia and Talia took an unconscious step backward, but Jase stepped nearer the darkness. "How do we destroy it?" he asked, ready to embrace the Power.

"We don't," Galiena said. "Any attempt to destroy it would kill Gideon, and that part of his soul would be forever trapped in the Void. He would be cut off from Eliara."

"How is this part of Gideon's soul still here?" Brysia asked. "The Veil collapsed. Maeon could have claimed him already."

Galiena smiled. "The Veil didn't collapse in this room."

She looked fondly at Gideon and added, "You are *El'kali*, the Soldier of God and Guardian of the Earthsoul. She wasn't going to surrender you without a fight. So, with the last of Her strength, She maintained Her hold on Maeon to protect you. Had Jase failed, the warding of Spirit over this room would have failed, and Maeon would have reclaimed this part of his soul and taken yours along with it."

Jase turned his back on the darkness and moved to stand before Galiena. "You said the Creator told you how to defeat this."

"He did. And He provided the means to do so." She turned her gaze on Elliott. "Show them."

Elliott reached up and took hold of the *chorazin* hilt rising behind his shoulder, then drew the Sword of Chellum from its scabbard. It came free with a steely hiss, and the Dragon-etched blade glowed from within as he held it before him. Jase's breath caught in his throat as his eyes fell on the etched symbols for Eliara.

"An Infinity Blade," Galiena told them. "Touched by the finger of God and endowed with Power from on High."

Jase stepped aside to give Elliott room to strike the darkness. "Then let's end this."

Galiena shook her head apologetically as she put out a hand to stop Elliott. "I'm sorry, Jase," she said. "This blade has but one purpose, and it isn't to dispel the darkness holding your father. Not in this manner, anyway."

Jase felt his patience starting to slip, but he kept his voice level as he spoke. "And what is its purpose?"

Galiena looked from him to Elliott and then back.

"To slay the Lord of Darkness."

*How great are the feet of he who entered the heart of the holy mountain; how great his blood as he awakened the Blood Seeds of the Rejuvenation.*

*How great is the love of she who died to open the way; how great the mercy of our God in restoring her life.*

*How great is the heart of he who carries the Sword of God; how terrible the burden of that blade.*

*For the path of the One Who Comes Before is at an end; while the path of the Sword of God has just begun.*

~ From the private journal of Galiena'ei to ul'Morgranon, Queen of the Rhiven.

# GLOSSARY

---

**Time:** is measured based on two important dates in history. The first, the Farewell of Elderon (A.F. 1), marks years in the Old World and was approximately 3000 years in length, though no one can be sure, since it's unclear just how long the people gathered before they went to battle. The length of the Great Destruction is even more vague. Estimates based on fragmented records indicate it may have lasted as long as sixty years. The New World is marked with the letters A.S. (After Solemnizing) and continues to the present, the year A.S. 2300.

**Calendar:** The Ha'lel Calendar has ten months of thirty-six days each. It was given to the Old World race of man by Elderon during the Age of Instruction. Every twentieth year, five days are added to Bashan and the Feast of Ha'lel is held. The names of the months are: Fayu, Hyr, Morshe, Elul, Corshem, Iathec, Bashan, Jad, Sewil, and Corlil.

**Distance:** is measured in leagues and miles with 1 league being the equivalent of 3 miles.

**Languages:** Because of Kelsa's location as the heart of the Nine Lands, the Kelsan language became pivotal in trading and economic development. In the year A.S. 486 the Unification Act was signed, and the countries of Elva, Zeka, and Melek adopted the Kelsan language as an official 'second language'. A century later, the Chunin nation signed as well, and the Kelsan tongue became officially known as the Common Tongue. The nations of Riak and Dainin became bilingual a half century later. Kunin and Arkania refused to take part in the Unification Act, and both countries have suffered financially because of it.

---

*arinseil*: Power-wrought metal of the nets used by the *Nar'shein Yahl*.

**Awareness:** The term used by Power-wielders to describe the mindlink a Dymas or *Dalae* must have if they are to successfully control the Power. It also allows a Dymas to see the spiritual realm of the Earthsoul itself. *See Ta'shaen*.

**Baalzebul:** The Kunin name for Maeon.

**Battle of Amnidia:** Also known as the Second Cleansing, this battle was fought in the year A.S. 1407 between an army of Dymas led by Siamon Fairimor and the legions of Agla'Con led by Throy Shadan. During this battle, so much Earthpower was used that the valley was left in ruin. At his death, Shadan unleashed one final onslaught so horrible it tainted every fiber of the valley, leaving it uninhabitable. The Elvan nation, recognizing this curse, relinquished their claim on the valley. *See also* Great Wall of Aridan; Shadan'Ko.

**Battle of Capena:** Fought in A.S. 2162 when a Riaki army led by sixty Agla'Con attacked and destroyed much of the city before marching north toward Chellum. They were intercepted in the Shellem Plains by Gideon and a small army of Dymas and were destroyed.

**Battle of Greendom:** Fought in A.S. 2280 on a hill overlooking the village of Greendom, it is known by many as *The Final Stand*. During this battle, the combined armies of Kelsa, Elva, and Chunin stood against the refleshed Dreadlord Throy Shadan and his Agla'Con.

*Book of Halek:* Old World book of prophecies written by Gamaleil Halek. It is one of the earliest known writings from that time, and though an exact date is still a point of debate for scholars, most agree it was written within the first fifty to one hundred years after Elsa was slain by Maeon.

*Chael'trom:* The Elvan name for refleshed. It means "deadman walking." *See* K'rrosha.

*chorazin:* An indestructible, Power-wrought substance.

**Cleansing Hunt:** What the *Nar'shein Yahl* call their hunt for an Agla'Con.

**Coercion:** Forbidden by the Creator, Coercion is similar to Thought Intrusion and is one of the most vile corruptions of Spirit *Ta'shaen*. With it, Agla'Con invade the minds of their victims and force them to do things against their will. Those foolish enough to use this forbidden talent often find themselves the target of a Cleansing Hunt.

**Communing:** The method by which Dymas are able to communicate with one another through their Awareness. Communing also allows Dymas to link their abilities and combine their strength in the Power.

**Con'Jithar:** The realm of darkness where Maeon dwells. Sometimes referred to as Hell by the different religions.

**Con'Kumen:** "Hand of the Dark" in the Ancient Language, it is an organization sworn to Maeon.

**Core, the:** The twelve members of the Kelsan High Tribunal who take over in times of war.

**Crux points:** Small spheres of Spirit that hold various kinds of wards and Power-wrought traps in place and provide the Power necessary to sustain them, sometimes indefinitely.

*Cynthian:* A history of the Elvan city Cynthia. Though most of what it chronicles deals with the secular and political elements of the city's history, it also contains many prophecies concerning the destruction of the Valley of Amnidia, the rise of Shadan as the first of the *chael'trom*, the death and rejuvenation of the Earthsoul, and the coming of the *Mith'elre Chon*.

*da'shova:* A collar-talisman used to keep a Power-wielder from embracing *Ta'shaen*.

**Dai'shozen:** Riaki word for First General. A Dai'shozen is the head of a clan's military force.

*Dalae*: "Gifted" in the Old Tongue. It is the name given to those who have received any one of the Seven Gifts of *Ta'shaen*. Except for Healers, most tend to keep their Gifts hidden because of the mistrust people have of those able to wield *Ta'shaen*.

**Death's Third March**: So-named in the prophecies, it is believed that this decisive battle will be proceeded by the arrival of the *Mith'elre Chon* and will lead to the final cleansing of the Agla'Con or the destruction of mankind.

**Defiling, the:** The desecration of the Temple of Elderon in Kunin when the Sons of Uri led the Kunin in rebellion against their Creator and used the Blood Orb of Elsa to try to bring down the Veil.

**Dragons**: Old World creatures believed to be extinct. Legend tells that they arrived in this world after being driven from their own world by Maeon. Sometime around the year A.F. 1000, a war was fought between men and Dragons which resulted in the expulsion of Dragons from the world of men. *See also*: Rhiven.

**Dragonblade**: Unbreakable, Power-wrought swords, some of which date back to the Old World. They get their name because of the Dragons etched into the blades and hilt. Even though the Dainin are able to craft these weapons in modern times, those dating from the Old World are prized by swordmasters since the hilts are constructed of *chorazin*. Legend says the Old World blades were forged in the fires of Dragons.

*Dy'illium*, **The**: An Old World book of prophecies.

**Earth's End**: A small, frozen continent at the bottom of the world.

**Earth's Heart**: Another name for the Soul Chamber.

**Earthpower**: A common term for *Ta'shaen*.

**Earthsoul, Rejuvenation of:** In order to keep Elderon's creations from becoming a part of Con'Jithar, and therefore subject to Maeon, it is prophesied that a firstborn son of Elsa will need to take up one of the Talismans of Elsa and use the reservoir of Earthpower it contains to instill new life into the Earthsoul. Although none of the records say exactly how this is to be done, they do say where it must take place: the Soul Chamber deep inside Mount Tabor in the Valley of Amnidia. *See also* Earth's Heart

**Elderon**: The name of the Creator.

**Eliara**: The place of peace where Elderon dwells.

*El'kali*: Old World term meaning "Soldier of God."

*El'shaen te sherah*: The 'Power and Light of the Creator' in the Old Tongue. It is the power Elderon used when He moved against the Void in order to create this world. It is the same Power that gives life to the Earthsoul and holds the Void at bay. It is Earthpower undivided into the seven individual Gifts.

*Eli'shunda Kor*: An Old World collection of writings.

**Elsa**: A righteous woman from the Age of Instruction who was slain by Maeon.

**Elsa, Blood of:** When she was slain by the hand of Maeon, Elsa's blood mingled with the dust of the earth and sprang forth in diverse places as Talismans of great Power. A link was created between her spirit and the Earthsoul which is the sustaining force behind *Ta'shaen*. The Talismans formed from her blood became the access keys to vast reservoirs of the Power. The Blood of Elsa is also a reference to those of her descendants who are prophesied to one day take up one of the Talismans to rejuvenate the Earthsoul. *See also* Earthsoul; Earthsoul, Rejuvenation of.

**Esielliar:** An ancient Elvan Prophet.

*Eved'terium:* A collection of Old World prophecies.

**Fist of Con'Jithar:** The predominate religion in Tamba. Founded by *Frel'mola* while she was still in the flesh, this "church" is dedicated to the worship of Maeon.

*Frel'mola:* "The Bride of Maeon" in the Tamban tongue. *Frel'mola* is a recently refleshed female Dreadlord who has once again seized control of the Tamban government.

*Frel'mola te Ujen:* "Fist of the Dark Bride" in the Tamban tongue, this dark religion was recently founded by *Frel'mola*.

**Galaron, Jeymi:** A young female Dymas and friend to Endil Fairimor.

**Gathering, The:** In the year A.F. 3000, the people of the Old World, led by two rival groups of Agla'Con, divided into two great armies and went to war against each other. Though the actual duration of The Gathering is unknown, it is speculated that it may have taken as long as ten years. The war resulted in the destruction of the Old World and the near decimation of the First Race of Man.

**Gideon:** A Dymas for more than 300 years, he is known as the Guardian of Kelsa and has served as warder-advisor to the Fairimor Kings for the past three centuries. His real name is Dunkin Fairimor.

**Great Destruction, the:** Worldwide battle between rival Agla'Con that resulted in the end of the Old World and ushered in the Second Creation.

*Holdensar Prophecies:* A book of Riaki prophecies.

**Imor:** A descendant of Elsa and father of the Fairimor bloodline.

**Imperial Clave:** The governing council of Riak. Members of the Imperial Clave are selected by the Emperor from among the Highseats of the most powerful clans.

*Jeth'Jalda:* The Tamban word for Agla'Con.

**Jyoai College:** A prestigious university in Trian.

*kamui:* Old World Dragonblades, these twin short-swords are the rarest of all Dragonblades.

**Kavet de'Leflure:** The capital of Dainin.

*kitara:* Traditional robe of the Riaki.

*komouri:* Black, tight-fitting uniform of the Shizu. Other elements of Shizu clothing include the *koro* hood-mask and the *kotsu* soft-soled boot.

**K'rrosha:** In the Old Tongue, "Refleshed."

**K'sivik:** A type of shadowspawn used as a mount for Throy Shadan.

**K'tyr:** A unique and very dangerous kind of shadowspawn. They are the rarest of all shadowspawn because their creation often kills the Agla'Con who helped spawn it. They are similar to Satyrs in that they have four arms and carry curved short-swords, but they also have wings and can fly. They have the ability to create voids in *Ta'shaen*, making it impossible for a Dymas to embrace the Power.

**Laureola Leaf**: The symbol of the *Nar'shein Yahl*. The Dainin see the seven foils of this delicate leaf as symbolic of the Seven Gifts of *Ta'shaen*.

*Lo'shaen:* "Power of the Void" in the Old Tongue, it is the power wielded by Maeon in Con'Jithar.

**Loharg Kala'peleg**: A half-Kunin half-demon Power-wielder.

**Maeon**: The name of the demon god who opposes Elderon and who rules in the realm of Con'Jithar. Always striving to take souls, he is the enemy of mankind. Other names include: the Great Deceiver, the Dark One, Soulbiter, Soultaker, the Destroyer, and Soulcrusher.

*Mae'kishon:* A rank within the hierarchy of the Con'Kumen.

*Mae'rillium :* A rank within the hierarchy of the Con'Kumen.

*Mith'elre Chon:* In the Old Tongue, "The One Who Comes Before." Prophecies in the *Cynthian* tell of the *Mith'elre Chon* going to battle against Shadan during Death's Third March.

*Mrogin:* A type of shadowspawn that resides in Amnidia.

**Myrscraw**: Giant birds from the Island of Myrdyn that are used as transportation by the Shizu.

*Nar'shein Yahl:* A Dainin phrase that means "Keepers of the Earth." The *Nar'shein Yahl* are Dainin warriors called by the voice of the Earthsoul to carry out Cleansing Hunts.

**Nine Lands, the**: A more commonly used title for the Temijyn Continent, which consists of the nations of Kelsa, Elva, Dainin, Chunin, Kunin, Melek, Riak, Zeka, and Arkania.

**Once-men**: *See* Shadan'Ko.

**Pit, the**: The desert valley where Throy Shadan's fortress is located.

**Quatha**: A type of reptilian shadowspawn.

**Refleshed, the**: *See* K'rrosha.

**Rejuvenation, the**: The act where a firstborn son of Fairimor must take up a Talisman of Elsa and revitalize the Earthsoul.

**Rhiven**: A race of Old World beings thought to be from another world. Also known as Dragons, their true form is the giant serpents spoken of in legend, but they are also able to take human form.

**Second Cleansing**: *See* Battle of Amnidia.

**Second Creation, the**: After the destruction of the Old World, Elderon returned to the Earth and created ten additional races of men. These new races included: Riaki, Meleki, Dainin, Chunin, Kunin, Zekan, Arkanian; and on the Jyndar Continent, the races Rosdan, Glendan, and Tamban. The Elvan people are believed to have been brought by the hand of Elderon from one of the many worlds He has created.

**Second Rise of the Agla'Con**: Took place in A.F. 2515. Much more wary this time, the Agla'Con kept their numbers secret until A.F. 2790 when they systematically destroyed all known Dymas. Eventually the Agla'Con separated into two rival factions that brought about the destruction of the Old World.

*Sei'shiin*: In the Old Tongue, "Spirit Lightning."

*sei'vaiya*: "Love-bond" in the Old Tongue. A rare Gift of *Ta'shaen* that allows those who are bound together to feel one another's presence.

**Seven Gifts of *Ta'shaen***: The Seven Gifts of *Ta'shaen* are Light, Earth, Fire, Water, Air, Flesh, and Spirit. Their names in the Ancient Language are *Shiin, Ta, Suzu, Nami, Tei, Sha,* and *Sei,* respectively. *See also* Earthpower; *Ta'shaen.*

**Shadan Cult**: A group of religious fanatics who worship Throy Shadan.

**Shadowhounds**: Dog-like creatures that scout ahead of K'rrosha. Other names include Sniffers and Hellhounds.

**Shadowlancer**: A name given to mounted K'rrosha. *See* Deathrider.

**shadowspawn**: Flesh and blood creatures created by the Agla'Con. Shadowhound come in hundreds of nightmarish varieties ranging from the very animalistic to the almost human. *See also* Darklings.

*Shel'tui*: The Kunin equivalent of an Agla'Con.

**Shey'Avralier**: Palace in the ruined city of Cynthia and gateway to Earth's Heart.

**Shomei**: Rosdan word for Dymas

**Solemnizing, the**: At the close of the Second Creation (A.S. 1), the Creator solemnized the marriage of Imor, a descendant of Elsa, and the Elvan Princess Temifair. He named their child Fairimor and placed him upon the throne of Kelsa.

**Sons of Uri**: Half-Kunin half-demon Power-wielders who head Kunin's dark religion. *see also*: the Defiling.

**Soul Chamber**: The sacred chamber of Elsa located inside Mount Tabor where the Rejuvenation of the Earthsoul can be enacted.

*Ta'shaen*: "Earthpower" in the Old Tongue. *Ta'shaen* is the power of God—the power by which all things were created—and is the life force of the Earthsoul. It is bestowed as a gift by the Earthsoul that it might be used to serve and help others. Like all things, however, it can be misused and corrupted. *See also* Seven Gifts of *Ta'shaen*; Agla'Con; Dymas.

*Tei'shevisar*: A Dainin book of prophecies.

**Temifair**: The Elvan Princess who became the mother of the Fairimor Bloodline.

**Temifair Palace**: Elva's seat of power in Andlexces.

**Thought Intrusion**: Forbidden by the Creator, Thought Intrusion is similar to the Gift of Discernment in appearance but is in actuality an evil corruption of Spirit *Ta'shaen*. Agla'Con foolish enough to use it often find themselves the target of a Cleansing Hunt.

*tres'dia*: "Fire Sword" in the Riaki tongue, it is the name of the newly formed

Deathsquad of the Gifted.

**T'rii Gates:** Also know as Veilgates, these reddish gates are constructed of *chorazin* and can be used to travel to other gates throughout the world. When using a T'rii Gate, the Veil is parted between two linked points in the spiritual fabric of the Earthsoul. Though some fragmented records mention T'rii Gates being used by Elderon to bring the Elvan people from their homeworld, there is no real evidence to support it. Another legend suggests the gates were used to facilitate The Gathering which preceded the destruction of the Old World. *See* Veilgate.

**Twisted Ones:** *See* Shadan'Ko.

**Valhan:** Glendan word for Dymas

**Valley of Amnidia:** Once a lush and fertile land, it was destroyed during the final battle with the living Shadan. Relinquished by the Elvan people, Amnidia became the home of the Shadan'Ko, former Kelsans corrupted by the taint left behind by Throy Shadan. It is now a wasteland of volcanic rock, ash, and soot. Only shadowspawn and a few of the boldest Agla'Con dare venture into the valley as the Twisted Ones have developed a taste for human flesh. *See* Great Wall of Aridan.

**Veil, the:** The spirit barrier that separates the world of the living from the realms of Con'Jithar and Eliara. It is, in a very literal sense, the Earthsoul—the spiritual sphere within which all life is sustained. As the Earthsoul weakens, however, the realm of Con'Jithar presses ever closer to the world of the living and will eventually swallow it unless the Veil can be strengthened or the Earthsoul rejuvenated.

**Veilgate:** Veilgates are mentioned in Volume I of the *Elvan Histories* but seem to refer more to the actual 'spiritual' gateway than the physical structure of the *chorazin* T'rii Gate. *See* T'rii Gates.

**Viewing:** A channeling of Earthpower whereby a Dymas can show images from the past.

**Waypost:** Small military outposts for Kelsa's Highwaymen. They dot the highways at thirty-mile intervals. *See also* Highwaymen.

*Zele'elre Shizu:* "The Shizu Born of Pain and Death" in the Old Tongue, this silver-haired Shizu is prophesied to help defeat Soulbiter.

# About the Author

Greg Park was born in 1967 in Provo, Utah, and spent much of his youth fishing the Provo River and camping and hunting in the Wasatch Mountains with his father and brothers. In 1986, he served a two-year mission in Osaka, Japan, then attended Brigham Young University where he received a Bachelor of Arts in English and a Master of Arts in theater and media arts.

A high school teacher for many years, Greg teaches English and Japanese and courses in creative writing, science fiction literature, and student government. He is the author of the young adult novel, *Sividious Stark and the Stadium Between Worlds*. His novel Veil of Darkness received the USA Book News Best Book Award for fantasy in 2007.

Still an avid outdoorsman, he spends much of his time fishing, hunting, and camping with his wife and children in Utah's backcountry.

# Praise for THE EARTHSOUL PROPHECIES™

USA Book News Best Books Award Winner

"Set in a richly detailed and varied world, this blend of coming-of-age
story and epic saga belongs in most fantasy collections."
– *Library Journal*

"The characters are rich, and the story is wonderfully told. The bad guys are truly
evil, deliciously dark. Park has the ability to weave a tale that's complex without
muddling the action."
– *Deseret Morning News*

"A wonderfully crafted, immersive epic fantasy."
– Midwest Book Review

"Sign up for the ride."
– *Deseret Morning News*

"Solid Storytelling."
– *Library Journal*

"Beautifully crafted... engrossing... I look forward to its sequel."
– *Leading Edge Magazine*

---

# BLADESTAR BOOKS

**Book One:** *Veil of Darkness*
ISBN-13: 978-0-9787931-8-0

**Book Four:** *Death's Third March*
ISBN-13: 978-0-9787931-5-9

**Book Two:** *Cleansing Hunt*
ISBN-13: 978-0-9787931-9-7

**Book Five: Blood Seed**
ISBN-13: 978-0-9787931-4-2

**Book Three: Children of** *Ta'shaen*
ISBN-13: 978-0-9787931-6-6

www.BladestarPublishing.com
www.GregPark.net